Tick Tock

More by Brooke Shaffer

The Timekeeper Chronicles

The Chivalrous Welshman
Time to Kill
Tick Tock
Windup (Fall 2018)

Tick Tock
Book Two of The Chivalrous Welshman
The Timekeeper Chronicles

Brooke Shaffer

Black Bear Publishing

Published in Michigan by Black Bear Publishing.

This novel is a work of fiction. Names, characters, places, and incidents are either products of the author's imagination or used fictitiously. All characters are fictional, and any similarity to persons living or dead is purely coincidental.

This novel contains an excerpt of *Windup* by Brooke Shaffer. The excerpt is provided for this novel only and may not reflect final published content.

ISBN:
        Hardcover: 978-0-9991392-3-3
        Softcover: 978-0-9991392-4-0
        eBook: 978-0-9991392-5-7

For L and D, still off on your own adventure.

Walter was just about to sit down to dinner when he got the call. He worked Missing Persons for Charleston Police Department, and he was the guy to call for any cases concerning children, or ones that fell a little out of the range of ordinary. He didn't always enjoy being interrupted at home for the calls, but he was bound and determined to wait as long as it took and weather every sleepless night it took to ensure that one child in particular was found.

He showed up to the hospital in his personal vehicle, but he'd changed back into his blues, hoping no one would mind the rumples too much.

"Oh, Walt, good of you to come," Lisa, the nurse who'd called him, greeted as he walked in the door of the emergency room. "Right this way."

"You said this would be interesting," Walter told her. "Anything I should know before I go in?"

"He's eight years old, and either extremely delusional, or...he's got a great fairytale to tell."

Now Walter was interested. This might just be the one. "What do you mean?"

"Well, he says his name is Tommen Forbes. Like, *the* Tommen Forbes, the one who disappeared into Forbes Cave a hundred and fifty years ago. He says he just went in the cave one day on an exploratory trip, came back out, thought it was night and his pa was going to switch 'im—" She grinned at this. "—and when he was coming back down the mountain, he was attacked by a demon. He was hit by a car, actually. But either way, he is extremely scared of everything and everyone. Half the time, he's not even speaking English."

"Let me guess, Welsh?"

"Yeah. And when he does speak English, it's with a lot of difficulty and a heavy accent. So, good luck getting through to him on that level."

"How is he, physically?"

"Well, wherever he comes from, he comes from poverty nonetheless. Doesn't know what electricity is, or running water. He's not starving, but he's suffering from malnourishment and several vitamin deficiencies. We almost had to sedate him to get lines in him for fluids and supplements. Otherwise, nothing to suggest physical abuse, no wounds in various stages of healing, no burns. Just cuts and scrapes like a normal kid, plus a broken collarbone, ribs, and pelvis from being hit by a car."

"Can't forget that," Walter said dryly.

By that time, they had reached their destination, and Lisa opened the door.

He certainly didn't look eight years old, as scrawny as he was, but he was every bit his father's son with the pronounced cheekbones, high forehead, and thick brown hair flopping over on his head. His eyes were his mother's, the purest chocolate brown you ever did see, always bright for one reason or another. Joy, love, curiosity, determination. Fear.

"Hi, Tommen, how are we feeling?" Lisa asked with all the warmth of a woman who had a ten year old herself.

The little boy looked like he wanted to shrug, but was presently unable. Instead, he just studied his hands and mumbled, "Good, ma'am."

"Tommen, I brought a friend with me. He wants to talk to you and ask you a few questions. Is that all right?"

"Yes, ma'am."

Walter took a chair from its position in the corner of the room and set it at Tommen's bedside. He sat down, trying to appear as unthreatening as possible. "Hi there, Tommen. My name is Walter. I'm a police officer. Do you know what that is?"

"Yes, sir," Tommen said, still not looking at him.

"Tommen, can you look at me?"

He did so, and for just a minute, Walter was sure he'd see the familiarity and the recognition. He was sure the boy would break into a grin; he would even take a cry of fear. But it never came. The boy just stared at him, wide-eyed and terrified. Walter continued on, heart heavy and twisting against the arrow that had just pierced him.

Tuesday

Tommen sat silently at Walter's bedside, watching the little blips of the monitors that surrounded him. Hard to believe that just twenty-four hours ago, he was alive and well and hugging him, both of them crying after being separated for two weeks when Tommen had been kidnapped by the madman Rifun Ndolo and his equally mad partner in crime, Cassius, both of them extremely powerful Time Agents—Rifun, a Timekeeper, capable of speeding up and slowing down time and manipulating it in almost perverse ways; Cassius, a Harvester, reaping the Potential Time from dying victims to extend his own years or sell in the industry of Time.

Originally, they'd set out to kill Lily Guile, the richest Harvester in Time, notorious for buying votes in elections, bribing officials, and generally being a bitch. Rifun and Cassius had failed to kill her because of a little magic trick she used, but her demeanor had changed. Most of the credit went to Walter, who had taken three bullets, first to save Tommen. Saving Lily had been a side effect.

But one of Rifun's accomplices was an alien species known as a Borelian, who were highly poisonous to all non-Borelians, their abilities ranging from stealing the senses, to total manipulation of the heart and lungs, or even worse. The only way to know which was which was by the color of their skin. Isthim was a special Borelian called a *vodrak*, capable of changing her color and so having all the abilities of all the Borelians, making her extremely dangerous. She'd dueled with Walter and incapacitated him long enough for Rifun to get a hold of him while she poisoned all the bullets in Rifun's gun.

Walter's only saving grace had been that only one of the

bullets had actually stayed in his body long enough for the poison to enter his system. But according to Lily, who knew and understood what had been done, it didn't matter. There was no cure for Borelian poison, and he only had a week to live, maximum. No amount of Harvesting, Banding, or Time was going to stop it or even slow it down.

So Tommen sat silently at Walter's bedside, watching the little blips of the monitors that surrounded him. He was still breathing on his own, and, for all intents and purposes, he was perfectly healthy. Sure, he'd knocked his head on the concrete floor when he was fighting Isthim, but that couldn't account for his comatose state which had been ruled as ideopathic. More like idiot-pathic.

Like his dad and Rifun, Tommen was a Timekeeper, and there were times he hated his abilities. How he wished he could just tell the doctors exactly what happened, exactly what was wrong. Except that it really wouldn't matter. Lily knew what was wrong, knew all the backstory, and she was even a doctor; even she could do nothing for him. Before she'd left, Lily had suggested using what time they had left together to come to terms that Walter was as good as dead.

Tommen wasn't willing to give up, but despair had settled over him. Time was not medicine, simply a tool used to accelerate the healing the body was going to do anyway. Except Walter wasn't going to heal. Even Micah and Micaiah Durvin—Walter's Timekeeper Lieutenants, Tommen's bosses at work, as well as now his legal guardians—couldn't come up with any tricks either, whether considered legal, illegal, or somewhat shady. The Borelians were used as Time's executioners. They were sought after *because of* their various poisons, and as Lily had put it, "No one sends a man to a poisonous execution with the intent of giving him the antidote."

That was even assuming there was an antidote. Even if there was, the Borelians were no friend to those they considered a "lesser species." And if they did manage to find someone willing to sell the antidote to them, they would never be able to afford it. It was like seeing a man dying of thirst in the desert and offering to sell him a bottle of water for a million dollars. There was just no point to it. Furthermore, according to Micaiah, the Borelians were very good at the slave trade, and they made slaves of just about anyone, so if they felt insulted by Tommen's pleading or a pitiful offer to buy, they would not hesitate to kidnap him and throw him into slavery. So while Walter was, yes, dying as they spoke, without enough foreknowledge of the Borelians or how to approach them and not get thrown into slavery or poisoned themselves, it wasn't a worthwhile risk.

So Tommen sat silently at Walter's bedside, watching the little blips of the monitors that surrounded him. He thought about what he was supposed to have been doing today. He was supposed to be working, running around the bakery with the twins like a trio of headless chickens, desperately trying to fill last-minute orders for Christmas rolls, biscuits, bread, pies, whatever people wanted. Because what better time to shop than Christmas Eve, right? Not like they had any plans to celebrate. No, they were more than happy to cater to the stupid and the forgetful and the poor planners.

What better time to have a Western-style showdown at a shipping yard, right? Not like things couldn't have been solved peacefully or avoided all together. No, they just loved a good life and death firefight, especially when one of the hostages was an officer's kid. Walter wasn't the only one who'd suffered, either. Five other officers had been killed, eight more severely injured, some not expected to live. Rifun and Cassius and all their little friends were easily at the top of Charleston Police Department's Most Wanted, but there was nothing they could do about it because Cassius had not been present at the yard when it happened, and Rifun and Isthim had just vanished. Reportedly, Tadashi had also escaped police custody and was deemed a criminal at large, but Tommen knew he would be long gone by now, run back to his masters like a faithful — or faithless — hound.

"Tommen?"

Tommen looked up to see his two best friends, Eric and Varad.

Eric was a senior, forced out of the traditional classroom into online classes in order to escape the bullying and even death threats of basically the entire school after he was accused of raping one of his classmates, which he hadn't. Varad was also a senior, an American-born Indian whose parents were now dead set on moving back to India in order to escape what they perceived as belligerent racism, and return to their families. The two of them had been taken hostage by Rifun as well, and they had been exposed to Time to such a degree that they could theoretically become Timekeepers themselves if they so chose. Except Time was a frightening thing to behold, and now they knew that he'd been living a secret double life. To call them his best friends now seemed a bit presumptive.

"Lost in your own little world?" Eric asked, trying to smile and muster up some old comradery, but it came out as forced.

"What do you mean?" Tommen wondered, but he knew exactly what they meant. They'd probably greeted him halfway across the room, but he hadn't heard them. Rifun had fired a gun next to his head and all but destroyed the hearing in his right ear. His left was a little iffy, too.

"We've said hi, like, four times," Varad told him, having a harder time of not outright sneering at him.

Tommen sighed and looked away. "I lost the hearing in my right ear," he confessed. "I just...I'm sorry. Why are you here?"

"The news had the whole story," Eric said. "About the warehouse and stuff. They said that some officers had been killed or injured. We came down to make sure it wasn't your dad, but...I guess it was."

"Yeah. But why come down at all?"

"Respect. Answers."

Too much had happened the last twenty-four hours for Tommen to continue to put up with evasive answers and bullshit. Grouchily, he Banded. When he'd been beside Walter in the warehouse, he'd broken through part of his next segment of training and begun Banding other people and things he did not have immediately in his hand, called External Banding. Now he Banded the three of them. More specifically, he started out Banding the whole room, then worked to narrow and strengthen the Band. It was kind of like trying to stuff a giant blanket back into a box, knowing that it only gets packed perfectly once, but darn it if it will still fit. Then it was just the three of them. It was a Fast Band, where they were in a Time faster than Base Time, so it appeared as though everything around them had stopped. It was a perfect Band to use when speaking privately.

"Don't do that!" Varad snapped. "It freaks me out."

"If you have something to say, you might as well say it, because it's only the three of us here now," Tommen told them flatly.

"So, that's just what you do," Eric said. "You just will Time to go faster or slower, and it does."

"It's not that simple. It's taking Time and...Banding it, is what it's called. Bending it around you or something or someone else in order that you move on a faster or slower plane than everything around you."

"And you just do this at your fucking will?"

"Well...yes."

"What about all those fights with Tyler, huh? How many times did he kick your ass?"

"Often enough. I chose not to use it."

"You do, but I don't!" Eric ran a hand through his hair and sighed, trying to stay calm. "Last week, I had to go into school and take a test. Toward the end, I wasn't doing so good, and I remember wishing that I had more time to finish. And somehow I...I saw something. And when I touched it, like with my mind, my will, time fucking stopped. I was so freaked out, I almost couldn't finish the test. I did, just to get my mind off it. After that, I had no clue how to stop it, or...make it go. I don't know. Somehow I did, though. I spent my entire weekend at work trying not to look at the clock because I was afraid it was going to, I don't know, spin out of control."

"I had a similar experience," Varad said, "but the opposite

direction. It was like my life around me was suddenly sped up like an old VHS tape. I didn't think it lasted very long, but my father said I had been completely still for nearly fourteen hours. He was overjoyed, thought I had finally received a vision from the gods and entered a trance in order to receive it."

"Timekeepers are trained for years to control Banding and learn other abilities," Tommen informed them.

"Timekeepers? Creative name." Eric folded his arms.

Tommen shrugged. "That's just how it got translated into English. There are other roles. Harvester. Merchant. Time is a huge industry in some parts of the universe. Earth is just...not engaged."

"Yeah, and an alien shot your dad, right?" Varad raised a brow.

"Rifun shot my dad, but his bullets were poisoned by an alien, yes. He's..." Tommen took a breath. "He's got about a week to live, tops."

That silenced the two of them for a moment. Eric broke the silence first. "I'm sorry."

Tommen rubbed his face. "Yeah. So am I." He looked at them. "I'm sorry you two got dragged into all of this. It's not fair, and it's not fun."

"You're right, it's not," Varad said, tears streaking down his cheeks though he tried to play tough. "And I'm done. I am moving to India with my head held high."

Even as he turned, Tommen released the Band from around him, and he seemed to freeze in place. Eric remained, studying him for a long moment.

"Tommen Forbes," he said.

"Yes?"

"You really are Tommen Forbes. *The* Tommen Forbes. From Forbes Cave."

"Yes."

Eric shook his head, but Tommen could see the information start to process. "Unreal. I mean, yeah, you read about this sort of shit in books or see it on, like, *Star Trek* or something, but you never expect it to actually happen. Just tell me one thing, Tommen."

"What's that?"

"Tell me I'm not crazy."

"Your mind has been expanded to a bigger universe and abilities beyond what the average person could comprehend. Of course you're crazy. But that doesn't mean it isn't true."

"Shit." He let out a breath. "What do I do, Tommen? I have a life. Not much of one since what happened at homecoming, but I have a life. I'm rebuilding. I don't want to deal with all this shit, Rifun and Timekeepers and all that. I just don't want to have this thing sneak up on me where I can't control it."

"I don't blame you. And I might know someone willing to help. Just stay here for a few minutes."

With that, Tommen released the Band. Varad stalked off without a word and without a glance over his shoulder. The door didn't even completely close before it opened again and Micah and Micaiah walked in. Micah looked over his shoulder as Varad went past, but otherwise they made for Walter's bedside. Micaiah set a small vase of flowers next to him. It was almost weird to picture Micaiah buying a vase of flowers. He wasn't a bodybuilder, but he worked out. Then, to distinguish himself further from his younger twin, as if he might get mistaken for Micah's thin, lanky frame, he also deigned to keep some tasteful stubble on his chin, cheeks, and neck, straight out of some men's magazine Tommen was sure.

"Eric," Micaiah acknowledged diplomatically. "Didn't expect to see you here."

"The news said some cops were killed or injured. Wanted to pay my own respects since Tommen said his dad wasn't doing too well," Eric told them.

"No," Micah said sadly. "But it's much appreciated."

"And I know this is probably a bad time, but I have something I want to ask of you."

Suddenly the four of them were in a Fast Band created by

Micaiah. "Does it have something to do with this?"

Eric shrugged and nodded. "Yes." He unfolded his arms and let them hang at his sides. "I don't want to be a Timekeeper or whatever. I just want to be able to control it."

To Tommen's surprise, the twins nodded. It was Micah who spoke. "There are those who have been exposed to Time in such a way who don't wish to really do anything with it other than keep it at bay as you describe. It's not a difficult thing to do if all you want to do is keep it from surprising you. But I will caution you one thing: The Hands who govern Time allow only this. If you start trying to strengthen it, control it, get better at it, you will be required to either become a Timekeeper or be treated like a Runner."

"A Runner?" Eric looked at Tommen.

"Like a bootlegger," Tommen told him. "Those who use Time illegally."

"Didn't realize you could use time illegally, but okay. No, I just want to get through my day without suddenly being surprised that everyone else is moving faster or slower than me."

"Makes sense," Micaiah acknowledged. "Well, we can either teach you to control it, or we can do something called Suppression. It'll basically take away the conscious ability, but you'll still see Bands and be susceptible to Time-related incidents."

Eric shook his head. "Too much shit going on for me to want to get rid of it completely. I mean, what if that fucker comes back?"

"Fair enough," Micah said. "How much time do you have?"

"I don't know, I have to be up tomorrow so we can travel early, so I was hoping to get home—"

"How bad is it?" Micaiah cut in. "Is it on you all the time, getting you lost and disoriented and everything else?"

"It was at first. My mom almost called the cops or the ambulance on me for a psychotic episode or something. But, I mean, now that I kind of get what's happening, I think I'm figuring out how to make it go away."

"Very good. But even this rudimentary training would take a

full day. Go home and enjoy Christmas with your family. When are you coming back?"

"Oh, we're just gone for a couple days."

"Come by the bakery when you get back, and then we'll set something up. Sound fair?"

"But what if I need it during dinner or on the road or something?"

"You're more apt to learn on the fly in high-stress situations," Tommen told him. He looked at the twins. "Which reminds me, I need to talk to you about something."

Micaiah just raised a brow but said nothing to that. Instead, he told Eric, "He's right. Just come by on your way back, and then we'll talk. Fair?"

Eric hesitated but nodded. "Fair." He took a few steps away then turned back. "And I'm sorry to hear about your dad, Tommen. I really am. He was a great guy."

Tommen could only nod.

Then Micaiah dropped the Band around Eric, leaving only three of them. "What did you want to talk about?"

"In the warehouse," Tommen said. "I made another breakthrough on my training. I was able to Band my dad. Like, I Banded him in order to essentially stall the bleeding until the ambulance arrived. Since then, I can Band other things, other people. I did it with Eric and Varad. Well, I started off with the whole room and then I narrowed it down, but I did it."

"Congratulations," Micah told him. "It's not an easy thing to learn, but it's the next logical step. Now you simply work at it like you did your normal Banding on yourself."

"That's it?"

"For all intents and purposes here today, yes. After your review, once you get into the Arena, then..."

He trailed off as they all began to realize what that meant. Yes, it meant that Tommen would be promoted to a full Apprentice, but it also meant that Walter would be dead. He wouldn't be able to take

Tommen to his review, would not see him become an Apprentice, would not be his mentor.

Quietly, Micaiah let the Band drop. "I'm sorry. I didn't mean—"

"I know," Tommen interrupted him. "I know what you meant."

The twins pulled up chairs for themselves.

"Is there anything you want to say or want to talk about?" Micaiah wondered.

Forget the crazy uncles, the twins were like Tommen's second and third fathers. They were just as responsible for him as Walter ever was. Now they were taking him into their home while Walter was out. In a week, they would probably start the process of taking him in permanently.

"It's not fair," Tommen said. "Maybe I shouldn't have provoked Rifun by following them from the museum or...maybe he should have just told me whatever secret Rifun thought he had so he wouldn't have been made to fight Isthim." He sighed, tried not to cry. "What secret does he have that is so important he would rather die than tell me?"

Micah and Micaiah glanced at each other. Tommen blinked. "You know it." When they only looked guilty, he continued, "Tell me. Obviously he's not going to."

"If your dad was willing to die for it, then we are obligated to keep it also," Micaiah told him sagely. "And I will not be the one to tarnish your opinion of him by telling you. Think of him only as the man you know him to be, not who he once was."

It was that sort of shit that spawned books and movies that usually had catastrophic outcomes for everyone involved. The secrets around a man everyone thought they knew. The secret life of the man who a family once called father and husband. Why did the twins not see that? Maybe because this was the real world, and in the real world, catastrophic outcomes were pretty limited to emotional turmoil and broken trust and relationships. No horrendous world-ending schemes here.

"So. What do we do now?" Tommen asked after a few minutes of silence. "We know he's going to die. Should probably stop pretending otherwise."

"That's not fair and you know it," Micah told him, struggling to put an edge to his voice. "He's still breathing on his own, and I count that as a good thing."

"Why? Because his directive states that if he ever becomes dependent on machines with no viable hope, to terminate treatment? He's got a week. Max. I'm not going to pretend like there's hope and wait for some miracle to happen, because it won't. It never does. There are no such things as miracles. Only science. And the science we have available and the science that could be available won't help him in time."

The only thing he got from the twins was a sympathetic look. Micaiah stood slowly, his knees cracking. "Well then, if that's how you feel about it, I guess we're going to lunch. Care to join us?"

Not accepting the invitation would make him appear to be a whiny child throwing a temper tantrum in the corner and refusing to eat until he got his way. Accepting the invitation and going to lunch, however, would make Tommen feel even more like he was giving up on his dad, just leaving and going about normal life while he labored away, the seconds and minutes counting down until the Grim Reaper swung his scythe.

In the end, Tommen did follow them out of Intensive Care. There was no way he was going to last a week without food, no matter how strongly he felt or how much he was determined to boycott everything but Walter's bedside. Wasn't like his dad would notice anyway.

They headed to a restaurant not far from the hospital and ended up waiting almost an hour to get a table. A few people recognized the twins as the owners of Bakery na hÉireann.

"I thought you guys were supposed to be open today?" their hostess wondered as she seated them. "I was looking forward to a cookie or something after work to treat myself."

Oh, she treated herself often enough, and the cookie had nothing to do with it. Tommen recognized her as a regular customer, but the only regular order she had was to see Micaiah and talk to him if she could. Micaiah was polite enough, but given that Time essentially made them ageless, he saw little point in dating. If he wanted to do something special for someone, he would, with no pretense. If he wanted to get in bed with someone, he was more apt to check out bars, clubs, and other one night stand possibilities.

"We thought we would be open today too," Micaiah sighed, not having to fake his exhaustion as he rubbed his eyes. "And what I wouldn't give for it right now."

She gave them an odd look but said nothing except to mention that their server would be right with them.

"Are you ever going to tell her to stop flirting with you and move on?" Tommen wondered.

Micaiah shrugged. "Probably not. Better she flirts with me than some asshole, I guess."

"And you're not an asshole for leading her on?" Micah asked.

"Micah, what ever happened between you and Lily?" Tommen cut in. When both twins fell silent and looked at him, he went on. "I mean, I never actually heard the whole story."

"Why would you want to?" Micah wondered nervously.

"I don't know, because you avoid it. Because it impacted you. Because she's changed in the last couple days?"

"Well, you're right in that, anyway; she has changed. I just don't think it will last."

Before Tommen could ask what he meant, their server came and took their drink orders. Only when he returned with the drinks and left the table to give them a few more minutes with the menu did Micah Band the three of them so they could speak.

"Why don't you think it will last?" Tommen asked.

"Because it never does," Micah told him. "Maybe this time will last longer because her life was at stake, but she always goes back to the same old Lily."

"What happened?"

"Lily was exposed to Time during World War II. Her mentor, Julianna, tried to Harvest her prematurely. Initially, Lily ran away from her, tried to get to her husband who'd gone missing overseas."

"Lily was married?"

Micah nodded. "She was. Her husband turned up dead, in the end. She spent almost two decades in Europe, trying to help them rebuild. She came back to America in 1962, just before the Dispersal. During the Dispersal, Julianna tried to hide her, keep her safe during the slaughters. That's how we ended up meeting. Julianna asked our mentors to keep her safe for a time since we were hiding out as well. After the Dispersal, we went our separate ways, but she and I always kept in close contact."

"Oh, come on, Micah, he's a big boy," Micaiah said. "Tell him the truth. You were fucking."

Micah rolled his eyes. "Fine, yes, we were sleeping together. But we did keep in touch after the Dispersal was over and things had returned to normal. Some years later, she wrote to me and said she'd gotten a job here in Charleston in NICU. Well, the District was short a couple Lieutenants, and we just happened to have completed our training around the same time. So we moved here and opened the bakery as a pretext. That's when we met your dad and became his Lieutenants. A short time later, I met up with Lily, and we started dating again."

He paused and sighed. "Our letters were not frequent, but often enough. She had long periods of self-righteousness, the bitch she usually is, as she developed her Harvesting abilities, got rich, got her college degrees, dated rich men, and so forth. Then she would have short periods of humility, most often after the rich men turned out to be abusive, or after periods of economic instability where her wealth, Earth-side or Time-side, was threatened greatly."

"So why date her at all?" Tommen wondered.

"I don't know. I guess I thought that if she dated someone

who, yeah wasn't rich, but was moderately successful and not an abusive asshole, it would help her find some stability. In the beginning it did, but she is a slave to greed and lust. She had her millions, but she always insisted on me buying everything. We were sleeping together, but apparently not often enough for her taste because after she got done with me, she would go out to a club and get laid with three more guys, and sometimes other women."

Tommen raised a brow. "I'm no expert, but that sounds like a sex addiction."

"Maybe," Micah admitted, "but love is blind. Stupidly, I thought marriage would fix it. Probably the best thing that ever happened was her pouring that wine on my head and storming out of the restaurant. It took me a while to get over it, but I see now that she never cared anything for our relationship, only its benefits. When that well ran dry, she just went looking for a new one."

"Oh."

"Take some advice from me, Tommen: If you want to date a girl, be friends with her first. If you want to sleep with a girl, date her for a little while first. Never jump headlong into a relationship with someone you know in your gut is unstable."

With that, the Band was released and life went on as though nothing was out of the ordinary.

Chapter Two
Sleeping Over

Lunch was good enough, Tommen supposed, wondering if he should be grateful or ashamed that his appetite and taste for food was returning. Did that mean that he himself was getting better as he recovered from his ordeal and was able to function semi-normally, or that he was already writing off his dad who was still technically alive, lying in ICU, his clock winding down?

"What do we do now?" he asked as the twins got the bill and they gathered their stuff to leave.

Micaiah appeared uncertain. "Well, we might as well head to your house so you can get a few more changes of clothes and whatever you need."

"Why don't one of you come to stay with me? Why do I have to come with you?"

"Because it's easier that way. Our house is bigger."

"So? If I'm the one getting tossed around like a football, it should be my decision."

"And until you're eighteen and have that legal right, what is and what should be are two different things. We don't like it any more than you do. And..." He sighed. "If and when Walter does die, then we can start talking about those decisions, because then it boils down to the will and estate."

Tommen took a breath, willing himself not to cry. "But not before."

"No. Not before. Come on."

They rode in a sullen silence to Tommen's house, a little rickety thing that had started out as some miner's shack and been

21

haphazardly added onto in the decades since, though the decor remained very, very 60's with a tiny kitchen, shag carpet, and a bathroom that looked like it had been vomited on by a paint monster high on shrooms. The newest part of the house was the kitchen appliances, oversized and stainless steel sorely out of place amid cabinets with six layers of paint in various stages of peeling and decay.

Tommen's room was the most-recently updated one, the same atrocious blue-gray, technically green, he'd picked out when he was eight years old. He had his dressers and his stereo and his TV and various video game systems he hadn't played in probably a year. His bed was the newest piece of furniture in the room, only a couple years old once he'd finally hit his growth spurt, only recently tipping him over six feet tall. He lay back on the bed, pleased that he was still able to fit with some room to spare.

It wasn't fair. None of this was fair. There was no one to be mad at except Rifun and Isthim, but they were long gone by now, and being mad at them wouldn't undo what had been done. He couldn't be mad at Lily except that if she had tricked her way into staying alive, she might have offered some assistance that would have helped stop Rifun and Isthim. But what could be done against a creature who excreted poison that could be felt just by sheer proximity? He could be mad at Micah and Micaiah maybe, but Micah had been incapacitated by Isthim, and Micaiah ran into the same problem Lily had—there was just no way to beat a Borelian. Tommen sighed. He couldn't even find it in himself to muster up the common, irrational self-hatred, that survivor guilt that so many people talked about. Would survivor guilt help the situation? He thought about it a minute and decided it wouldn't.

Not that his irrationality was limited to such guilt. Unfocused anger and toddler-like outbursts were just as unhelpful. But why did any of this have to happen at all? And why to him? Why was it that he had no control over these circumstances? First he waltzed into a cave that catapulted him a hundred and fifty years into the future, ended up in foster care, and finally had Walter adopt him. Now Walter was being taken from him just as suddenly as his biological family. By technicality, he would probably end up in some kind of limbo foster care for a time until the twins took full legal custody of him. But it wasn't fair. Didn't he get any say in it? He was the one being tossed around like a football. But then, no one ever stopped the Super Bowl to ask what the football thought.

He sat up. Might as well get moving. There was no point in stalling the inevitable. Sure, he might buy time today and tomorrow, but they were all scheduled to work the day after that. Christmas Eve, they might get away with being unexpectedly closed—much to the dismay of a few people, but shit happens—but there were even higher expectations for the day after Christmas. People were out returning gifts and spending gift cards and cash, and they would be hungry while they shopped. It was a time for them to put their emotions aside and think of the business side of things. The bakery had bills to pay. The twins had their personal bills to pay. And Tommen knew that the mailman would still bring Walter's bills and put them in the mailbox at the end of the driveway with no regard for his current physical location or well-being.

The only thing that would change that was his death.

Then it would all fall on Tommen. He knew that Micaiah was the Executor of the Estate, but it wasn't as though Walter had four siblings and six kids and twelve grandkids all squabbling over his possessions. More than likely, whatever Tommen didn't want to keep would be sold and the money put into a trust. Briefly he wondered if there was such a thing as a Time will. Walter got a pretty good salary of turns for his work as a Timekeeper Captain. Would his salary get turned into cash and handed over to Tommen, or simply get put back into the Time industry economy?

Tommen shoved a few pairs of pants into a bag. It was only Tuesday. Walter wasn't due for death until Monday, maybe sooner if he stopped breathing on his own, but either way, he wasn't dead yet, and there might still be a solution to all of this. He didn't know what, but he found it impossible that a Borelian had never, ever accidentally poisoned someone. Surely they had to have antidotes handy. But how did he approach a Borelian and ask without being dragged off into slavery?

He zipped up his bag of clothes and headed to the bathroom. For as much as he loathed the decor, he found that he was oddly attached to the house itself. Maybe because he could still very clearly recall the tiny cabin he'd lived in up until he was eight. He had many fond memories of that cabin. He had many fond memories of this house, too. He remembered the first time he walked inside and was stunned at all the space just for one person. He remembered being told that his room was all for him to do with what he wanted. Lord above, what was he going to do with so much space? And taking a bath without having to go to the creek and lug water up one bucket at a time? Probably one of the many times he'd burst into tears just from being overwhelmed and overjoyed and not knowing how to express it any other way.

Tommen wasn't exactly sure if he wanted to just sit right down and drown in the memories and become some crabby old hermit man living solely in the past, or run away as far and as fast as he could, as if putting physical distance behind him would somehow make the memories go away. He'd always scoffed at people who did that, usually from divorce or death of a loved one, but now he could understand what made them run. Though when the pain was emotional, there was no way to outrun it.

By the time he was finished, almost an hour had passed, and the twins were patiently waiting in the cramped kitchen, pilfering some chocolate out of the candy dish.

"Ready?" Micah asked.

Tommen shrugged. "I guess."

"We know it's not fun. It's hard for us, too. But if we do this now, then it's just one less thing we have to figure out later on."

"I know." Didn't mean he had to like it, but it was good to know they were having their own struggles, too. And why not? They were good friends with Walter, as his Time subordinates. If and when Walter died, who knew what the new Captain would be like, or where he would be stationed out of? For all they knew, they could be the ones running the show in Charleston.

Wherever Tommen went during that time, it always felt like he spent far too long in any one place. He spent too much time at the hospital, brooding over his circumstances while Walter lay dying. He spent too much time at home, stalling, as if by being lazy, he could somehow prevent Walter's death. He spent too much time in the car, driving, driving, always driving but going nowhere. He spent too much time at the twins' house, feeling very out-of-place in a home that was not only extremely familiar, but was probably going to be his permanent home come next week.

Really, it wasn't a bad home, and certainly there were worse places. Normally, Tommen lived south of Charleston across the river in a neighborhood that wasn't bad, but the occasional stupid break-in or graffiti by a couple of kids wasn't a huge surprise. The neighbors made small talk and there was the ubiquitous rivalry; when one neighbor mowed his lawn, they all had to. If Mrs. Wilson put out one hanging basket of flowers, Mrs. Lawson inevitably had to put out two.

Micah and Micaiah on the other hand, they lived north of Charleston in a neighborhood that had once started out as posh, rich, gated community development for the two-months-out-of-the-year vacation homes for celebrities and politicians. It had been a huge undertaking that brought applause and support and attention from around the country. But that plan fell through when trying to turn mountainous terrain into the gently rolling hillside of such a gated community became not only expensive, but dangerous, as crews battled snowstorms, rockslides, and everything else the mountains had to throw at them to stop such monstrous construction.

So there were no gates or walls to be found here, just a meandering road that followed the only stable path through the valley before degrading into some old two-track at the end. The driveways branching off the road were steep and winding. Furthermore, while one might boast about having twenty acres, most of that was straight up or straight down, and very little could be done with it. A few houses managed to keep both their size and have enough room for a garden, but other homes, when they were being built, elected to forgo the fourth bedroom and instead build a greenhouse or some such thing.

Only about half of the homes could be seen from the road anyway; the rest were tucked way up into the mountains, the driveways a mile long or more. They were simple homes, one-story, squat things, like turtles huddled against the wind and the snow. They might get covered in snow, but they would still be there in the spring. Given the general value of the neighborhood, it was fair to say that most of them probably had full, if not finished, basements and at least two bedrooms. With exception of the ones that were tucked too far back, most of the homes also probably had electricity and running water. A few had attached garages.

The twins lived about halfway down the road. As the crow flew, it was maybe three-quarters of a mile from the main road to the end of their driveway. With all the twists and turns in the road, it was more like three or four miles, or so it seemed. Similarly, their driveway was not terribly long. With exception of some carefully planted and trimmed hedges and trees obscuring some of the view, their house could almost be seen from the road. But the actual distance following the driveway to the garage felt like another mile, though Micah had once made the comment about it only being half a mile in actuality. At any rate, it was easy to shovel going downhill, but climbing back up was a nightmare. Tommen had been "commissioned" more than once to keep their driveway clear during the winter, and never once had he thought the work worth the pay, even if that pay was getting out of a grounding. He would have rathered sit and stare at a wall with none of his electronics for an entire weekend, than have to shovel this driveway.

But that was neither here nor there as Micaiah's car slowly but faithfully plugged and chugged its way up the drive into the garage.

Well, it wasn't necessarily a garage per se, more like a small metal pole barn that was barely big enough for two cars and just happened to keep the snow off their vehicles. Plus it was a good thirty feet from the house anyway, and it had started snowing and blowing like crazy as they got higher up into the mountains.

Tommen grabbed his things and prepared to make a dash for the house. The trees and shrubs they had planted around the yard helped to cut down on the wind, but nothing could stop the cold. If the trees weren't there, they would have had a million-dollar view of the capitol building and Charleston lit up for Christmas, but stunning views did nothing to keep men warm or the snow from blowing in sheets up the hill. So, while the view was pretty from the other side of the trees, Tommen was presently more appreciative of the protection they offered.

He made it to the front door and almost ran smack into it in his eagerness. Of course the door would be locked, why not? It was only freezing outside, and it wasn't like he could Band or anything to help himself. Fucking hell, but where were the twins? It seemed to take forever for the twins to get from the garage to the door.

"Sorry," Micaiah said humbly as he picked a key on his keyring and slid it into the lock. "Forgot where I put the key."

It was not a comfort, but the warmth emanating from inside was, and Tommen hurried inside, kicking his boots on the steps.

From the outside, the house didn't look like much, at least nothing out of the ordinary. Well-kept, windows clean, shutters clean, beige siding, lawn and shrubs well-groomed. The poorest thing they had in appearance was the garage, but they'd been told multiple times by various builders that there was no safe way to build a permanent garage on the same site, so they had to make do.

Once inside, however, it was easy to imagine the scale of rich smugness that would have gone into the original construction plans for the neighborhood. The twins had not been part of those original plans, but the developers, in an effort to continue with the gated community idea while minimizing the dangers of trying to literally level mountains, had built several model homes that were smaller but still very, very rich. Only one of those houses had been deemed "acceptable," and reportedly, that same Senator from Alabama still vacationed in that home, farther up the road.

As for the rest of the houses, four in total, they had gone up for sale or auction when the gated community plans fell through. The twins bought their home, and so far the only changes they had made were to change the siding, from solid brick to vinyl, in order to make their home less of a target. Everyone called them idiots for doing it, but the Senator's house had security on it at all times, and all the other houses had been broken into during a string of thefts that plagued Charleston a couple years back, except for the twins' house. So most of the critics had shut up since then.

Despite the average-looking exterior, the interior was as true to form as the day it was built. The front door took them into the kitchen, though one corner was set aside for shoes and coats. Shining tile graced the floor, the light color reflecting the light from a dozen pendant lights that hung over both an island and a peninsula. An enormous, beautiful, custom-made window sat over the sink, providing an exquisite view of, well, trees. And rock. The last remaining evidence of the excavating that had been done to bring the ground to something resembling level. But the curtains around the window were nice, as were the granite countertops and solid oak cabinetry. All the appliances were stainless steel. The island held the dishwasher, and a double-stacked oven sat in one corner—because some people like to take their work home with them? The refrigerator was a double-wide sitting across from the end of the peninsula like the gatekeeper to the rest of the house.

On the other side of the peninsula was the dining room, the oak table and chairs overseen by heavenly light from a seven-light brushed nickel chandelier. A short distance away, stairs led down to a tiny basement that only spanned about half the house. It was unfinished—the developers wanted to make sure they could proceed before they did, and were ultimately shut down—but the washer and dryer and Micaiah's gym equipment didn't care much about their surroundings.

Opposite the dining room and hidden by the interior kitchen wall, was the living room. It sported the same dark hardwood floors that graced the dining room and ran down the hall, but several area rugs brought color and life into an otherwise dull room whose only flaw was harkening back to a brief interior design fad of textured, multi-colored walls. It was supposed to be a bronze base with a textured overlay of black and gray. It was, in Tommen's opinion, hideous, but the twins liked it well enough and made it their own. The south outside wall was mostly giant bay windows, while an enormous mirror spanned the entire east outside wall. Heavy curtains draped the room in shadow, but even on a cloudy day, with the curtains open and the mirror in its place, the whole house lit up. In the summertime, it also turned the house into an oven. Micah joked that with such a system, it helped to cut down on the electricity bill. Opposite the mirror was the TV, big, but, as work demanded, used very little.

Down the hall were three bedrooms all in a row, two off the left side and one on the end, the bathroom sitting off the right side of the hall. The bathroom was unusually small for a rich house, but had no less vanity and money put into it. The same glorious tile found in the kitchen was also found in the bathroom, and a white marble countertop graced the vanity, the cabinets made of the same dark wood as the floors in the rest of the house and expertly matching the dark-painted walls. The shower was the epitome of bathroom luxury, featuring every unnecessary option known in the bathroom world at the time. More than that, it had also been the first installed model of that shower type, featured in a dozen or more magazines and commercials, showing off the wavy showerhead patterns and the soothing jets and water streams and whatever else they had come up with.

Tommen had only ever caught glimpses of Micah's and Micaiah's bedrooms as the doors were usually closed. He knew that they both had hardwood floors covered in area rugs that they changed out every few years, and they both slept in queen-sized beds with bedding that also changed every few years, but that was about it. Not that it mattered. Not like he was expecting to go running to them in the middle of the night with some scary nightmare, or because of some scary noises outside. He was vulnerable, but he wasn't stupid.

Instead, he made for the bedroom he would be using; he still refused to think of it as his room. For one, it was the only room in the house that wasn't pristine. Boxes and bags littered the area, accompanied by a multitude of instruction packets and owner's manuals. Only the little bed and a desk were cleaned off, and even the desk was questionable. Take-home paperwork from the bakery sprawled out across the surface, and a tiny trash bin on the floor was filled as much with dry pens and broken pencils as actual trash, which amounted mostly to snacks and candy bar wrappers. Did the twins ever actually sleep, or did they just Band each other so they could rest eight hours in only a few seconds' time before continuing in what appeared to be twenty-four hour days?

He tossed his bag on the bed, wondering if he shouldn't make an effort to clean the room and keep things in order. His mind wandered to how clean his room had been, how spotless Walter had made it in his worry. He looked at the boxes and bags. How long had some of this stuff been there? Should he try to keep instructions and manuals together? Should he keep the boxes? Should he just get rid of everything?

He'd barely picked up half a dozen tiny bags—the kind that the screws and hardware come in—when Micaiah stopped in the doorway.

"You don't have to worry about that now, if you don't want," he told Tommen. "We'll get it cleaned up. Might find a few things while we're at it."

"Just helping to clean the house," Tommen answered stiffly.

"Tommen."

Tommen stopped, dropped the stuff in his hands,

straightened, but did not look at him. It was a moment before Micaiah went on. "It's not your room. Yet. I know you don't want to give up on your dad. Neither do we. So until he's six feet under, let's you and us go about this like he's coming back. You're a guest here, and we're not holding you to more than that. Fair?"

Tommen sighed. It would be like the time Walter had gone to some police conference in Philadelphia, leaving him with the twins for four days, which was about all they had left now anyway. He'd been thirteen—well, close enough. Walter had been gone for his actual birthday, but made up for it by bringing back all sorts of goodies from Philly. The twins had been good to him, like crazy uncles. They wouldn't try to be his parents, but they would still exercise authority over him. But not until Walter was, as he said, six feet under. Finally Tommen nodded. "Fair."

"Good. That's all we can ask."

"But this room is still a mess."

"I don't deny that."

"I need to do something."

It was barely dinnertime but dark as midnight, damn daylight savings and axis tilts and all that. Micaiah shrugged. "All right. Fair enough. Just don't throw away any instructions or manuals or anything; leave those out so we can sort through them."

Tommen agreed and, once Micaiah left, set to work on picking up the clutter. He found the box and all the paperwork for a new toaster oven, for some kitchen handheld slicer doo-dad, for the desk in the corner, and various unmarked boxes and bags. At some point, Micah brought him a large garbage bag, and he stuffed everything he could into it.

It was good to have a task, something to keep his mind occupied. He didn't feel odd about cleaning the room either as long as he kept telling himself that he was just helping out the twins. They worked long and hard and didn't have time to do absolutely everything. This was just the room where they stuffed all the things that weren't quite as pristine as the rest of the house.

That was all a lie of course. Tommen was cleaning the room as much for himself as the twins, who did, in fact, have enough time to do just about anything they wanted. And there was no real excuse for not cleaning this room except just loafing and being lazy. Not that Tommen blamed them necessarily. All work and no play and all that.

"Tommen!"

Just by the tone, Tommen knew that Micaiah had been standing in the doorway for a while trying to get his attention. He probably didn't want to yell and make him feel bad about his hearing loss, but Tommen also knew that the elder Durvin twin had much less patience than his younger counterpart. This was probably testing his limits a little, too.

"What?" Tommen asked, trying not to sound either annoyed at being yelled at, or guilty that he hadn't heard.

"Why don't you take a break? All the Christmas movies are on."

"But I'm not done."

"Believe me, this room is cleaner than it's been in probably six months, if not longer. You've done a fine job. Take a break."

Tommen was hesitant, but stuffed the last of the trash in his hand into the larger bag and headed out to the living room with Micaiah. Micah was in the kitchen. Judging by the smell, he had the extra buttery popcorn in the microwave.

Micaiah picked up a smaller bowl of caramel corn and chose one end of the couch. Tommen elected for the recliner. When Micah walked in, he'd divided the butter popcorn into two bowls, handing Tommen one of them. It was extra buttery with a light dusting of cheese. All of it was entirely fake, but fake, sugary, and disgusting made for the best stress foods.

They watched several movies, some of them simultaneously by flipping back and forth during commercials, from *How the Grinch Stole Christmas* to *A Christmas Carol* to *Miracle on 34th Street*. By the time they got around to *National Lampoon*, Tommen was pretty sure he was on the out. That was the terrible thing about not being able to

Band things like TVs, phones, computers, and so forth. They had to watch everything in real time, which included having to endure commercials. Tommen was pretty sure he dozed off at least once during a commercial because when he blinked back to wakefulness, he knew he'd missed a scene or two in the movie.

It was past midnight before the major family Christmas movies ended and the only thing left was a string of B-movies, a marathon of R-rated Christmas movies, or a twenty-four hour feel-good reel of Hallmark movies. B-movies were fun to laugh at when one had the energy to laugh at them. Hallmark movies were nauseating. And while Tommen knew that the twins—that is, Micaiah—might enjoy the highly sexualized and vulgar R-rated movies, he was still decent enough to not subject Tommen to them before the age allowed by the movie rating bureau. Even if Tommen heard worse in school, watched worse online, and amused himself with worse fantasies. Fantasies he was still too afraid to attempt to entertain after being dream-raped by a white Borelian.

"You done?"

Tommen jumped, not sure if he had been asleep or not, but his jump made Micah jump.

"Sorry," Micah mumbled. "Are you finished?" He nodded to Tommen's popcorn bowl. All that was left were a few small pieces and a handful of kernels.

"Yeah." Tommen handed him the bowl. "Thanks."

"You look tired."

"A little."

"Might as well get some sleep. All the movies are over; no point in trying to stay awake."

Tommen shrugged and yawned. "I guess."

He dragged himself out of the recliner and glanced at Micaiah who was asleep on the couch, a blanket draped over him.

In that instant, Tommen suddenly found himself jealous of the twins. What he wouldn't give to have his older brother Teo with him now, to give him brotherly advice, to grieve with him in the loss of his dad, to tell him everything would be all right. What would he say right now, if he saw him? Would they even recognize each other? Would Teo grieve for Walter the same way Tommen did? Maybe not, but would he grieve at all? Would he understand how much Walter meant to his younger brother? Maybe not, but at the same time, Tommen knew Teo had always been compassionate. He might not understand, but he would understand.

How had they grieved when he, Tommen, disappeared? Did they have any idea where he'd gone? Had they searched? Had anyone else gone into the cave looking for him? Had they emerged after an hour, only to find that fifty years had passed? Were there still people in that cave looking for him, who would not come out for another hundred years? When had they given up? When did his pa finally admit defeat and call everyone home, saying, "It's no use. He's gone." Did he even have a grave or some kind of marker, hidden somewhere in those hills?

What had it been like—that first night, when they hadn't set a place for him at the dinner table; that first harvest, when they didn't have to scold him for picking on the girls; that first Christmas, when his ma didn't have to check that his clothes didn't have holes to let in snow? When did the hurt finally callous over?

Was that what this Christmas would be? They didn't normally spend it with the twins, but in his, Tommen's, absence, plans had changed and everything had been moved into their living room: the tree, the gifts, all of it. Would they open gifts? Probably. Would they open gifts that had been from Walter, even though they couldn't properly thank him? Maybe, depending on how they felt about it. What about the gifts that they'd gotten for him? Would they remain unopened? Should they be opened? Should they be returned? What was the protocol in this situation? How did other people do it when they lost loved ones so close to Christmas?

There was no good answer to those questions, Tommen decided as he got his toothbrush and toothpaste and headed to the bathroom. Sympathy, mourning, those were standard for any death—and some families couldn't even manage that. But there was no good way to handle the grief around a holiday or a birthday or any other special day. So what was there to do?

When Tommen had been around nine or ten, finally coming to realistic terms with his separation and what had happened, Walter tried to explain it using the analogy of him losing his first officer on the job, a car chase that ended in a shootout. Walter had gotten out unscathed, but his partner had been killed. Dead on contact; not even Walter's Banding could save him.

"You never forget," Walter had told him. "Sure, the specifics will fade, and maybe one day you'll forget their faces completely. But you never forget who they were, what they meant to you. And sometimes, far into the future, long after the wound has healed, something will suddenly remind you of them. A smell, a sound, a bit of déjà vu, or someone you could swear looks just like them. And you remember. And that memory is like a warm blanket on a cold winter night. And just like in the winter, the night is long and dark, and it seems like it will never end. Then it's okay to hold onto those memories. But when the summer comes and the sun breaks the clouds, it's time to let them go again."

Tommen rinsed his mouth and headed back to the bedroom, momentarily pausing in the doorway, stunned at how clean it had gotten. Not perfect, but a lot better. *Did I do that?* Then he shook his head, closed the door, turned out the light, and got into a bed covered in cold, cold blankets.

Chapter Three
Staying Up

It was like walking through the portal to the Wheel, except not. The portals to the Wheel just made Tommen feel like the wind had been forcibly sucked from his lungs. This...this was like having the wind sucked from his lungs, the blood from his heart, and his body stretched and twisted as if he was being tanned, his skin pulled and stretched and softened. He offered no resistance as Rifun grabbed him and started moving. His thoughts were sluggish, sensory input struggling to make sense of it all. It was dark, of that he was sure, but he could hear nothing but the ringing. Well, that wasn't entirely true, but when the only things to hear were heavy footsteps and heavy breathing, the ringing held a certain appeal.

By the time his brain realigned itself, a gag was shoved into his mouth, and his tongue was overwhelmed with the taste of used motor oil, dirt, and blood. He was bid move only when told and speak not. Or at least, that's what he was pretty sure Rifun was saying; he couldn't be certain, even in such close proximity.

Speaking of proximity, where had that bitch Isthim gone off to? He knew they'd gone through whatever portal or temporal distortion together, but since then, she had disappeared, taking Lily with her. Was she killing Lily? Had all this bravery and hostage negotiation been for naught?

Immediately, his thoughts turned to his dad. He would be coming. Deep down, something told him that this entire warehouse was rigged, booby-trapped; Walter would be walking right into it. He doubted that Rifun would let any backup get in. It would be him and Walter alone.

The warehouse hadn't looked that large from the outside, but from the inside with its high ceilings and maze of cargo destined for the ship that was conveniently late, it might have well been the Minotaur's labyrinth. Tommen wasn't sure where he was in relation to any exit, but his heart leapt with hope when he saw a flashlight beam shining up through the darkness. It turned off for a moment, then reappeared somewhere on the catwalk. Tommen prayed that Walter would be able to shine his light down and see him, even as he knew that would be impossible. The shadows cast by the cargo containers would fall far over him.

Walter did not stay on the catwalk for long, and when the beam flickered out so he could climb back down the ladder, Tommen did not see it reappear. For a minute or two, he might have thought that he could see the very outer edge of the beam, track his dad's movements from here to there, but in the end he was sure he was fooling himself.

He did not hear Rifun walk up behind him, did not hear anything that was said, though the ringing had gone, and he could hear the more bass sounds. As they walked, the hearing in his left ear gradually improved to give him mid-range sounds, enough to make out words as long as they were spoken loud enough and clear enough from a pretty close distance. Rifun right behind him was very much close enough to be heard and understood.

"Now, I'm going to take this gag off you," Rifun hissed in his left ear. "Do not yell, scream, or say a word. Daddy is on his way, don't worry. So we'll have a nice little chat without you sounding like an idiot trying to talk with no way to hear yourself. Got it?"

He could only nod. He hoped he was allowed to spit at least, which was the first thing he did when the gag was untied. Rifun only chuckled as he spit several times, trying to muster up enough spit and phlegm and whatever else to get that awful taste out of his mouth. He would be tasting that for a week, he was sure.

They met up with Isthim in a spot between a row of containers and an outer wall. Two chairs were set up. One was occupied. Lily sat tied to it, but slumped forward. He knew in that instant that she was dead. They'd succeeded. They had completed their mission to kill Lily Guile. All that followed with him and Walter was mere folly, a game that they had started and were going to finish, a side bet to be collected on a poker game, a significant sum but having nothing to do with the actual game at hand.

Then there was the flashlight beam, and he saw the electrical panel. Rifun gently maneuvered him into the chair, a slight squeeze of the shoulder reminding him not to make a sound. Walter walked up to the panel and opened it, first trying one switch, and then another.

Light burst into the warehouse, row after row of huge industrial lights switching or flickering on. Tommen was momentarily blinded, but tried to blink fast enough to clear his vision so he could see what was going on. His dad had come for him. He was here. He looked strained from the events of the afternoon, and why not? His blues were dark with sweat, hairline slick. He fought to control his breathing, his reflexes. Tommen knew Walter didn't like the dark. He knew Walter slept with a night light. He'd always assumed it had to do with too many scary calls at night; he had to see what was going on.

But as Rifun taunted him, challenged him, he was forced to wonder whether that was the full truth. He couldn't hear everything that was being said—he got most of what Rifun was saying, but only about every fifth word from Walter—but he was starting to get the feeling that Walter had never been fully honest with him. Sure, everyone from Time had a story, but he was forced to wonder about Walter's story. He'd never gotten it. As a kid it didn't matter, and so it seemed to be. But if it was strange enough and dark enough to kill for, what could it possibly be?

Whatever it was, apparently it was worth dying for, too, as Walter refused to divulge it, even as he looked on the verge of doing so. Instead, Rifun sighed and nodded to Isthim. She began changing colors. He thought he was seeing things, maybe the gag had been dosed with some sort of hallucinogen. Then Rifun started explaining that Isthim was a special kind of Borelian, one who could not only change colors, but change into any color, and she harbored every poison. She was the epitome of a Borelian warrior, so feared even by her own people that she had been pursued.

Fear coursed through him, but as he tried to shout and tell his father what colors did what, the gag was forced back into his mouth. But then, did it really matter which color did what, since they were all considered to be lethal? Even just being in proximity to her would have some nasty side effects.

Walter was no rookie boxer, but how did you beat an opponent you couldn't touch? How did you beat an opponent who could simply grab your gun and melt it? He bobbed and weaved, ducked and slipped behind, getting in blows where he could, but he would wear out far sooner than she would. She was practically playing with him.

The game he could stand. In the game, there was always a chance. It was when the game got boring that the fear turned to screaming, agonizing horror. Tommen wrestled against his restraints, chewed on his gag, did everything he could to break free. *Come on, let's go! This is the part in the movies where the underdog breaks free of his chains and runs to the rescue, surprising the bad guy from behind and saving the day.*

But this was no movie, and he was no underdog hero. He was the underdog who stayed an underdog and was forced to watch the bad guy gloat his victory, standing over Walter and pointing a gun straight at him, poison bullets at the ready. He saw the Band, how Walter tried to move Fast enough to dodge the bullet. He saw Rifun tear into that Band, at least forcing the bullet into Walter's shoulder, if not his head. Walter tried to hold the Band, but then the pain hit, and he couldn't do it. A second shot to the chest, a third in the thigh. The whole exchange lasted hardly a second.

Then Rifun turned the gun on him and fired.

Tommen tried to sit up in bed but found that he was caught,

tangled. He panicked, realized it was only the bedsheets, relaxed a little. Slowly, deliberately, he got his legs untangled and lay on his back. He was drenched in sweat, and the sheets were, too. He let out a breath he hadn't realized he'd been holding, found that the low rumble that tickled the edge of his hearing was only the furnace kicking on, the wind from one of the little vents fluttering some papers in an unknown corner he hadn't gotten around to cleaning yet.

He'd heard of PTSD of course—everyone had—but mostly that kind of stuff was reserved for the military or emergency personnel or survivors of catastrophe like 9/11 or something. The fuck was this? What was he, a coward? At the same time, he'd been kidnapped and involved in a shootout. He had been among those emergency personnel who put their lives on the line. Five of them had crossed that line. Five families would be celebrating Christmas without their loved ones. It might have been easier to bear except that was only two days ago that all this happened.

So it was certainly possible that he wasn't experiencing PTSD, but simple nightmares about a recent scary event. They would go away in time, he was sure, the same way his memories and nightmares of being separated from his family had died down to a dull ache and a collection of short stories in his notebook. Nothing terrifying or crippling there.

He took a breath, focused on the noise of the furnace, tried to use that as a sort of white noise to lull him back to sleep, but every time he reached that cusp, his body would jump into red alert mode, heart rate skyrocketing, skin breaking out in sweat, mind completely convinced that he was being watched or some sinister thing. He glanced around the room more than once, looking for anything to indicate that someone else was in the room, not the least of which would be some kind of wake from a Band. But there was nothing to be found.

Tommen sighed and closed his eyes. He needed to sleep, but his mind was awake now. Worse, his mind was wandering off into a realm he didn't want it to go. First, what did he think of his new room? It was bigger than his old room, could accommodate his furniture if he wanted it, or he could just upgrade to the nice furnishings in here. But he would have to make up his mind quickly and finally about that since, if he didn't want it, chances were it was going to be sold or donated. Because, you know, Walter was dying as he even thought about these things, what he thought about his new room and all that. *How selfish, to be thinking about getting new furniture while your father lays dying in the hospital. How cruel and thoughtless. Look at Micah and Micaiah, how they take you in so calmly, treat you as their guest, talk about how hard Christmas is going to be and everything that follows. Look at how they loathe the thought of going back to work because they have nothing to offer, no answer or cure for Walter's disease to draw them away. And you're thinking about new furniture.*

He squeezed his eyes shut and even put his hands on his head as if he could shut out the things that were already inside. He struggled to corral his racing thoughts, but he might as well try to catch minnows bare-handed. *And speaking of bare hands, how long has it been since you've had a little fun, hm? It's the middle of the night. You have your phone and the Internet password. Or, barring that, why not go back to that dream about the white Borelian? Why not let him touch your brain and tease you a little, make you sensually helpless? Wouldn't that be fun?* Tommen felt himself involuntarily grow hard, and he groaned and rolled over. He did not want to do this right now. All he wanted was to go back to sleep.

But his mind was a beast, chained, caged, and enraged. It was not a lion, prowling back and forth, looking for prey to devour necessarily. It was more like a hyena, going, going, laughing at him and mocking him. It was like a monkey, swinging back and forth from one thing to another, throwing all manner of things at him until it found the one arrow that struck true.

That's right, I've got you now, his mind said. *I control you. I control everything about you. And I get what I want. Because otherwise I'm going to keep running and racing and never let you get back to sleep. And right now, I want either the phone or the dream. Not that you can control your dreams, but I can. So which would you prefer? Watching someone else be rendered helpless, or being rendered helpless yourself? Because you like that. You know you do. Because I know you, and we like that.*

Was this more like talking to himself or hearing voices? Fuck, he was insane. Worst part was, he knew it was true, what his mind was saying. He was an addict of the worst kind, and because he had been cut off for weeks, his mind was reeling, unable to compensate. All the fantasies stored up in his brain were not sufficient. He needed more. Needed new ones, old ones, reimagined ones. Always, more, more, more. Feed the monster.

In an insane move, Tommen threw back the covers and sat up. For a moment, his mind was quiet, stunned by his move. This wasn't supposed to be part of it. He wasn't supposed to resist, wasn't supposed to grow stronger.

Oh, right, because he wanted to go out and watch some "TV" right? A little late night action?

Again, Tommen surprised himself by going to the bathroom instead. He went to the sink and splashed himself with cold water until his mind couldn't hold onto any kind of fantasy other than being cozy and warm—his whole body, not just his penis.

Fuck, but I am despicable, Tommen thought ruefully. *What would my pa think? Or Teo? They would probably take me out back and both give me a good switchin' followed by a long lecture and then a visit to the nearest priest for absolution. And I probably deserve it, even the last bit.*

In that moment, Tommen had to chuckle. Rifun was many things—a murderer, a thief, a lunatic, a zealot—but he was also very good at breaking people of their habits. Or maybe that was just a side effect of captivity, that Tommen had finally realized his glaring addiction and character flaw, enough to recognize it, be ashamed of it, and want to change it. So maybe that was a little bit of silver lining in all this darkness.

Of course, by that same token, Tommen would gladly have been addicted to any of a thousand things—sex, drugs, alcohol, video games—just to bring his dad out of the hospital not in a casket.

Walter would probably roll his eyes and say he would rather be dead and Tommen well and healthy, but given that he was currently in a coma, Tommen figured he was calling the shots right now. And if being a homeless heroin addict would have made Walter rise again, he would have done it.

Foolish fantasy, of course, and it did nothing for his morale. He couldn't trade places with Walter in any way, shape, or form. Somehow, he doubted that the Borelians would accept a lifetime of slavery in exchange for an antidote; more likely they would palm the antidote back into their own pockets and take him into slavery anyway. But what if his slavery was conditional upon Walter getting well? Were the Borelians that reasonable? All testimony to the contrary. So his best option was to come up with a solution that was more realistic.

If Lily said the toxin was like a poison that had entered the bloodstream, would any kind of CT or MRI show any kind of abnormalities in Walter's brain? Could that motivate the doctors enough to keep him comatose past his directive, at least long enough to give an antidote a shot? Something told Tommen that they'd already done such scans when he went comatose. As he'd had no brain injury—and apparently smacking his head on concrete didn't count—they would have to do a scan for an ideopathic coma. Wouldn't they? Was that a thing? Or if it was in the blood, what about cultures? Isn't that what they did on TV? More to the point, wasn't that what most doctors did anyway and what most patients complained about, a whole array of unnecessary tests and cultures and waiting, all to avoid litigation? Or were the doctors not worried about retribution from Tommen because he was a stupid teenager, or the police department because it could be written off as just a casualty of the firefight?

Or what if they had done everything, and to their eyes, it truly was an ideopathic coma? What if their tests just showed everything to be completely normal, except for the dying part? They would do what they could, maybe push the limits a little with his directive in order to pursue one treatment or another, but if there was no real hope to cling to, and Walter stopped breathing, they would pull the plug. And he would be gone, just like that. Game over.

Tommen found that he had sunk to his elbows on the countertop. Sometimes the only thing worse than his thoughts running wild was them being hyperfocused. And it always came back to this: what could he do? The angry, cynical side of him said nothing. He was powerless. He won the battle, got away from Rifun. But he lost the war. In the larger Time industry, even the battle had been lost. A Timekeeper Captain was dead, and the Runner responsible had not only gotten away, but he was in league with the Zero Hour who had granted all of them immunity. Battle, lost. War, hopeless.

But there was still that smaller, more feeble part of him that clung to hope, to reason. If there was an evil, there had to be a good. He was no philosopher, but there were some truths that were just fundamental. Darkness, light. Cold, heat. Poison, cure. It was a puzzle. It was just a matter of figuring out what the picture was, what the pieces were, and how to make them fit together to form that picture. The end was easy, once the picture started coming together and the pieces became fewer and fewer. The beginning was easy, too, just finding all the border pieces. But it was the part in the middle that was a bitch.

Problem was, Tommen felt like he had gotten a puzzle that either didn't have a picture, or it was one where it was just one solid color, and out of a thousand pieces, he'd only been given a hundred. All center pieces. And none of them fit together. He was going to have to manufacture his own pieces in order to make this work.

He ran a hand through his hair. He was exhausted. His mind was exhausted. He figured that he was pretty well-removed from the nightmare to go back to bed. But he just knew he would never be able to sleep.

He almost jumped through the roof at a gentle tap on the door.

"Tommen?" Micaiah asked from the other side.

"Yeah?" Tommen wondered.

"You...almost done?"

"Oh." Right. He was in the bathroom, and it was used for more things than midnight musings. "Yeah."

He opened the door. Micaiah stood there in a worn T-shirt and boxers, looking impassive and yet slightly strained.

"Yeah, sorry, go ahead," Tommen murmured, slipping past him.

Tommen did a few paces up and down the house, trying to be quiet but secretly wishing he was louder, because as he passed the bathroom once, twice, he found that the hardness he felt now was not from his mind screaming for addiction food. Rather, it was his bladder pleading for relief. When Micaiah finally came out after what felt like forever, he all but bulldozed him to get in to relieve himself.

Something about it also seemed to put his mind at ease. Maybe it was the simplicity of a normal bodily function. Something simple, primal, nothing that required extensive use of the more evolved parts of his brain, the ones that made him worry so fervently about his dad. Well, not quite true, since most animals experienced some kind of stress when herd or pack members disappeared, most especially if they were close kin. A mother dog having her puppies taken away for instance, or two old cats who had been together since kittenhood and one suddenly dies. Animals could get stressed over things, too.

He shut down that line of thought before it ran away and instead tried to somehow equate one bodily function with another bodily function, that is, sleeping. Something he needed to do in short order or else it would be morning already.

Whatever thoughts he'd been having about sleep quickly disappeared as he opened the door and found Micaiah leaning against the wall opposite the door, arms folded.

"Hi," Tommen said awkwardly, turning to head down the hallway.

"*Mar sin, céard atá ort?*" Micaiah asked. (So what's up?)

"*Am ait le haghaidh cuairt sóisialta.*" (Strange time for a social call.)

"*Tá a fhios agat céard atá i gceist agam. Seasann tú ag an doirteal ar feadh fiche nóiméad moill a chur ar fear, agus ní cheapaim go bhí sé mar bhí deacrachtaí agat a cac. Mar sin céard atá ort?*" (You know what I mean. You stand at the bathroom sink for twenty minutes keeping a guy waiting, and I don't think it was because you were having problems pooping. So what's up?)

"*Rud ar bith. Ach deoch an huisce uaim.*" (Nothing. Just needed a drink of water.)

Micaiah raised a brow. Tommen sighed. "*Rud ar bith. Ach...tromluithe.*" (Nothing. Just...nightmares.)

"*Faoi?*" (About?)

"*Rud ar bith.*" (Nothing.)

Micaiah frowned in a special way he had, one that almost made Tommen consider that there might be some kind of wrathful god out there somewhere waiting to strike him down with lightning at the slightest infraction. It was a frown that Tommen knew meant that it was too late. He should have just told the truth in the first place. Micaiah did not yell, did not raise his voice, did not get any kind of violent, but he had a way of talking that was brutally straightforward and cruelly honest. And it was always preceded by this frown.

"Tommen, you know us ninety percent of the time as simple bakers. We get up early, go to work, and bake a shit ton of food, more than we should be able to crank out. We work hard. So do you, when you work. But we're also Lieutenants of Timekeeping. It's easy to dismiss as some cute rank of some fictitious army in some fairy tale, but we are officers of a very real policing force of a very real dimension, even if that dimension is hidden to most human's eyes. As such, we have training that goes beyond mere Timekeeping abilities. It is training in hand-to-hand combat, a variety of weapons, a number of cultures and political systems. It is training in disciplines not even fathomable at the highest level of Earth-side education. But it is also training in some very basic elements of managing people, the grunts under us, the Masters, Journeymen, Apprentices, even probies like you. Some of these elements include psychology, which further includes how to spot a liar. And even then, I think even a common human with no training could say with confidence that you are lying to me right now.

"Under normal circumstances, I might dismiss it, say that your dreams are your dreams, same with nightmares. I'm not your mom to go crying to. But you've just been through a horrifying ordeal, and your dad is dying in the hospital. It's eating you up inside; I know it is. Playing tough guy isn't going to help, and it won't just magically go away. Time is not medicine, Tommen. It does not heal all wounds. Sometimes it just gives the infection a chance to fester." He let that sink in. "Now then, I'm going to ask again. Nightmares about what?"

Tommen took a measured breath. "Can we not stand right here in the hallway?"

"Fair enough. Where to?"

He certainly didn't want to go to his room like they were going to have some kind of father-son chat, and if they sat on the couch, he knew he'd be asleep instantly. The thought was mildly appealing until he realized that Micaiah would only wait until morning before again pursuing the conversation, this time with Micah. So he opted for the dining room table. The elder Durvin twin did not say anything as he sat down, just waited patiently for Tommen to speak.

So speak he did. He started out just recounting the nightmare. As he spoke, he realized that some elements of the dream were not quite true to what really happened, so he ended up having to go back and retell or clarify or admit that he just couldn't be sure about something. Sometimes he had to pause and think for a second, trying to separate the reality from the nightmare which had been too close to reality for comfort.

"But it was the very end," Tommen said finally. "After he shot my dad, he looked at me, pointed the gun at me, and fired. I mean, he didn't do that. Obviously. He just untied my gag and left me to watch him die. Why would I dream that he killed me?" He ran his tongue over his teeth. "Maybe, in killing Walter, he also killed me, or a piece of me. He's the only family I have—well, other than you two, but you know what I mean—and I really haven't known anyone else since I came into this Time."

Micaiah nodded thoughtfully. "Did you die in the dream?"

Tommen searched his memory. "I don't think so. I think the shot just scared me awake, but it was only the furnace kicking on."

"Just because he pointed a gun at you and fired doesn't mean he killed you. Maybe it was only a wound. Or perhaps a deliberate miss."

"Deliberate miss? Cai, we're talking about a dream. Well, a nightmare. It's terrifying, but other than some obvious components and psychological elements—like killing Walter also kills me—they don't mean anything. I mean, let's say that in the dream, Rifun deliberately missed when he shot at me. That would theoretically mean that he somehow spared me from something, for something, and I somehow subconsciously know this."

"Or that he also somehow is going to spare Walter. None of the wounds he inflicted on Walter were instantly lethal. The final shot, the one at you, missed."

"Again, somehow I would have to subconsciously know of some kind of plan that he has to spare him, and he made it abundantly clear that he intended to kill Walter. Kill Walter, kill me. That's all there is to it." Tommen stood. "Dreams are great, but they're only the products of our own overactive imaginations, not some subliminal message from God. Sorry."

With that, he headed back to the bedroom and got back in bed. The sheets had dried, but all the blankets were cold again. He stayed awake for a few minutes as his body heat warmed the bed, and even then, it was a minute or two before fatigue started creeping over him. Talking about his nightmare had eased the burden a little, and recounting what actually happened had helped to set his memory straight, or as straight as it could be. Even mulling over the psychology of it had been a welcome relief, like solving a puzzle. But there were no secrets or philosophies or messages hidden in dreams. It could seem that way, as the mind tried to present information that had been lost in the depths of time and memory, but there was nothing in dreams that happened that the person didn't already know or could come to understand. Such as killing Walter meant killing Tommen.

Wednesday

Chapter Four
Coffee and Christmas

Tommen woke slowly, feeling like he hadn't slept at all. He glanced at the little digital clock on the desk. Not even eight o'clock. If he went to bed at one, had a very unrestful sleep, and then spent an hour or so awake in the middle of that time, that meant that he got about six actual hours of sleep, but only a couple of truly restful sleep. Which meant that today was probably going to be miserable.

Merry Christmas to me. And fuck the rest of you, Tommen thought bitterly, pushing back the blankets and stumbling out of bed.

He made his way to his suitcase and pulled out a fresh set of underclothes before heading off to the bathroom. For as awful as he felt, a hot shower could usually do wonders to get him motivated for a few hours.

And hot damn, but that shower. For just a few minutes, Tommen forgot his problems and felt more like a little boy as he played with all the little knobs and controls, turning on this jet or that one, changing the water patterns, and generally having fun. At least until common sense got the better of him, that is, best not use up all the hot water before the twins had to jump in. He imagined they would be waking soon, if they weren't already either lying in bed or standing in line at the door, waiting their turn. One didn't just go from waking up every single day at four a.m. to sleeping in until noon. Force of habit would have them up before eight.

But to his surprise, there was no angry Irish mob pounding on the door, demanding to be let in. In fact, Tommen heard no signs of life whatsoever on the other side of the door. No moving around in the hall or clanging of pots and pans in the kitchen. Everything was

53

completely silent.

By the time he got back to his room—no, not his room, the room he was using—and got his clothes out for the day, the joy from the shower had gone, and he was back to being as melancholy as ever. The fun of the shower would ebb, as such things always did when they were experienced routinely. And if he was going to be staying here, he would use that shower routinely, with all its jets and water patterns. And so what?

With the motivation from the shower already burned out, Tommen slogged out to the kitchen and rummaged around for the coffee pot and assorted necessities. He was surprised to find an entire cabinet dedicated just to coffee. Not just the maker, but bags and bags of coffee. These weren't no run-of-the-mill bulk-buy coffees either. These were the ten dollars a bag, two pots per bag, kind of coffees. They seemed to have over two dozen different flavors from a number of brands and even a few foreign countries.

In Tommen's opinion, there were no "masculine coffees." Unless he was talking about just taking his coffee black, or maybe with a cream and sugar, there was no way any guy could say that he drinks the "Romantic Peruvian Sunset with Peppermint Ocean Breeze" and still retain his man card. That was just not going to happen. When brewed, coffee pretty much looked all the same. Call it black with cream and sugar, no matter the flavor, and carry on.

But still...what the hell?

Tommen knew that the coffee he was looking at was really expensive, and he felt guilty for taking a bag out—"Pumpkin Pie Christmas Latte with Caramel" sounded the most festive and thus less gay—but what was the point of having it if not to brew? After all, the name sounded festive, and it was Christmas.

Within seconds of the liquid dripping into the pot, the house was filled with the smell of pumpkin pie, as if one had just come fresh out of the oven and was just waiting for whipped cream and ice cream. It was uncanny. Tommen took a deep breath. Seriously, if coffee flavor names could just have simple names—for instance

"Peruvian Blend with Peppermint" or "Pumpkin with Caramel" — and not be marketed towards women, he might actually consider buying some of these nice coffees. Not that he necessarily drank coffee religiously, or even bought it. Mostly he just took a cup here and there from the bakery when it came time to throw out the old pot and make a new one. But damn, did it smell good. Holy shit, even the odor was caffeinated, and all that motivation that he'd lost suddenly came roaring back like a tidal wave. He could do anything. But fuck, he was wary of trying to drink the stuff directly. It was the difference between proximity and direct contact.

Despite the sudden connection to the Borelians, Tommen was largely unmoved, instead remaining intoxicated by the smell. Trying to tell himself it was curiosity and not an addiction-like jittery need, he found himself a mug and filled it just as soon as the last drop had fallen into the pot.

If there was a god, his name was Coffee. And not just any coffee, but—Tommen looked at the label on the bag—Jungle Gold, product of Belize. And he came in so many different flavors, dozens of tiny coffee religions all with their little nuances, just find the one that works for you. And right now, Pumpkin Pie Christmas Latte with Caramel was Tommen's religion of choice. And if all that were really true, it might have been enough to make him a believer. Maybe not in a God-type-god, but Coffee-god was close enough, right? Hot damn, but this was heaven.

"So you like the coffee?"

Tommen almost dropped his mug when Micah spoke. The younger twin was crossing the dining room and had an expression that was a mix of humor, trying not to laugh when he saw Tommen startle and almost spill the coffee, and guilt, startling him because he probably didn't hear him coming. Tommen hadn't heard him coming, but the intoxication of the coffee made it so he was practically unable to be cranky about it.

"What is this stuff?" Tommen asked.

"Good, isn't it?" Micah went to the cupboard, found a mug,

and poured himself a cup. "It's our little secret stash."

"How do you get this?"

"Through a Belizean Timekeeper—or Peruvian, or Brazilian, or whoever. They trade good coffee, and we provide bread and food for them for their families or their villages."

"So that's what you do with the leftovers at the end of the night," Tommen said.

Micah nodded. "Exactly. We consider it a fair trade."

"But...how is it this good? I mean, I've smelled and tasted so-called 'refined' coffee or just expensive coffee, and it was never anything like this."

Micah shrugged. "I don't know. I've asked, but all we get told is that it's a trade secret. I think they do it just to spite us and feed our addiction to it."

"No shit."

"So. Hungry?"

Tommen hadn't realized it, but the coffee also apparently gave him the munchies. He wondered if that was one of their "trade secret" secret ingredients. Maybe it was just him. "Sure."

Tommen knew there had to be something in the coffee, something that both heightened the senses while dulling any emotional pain. He became acutely aware that he was supposed to have been responsible for the Christmas ham. Like the Thanksgiving turkey, he was supposed to prepare it the night before so it would be ready to eat in the morning before his dad had to go to work. And yet, even as he knew this, he found that he couldn't quite muster the same soul-crushing emotion as he should have been able to. This was Christmas. His dad was dying in the hospital. He felt the twisting hurt in his heart, and yet it didn't slow him down or dampen his spirit much. It was way too soon for this to be the day that he just woke up and everything was better, hope had returned, and yet, Christmas wasn't that festive or important to him.

"You sleep well?" Micah asked, his tone suggesting he was speaking loud over the hissing of butter in a pan, but Tommen just heard him normally, more or less. The butter was almost invisible.

"Not really," Tommen answered, deciding to play it safe and assume that the twins would talk. No use lying to him if Micaiah would just tell all about their little chat the night before—or earlier that morning, depending on how one wanted to look at it.

"I'm sorry. But one bad night usually means a better second night, am I right?"

He was trying to play it off, play it safe, and again Tommen found that his emotional response was muted. He knew the implications, knew what Micah was really saying he was sorry about, and yet he wasn't mortally wounded.

Or maybe he really was getting better, just a little bit. Enough that he could function without having to tiptoe around every word.

Nah, he still blamed the coffee.

Tommen had only ever really seen the twins bake. Measure ingredients, mix, beat dough, cover for the first rising, put in the oven to bake, decorate. He'd never really appreciated their cooking abilities, like how Micah forsook all recipes and measuring utensils, instead flying by the seat of his pants in a whirlwind of ingredients. This thing needed more onion? Okay. More onion. How much? Who cares! *More!* That dish needs more sausage or cheese? Go for it! No need to weigh and measure and consider how to price it out. Just toss in a pinch or a whole handful. It was the joy of just being able to cook for its own sake because something tasted good, and doing it all in real time. No Banding here; if something burned, it was your own damn fault.

At some point, Tommen noticed the bathroom door was shut and the light on. A moment later, Micaiah emerged, still wiping down his hair with a towel.

"*A Mhicah, chan eil barraí sopa againn,*" he said. (Micah, we're out of bar soap.)

"*Beidh ort fanacht go dtí amárach,*" Micah told him. (It'll have to wait until tomorrow.)

"*Shíl me go cheannaigh muid sopa.*" (I thought we just bought some.)

"Ní cheannaigh muid." (Nope.)

It was easy to forget which day it was, especially when there was a lot of Banding involved, Tommen figured. Still, he found it amusing as Micaiah scowled and tossed his towel back in the bathroom.

"I hate shopping the day after Christmas," he grumbled as he entered the kitchen and went to the fridge for the orange juice. "Don't like working it much either, but it's a good day for business." He drank straight from the carton.

Tommen simply shrugged. "Coffee?"

Micaiah put the orange juice back and glanced at the coffee pot, only about half empty. He raised a brow at Tommen. "So you found our stash?"

"Yeah."

The elder twin got a mug and poured himself a cup. "Horrible stuff."

"Come on, Cai, you drink it more than I do," Micah said from the oven as he pulled out a pan of biscuits.

Micaiah just shook his head and rolled his eyes, but he did not disagree.

"All right, gentlemen, breakfast is served."

Breakfast was a beast, each person given enough to feed five more people. It was like the world's biggest five egg omelet stuffed with every ingredient imaginable—from the routine sausage, cheese, onions, and peppers, to the more unusual olives, banana peppers, carrots, orange chunks, and spinach, even crispy chicken strips cut into chunks. This was set in a bed of tiny cubed hashbrowns of both russet and sweet potatoes, heavily seasoned, and layered in cheeses of all varieties. Then the whole thing was surrounded by small homemade biscuits and drowned in peppery sausage gravy. Then there was a second plate of three huge pancakes with melted butter on them while a bottle of real maple syrup sat in the center of the table. And as if that wasn't enough, there was also a saucer off to the side with a bagel and cream cheese as well as an English muffin.

And Tommen was accustomed to leftover pizza or peanut butter toast.

"How do you expect us to eat all this?" he asked incredulously, taking a seat and staring at the bounty before him.

"With diligence and joy," Micah replied with a smirk.

Micaiah sat in his seat but only frowned at his food.

"Did I forget something?" Micah asked.

Micaiah seemed uncertain for a moment, which almost made Tommen afraid. He was never uncertain. Pissed, exasperated, annoyed, but never uncertain. Finally he said, "I know Tommen doesn't want anything to do with it, and neither of us is particularly religious or have the faith that Walter has...but for Walter's sake, I don't think it would hurt to pray over the food."

Tommen's stomach leapt as Micaiah managed an awkward, halting prayer. He wasn't uncomfortable from the prayer itself, but from some irrational hope that something might come out of it. He hated the hope, hated the fear of that hope. If Walter got better, did that mean the prayer worked? If they didn't pray and he lived, was it just saving God the bother of looking down? If they didn't pray and he died, would it have made a difference? There were all sorts of stories of people who claimed that prayer healed them or made things go smoothly, but there were just as many people who prayed and weren't healed. Who made the rules on these things?

Simple: biology. Biology made the rules. Tommen did his best to swallow the fear, the hope, and the irrationality. It was biology that had poisoned Walter, and biology that would either save him or kill him. There was no intervention to be found here. No one was coming to magically save the day. There was no use hoping or crying or praying, because no one was listening.

He came to that conclusion just as the prayer ended, digging into the food laid out before him and being almost unable to comprehend it just as he was unable to comprehend the deliciousness of the coffee. Why were they bakers and not restaurateurs? They could be mistaken for master chefs.

Well, it really could have been an exaggeration. Maybe he really was healing just a little bit, enough that taste and his appetite had come back, though no appetite was great enough to finish all the food Micah had put out before him. In the end, they all had dishes in the fridge with their names written in black marker. It was probably going to be their lunch and dinner, if not their breakfast the next morning, too.

Okay, so that was an exaggeration, too. Lunch, maybe dinner if they really couldn't stomach it all. Dinner appetizer. A snack. But between the coffee and the food, Tommen was feeling rather giddy, drunk even. Maybe that's what festivity felt like.

Except the next order of business in their regularly scheduled festivities brought the real world back to the front door. Presents.

Years ago, it was cute to have Tommen hand out the gifts to everyone. These days, it was pretty much just habit. Tommen was able to kind of tiptoe around the uncomfortable part of the gift-giving by handing out the cards and getting out the presents that the twins had gotten for each other or gotten for him.

The cards, not surprisingly, were nice little well-wishing things, but the real prize was the gift cards stuffed in them. For Tommen, that meant $25 to spend on downloading music and another $25 to go clothes shopping. Not exactly a subtle hint. *Okay, Dad, I get it. And I need a haircut, too.*

For some reason, it was easier to open the card from Walter, maybe because mail felt a little more impersonal, like a note left on the fridge saying something like, "Sorry I couldn't make it, be back soon."

Presents, though, they demanded to be opened in the company of those who had sent them. Excepting people separated by great distances, this was like an unwritten rule. It was respectful to the gift-giver, and it made them feel good. For example, Micaiah opening his gift from Tommen—a deluxe platinum super extended cut whatever-else edition of all the *Star Wars* movies (so far)—made

Tommen feel pretty good. Micaiah was happy to get it, and Tommen was almost just as excited to see him get it. He was also just as excited when Micah opened his present, a similar deluxe platinum et cetera et cetera *Lord of the Rings* set.

"We're not going to leave this house for days with these," Micah said, grinning, as he and his brother compared features and run time and everything else.

"Dude, we don't have to," Micaiah chuckled. He looked at Tommen. "Thank you."

It was nice to see the twins in a mood other than "business." To see them now was like watching a couple kids his own age geeking out about some nerdy fad. Personally, he was more into *Star Wars* than *Lord of the Rings*, but hey, they were kids. Let them have their fun.

"So, go on, open up your presents," Micah prompted.

The twins' idea of wrapping presents really didn't go much beyond putting the gift in a bag and stuffing it with enough tissue paper to choke a horse, and Tommen went digging for China, or so it felt.

Confusion met his fingertips a second before the fabric did and he pulled out a T-shirt, tied around the neck and the waist with a ribbon. It was beige with a picture of white sunglasses and "Yes, I'm a nerd. I'm also your boss." Beneath that was a long, complicated mathematical equation. Curious, Tommen turned the shirt around. On the back was an illustrated and somewhat exaggerated picture of a graph depicting one stick figure on one side in sunglasses, throwing something at another stick figure on the other side with a big "Boom!" and the line on the graph following the path of whatever projectile was supposed to be drawn. It might have been a basketball. Or a nuclear bomb. He really couldn't decide.

As he moved the shirt around, he flet something moving inside, held fast by the ribbon. He laid it down and undid the ties. Then he reached inside and pulled out three magazines, *Popular Science, Popular Mechanics,* and *Scientific American.*

"Whoa, nice!" Tommen exclaimed.

"Full year subscription to each of them," Micah told him.

"That's awesome. This is great. Thank you."

It didn't occur to him until about ten seconds later that the magazines would be sent to his house, the one that was probably going to be sold in a couple months. He quickly chased down the nausea by simply trying to figure out how to set up a mail forwarding at the post office. After all, it was just a simple move, and magazine subscriptions could be treated as impersonally as greeting cards, right?

They sat there for a moment longer, nerding out over their respective presents, but after a minute or two, it became forced, like someone pretending to be really interested in their work and ignoring something else going on. The white elephant. And this white elephant was as big as the room and, Tommen thought, more reminisce of the COPD commercials he saw with the person with an elephant on their chest.

"So, what about the rest of the presents?" Tommen asked finally.

The twins looked at each other uncomfortably. It was Micaiah who spoke, setting aside his gift and leaning on his elbows. "I think...we could open the ones from Walter. He got them for us and meant for us to open them and have them to use and enjoy. I think he would want us to celebrate with or without him. He was scheduled to work today after all, so we ought to treat it as such.

It was a thought to hang onto, and Tommen slowly distributed the next round of gifts. Walter had a magic touch when it came to wrapping presents. The twins preferred bags and tissue paper, and Tommen knew he wasted more paper than he needed to use as he haphazardly wrapped and layered and frantically taped. Walter, however, was a master of crisp edges and perfect lines, ends folded over neatly and cut straight, using only just enough tape and being able to hide even that, so it looked like he picked them out of a magazine or something.

For the twins, he got two gifts. The first was a set of T-shirts, ripping on Thing 1 and Thing 2 from Dr. Seuss, instead reading Baker 1 and Baker 2. Then, as the twins unfolded those, there was a second set of shirts, the second set being green, presumably, and reading Báicéir 1 and Báicéir 2, the same as the first but in Irish, appropriately.

The second gift was a box of snacks from some online snack company along with a $25 gift card to use on the company's website. Something about picking out different snacks and having them shipped directly to their house every week or every month. Tommen didn't understand it, but the guys thought it was pretty cool, and they apparently understood how it worked. It suited them, actually, since they survived more on snacks than food while they worked.

Tommen couldn't deny he was a little hesitant about opening his gifts. Truthfully, he was always a little anxious about destroying Walter's pristine wrapping job, but now he wasn't sure he ever wanted to know what lay beyond the paper. It was like, this was the last time Walter would ever give him a Christmas gift. Did he really want to open the packages now and ruin all the joy and the magic forever? Could he save them until next Christmas when he might be a little more ready for it?

His fingers found the tape before his mind could brood too much longer, and he made at least a semi-conscious effort to not completely rip off the paper like an excited child. The box itself was fairly small, maybe four by four by four, and when the paper came off, it more resembled some kind of box that jewelry came in, hard and supposed to resemble leather or something. When he opened it, he was even more confused.

"A watch?" he wondered, taking it out of the box.

It wasn't even an expensive-looking watch. Not that he expected—or wanted—a Rolex or anything, but it looked pretty much like any watch sold in, say, Walmart. Sure, it looked pretty with its braided brown fake-leather band and fake rhinestones around a bright white face and shiny hands, but it was cheap. Walter didn't do cheap gifts. Inexpensive, but not cheap. If Walter gave a cheap gift, it was secretly an insult.

But Micah seemed to understand. "That's not just a watch, Tommen. That's a Time watch."

"Don't all watches keep time?"

"No, Time. Capital T. As in the Time industry."

"Oh." Which meant this thing was probably, relatively speaking and accounting for currency conversion, probably uber expensive and cost Walter a few months of his Captain's salary. "So what does it do that a regular watch can't?"

"It can tell you the time of any place anywhere. In the event that you ever went to the Wheel and visited another world, you would always know what time it is on Earth. If that world keeps time, it would tell you that local time, too. And it would tell you the local time or time of day of anywhere that the Time industry touches."

"Wow." Tommen put it on his wrist and started fumbling with the little buttons on the side. Presently, it looked like any regular watch, but as soon as he started messing with it, it came to life like a smart watch, giving him menu after menu after menu, and option after option after option. He even found, somewhere in the depths of the settings and customizations, a way to change how it physically looked. He could change the color of the band, the style, the color of the face and hands, even make it digital or analog. He could make it look like some cheap kids plastic watch, or the most expensive and modern Rolex on the market.

"He was going to get you that after your review once you'd become an Apprentice," Micaiah told him.

"Why did he change his mind?" Tommen wondered, not sure if he wanted to know the answer.

"After you disappeared and it became more likely that he might have to sacrifice himself to get you back, he wanted you to have this when you went into your review, so it was like he was still there with you when you stood before the Hands."

If not for his own selfish pride, Tommen might have burst into tears right there, maybe torn the watch off and stormed off toward the bedroom or bathroom like a petulant child. But he didn't, instead just looking down at the watch and wondering if this might be the only thing he would ever have left of his dad. Goodness knew he had nothing left of his pa or brother, nothing but their memories.

"It looks good on you," Micah told him. "But then, you can customize it however you want. And where he got it from, those watches are pretty much guaranteed to last a thousand Base Years."

"Do I have to take it to the guy to get it wound up or something after that?" Tommen asked, unable to stop a grin.

"Nah. Even better that it doesn't need batteries either."

"So how does it run? What's the power source?"

"Watchmaker's secret." Micah shrugged.

Tommen looked at the watch again. It was an unassuming thing, ticking away like any ordinary watch.

"I want to see him," he said.

The twins agreed wordlessly, but they didn't just up and leave like a bunch of zombies. There was still stuff to clean up. Micah got a trash bag while Micaiah and Tommen rummaged around and collected all the wrapping paper scraps, big and small, tiny pieces of tape that went unnoticed until they got stuck on the bottom of a sock, a barcode sticker with the price inked out that labeled someone as having an unknown price (there were not a few jokes about that one).

Then they gathered their scattered gifts and scurried away to add it to their piles of loot. Tommen hadn't even opened the second gift Walter gave him. Compared to the watch it seemed unimportant. Maybe it was a just-as-important Earth-side gift, but he had no real wish to open it just yet. Maybe he would save that one until after his review. He would take Walter with him in the form of this watch, and then save the congratulatory gift until afterwards.

By the time he got back out to the living room, Micaiah was just putting away the vacuum cleaner and Micah was pulling on his boots.

"Should we take his presents?" Tommen wondered. When the

twins looked at him blankly, he clarified, "Maybe it will help him. Just a little. Maybe we can open them for him. Or else they'll never be opened until we decide to toss them, and then it won't be Christmas and—"

"Tommen, slow down," Micaiah said forcefully, but not unkindly. "Okay, we'll take the gifts."

Once again, Micah got a bag while Micaiah and Tommen gathered up the gifts. There were only two real wrapped or bagged presents and a single card. Once everyone had gotten their boots and coats and hats on, Tommen took the bag of gifts and followed the twins out to Micah's car this time.

The snowing and blowing had ebbed to a gentle floating snow, the kind where the flakes stay in the air forever and never actually quite hit the ground. The sun was just at an angle where it lit up the mountainside and pretty much the entire subdivision. It didn't matter whether a person were driving north, south, east or west, the snow was pure crystalline beauty and, as they say, love is blind. Tommen ducked childishly behind the front seat as the twins fished out sunglasses before Micah finally started the engine. The car gave a hesitant cough, paused to see if he would give up, then reluctantly came to life in a grumbling, whirring, buzzing kind of way.

The blinding white snow became less of a nuisance the closer they got to the city, where dirt, salt, sand, and all manner of oils and fluids were spilled on the road and scraped up and thrown every which way by the snow plows, turning rolling white hills into small piles of black slop.

The city was less busy than it usually was, but it was still busy. People were still traveling which meant gas stations were open, a few chain restaurants were open, and about half the retail stores in town were gearing up to open later that night. Preventative maintenance, some said, relieving the pressure of people who just had to go out and spend their Christmas money or exchange an ill-fitting shirt or pair of pants. Because December 26th would be too late. They had to show off everything right away or else be thought poor and destitute. Gift-giving and peace on Earth was nice and all, but buying stuff was what it was really all about. Like a Black Friday for Christmas.

In the middle of it all, of course, were the inevitable accidents and other assorted activity. Cars in ditches or sliding through red lights notwithstanding, the holidays were prime time for domestic violence, theft, vandalism, even rape. Tommen remembered thinking once that if there was slightly less emphasis on being with family during the holidays, some of the problems might be solved. After all, how often did people get shamed for not going to visit their parents for Christmas, never knowing that to do so would be to invite a beating or a screaming match that would only end in tears? When was it better to simply stay away from family over the holidays? It wouldn't solve all the problems, true, but maybe a few of them.

They were slowed down briefly by a car accident that had reduced traffic to one lane, being directed by a very cranky police officer, one Tommen didn't recognize. He followed all the rules of directing traffic, but just barely, only allowing a few cars through at a time despite the backup both ways. It was a battle he couldn't win anyway. Let one through or all of them through, no one was going to be happy about the delay.

They slowly moved forward and were forced to stop, the first in line for the next go ahead, sitting almost right next to the officer. Micah rolled down his window. The officer did a poor job of disguising his disgust, obviously thinking Micah was going to bitch at him about the job he was doing. But instead, Micah simply said, "Merry Christmas, officer."

The officer sighed and nodded once. "Merry Christmas. Be safe out there."

"How's the department doing after Monday?"

Now the officer paused and he gave Micah a wary look. Finally he said, "We're still trying to process it. Holidays aren't giving us a lot of time to do that."

Micah nodded. "We're on our way to visit his dad in the

hospital." He jerked his thumb towards the back seat. "Walter Forbes."

The officer had been walking, and as soon as Micah mentioned the name, his legs just about went out from under him. Once he got himself steadied, he slowly approached the car and glanced in the back. Tommen could only stare.

"Your dad's a hero, Tommen," the officer told him, his voice slightly muffled. "Everyone in the department is rooting for him. You tell him that when you see him, all right?"

"I will," Tommen told him, his voice straining.

Then the officer backed up and motioned them on. They were only about two blocks from the hospital and made it there without further incident. Christmas or not, the parking lot was always full, and it felt like it took longer to find a parking spot than it did to get to the hospital. When they were finally parked, Tommen grabbed the gifts, and they went inside.

Nothing had changed since the previous day. The hospital itself was still festively decorated with little plastic wreaths and garland, shiny tinsel and ornaments galore, from angels and baby Jesus to Mickey Mouse and Darth Vader wearing a Santa hat, holding a candy cane lightsaber. Nametags were written in multiple colors and decorated, and any staff members who weren't in scrubs wore the ever-popular ugly sweaters, probably for some office contest.

They made it to ICU unopposed, and that was where the holidays seemed to stop. Intensive Care, with exception of the reception desk, was as cold and uncaring as ever. No ornaments hung from door handles, no tinsel hung from the lights. Even the single strand of scraggly garland that sat on the reception desk made it feel oddly underdressed. The receptionist had on a tasteful Christmas sweater and a little sparkly barrette in her curly hair, but that was all.

"Forbes, Walter," Micaiah said, walking up.

She nodded. "I remember."

"How's he doing?"

"Why don't you see for yourself?"

She did not say it reassuringly, with a knowing twinkle in her eye and a grin in her voice, suggesting that maybe Walter was up and around and recovering, and it was like some little Christmas surprise the hospital was waiting to spring on them, like the end of some Hallmark story. Rather she spoke coarsely, as if they were interrupting her Christmas, as if they were the reason she was working and not at home with the grandkids, and by getting them through the door and out of the reception area, she could go home.

They moved past the reception desk and headed down the hall toward Walter's unit. When they entered the room, though, they were surprised to find Lily already there, sitting at Walter's bedside, staring at nothing.

"Lily," Micaiah acknowledged. "What are you doing here?"

"Paying my respects." She sounded exhausted, like she'd been up all night. "Praying for a miracle."

"Is he worse?" Tommen asked fearfully.

"No. Actually, by Harvesting standards, he's doing very well. He's maintaining. His clock isn't ticking down, or not as fast, which suggests that he is fighting, or trying to."

"How long does he have?" Micah wondered.

She sighed and looked longingly at Walter. "Six days, twenty-one hours, eleven minutes, fifty-eight-point-seven-three-four seconds."

"That's good, though," Tommen said. "I mean, maybe he'll pull through. Have the doctors done any sort of treatments on him?"

"Not since I've been here. But it's still highly unlikely he'll recover." She went on before he could continue. "It's just like any foreign body disease, Tommen. All of us here, we're accustomed to the diseases found here. We've all experienced probably the same strains of cold, flu, and cold sores. Any of us travel outside the country, that's a whole new set of diseases and strains, and we're going to get sick because we don't have he antibodies to fight them off yet. This is like that, except it is a far more deadly poison, one that he can fight and strain against, but in the end, it will win."

Tommen shook his head. "No. I don't believe you."

"It's not a matter of believing me, Tommen. It's going to happen."

"No." Fuck, were those tears? "Comatose patients are helped best by touch and having those they love around them. And we brought his Christmas presents. We're going to open them for him, and maybe we'll leave them here so he always knows we're here, even when we're not. Just like he got me this watch to take into my review."

Lily glanced at the twins but said nothing, instead standing up and moving out of the way. "Very well, then. Unwrap away."

"Why don't we unwrap each other's gifts for him?" Micah suggested. "Tommen opens the ones from us, and we open the ones from him? That way it doesn't feel like we're just unwrapping our own gifts."

So Tommen went first, opening the card envelope, reading the front aloud and then being momentarily distracted as something fell in his lap. He picked it up and raised a brow at the twins. "A gift card to the bakery? Really?"

The twins grinned, and Micaiah spoke. "It was supposed to be a joke."

"He's your best customer, and half the time you let him just take stuff on the house."

"Like I said, it was supposed to be a joke. Keep reading."

Tommen finished reading the card, although the seriousness of the words had lost all meaning as he could barely keep a straight face. A gift card to the bakery. It was like giving someone a hundred dollars so they could go and buy you a one hundred dollar birthday present. Joke or not, Tommen was forced to wonder what possessed them to choose that; they had no shortage of pranks they could pull. He'd been on the receiving end of those pranks more than once.

It didn't matter, he supposed, and moved on to unwrapping the gift, or rather, fishing for it amid a sea of tissue paper. There were a few things in the bag, the first being a blue coffee mug with some snarky, sarcastic remark about coffee and police officers. The second was a police magazine that Walter got sometimes, probably a year subscription. With that was a baseball cap with a generic sheriff badge printed on the front and the name of the magazine on the back.

So Tommen put the mug near Walter's right hand, and the magazine near his left, choosing to let the hat rest on the uninjured shoulder as his head was still taped with gauze in the back.

Micah got the honor of unwrapping Tommen's gift while Micaiah took it out of the packaging remains and lifted it out. It was a set of various iron-on patches. Walter had a large sheet of old burlap he kept hung in his room, and he sewed or pinned patches onto it from places he visited, things he'd seen, people he'd met, things he'd done. This particular set of patches Tommen had found just by chance on the Internet one day, and he'd managed to convince Eric to use his credit card to buy it and paid him back.

They were police patches, from 1* to World's Greatest Police Dad to I Pulled My Own Kid Over Yesterday How Lenient Do You Think I'm Going To Be With You? Walter had never put up any police patches as they referred to himself. Conferences, symposiums, trainings, other police departments, sure, he collected those, but never anything that he felt glorified himself. Tommen was proud of his dad and figured that maybe if he bought the patches, then Walter would have to add them to his canvas. These Tommen elected to put inside the hat and set it back on his shoulder, careful that the patches didn't fall out.

Nothing happened then. There was no miracle. Walter didn't suddenly take a deep breath and open his eyes, and the vital monitor did not show anything else going on. Though Tommen thought the EEG might have caught something, he was no doctor. He couldn't be sure.

"You did good," Lily said from the end of the bed. "You actually managed to buy him four more seconds."

Tommen reached for Walter's hand. "That's good, though,

right? He has a chance."

"All Time is borrowed, Tommen. Borrowed or stolen. The only time when Time is actually created is when new life is created. Your dad is no spring chicken, and his time is coming."

Tommen shook his head and threw up a Band so fast and so tight, he thought that the twins might visibly flinch once he released it and went back into Base Time. He looked at Walter's face, expressionless and yet peaceful.

"I will find a way to bring you back, Dad," he said, fighting the urge to cry and bury his face in his father's chest. "You just keep fighting, keep holding on. I'll find a way, even if I have to sell myself into Borelian slavery."

Chapter Five
Forbes Cave

Tommen wasn't sure how long he waited in the car, wasn't sure how long it was before the twins finally left Walter's bedside and came looking for him. He spent his time in the car watching the snow fall, occasionally Fast Banding so he could study a snowflake up close, or alternately Slow Banding to make it seem like a blizzard. Eventually, though, the twins found him. Micah opened the driver's door and stopped.

"Can I help you?" he wondered.

"Can I drive?" Tommen asked.

Micah raised a brow. "Normally, I would consider it, and probably say no because of how icy it is. Given your present emotional state, I would say no even if it was the middle of summer. Get in the back."

"I'm fine," Tommen protested. "I mean, I know where I want to go and what I want to do."

"I thought we were going home."

"Well, yeah, eventually, but there's something I want to do first."

"Then give him the directions," Micaiah said as he got in the passenger seat and clicked the seat belt. "Get in the back."

Tommen wanted to protest and remind him of his words to treat him as a guest until Walter died, but he knew that would get nowhere. For one, many guests would be pleased at being driven around, especially when the roads were icy. But there was the matter of Tommen not having his license and not being familiar enough with the vehicle to drive halfway decently on the roads, especially

73

considering where he wanted to go. So, reluctantly, he got out of the driver's seat and into the back seat.

"So, where are we going?" Micah asked, starting the car and letting it warm up for a minute or two.

The accident where they'd spoken to the grumpy officer was just cleaned up and the road just being reopened for normal use. Micah waved to the officer as they went by but did not stop. Short days and tall mountains meant that everything had melted while the sun had been overhead and blinding everyone. Now everything was starting to refreeze as the sun disappeared.

Tommen was just as secretive about their destination once they got on the highway out of town. It wasn't that far away, the place they were going, not really any farther than the twins' house, though it seemed farther just because it was unfamiliar. It was kind of like they were heading home, but making a right instead of going straight.

He wasn't sure why he was keeping it a secret. On the surface, it was just a little strange. Most of the parks were technically closed, but they still had trails for cross country skiing and snowshoeing and such. It was only if the twins got smart enough to look at a map that they might get worried. With any luck, Tommen could just Band and be out of the way and have some time to himself before they realized where he went.

"Those were some nice patches you got your dad," Micah said conversationally.

"Yeah, I found them online," Tommen said. "I thought maybe if I got them for him, he would have to put them up on his wall."

"So where are we going?" Micaiah asked irritably. He was not a fan of surprises. Few people were, but few people were as vocal about it, too.

"It'll be a left up here."

Tommen had only been out this way a couple times, usually with Eric and Varad. Eric was better at cross country than downhill, and every so often he managed to talk the rest of them into it, too.

The bribe to do it was usually booze and weed; they would go out cross country skiing up one trail and down another until they were out as far as they could go on the trails. Then they would take off their skis and go a short distance to some pine trees or bushes or something, get high, get a little tipsy, return to the trail, and keep going like nothing ever happened. Fuck, that felt like so long ago. Tommen couldn't even remember a time when his biggest worry had been getting caught and Walter taking him out to the woodshed.

They snaked their way up the mountain, the valleys becoming draped in shadow and ascending to the peaks like an angry cloud of despair.

"Are we going to be here long?" Micah asked. "Wherever we're going? It's getting dark."

"Nothing a little Banding won't take care of," Tommen said smartly. "And it shouldn't be too long."

Strictly speaking, in a Band, he could be here for hours, or at least until he couldn't feel his toes anymore. Contemplation and reflection was like that. It took time; it wasn't on demand. Hopefully the cold could motivate it just a tiny bit so he wasn't forced to come back to continue his reflection and contemplation. It was good that Walter was fighting and holding on just a little while longer, but Tommen didn't mean to squander that time. If he was going to come up with a solution to the problem, he meant to do it as quickly as possible.

You hear me, Contemplation and Reflection? You better come to me pretty quickly, and bring along your friends Idea and Solution because otherwise I'm just some so-called wise man sitting on top of a mountain.

"Intersection," Micah said. "Which way?"

Tommen looked out the windshield, trying to get his bearings. Funny how he knew this place better in the summer, when the last time he'd been here in the summer was years ago when he was a child. Micah slowed down and he and Micaiah looked at him expectantly.

"Left," Tommen finally decided, and instantly he knew it was the right direction.

The park looked much bigger during the summer when all the picnic tables were set up, the playground was cleaned up and bright with color, the maps were dusted off and set out in the open on display, the trail signs were freshly cleaned, and the paint on the various directional arrows was touched up. But now, all but one of the tables had been put away, locked in a storage building. The playground was little more than a giant snowy lump in the middle of a snowy landscape, only the faintest hints of color peeking through the ice built up on its rails and assorted obstacles. The maps had been moved under the main pavilion and set up so they somewhat formed two walls and a windbreak, but still they were crusted with snow. The trail signs had the rough brush marks of snowshoers and skiers kind enough to keep them clean, but the taller signs with their directional arrows were all gone, disappeared behind a crust of snow and ice.

Only the parking lot gave any indication that the place was cared for, or at least acknowledged by the city during the winter. It was reasonably plowed, the snow banks pushed back to fill in a depression just off to one side. By winter's end, it would be a roaring, foaming beast, creeping its way into the lot. There were two other cars in the lot, both of them covered in a light dusting of snow. As they climbed out of the vehicle, Tommen saw brightly colored jackets through the trees, and a couple skiers made their way off the trail and back to the main pavilion.

There were half a dozen pavilions of various sizes and amenities scattered about the area. The main pavilion had a small building, big enough for one picnic table, a snack machine, and bathrooms, as well as outdoor lighting and an outdoor water spicket. A couple other pavilions had lighting, but some were little more than a propped-up roof. A common hand pump serviced those pavilions.

"What are we doing here?" Micah asked, looking around. "It's dark, and we don't have any gear. We don't even have proper jackets."

It was true, they were without gear, and the clothes they wore were pretty limited in their usefulness. They were good enough to get from a warm house to a warm car and back again, but not for any kind of hiking. Tommen began doubting his decision. Banding only let him step into Time Faster or Slower than Base Time, but air was immune to its effects. No matter the speed of the Band, cold was still cold. He'd learned that very well just a couple weeks ago when he decided he was going to walk home from work.

At the same time, he'd dragged them up here. More to the point, he'd tricked them up here. If Micah wasn't going to let him drive, there wasn't going to be a second chance at this; if he was going to move, he would have to do it now.

So he did. He Banded, a Fast Band that made everything else appear slowed down, stopped. The twins were just closing the doors of the car, and the skiers were just stepping out of their skis under the main pavilion where a bird was stuck, mid-fight, as it swooped down from the rafters. The snow had ceased to fall, instead hovering in mid-air. When Tommen touched a snowflake, it melted. Air and heat, immune to Time.

He went to the pavilion and studied the maps. He knew the trails he, Eric, and Varad usually took. They wound down through the valley, taking them along clear mountain streams, through tall majestic pine groves, and across open fields where the trails disappeared as the wind shifted the snow and created drifts as tall as he was. That was not where he needed to go now.

He needed the more difficult trails today, the ones that took him up the mountain, along clear mountain streams that made the rocks and snow slick with ice, out of the tree line where only bushes grew, and across open face where the wind would burn him as soon as cool him down from the exertion.

Well, all that wasn't entirely true. The Appalachians weren't that tall. Trees still grew, even at the very tops of the mountains, but where he needed to go, the streams were rocky, and the water flowed fast, splashing the banks with freezing water, and the view from the ledge was open and had ferocious winds that swept up the bare face, smoothing the stone and burning bare skin like no fire could.

Tommen began to sweat even as his skin prickled with goosebumps. He thought about turning back—why had he come here anyway? To have an existential crisis?—when his eye caught the marker he was looking for. It wasn't well-marked, and it certainly wasn't labeled. Only because of its historical lore was it marked at all, but ghost stories and other odd occurrences there prevented the map makers from actually putting a name to the little symbol. But Tommen knew what it was, and now he knew exactly where it was.

Strange to think that he'd ever actually forgotten, considering how many times he'd watched it from afar, like an animal too big to hunt. But that was over a century ago, before the trails and the parks and the pavilions. In a century, trees had fallen and new ones grown up in their place, or in new places where trees had not been before. It had confused the hell out of him that first night, sending him straight into the path of a speeding car.

Now he turned and looked around for the trail he would use to get up there purposefully. A roughly brushed sign pointed him in the right direction, and he started off, hunching his shoulders against the cold and hoping the hike would warm him up some. Actually, according to the map, it wasn't as steep a climb as he'd thought, at least as long as he stuck to the trails. Though he was forced to wonder if he would actually remember the area well enough to know when he was close, or if he was going to have to hope that they'd marked the area in some way.

Strictly speaking, it wasn't too far away, or it didn't look like it on the map. It wasn't tucked way far back at the farthest corner of the trails. Some of the spots he'd escaped to for weed and booze had been farther out. In a way, he was grateful because it meant a much shorter distance if he had to come running back and jump in the car. But in another way, it was also worrying for him. He knew how dangerous it was, but there was no way to tell anyone about it, at least not anyone who mattered. Literally, he, the twins, Walter, they were all relying on campfire ghost stories and general fear to keep people away. But it never kept everyone away, and it wouldn't keep everyone away for long.

He trudged through the snow. The trails were rarely groomed by a professional, motorized trail groomer. Mostly it was left up to the cross country skiers or snowshoers to keep the snow packed down and the trails clear. This trail had not seen many of either, so Tommen was left to force his way through calf-deep snow which turned to knee-deep snow once he turned off the main trail and onto a smaller trail. A tertiary trail snaked off another direction to go all the way around the mountain, but he continued on his path.

Overall, they were nice trails, though, very unobtrusive, and Tommen passed by a number of deer and elk. When he cared to stop and take a look around, he also spotted dozens of birds of all kinds. Squirrels dug for their winter stores at the base of a large fallen oak, and large paw prints crossed the trail, came back, walked down the trail for a while, then went off again. One rabbit poked his nose out from under a bush while another made a bold dash through the open, his path taking him to the safety of another bush.

Soon enough, Tommen found the stream, rushing hungrily around and over rocks, water droplets suspended in the air. Ice glistened on the banks, the rocks and snow on either side of the river. Tommen picked his way carefully toward the river, getting down on his hands and knees, gritting his teeth at the cold. Sticking his hand in the water was like sticking it in a bucket of ice right after getting out of a sauna or something. Every muscle from his fingertips to his shoulder suddenly seized with cold, and he jerked his hand back, shaking off the water, as if it would help.

The second time, he mentally prepared himself for the shock of cold as he plunged his hand back in the river and clumsily brought a few handfuls to his mouth to drink. The water was cool, clean and refreshing, a real mountain spring, nothing like the shit that got bottled and sold in stores for a dollar and a feel-good gimmick. This was the real deal, the stuff he'd been raised on.

Unfortunately, with a cold mountain spring also came the cold mountain air. Trying not to stick his hand in the snow, Tommen backed away from the edge of the river and stood, wiping his hands on his pants and thrusting them into his coat pockets. He had to keep moving. He was getting very cold and didn't need to put himself in the hospital next to Walter. Silently, he resolved that he was probably going to run back down the trail.

As he walked, old memories toyed with him, warning him of a rock or a tree stump that he needed to watch out for. Instinctively, he stepped over something or moved to one side, even though he knew there was nothing there anymore. The trail was clear; there was no rock there to trip him up, and all the stumps had been removed. The pine trees whose branches seemed to come together like a couple of billy goats ramming and locking horns had been cut down and hauled away, and the maple with a knot in it like an owl had fallen decades ago, leaving only a rotting corpse behind. He remembered that knot, how it always fooled him into thinking he was being watched. He remembered talking to that owl on more than one occasion, as if it was his friend.

Everything he had once known by heart had changed, cut, cleared, commercialized, open to the public. They came out here to snowshoe and ski and be one with nature without even realizing what that meant. It meant squatting in the snow, waiting patiently for a rabbit to walk into a trap that was only three feet in front of you. It meant using the entrails of that rabbit to lure in larger prey. It meant surviving on roots and berries while you tried to fill your meat stores. That's what it was to be one with nature, and it had nothing to do with brand new Salomon skis or snowshoes that had been marketed as hand-made and supported Canadian Natives when they were just manufactured like everything else. Swap out the shiny, new, fancy snow jackets with "thermo-trapping technology" for a coat made of deer fur, and that might be a good start. But there was nothing natural about the granola bar wrappers left in the snow.

At the same time, if not for the granola bar wrapper and him bending down to pick it up, he might not have noticed the opening in the trees. The trail veered to the left, to go below the ledge and back down into the valley where it would meet up with another trail and return to the pavilion. But his interests lay straight ahead.

There was no podium with a little plaque on it, marking what this cave was or its significance, no laminated book detailing the history of the cave and the local legend surrounding it. There wasn't even a rope with a keep out sign to separate hikers from the cave. The best that the park makers had done was to dig out the rock, drop the trail a good four or five feet from the ledge and hope that no one climbed up there.

Climbing up onto the rock, however, proved more difficult than it initially looked. First, there was the height itself which Tommen was going to have to haul himself over, and he was no weightlifting champion, or even a runner-up. Second, there was the fact that it was quite icy on both the top and the face, providing very little traction, assuming he got a good enough finger hold to even worry about traction.

Eventually, though, he managed to clumsily pull himself up high enough to roll his way onto the top of the rock, exhausted from the effort and acutely aware that getting down was going to be no easier. Well, that, and the fact that it really was not a good idea to just lay there in the snow, especially since he knew he'd been sweating, and he didn't need the sweat to freeze to his body.

Groaning, Tommen picked himself up and meandered up the trail that had been cut off from the rest of the trails, untrodden for who knew how long. It wasn't much different from the rest of the trails until he broke the tree line and was nearly toppled by a sudden blast of icy wind. First he stumbled sideways, arm out to hopefully catch himself on the rock face, then as he brought his foot down, he slipped on hidden ice and went tumbling into the snow a second time.

Go back, he told himself. *There is nothing for you here.*

But he got up again, more prepared this time. And he went to stand and face the old, abandoned salt mine for the second time in three centuries.

The outside of it was a little more worn, more weathered, more battered and smoothed by the wind. The log with "Beware Keep Out" carved in it had long since rotted away, and the crudely carved warnings in smaller signs and on the rock had all been weathered away. Instead, a new, plastic keep out sign had been posted, hanging on a thin wire, citing something about dangerous gases in the old mine and giving some history lesson about the phrase "canary in a coal mile." It was a plausible excuse. At some point, eons ago, the cave had been the entrance to an old mine, but in a century and a half, anyone might start to question just how dangerous those gases really were.

But there was also something very new, a plaque hung to one side of the mouth of the cave.

"Forbes Cave, dedicated April 6, 2005, by the Forbes Family of Charleston, West Virginia

"On April 6, 1855, 8 year old Tommen Forbes, a well-known explorer in his day, entered this cave and was never seen again. This cave was a legend even among its settler residents as people went in the cave and did not reappear for months or even years, claiming they had been gone only a few minutes. Eventually, the cave was sealed off, but that did not stop young Tommen from exploring. He was the youngest person to vanish into the cave. This cave is dedicated by the Forbes family, who are the descendants of Tommen's older brother Teo."

Tommen backed up a few steps and might have slumped into the snow if another gust of wind hadn't come along to keep him upright. Forbes Cave. Sure, it was the family name, but ultimately it was named after him. This was his cave. This was his mark on history, and no one would ever know it.

Curious, he went to the rock in front of the cave and peered over it. He was nearly blinded by the temporal distortion inside, the Band that encompassed the cave. As a child, this cave had merely been a pitch-black cave. Now it was a swirling vortex, supposedly of red, the color of a Fast Band, the wake leading ever deeper until it overtook its victims in the darkness. It moved and writhed in every shade from red and orange to purple to black and white, like a giant snake writhing in a cage too small. He squinted his eyes and tried to make it out better, tried to distinguish the colors, tried to guess the ratio of the Band. The best he could come up with was half an hour to half a century. Every half hour spent in the Band meant that half a century passed in Base Time.

Did that mean that he'd really only spent an hour and a half in the cave? Or was it possible for Bands to change and weaken over time? Well, normally they did, and those were called wakes, but this was no normal Band. It was mystifying even to Walter and, according to him, even for the Gatekeeper who had come to inspect the Band herself. And even the Gatekeeper had been unable to penetrate it and shut it down. So for whatever reason that the Band had been created, that reason was now lost, along with the identity of the one who created it. A PSA had been posted about it for anyone who deigned to visit the area, but there was little else that anyone could do.

Tommen stepped back and rubbed his eyes, trying to make the black spots go away as he blinked back to reality. Why had he come up here anyway, to torture himself? To have an existential crisis? What good did it do to come back and look at the gateway that had brought him from his birth home to his new home, knowing that the gateway was only one-way? Was it just looking back on everything he'd lost, knowing that soon enough he would just have to add Walter to that pile of bodies?

An evil thought crossed his mind: What if he went and approached the Forbes family who had dedicated the cave, tell them he was Tommen? What would happen if he tried to explain the whole Time Portal thing to them? Well, they would probably call him a lunatic and call the cops to deliver him to the mental hospital.

Slowly he turned around, minding the wind which was not so much a constant breeze but bursts of angry, icy wrath. He looked out over the valley. As long as he didn't focus too much on any one tree or rock formation, and instead took in the valley as a whole, it hadn't changed a whole lot, really.

That was a lie. The part that was owned by the state or the city and had been turned into trails and preserves, that was pretty well the same, but the rest was unspeakably unfamiliar. Here and there were little neighborhoods, ranging from trailer parks to normal suburbs. Roads crossed the valley, moving up and down and curving every which way, some following old wagon trails, others being new construction. The highway dipped down one side of the valley and rose on the other side, little ant-sized cars moving back and forth — or they would be, in Base Time.

No one saw him up here, on the ledge. The most evidence he would leave behind was his tracks in the snow and the rather obvious blunders he'd made trying to pull himself up onto the ledge. But even those would be covered over by wind and snow eventually.

He sighed. Tracks in the snow were covered up eventually, but memories stay for much longer. He knew this valley as it had been over a century and a half ago. He knew it now, as it was in the present. He still remembered his ma and pa and big brother — and to an extent his sisters, but he was fairly certain they were much, much younger when he vanished. Was he really going to be forced to keep Walter only in his memories, too? Was it just chance that he was that good at losing his family? If the twins became his legal guardians — and they were already like his crazy uncles — was he just destined to lose them, too?

Was there such a thing as destiny, or did he just have shit luck? Did the universe hate him for some reason? Well, for one thing it brought him puberty, which was probably the real root cause of his existential crisis, a young man breaking into adulthood and trying to figure out his place in the world.

At the same time, there was nothing fleeting about loving his dad and wanting to save him. There was just the problem of sorting out wishes, fantasy, and reality. Tommen wished he knew of an antidote to the Borelian poison. Fantasy was walking up to a Borelian, asking for the antidote, and being given it for free with no strings attached. Reality was being thrown into slavery.

Was there no other way to do this? Why were his only two options slavery or losing his dad? Yes, he would gladly get thrown into slavery if he could get some kind of guarantee that it would help things. As it was, it was still too uncertain.

He paced back and forth on the ledge, feeling the wind bite and burn his skin and his feet go numb in the snow. Air and heat, unaffected by Time. He'd gotten over the Contemplation and Reflection part, now he just needed to get moving on the Idea and Solution part. Preferably before he froze to death up here or lost a few layers of skin to the wind.

Walter was his mentor. If he died, would Tommen be reassigned to the twins? Was it possible to be assigned to someone who didn't actually live in the area? He didn't think so, but no one had ever told him otherwise. Maybe problems like this didn't happen often because Runners were usually no more skilled than he was, generally unthreatening to any officer. Was this a precedent case, then? He doubted it. The Time industry had been around a lot longer than that; they'd probably seen it all, done it all.

Another gust of wind buffeted Tommen as he paced. Shivering, he moved a little farther down the hill to the tree line. He turned and looked back up at the cave and the little keep out sign flapping in the wind. Why had he come up here? He didn't need to look at some painful emotionally-significant landmark in order to have an existential crisis. And the fact that it seemed to amplify his crisis wasn't helping either. He could just as easily go home and stare at a wall while having his crisis. At the very least, it would be warmer. His thoughts on that were interrupted by the realization that he would not be going home-home, but to the twins' home. Until Walter died, it was not his home and not his room. He was their guest, not their son. He was just on some kind of short vacation or something, staying with them while Walter recuperated.

But it was a lie, and the mouth of the cave laughed at him as he turned his back and walked away.

Chapter Six
Down the Mountain

There was a time when Tommen was about seven or eight years old, early in the autumn, the last winter he would see before wandering into the cave, he'd found an old log that had rotted from the inside out, so the core was mush, but the outer bark was still fairly tough. He'd sneaked away for weeks to dig out the center, scratching and scraping at the fine pulp fibers, getting distracted more often than not by the variety of bugs and grubs that had moved into the rotting log.

One day, Teo found him with his new treasure. Tommen was afraid his big brother would destroy it or take it over or go and tattle to their pa (usually he was shirking responsibilities when he sneaked off to his log). Instead, Teo began to sneak away with him and help him hollow it out, his strength coming in handy to get past the obvious mushy rot and scrape the wood down to only the last few layers of bark and hard pulp.

Then Teo came up with a brilliant idea. He told Tommen to stay put while he went to retrieve a saw. It was painstaking and took most of the afternoon, but big brother Teo cut the log in half. At first Tommen was horrified, especially when Teo said to leave the two halves and wait until winter before going back to them.

It was a long rest of the autumn and early winter. When the snow began to fall, Tommen begged Teo to go back out to see the logs, but Teo made him wait until the snow was almost thigh-deep. Then he grabbed a couple lengths of rope and some small tools, and together they slipped out of the cabin and through the woods.

It took them most of the day, partly just trying to find the logs since they were buried under the snow, but Teo put holes in the front of the logs and Tommen got to practice his knots as he threaded the ends of the ropes through the holes and tied them off. Then they dragged the log sleds back to the cabin for the evening.

Their ma had been impressed by their creativity, while their pa just shook his head and said something about, "So that's where you boys have been getting off to."

The following morning, the two of them grabbed their sleds and raced up the mountain. Well, "race" was a relative term as Teo had to break through the icy crust so Tommen could follow in his wake. But they made it up the mountain nonetheless.

They started on small knolls and hills as they worked out the design flaws and how to handle the sleds. There were a number of failures that mostly resulted in stopped or toppled sleds and snow getting down their shirts and pants, but in their mirth, they noticed none of it.

The last run of the day was the longest and most dangerous. They went higher up the mountain to a spot just out of sight of the cabin. Tommen was cold from the snow and gathering darkness and tired from all the trudging back up the mountain. But he dutifully followed his older brother up for one last run which Teo promised they could ride all the way back to the cabin; there was a trail from top to bottom, and with the height, they would get enough speed to make it all the way back.

It was still light at the ledge where they started, but the shadows crept up from the valley like a wolf stalking its prey. Tommen found it hard to be excited about the ride given how sore he was, but he had no trouble being afraid of the height and the trail down. It might not have been so bad if he could see the cabin, but this trail required a turn, and they hadn't quite mastered turning in these sleds yet.

"I'll give you a headstart," Teo told him. "And I'll be right behind you the whole way."

It was meant to reassure him, but Tommen only felt dread. He didn't like having Teo out of his sight like that, even if he knew he'd be right behind him. Still, he was cold and wanted to be next to the fire more than he wanted to be at the top of the mountain. So he wiped the snow out of his sled and got in.

A moment later, Teo pushed him over the edge, and he was flying, soaring, absolutely and utterly free. His sled cut through the crust of the untouched snow, sending icy shards spraying left and right and some right back into his face. Wind bit at him and burned his skin, but he was free, at the mercy of God and the elements as he flew down the hill, the open face of the mountain.

He wasn't sure where the tree came from or how he got tangled up in it. He remembered seeing his sled break into pieces, and then a second log sled go sliding by. Teo had seen him go into the trees and jumped out in order to slow himself down and get to Tommen without crashing into him.

"Help!" Tommen cried, more out of fear than anything. If he'd just calmed down and thought about it, he probably could have wiggled his way out just fine. But what eight year old thinks about that?

"Tommen!" Teo exclaimed, picking his way as close as he could, but unable to get his mass into the little nook where Tommen had landed. "You okay?"

"Help me!" Tommen cried again.

"I'm going to get pa, okay? You hold tight."

"You did this, you help me!" Tommen screamed angrily.

Teo reached one arm through the tangled mess of branches and took Tommen's hand. "I know. I did this. But I can't undo it, not by myself. I need help. Now I'm going to get pa, and we'll get you out of here. I won't abandon you. Just hold on."

Tommen had managed to get partially free by the time Teo and their pa got back with axes and saws, and it was long past dark when they got back to the cabin, shivering and blue. Tommen wasn't hurt beyond some bumps and bruises, but he still got a bowl of warm soup and a couple blankets while Teo got a switchin' and sent to bed without supper.

It was probably one of the few times the two of them had done anything brotherly, given their age difference, and, once Tommen finally forgave Teo for making him go down that trail, they laughed about it until the snow finally began to melt.

Tommen stopped his trek down the mountain. No time had passed since he'd stayed Banded the whole way; it was still sunset with the shadows long in the valley, creeping up the mountain like a wolf stalking its prey.

"A hundred years dead, and he's still teaching me things like a brother should," he said aloud to a rabbit, frozen in the snow, as if it could hear him or would care.

Scenario one: Walter was Eight Year Old Tommen, and Isthim was Teo. Isthim had done something awful to Walter and she couldn't undo it.

No, that wasn't right. Tommen had a great suspicion that Isthim, or the Borelians at least, could undo it if they really wanted to. But they didn't want to.

Scenario two: Walter was Eight Year Old Tommen, and Sixteen Year Old Tommen was Teo. It was Tommen's fault that Walter was in this predicament, but he couldn't undo it by himself. He needed help, and he had to do it before Walter-slash-Eight-Year-Old-Tommen froze to death in the dark and cold.

Micah and Micaiah were unable or unwilling to help, likelihood on the former. They had greater Timekeeping abilities than Tommen and they were just as powerless. Walter's disease was also immune to Time and Banding. Therefore, Timekeeping was not what would save Walter.

Lily was also unable or unwilling to help, and the jury was still out on which one was more likely. She was a Harvester who was basically already giving Walter a time of death. This could be either force of habit from her work, or an indication that Harvesting was no use to Walter either. For the sake of Tommen's sanity, he elected to consider it useless and omit it completely rather than play the what-if game.

Tommen sat down where he was on the trail, in the snow, heedless of the cold now that he'd gotten some semblance of clear thinking and maybe even a plan.

Ultimately, Eight Year Old Tommen had gotten stuck and tangled in the lower limbs of a pine tree. Those were easy enough to get untangled, except he'd also managed to crash through a tangled mess of bushes, brush, and undergrowth. The limbs weren't the problem; it was everything around it. He'd crashed through, so Teo and their pa had used axes and saws to clear the rest of it.

He rubbed his face. No, he couldn't think of this as a one-for-one analogy. The memory had only served to get him thinking realistically, nothing more. He couldn't rely on it to solve everything.

Abstract thinking then. He needed to find someone who wasn't a Timekeeper or a Harvester with the tools to break through a very tough barrier without hurting the person who was trapped behind it.

Medically, Walter was already getting the best care available. He was in ICU with cutting edge technologies and treatments and medicines. Medically, he was fine, he was as healthy as could be.

Or maybe that kind of help was like Teo bringing a botanist to help cut Eight Year Old Tommen out of the brush. A botanist would be able to tell what kind of tree he was in, what kind of bushes and brush and stuff was trapping him, but he wouldn't have the ax to cut him out.

So, who had an ax?

Tommen almost could have slapped his forehead if he didn't think the move to be very childish. Pa. The Hands. It was so simple. Cassius was the Zero Hour Impostor, who used the confusion in the system to have access to all the resources of the Zero Hour and was able to use the influence of the Zero Hour, but Micaiah had said something about him not doing all the boring stuff, the politics and the court and the Coliseum. He was in it for the power, not the politics.

If Tommen could get an audience with the Hands, he could bring up the matter with the real Hands, the real Zero Hour, and get around Cassius' influence, like dialing 0 to talk to customer service instead of having to go through computerized menus. He could get in and out of the Wheel and save Walter before Cassius ever found out what was going on.

He stood then, mindful of the slippery trail, and continued down the mountain. The problem now was how he wanted to approach the matter. How much attention did he want to bring to the Borelians? Yes, he would mention it as being the cause of Walter's affliction, but did he dare demand retribution from the Borelians, or make a request of the Hands? Truthfully, he wasn't sure how all that would work. He'd never gone before the Hands for such a formal petition. Actually, he'd never gone before the Hands at all except when Walter introduced him as a probationary Timekeeper.

Well, he had to hope that the twins would help him somewhat. If nothing else, they were the ones who were going to have to take him to the Wheel. Since he was still only probationary, they would have to accompany him pretty much everywhere anyway.

He trudged back through his own tracks until he got back to the main trail where it was a little more packed down from all the cross country skiers. He couldn't suppress a grin and a little self-satisfaction. Finally, he had an idea. He had hope. And even if Cassius caught wind of what he was doing, he couldn't control all of the Hands, could he? Not with an election coming up, and it would be especially difficult if there was even half the shake-up that the twins had reported because of their brown-nosing beforehand, trying to find Cassius and Rifun and spreading rumors about there being a false Zero Hour. All those Hands or candidates who had pledged support but had been unable to deliver might be good for something. Time or no Time, politics was politics. Regardless of their true loyalties, politicians had to at least pretend to like their peacekeeping force or else be at risk of a mutiny.

Yes, Tommen was feeling very pleased with himself as he

stopped briefly to take his shoe off and dump a small snowball out of it. So basically, all he had to do was go to the Wheel, get an audience with the Hands—only the most powerful figures in the Time industry—and petition them to help a Timekeeper Captain because the False Zero Hour had set out to murder him in order to stay in power.

Cassius might not do the boring politics, but even if he was there, he wouldn't be able to reveal himself there because that would be revealing himself. His cards didn't work until after the elections. Until then, he still had to play along, play by the rules, and do his part to help save this dying Captain. Right?

Tommen didn't want to consider the alternatives. First, Cassius would kill him either on the spot or as he tried to leave the Wheel. Second, Cassius would send someone to kill Walter outright and thus sidestep the whole thing. Or third, there was a way for him to somehow veto the whole vote, somehow deem Walter too unimportant to save. Politics with the Borelians and all that. Earth was not openly engaged in the Time industry, so there would be no huge upset in the markets.

He shook his head, trying to stay optimistic. *It's not over until it's over.* Until the Hands told him that they couldn't or wouldn't help, he had to have some faith that justice would be served. Corruption was bad by many accounts, but there were ways to play on the self-serving narcissism of most politicians. Problem was, that was how governments became corrupt, and those who played that game were veterans. Cassius was one of those veterans, and in his world, you win or you die. He was poised to win the elections and kill all who opposed him. Tommen would just have to be that last elusive golden egg and stay one step ahead of him.

Mind whirling with a thousand thoughts and plans, Tommen finagled his shoe back on over a wet sock and headed back down the mountain. He'd gone up the mountain to have an existential crisis, and now he came back down with the plan to save his dad. All in a day's work, right? No big deal. Now he just had to complete his plan within six days and all would be well. What could possibly go wrong?

Once the pavilions came back into view, Tommen dropped his Band. Immediately, life on the mountain came roaring back to life. Squirrels jumped from branch to branch overhead. Birds swooped down from the rafters of the pavilion while the cross country skiers laughed and chatted eagerly about something or other. A gust of wind stirred up some snow in Tommen's face, and he was momentarily blinded until he took refuge under the pavilion roof and ducked into the tiny building.

He fished around in a pocket for some change and bought a bag of chips which he ate while he took ten seconds to warm up, at least until the twins got to the pavilion. They looked a little confused and a lot exasperated. He'd run off on them. Again. Silently amused by the prospect but not wanting to keep them waiting — and knowing that the best time to ask for help and a favor is when someone is in a good mood — he finished his bag of chips and went out to meet them.

"That's got to stop," Micah told him severely as he Banded the three of them. "Something happens to you out here and that's a lot of ground to cover."

"Well, you could have followed my tracks," Tommen pointed out. "But that's not the point."

"No, the point is, we're going home," Micaiah told him decisively.

"You don't even want to know where I went?"

"No."

But Micah first gave Micaiah a look, then Tommen. "Fine. Where did you go?"

"Forbes Cave," Tommen answered proudly.

Now they gave him a hard regard, as if they were looking for the punchline to a joke or some terrible news. Funny how they got the same expression when they were looking at something incredibly hilarious or incredibly not hilarious.

"And what did you find there?" Micaiah asked cautiously.

"The answer to our problems, hopefully, and a cure for my dad," Tommen said, hoping he sounded optimistic and not childishly naive.

The twins synchronously shifted their stance and folded their arms. It was Micaiah who spoke. "Do tell."

"We can't help Walter, as Timekeepers. This disease is immune to Time," Tommen told them, hoping it sounded like he was outlining his thoughts and not treating them like idiots. "And if Lily's attitude is any indication, Harvesting can't help him either."

"We know this," Micah said, a little more sharply than was probably intended, but Tommen didn't like it either, being reminded that for all their power, they were helpless against this.

"We can't get through the brush on our own; we need help from someone with an ax."

Admittedly, his excitement won over him there because that was pretty much where he lost the twins in his train of thought. Their expressions went from interested, cold, calculating, and a little wounded, to completely baffled.

"What about brush and axes?" Micah wondered.

Tommen shook his head and gave them the abbreviated version of his encounter with the lower limbs of a pine tree. "Walter is tangled up in those limbs. The sled is gone, and the snow will kill him. Branches, brush, and undergrowth are keeping us apart. We need to find someone with an ax to just chop the shit out of it and pull him out forcefully."

"And hopefully your wise man existential reflections on the top of the mountain pointed you in the right direction," Micaiah said.

"Yes, at least I think so, I hope so, and I'm going to need your help to do it," Tommen told him.

"You always have our support," Micah said. "But given that Walter's only got about a week left, unless your plan works instantaneously, I wouldn't waste my time on mystery games."

Well, he had a point.

"I want to petition the Hands," Tommen said.

He wasn't sure exactly what he'd been expecting. In the movies, something like that was usually some sort of defining line or moment and one of two things would happen. First, there would be epic music as the hero realizes the path to his destiny, and then there would be a cutscene to somewhere else. Second, the audience that the hero was speaking to would erupt into protests and arguments, telling him he was crazy and foolish, that it would never work. Then the hero would either tell them to shove it and carry out his orders anyway, or he would sway them to his side. Either way, they were walking down the path of destiny.

What he wasn't expecting was for the twins to just give him a look and a shrug and Micah to say, "Okay. Petition them for what?"

"To help," Tommen answered. "One of their Timekeeper Captains is dying because a very powerful Runner—who is also in league with the False Zero Hour—got in cahoots with a Borelian, a *vodrak* Borelian at that. What is to stop them from going after other Timekeepers, or even the Hands themselves?"

"You make a good point," Micaiah admitted, "but if you're going to make an argument before the Hands, you have to understand how to appeal to them, each and every one of them. You have to understand how the petitioning works."

"That's why I need your help. We all want Walter to live, so I know you'll give it your all. I'll even let you go before the Hands if you think it would increase our chances."

Micaiah shook his head. "No, it wouldn't. After all the trouble we've caused, another appearance by us would only weaken our chances."

"And," Micah interrupted, "many species place great value on family structure. Most place great value on societal and military structure. With you coming forward as his son, his societal lesser, and his subordinate, you'll at least win some brownie points."

"So you'll help?" Tommen wondered. Why was he surprised?

"Of course we'll help," Micaiah told him, dropping the Band. "We love Walter just as much as you do."

They paused in their conversation as the skiers gave them some sly looks as they gathered up their things and made for the parking lot. Tommen couldn't hear their hushed words but he was pretty sure he could lipread well enough to make out "cute couple," "boyfriend," and "adorable." He shook his head as they got in the car and drove off.

"One more thing you can help me with," Tommen said before they headed back to their car. "Can you fix my ears?"

"Fix them how?" Micah asked.

"Fix the hearing. I don't like the...imbalance. It's confusing."

The twins frowned.

"Tommen, Time is not medicine. It doesn't heal all wounds. It has no medical properties in and of itself. Using Time to, as Walter generally does, fix your face when you get into fights was essentially just speeding up Time to allow your body to heal itself as it naturally would, condensing a few days into a few seconds. I shouldn't have to explain that. Pinpoint Banding your ears for even, say, six months in just a few minutes, it would not restore your hearing unless in that time your hearing would naturally come back on its own. Okay, if you'd lost an eye, Banding wouldn't make an eye grow back. It would just speed up the process of growing scar tissue."

Tommen sighed and rubbed his face. "I know, but I have to hope that it will come back. World War I, victims of mustard gas would go blind for weeks, but their vision would return."

"Sometimes," Micaiah reminded him. "Not all the time, and rarely was it a complete restoration or free of side effects."

"I have to hope. Will you try at least?"

The twins still looked skeptical but finally they nodded. Tommen couldn't tell exactly, but he was pretty sure they both got in on the Banding, one doing the pinpoint Band while the other did the double Band. Immediately, his head exploded with a headache, and it felt very much like he'd contracted an ear infection in both ears with the amount of pain that lanced through them. He gritted his teeth, tried to find a sound to focus on—a bird, a squirrel, a car down on the road — to see if his hearing got better. Then, after about thirty seconds, both Bands were dropped.

"That was approximately six months," Micah told him.

"It hurt," Tommen said. "It was like a severe ear infection, but it doesn't hurt anymore."

"Does your hearing still feel imbalanced?" Micaiah wondered.

Tommen looked around, tried to pick out a sound, but that was the problem with being alone at the park; they were the only ones around and the wind made it difficult to hear anything else. But at the same time, the wind sounded different coming from either direction. Finally he sighed. "I don't think it changed at all."

Chapter Seven
A Plan of Action

The drive home was quiet. The twins did not speak. The radio was on, but it was so low than Tommen could really only hear the bass noises in one ear, and he could barely pick out the lyrics in the other ear. Six months they had Banded his ears, plenty of time for his hearing to go through its ups and downs of healing and realigning and readjusting and whatever else they would normally need to do in order to heal. They'd been in a quiet environment, so it wasn't as if he could have lost more of it due to outside noise. Was this how he was doomed to spend the rest of his life?

There were several deaf students at school, he knew. They took their classes mostly online, but a few attended normal classes. One was a master lipreader, and another had cochlear implants; he wasn't sure about the rest. He did not think less of them, maybe pitied them for being forced into a system designed for so-called "normal" students, but was usually impressed at how well they adapted.

Where was he in this? He wasn't completely deaf. He'd grown more accustomed to the imbalance in his hearing, knew how to control his voice and tone, and he could hold a regular conversation with the people around him. But he couldn't hear someone walking up behind him or talking to him across the room. What would happen when he went back to school? What if the class got noisy and someone needed him? How long could he hide his hearing loss? When he took Spanish next semester, could he fudge his way through the speaking and listening portions? What if Tyler Freeman found out and decided to take advantage of it, sneaking up behind him and attacking from behind?

What if the audiologist told him he needed a hearing aid? What then? He would be mocked. He would be chasing hearing aid batteries like some old lady. He would be the butt of every joke if he ever misheard something, which he inevitably would. Perfect hearing or hearing loss, he would inevitably miss something, but the hearing loss and the hearing aid made it funny. To everyone else. He'd just clawed his way up from the land of idiots into the land of intelligent AP students. Somehow, the hearing loss made them seem...unimportant, as if that achievement suddenly meant nothing if he wasn't whole.

Could he make friends with the deaf students, or would he be excluded since he wasn't entirely deaf? Even if he was accepted, he didn't know sign language—or at least, not any signs that weren't considered vulgar—and outside of classes, that was the only way the deaf students communicated, at least that he'd seen. He could learn, he supposed, but...why? Why did this have to happen? Why was it not going to get better?

"You're quiet," Micah observed.

"Yeah," Tommen murmured.

"Going over what you're going to say to the Hands?"

You are too kind for your own good, Micah. "Sure."

"Well, when we get home, we can talk a little more about how the process works and what you'll need to do to prepare."

"And just something to consider," Micaiah interjected, "humanitarian reasons don't work well with the Hands. Doing things for the common good, the greater good, out of the goodness of their hearts, go in assuming that they don't care about that. If a few are swayed by it, all the better, but you have to show them some sort of personal gain."

So basically, Tommen was going up against the CEO and ruling board of the world's biggest and richest corporation and asking them to have mercy on some poor low-level manager, like going before a fast food chain CEO and asking them to pitch in to save the life of the manager of some little podunk restaurant in the middle of the desert. They sympathized, would put on a good and sympathetic face, offer their condolences and sympathy, but ultimately refuse. If they did it for one, they would have to do it for all, and how would that look to everyone they had snubbed thus far? They would have to come up with some pretty good reasons and excuses why they cared for that manager and not other managers, especially the more high-level managers.

Putting it in those terms helped Tommen to better define what he was working with, and he found himself wondering just how far from the truth that was. The Hands were the government of Time, but it was only a business to them, a profit. Given the complexity and diversity of the races involved in Time, it was a feasible model, until the greed started. So he was going to have to come up with a way that saving this low-level manager of some podunk desert fast food restaurant was going to start raking in the dough better and faster than letting him die and simply replacing him.

Truthfully, he couldn't come up with anything. In no scenario he concocted was he able to conjure up more Time and more turns—the currency of the Wheel—out of thin air. Mostly because he wasn't sure how this would be accomplished, the Hands helping Walter. If they went to the Borelians, Tommen couldn't make any promises on their behalf. If the Hands just produced an antidote from up their sleeves, the only thing he had to offer was his Timekeeping salary, which was mere pennies, comparatively speaking. And none of them, truly, would do this out of the goodness of their heart?

"You said that some of them hold family and societal values in great esteem," Tommen said suddenly as they pulled in the driveway. "But you said that none of them cared about humanitarian reasons. What gives?"

"The family and societal values are what's going to get you an audience with the Hands in the first place," Micaiah told him as he got out of the car. Tommen followed suit. "The Hands are petitioned literally thousands of times a day. Most of them are complaints and requests with little and less merit than your petition—and I'm speaking honestly, not just to flatter you or give you false hope. Using the family and societal values as a reason to be seen simply lets the Hands know that your petition is less likely to be run-of-the-mill; there might be something interesting and worth hearing. That's all. Once you go before them, it's all about gain and profit."

That was what Tommen was afraid of. That was where he knew he was at a disadvantage. Hundred and fifty year leap into the future notwithstanding, Tommen had been raised in a culture that was all about humanitarian reasons. Food, water, warmth, survival. If you saw someone starving or struggling to keep warm, you helped them because it was the right thing to do, not because they had anything to give in return. If they did have something to give—a particular skill or craft or maybe a little money—then that was simply a bonus. But you didn't hold out on life-saving food or furs because they had nothing to give. Help now, ask questions and figure out payment later.

In this situation, he was going to have to learn how to be a hard ass. He was going to have to learn to think coldly, as cold as the hearts of the Hands, as cold as the money that lined their pockets. He was going to have to show them not just a carrot, but a gold carrot—carrot, carat, ha ha?—and make it so irresistible that they would walk over a cliff for it. Somewhere in there, he was going to have to get a little something for himself, that being the antidote. And hopefully not get thrown into slavery for the Borelians.

"There has to be something I can bribe them with," Tommen said as he pulled off his shoes and coat.

"You're not going to be able to bribe the Hands," Micah told him. "Not with your paltry salary."

"What about Lily? She's changed her attitude for the time being; can we take advantage of it somehow?"

The twins shook their heads. "We spent most of our credibility and bribery influence trying to flush out Cassius and Rifun. Lily will be lucky if she can recover that credibility and influence by the next election."

"Okay, so maybe there's something I can use that has to do with the election. Votes? I'm fishing for something here."

"Move to another part of the river, then," Micaiah told him. He sighed. "Tommen, the best we're going to be able to do is steer you in the right direction with the process and the paperwork. We have no influence right now, and our votes have pretty much been spoken for, even Walter's. You're not an officer, so you can't be bribed; politically, you're worthless."

"So what do I have to go on? I need a better narrative than humanitarian reasons; you said it yourself."

"A better narrative?" Micah raised a brow. "This isn't an essay contest."

"Good, because I suck at public speaking."

"So maybe instead of English, you can think in terms of math," Micaiah suggested. "You have to benefit enough Hands to make it worth their time."

"Okay," Tommen said as they went to sit at the dining table. "How does this whole thing work?"

"In order to petition the Hands, you have to see the secretaries to file for a hearing. That's where most of the bullshit cases are either resolved quickly or dismissed, taking things to a lower court before they go all the way to the Supreme Court as it were. After the hearing, you will know your results immediately whether you are going before the Hands and when. Most often they try to schedule it within thirty hours, but it depends on what the Hands are doing.

"When it is time for you to go before the Hands, you will go before them alone. It works just like a review, being admitted into the inner sanctum of the Coliseum, so remember well how it goes. There you will have fifteen minutes to present your initial case. The Hands may question you, and that will last as long as they think they need information to make a judgment."

"Do they rule on it immediately?" Tommen interrupted.

"Sometimes," Micah answered. "Some cases they may rule

right there, others they may retire for deliberation, like a jury."

"If they decide to deliberate," Micaiah picked up, "you will be escorted to a special waiting chamber. Food and drink will be provided as necessary until you are called to hear the verdict."

"Once the Hands have delivered the verdict, that's it," Micah warned severely. "There are no appeals, and you cannot file another petition for the same exact issue twice. They deliver the verdict, and you leave the Coliseum. If they suspect any kind of upset or resistance or belligerence, you'll be spending the night with the Grandfathers."

"Well, what if they rule favorably?" Tommen wondered, shifting uncomfortably. "What if they agree to turn over an antidote?"

"Then that's what they'll do. They will inform you of the manner and method of the delivery, and as long as everyone follows the orders, there are no problems. Case dismissed; thank you, ladies and gentlemen of the jury."

"Okay, so how do I convince them of that? How do I turn this into profit for them? You know the Hands; you must know their weaknesses."

"This isn't a video game, Tommen," Micaiah said. "The Hands are always shrouded; you know that. It's supposed to prevent favoritism, but take that how you will. You have to benefit each Hand without letting the other Hands know which Hand you're benefiting."

"Tell me what I need to do, need to say. I don't have enough time to learn all the nuances, and you don't have the influence to be able to go before them. Give me the words, and I'll be your eyes."

The twins glanced at each other. Micaiah shrugged. "It could work."

"All right," Micah said. "Fair enough. We'll work out a rough sketch of the points you need to hit and the promises you are able to make. It's up to you to decide how you go about it, that way it doesn't sound like we're doing what we're doing. It will seem sparse, but it will not have more information than you are reasonably expected to know, being a probie. Fair?"

"So, all the Hands and candidates who promised to be with Micaiah and help Walter...?"

"You don't know that," Micah admitted sadly. "In the same way you don't know the extent of our bribery and trickery beforehand with Lily. I don't think you know enough to hurt you, but just to be safe, you know less than that." He stood and went rummaging in drawers, looking for paper and pencils.

"How much do I know about the False Zero Hour?" Tommen wondered.

"You were held hostage by him and his henchmen. How much *do* you know about him?"

It was the closest thing to a green light as Tommen was going to get, even as Micaiah turned that green light into a cautionary yellow one, saying, "Cassius isn't too interested in the boring politics like the hearings and the petitions, but that doesn't mean he isn't keeping an eye on things to see if you do try something like this. Best advice, keep the main focus on the profits and the gains. Obviously, keep Walter in the spotlight, but only mention the Borelians, Cassius, Rifun, all of that, only as necessary. You are just a probie trying to save his Captain and his father, not some arrogant prick trying to stir up the political pot and potentially anger the Borelians. You save Walter, they make money. Got it?"

Tommen nodded. Money and Walter, Walter and money. It was nice to have a focus, except he still found very little substance to back it. He hoped the twins could come up with a list. Personally, he would rather make it to the end of the fifteen minutes and have the Hands think he could offer even more benefits to them if only he had the time, rather than finish in two minutes and make them think he had nothing to go on substantially, instead relying on humanitarian reasons that didn't mean jack shit to them.

"What's the worst the Hands can actually do if they don't like my case?" Tommen wondered, not sure if he really wanted to know the answer.

"Officially, they can laugh you out of the Coliseum, maybe

have you spend the night in jail," Micah told him.

"And unofficially?"

"People have died," Micaiah answered bluntly. "Mysteriously. Most often, everyone knows it was a Hand who did it, or at least ordered it. Sometimes people even have a good idea which Hand it was, and why. But nothing can ever be proven, so it just kind of goes away."

"Would Cassus or Rifun be likely to kill me?"

"They might, but I doubt it. If the Hands rule against you, they get the joy of watching you watch Walter die. If the Hands rule in your favor, you turning up dead would be mighty suspicious, and any mention of the False Zero Hour would only be given credence, thus upsetting the elections even more. This is probably the best time to do this because Cassius still has to play, somewhat, by the rules, at least until after the elections when the new cards are dealt."

"So I save Walter, and then I get three weeks to live until after the elections. Then Cassius kills me."

"Not if we have anything to say about it."

It should have been a comforting thought, knowing he had the twins behind him—and Walter, if he survived—but it wasn't. Tommen was already risking life and limb and honor by petitioning the Hands. If things went awry, and Cassius made a move, thus putting them all in danger again, what was the point of diving into the maw in the first place? It was like bungee jumping to save someone who was free-falling, only to have all his bungee jumping companions have their ropes cut, and then have them pushed off the platform while he was halfway down after the first guy. He wouldn't be able to save them all. Most likely, it would all happen so fast that he couldn't process it fast enough to even know his companions' ropes had been cut and they needed saving. And another thing, would his companions even know their ropes had been cut?

Tommen rubbed his eyes. It was too much, too fast. He had six days to do this, and yet it felt like if he didn't do this right now, Walter would be dead by midnight. He almost wanted to call Lily and get an update, but he was both too afraid of calling her and too afraid to know the answer. What if Walter had gotten worse after they left? What if his clock was ticking down faster than anticipated? What if there was a tipping point where, even if he did have some good time left, there was just a point of no return?

"How about we take a dinner break?" Micah suggested, sensing Tommen's distress. "Some good food might help us think a little more clearly."

It ended up being leftovers from breakfast which felt so long ago. Still, it was delicious, and Tommen felt some semblance of hope and clear-thinking returning to him as he ate.

"So why is it that with access to the Wheel and the free food in the Food Court that you guys still insist on buying food and cooking it and stuff?"

"We're cooks, Tommen, it's what we do," Micah said. "It's what we love to do. Well, what I love to do," he added at a raised brow from Micaiah. "Some things you shouldn't give up just because there is something more convenient. Take you, for example. Why do you still trap animals for meat when you can just go down to the grocery store?"

"It's cheaper and healthier and I don't want to forget how to do it. I keep the furs, too, tan them and stuff."

"So there you go. Not everything that's new is good. Not everything that's old is bad."

Tommen grinned and shook his head. "Yeah, every spring my dad thinks we're getting chickens. Fresh, delicious eggs every morning, and nice healthy white meat whenever we need it, more or less. Problem is, he never gets around to buying or building a coop, and we're really not home enough to take care of them like they need."

And, personally, Tommen hated chickens. Maybe it was because he'd been attacked by his ma's favorite rooster, Welly, every time he went anywhere near the chicken coop or one of the hens if they wandered off. He was always there, waiting to attack. Really

Tommen preferred ducks and geese. He'd liked to watch them swim around in the river and little pond and preen themselves on the banks and build little nests in the spring. The drakes and geese were never as mean as those damn roosters, especially Welly.

"What kind of chickens does he want?" Micah wondered pleasantly.

"Americaunas, the ones with the little blue and green eggs." And very tiny chickens, barely any meat on them at all, hardly worth the effort to butcher and pluck sometimes. At least Tommen's ma, though a prized chicken breeder she was not, knew enough about breeding to get her chickens plump and fat, breeding them bigger every year, culling the small ones, and introducing as much color as she could. She liked colorful animals, the more colors and unusual patterns, the better.

"There's one neighbor down the road has got those," Micah was saying. "He's got one sneaky hen, though, and every spring she manages to hide a nest on him and hatch a clutch. If you wanted a starter flock—"

"Not until after the new year," Tommen cut in.

He knew Micah was trying to be friendly and helpful, make polite conversation, but Tommen did not appreciate the implications. They were gearing up to go before the Hands to present a case and win the antidote to the poison that was slowly killing Walter. He didn't need to be reminded that his chances of winning were slim, and he should realistically be planning for the logistics of moving in with Micah and Micaiah.

Dinner was pretty quiet after that as they all pretended to be interested in the last remains of their food. It wasn't too difficult to be interested, considering it reheated almost as good as it was cooked fresh. Eventually, though, they were forced to admit defeat and got up to wash their dishes. Despite having a dishwasher, the twins rarely used it as they were home infrequently and usually didn't have enough dishes to make a load before needing those dishes again. It was hard when there were only two in the house, or so they liked to joke.

Tommen made an excuse to go to the bathroom, if only to buy himself time to think alone without seeming rude and aloof by heading to the bedroom. He wasn't sure why he was so worried. Anxious, yes, as he considered everything that he had to do in order to go before the Hands,to speak to them and present his case, but this was worry of a different kind. He couldn't quite pinpoint it. It was related to the situation at hand, and yet there wasn't any single issue he could identify as being so much more worrying than the rest.

Walter in a coma? Definitely frightening. Definitely worrying. But a tiny bit less so since there had been evidence that he was in there somewhere, fighting back, winning back his life one second at a time.

Petitioning the Hands? A little frightening since he was, morally, very far removed from them. He was a newcomer to their game. Even if the twins were writing the script, he still had to deliver the lines.

Eventually, Tommen could only conclude that he was so overloaded and overwhelmed by the whole thing that he was worrying about phantoms. It was unfocused worry, probably the worst kind. At least if the worry had a cause, like Walter in a coma or petitioning the Hands, there was usually a way to deal with it. Unfocused worry was the worst because it was a phantom, chewing away at his clear thinking and his sanity. The only way that he knew of to deal with unfocused worry was to get rid of all the normal, focused worries and make things right again. The only way he was going to do that was by going back out to the dining room, sitting down with the twins, and going over his script, like an amateur actor getting ready for his first lead role in a major Hollywood feature film. Except Tommen had never acted before in his life, not like this.

When Tommen emerged from the bathroom, the twins were deep in conversation at the dining room table. Neither appeared to be writing much, but judging by their expressions and body language, they were having a hard time deciding what to write. It was a long jump from probationary to Lieutenant Timekeeper, and there was a lot of knowledge that went with it, too. How much did Tommen know, how much was he going to present before the Hands, how much would be too suspicious? And with that knowledge, how could he come up with a convincing argument, a way to make the trade seem profitable? How much could they pass off as him just being an educated speaker and master of persuasion, and what would be considered him reading a script that someone else gave him? How could they give him words, and him give them eyes, without anyone else knowing what they were up to? What could they do so they had the appearance of just being there to open and close the portal?

"Bhuail, i dtús báire," Micah was saying, *"Ní féidir linn a feictear leis nuair a réitíonn sé a achainí."* He looked up to see Tommen hardly three feet away. *"Tar, suigh síos sa chaoi is féidir leat sinn a chloisteáil."* (Well, first thing, we can't be seen with him when he files his petition. Come, sit down so you can hear us.)

It wasn't meant to be a slight, but Tommen still inwardly flinched at the comment. He sat obediently and waited.

"The nice thing about petitions is that they are open to everyone," Micah went on as though there hadn't been a break in the conversation. "So you can approach the secretaries without us, and it won't be suspicious. Unusual, maybe, but not suspicious. We are going to do our best to not be involved at all once we get to the Wheel."

"But, what if I have questions about something and—"

"The secretaries can answer all your questions about the process itself," Micaiah promised. "But before we leave here, you must know by heart everything you must say. If we interact at all, it will be as officers and probationary. Not as mentors and student, especially not as friends. Strictly formal."

"So what will you be doing?" Tommen wondered.

"Politicking elsewhere, most likely. But don't worry about us. Worry about here, now, what we're telling you."

"I'm listening."

And he did. Micah did most of the talking at first as he explained the importance of the introductions and the formalities, how Tommen was to introduce himself and formally bring about his case to be considered. Some things were not absolutely necessary, but by showing deference to the Hands and acknowledging such formalities, he might be able to gain their attention just a little bit more. Not much since the Hands heard cases all day, but it never hurt anyone to flatter the Hands a little and play on their narcissism.

"Make them feel important, and they will feel less threatened by you," Micah told him. "The less they think of you, the less they think your case is anything more than giving the dog a bone as it were, as opposed to giving a homeless person a six-course meal. It's a cruel analogy, but it takes less effort to give the dog a bone, and it's something easily forgotten. Remember, you are not only going before the Hands, but you are also crossing the Borelians and, in effect, the Grandfathers. Be the dog, ask for a bone, and be easily forgotten."

Tommen wasn't sure how he felt about being told to be a dog, to be treated like a dog, to have to beg and live in fear of being whipped. But as long as he said he would throw himself into Borelian slavery to save Walter, he figured he could take a little whipping.

"As far as bargaining chips, you don't have many," Micaiah began. "And you certainly don't have any trump cards to hold over anyone. Avoid naming Cassius as the False Zero Hour or otherwise associating them. Mention you were kidnapped by Cassius and Rifun, mention that you understand that there is a False Zero Hour among them somewhere, but do not put them both together."

"Don't tell them I was kidnapped by Cassius who is the False Zero Hour."

"Precisely."

"So how do I make this profitable for them? How do I make them money off of this?"

The twins looked at each other and Micaiah squirmed just a little bit, enough to make Tommen nervous. "It's a dangerous play, one that I'm hoping comes off sounding like probationary naiveté, while secretly getting the wheels turning in their minds of how to make it work for them." He paused for just a split-second. "Tell them that by allowing the creation of antidotes to Borelian poisons, the Hands stand to gain power over the Grandfathers. It would allow them to better control the prosecution of Runners.

"If Cassius takes the bait, he'll be able to save his friends from damning prosecution while crippling one of the most terrifying races involved in the Time industry. With Isthim already allied to him, he'll be able to potentially hold them over the barrel to do whatever he wants in exchange for not distributing antidotes, thus creating a secondary product market that he can control and make money on."

"That's what you call probationary naiveté?"

"What do you think it is?"

It was so evil and yet so perfect. Tommen briefly wondered why it hadn't been thought of before, then decided he didn't want to know. It probably had been thought of before, but there were reasons why it never took off. Maybe because the Borelians were just that fearsome. Maybe because no one as evil as Cassius had ever been Zero Hour and thus able to control the Borelians in such a way. Either way, Tommen was determined not to question it until he had the antidote and Walter was safely recovering at home.

"So can we go to the Wheel now?" Tommen wondered. "Or is there more?"

"No, we're going to wait an hour," Micaiah told him. "I suggest you use the time to rehearse what you're going to say. Chivalrous Welshman you may be, but I don't think grand public speaking is one of your strong points."

It was true, and Tommen slunk off to the bedroom to practice his speech. In his head. Because he couldn't stand the thought of the twins listening on the other side of the door and hearing his every "um," "uh," "well," as he more than occasionally stuttered and tripped over his words. In the movies, the hero always knew what to say, but only because the screenwriters told him what to say.

An hour felt like a dreadfully long time to put off going to the

Wheel and getting the cure for Walter's ailment, but at the same time, as Tommen watched the clock more than he practiced his speech, an hour also felt like not enough time to get anything done. He ended up continuing on his quest to clean and organize the room a bit, whispering his speech to himself, going over the profit plan, trying to word it so it sounded irresistibly enticing. Was that redundant? He tried to recall anything he learned in his English classes about speaking, but it all had to do with how to speak rather than what to say. They spent weeks on perfecting their speech essays; here, he had an hour. And he wasn't doing this for a grade, but to save his dad's life. No pressure or anything.

The hour that was endless and yet too short ticked by in regular little blips of a digital clock. Tommen could have Banded to give himself more time, but he knew there would be no point. It would only give him more time to be distracted and completely fumble his words. Still, he nearly jumped through the roof when there was a knock on the door and Micaiah entered.

"Ready?" he asked.

"No," Tommen admitted.

"You know the plan?"

"Producing an antidote gives the Hands more power over the Grandfathers and a way to control the Borelians, while also giving them a new product market that they can control."

"Exactly. Do you have some kind of idea how you're going to deliver it semi-eloquently?"

"I don't know. Kind of."

Micaiah looked somewhat annoyed, but Tommen chose to take it as concern. "At this point, if you need more time, you can Band. Otherwise, Walter's running out of time and we need to go. I'll give you five seconds to Band and take your time if you want."

While Tommen did want, he knew it would do no good, so those five seconds ticked by normally. Micaiah studied him for a moment longer before finally nodding and moving out of the doorway. "All right, let's go."

Tommen followed the elder twin out to the living room where Micah was already waiting, mentally preparing for the strain of opening a portal to the Wheel, which was nothing short of tearing a hole between dimensions. Then the twins stood together, and, in just a matter of moments, the portal appeared, and they stepped through.

Chapter Eight
The Wheel

The Wheel was not a spaceship or any man-made celestial body. It was not another planet or any natural celestial body. It was, for all intents and purposes, another dimension, supposedly an artificially-created dimension, designed millennia ago by the first Council of Hands. Since then, it was run and maintained by an army of secretaries. Not limited to just desks and paperwork, the secretaries handled all the day-to-day operations of the Wheel, from general cleaning and janitorial, to maintaining the portal room and making sure the portals didn't close on anyone as they went through, lest they disappear into some halfway dimension and never return, as was the common plight of humans half a century prior.

But Tommen and the twins passed through their portal safely, though not without side effects. It was only a brief ride, less than a second, like walking through any door, and yet it was like being tossed around in some kind of astronaut basketball tournament where the rules of physics alternated between zero G and super G. For Tommen, it was as if his limbs had turned to jelly and the air sucked forcibly from his lungs. For the twins, he imagined it was much worse, both the ass-kicking they got from going through the portal as well as the exertion from just opening it.

They entered into what was known, creatively, as the portal room. A thousand rows and a thousand columns of portals to thousands of worlds, all lined up like doors in an enormous corridor, except these portals looked more like they were suspended from a metal shower curtain rod or something. Once the portal was locked into the Wheel and held open on the super long shower curtain rod, the burden was off the portal opener, and the portal would stay open until the portal opener went back through it. Portals could be opened arbitrarily by the Hands or anyone qualified to do so, but rarely was there a reason to do so, at least for Earth. Some planets, Tommen was sure, had portals permanently open so Time Agents could move freely back and forth.

Once they had recovered from their ordeal, they headed to the front of the room to something that looked kind of like an ATM, but actually dispensed translators. It only required a small sample of flesh to determine the species of the person requesting a translator, and it gave them the appropriate device. For humans, a collar went around the neck to read the vocal chords, and an earbud went in the ear in order to receive translated messages.

Tommen instinctively went to put the bud in his right ear, then paused. Was that a smart idea? Should he put sound so close to his damaged inner ear? Would he be able to hear better, or would it just make it sound worse than garbled? Eventually, he moved the earbud to his left ear, trying to convince himself that he was totally comfortable. It was just like wearing normal earphones in his mp3 player, just in one ear only. Then he and the twins adjusted the language settings and headed into the Wheel itself.

The atmosphere in the portal room was somehow designed so the person coming through the portal could carry enough of his own atmosphere with him to reach the translator dispenser. The translators themselves were also capable of generating a tiny personal atmosphere that the wearer could take with him. This saved the secretaries from having to accommodate thousands of different species within the Wheel, some with vastly different and sometimes contradictory atmospheric needs. So Tommen and the twins could comfortably breathe the oxygen-nitrogen mix of Earth's atmosphere while everyone else could comfortably breathe their own atmosphere.

And it wasn't like *Star Trek* either, where 95% of all the alien species were humanoid and breathed oxygen. The alien diversity of the Wheel leaned more toward the *Star Wars* alien universe. Sure those aliens all still breathed oxygen, but there was more physical diversity. Extra limbs, funny heads, no eyes. Hell, the last time Tommen was in the Wheel, he'd spoken to an alien that looked like a spider had sex with a jellyfish.

There were a multitude of alien species, some Tommen couldn't even put a name to. Some walked, some flew, some seemed to play tricks on the mind to make him think they weren't even there when he knew they were. Humans were not the biggest boys in town either, as he jumped out of the way in order to avoid being stepped on by what he could only describe as a giant. But neither were they the smallest. Mouse-sized aliens scurried to and fro, darting in and around and between and through the legs and appendages of other aliens. They moved too fast for Tommen to tell exactly what they looked like, then figured it wasn't all that important. The best advice when visiting the Wheel was to just not try to figure it out. It was a mind-fuck and leave it at that. There was no logic here.

There was even less logic when it came to how the Wheel actually worked, how it was laid out. The only rooms with any semblance of order, with defined walls, floors, and ceilings, were the important ones such as the portal room, the Coliseum, the Judgment Wing, and so on. When it came to the marketplaces and rooms of considerably less importance, all logic of architecture and physics went straight to hell. There were steps and stairs that appeared to just lead straight into a wall, going nowhere, but if a person went up those steps, gravity would change and one would be walking on the wall. No awkwardly fighting gravity, not even a head rush. It was just turning the world on its side. Then there were steps from the wall to the ceiling, doing the exact same thing. It was like the biggest mind-fuck hamster wheel anyone ever saw. So even though the walls were all a translucent gold color and the ceiling was blue and the floor gray, a few trips around the hamster wheel and it would all be meaningless.

If that wasn't enough, the Wheel also didn't have what might be considered normal rooms. Everything was its own room, and to get from one room to another, it was all done via portals. Unlike most science fiction portals where they were "projected" on a wall or other surface, or suspended via a frame or a gate, portals between rooms in the Wheel just stood in midair. No frame, no surface. What was even more fucked up was that going through a portal one way took you to one room, but going through it from the other side took you to a different room. It was the same for every portal, whether they were on the floors, walls, or ceiling, and there was no guarantee that a portal on the floor of one room was going to open to the floor of another room; it would just as likely open on the ceiling. The only saving grace was that the portals did not change; once a person learned his way around the Wheel and knew which portal was which, everything was easy-breezy. Just going through the portals within the Wheel was less excruciating than going through a portal to get to the Wheel.

In a nutshell, the Wheel of Time was kind of like the garbage bag of science fiction ideas, from the inception to the portals to the physics to the aliens. Tommen couldn't decide if it was the garbage bag of really bad ideas that any sane science fiction author or director would reasonably discard, or the garbage bag of really awesome ideas that those authors and directors kept going back to so many times that it was always a surprise and yet not a surprise to see these elements together. The Wheel of Time was a mind-fuck and best left alone when it came to logic or sanity.

Speaking of sanity, while the Wheel also had its own calendar and did things by scheduling and was, in fact, the central hub for the Time industry, once Tommen and the others went back through the portal, it would be as if no time had passed at all. It was like six-something when they went in, and it would be six-something went they came out. Same day, same time.

Tommen had his suspicions that that rule could be tweaked a little. When Rifun had kidnapped him, there had been a delay between when they got out and when Walter, who had opened the portal, also got out. But that didn't concern him too much right now.

For now, they would all be traveling together, in and out of the Wheel together.

Or so they tried, as the Wheel was crowded, and Tommen lost sight of the twins more than once. He followed them across rooms, up walls, through portals, through crowds, and through at least one marketplace before finding a slightly less-crowded room where they could speak and not shout or risk being separated.

"What do we do now?" Tommen wondered.

"Now you head to the Coliseum and start your petition," Micaiah told him. At first Tommen was a little put off by his callous tone, until he realized they were in the Wheel only as officers and probationary, not mentors and student, and certainly not friends. "If you need us, we'll be in the Archives."

And like that, they turned and walked away, disappearing through a portal and leaving Tommen alone to find his way.

That was another thing; there was no universal system of writing in the Wheel, unless one wanted to count the linguistic programming that the secretaries had to do to keep the translators updated. Otherwise, anything that had to be displayed universally was done in simple pictures, or somewhat simple pictures. An eye was an eye, but would the Hands use an image of the Coliseum? The Coliseum was just a name, how the term was rendered in English in order to describe the Sanctum of the Hands. What the symbol was for it, inlaid on the floor, Tommen wasn't sure.

He knew the symbol for food, leading to the Food Court. He knew the symbol for portal, taking him back to the portal room. He knew the symbol for the turn currency and for Time Capsules, directing people to the marketplace hub where more symbols would direct them to the lower marketplaces, the intermediate marketplaces, or the auctions. So by process of elimination, he knew he was not where he wanted to be.

Figuring that if nothing else, he would simply learn all the symbols before finding the one he wanted, Tommen picked a symbol and went with it. It was a triangle that looked like it was some kind of rendition of the scales of justice. So he followed it, across a room, up a wall, across a ceiling, and down a corridor-like room before finally being presented with the symbol much larger on a wall above a portal; this was the room of that symbol.

It was, lamentably, not the room he was looking for. He knew that as soon as he stepped inside. If he had to hazard a guess, this was the Judgment Wing, the Seat of the Grandfathers, where Runners went to be prosecuted and punished.

A strange thing happened as Tommen entered the room. He couldn't really describe it other than being stripped of one of his senses, and not an obvious sense like sight or...or hearing, but it was like losing a sixth sense. Only after a moment of consideration did he realize he did not perceive Time as acutely as he normally did. As part of the Time industry, and especially as a Timekeeper, he was far more aware of the passage of time, each second and split-second that ticked by. It was how Timekeepers could break into incredibly narrow Fast Bands that lasted less than a Base Second, because they were able to perceive that small of an increment of time and act on it.

Tommen had no such instincts now. He could count off seconds, but he couldn't feel the threads of Time, couldn't manipulate them. He'd been stripped of his abilities. He might have panicked except he knew that sort of stuff happened in the Judgment Wing, and it would happen again when he went into the Coliseum.

"Are you lost?"

The Hands were not the only ones who were shrouded. The secretaries here also wore basic cloaks that did not conceal their identity, but made it impossible to tell from a distance their species. There were various colors and pins that denoted their function, but Tommen did not know all of them. This one wore a beige cloak with some kind of dark brown lining along the seams and a pin whose symbol matched the one above the door.

"Um, I'm looking for the Coliseum," Tommen told the secretary.

The secretary sort of resembled an ewok, Tommen thought, as

it looked up at him through bright green eyes set deep into a furry face. Finally it nodded.

The secretary gave him odd directions as only directions through the Wheel could be. Back through the portal, up to the ceiling, down the hall, third portal, then across the wall through the second portal, following the symbol that looked, to Tommen's eyes, like compass points.

"Thank you," Tommen said. "If I may ask—I'm only a probationary Timekeeper—where am I? Is this the Judgment Wing?"

"It is the Judgment Wing," the secretary confirmed. "This is where Timekeepers bring Runners for processing. They will be prosecuted and punished according to the Laws of Time. When you are an Apprentice, your mentor will bring you here, and you will talk to one of the Grandfathers to better understand the process."

Given that the room looked like it was made out of a single solid block of steel, Tommen was afraid to know the rest of the process. Still, he thanked the secretary, confirmed the symbol with him, and left the Judgment Wing, more than grateful to have his Time senses back and be able to feel every microsecond that passed. It wasn't even a huge thing, as if every second passed like a day, but it was a subtle awareness he never knew he'd developed or missed until it was suddenly taken away. He shivered.

He followed the symbol through portal after portal, both relieved to find the Coliseum door, thus not having to wander around looking like an idiot, and afraid to go through it and actually have to follow through with his mission. This could get him killed, or the twins, or Walter at a later date. At the same time, if he didn't try, Walter was going to die anyway. Tommen hesitated for just a moment before finally resolving that there really wasn't anything he wouldn't do to bring Walter back if he could help it. So he took a breath and stepped through the portal door to the Coliseum.

It didn't really look like the Coliseum in Rome, but Tommen could figure how it got its name. He stood outside a massive structure that looked like it was built out of millions of tiny windows or maybe solar panels, and then spray painted with something that was supposed to give a faux textured appearance, a stone facade. He wondered if people inside could see out through the tiny windows while the people outside couldn't see in.

He stood on what felt like the same strange floor as the rest of the Wheel, though it, too, was spray-painted to look like stone despite the inlaid metal. The whole structure rose high above his head until it appeared to go right through the ceiling, the walls were curved like the Coliseum, seeming to disappear just from sheer size, rows of arched windows lining the top that he supposed looked like they might have belonged to the Coliseum. So it was like a high-tech, modern, digital Coliseum.

It was probably the first place in the entire Wheel that used normal doors and arches instead of portals. At the same time, when the whole place was covered in the same Time ability hampering technology as the Judgment Wing, it probably made more sense to keep a potential villain better contained in a single controlled environment.

Not wanting to stop and stare like a dumb tourist, Tommen headed for the first door he saw, the one that looked like it saw the most traffic as aliens of all varieties walked, ran, scurried, or flew in and out. There were no symbols here that he saw, but there had to be someone around who could point him in the right direction, right?

Only when he was halfway through the door did Tommen realize that there were guards there. It was like a couple of tiny dimensions had been built into the door frame so the guards were invisible until a person was literally right in front of them. If Tommen had to hazard a guess, those guards would have no trouble breaking through the sliver of a dimensional wall to apprehend a perpetrator. As he went along, he saw more of the tiny dimensions with guards in them, but never until it would be too late.

The little bit of the Coliseum that could be seen from the outside did not do justice to the magnificence of the structure as seen from the inside. There was a track on the outer edge of the Coliseum that stood probably as wide as a football field and three or four stories tall. By the time Tommen had finished one lap of the track—because he was both an idiot and a tourist—he felt like he had gone back out and climbed the mountain to Forbes Cave at least twice, in thigh-deep snow, with weights on his ankles.

All around the inner wall of the track were doors, huge arched wooden double doors fifteen feet tall and ten feet wide. About every six doors was another set of doors, twice as big and twice as heavy with more metal gadgets and gears than the smaller ones. Twice in the outer track he came across gates that looked like they were a single piece of solid cast iron, fifty feet wide and fifty feet tall, held in an iron track with iron chains made of links as big as Tommen and as thick as Micaiah. Where in the universe did a race so advanced as to create the Wheel and all its mind-fuckery get the idea that its central governing building should be modeled after something from Ancient Earth? Or maybe the Coliseum was modeled after something from the Wheel? Whoever got the idea first, Tommen still couldn't figure out why all the technology suddenly seemed to cease in favor of stone and iron.

Having made it all the way around the outer track, Tommen had made several observations about the activity and goings-on. First, the larger wooden doors were most likely the smaller courts, the hearings for petitions before they went to the Hands. He guessed that from both glimpses he'd caught as the doors opened or closed, as well as a recurring symbol above the doors. Some of the smaller doors had recurring symbols, but not all of them, which meant it was going to be a treasure hunt to find what he was looking for. On the one hand, he could just ask. On the other hand, he could play dumb and do a little exploring first, see if he could find anything.

He doubted it, since any good evil villain didn't just leave shit lying around for any grunt to find in an otherwise unrestricted area, and Tommen walked into a number of unimportant rooms in his mini-adventure. He found what amounted to a janitor's closet, a mechanical parts room, several sitting rooms, a couple classrooms, even a break room for secretaries who did not look pleased at being interrupted. It was then that Tommen learned the symbol for Secretary.

"What are you looking for?" the angry secretary demanded as it shooed him out of the room.

"Um, the petition room to file...a petition," Tommen answered dumbly.

The secretary grunted and, in a manner that Tommen couldn't decide if it was just part of this alien's custom of imparting information or a rude slight, scratched the appropriate symbols into his arm, giving him the meanings for each, and then telling him to get lost.

Tommen stumbled out the door which was slammed and locked behind him. He held his arm, waiting for the throbbing to stop before daring to look at the symbols again. At least he wasn't bleeding. Time to make another trek around the building.

It didn't take as long as he'd feared, only about thirty doors from the main entrance. He wasn't sure if it was an appointment thing or more like the DMV, but the only way he was going to find out was by opening the door.

Truthfully, he wouldn't have minded if it was like the DMV, either waiting in a freakishly long line or else taking a number and waiting to be called. It would give him time to organize his thoughts and go over the plan in his head one more time, make sure he had all his points correct. Get the antidote, open a new market. That's all he had to remember and the rest would come to him. He hoped.

What he didn't expect was a triage setup refugee camp. The line was not long, and a team of six secretaries went to each person in line, spoke to them for about a minute or so, then directed them to one of a dozen or more waiting areas. Tommen was seen to within only a few minutes of walking in.

"Personal Designation, Rank, Celestial Position," the secretary said with the dull boredom of someone who did nothing but ask the same questions day in and day out.

"Tommen Forbes, probationary Timekeeper, Quadrant One, Parsec Eleven, Sector Five, System Four, Planet Thirty-Eight, Region Four, District Four," Tommen recited.

"What is the nature of your visit?"

"I need to file a petition with the Hands."

"What is the nature of your petition?"

How should he word it? A complaint? A request? A chat? "I want to make a bargain with the Hands to save my dad and Captain."

In the movies, the whole room, or the immediate vicinity, would come to an awkward pause as the other average people stared at him like he was crazy, the underlings of the Powers That Be would glance uncertainly at each other, as if they held a great secret and had to protect it and their masters. But this wasn't a movie, and the secretary did not seem affected one bit by Tommen's slightly cryptic response. Was that a normal response, then? Did many people walk in here looking to petition the Hands and make bargains with them? They might, he supposed, but he couldn't imagine anyone less than a Master in any Time Agent discipline doing so. The CEOs of McDonald's and Burger King might get together to make bargains, but this was like sending the part-time guy from some podunk desert Burger King to meet with the CEO of McDonald's. Did no one find it a little strange?

"All right, you'll be waiting in section seventeen," the secretary said, briefly pointing Tommen in a general direction and moving on.

There was a section for him? They had a section for people waiting to meet with the Hands in order to make bargains with them? Maybe it wasn't as uncommon as he thought. On the other hand, maybe he hadn't worded it quite right to fully get the scope of what he wanted to do. What if he got sent to the wrong court? What if the judge didn't know what to do with it so they threw him out?

Tommen found the section on the floor marked with the symbol for 17. Numbers were about the only thing that were fleshed out in the system of symbols used in the Wheel. Thankfully, they were on a base 10 system, or else it would be hell trying to convert the numbers back and forth. There were no chairs, just a simple box-like structure which was already occupied by five other aliens waiting their turn. One was humanoid with pale white skin that appeared almost translucent and seemed to glow, white tendrils floating around its face like hair, eyes closed. One was small and kind of resembled a gerbil, but only if a gerbil and a hairless cat got together and had a kid. The others were too difficult to describe and did not take kindly to being stared at to get a good look anyway.

He sat on the floor and waited. The hairless gerbil cat was taken first. He looked around. It was like a refugee camp, but without all the sickness and the weeping and the children running around naked. Maybe it was more like an airplane layover, but without the sickness and the weeping and the children running around naked. There was very little conversation, just a constant din of activity. One set of secretaries interviewed people as they came in while another set of secretaries came and went freely, pulling people and escorting them to their appropriate courts, or that was the best that Tommen could gather.

"I've never done this before," he said, turning so the white humanoid might hear him without having to stare and have a formal face-to-face conversation. "What happens now?"

The humanoid opened its eyes, which were almond shaped and completely black with no distinction between white, iris, and pupil that Tommen could see, like the eyes of the little green Martians in retro posters and bad B-movies. It looked at Tommen and regarded him for a moment, its forehead pulsing gentle colors for a moment before it opened its mouth to speak. "We wait until a secretary comes and brings us to our respective court where we will give a brief account to the candidate so they will determine if we will go before the Hands."

"And if they do determine that we should go before them?"

"The candidate will assign a time to go before the Hands. Then we are free at our leisure until the appointed time."

Tommen nodded. So it was pretty straightforward, about as much as he'd begun to suspect. He couldn't remember why he'd been so worried about the whole thing. Now that he was here in the middle of it, it almost felt too simple. Could this really be all there was to it? Just file a petition, wait, make your case, wait, go before the Hands? No monsters to fight, bosses to beat, boobytraps to disarm? Would he ever experience an adventure like Indiana Jones? Well, come to think about it, maybe Indiana Jones was a little much. Forget Holy Grails, he was after something far more practical, like an antidote for his father's illness.

"So what are you here for?" Tommen wondered, hoping he sounded friendly and conversational, and also very much needing to shake off the jitters.

The humanoid regarded him again momentarily before looking away and closing its eyes. "It is improper to inquire into the affairs of others who are waiting."

"Oh. Sorry." Pause. "So where are you from?"

Tommen was no great reader of alien expressions, but he got the impression that this alien was becoming annoyed by his persistent chatter. Still, it answered, "Quadrant Three, Parsec Four, Sector One, System Seven, Planet Ninety-Two, Region Three, District One."

Tommen nodded like he had any clue where that was. "I'm from a planet called Earth, live in the mountains of West Virginia, city called Charleston."

A secretary approached them but took one of the other aliens. The humanoid looked back at Tommen, then looked away and did not answer. So Tommen liked to talk, so what? He needed to talk, needed to have a conversation and relax before being taken before the...candidate?

That was the thing about translators. They were good, but they would never be one hundred percent just because of slang and nuances and personal word choice. But it was a fascinating mini sociology study, Tommen thought, as he mulled over possible reasons why the translators had rendered the word "candidate" when the intended word was probably something more like "judge" or "mediator" or something of that sort. What sort of judicial structure did the humanoid's planet or region have that made a judge a candidate? Perhaps being a judge made them a candidate for other government positions. Maybe being a lower court judge made them a candidate for becoming a higher court judge. Who knew? But it was fun to speculate.

The secretary returned again and took another alien. A few minutes later, someone else joined them, in line behind Tommen. Were there really that many people looking to strike up a deal with the Hands? Shit, he thought he was doing something special, that it would somehow give him an edge. He had nothing.

Then it was the humanoid's turn to go. It stood, but before it followed the secretary out, it turned to Tommen.

"Rudlash," it said.

"What?" Tommen wondered.

"My city, it is called Rudlash."

And then it just turned and followed the secretary out of the waiting area without another word. Tommen watched them leave, suddenly aware that the whole waiting area was alive with aliens, many of them having conversations that he couldn't hear. Some of it was because of the translator, limiting the range of sensitivity so as not to be overwhelming. But some of it was simply because he couldn't hear it.

It was a terrible thing to think about, and he wondered if it would affect his court hearing. What if he couldn't hear the judge? What if he had to ask for something to be repeated? Would he be looked down upon? It was a silly, irrational fear; he could just adjust the settings on his translator. But he didn't like being left without his other half. He needed his right ear in its full capacity. He needed the translator to understand what others said, but he needed his free ear to pick up on what others did, figure out where things were, how people were moving, if there were any surprises waiting for him. Fucking hell, he needed a hearing aid.

Gingerly, he moved the translator ear bud from his left ear to his right. Immediately he was overwhelmed, and he jerked the volume controls to the lowest level they would go. He gradually increased the sound, but the translator was not a hearing aid. It was an earpiece. It simply transmitted what was put into it. It didn't have built-in technology to compensate for increasing external or internal sound. Actually, Tommen wasn't sure what the difference was between the translator and a hearing aid, but it sounded pretty good. How could he petition the secretaries to come up with a translators that had a built-in hearing aid?

So he switched the earbud back to his left ear. Better to have sharp hearing in one ear than garbled conversation in one ear and nebulous noise in the other.

The last of the aliens who had been sitting when Tommen arrived was taken out. Tommen's stomach did a flip. Next one was his, and he was going to have pitch them a good one. This was the marketing stage, the street conversation where he had ninety seconds to sell his revolutionary product that was going to change the world. As seen on TV, the only thing that matters is the flash, the visual appeal, the benefits, and of course, a low, low price. And never underestimate the power of "But wait! There's more!" That's what he was going to have to come up with, but in a more formal court setting. How did one go about Billy Mayes-ing in front of a judge?

Or maybe it wasn't about being Billy Mayes, but Jack McCoy. He always had a good closing argument, one that made the jury squirm, one that laid everything out in plain detail. Skip the trial, go straight to the closing argument.

He didn't have a whole lot of time to consider it before the secretary approached the section.

"Tommen Forbes," it said blandly.

Tommen stood. It was like being called back to go to the dentist...when the appointment was to get all his teeth pulled...without anesthesia. But the secretary was not the friendly assistant in pink Minnie Mouse scrubs who smiled and welcomed him back and asked how he'd been in the last six months. No, the secretary was as passive as ever, like most of the people who worked fast food or shitty retail stores. There was no life there, just a body who went through the motions to do a job to get a paycheck.

They exited the room through another door at the back of the room in order to bypass the line of people walking in to start the petition process, and they ended up in another track. This track was narrower than the outer track, maybe half as wide as a football field, but just as tall. On the outer wall were pretty much all the same doors as the outer track, the little wooden doors, the big wooden doors. The only thing that was really different was the path that was gated by the two enormous iron gates. The wall itself on either side was made like the gates, but as fixed walls. The path itself did not lead up to those walls, instead dipping down and moving under the path and through another set of smaller iron gates, which basically meant that passage through that path was restricted, and Tommen bet that there was some measure that prevented flying aliens from getting through as well.

"How many courts are there?" Tommen wondered aloud.

The secretary looked back at him. It was a dog-like alien except it had six legs and, if Tommen guessed correctly, a modified wrist bone similar to a panda, kind of a thumb to hold things, but not really opposable. It had mottled gray and yellow skin that looked a bit like a hide that's been cleaned and yet still very wet and slimy on the flesh side. The face put Tommen in mind of a Great Dane or Labrador, though instead of whiskers, there were spiny fleshy appendages. It did not have a tail that Tommen could see, but it was wearing a cloak after all, this one white with blue trim, bearing the symbols for Court and Secretary and a couple others he did not know.

"There are fifty-one courts," the secretary answered after a moment's pause. Tommen was beginning to get the feeling that talking was frowned upon outside of normal operations. "One for each of the Hands and so at least one for each of the candidates. This one is yours. For the time being."

They stopped in front of one of the larger sets of double doors and the dog-alien stood up on its hind legs with perfect humanoid balance, about nine or ten feet tall.

"When you are ready to begin the hearing, stand between the columns," the secretary informed him. Then, using its modified wrist bones, it opened the doors for Tommen. As he stepped inside, the last thing he remembered thinking about the dog-alien was that it did, in fact, have a tail.

The courtroom was not like any courtroom Tommen had ever seen. The double doors on either side made up the entire wall. Like most of the Coliseum, it had the appearance of being made of stone. Two stone podiums stood in the center of the room, the only thing that kept the room from being a solid stone box. There was nowhere to sit, and the podiums were too tall for anything but a casual lean, that is, unless Tommen wanted to act the child and climb on top of one. But he was determined to be as mature and professional as possible, dredging up little tidbits of manners and respect that his ma and pa taught him even before Walter had entered his life.

Stand up straight, feet together, keep your arms at your sides, look the other person in the eye, speak clearly and concisely, be confident but not arrogant, better to use a simple word you know well than a sophisticated word that doesn't fit, and above all, speak only the truth. Wishes and speculations are fine, but when reporting facts, speak only the truth. Not exaggerations and especially no half-truths.

Tommen went to the podiums and hesitated. When he was ready, stand between them. That's what the secretary had told him. Was he ready to speak now and get the ball rolling? What if he just walked out, pretended this never happened?

Well then, that would make him a coward and far less chivalrous than he ever wanted to be accused of being. Not only would he be failing the weak and defenseless, but he would be abandoning his own father, condemning him to death. That was less than chivalrous, that was murder. No one on Earth would ever know, and he didn't even have to tell the twins—he could just say it got thrown out—but he would always know. He let his father die. And he could never live with that kind of guilt.

So, even if Cassius killed him or had him killed. Even if Rifun came after them again and Walter died anyway. Even if Cassius did gain control over the Borelians. Tommen would not be the one to murder his father by his own negligence and cowardice. He stared at the two podiums in the middle of the room for just a moment longer before finally taking a breath and stepping between them.

He wasn't sure what he expected would happen. Nothing exciting certainly. Maybe elsewhere in the Coliseum, someone was getting the little servant bell rung, signifying that their lunch break was over, but in the room itself, Tommen just stood there between the podiums, looking around. Was he facing the right direction? Did he miss some kind of "Enter this way" symbol? He looked around on the ground, but nothing stood out to him.

Then the door opened, and the first thing through Tommen's mind was the realization that both the humanoid alien and the dog-alien hadn't been misspeaking when they said he would be speaking to a candidate. The judges in these lower courts were the Hand candidates. His judge-candidate was dressed in the same shimmering white cloak that shrouded the Hands, but candidates wore their masking hoods down. Until they were elected as Hand, candidates had to wear them down and show their identities.

This judge-candidate was humanoid, and Tommen might have believed him human except for the abnormally large eyes and vine-line things that snaked across his skin.

"Tommen Forbes, probationary Timekeeper, Quadrant One, Parsec Eleven, Sector Five, System Four, Planet Thirty-Eight, Region Four, District Four," the judge-candidate recited, apparently from memory.

"Correct, sir," Tommen said, unsure of how he was supposed to respond.

"Liron aq Shoren aq Pelin, Triage Harvester, Candidate for Hand of Flora, Quadrant One, Parsec Six, Sector Two, System One,

Planet One, Region Nine, District Seven."

Hand of Flora? A Hand that represented plant life? That was a thing? Thankfully Tommen was either too nervous or smart enough to keep his mouth shut. Never insult the judge when you're trying to win your case; that much Tommen knew even if Walter wasn't a cop.

"You have indicated that you wish to strike a bargain with the Hands," Liron aq Shor—whatever continued, sounding every bit as enthused as anyone else who worked in the Coliseum. "Indicate the terms of your agreement."

"I want them to give me the antidote to one of the Borelians' naturally-occurring poisons. In return, they gain control over the Borelians," Tommen said simply.

Had Candidate Liron been the bad guy in a movie and Tommen the hero delivering some kind of ultimatum, Liron's eye brows would have gone sky high, his expression would turn long and thoughtful. He would probably nod slowly, begin to pace, maybe tell him what a tempting offer that was, maybe compliment him on finding his one weakness, that one thing he could never have that Tommen was offering him now. Probably he would go on for a bit, detailing his failed attempts at doing such a thing, commenting on how difficult it was and how he had ultimately failed. Then he would grow suspicious and ask how a mere probationary Timekeeper could possibly offer him that impossible thing.

But Liron was not the ultimate bad guy, though that wasn't to say that Tommen hadn't piqued his interest. He was no master of alien expressions, but he knew when Liron got a glimpse of that golden carrot.

That's right, big boy. What would it mean if you didn't have to worry about the Borelians if you became Hand?

"Are you yourself suffering from such an affliction?" Liron inquired.

"Not me, but my father who is a Timekeeper Captain and my mentor," Tommen answered, hoping he sounded confident without brushing off the severity of the situation, while still letting enough emotion bleed through to make an impact on him. Damn, that sounded sappy, like something out of a bad novel. And impossible to boot.

"How long does he have?"

"Six Base Days." Tommen tried not to sound too desperate, but also not too excited. Was it good when the candidates asked questions? Did that give him better odds that he would get before the Hands? Or was Liron just gathering more information in order to make his ruling?

For a long moment, Liron regarded him. Then he dipped his head once and the vines on his face continued to writhe and slide across his face. "Very well. You will present your case before the Hands. As you are a probationary Timekeeper, you cannot have gotten here by yourself. Who accompanies you?"

Tommen gave him the information for Micah and Micaiah. He struggled to judge his expression and his feelings toward the twins, but the man was a statue.

"Very well," Liron said. "Place one arm on a column."

Tommen did so and was rewarded with what basically felt like a needle stabbing him straight through the arm. He jerked his arm back instinctively and found a glowing blue tattoo on the inside of his arm with a variety of symbols, most of them numbers.

"You will go before the Hands at this time. Your mentors will show you where to go. Have you any questions?"

"Not that I can think of."

"Then go in harmony."

With that, Tommen was free to go. Liron watched him the whole way out the second set of doors to the outer track. And just like that, he had an appointment to meet with the Hands. Problem was, he didn't understand the Wheel's calendar system well enough to actually know when that was. Well, at the very least, he figured he had some time, enough to find the twins and ask them and make sense of it all.

It took a little time, but he found the exit and left the Coliseum, still slightly disturbed by how well the guards were hidden. Then he was out. Once he went through the portal, he was back in the main Wheel. He looked around, slightly disoriented after spending so much time in Ancient Rome in the middle of a man-made dimension. Well, the twins said they would be in the Archives, so that's where he figured he ought to start searching.

Chapter Nine
Research

The symbol for the Archives turned out to be a vertical rectangle, and it took Tommen on perhaps the longest chase he'd been on, trying to track it down. The chase finally came to an end outside a portal-door whose wall facade put him in mind of a building that's been through a fire and yet still stands. He couldn't pick out the material that the wall projectiong said it was made of, yet it was blackened and charred unevenly, fire burning hotter in one section or simply smoking in another. Tommen found himself wondering if this was simply part of the facade or if there had really been a fire here. He guessed at the former since maintenance crews could fix up any problems in almost no time at all.

When he finally stepped through, his throat closed, his heart seized, and his first thought was that he had stepped into some kind of horror movie and he was about to die. Not like a *Psycho* horror movie, more like *Saw*.

As his mind slowly put together the image before him, he felt foolish for thinking such a thing, even if he knew why. The initial lobby-like area was very poorly lit, and what lights there were, were gold. Like, Midas gold. The room itself was styled lavishly and reminded Tommen of pictures he'd seen of Victorian England or Imperial Russia, yet mixed with freak science fiction. The sconces, for example, appeared to be, at first glance, like any modern Earth-side sconce. Upon closer inspection, he realized that the light was not any kind of bulb or electricity or anything he'd ever seen. It was simply...light, a little ball of gold light. No colored glass or filters, not even any filament or bulbs, but gold light.

The walls were also decorated with massive paintings, not of anything specific, really. One was of a shrouded Hand, but without a label or a biography, one Hand was as good as another. Another was an apparent watercolor of an alien jungle. Still another was a landscape but with a secondary image of the symbol of the Hands hidden within the picture. A fourth was similar in style, but this time it hid the symbol of the Archives.

At the opposite end of the room was an enormous arch, and on either side of the arch was a desk, each with a secretary and a little machine that seemed to resemble the translator dispenser in the portal room. Trying to appear confident and not completely lost, Tommen approached one of the desks.

"Excuse me, I've never been to the Archives before," he told the secretary.

"Then first you will need a chip," the secretary told him, indicating the dispenser.

It worked just like the translator dispenser, needing only a sample of flesh before spitting out a chip that looked somewhat like an SD card. As he looked at it, the secretary went on, "That chip will translate any record into any of the languages of your home planet that we have on record. If it is on your translator, it will be on that chip."

"That's handy," Tommen commented.

"What are you looking for today?"

"Actually, I just came to find the people I came in with."

"I cannot speak to the exact whereabouts of anyone in the Archives. Do you know what they came here to look for?"

"I don't."

"Then you will have to look for them."

"I was afraid you'd say that."

"The Archives are through the arch here. Insert the chip into the end of a row to view topics or titles in that row, then simply insert the chip into any glass. You will only have to choose your language once, and the chip will remember for the rest of the visit. Every glass also has a map built into it if you become lost. We ask that noise be kept to a minimum and all glasses returned to their appropriate positions when you are finished. Any questions?"

"Not until I need help, I suppose," Tommen said.

The secretary nodded, and he stepped cautiously toward the arch, as if great steel doors would slam shut once he was through and trap him inside forever. But what he saw almost made him not care if steel doors did slam shut.

It was like the biggest library in the universe. Bigger than the Library of Congress, bigger than any library he'd ever seen or imagined. Bigger than the fantastical fantasy libraries of fictional fantasy castles or the library planets of science fiction. Bigger than...life. It was like taking every number on the Dewey decimal system and giving it its own four-story library, and then expounding on that with all the information and knowledge and histories and sciences of a thousand thousand galaxies with a thousand thousand worlds each. It was like Library-ception, a dizzying tessellation of a library within a library within a library, corridor after corridor, row after row, floor upon floor upon floor, and he stood only in the middle of it all. Connecting it all was a series of stairs and lifts, and not just ones that went up and down, but from one side of the great room to the other in an intricate carousel of moving platforms. Tommen jumped as some flying alien swooped past him on its way to somewhere else in the library. It was like an entire library planet stuffed into an infinitely enormous room, so much bigger on the inside.

Tommen realized he was standing there looking over the balcony with his mouth open. He quickly snapped it shut and decided just to move before he froze to the spot in sheer wonder. Once he got past the walls of the lobby, the Archives again unfolded before him, three times the size of the original view from the lobby balcony. Aliens of all shapes and sizes browsed up and down rows, picking out tablet-like things and inserting their chips.

Tommen's first thought was that he was never going to find

Micah and Micaiah in here. It was far too big. It was probably a week's journey from one side of the library to the other. He would hate to play a game of hide-and-seek in here, except that's what this was going to turn into pretty quickly.

Every glass has a map, the secretary had said. Curious, Tommen went to the first glass-tablet he found and inserted his chip. After browsing through at least a bazillion available languages, he found Welsh and selected it before going to the map feature.

Shit, the Archives were even bigger than what his gaze could take in. And yet, once he figured out how to use the tablet and navigate the map, he also found that the organization was astoundingly precise. The tablet books were arranged in a Dewey decimal-like system—that is, they were arranged by topic—but there were several subsystems within that system depending on what one was looking for or how one wanted to search. For example, in "Science" he could browse by General Astrophysics or by the astrophysics of a specific planet or system. History he could go by the history of a specific planet or by, say, the history of a specific disease that may have traveled from planet to planet. There were an infinite number of permutations for searching that would lead him exactly where he needed to go.

Tommen found himself grinning and thinking, with a little cheekiness, that this was the ultimate search engine, far more informative and refined than any standard Internet search engine. He could get almost down to the exact book where certain information would be stored. Holy fuck, if he learned how to open portals to the Wheel, he would have access to all the resources he would ever need to write papers in college. Citations might prove a bit of a challenge, but he could find information that was so much more thorough than anything he would find on the simple Internet. Hell, even the Internet might as well have been a collection of old stone tablets.

He spent probably a good half hour just playing with the map, trying to get himself oriented even a little with the layout of the Archives. At least if he got a rough idea which sections were where, he might have an easier time of it in the future. From the lobby balcony, the section immediately to the left, where he stood now, was reference. Where he presently stood was the map area. Here were maps of millions of worlds and millions of regions within each world, star charts, sea charts, ancient maps, digital maps, maps in infrared. Directly across from the lobby balcony was the history section which also extended around to the right side of the lobby balcony. And that was just one floor. The next floor up, sciences, plants and animals mostly. The next floor down, more reference, almost exclusively devoted to language.

Eventually, Tommen got an idea of what to look for. He knew it was probably a dangerous thing to enter such a broad search term, but he did it anyway. TIME.

He did not get hits the useless way that most search engines presented them, ordering them by who paid the most to be sponsored and who was the most popular. Instead, it let him search in sections. He chose "Reference" and "Math," figuring the second might be useful. He went through several more menus before finally coming up with a more specific location. Reference, three floors up. He almost took the tablet with him until he remembered the secretary's words, both about returning the tablet to the right spot and about every tablet having a map.

While the lifts and other assorted moving platforms were cool, Tommen had to go with the nostalgia of taking the stairs, running up the spiral staircases two steps at a time until he reached the appropriate floor. There he went to the section he thought was correct and picked out another tablet.

This time he was sent to a subsection of rows far back into the section, almost out of sight of the open atrium except for the rows all lining up and allowing him to see out. There were several open areas where various aliens sat quietly to read, and this subsection opened up to one of them.

The rows themselves were metal, but they were shaped just like racks at the library at school. When he inserted his chip into a slot at the end of a row, it did what the library rows at school couldn't do. It lit up and presented him with a list of all the tablets in that row. When he tapped on a book, it opened up a description of the book including all important points and search terms. When he tapped on a button that said, "Show Me," the tablet in the row would light up gold, indicating its position.

It took several tries, but eventually Tommen found what he was looking for. He took the tablet to a spot in the reading area and sat down cross-legged. He inserted the chip and, as the book was loading, rolled up his sleeve where the blue tattoo still marked his arm. He wondered momentarily if it would come off after the time was past, or once the hearing was over.

What he wanted to do was very simple. He wanted to convert the date on his arm, written in terms of the Wheel calendar, to its Earth-side date counterpart. He was curious to know if there was a simple method of conversion, like Fahrenheit to Celsius or some such thing.

First thing he had to do was go through all the preliminaries in the book, selecting his quadrant and parsec, all the way down to his planet. And even then he had to go through a small dog and pony show about the date and time when he'd left. It was a little frustrating until he considered that with the International Date Line, that could make a big difference in whether he was supposed to go before the Hands in two hours or twenty hours, and he certainly didn't want to be late.

Unfortunately, the equations for date conversion were not so simple as Fahrenheit to Celsius. First off, he wasn't entirely familiar with the higher and more complex number symbols used in the Wheel. Second of all, he wasn't entirely familiar with the calendar system of the Wheel either, both of which were necessary to even begin the conversion. And assuming he even understood all that, the equations were of a level far, far beyond his comprehension as it employed both math and physics, having to account for "dimensional dissimilarities" and other such things which Tommen was pretty sure were nonsense. And even if they did make sense and were relevant, there was no way he could even fudge his way through the equation. If the conversion wasn't as important as meeting with the Hands, he might have given it a shot and hoped for the best. But as it was, he knew when to admit defeat and ended up using the converter. Conveniently enough, there were several to choose from, including one labeled, "The Courts Gave Me a Time to Meet With the Hands; What Time is it At Home?"

"Today is December 25, 2013," Tommen whispered as he entered the date. "We left at...six-fourteen?" He hoped that a few minutes off wouldn't make a huge difference. He looked at his arm and had to keep going back and forth between the converter and the number cheat sheet. "Four, eleven, twelve...nine, six, seven, one..."

He wasn't sure what difference it made between what time it was when he left home and the time on his arm, but he figured that as long as he did everything true to form, there would be less room for error. When he finished, he checked and double-checked everything before finally tapping "Convert."

"December 26, 2013, at 0412" the tablet read.

Tomorrow at four in the morning? Tommen stifled a groan but still rolled back on his back on the floor. Fuck. He wondered if the judge-candidate had done that on purpose or if it was all just the next available appointment. That meant that his best bet would be to go home now and get some sleep before going before the Hands. But he wasn't tired yet.

He sat up. He was in a dimension where no matter how much time he spent here, it was as if no time had passed at all at home. And he was in the biggest library in probably the entire fucking universe. There was no guarantee that the Hands were going to help him. If they didn't, he was going to need a backup plan.

Tommen stood and went back to the row. All the tablets looked the same, not even titles on the spines. He inspected the tablet, looked at several open spots in each row of books, trying to decide which one was his open spot. He paused as his finger found a button on the tablet. He pushed it. Instantly the tablet lit up and a corresponding empty slot on the row also lit up. Relieved, he slid the tablet back into place, and all was normal again.

He immediately took the tablet back out, seeing how he needed a map to continue. It took some finesse with his searches as he walked, ran, or floated his way from one part of the library to another, grabbing tablets and consulting maps until he finally narrowed his search down to subsection of rows. Even then it was difficult to find what he was looking for, given that the entire floor was dedicated to medicine. Seeing how many alien species there were, and then considering that there were even more, medicine was a very big deal, and very thoroughly accounted for.

Eventually, Tommen picked out several tablets and found a quiet corner to sit and read. He was never a big reader. He barely read the novels assigned in English class, and long technical scholarly papers were equally as boring. If he read, it was magazine articles. If it must be technical, make it relevant and to the point, or don't bother with it at all, in his opinion. If he needed something, he would look it up. Look it up enough times, use it enough times, and he would learn it. If he wasn't going to use it in some way or use it to build on something that he would use, he saw little point to it.

The information collected and put into the tablet books was not his kind of relevant-only reading. They were the long technical scholarly articles. Mercifully, whoever compiled the information also saw fit to vomit hundreds of images and diagrams to go along with the text, but he was looking for Cliffnotes and found the Encyclopedia Brittanica.

Tommen wished he had brought a notebook of some kind to write down what he found, but it was no use wishing for what he didn't have. He would just have to commit as much as possible to memory.

"The difference between a vaccine and an antidote," he breathed, scrolling through the information. "A vaccine is a dead or weakened strain of a disease that is introduced into someone's body for the immune system to attack and build immunity to, without the disease doing any lasting damage to the body, for example, a flu vaccine." *Yeah, right. Not always true, guys.* "An antidote is a cure to a non-viral or bacterial disease usually caused by adverse reactions to toxic chemicals that often cannot be defended against by the immune system, for example, an antidote to snake venom."

Tommen leaned back against a wall. So if he treated Walter's disease like snake venom, he would still be susceptible to it in the future. But at least they would have an antidote. Question was, how did he go about finding one? How did he make an antidote to snake venom when he couldn't ask for it from the snake, or even approach the snake?

"In order to effect an antidote, one must first understand the nature of the toxin or chemical and how it affects the body. Then one must produce an antidote that not only works against the toxin but is toxic to the toxin itself without it doing further damage to the body. For example, for a toxin that attacks the nervous system, an antidote must not only destroy the toxin, but protect and even restore the nervous system, and not shut it down."

Well, no shit. Whoever wrote this was a genius. But it was all true. Tommen wasn't going to cure Walter's poison by injecting him with juice from poison hemlock. Yeah, it would kill the poison, but it would also just as readily kill Walter.

Problem was, how was he going to discover the nature of the poison? It didn't even register on all the tests and scans and instruments that Walter was hooked up to. Everything said he was fine; he was in perfect medical health less the three gunshot wounds, but still. No, Earth might not be an engaged planet, but Tommen would say it had pretty good medicine all things considering. And poison was poison, one of the oldest killing methods, and it was a ghost on the machines.

Sighing, Tommen gathered up the tablets and, after much frustration, finally managed to return all of them to their rightful spots on the shelf. He rested his head on one of the shelves. The poison wasn't a viral or bacterial disease, so there would be no vaccine for it. Anyway, a vaccine would take months or, more likely, years to develop. An antidote was equally as unlikely without knowing the nature of the poison which he couldn't get because it was entirely invisible.

Was he really going to be forced to hope that the Hands would be merciful and help him out? Were all his hopes going to be pinned on his leaden-tongued speech that he was going to give in however much longer it was until he went before them? Was there no other way, no Plan B that he could fall back on if this plan failed?

He went to the balcony and looked over the railing. He thought he could see the bottom floor, way far down there with aliens running around like little ants going about their business to build a bigger, better colony.

Tommen rubbed his face. Lily said Walter was fighting back, hanging on, making his countdown go just a little slower, buying him some time. They'd managed to give him four seconds more just by having Christmas with him. What did that say about the nature of the poison? Was it a matter of willpower, mind over matter? Walter had once gotten the flu, and even though the department made him stay home, he still powered through it like it was no more than a bad cold. It had to have destroyed his body internally, but he never let on how bad he hurt. He simply steeled himself against it and bulled on.

A thought occurred. Tommen was no doctor, that was for sure, and he had very little exposure to medicine beyond Walter having to renew his emergency responder license every few years, but he'd watched enough *Grey's Anatomy* and *House* to make a few connections, at least enough to get started in the right direction.

Borelians of all colors and all toxins also had side effects that affected others just by sheer proximity. Did that mean that the toxins were like gases? And if it had to enter the bloodstream in order to be effective, that meant that the poison was blocking the oxygen from bonding to the red blood cells. And if the toxin acted anything like carbon monoxide, it would not be detectable on his oxygen stats because they would appear normal. Walter would have been on oxygen during the surgery, and been receiving units of blood, probably putting off the effects of the poison. And because he was breathing on his own, he had little more than a nasal cannula on in ICU, which probably didn't give him enough oxygen to counteract the poison entirely, but enough to "fight back" as Lily put it.

Tommen might have prayed to God that he was right if he believed it would help. He wasn't about to cancel his meeting with the Hands, but it was a theory he could test if they did refuse to help him. And just to be sure, he picked up a tablet and went back to the map.

The Biology floor was the bottom floor, or what passed as the bottom floor. Tommen still wasn't sure how many floors there were in the Archives, seeing how he couldn't even see the top, standing on the first floor and staring up at the atrium at a light that seemed to come from nowhere and yet lit up the entire place. It was like it just kept going. Maybe it did. Forever. Endless information.

No time for that now. He had work to do. It took several tries and what felt like hours of just looking, but he found the subsection he was looking for. He searched through hundreds of books at the end of the row, finally picking just one and going off to a secluded corner as if he was doing something evil and secret.

As Tommen inserted his chip into the tablet, he wondered if he was being followed, his movements tracked. He wondered if Cassius somehow had his chip bugged and knew exactly what he was looking for. Was he just being paranoid? Not if it was true. He looked around, saw no one, saw no obvious indications of security cameras. He shifted position and tried to tell himself to relax. No one could see what he was reading, and even so, he was just a probationary Timekeeper studying up before his review. Though if that was his story, he really should be in History.

Either way, didn't matter. No one had questioned him so far and he wasn't about to give anyone a reason to do it now. *Sit down and be good.*

" 'Borelians originate from Quadrant One, Parsec Eleven, Sector Nine, System Three, Planet One,' " he read quietly, " 'a world called Brelix in the Surg...Surog...' um, Something-or-Other 'system.' " *Just read it quickly and move on.* He skipped over the bits about their involvement in Time. " 'Within the last two hundred years, Borelians have achieved space travel and have gone out among neighboring systems. The Borelians are a unified race, though violent and war-like, famous for their cruelty, casual use of torture, and vicarious slave trade. They believe themselves to be superior to most all other alien races in the universe. At best, they will simply ignore someone they believe is bothering or insulting them. At worst, they will kidnap that person and sell them into slavery which, by all accounts of surviving Borelian slaves, is a fate far worse than death.' "

Lovely. So it was cyanide or bust when dealing with Borelians. But this was a biology book, and pithy introductions meant little to Tommen right now.

Originally he was just interested in the poisons and how he might counteract them. But as he thought about it, scrolling through exceptionally detailed diagrams, it might be useful to know a little about their physiology. It might help to find a weakness in the event they encountered Isthim or any hostile Borelian in the future.

" 'The horns of a Borelian serve many purposes and are as vital an organ as the heart and lungs as they are connected to several bodily systems. First, they are connected to the circulatory system, and a major artery runs through them, helping to regulate body temperature. The horns themselves have a hollow core which is part of the respiratory system, especially the sinuses, providing a greater sense of smell, a greater sense of deep vibrations which help them to predict earthquakes which frequent Brelix, as well as extra air sacs in which to store air, much like storing air in the lungs. The artery in the horns surrounds this hollow core, keeping the air warm. The artery is encased in a spongy, porous tissue surrounded by a much harder bone-like structure which is part of the skull and visible on the outside. The horns are also covered in millions of micro-hairs that are so sensitive, they can detect atmospheric displacement down to one micrometer.' "

So, horns, very important. And if they were made of bone and Borelian bones were anything like human bones, best bet was to break one and break it good.

He kept going through each of the systems. Fundamentally, they were very similar to humans. Heart and lungs were basically instant kills. Food went to a stomach that digested a little differently, but not in any way that mattered to Tommen. Sexually they were very similar, though apparently instead of bloody menstrual cycles every month, female Borelians instead, once or twice a year, became exceptionally irritable and enraged and would literally lock horns with a chosen mate while they mated, over and over again for several days until she became calm once more. Tommen was intrigued until he came to the part where it said that was the only time that Borelians had any form of sexual contact with each other. Shit, that had to suck. No wonder the entire species was violent and war-like.

Then he finally got to the part he'd been looking for. He originally thought it might be part of the integumentary system diagrams and explanation, but the toxins had their own section, and probably for good reason.

" 'The Borelian toxin system is as much about thought as it is proximity and touch. Borelians consider it a muscle to be trained and honed as much as any physical muscle. For example, any yellow Borelian can stop a heart at a touch, but a highly-trained yellow Borelian can control its abilities and effectively "reach into" a victim in order to manipulate his circulatory system, anything from causing the heart to burst to boiling the blood or reversing its flow.

" 'A Borelian is immune to his or her own toxin and, most often, the toxins of the parents (color is usually random, though two parents of the same color have a higher chance of having a child of the same color). It is possible to expose infants to the other toxins and grant them some immunity.

" 'The toxins are not part of the skin, but rather a separate "skin" on top of the protectorate skin (see Chapter 6). The toxins are pushed into this top layer of skin through several ports found at the following locations. Once the toxin hits the air, it is given off as a gas, causing side effects.' "

If Tommen was reading the diagram correctly, those ports were at the base of the neck, the armpits, the groin, and the small of the back. Briefly he had a revelation, more of a memory, of his ma butchering a duck. Once she'd plucked it, she had to cut the oil gland off the tail. So the Borelians were a bit like ducks with their poisons.

" 'Sometimes, a Borelian child is born with the ability to "push" two or more toxins. These are called "bitoxic Borelians" and come in two subsets, adjunct and disjunct. An adjunct bitoxic is able to push two toxins that are similar in nature, for example, a child who can change from gray to green (see chart), would be considered an adjunct bitoxic, where a white and gold Borelian would be considered a disjunct bitoxic.' "

So it wasn't about the color like Rifun had assumed, but the nature of the toxin.

" 'Rarely, a Borelian is born with the ability to push all the toxins and is called a *"vodrak"* which roughly translates to "all deadly." These *vodraks* have more concentrated toxins than any Borelian of a single color, however, they typically have a much shorter life span, up to 60% shorter, due to the effort of storing, changing, and pushing all the different toxins.' "

Then there was the chart detailing each of the toxins, the color, the side effect, and the poison, all arranged in order for the reader to understand which toxins were considered adjunct and disjunct. There were literally dozens of colors, most of them with their Borelian names since there was no word for them in Welsh or English or any other Earth-side language because humans couldn't see most of those colors. And the things they could do were...unspeakable, how they could just reach into someone and turn their own body against them.

Tommen rubbed his eyes. It was useful and yet useless. Where was the part about what to do if someone accidentally touched a Borelian? He sighed and kept scrolling.

" 'Borelians are very aware of their deadliness to outsiders. Because of the slave trade, they go to great lengths to cover themselves to prevent any accidental touches. However, there are occasional accidents. While Borelians claim that they have an antidote for every poison they produce, they refuse to share it with outsiders, or even show proof of its existence, instead reserving the antidotes only for their own species, if indeed they do exist. So far, anyone who has attempted to search for one and steal it has been killed. Anyone who has tried to bargain with or bribe a Borelian for an antidote has been sold to the slave markets. Anyone who has attempted to develop an antidote themselves has been killed or gone missing with no trace. Therefore it is advisable that, if one wishes to avoid needing an antidote, one should stay away from Borelians in the first place.' "

And that was that. The text simply cut into a new chapter, and no matter how far Tommen scrolled or what words he looked for, that was it. No hints or reassurances, no stories of survival. Just, "this is the color, this is the toxin, this is what's going to happen to you if you come in contact, and if you do, kiss your butt goodbye."

There should have been something. Anything. Surely in this vast Archive of knowledge from all around the universe, there had to be something. The Borelians couldn't have clamped down that hard on that kind of information. It was like the government. They could classify stuff and shred all the files they wanted, but there was always a whistleblower somewhere. What about the poor and insignificant vessels that went where no Borelian went before, peacefully? Would none of them give up such information? Wouldn't they want to help those who had been captured and enslaved by their own people?

Tommen went back to the shelves, picking up any tablet that was even remotely about Borelians, but to no avail. He went back through the map of the Archives and did a search for poisons and cures. Maybe "gold Borelian of doom" was secretly lodged somewhere between "nightshade berry" and "poison ivy."

He found the subsection and did a tearing search through

every tablet, one at a time, poring over the information. Poisonous plants, poisonous animals, poisons of the species of other worlds. It looked promising, but the section on Borelians was less so.

" 'Every Borelian is poisonous to outsiders, the toxin determined by the color of their skin (see chart). The glands controlling these toxins are located at the base of the neck, the armpits, the groin, and the small of the back. When the toxins are exposed to air, they turn into a gas, thus causing side effects when in proximity to a target. Some toxins kill more quickly than others, but all are considered deadly. The Borelians often make claims that they possess antidotes to each of the toxins, but have never shown any proof to outsiders.

" 'Any outsider who has attempted to make his own antidote has been killed. It is the observation of this author, however, that the toxins are secreted as an oil. Skin-to-skin contact is lethal, if not deadly, however, if the gaseous toxin is absorbed into the blood stream directly via an open wound, it is certain death.' "

Certain death, always certain death. And what was it about the oil that killed just by touching the skin, that the gas had to infect the blood? Did that mean Tommen's theory about the toxin inhibiting the oxygen was false? Or was it just the method? Like drinking toxic cleaners versus just inhaling them? He put the tablet back and vigorously rubbed his face. What was he missing? What were the doctors missing? The doctors, who went to medical school and knew helpful stuff, what were they missing? What kind of test would show this stuff and motivate them to act?

He couldn't think of anything. He was tired of thinking. He was tired, period. And he still had to go before the Hands tomorrow. Fuck, what was he supposed to give them? They probably already knew all this shit. They'd probably been trying to do this for years. Maybe they had already sent people out to try and steal or develop an antidote.

Did Micah and Micaiah know about all of this, too? Had they sent him out, knowing that it would be a failure, just to placate him in his quest to do anything to save his father? That didn't sound like something they would do. Well, it did, but not on something so serious. They would let him touch a hot pan to prove a point, but they wouldn't juggle him around like this and toy with him. They played pranks, but they weren't cruel.

Slowly, he replaced the tablet and headed out of the rows. Time to find them, Tommen supposed. They'd go home, and then he could get some sleep before dragging his sorry ass in front of the Hands in the morning and making a fool of himself.

And why had the candidate approved him to go before the Hands? Surely he must have known all this. Maybe he was just trying to make him feel like a fool. Well, it was working. He was probably the biggest fool in the whole Time industry right now.

His search for the twins was more passive than active, and he stumbled across more than found them. He wasn't sure what section he was in, either.

"You look like hell," Micaiah told him quietly, looking up from his tablet. "You get rejected from seeing the Hands?"

"No, I got an appointment," Tommen said, rolling up his sleeve and showing them the tattoo.

"That's not too long from now," Micah said. "We should get you home so you can get some sleep."

The twins put their tablets away, and they started for the lobby.

"So what's got you down, then?" Micah asked. "You got an appointment with the Hands, but you look like someone just kicked your puppy."

Tommen hesitated but told them the bad news first, that nothing in the Archives had anything good to say about Borelian toxins, except that the Borelians claimed to have them, but any outsiders who sniffed a little too close to home were killed or sold as slaves.

"Did you know?" Tommen asked when he'd finished. "Did you know it was useless?"

Micaiah gave him a sympathetic look. "No, we didn't know. The judge probably did, and him sending you to the Hands means that something might be able to be done."

"Or he wants to make a fool out of a fool probie Timekeeper."

"Or maybe one of the Hands is a Borelian," Micah pointed out. "Or maybe the Grandfathers have an in on it. We don't know. But the best you can do is go before the Hands as planned and give it your all, fight for your dad with all the zeal you've been hitting us with lately. Okay?"

Tommen hesitated but agreed. "I did think of something else, though, and I want to try it if the Hands don't help."

"We're all ears, but wait until after we leave."

They'd reached the lobby by that point, turning in their chips and leaving the Archives quietly, emerging into the sci-fi chaos that was the Wheel.

"So what's your idea?" Micah asked, seemingly grateful that he didn't have to speak softly anymore. Tommen was glad too, because that meant he could actually hear them, and not just through the translator.

He gave them the rundown of his thoughts and observations about the toxins inhibiting the oxygen in the blood. He tried to include as many details and as much knowledge as he could to made sense, but really it just made him feel like a charlatan, a TV doctor throwing around some medical word salad to make it sound convincing.

"It's an interesting theory," Micaiah admitted as they got back to a place that was more familiar, not far from the portal room, "and I wouldn't discount it."

"But what kind of toxin would kill instantly at skin contact, yet the gas would need to permeate the bloodstream?"

"I think you may have misread something," Micah said. "The gas causes the side effects. The air dilutes the oil's potency. When Isthim handled the bullets to poison them, she was wiping oils on them, and those permeated the bloodstream."

"Which makes my previous theory worthless."

"Not entirely. It's a good thought, and since we don't have any better ideas, I would be willing to try it."

They reached the portal room and removed their translators. Tommen's ear felt a little funny after removing the earbud, and he was surprised to find comfort in the muffled silence. Fuck, was he in the acceptance stage already? It had been, like, two days. Maybe three. How was he over this already? Except that he had bigger problems than his pettiness. He would give up all his senses to bring Walter back.

"How do you expect to try that experiment?" Tommen wondered as they headed down a row of portals.

"I'll show you when we get back," Micaiah told him.

It was comforting to have Micaiah take the lead, and have him be almost confident in the idea. Even if he was just confident in the thought of having an idea to try, Tommen took comfort in it, and a little pride, too, that it had been his idea in the first place.

They reached the portal and took a moment to mentally prepare themselves before walking through. When they did, there was the familiar yet terrifying sensation of having the air sucked from their lungs before being deposited most ungracefully of the floor of the living room in the twins' house. Gradually, they picked themselves up off the floor. Tommen and Micah made it to the couch while Micaiah stumbled into the dining room to grab his phone. He dialed a number and headed weakly back into the living room to relax in the recliner.

"Lily?" he wondered breathlessly. "It's Micaiah. Yeah, we just got back from the Wheel. Yes, Tommen made a petition and he's going before the Hands tomorrow. Yes. Yes, I know. I...I know. Listen, we spent some time in the Archives and Tommen did quite a bit of research. He—No. No, he didn't find anything out about the Borelian toxins specifically, but in his sleuthing, he may have discovered some amateur medical school dumb luck. And I'm willing to try it. Are you at the hospital or can you get there? Good. Let me tell you the theory and then you can talk." Briefly he relayed Tommen's theory. "How does that sound to you?"

He was silent for a good five minutes, and Tommen could feel his hopes crashing and burning with each second that went by. It was stupid. Worthless. She was ripping his theory to shreds like a movie critic tearing into a shitty movie. Finally, Micaiah spoke again.

"Uh-huh. Okay. I understand. But here's the thing: we don't have any other ideas. We have no options right now. I consider this thing with the Hands to be a last resort. What's the worst that a little extra oxygen is going to do to him? You have Harvester-vision; either it works or it doesn't, and you'll be able to tell the difference. Help us out here, Lily. Help Walter." Pause. "Okay. Thanks, Lily. Uh-huh. Bye."

He hung up and rubbed his eyes.

"What's the word?" Micah dared to ask.

Micaiah sat up and leaned forward on his elbows. "Walter is still ticking down, almost at a normal rate, just a tad slower. She doesn't think Tommen's theory is entirely correct or that the oxygen will help," he answered honestly. "But, just like us, she has no other ideas or options, so she's willing to give it a try."

"When will we know if it's working?" Tommen wondered.

"You go to bed," Micaiah told him. "You're exhausted, and you have to get up early. We'll wait up for her call back."

"And you'll tell me before we go?"

Walter would either be improving or he would stay the same. Either way, Tommen was going to be worried sick and it was going to affect his speech. He knew it, and he could see the twins knew it, too. Finally, Micaiah nodded. "Yeah, we'll tell you before we go. Assuming she calls back. Now, off to bed."

Thursday

Tommen jolted awake at a hand on his shoulder. He grabbed the blankets like a fearful child and looked around, but it was only Micaiah kneeling beside the bed. Trying to calm his racing heart, Tommen let out a breath that turned into a yawn and stretched.

"What time is it?"

"Quarter after three," Micaiah told him. "We think it would be best if you took a shower and made yourself presentable."

It made sense, but it didn't make him want to do it. "What about my dad? Did Lily call back yet?"

With only the light from a lamp in the living room, it was difficult to judge Micaiah's expression, but his hesitant pause was enough to put ice in Tommen's veins.

"Lily got the doctors to up the oxygen," Micaiah told him slowly, "but it made things very bad, very quickly, and it almost killed him. They were able to get him back about where he was. Lily estimates he's got about four days."

Tommen tried to sink back under the blankets. He wanted to cry. He wanted to have never woken up. He wished he could go back in time and tell himself to keep his mouth shut about his stupid theory. Micaiah kept talking.

"The good news, though, is that it got the doctors back on the case, investigating different possible causes of the coma and why the extra oxygen made it so much worse. According to Lily, they're doing dozens of labs and tests, but they're going to have to find something pretty quick in order for it to be effective."

"What are they doing that they didn't do before?"

"Ah, she explained it but I really couldn't tell you. Basically it sounds like they've moved away from the brain and neurological causes to the heart and lungs. It sounds like it's a step in the right direction."

"I guess."

Micaiah looked away for a moment before standing and sitting on the edge of the bed. "Tommen, I know it looks very bleak, even hopeless, but you've got a lot of fight left, and so does Walter. And I'd be willing to place a bet that one or both of you is going to come up with something. Four days is more than enough time for that."

Tommen scoffed. "Cute speech, but we're nothing. We're just a couple of guys on an insignificant world dealing with an extraterrestrial poison whose antidote is worth killing for. And I'm going to a meeting for it." He shook his head and threw the covers back. As he got out of bed and left the room, he said, "And don't sit on the edge of the bed and talk to me like you're my dad!"

Somewhere in the more rational part of his mind, Tommen knew he'd cut Micaiah deeply with that statement, knew that it had cut a rift in their friendship even. It was a statement reserved for righteous anger, and not supposed to be flung about carelessly in a moment of hopeless despair. He knew he would have to apologize even before they headed to the Wheel, but things had just changed. He'd just created a war on another front, lost an ally he couldn't afford to lose.

He couldn't decide how much of his growing fear was justified and how much was exaggeration, but he stayed in the shower as long as he possibly could before there was a banging on the door and he was forced to hurry up, jump out, and get dressed. When he got out to the living room, the twins were waiting for him, Micaiah's face a mask of stoic determination, Micah looking helpless in the whole thing.

"Ready?" Micaiah asked sharply.

"Cai, I am so sorry for what I said," Tommen began, the

words falling out of his mouth. "I didn't mean it like that, I mean, I shouldn't have said —"

"I asked if you're ready." His words were as cold as his gaze.

Tommen sighed. "Yes."

Then the portal was open, and they stepped through. It was even more brutal than before. It could be dangerous to go through all these portals through dimensions too many times in a day. When Tommen finally stumbled through, he almost fell into another portal leading who-knew-where. Slowly the room stopped spinning, and Micah helped him to his feet. As he turned to follow the younger twin to the front of the room, Micaiah grabbed his shoulder and spun him around. Tommen shrank back under his dark stare.

"I know you're hurting, Tommen," he said, "but you seem to think you are the only one who is. Micah and I are just as worried and just as helpless. We don't have the ability to go before the Hands and influence them. You do. And we're trying to help you. So, assuming that the Hands grant your wish and we all go back to the hospital and bring back your dad, don't go standing on your soapbox and brag about how you did this alone. Got it?"

"I would never —"

"Wouldn't you? Maybe not to anyone in Time who knows you don't have that ability, but what would you tell your friends at school? What story would you tell them? Don't make a bigger man of yourself than you are, because the weight of all the pride and all the lies weighs you down in a fight. We don't ask a lot from you, Tommen, just enough. If we ask you to walk a foot, don't brag about walking a mile."

Tommen lowered his gaze. "Yes, sir."

"Good." Tommen was suddenly caught off-guard as Micaiah pulled him against himself and hugged him. "We're all hurting, Tommen. We all want Walter to pull through. You have the ability to try and help him where we can't." He released him. "So let's go."

Tommen nodded and numbly walked to the front of the room where Micah already waited with a translator. Had Micaiah just hugged him? Steely-eyes, rigid posture, no shit, no holds barred, sometimes-playboy Micaiah hugged him? There were no words to describe the shock and emotion that went through Tommen at that moment, even as he got his own translator. He didn't think the elder twin was capable of such an act.

The twins saw Tommen to the front entrance of the Coliseum, that is, the portal-door just outside, and made him continue on his own. Better if they weren't seen hanging around there too long. They were already taking a chance just by being seen with him.

"I do have one question, though," Tommen said before they vanished. "How is it that the Hands hold court, the candidates also hold court, and yet they all have time to campaign for the elections? And how would they know if you're hanging around here?"

"The Hands and candidates don't hold court every day," Micaiah told him. "Most days, but not every day. They schedule their campaigning days and send messages far and wide to the voters to come on those days to meet the candidates. As for how they would know, the secretaries are not as innocent as they all claim to be, and they're not the only staff the Hands have access to."

"You mean spies?" It sounded so cool, and yet also very dangerous considering they were the object of the spying, and not in a good way.

"When you're done, check the marketplaces. We'll be around."

With that, Tommen watched them walk away and disappear through another portal. He looked back at the portal-door to the Coliseum. Here he was, standing inside a man-made dimension among aliens and technology hundreds of years in Earth's future, and he was about to pay a visit to Ancient Rome. Still, he was on the Wheel's calendar now, and he had a time to keep.

He still had no idea where to start, but at least he knew where the entrance was and had a general idea of what to look for and where to go. A thought occurred to him that he probably should have done a little studying up on the various symbols so he could avoid any unpleasant or embarrassing encounters or intrusions. But he hadn't.

Should he just start trying doors and hope to get lucky again? Should he go back to the waiting room from yesterday and get directions? Should he find a secretary and ask? He looked around, feeling helpless and alone, like a child separated from his mother at a shopping mall.

He made one loop of the outer track before deciding just to go back to the registry and waiting room that he was in yesterday. The worst that would happen was they sent him on another loop of the track to another room. He found the room and waited in line behind a couple others. It didn't seem as busy as before and a secretary got to him quickly.

"Personal identification, rank, and celestial identification," the secretary began.

So Tommen repeated the information.

"Nature of your visit?"

"I was here yes—earlier, and I'm supposed to go before the Hands." He rolled up his sleeve to show off the tattoo which, in his opinion, had begun to glow again. Did that mean it was almost time, or that he was late?

"Ah, then you're not in the right spot," the secretary said, though it sounded no more enthused for the fact. It—a short, squat, orange creature—turned and motioned for another secretary, the same dog-like one from before. This time it moved on its hind legs instead of all—sixes. Still, it moved with the grace of a long-legged dancer.

"He has a meeting with the Hands," the orange secretary said blandly.

"When?" the dog secretary wondered. When Tommen showed it the tattoo, it nodded. "Very good. Follow me."

Tommen followed the dog-like secretary through the back door and to the inner track of the Coliseum. As they walked, it spoke. She, if it was a she, had a beautiful voice. For a dog, that was.

"With the elections coming up, the Hands have been hearing

fewer and fewer cases, and more often than not, they've been retiring to deliberate. The time that was given you is only an estimate. As it stands, they are still in deliberation for a case, and then there is another case to be heard before yours, so the wait may be some time. Food and drink will be delivered if desired."

"Thank you," Tommen said. "Do you mind if I ask your name?"

"Harshi," the secretary replied. "Quadrant Two, Parsec Nine, Sector Twelve, System Forty-four, Planet Three. I am from Region Seventeen, District Two."

Tommen made a mental note that if he was going to be asking people's names and where they were from, he should probably at least have the decency to go to the Archives and look up some of these places.

Harshi ended up taking him to a room on the inside of the inner track. It was small, empty but for a raised platform which Tommen might take for a bench of some sort.

"The next case must be in session," Harshi commented. "Your wait may be long or short, depending on how the Hands handle it. Would you care for food or drink?"

"Yes, please," Tommen answered. "Water at least."

"It will be done."

And like that, she was gone, and Tommen was alone in the room, sitting on a rock bench. Fuck, but it felt like he was sitting and waiting for a guard to come by an escort him to his death. Not even a hanging, either. This was the Coliseum; he was going to be delivered up to some motherfucking lions, man. Or a bear. Stand there in the middle of a roaring crowd and wait for Caesar to give the signal.

He tried to think and go over his speech which had been so well-rehearsed in his head, but now he couldn't find the words. He remembered the gist of it, but he couldn't recall why he'd thought it was such a wonderful idea, why he'd been so sure that they had this in the bag. He was nothing, just a stupid teenager from an insignificant planet, a probationary Timekeeper going before the

Hands with an offer they couldn't refuse. Except they could refuse it. Worse, they could refuse it and still act on it. They didn't have to give him the antidote in order to take it for themselves and bring the Borelians to heel. They could refuse him the antidote, go after the Borelians, then turn on him and try to sell him the antidote. Like Micaiah said, it was all about profit.

How the fuck could they have been so stupid? Love was blind, but apparently so was grief and desperation. And now he was about to go before the Hands and make a fool of himself. Worst case scenario, he broke down into an inarticulate, blathering idiot, and Cassius would be the Zero Hero to watch him have a meltdown, basking in his own victory.

Sweat broke out on the back of Tommen's neck. He'd elected to wear his darkest jeans and a button-down shirt, the only one he'd packed in his bag. He looked good, maybe business casual, like a moderately successful salesman gone out to a comfortable lunch with his friends before they went out and played eighteen. Although, if he continued sweating as bad as he was, he was soon going to look like that salesman after he got his ass handed to him, before he and his pals even reached the back nine.

He went to the door opposite the one leading to the inner track. He couldn't hear anything. Was the Seat of the Hands just on the other side, or was there something more, some tunnel or passage he had to walk through? He was pretty sure someone would come to get him when it was his turn. Would he hear them come? Where were they now? Was the case now still going on, or had the Hands already retired to deliberate? Had it been fifteen minutes yet? Was there a time limit on the deliberation, or did they just keep going until a consensus was reached? Did it have to be a consensus, or would a majority do? Another passing thought told Tommen he probably should have read up on this, too, while he'd been doing all his other research. Oh well, experience was both the best and worst teacher.

He sat. He stood. He walked around the room. Quickly, then slowly, then deliberately putting one foot in front of the other and trying to make perfect turns like in the Army or something. He failed miserably, and he knew it. He tried counting off the minutes, lost interest. Went back to the bench and sat down.

He jumped as, at the same time he sat down, the door to the inner track opened and a secretary walked in, bearing a platter of fruit and a pitcher of water.

"You will forgive the delay for food," the secretary said. "When such is ordered, we must research the appropriate food to bring. This was deemed acceptable. Is it?"

Tommen stomach rumbled. "It is, thank you."

The secretary tilted its head and left then. Tommen gave it a three-count before descending on the platter with all the ravenous hunger of a pack of wolves, or at least a starving teenage boy, whichever was hungrier. He wasn't even much of a fruit fan, but he was hungry, and it tasted good. The water was cool and fresh, and he soon found that everything was gone, cleaned up like giving the dog the plate to lick clean. Damn, but he should have put in an order for a bacon and sausage biscuit or something.

He turned as the opposite door opened now and a secretary stood there, taking up pretty much the entire frame. At first Tommen couldn't figure out why the secretary's cloak was black. Then he realized that the creature itself was like a giant bat, and it was using its wings as a cloak. It studied him through beady gold eyes, ears pricked forward like a cat, listening.

"Tommen Forbes," it said.

"That's me," Tommen confirmed.

"Follow me."

So Tommen did. He followed the giant scary bat creature out into yet another track, about the same size as the middle track, though obviously smaller in terms of distance. But where the middle and outer tracks had been whitewashed stone, this track was some kind of gray and black stone, making the whole thing feel like a dungeon. Sconces dotted the walls, of a similar style as the ones in the Archives, but these glowed white instead of gold.

I've been brought to a crypt, Tommen thought. *The Hands are reminding me and any who come before them that they basically hold my life in their hands. More to the point, they hold Walter's life in their hands.*

How daunting.

The secretary stopped suddenly, and it was then that Tommen realized that the creature was blind. Blind as, well, a bat. It had been listening for Tommen; that was why it spoke and asked for him by name first. Maybe it was truly blind, or maybe just light-sensitive. Maybe it could use echolocation, maybe not. Tommen was betting on the echolocation as the door they came to was a tunnel with an iron gate on either end. The echo would sound differently as it headed down the tunnel versus just bouncing off the stone walls. The bat-secretary reached slowly, deliberately, for the wheel to heave over and over to raise the gates. When it was finished and a stopper set on the wheel, it turned to Tommen and looked at him with those same golden eyes, almost as if it could see him.

"The Hands await you," it said.

Tommen swallowed involuntarily but forced himself to walk down the tunnel toward the light. He was going to die. That was all he could think about. He was going to die. Or maybe he was already dead and now heading towards the proverbial light at the end of the tunnel. Then it would be all over. Or if the loonies were right, his death was only just beginning, and now he was going to be tormented forever.

He was momentarily blinded as he emerged from the tunnel, and he put a hand up to shield his eyes. Once he'd adjusted to the light, he could not stop a soft gasp of awe as he adjusted also to the sight.

The entire Seat of the Hands was solid white marble, or so it looked. Maybe it was glass or metal covered in the same spray paint as the outside, but he was fairly certain that this was solid marble, impossible to say how thick. He went and stood in the center of the Seat, the floor looking like it was cut from a single, solid block. There was not a single imperfection in it, save for a deliberate carving of the symbol of the Hands in the center where he now stood.

The wall around the outside leading to the tiered seating was about fifteen feet high. It was not so perfectly cut from a single block, but it would not have mattered anyway as it was intricately carved with all manner of flora and fauna. If there was any significance to the scenes depicted, it was lost on Tommen, to his shame. The only interruption in the art was the little iron gate he had just come through. Each of the tiered seats, eight rows in total, and the lip of the benches were also carved while the seats themselves were inlaid with metal leaf. The seats were not like stadium seats made for humans, but bigger to accommodate all manner of aliens large and small. But still they were beautiful, broken only twice by the enormous iron gates that led straight to the outer track.

Around the top of the Coliseum were the ever-famous arch windows. Light came in through these windows, but from where, Tommen did not know. Around the very top of the windows was an inlay of what looked like gold, shining in the light, reflecting it around the entire arena, and bathing everything in a soft golden light.

All of this took only a moment to take in, but Tommen knew he would not easily forget it. Except he knew he had. He'd been here before, as a boy, being presented to the Hands, and he'd forgotten the majesty of this place. He briefly remembered standing beside—well, more hiding behind—Walter as he was introduced to the Hands. He remembered clinging to Walter's leg, terrified, and feeling that no matter what, he would be safe with his dad. And for just a moment, Tommen almost felt like Walter was standing there with him now. He touched the watch on his wrist.

Just as he was feeling all this, he got the sense that he ought to turn around. The whole idea was that when he walked in, he walked away from the Hands. It was a way for them to observe him, see what he would do before he realized they were watching him. So he turned to face them.

The Hands varied in size from almost a hummingbird to a monstrosity easily sixteen to twenty feet tall, whose shape beneath its shroud put Tommen in mind of a giant centaur. Other than obvious bulges here and there and general shapes, it was impossible to tell the species of any of the Hands with certainty. The shrouds were not like regular cloaks where movement might kick up the hem to expose the leg, or a light shined at the hood might reveal the face. The shrouds of the Hands were absolute, always touching the ground no matter what they did or how fast they moved. For any flying species, it was the same technology that kept the face covered. Any light shined in the face of the Hand would only yield blackness. By all accounts, the Hands could see and hear and sense just as well as if they were not shrouded, and there was speculation that the shrouds themselves were not real, but a projection.

But in this moment, it did not matter if the shrouds were real or not, because the Hands beneath them were real. And they were probably going to be the ones to decide Walter's fate. Tommen gave each of them at least a once over, his gaze settling on the Zero Hour. All the other Hands had cloaks of a soft golden color that shimmered and sparkled. The Zero Hour, however, wore a cloak of silver that reflected more than it shimmered. And where the regular Hands' shrouds were trimmed with blue, the Zero Hour's shroud was trimmed with gold leaf.

Was this the true Zero Hour, or was that Cassius looking down upon Tommen from behind that black mask? Was this an alien who would be actually interested in helping him find a cure for Walter's ailment, or the man who would squirm and giggle with ill-contained glee when Tommen revealed just how sick he was? How many of the other Hands would come to his aid? Would this be a war of sides, Tommen's or Cassius', or was this solely for self-interest and personal profit? Somehow, Tommen had the feeling that he would have better luck if all the Hands were in it for themselves versus having to try to sway them to his side or risk losing them to Cassius.

But all of that was pushed to the side as soon as the Zero Hour spoke.

"Tommen Forbes."

The acoustics in the Coliseum made it impossible to determine if the voice belonged to Cassius or the true Zero Hour, at least to Tommen's ears—that in itself didn't mean much—and Tommen tried to judge which Zero Hour might be hiding beneath that shroud based on the reactions of the other Hands. He had no benefit of facial expressions, but body language was still visible beneath the shrouds. He tried to gage a shuffle of a foot, a movement of the arms. What was normal for someone who'd been standing for a while and trying to stay upright, and what was the uncomfortable shuffle of the realization that the Zero Hour was not who he was supposed to be? But he had a case to plead, not to study.

"Great Hands of Time and Lord Zero Hour," Tommen greeted, trying to remember everything about the long, formal introductions, fearing that he would fail miserably. "I come before you, Lord Zero Hour, overseer of the government. I come before you, Hand of Scientifically Advanced and Openly Engaged Civilizations. I come before you, Hand of Scientifically Advanced and Reserved Civilizations. I come before you, Hand of Scientifically Advanced and Unengaged Civilizations. Hand of Scientifically Advancing and Openly Engaged Civilizations."

Fifty-one Hands, each with its own title, its own representations and duties associated with that representation. Tommen knew that once he started in on the titles, he was going to have to go through every single one of them, no stopping in the middle or lumping them together or hoping that someone thought that they'd just missed their call. They would be paying very close attention, and they would know if he missed a title. Thankfully, it was one of the things he had to know for his review, so if nothing else, this would be practice for him.

Trying to envision this as merely practice for his review made the recitation a little easier, and there was something soothing about the rather similar titles, naming them off as if checking items off a grocery list.

There were some unusual titles and representations, too. Like

Candidate Liron aq-whatshisface representing the vegetation of worlds. All the worlds apparently, as the title only came up once. Apparently it was a big thing on some worlds. But there was also the Hand of the Mountains and the Pebbles. So...rock guardians. Like Donojok, sentient alien creatures made of rock? Or did he literally represent rocks, like, the Himalayas basically had a lawyer?

And what was their influence over unengaged planets like Earth? Did they inspire environmental protests, or were they only interested in engaged planets? How did Time affect rocks and trees anyway? How did they negotiate with the other Hands? Fuck, but Time politics were confusing.

The only Hands who were representative of Time itself, as far as Tommen was concerned, were the Hand of the Timekeepers, the Hand of the Harvesters, and the Hand of the Merchants. Each of those Hands was required to be of the order they represented. Tommen had once inquired as to why the Grandfathers did not have a Hand, to which Walter had grimly replied, "Oh, they have a Hand. They have a hand in everything, don't worry about that."

Thankfully, the introductions were not part of his fifteen minutes to pitch his problem, or else he would have been screwed out of at least ten of those as he fought to remember the last few Hand titles without giving away that he was struggling to come up with the titles. Eventually, though, he must have hit all fifty-one, because the Hands took his pause and did a collective murmur of greeting. Relief flooded Tommen. He wanted to flop down in a chair, but he knew the fight had only just begun.

"Timekeeper Tommen Forbes, you do yourself and your mentor credit with your knowledge, formality, and acknowledgment of tradition," the Zero Hour said. "You come before us now with a case that we may hear and act upon. You wish to ask a favor of the Hands and strike a bargain."

"I do."

"What do you ask of us?"

Tommen thought they might have told him about the fifteen

minute time limit seeing how this was his first time appearing before them, but maybe they expected him to already know about it since he'd made it this far and made such formal introductions.

There was also another sense that Tommen got. Walking into the Coliseum, he'd been stripped of his Banding abilities, reduced to a normal person. But now he could feel a sense creeping up on him, his sense of Time, of the mere passage of time, one second into another, one minute into another. That was his fifteen minutes starting; he would simply know when those fifteen minutes was up. Which meant it was time to start talking. Good old Tommen Forbes, the Chivalrous Welshman with the Silver Tongue.

Yeah, right.

"Good Hands, in recent weeks on my world, my father, mentor, and Timekeeper Captain Walter Forbes had been pursuing two very dangerous Runners, Cassius Hand and Rifun Ndolo, whom I believe you are familiar with." *Just let the names hang there. Let them come to their own conclusions of what Micah and Micaiah told them.* "He sought them out adamantly with the help of his Lieutenants, using every resource he had available to him on Earth and in Time." *Probably better not to name the Lieutenants. Pause for effect. Was that the right place to pause?* "I myself was captured by these Runners and held for two weeks." *Another pause. Are they getting the effect or do they just think me an incompetent speaker?* "Captain Forbes pursued them all the more and eventually confronted them, but Cassius and Rifun were not working alone." *Pause to let them think the network of Runners might be bigger than anticipated, and given how powerful those two are, what might their friends be capable of. But am I overusing the pause?* "Among their helpers was a *vodrak* Borelian named Isthim." *Will that name ring a bell with any of them, or is that just useless information?* "Rifun, being too cowardly to face Captain Forbes himself, sent Isthim to fight him instead." *Use Walter's title, call Rifun a coward to make it sound like there is a fighting chance here. Isthim...is Isthim?* "In the end, Isthim was unable to kill Captain Forbes by herself." *Make Walter look as good as possible, give him the upper hand in the fight.* "Instead, she poisoned the weapon that Rifun used to attempt to kill Captain Forbes. And Rifun and all his helpers got away."

Tommen didn't like talking to invisible men in bedsheets. He knew it was supposed to prevent favoritism, but it was wildly unnerving not to be able to see facial expressions. Even if he couldn't understand the facial expressions or subtle twitches and movements of most species, he liked looking his audience in the face at the very least.

"Captain Forbes was rescued and taken to a medical facility where his major physical wounds were treated." How technical did he want to get? For being in a man-made dimension surrounded by technology far superior to Earth's, Tommen felt strange about using words like "hospital" or "bullet wound" as if the words wouldn't translate and he would end up sounding like an imbecile. "However, the poison that Isthim used to taint Rifun's weapon found its way into his bloodstream. He's dying."

Pause for effect, but how much did they care? Tommen shifted his stance because he was uncomfortable, but tried to make it seem like he was trying to stand straighter, like he was coming to the real point of his speech.

"I have been told and read many times that there is no cure for Borelian poison, or if there is, they keep it under heavy guard. But just yesterday, my people made their annual celebration of gift-giving, and when we presented Captain Forbes with his gifts, a friend of mine who is a Harvester confirmed that his countdown reversed." Fuck, but he wanted to see their faces. Shock? Apathy? Outrage? He was probably the most shocked out of all of them, calling Lily a friend, but he had to swallow his pride on that one. "It was not a large reversal, only a few seconds, but for a few seconds, Captain Forbes was able to fight the poison that invades his system. It can be done."

He paused again, as much for effect as to feel out the timer. He'd only used between five and ten minutes. Fuck. What happened to his grand speech with all the evidence and the science and the plan to get it all done and everyone went home happy? It was dissolving into this pitiful, sentimental mewling.

"My world is scientifically advancing, but unengaged. The doctors treat him the best they can, but with no knowledge of Borelians or their poisons. One of their treatments unwittingly undid the small progress that was made and even made Captain Forbes worse. My friend who is a Harvester says he went from six days to four days to live."

He tried to put on a tough face. "I have been told, and I have seen that Cassius and Rifun are very powerful Time Agents, a Triage Harvester and a Warden Timekeeper. And they have a powerful ally in a *vodrak* Borelian. This concerns everyone, regardless of any rumors. They are not the average Runner who may be pursued and turned over to the Grandfathers. They are cunning and bloodthirsty and may go after whomever they please with little or no resistance. And a *vodrak* Borelian will be immune to even the greatest torture the Grandfathers may inflict upon them." *Pause. There's one bargaining chip*, Tommen thought. *Tell them that even their most fearsome tortures will mean nothing. You can't touch her to beat her and make her talk, and you can barely stand in the same room as her, so what do you do?*

"My proposal is a simple yet profitable one," Tommen continued. "You, Great Hands and Lord Zero Hour, are very powerful, and your influence reaches to the ends of the universe to civilizations untouched. I want only one thing. I want the antidote to the Borelian poison. I cannot say which poison she used as she is a *vodrak* and it was poor light when the incident occurred." *And I'm color-blind, but this isn't about me.* "Perhaps the acquisition of the antidotes will shed light on which one I need.

"I realize this sounds a steep proposal as the Borelians are willing to kill to keep the antidotes secret. But they also cast out Isthim because she was so volatile that even her own war-like race feared her. Now look what she has the power to do. I propose that the Hands—and perhaps the Grandfathers may be interested—devote all resources to the pursuit and capture of the *vodrak* Borelian Isthim—Cassius and Rifun being mere extras. The Hands will turn her over to the Borelians so they may dispense their own justice in exchange for the antidotes to each of their poisons.

"Now, you have an excellent opportunity to expand your market. People all over the universe will pay anything for a little extra Time, minutes, seconds, all precious. Borelian poisons transcend Time, making all those Time Capsules in the marketplaces and the auctions utterly worthless. How much more would someone pay for that antidote if they needed it? I have no doubt that once you get your hands on one antidote, you will find a way to make more and make money from it.

"And not only do you open a new market, but you hold the Borelians hostage to their own terror. They consider themselves superior, invincible, what wouldn't they give to remain that way and not have those antidotes distributed? What could you make them do? What could you make the Grandfathers do, since they rely on the Borelians for their staff?"

Tommen took a step back, clasped his hands together and nodded once, indicating he was finished.

For a moment, the Hands were silent. Fuck, fuck, *fuck*, but he wanted to see their faces. Knitted brows, icy glares, the light of prospecting, anything at all, just not black masks. Tommen could feel his Time sense evaporating as his time was up. Now it was time for the questions and clarifications, but they were still silent for several minutes. Finally, the Zero Hour spoke.

"And you expect that we would just hand over a vial of the antidote to you? Why?"

Tommen found it in him to smirk. "Because it was my idea. All the rest goes to you, but I only want the one. Because after all, if you had this idea yourselves, I have little doubt it would have been done already."

"You expect us to simply divert all available resources to hunt down Isthim?" another Hand inquired.

"Yes, I do, seeing how simply sending in three Timekeeping officers and twenty men of the local policing force was already inadequate."

"You said that Captain Forbes has approximately four days to live," a third Hand said. It was impossible to tell which Hand was speaking. "Have you any idea where they might be, where we should send our forces to look?"

"I do not," Tommen admitted. He thought about saying something about Cassius being the False Zero Hour, but figured that would do little good to find Isthim. She'd spent more time with Rifun anyway.

"What makes you think the Borelians will trade the antidotes for Isthim?" another asked.

"Because they know how dangerous she is. That was why they sent her away in the first place—or lost her in pursuit—either way to their shame. They cannot afford to simply let her go a second time. She once told me that only the highest officers are engaged in Time, so they understand the higher stakes if she is not dealt with. And the only way to deal with her is to execute her."

"We cannot simply let her go either," someone else pointed out. "They would call our bluff."

"Then don't bluff."

"Are you suggesting we actually let her go?"

"Set it up however you want to falsely release and then recapture her, enough to unsettle the Borelians and make them believe that you would do it, that you would release her again into the larger universe, into Time."

He still couldn't see their expressions, but now the Hands glanced uncertainly at one another. He wondered if they had the ability to see through the masks and actually look at each other. And they fell silent again. When a minute or two had gone by that no one said anything or asked anymore questions, the Zero Hour spoke again.

"Your proposal is a unique and perplexing one, Tommen Forbes," he said. "We will take your story and your proposal under advisement and retire to deliberate."

"That is all I can ask," Tommen replied.

The Hands did not turn and move in unison, instead resembling the common exiting strategies of everyone at every football game ever. Stand, turn, and shuffle awkwardly off the bleachers. This was made even more comical by the size differences in all the different Hands. The small iron gate in front of Tommen also opened, and he saw just the little beady eyes of the bat-secretary standing there at the end of the tunnel.

Tommen took it as a cue and headed for the tunnel, stepping under both iron gates and watching the secretary lower them gently to the ground, without so much as a crash, clang, or even a squeak from the wheels. Then he began walking away and Tommen dutifully followed.

"You will return to the waiting room until the Hands have finished deliberating," the secretary said.

"How long will that take?" Tommen wondered conversationally.

"There is no set time. They will finish when they will finish and not before. And their judgment is final."

"Right."

They walked in silence through the inner track until they reached the door to the little waiting room. The secretary opened it with all the formality of a Victorian butler. Tommen walked into the room, unsure of the protocols.

"I heard your case, and your proposal," the secretary said once Tommen was inside.

"You did?" Tommen echoed dumbly. *Of course he did, he's a bat.*

"I did. It's madness you know, to cross the Borelians. That's why they're used as Grandfathers. Likely they will take it as an act of war."

"An act of war, for what?"

"Theft. Their poison is their pride. Stealing and distributing antidotes would be theft of pride and their every advantage against every other race in the universe."

Tommen folded his arms. "Should you be talking to me like this? Won't the Hands get mad or think you're, I don't know, trying to influence me? Tamper with a witness or something?"

"How so? Your piece is spoken. The only thing left is judgment. And I expect it will be some time before they return from deliberation. Would you like food and drink? It will be delivered to you."

"Actually, I kind of want to go to the bathroom. Um, my people see it as kind of personal and a matter of sanitation."

"Understandable. A bucket will be brought, with the food and drink."

I'm in a man-made dimension surrounded by astounding technology that can recreate ancient architecture, build libraries within libraries, and I'm going to be using a chamber pot like some bloke in the sixteenth century.

"Thank you," Tommen managed stiffly. "And I don't know how this whole thing works with the food and the drink, and I don't mean to impose or sound rude, but if it's possible, I'd really like a cheeseburger with all the fixings, a side of fries, and a strawberry milkshake."

It was difficult to gauge the secretary's expression, but after a moment, he simply said, "Of course. It will be done."

Then he shut the door and left Tommen alone in the room.

Chapter Eleven
Between Truth and a Hard Place

There was a time, when Tommen was in sixth grade, that he had to give a speech in front of his class. It was the 2008 presidential election, and all the classes were geared up for it, all the teachers thrilled to have the opportunity to teach all the little pupils about the wonders and workings of American democracy. This included everything from mathematical probabilities and algebraic equations, to extensive history projects, to the biggest class council campaigns ever seen, as class presidential candidates were encouraged to try and campaign like the national presidential candidates, where they would be judged at the end of the year how those winners compared to whomever won the national election.

In English class, it was the year of speeches, a joy for the teachers as the curriculum focus for that year coincided with the elections. For the students, it was less than thrilling as they had to recite famous speeches and come up with their own, both on assigned topics and topics of their choosing. For Tommen, it was a nightmare. Even at that time, three years in to his being deposited in the modern era, he still struggled with English, both written and spoken. Public speaking was not even close to being an adequate talent, never mind a strength. He still had an incredibly thick accent that marred most of his words, and when he got nervous, he would default back to Welsh. His grades for that year on all those assignments were dismal, even with the teacher being generous and trying to account for his very real attempts at mastering English.

The last speech of the class was the open topic speech; they could write and speak about any issue they cared about, from the national election and foreign wars to a dumb local ordinance. Tommen had chosen to write about discrimination against people with accents, how it seemed to automatically brand them as dumb immigrants when they—and by they, he was really writing about himself—could be just as American-born as anyone else, just having a little different home life. His written speech, that they all had to turn in prior to speaking, had been his best grade all year, almost a hundred percent. But he couldn't get over his fear of the actual public speech, and they had to speak from memory; every prompt by the teacher got marked down.

The night before Tommen was due to deliver his speech, Walter sat down with him, and together they watched a bunch of movies. Or rather, parts of movies, all with speeches. Some were famous, others were obscure; some came from kings and knights and soldiers, others from children and homeless men and people whose names were never told; some were spoken with English so perfect the audience could almost hear them verbally dotting the i's and crossing the t's, others were in poor English or accented English or not in English at all and they had to read subtitles.

They must have watched two hours or more of just speeches, until Tommen was practically falling asleep on the couch. Then Walter took him to bed and sat him down.

"Not everyone is a great speaker," Walter told him. "Not everyone has the physical stature of a king to command men's attention, or the voice that carries and echoes regardless of the acoustics of a room. Not everyone gives a speech to an army of a thousand soldiers looking for inspiration. And not every speaker will speak to everyone in the audience. Not every speech is spoken the same way.

"Don't worry about what your teacher is writing on her clipboard. Don't worry about Jackie and Katy whispering to each other. You are speaking about an issue that you care about. You can't make everyone care, and don't try. Just try to make everyone see that you care about it. You know how you want to sound and what you want to say. Now, we watched a lot of speeches in the last few hours. If all else fails, pick one of those speeches or pick one of those actors, and try to model yourself after them. It's only for a short time, and then it will all be over. Every speech has an end."

So Tommen walked into his English class the next day and volunteered to go first. He'd thought about all the different speeches they'd watched, and he decided he wanted to sound like a king. In the end it was a poor choice for a model—trying to inspire an army to pick up their swords and go against the odds was not the same as talking about discrimination—but it got him through the speech. His accent still jumbled some of his words, and several times he lapsed into Welsh when he couldn't think of the English word, but eventually, like all speeches, his came to an end. He ended up getting a B- on it, shamefully his best speech grade of the year.

He was more than happy to get out of the class, and, over the summer, he ended up taking a few ESL courses just to improve his accent, if not help him with basic English.

Now, as Tommen sat alone in the room waiting for the bat-secretary to retrieve him, he thought about the speech he gave the Hands. He hadn't picked out a model beforehand, despite how nervous he'd been, and as he'd programmed the translator to pick up his Welsh, he figured he'd done the best he could at giving himself every advantage he could.

He wondered how he'd done, what impact he'd had. He found himself again thinking about all the speeches they'd watched that night, so long ago. He couldn't remember all of them, but some. And he considered all the speeches he'd heard since then, both in movies and in real life. The 2012 elections had been another glorious opportunity for the schools to showcase the brilliance of American democracy, and Tommen had narrowly avoided having to give another speech just by sheer luck of having strep throat for a full week, and the teacher had been unwilling to wait that long for him to recover. So he just took the written speech and called it good.

Did any other species care about heart-felt speeches delivered with the right tone and amount of power? Or was it all about the profit? Was his preparation all for naught? He hoped not, considering how much sleep he'd lost over it.

Tommen was pleased to see that when the food came, it was what he ordered, and he devoured the burger and fries as readily as he'd devoured the fruit beforehand. He was just starting on the milkshake when the door opened again and the secretary walked in, gold eyes blindly looking at him. Now he saw that the bat's mouth was just open, enough to echolocate the room and probably the inner track, but he wasn't hunting for insects in the dead of night. At least, not that Tommen knew of.

"The Hands are ready to deliver the verdict," he said.

Tommen almost protested, saying he wasn't finished with his shake, then realized that it would come off as childish. He wasn't here to be fed and served and waited on with good food and tasty milkshakes; he was here to win his case and win the cure for his father's ailment. So he set the glass down as casually as he could and followed the secretary out of the room.

"Do you know how they ruled?" Tommen wondered. "Just so I can take the time to process it before I get in there and they spring it on me?"

"I do not know," the bat replied, and Tommen had a hard time judging whether he was telling the truth.

"Are you telling me the truth or just keeping me in suspense?"

"I do not know how they decided. I do not join them in their deliberations."

"How long has it been, anyway? It felt like a while."

"Approximately three Base Hours."

Three hours? That was all? Fuck, some Earth-side juries took days to come back from a verdict. Either that boded well, that they saw the money and decided to jump on it, or it boded ill, that they took his proposal and ripped it to shreds in record time. Brooding too much on it, Tommen almost walked right past the small iron gate even as the secretary stopped to open it.

"So, are you like the only secretary here to do this, or what?" Tommen inquired.

"I am the secretary of the night," the bat replied. "There is another secretary of the day." The gates opened. "The verdict awaits you."

How was it that a damn bat had better luck coming up with cool yet cryptic parting lines? Of course, he probably had quite a bit of practice under his belt. After all, he was a bat. And he worked very close to the Hands, probably see — er, hearing all manner of cases and verdicts, questions and arguments, plots and schemes. Was it any real wonder that he would be good at instilling fear into people as they went to hear the verdicts on their cases?

Tommen walked through the tunnel and emerged into the Seat of the Hands, still dazzled by the marble and gold. He was forced to wonder, as the thought had occurred to him in his solitude, why the Coliseum? There were no gladiator fights here, and there were only fifty-one Hands. If they spaced out far enough, they could surround him in the ring, but bunching together was more practical. So why the circle? A philosophical person might propose that the circle was a representation of time, always moving in circles, but then why the mind-fuckery of the rest of the Wheel? Why was everything about the Wheel so fucking contradictory?

He thought all of this in about the time it took for him to turn and face the Hands who were just getting settled and preparing for the delivery of the verdict. Facial expressions were again out of the question, and body language was dubious at best. At that moment, Tommen would have really rather preferred to receive a written notice of the verdict. Yup, just mail it to 5555 S. Deering Rd., Charleston, WV, USA, Earth, System Four, Sector Five, Parsec Eleven, Quadrant One. He would have rathered been anywhere but there at that moment.

"Timekeeper Tommen Forbes," the Zero Hour began.

Right, more formalities. "Great Hands of Time and Lord Zero Hour, I thank you for taking the time to hear my case and for the time spent in deliberation. I hope all arguments were constructive and a consensus was made in fair and just due order." It sounded a little awkward, that last part, but it was the way it was rendered. Damn translations anyway.

"And we, the Hands of Time and the Zero Hour, thank you for your time as well, for the time spent before the lower courts, as well as your forethought in your case and proposal, your patience in waiting for our deliberations, and your participation in the courts as a whole."

Tommen had to wonder if the Hands had to go through all the bullshit formalities before and after their deliberations, and how long it took compared to how much time they'd actually spent in deliberation. Or did they simply retire to a room, plop down at the table, pass around the coffee, and say, "Okay, boys, what do we do with this one? Let's flip a coin."

"Our arguments were few but severe, yet our deliberations were swift." That could be good or bad. "But in the end, we believe justice, reason, and common sense have prevailed."

There was either a severe logical flaw in that statement, or else common sense was the same, literally, throughout the entire universe. For example, common sense, as well as common decency, for a human meant helping one's fellow man when he needed help and one had the means to help. Common sense for a Borelian meant protecting the antidotes to their poisons at all costs and murdering anyone who tried to learn the secrets of the antidotes. So either none of the Hands were Borelian and thus the same common sense prevailed throughout the rest of the universe, or else "common sense" was simply a code word for "common interest" which ultimately alluded to money and power. Thinking about it that way put a rock in Tommen's gut.

"Your proposal was a unique one, cunning and deliberate," the Zero Hour went on. Was this part of the introductory formalities or was he stalling? "No doubt you as a human are considered brilliant and persuasive among your people, a leader with a satin voice."

Either the Zero Hour actually believed that and was impressed by Tommen's proposal, or else he was trying to flatter him and soften the blow. Still, Tommen did not bother to correct him. "It is not easy to come before us and speak, let alone deliver such a...controversial case."

The Zero Hour shifted his stance and Tommen grew more nervous. "What you have proposed, many of the Hands would stand to gain from. Arguments were severe on both sides." So it was about sides, yea and nay versus self-interest. This did not bode well. "Verdicts are made from a majority vote of the Hands. As Zero Hour, I am tasked with presiding and do not vote unless there is a tie vote that cannot be resolved."

Tommen felt the blood thundering through his ears and his heart leapt into his chest.

"I have not needed to cast a vote in nine years, and today I have needed."

If not for the fact that a losing vote meant losing everything, Tommen might have been immensely proud of himself that he was able to tie up the Hands like this, the first true tie vote in almost a decade. He felt sweat break out on his neck and under his arms; he probably looked a wreck. Still, he forced his body to stay still. He was not picking a speech-giver to emulate now, but a man listening to an enthralling speech. A soldier, listening for his commander's orders.

"And so, in the case proposal brought by Timekeeper Tommen Forbes, bringing to light the circumstances of Captain Forbes' health as well as proposing the capture of the Borelian Isthim and the trade and distribution of Borelian antidotes, we, the Hands of Time and the Zero Hour..." Fuck, but he knew how to master the pause for effect better than Tommen. "Reject your proposal."

It was like a dream that Tommen had once, when he was still fawning after Emily. In the dream, he was at a school dance. Suddenly the doors flung open and a heavenly white light flooded the room, and an angel walked through them, except the angel was Emily. She was dressed in this beautiful white silk gown with lace and ribbons and small buttons, and her hair was done up in a dazzling display of lace and a diamond tiara. Everyone at the dance was gaping, but she brushed past all of them, instead heading straight for Tommen who found he was wearing grubby clothes as if he'd been out working on the farm. With a teasing grin, she giggled at his clothes and then touched his chin with a single delicate finger, her nails painted white with glitter. Then, she raised her chin and just before she put his lips on his, she slapped him. Hard. Like, Catholic nun schoolteacher with a ruler to your knuckles kind of hard. Then Tyler Freeman and his goons grabbed Tommen under the arms and hauled him off for a beating.

This was like that. The Zero Hour had done a superb job of manipulating his language in order to not give away one side or the other, instead making statements that might lean toward either. Then came the slap and being hauled off for a beating.

No one spoke for a long moment, probably giving Tommen time to process the information. How he wished he could Band and take even more time to just stand there quietly and think about it. It hurt, the slap had come, but he just didn't really realize it yet. He felt his knees weaken, but he forced himself to remain standing.

They weren't going to help Walter. They were not going to go after Isthim and get the antidotes. They were going to do nothing.

Well, that wasn't entirely true. The proposal had included giving him the antidote needed to save Walter. That was what they were rejecting. There was every chance they would carry out the rest of the plan, and then try to sell him the antidote at a later date. Fucking swindling assholes. It was like punching himself in the stomach over and over again the more he thought about it.

"If I may beg the Hands for an explanation?" Tommen found himself asking.

"We are aware of the circumstances of Captain Forbes' ailment," the Zero Hour began. *Translation: We were playing dumb to see if you would play it up. Question: How did they find out? Answer: The twins. Therefore, they knew Micah and Micaiah were helping him.* "And while we are sympathetic, not only for the impending loss of your captain but your father as well, incidents with Runners happen every day. They are not always as powerful as Rifun and Cassius, but neither are they always without loss." *Translation: You are insignificant, and there is nothing special about you to warrant our time or even giving you an antidote if we did pursue this cause. Question: Did that mean that Cassius was the Zero Hour here and wanted to see Walter die, or was this the true Zero Hour and he really didn't give a fuck about a mere human being?*

"As for the method of your proposal, while the pursuit and capture of Isthim—with the potential 'consolation prize' of Cassius and Rifun—would represent a significant victory for the Hands and Timekeepers...that is why the Hands have Timekeepers." *Translation: That's what we have you guys for; you're our pawns to burn up on the frontlines. Question: So did that mean that the Hands were not as powerful as everyone assumed them to be, or were they more afraid of the repercussions from Cassius since he had granted himself immunity?* "It is up to the next Captain of District Four to be more judicious with his pursuit and attack, and learn from Captain Forbes' mistakes." *Translation: Walter fucked up. Better hope the next guy doesn't do the same.*

"Furthermore, it is the judgment of the Hands that the gamble of trading Isthim for the antidotes is too much risk for the safety of everyone involved." *Translation: Too rich for our blood. Better to keep her as a renegade; then we can wash our hands of any of her actions.* "The Borelians are violent, war-like, and extremely unpredictable." *Translation: They're a wild card, and we don't want to risk that they're also a trump card.* "They are as likely to accept Isthim back with honors as much as execute her, which would put her in a position of potential retaliation." *Translation...well, no, that was pretty clear and did make some sense. Fuck.* "And even if they did agree to execute her, there is no guarantee they would hand over the antidotes." *Translation: Better to make bets we know we can win, rather than risk all and potentially gain all.* "Furthermore, they are well-documented to kill or make slaves of anyone who tries to steal or concoct their antidotes." *Translation...nope, that one was pretty straightforward, too. Question: Were the Hands really afraid of the Borelians? Don't they have anyone expendable to send after the antidotes, someone they could bribe handsomely but who would be no great loss if they were captured or killed? They treated Walter like that, surely there must be others.*

"As to the proposal of opening up a new industry focused on the antidotes, the price that the antidotes must be held at in order to both maintain demand and maintain control over the Borelians would limit the market and so outweigh the cost of efficiency, assuming we held the market ourselves." *Translation: Our target audience would be so small, we'd lose money. And if anyone else ever discovered the secrets of the antidotes and opened a secondary black market, it would be all over. Question: So then how did they keep such a hold on Time?*

"We were most intrigued, however, about your proposal to control the Grandfathers. While it is true that they rely on the Borelians for staff, there is no strife between the Hands and the Grandfathers to warrant such a binding." *No two departments in any company ever worked so flawlessly together. Translation: There is no strife that we're going to tell you about, so stay out of our business. And we'll be sure to keep your proposal in mind so we might profit off it later.*

The Zero Hour paused briefly. "We appreciate your loyalty to your Captain and your love for your father. We appreciate the forethought you put into your proposal and your desire to see that everyone benefits, and the industry—and indeed the universe—is rid of a grave evil."

"Then what's the problem?" Tommen cut in. Fuck formality. They'd made their judgment and they could rot in hell for all he cared now. "Why won't you help?"

"To speak candidly, Tommen Forbes," another Hand said, "and with your pardon, Lord Zero Hour—" The Zero Hour nodded. "—even if we did agree to help, what do you think are the odds of us finding and capturing Isthim within the four days that your father has left to live? If it were that easy to find and capture her, you think she might not have already been captured by now, before all this began? Furthermore, the Borelians are no real threat to humans. The

Borelians terrorize other systems and other planets with far greater force and brutality. On some worlds, people would rather die trying to steal or develop an antidote than be captured and sold into slavery. Once, a small black market did crop up, but the only thing that remains of it now are the stories of how it was destroyed. And it was not a beautiful thing to behold."

"Well-spoken," the Zero Hour said. "So you see, Tommen Forbes, it is a brilliant plan on paper and in speech, but in practice, it is wildly impractical and even deadly."

Tommen sighed, racked his brain for anything he had left, any excuse at all. In the movies, this was where the hero would pull something from way out of left field. A favor, a benefit, a piece of blackmail, something that would shock the audience and bring them all inevitably to his side. But he had nothing.

"Is there nothing you can suggest?" he wondered, feeling suddenly weary. "Are there no survivors who can share their secrets? The Harvester can attest to him gaining ground, before our doctors bungled it all up. There must be a way."

"There are survivors," the Zero Hour admitted, "but they are slaves, far out of the reach of Time and inaccessible to most everyone else anyway. We are sorry, Tommen Forbes, but the Borelian poisons are unique toxins, and they alone hold the key to unlocking the antidotes."

After that, Tommen was silent. He wasn't sure if it was more formality as the Zero Hour then went through which Hand voted which way. The Hand of Scientifically Advanced and Openly Engaged Civilizations voted for it, probably because they had the most to gain by offering an antidote to their space-trekking people who may have had encounters with the Borelians. The Hand of Scientifically Primitive and Unengaged Civilizations voted against it, probably because they had no real stake in it. Maybe they understood slavery and were too afraid of the risks. The Hand of Fauna voted for it, maybe because they wanted to prevent their woodland animal friends from dying of accidental poisonings. The Hand of Flora voted against it, maybe because of some ethical reasons that plants might be cut down for the making of the antidotes.

It was all cynical speculation, like a child throwing a temper tantrum and coming up with stupid reasons why he shouldn't have to clean his room, and Tommen knew it. His mind warred. He would get no help from the Hands, that much was clear. But he refused to believe this was just the end of it, that he would have to spend the next four days coming to terms with his dad's impending death as the Zero Hour put it. There had to be more. Fuck the stages of grief, he knew there had to be more. As long as Walter was still alive, there had to be more.

The Zero Hour finished up with his recount of all the votes, and then the Hands stood. Tommen stood at attention as the Zero Hour spoke again.

"This case, being of Timekeeper Tommen Forbes inquiring of an antidote for his dying captain and proposal to the Hands for the capture and ransom of the Borelian Runner Isthim, is closed, having been rejected by a vote of twenty-six to twenty-five. This case may not be reopened or appealed, and a case may not be brought against it again in these circumstances. I, the Zero Hour, thank the Hands for their time and prudence in this matter, and thank Tommen Forbes for his time and forethought in his case. This will be the last case we will hear today, and we will reconvene for another session in due time."

And that was that. It was over. The Hands filed out of the Coliseum while Tommen waited for the iron gates to open, which they slowly did. He remained where he was for just a moment longer, maybe under some delusion that as long as he stayed in the Coliseum that the decision might be reversed. Someone would have an attack of conscience and run back into the Seat, wishing to change their vote.

It never happened. No one came running in screaming, "I object!" The Hands left the Seat and Tommen alone in the center. Eventually he moved, meeting up with the bat-secretary in the middle of the tunnel, as if he were coming to remove Tommen by force.

Neither said a word as they returned to the innermost track, and he waited patiently for the secretary to close the gates once more. As the gates hit the ground with just the tiniest clack on the stone floor, Tommen spoke.

"Did you know?" he asked.

It was tough to judge the Bat's expression, but Tommen liked to imagine it was something resembling guilt. "I did know. The Hands make the verdict official on the case record before summoning the applicant for the verbal telling."

"How do they deliberate? Do they spend as much time on formality and bullshit as we did out there?"

The Bat fluttered his wings, maybe embarrassment, maybe a shrug. "Sometimes. They would have, if this is the last case they are taking today."

"So in three hours, they probably do something to introduce it, and then they have to go through some shit to close it, so it really didn't take them very long to decide my case was worth nothing to them. Not profitable enough I suppose."

"The Hands must make decisions based on the good of the industry," the secretary said.

"Of course. The good of business, the best bottom line. Fuck the people."

They walked in silence after that, the bat-secretary taking him only as far as the middle track and leaving him there. Tommen stood in the track in silence, thinking, wondering. Had all that really just happened? He'd spent days preparing for it, and now it was all over, gone, and nothing to show for it. Except giving evil, greedy Hands a plot to increase their own wealth without having to actually give him anything.

He must have looked lost enough as another secretary approached him and offered to lead him out, which he accepted if for no other reason than if he wasn't led out, he probably wouldn't otherwise leave, at least not yet. It was too soon, too sudden. He needed time to process it. Fuck, if only he could Band. Well, he could

Band once he got back into the main Wheel.

The outer track was far less crowded now. Maybe it was some sort of collective nighttime, when everyone just knew it was time to go home and sleep. Maybe it was because some word had gotten out that the Hands were not hearing anymore cases today. Whatever the reason, Tommen didn't like it. Now was the time to get lost in a crowd, lost in the anonymity, being able to sit down and think without anyone bothering him. Or if they did bother him, it was easier to talk to a stranger than a familiar. Tommen would have rather talked to a secretary than even the twins. The twins knew too much. They knew him too well. The worst part was that they would have advice.

He didn't want advice. Not yet. He just wanted to talk and lay it all out. That was how he came up with the plan to go before the Hands. As much as Tommen wasn't a talk-about-your-feelings kind of person, he knew it had some merit in some situations. This was one of those situations. And talking, combined with good food and a good night's sleep, could bring out the answer he needed.

Tommen realized he'd stopped right in the middle of the track. Another secretary was making a beeline for him, probably to ascertain his purpose for being in the Coliseum and direct him on his way. He shook his head and kept moving. Move with a purpose and people tend not to question it.

He wasn't sure quite where he was in the grand scheme of the Coliseum and the tracks and his relation to the entrance, but he found his way out eventually, walking past the hidden guards and struggling to suppress a shiver. What would it take to simply hide in there and wait for someone to pass by, then, *wham!* Off with his head! Or a stab in the gut. Or even just a fist to the face.

So he left the Coliseum, left the windows or solar panels painted to look like old stone architecture, left the facade of arches and craftsmanship. His eyes told him he walked along a cobblestone street, but he did not scuff his shoes along dry rock. Instead he clicked along some kind of metal plating, like the rest of the Wheel, almost as if he was wearing high heels.

When he reached the portal-door, he turned. It was a beautiful illusion, the whitewashed stone and arches just starting to show signs of crumbling, a mesmerizing feat of man-made brilliance just beginning to succumb to the inevitability of time. Could almost make a person believe he was stepping into history. But Time was less about the past or the future and more about the present, how much money could be made now.

There would be no help for him here. Not now. Maybe not ever. Maybe he was being cynical and a bit childish, either in thinking the Hands were worthless, or for thinking they would help him in the first place. Maybe he was being foolish for continuing down the path of trying to find a cure when every source told him it was hopeless. But he wouldn't give up. He couldn't. Not until Walter was six feet underground, even if Tommen had to bury him himself.

Chapter Twelve
The Offer

As promised, Tommen found Micah and Micaiah in one of the marketplaces, though it took several tries and quite a bit of pushing and shoving in the various markets to spot them. Even once he spotted them, it took at least ten minutes to be able to get close enough for them to notice him so they could push and shove their way back out of the market and find a more private place to speak.

"And?" Micaiah wondered.

Tommen opened his mouth to say something, but he just sighed and shook his head.

"What happened?"

So he detailed the case, from the beginning with all his recitals and formalities and the hoops he had to jump through, to every point he made in his case. He tried to watch the twins' expressions for signs of approval or disapproval, if he did good or bad, but they betrayed nothing. Not that it would have mattered, since the case couldn't be brought before the Hands again. He told them about how close the vote had been and as much as he could remember about who voted which way.

"If the Hands are divided so perfectly, it could mean either fear or bribery," Micah commented.

"Either one is bad for us," Micaiah said grimly. "Go on."

Tommen did so, repeating the reasons the Zero Hour had given for not helping.

"It's unlike the Hands to turn down such an opportunity," Micah pointed out. "They're not just fearless when it comes to a money-making opportunity; they can be reckless. Damn the danger.

And as far as the target market being too small, that's just bullshit. They make more money off the auctions alone than all the lower marketplaces combined, and some of the intermediate marketplaces, too."

"So, is it fear, or bribery?" Micaiah wondered.

"Are the Borelians really that fearsome?" Tommen asked.

"If you knew Genghis Khan was marching your way to kill your men, rape your women, and burn your village, what would you think?" Micaiah let that hang there as he folded his arms. "Which makes me curious to know why they wouldn't jump at the opportunity to control the Grandfathers. They've been warring for years; it's unlike them."

"I don't know, but I can't ponder and scheme on an empty stomach," Micah said. "Why don't we get something to eat and talk about this like rational men?"

That was the last thing Tommen felt like doing, actually. He'd already eaten twice, once recently, and he was so riled up over the whole being rejected thing that he was more afraid of getting sick. Although, he never did finish his strawberry milkshake. Maybe that would be his excuse.

Where Time was an industry, food was not, and it was provided free of charge. The Wheel had many so-called Food Courts catering to any and all sustenance needs, from sunlight and water, to vegetation, to meat both raw and cooked, to rocks and minerals, even waste and carrion.

The Food Court where they dined greatly resembled a food court as if it came straight from a mall or outdoor festival, with a variety of little "shops" set up to form a semi-circle while the world's largest salad bar dominated the center of the circle. There were some tables and some open areas to sit, and it was all very much like a nice little picnic. As long as you didn't mind that your server came from the planet Marex and had four eyes and striped skin.

When they weren't working, Tommen never saw the twins touch anything that even resembled what they baked at the store, with the exception of an occasional slice of bread for a sandwich. Otherwise they stayed away from most anything baked, sight-sick of it after years of doing nothing but bake. From the Food Court they both ended up with a breakfast platter as well as a salad generously topped with bacon bits and ranch dressing.

Tommen just wanted his strawberry milkshake, but as he tasted it, all he could think about was sitting in that little waiting room. Waiting, waiting, waiting for his dad's fate to be decided. He remembered just tasting the shake when the secretary interrupted him and told him to follow, the verdict was to be delivered. Tommen pushed the milkshake aside.

"No appetite?" Micah asked solemnly.

"You know they enter the verdict for the case into the record before they actually deliver it?" Tommen said. "What kind of shit is that?"

"Did the Bat tell you that?" Micaiah wondered. When Tommen was silent, unsure of his expression but pretty sure there was shock on there somewhere, he went on. "No one knows his name or his species or where he comes from. Or even if he is a he. Bat's been working for the Hands for as long as anyone can remember. He's probably their most trusted worker, if the Hands trust anyone. He's privy to most of their dealings, their cases, and their verdicts. He is the one they deliver their verdict to when they're done. He enters it into the record, then goes to retrieve whoever is waiting."

"Fucker lied to me when I asked if he knew how they'd ruled."

"He's not permitted to tell," Micah told him. "Only the Hands may deliver a verdict, and none may speak of it beforehand. He does his job well."

Tommen gave them a look. "Something tells me his job isn't limited to being an errand boy."

"The best advice you will get about him is to watch what you say, and assume that everything you say will be reported to the Hands, every question you ask, every answer you give, even the food you order if they offered you food."

Tommen let out a breath and stared at the milkshake for a minute. He might honestly be sick right now. "Doesn't matter, I guess. He's in the Coliseum, and we're out here. He can't hear us now."

"Doesn't mean there aren't others," Micah said even as he stuffed his mouth full of salad, ranch dripping down his chin.

"Honestly, Micah, you're disgusting," Micaiah complained.

"No worse than you."

"You think so?"

"How many times have I had to clean up snack crumbs and wrappers that you leave all over the office floor, hm?"

"No more than I've had to clean up after you in the kitchen."

"We had an agreement. One cooks, the other cleans. I don't intentionally try to create work, but I get...enthusiastic."

"Sloppy."

Tommen shook his head and let them argue. He looked out across the Food Court, at all the alien species going about their lives, on some errand or another in the Wheel, just grabbing a bite to eat before going home probably. Back to jungles and cities and spaceships. Back to friends and families and daily lives. For some, it was as simple as getting up and going to work each day, pulling a nine to five at the office. For others, it was a secret double life, having to steal away in order to do their duties, lie to their superiors about incidents and shenanigans.

Walter did that, frequently. Usually, for most Runners, he could fudge it, how he or the perpetrator moved with such speed or had such awesome reflexes. Sometimes he had to get creative. But fuck, how was he going to explain a rock monster and a neon yellow Viking chick to his superiors?

Didn't matter. Those logistics had probably already been covered, the paperwork filed away. Halloween costumes, most likely. Mentally depraved individuals, high on something, decided to be superheroes or supervillains and got all dressed up for the part. And looking around the Food Court, the Wheel itself, it was kind of like a living advertisement for Halloween costumes. Not all of them certainly, just the humanoids. Maybe the quadrapeds showcased animal costumes. But costumes still. Fake. Pretend. All folly.

But the one thing that wasn't folly was Walter still lying in his hospital bed back on Earth, still in a coma, with only four days to live. That was real. And unless Tommen could come up with something and fast, he would be really dead, too. He looked back at the twins who had given up on their bickering, instead choosing to concentrate more on their food before it got cold.

"This will probably be the first real breakfast I've had before work in a while," Micaiah commented.

Yeah, right, they still had to work. They all did. Day after Christmas, they had to be up and around early so they could get started early so they could open early. Real life. Things went on. But Walter wouldn't unless they found some kind of cure.

"So what do we do now?" Tommen interrupted irritably.

The twins stopped talking and looked at him. Micah frowned. "Tommen, we know you want there to be more. We know that you're hoping to just think of something out of the blue and have it be a miracle cure, something that you can rub in the faces of the Hands and walk away victorious. But..." He sighed. "The Hands, the Archives, these are the greatest resources available to us. When they fail...they fail."

"You're giving up."

"What do you want us to do, Tommen?" Micaiah asked. "What more can we do? What more do you want us to do? The Hands won't give it to us and neither will the Borelians. Earth-side doctors are all but useless in this, and even if they did find the poison and decide to work on an antidote, chances are, it would take far too long to develop. You know that."

Tommen fought tears. He wasn't going to take it. He couldn't. He couldn't have failed. He still had four days left. There had to be something. But there was nothing. Nothing at all. It was all over.

"So there is really nothing we can do?" he said softly.

"I'm sorry, Tommen. We've done all we can."

"Excuse me, hello. Perhaps I can help."

They all looked up as a Hand walked toward them. General shape put Tommen in mind of a humanoid, and the voice was very feminine, being in such close proximity. The Hand walked up to their table and knelt beside it rather than pulling up a chair.

"Greetings, Hand," Micaiah said. "Lieutenants Micaiah and Micah Durvin, Probationary Timekeeper Tommen Forbes, Quadrant One, Parsec Eleven, Sector Five, System Four, Planet Thirty-Eight, Region Four, District Four."

"I know, I saw Tommen at his case," the Hand replied. "I am the Hand of Scientifically Primitive and Unengaged Civilizations."

Tommen gave the Hand a hard regard. "You voted against my case."

"Yes, because I saw the greed of the other Hands who voted for it, and the dangers it possessed. I would not support such a catastrophe when I knew of a much simpler, easier way. I have a cure for your father's illness."

"Your father," not, "your captain." Her word choice was not lost on Tommen.

"How do you have a cure when no one else does?" Micaiah wondered.

"I study poisons and medicines for my people," the Hand explained quietly, as if someone were listening in. "The poison inflicted upon your father is in the same family as a toxic plant that is native to my world. It is a very common poison, but lethal to my people, and we have a cure for it."

"How do you know it's in the same family, or that this cure will work?"

"Since entering into Time, I have spent many days looking more in-depth at the various poisons of my world and of other worlds, trying to find cures for poisons that are very lethal to my people. I have been to visit the Grandfathers more than once, to observe their punishments of Runners. When I saw that some of the poisons were similar to ones I have encountered, I began to research them. When I discovered that doing so was dangerous, even forbidden by the Borelians, I have made it my mission to develop cures for just such a situation. I do not know that it will work, but it is my only chance to help. And it sounds like you are out of options."

Tommen sighed. "We are."

"How do we know we can trust you?" Micah asked.

"You do not. But what good would it do me to poison a man who is already condemned to death?"

Micaiah shifted in his seat. "What do you want in exchange for this poison?"

The Hand shook her head. "The greed and backstabbing lies of this place have made many people mistrustful and quick to suspicion. I ask nothing in return. The journey will be hard enough."

"Journey?"

"My people do not possess the cure. It belongs to another tribe called the D'Bok. They are good enough to trade for the cure; we are at peace. But the journey between my people and the D'Bok is seven days." When they sighed, she went on. "As Timekeepers, you could condense the time and make it."

"Seven days condensed is still seven days for us," Micaiah pointed out. "Even if we double-Banded, we would still be up for seven days. And anyway..."

"I'll do it," Tommen said. "When do we leave?"

"Tommen, you can't double-Band," Micah reminded him.

"But I can stay up for the seven days. I've done it before. Once."

"With catastrophic results, if I recall," Micaiah said severely. "You almost put yourself in the hospital."

"You can go home and work. I'm going to save my dad."

The Hand looked back and forth between Tommen and the twins. Finally she spoke. "I have work I must do yet here in the

Wheel. If you are interested in coming with me, wait for me in the portal room."

"Why don't you come with us, just for a bit, so we can talk without being...monitored?" Micaiah suggested. "We can talk about what this entails. Then we can decide if it's a venture worth taking."

Tommen shifted in his seat, wanting only to jump through the portal with the Hand and run as fast as he could to wherever these D'Bok people were to get the cure. But it was a sensible thing to do. The Hand nodded. "Very well. I will first come with you to your world, and we will speak of this adventure. Is it possible to introduce me to your father?"

"Not unless you're human," Tommen said regretfully. "How long until you're ready?"

The Hand produced a piece of paper and set it on the table, reaching beyond the cloak of the shroud. Her hands were slender and human-like, but they were also striped black, gold, and white. "I will be at the portal room at this time. I will see you."

With that, she departed, vanishing into the crowd as if nothing had happened.

"What do you think?" Micah asked Micaiah.

"I think it's a good prospect, but we'll have to check the Archives," Micaiah answered. He looked at Tommen. "You'd best come with us."

"Why are we going to the Archives?" Tommen wondered as they hastily departed the Food Court and headed for the Archives.

"To research this Hand, for one, and to research her world, to see what you could be going up against." The twins could move quickly when they wanted to, and Tommen had to speed walk to keep up. Only because of the translator could he hear what they were saying.

"I thought you couldn't see the Hands or know their race or anything like that?" Tommen said.

"You can't," Micah confirmed. "But elections are very well-documented and include all information about the candidates, which will be more than enough to get a good start."

"So if you can just do that, why do the Hands need to be shrouded?"

"They hope that most people will just forget, which many do. Most of the time, it really doesn't matter, but it's in these rare instances when that information can be helpful."

Tommen was ready to ask more when they reached the portal-door to the Archives. It made sense, really, doing the research beforehand. What if the air wasn't breathable or the water was toxic? Would he be walking into a blistering desert or a frigid snowstorm? He sighed as he mentally admitted that the twins had the right of it. They needed to stay calm and think about things with a level head. The Hand had given them a time to meet if they were interested; now was their time to decide if they were.

They crossed the Archive lobby and gave another sample of flesh in exchange for the chip that let them read any of the many tablets in the Archives. The twins gave a curt nod of thanks and headed in, Tommen trailing.

"I have a couple questions," Tommen said as they hopped a platform and began going up, up, up.

"There's a shocker," Micaiah chuckled dryly, but nodded for him to continue.

"Why is it that we're wandering around in a man-made dimension with obscenely advanced technology, and yet the Coliseum is a literal Coliseum and has the appearance of stone, and the Archives are like the biggest library in the universe? And why is it that Earth has the Internet which lets us go from page to page to page of infinite topics, but here we have to insert chips into a specific tablet like we're loading old Gameboy games?"

"The tablets is an easy answer," Micah told him as they got off the platform after what felt like ten or fifty levels. "Each one of these tablets, as you may have guessed, is a book. Except it's not a book per se, which is published and printed, but a specific set of information that is coded fluidly. I don't know how to explain it, maybe like AI, but that information is not set until a chip is inserted and the reader chooses a display function, the language you want to use. Basically, that is a lot of information to contain, and the builders of the Wheel apparently found it more efficient than trying to build a single supercomputer like the Internet. Maybe because if one tablet fails, one tablet fails. One supercomputer fails, everyone's shit out of luck."

Made sense.

"As for the layout of the Coliseum and Archives," Micaiah went on, "no one knows. Builders' prerogative, I guess. Maybe they were fascinated by Earth-side architecture. Maybe such libraries are very common around the universe and they decided to pick something that was a common theme to make it easier on the races. Who knows? The Coliseum? Not a clue, but there are conspiracy theories."

"What kind of conspiracy theories?"

"None which are relevant here." He turned into a subsection and kept going through several subsections until they hit an outer wall. Then they turned again and headed to a single row among thousands.

"How do you remember where stuff is in here? It's huge," Tommen commented.

"Just depends on what you need to look up, and how often you come here, same as learning every new place," Micaiah told him, inserting his chip and scrolling through a long list of books. He picked one and Tommen saw it flashing orange on the shelf. Micah retrieved it.

"These are the last election results," Micah explained as he scrolled through. "Looks like the Hand of Scientifically Primitive and Unengaged ran unopposed."

"Makes sense, considering how few of them there are," Micaiah said, half to himself. "Name is Sifura. Quadrant Two, Parsec Nine, Sector Five, System Twelve, Planet Nineteen."

He did something—tapped the screen or hit a button—and the map came up on the screen, moving crazily until it showed a section of a floor blinking orange. Then Micah removed his chip, returned the tablet to its place on the shelf, and they were off again.

The twins were surprisingly efficient, Tommen thought as they moved through the library. He had heard stories and read articles about twins being able to move with scary efficiency and synchronization when they were of a mind, but he'd never quite seen it in action. At the bakery, Micah worked in the kitchen and, once Tommen got off the bus, Micaiah worked in the office. What did they do when they were both in the kitchen? Tommen decided he didn't want to know.

They got off on another floor, and Tommen dutifully followed Micah who followed Micaiah to a subsection not far away. Then it was a matter of trial and error as they searched the rows for any tablets regarding the Hand's world. Micah was the first to find the row, and Tommen was sent to retrieve several tablets so they could all sit down, read, and discuss.

" 'The name of the planet varies from tribe to tribe based on various spiritual beliefs and mystic rituals,' " Micaiah read quietly. "Well, that's lovely."

"Here's one," Micah interrupted. " 'The people groups are divided along lines that are both ethnic as well as racial. Each tribe has what may be referred to as a "spirit animal" though the religious implications are unknown since the tribes have been known to hunt and kill members of the animal species with no more regard for it than any other species. It may have to do only with physical appearance. For example, the Gin Jor people of the northwestern continent bear a striking humanoid resemblance to the gin jor animal, the Selak people have an appearance of the selak animal, and so forth.' "

"I think I found the one of our Hand," Tommen said and turned his tablet around in such a way so they could all see the picture and he could read the text aloud. " 'The Xur people are extremely isolated compared to other tribes, choosing to live in the Red Desert among the xur for which they are named. The Xur are divided into three factions, the Xurdok, which is the largest faction, boasting eleven thousand members; the Xresa, with four thousand members, and the Xorik, with only a thousand members.' "

" 'Each tribe,' " Micaiah read from another tablet, " 'is divided into factions. The Gin Jor has the most people, one hundred thousand, but only eleven factions, while the Da Leio have eighty thousand people and twenty-nine factions. Each faction is led independently with no one person claiming leadership of the whole tribe. Each tribe has their own politics of how leaders come to power, but most often the ritual is the same within each faction. The only known discrepancy is among the D'Bok people. Four of the seven factions are democratic in nature, while the remaining three require combat tournaments.' "

"We'll have to find out which one Tommen is going to be visiting," Micah said, taking a pad of paper from his pocket and making a note. "The Xur and the D'Bok may be on good terms, but I don't want to send Tommen into some warrior combat tournament to prove his worth and the worth of his people."

"God help us if he does," Micaiah said, grinning. Tommen could have punched him.

"I'll keep reading about the D'Bok," Micah told them. "Tommen, do more research on the Xur. Cai, keep an eye on the time and see if you can't find out more about Sifura."

"I think I just did," Tommen interrupted. " 'The current leader of the Xresa, a faction of the Xur, is a female named Sifura. She came to power after the former leader, Asik, was killed on a hunt. Xur tradition for choosing a new leader is for all candidates to declare themselves and boast of both their warrior skills and survival skills in the desert. Sifura gained an edge over her opponents as she studied the medicine of the desert and other regions of the planet in addition to numerous victories in battle and on the hunt.' "

"So she's no fool," Micah said. "Cai, see if you can't find her record as Hand. Tommen, more on the Xur and on the planet in general."

They separated to their assigned tasks, but there was precious little information about the Xur, at least anything specific. They were largely nomadic, traveling and returning to various oases at certain times of the year. The nomadic paths of the different factions crossed only rarely. If they saw each other at all, it would be on a hunt because two factions were hunting the same animal. Other than squabbling over kill rights, they weren't at peace so much as they were completely passive and indifferent to the existence of other Xur factions. Once a year, they gathered to trade and make peace and tell stories of the various other tribes they ran into, but they were, as the book said, extremely isolated.

Tommen returned all his tablets to their places on the shelves and started hunting for books about the planet itself. On that, there was more information. Geographical, geological, astrological, biological, all the other -ogical information could be gathered easily without having to interfere with the tribes, and straightforward facts were easier to digest than distant speculation.

Tommen quickly found a setting on the tablet with such information that allowed him to compare it to any other planet, namely Earth. He scanned through it, and he thought it seemed promising.

" 'The atmosphere is comparable to Earth's and may be tolerated by humans. The hottest recorded temperature was in the Red Desert, measuring 135° Fahrenheit, and the coldest temperature was measured at -70° Fahrenheit in the Broken Ice Lands.' " Tommen ran his tongue over his teeth. So basically he would be vacationing in Death Valley for a week. " 'The water is high in minerals, specifically copper and iron. Some inland lakes have been known to also contain deep pockets of liquid methane and other gases and chemicals, making them toxic. Typically, however, if an indigenous person is drinking the water, it may be considered safe within reason for human consumption.' "

He did not have to go far to find a tablet with similar information on the Red Desert, though it was sorely limited. "

'Temperatures vary greatly in the Red Desert, from an average of 120° Fahrenheit during the day to 0° Fahrenheit at night. While the desert is littered with oases, most of them contain toxic water owing to pockets of liquid methane deep beneath the surface.

" 'Aside from the native tribe called the Xur, the Red Desert is far from desolate in terms of wildlife. A number of herds move across the desert to get from the Great Plains of the Ouin to the Snakevine Jungles of the D'Bok and the Skytouch Mountains of the Rupi. The only animal who calls the Red Desert home year-round without exception is the xur, for which the Xur people call themselves.' "

The Snakevine Jungles. That did not sound reassuring, and Tommen found himself hoping it was just a name meant to scare people. The comparison information, however, was less than comforting.

" 'The Snakevine Jungles, home to the D'Bok tribe, are considered extremely hazardous to humans as most of the plants are poisonous at the touch, some giving off invisible toxic gases which can paralyze and kill within ninety seconds.' "

Ah, fuck. Well, it would make sense that if all the plants were toxic, then they would have cures for them. And if one of them truly was similar to the Borelians' poison, all the better for it. But how was he going to protect himself? Long sleeves and long pants could do well for the contact poisons, but was he going to have to take a gas mask with him, too?

Tommen jumped at a hand on his shoulder. Only Micaiah.

"Sorry," the twin said, though it was more of formality than true apology. So he was still mad about earlier. Understandable, but at least he was still helping. "Find anything useful?"

"Sounds like I'm going to be vacationing Death Valley for a bit before stepping into a wildly poisonous Amazon rainforest," Tommen told him. "And it's not just plants that are poisonous on contact, but they give off toxic gases, too."

Micaiah grunted, his expression clearly displeased, but he said nothing aloud. Probably just one more thing to talk to Sifura about.

"Did you find anything on Sifura as a Hand?" Tommen asked. Out of the corner of his eye, he noticed Micah walking up, the same question spelled out in his eyes.

"Not a lot," Micaiah answered. "But that's not a bad thing. She's a Harvester, actually, Triage, been training for probably twenty years and is exceptionally bright. On many issues brought before the Hands, she is one of the last to vote. If the vote is decided, she refuses to vote. And if the vote is close, she votes very...humanely. She usually refuses to vote in favor of something that would be very damaging—and very profitable for the person bringing the case—and so far refuses to endorse anything that results in someone getting killed."

"Except my case," Tommen growled.

"Except your case," Micaiah confirmed.

"But if she's right," Micah told him, "this will be much easier and much safer."

"I still handed my incredibly profitable and extremely 'damaging' plan to the Hands which they could still use, just without getting the antidote," Tommen complained.

"But if you hadn't gone before the Hands in the first place, she would never have been made aware of Walter's plight and would never have come to us. Furthermore, which one of us, having access to the greatest vault of medical information in the universe, would have paid any attention to some little primitive, unengaged world with highly toxic plants?"

Tommen shrugged. They were right, of course. Didn't mean he had to like it, but they were right. They were all guilty of that one. And Walter would have died without ever knowing that there might have been a last chance somewhere out there in the universe. With Tommen leaving and needing to be able to Band for seven days, this truly was their last ever last chance to do something for him.

"Is it time to go?" Micah asked.

Micaiah simply nodded and turned to leave. Tommen quickly returned his tablet to its place and hurried after the twins, twisting and turning through the subsections until they reached one of the platforms and returned to the lobby to return their chips.

"Why not have the tablets somehow connected to the translators so we don't have to get chips?" Tommen wondered as they crossed the lobby toward the portal-door.

"I don't know," Micaiah said as they stepped into the main hub of the Wheel, his tone suggesting he was growing very irritated. "Maybe the secretaries in there will have heard your off-handed comment and act on it."

Tommen wanted to inform him that his snippy attitude was not fair or welcome and he wanted to move on, but he knew that the elder twin would only come back on it, pointing out how often Tommen made comments that were not only unfair, but also very rude. Best to just let it slide and ride it out. Even being Irish, Micaiah couldn't hold a grudge forever.

"There's a lot going on here," Micah said softly. "We should move quickly."

Tommen looked around as they headed from portal to portal. The Wheel was usually always busy to varying degrees, but now he also felt a sense of urgency, as if the room was starting to fill with smoke but people were trying to pretend it wasn't there and go about their business while also trying to make a discreet exit.

"What is it?" Tommen wondered lowly, moving closer to them.

"I'd say word's gotten back to Cassius about your case," Micaiah growled. "It's only a matter of time before he starts connecting dots. Come on."

So they picked up the pace just a little trying to move just a little faster without drawing attention like a trio of arsonists. Tommen picked out a couple Hand shrouds and also some other kind of shrouded uniform. A troupe of alien soldiers, or something far more sinister from the Wheel itself? The Grandfathers, maybe?

They reached the portal room where, as promised, Sifura was waiting for them. Well, a Hand was waiting for them, but they made no assumptions until they walked over to the dispenser.

"Wait," Sifura said under her shroud. "I am here."

Micaiah refrained from dropping his translator in the dispenser. "Good. We can't be too careful, but we also don't have the time."

"Agreed. I will follow you."

"What about the translators?" Tommen wondered.

"How do you expect to understand each other?" Micah said as they headed down a row of portals.

"Won't they know we took them?"

"They'll know they went missing, but it's hardly a felony. People forget all the time. We just bring them back when we're done."

"Where we are going," Sifura interrupted, "is there anything I must know or do?"

Micaiah looked back at her and shook his head. "No. It's the middle of the night, and it's our house. We may speak freely for a short time until we have to work."

It was easy to forget that it was the day after Christmas, at four in the morning. Technically, the twins should have been on their way to the bakery already, ready to get baking and be open by six. But that was what Banding was for, wasn't it?

They reached the portal that opened up to the twins' living room, lit only by a single lamp that cast shadows over everything. Micah went first, to make sure everything was clear. Then Tommen went through, followed by Sifura and then Micaiah.

Chapter Thirteen
Sifura Three-Heart

Tommen always hated going through the portals, hated the feeling of having the air sucked from his lungs and the strength sapped from his entire body. He'd always hated it, but now as he thought about it, it also reminded him too much of the night he pursued Cassius and Rifun after the museum break-in. It wasn't about the pursuit or even the fight where he'd gotten shot, albeit superficially, but it reminded him of the swim. He'd attacked Rifun in the boat and made it capsize. While Rifun was disoriented underwater, Tommen had taken the opportunity to seize the journal he'd stolen and make a swim for it.

That had been a long, cold swim. The dive had been like a haphazard bellyflop into a pit of knives, and the swim itself was like being caught in some kind of bear trap or iron maiden, the spikes slowly closing in and piercing flesh. He'd been soaked through well enough just by being underneath, but as he swam, the cold water sent icy tendrils through his skin to his core. He remembered his limbs stiffening and his fingers freezing as he told himself to just keep swimming. But he was no athlete; he barely merited participation ribbons. And still the cold closed its icy jaws around him.

By the time he'd gotten to shore, he was grateful just to have his shoulders and hips moving well enough to propel him through the water, never mind trying to drag himself up onto shore through the slushy snow, the top of his head frozen with icicles in his hair while frigid water began to freeze on his face. The weight of the water soaking his clothes added probably fifty pounds or more as it, too, began to freeze. Then, in his suffering, Cassius had managed to walk right up to him and sucker punch him twice in the gut before he got his bearings, driving the air from his lungs and the remaining strength—fueled almost solely by adrenaline and the bestial need to keep moving and survive—from his limbs.

That was about how it felt to go through the portal either to or from the Wheel, less the freezing cold and the wet. Walking into the portal was like trying to drag himself up that slushy boat ramp, the weight of the water dragging him down, forcing him to use all his strength to keep going. Then, as he passed through that dimensional threshold, it was like Cassius had come out of nowhere to punch him twice in the gut. Tommen found himself on the floor of the living room, gasping for air, all strength sapped from his body and will from his mind.

Maybe he really ought to join Drama Club. There were times when he could be really dramatic. Walter and the twins all said so.

Even as he thought it, a hand came under his arm, and he was drunkenly helped to his feet by Micah.

"You okay?" Micah asked, not sounding quite up to snuff himself.

Tommen nodded dumbly, aware that his mouth was hanging open and he was probably drooling, but unable to do anything about it for a long moment. Micah got him to the recliner and handed him a paper towel and a glass of water.

"It's not good to go through the portals so many times in such a short span," Micah said. "But I have a feeling you'll be going through them a lot more before today is over."

"So you think I should go with her?" Tommen's jaw felt numb, like he'd been out in the cold for too long or maybe gotten in a fight.

"I don't know, but that's what we're here to discuss."

Somewhere in Tommen's sluggish, drunken thoughts, he remembered thinking that normally it was the girl's family, specifically her father, who had to interview the guy before they went anywhere together and alone. Did that still happen these days? He churned through his memories of past girlfriends but either could not recall or else it hadn't happened. At the same time, he'd never dated a girl long enough to go anywhere together and alone. Outings with friends or an occasional dinner-and-a-movie date, but never anywhere alone, like alone-alone. And certainly no sex. Part of this had to do with his lack of driver's license, which he was working hard to remedy. Part of it had to do with his girlfriends either being so superficial he didn't want to do anything with them, or they didn't want to do much more than play him for a couple free meals. And part of it had to do with him not believing in sex on a first date. Three months, minimum, maybe a little more if she was really good and he was really interested, maybe a little less if she was really willing and he was really desperate.

Of course, Eric had said Michelle had been more than willing—willing enough, or drunk enough, to go for it in a fucking janitor's closet—and look what had happened to him. True, they hadn't been dating, and it had probably been a cover-up for her other activities and her pregnancy, but still... And there was that whole bit about his own addiction which he was still trying to break away from, and his nightmares about the white Borelian.

The serious nature of his thoughts now killed his arousal, not that he'd been terribly interested anyway, even if a hot girl had taken the opportunity to walk up and sit on him. His mind seemed to come back to him from wherever it had been, and he sat up in the chair, taking a drink of the cold water, wiping his mouth, and hoping that Micah hadn't seen him lounging there like a drunken, aroused pig.

Thankfully, Micah was turned the other way, toward the portal, waiting as Sifura and Micaiah came through.

Tommen had once had it explained to him that once a Hand was named, they were entered into a special database and their DNA was also recorded, so that upon opening a portal to the Wheel and entering, they would automatically be shrouded. No muss, no fuss. Theoretically, this process also worked in reverse, and it did now as Sifura walked out of the Wheel and into the living room, her shroud coming off her like scraping dirt off the bottom of a boot.

The creature that stepped into the room before them had an effect on all of them, Tommen saw, though the twins were a little more adept at hiding it and keeping it under control. Tommen was not, and, while their attention was taken, he Banded and slipped down to the bathroom.

That whole bit about his arousal being killed and nothing could help it even if a hot girl walked in and sat on him? Yeah, apparently not true. Not true at all. He remembered seeing her picture on the tablet, but it had been small and very brief. To see her here before them now was like the difference between seeing an ad for Victoria's Secret and actually seeing one of the models in person.

But then, that brought back all of his new addiction struggles. A month ago, Tommen wouldn't have thought twice about taking himself in his hand and coming up with all number of fantasies about that hot goddess out there. Even as he thought about it, he twitched and groaned. Fuck. He wasn't sure if that was a pejorative or a command. But now, having realized his shame and still haunted by the white Borelian, his mind was torn.

He really had no moral reason not to. No god was going to judge him and tell him it was wrong. He was sexually maturing; he had the energy and the desire. Strictly speaking, he ought to be fucking every female in the herd, trying to pass on his genes. Medically speaking, he knew he should be cautious lest he amass a whole book of diseases. But he was there, he was ready.

And yet, some small part of him still clung to the idea that there was more, he was more. Maybe it wasn't some spiritual thing, but just that he was not just an animal in the herd who went into rut every fall; he was a human being, above the animals, capable of true love and compassion and creativity and innovative thinking and the drive to do whatever it took to save a loved one from certain death.

There was also the fact that he was probably going to be among Sifura's people for at least a short time, and he was going to have to get used to them lest he shame himself in front of them.

Cold water did wonders for killing arousal and bringing his

mind back to itself, and Tommen returned to the living room, intent on thinking things through strictly scientifically and only as a matter of principal.

But fuck, it was hard. And so was he. *No. Fuck. Stop! Dammit!*

He dropped the Band, and Micah helped his brother, nearly unconscious, to the couch while Sifura picked herself up off the floor. She stood about six feet give or take, with a body structure that was both curved and yet solid steel, like a ballerina who was also a weightlifting champion and a kung fu master. Just like the picture, she was humanoid with two arms and two legs and walked upright, but she also had a tail that came down as an extension of her spine, just a little longer than her legs, hovering over the floor and twitching like a cat's tail. Her ears were not human ears, but pointed cat ears perched on top of her head with all apparent range of motion as they twitched and twisted and turned like a couple of satellites. Her pupils did not dilate, but rather widened and narrowed into slits; her irises were bright orange. The end of her nose was leathery, like a cat's, and she had whiskers on her cheeks and above her eyes, with only the faintest hint of anything resembling eyebrows.

She was also stark naked, though it was difficult to tell. She was black, gold, and white but not striped like a tiger. Rather, it was like an artistic swirling of paint. Her face was mostly gold with a bit of white on her chin and black on her forehead. Her neck was black, giving way to a gold and white torso except for her right ribs and part of her right upper arm which were black. Both breasts were gold, one with a white stripe, and her gold nipples were nearly invisible. The rest of her right arm was almost equal parts gold and white, her hand striped black, gold, and white. Her left arm was gold at the shoulder followed by a ring of black, and then a mix of gold and white the rest of the way to a nearly solid gold hand accented in white. Her hips were gold as well. Her legs were the only thing really disproportionate from the rest of her body. Instead of being long and slender, they were very muscular, like the legs of a tiger, with massive paws instead of feet. Her thighs were mirror black and white, returning to gold at the hock, then mixing with white the rest of the way down to striped paws. Her tail was gold part of the way down, turning to white to the tip and messily ringed with black three-quarters of the length.

Her hair was also a beautiful mess of black, gold, and white, and it took a second for Tommen to realize it was braided. It wasn't quite like any braid he'd ever seen as it wasn't just three strands woven together, more like a network of dozens of braids. Not cornrows, but maybe...a fish net? How could hair be done in such a way, and why did it make her look so damn beautiful?

Perhaps the most peculiar thing about her, however, was that she had diamonds embedded in her abdomen, or at least they looked like diamonds. There were six of them, following a swirl of white that started below the breastline and ended about where her navel should have been, except she didn't have a navel. Not born then? Then what was the purpose of the breasts?

Tommen told himself to be objective and think things through scientifically, mission-oriented. She was going to help him save his dad by taking him to another people who had the cure for his disease.

Would those people be just as hot?

No! Snap out of it! She is here to help, not to show you a good time. The only good time you are going to have is when your dad wakes up from his coma and you are back together again.

Fuck, this was going to be harder than he thought.

"Are you all right?" Micah asked Sifura, Banding the group and cutting in on Tommen's thoughts.

"I am well," Sifura replied calmly. She glanced at Micaiah on the couch; he'd passed out. "You have opened many portals, been through too many portals, in only a short amount of time."

"We have. It's not good for us."

"He will be all right?"

"Yes, in time. Would you like something to eat or drink? I will see what we have to offer."

"I have heard that the water here is safe for me."

While Micah got the water, Sifura took a few tentative steps and looked around the room. Tommen saw claws poking out from the end of her toes with each step.

"This is your home?" she wondered.

"Aye, it is," Micah said, returning with a cup of water. "Cai and I live here."

"And Tommen Forbes?"

"He...lives with his dad. If his dad dies, he'll stay with us for a time."

"I see. You do not have mates?"

Micah flushed red. "Ah, no. No, I don't. It's hard to find a girl when you are what we are. Time and Timekeeping and all that."

Sifura looked confused, but she said nothing more about it. Probably just weird alien customs to her, Tommen thought, and they had no bearing on the situation at hand. As he thought this, Micaiah moved on the couch and fought to sit up, rubbing his eyes and yawning.

"You okay, Cai?" Micah wondered, handing him a glass of water also.

"Fucking hell, I can't keep doing this," Micaiah sighed and took the water.

"Well, hopefully you won't have to for much longer. Think you can get up and talk?"

"Sure, sure."

"You are twins," Sifura observed as they moved to the dining table.

"Aye, we are," Micah said, helping Micaiah from one seat to another. "Technically, he's older."

"Twins are good luck."

"That's relative when you're talking about us," Micaiah said, grinning like he was drunk. He took a breath and tried to relax without lapsing back into slumber.

"We will begin formally," Sifura decided. "I am Sifura. In my tongue, it means 'Three-Heart.' I am the leader of the Xresa, a faction of the tribe of Xur. In Time, I am also a Triage Harvester, and the Hand of Scientifically Primitive and Unengaged Civilizations."

Neither twin saw fit to inform her that they already knew all this. Instead, Micaiah took a breath and went next. *"Is mise Micaiah Durvin, nó Micaiah, nó Cai. Is an leathcúpla mór Durvin mé. Le cheile, tá bácús againn. San Am, is Leifteanant Amcosaineoir mé."* (I am Micaiah Durvin, or Micaiah or Cai. I am the elder Durvin twin. Together, we own a bakery. In Time, I am a Lieutenant Timekeeper.)

Next they looked at Micah. *"Is mise Micah Durvin, nó Micah. Is an leathcúpla beag Durvin mé. Le cheile, tá bácús againn. San Am, is Leifteanant Amcosaineoir mé."* (I am Micah Durvin, or Micah. I am the younger Durvin twin. Together, we own a bakery. In Time, I am a Lieutenant Timekeeper.)

Then it was Tommen's turn. He swallowed. *"Tommen Forbes dw i, o Tommen. Dw i'n mynd i'r ysgol a dw i'n gweithio i Micaiah a Micah Durvin yn eu bacws. Yn Amser, Amseramddiffynnydd prawf dw i."* (I am Tommen Forbes, or Tommen. I go to school and I work for Micaiah and Micah Durvin in their bakery. In Time, I am a probationary Timekeeper.)

"Very good," Sifura said.

"So, let's talk about this disease and cure of yours," Micaiah said, his stern, slightly surly attitude returning. "What is it on your world?"

"We call the plant hasax, and sometimes we use it on our spears or arrows to wound an enemy, but we cannot use it in a hunt or it will taint the meat."

"What does it do to your enemies?"

"It puts them into a deep sleep, a coma as the tablets call it. With the antidote, they will usually make a full recovery. Without it, death is almost certain."

"How do you know that this is in any way similar to Borelian poison? The Borelians have a number of toxins."

"I have studied the effects of the Borelian poisons as their victims die, the way they die. There is only one that corresponds so cleanly between the poison I know and the symptoms Tommen described before the Hands. I know this because I analyzed the chemical makeup of both the plant toxins and the Borelian toxins from the Grandfathers."

To hear that sentence come from a wild she-cat who led a primitive tribe who still used spears and bows and arrows to hunt and defeat enemies was honestly hilarious, and Tommen had to fight even a smile, never mind a laugh.

Sifura went on, "They are similar. Not the same, but in the same family. I meant to test the antidote on both of them and watch the reaction, but the Grandfathers discovered my work while I was away and destroyed it." Her gold eyes blazed with fury. "They did not know it was me, but I have seen the punishments, and I have not tried again, not until I have found a way to do so without being discovered."

"Fair enough," Micah said sympathetically. "What is hasax exactly?"

"It is a flowering plant with enormous leaves. Ironically, the flower is the antidote, but to get to it, one must go through the leaves which are covered in the toxic oils. Gathering the antidote requires at least two people, one to risk the leaves, the other to get the flower, and part of the flower must go to the person who braved the leaves."

"Nature's little ironies," Micaiah murmured. "What will it take to get it? What will you and Tommen be doing?"

"My portal to the Wheel is not far from my people. I must take him there and introduce him. He will be a representative of another tribe, come for help for his dying faction. It is customary that a man requesting must bring a gift, where a man invited must take a gift. You are coming to us for help, and we are going to the D'Bok for help. We will require gifts. For my people, you will bring the translators as the gift of language."

"How will you explain that kind of technology?" Micah wondered. "What will you tell your people?"

"I will tell them whatever I wish. It is not your concern," Sifura told him dismissively.

"What would be appropriate to bring?" Tommen asked.

"Something unique to your people that we may trade in the future. It may be furs or jewelry or exotic foods. The tradition is the same for most tribes, and it will be for the D'Bok also."

"So what happens next, when you introduce him to your people?" Micaiah inquired.

"Normally, in such dire circumstances, we would set off immediately." She sighed. "Unfortunately, it is the Day of the Sun, and I cannot be absent for the feast. Tommen will join us for the feast and become part of us, and we will make merry talk of a future of trade of kinship between our tribes. In the morning, we will set out at once."

"And it takes seven days to reach the D'Bok?"

"It does, and that is taking the sand skimmer. On foot, it takes nearly thirty days."

"Sand skimmer?" Tommen wondered.

"A vehicle you will learn to operate," Sifura informed him. "If you can Band for seven days, we will reach the D'Bok swiftly."

It hadn't occurred to Tommen until just then that he probably should have checked to see just how long days were on her world. For all he knew, he could be Banding for three Earth days or fifteen.

"When we reach the D'Bok," she continued, "we will present gifts to their leader and council. I will try to convey the urgency of the matter, but I make no guarantees about how things will proceed after that."

"I thought you said the Xur and the D'Bok were at peace?" Micah said.

"To be at peace means we are not at war. My people do not commune with outside tribes often. The D'Bok themselves are great hunters and warriors, and they often mark their territory at the end of the jungle and challenge those who would cross it to prove their worth. It is no great feat to meet with their leader and council, but it is very trying when it comes to negotiations. It is equally likely that they will just give us the antidote as make us go and fetch it ourselves."

"Which is how you know what the plant looks like and its properties," Tommen concluded.

"Yes," Sifura confirmed. "When I was a healer, before I was the leader, I went to the D'Bok and asked for permission to gather and study their poisonous plants. They told me I was welcome to all the poisonous plants I liked, and if I was able to take any with me, they were well-deserved." Her words dripped acid.

"How is their attitude toward unfamiliar outsiders, like Tommen?" Micaiah asked.

"He will be challenged, undoubtedly. Many may try to fight him. I would not advise engaging all of them as it is merely fun sport, but neither should you walk away from all of them either."

"Fuck," Micah hissed. "He gets in trouble at school for fighting, now you're telling him he's going to have to fight?"

"It is the only way to earn respect from the D'Bok, the only way they will allow us to have the antidote, however they offer it to us."

"So I guess all my fighting wasn't completely worthless, right?" Tommen said, trying to find humor. The twins, however, did not find it humorous at all.

"If we must retrieve the flower ourselves, we will do so swiftly, and return swiftly to the D'Bok village," Sifura continued. "Once we leave their territory and are fair distance from everything, then I will open a portal to the Wheel, and you will return home."

"And what will you tell your people about why he didn't come back?" Micaiah asked.

"I will tell them he left quickly to save his people. I will tell them whatever I wish. It is not your concern or relevant to the matter at hand."

Tommen couldn't tell if her attitude came from being a badass leader and part tiger, or if it was just a Harvester thing. Well, it really didn't matter, did it? He was going to have to put up with her for the next week or so; he might as well get used to it.

"Sounds simple enough," Micah said, looking at Micaiah. "And it might be our last chance to save Walter."

Micaiah nodded grimly. "Aye, it might be. But I have other worries, too."

"Their atmosphere is tolerable," Tommen jumped in. "And the translator generates a small atmospheric shell. And I read that their water is safe, too. Well, for the most part."

"That's not what my worries are." He folded his arms and gave Sifura a hard regard. "No doubt you noticed the...urgency in the Wheel as we left, the other Hands and even the Grandfathers out and about."

Tommen thought about the strange figures moving around with the Hands. He hadn't gotten a good look at them, but they'd almost looked like the Hands except shrouded in black instead of white.

Sifura dipped her head. "I did see." She shifted uncomfortably in the chair and spoke before Micaiah could say more. "After Tommen Forbes' case was closed and he left the Coliseum, some of the other Hands met secretly in the deliberation chambers. I do not know if they are unaware of the listening holes in the room, or if they thought the others were gone, or if they thought the others did not know about them. But I knew, and I listened."

The deliberation chambers of the Coliseum had convenient listening holes. Of course they did.

"What did you hear?" Micah wondered.

"I did not hear everything, but I heard enough to make me flee even before they were completely finished, and I sought you out. There was mention of Tommen's plan, to capture the Borelian Isthim and hold her against the Borelians. Some wanted to do it anyway and claim they were not going against the ruling by pointing out that you would not be given the antidote in exchange. Some wanted nothing to do with it. There was mention of Cassius the False Zero Hour, and of you two—" She looked at the twins. "—and of your captain. There was mention of Rifun. Some thought to ally with the Grandfathers, others to fight them. I left when they started shouting and getting very angry."

Micaiah sighed. "The Hands are descending into civil war." He frowned. "The Time industry has long been corrupt, but it was manageable as long as the Hands were many islands fueled by greed and self-interest; it was how the Dispersal was kept from being any bloodier than it was."

"If the Hands begin to form factions, it could tear the industry apart," Sifura concluded. "It would divide the Time Agents."

"Worse," Micah growled. "It could force the Timekeepers to move against the Grandfathers. The Timekeepers are the peacekeepers. If the Grandfathers favored one faction over another and tried to bring it into greater power, it would be our job to make sure that didn't happen."

"The Grandfathers are not as feared as they are for no reason," Micaiah said obviously. "We might as well stand aside and cut our losses."

"What about the elections?" Tommen wondered. "I thought everyone had to play nice until the elections are over?"

"They did, until we stupidly planted this little idea in their minds."

"It could be worse than that," Sifura said, as if anyone really wanted to hear how much worse it could actually get. "The Hands who are voted out may regroup in order to pursue Isthim and the Borelian poisons and antidotes. They could form a separate industry while still maintaining ties to the Hands of Time and the Grandfathers."

"Thus further dividing the Time Agents," Micaiah finished. He leaned back in his chair and shook his head. "We never should have come up with that idea."

"Come on, Cai, this was bound to happen sooner or later," Micah consoled. "The Hands are always on a cycle of civil war."

"Except this time we gave them a nuclear bomb to fight over. It's not going to end well for anyone."

"So what does that mean for this little venture to find Walter's cure?" Tommen asked.

"The adventure itself? Very little once you're with her on her world or back home here. It's the time in between, those few moments running from one portal to another that make me nervous."

"What could they actually do, though?"

Micah shifted in his seat. "Cassius—well, Rifun, but Cassius knows what's happened to Walter. He knows he's been poisoned by a Borelian. Regardless of how it got in his system, Walter is dying from Borelian poison. You made a petition to find a cure, and you were rejected. Next thing you know, you're running off to some alien world. Fine and dandy, but you bring something back from that world and suddenly Walter is cured.

"That is not an isolated thing. Okay, we already sent word to the other Timekeepers in the District and the other District Captains and the Regional Manager that Walter is dying and to come pay their final respects if they choose. Everyone knows Borelian poison is the end. Suddenly Walter gets out of bed and is miraculously cured? Word will get around.

"Immediately, you, me, Micaiah, we're all implicated. And it won't take long before they figure out who helped us, Sifura. Basically, we just cured Borelian poison. That means that we're not only going to be celebrities among the peasant folk, but wanted among the higher folk. The Borelians will undoubtedly want retribution, which may trigger a move by the Grandfathers. The Hands may get greedy, recalling your plans to make them obscenely rich by selling the antidotes. And with the elections, Cassius will not pass up an opportunity to seize power for himself, however that happens. But you can bet that this good deed will not go unpunished. And there are fates worse than death when you're talking about Time."

Immediately Tommen's mind went to having his clock broken,

that innate sense of the passage of time, simply erased, where a day was a thousand years and a thousand years was a day and all that.

"Why pursue this at all, then?" Tommen wondered.

"Civil war is coming, Tommen," Sifura said gently. "There is no getting around that. But bringing your father back will make weathering the storm easier. And you will need all the help you can get if it does come to bloodshed. Probationaries and even Apprentices rarely survive without a Master at hand."

The twins nodded, their expressions difficult to read.

"What happens to Walter, then, if he makes his miraculous recovery?" Tommen dared ask.

"Then he makes a miraculous recovery," Micah answered. "He's in a coma, dying of Borelian poison. The Hands and the Grandfathers may conjure up some very strange crimes and very sketchy evidence, but this is their catch-22. Either Walter is dying of Borelian poison and thus cannot be a conspirator in the development of the antidote, or else he is not dying of Borelian poison, thus he couldn't be a conspirator to anything truly criminal and thus the Hands have sticks up their asses over nothing. So either way, he is not on the hook for any crimes here. Just us four."

It really wasn't much of a comfort.

"What about my review? Will they keep me from being an Apprentice?"

"They could," Micaiah answered honestly. "And at the rate your skills are developing, we would have a hard time convincing them to simply let you go and not train you further, versus having to break your clock, even a little."

"A little? There are degrees to that kind of torture?"

"There are. So I suppose this all really boils down to how much we're willing to risk for Walter. The Hands are always on the brink of civil war, as you said. So, are we willing to risk alien cultures, poisonous plants, giving a nuclear bomb to the most corrupt politicians in the universe, and risk starting an intergalactic war that transcends time and space, potentially branding ourselves outlaws and criminals at risk of having our clocks broken so we may never function normally ever again?"

Well, Cai, when you put it like that...

It almost wasn't fair. Actually, it really wasn't fair. Why did they serve a government that was so corrupt, that just by the actions of one boy trying to save his dying father, it could ignite such a war? Why were they content with a government that was just "manageable" as long as the politicians were petty, self-serving little lordlings of their own castles? Was there no one who believed in a government of the people, by the people, for the people?

But this wasn't Earth, and the Time Agents were not united in anything but duty and possibly rank. They came from a wide variety of backgrounds and histories and cultures and opinions. What was holy and just to one person was evil blasphemy to another, which was why they only had to govern their own worlds and leave the higher governmental functions to the Hands, because there would be no Continental Congress here. It was like trying to put together a council that governed birth control and have it enforced faction by faction. The Catholics would want it one way, the atheists another. When they each governed their own affairs, they did well. When it came to the higher government, there was no reconciling. Only power struggle.

Well, like all analogies, this, too, sounded better in his head. But the idea was still there. The Hands were on this eternal cycle of bloody civil war, tired peace, and then tension, which led to another civil war. Everyone suffered, but the best the underlings could do about it was weather the storm and hope they weren't the target of anything malicious. Maybe it really was better to be part of an unengaged world, less likely to be a battleground. Well, except that the ones to potentially start this war would be from Earth, an unengaged world.

"I'll risk it," Tommen said, breaking the silence that had blanketed them all. "My dad risked his life to save me from Rifun and fought a Borelian to do it. If I die, I'll die knowing that I did all I could to help him instead of hiding under the bed like a child."

He looked at the twins, daring them to oppose him. Finally Micah nodded.

"I'll risk it. Walter's a good friend and a damn fine fighter, and we'll need him in the future, whatever comes our way."

"And I'll risk it," Micaiah agreed. "Walter has been nothing but good to us, and there is no reason I can find why he should be left to die when there could be a cure out there somewhere."

"I, too, will risk myself," Sifura said. "To see a boy willing to come before the Hands and risk everything, even war, to save his father is the embodiment of purity and goodness, and I will support it and help him."

There was, though, too, the thought that some wars started for some very pure but very stupid reasons. Love of a woman, for example. Helen of Troy. The pursuit of love was a noble one, by most standards. Was starting a war over love really a smart thing to do? Would they look back on this one day and say, "What the fuck were we thinking?"

But the matter was settled. Tommen was going with Sifura. They were going to cure Borelian poison. And if the war followed, so be it.

They stood from the table then. Sifura regarded Tommen with her large golden eyes, pupils moderately narrowed.

"You will bring the gift of language to my people, but you will need another gift to bring to the D'Bok. Consider your choice wisely." She paused. "The water will be provided by my people as you are able to drink it. I have heard that you also eat cooked flesh, and so we will have it. However, if there is anything you require, it is best you bring it yourself; I make no guarantees that what we have will satisfy." She turned as if to go, then stopped and looked back at Tommen. "One more thing. Our home is very hot, but the jungle is cold in the cover of the trees. You cover yourselves for reasons I do not know, but among all the tribes, it is considered deceitful, shameful. You must not cover yourself among my people, except under the night furs.

Among the D'Bok, not at all."

"But I'll freeze," Tommen protested.

"You must endure and know yourself."

It was then that Tommen saw that her different colors of skin were textured differently as well. The black was as leather, tough and worn. The white looked like suede or maybe velvet. The gold resembled human skin. So they regulated their body temperature with the various types of skin covering. Well, Tommen had pretty thin skin in that department, and he had no fat to pad him in the cold. First he was going to burn in the sun, then freeze in the shade.

At the same time, the thought of being naked with this hot wildcat chick for seven days in the desert was pretty appealing. Actually it was more than appealing, it was arousing, but he forced his thoughts to other things.

"I'll put a change of clothes in a bag at least," Tommen said. "Is that acceptable?"

"It is," Sifura conceded after a moment of thought. "But show them to no one."

She went to the living room and turned back. "You have paper?"

It took Micah a second to comprehend her words, but he nodded and went to grab some scrap paper and a pen. Sifura knelt beside the coffee table and wrote something down. She handed it to Tommen. "I will go before you, to test the waters of hostility in the Wheel. Come to the Wheel at that time. Go to the translator dispenser where we met before. If I am not there waiting for you, do not wait for me even a moment. Run straight back here; it means something bad has happened. If I am there, we will go straight to my world. Be prepared for a swift departure."

"I understand," Tommen said, taking the paper.

"We'll make sure he gets there," Micah promised, but Tommen did not miss the look on Micaiah's face, an expression that screamed agony and pain and righteous fury that he did not want to open any more portals and you can't make him. But he would do it.

Tommen knew he would.

"I will see you, Tommen, hopefully," Sifura said.

With that, she bade them step back, which they did. Sifura took a breath and readied herself like a weightlifter judging her bar. Then she opened her portal to the Wheel and stepped through. Tommen watched as he caught a glimpse of the shroud closing in around her, obscuring her features and hiding her from the world.

"Doesn't she have to come back through in order for—?"

Then the portal closed.

"Hands and other high-level Time Agents can also close them," Micah told him.

"What time did she write down for you?" Micaiah wondered, holding his hand out.

Tommen surrendered the paper. It was written in Time notation, which meant nothing to him. Micaiah grunted and went down to his room. Micah followed at a distance.

"Where is he going?" Tommen asked.

"Oh, he copied down the formula to convert time notations back and forth. It's next to impossible to just memorize it and do the conversions in your head. Even your dad has to use the formula, such as when he had to convert the date and time of your review into something more understandable."

"Oh, right." Beat. "How long will it take him?"

"Not long, I think. Most of the variables are pretty constant as they relate to interdimensional distortions, but geometry was never my best subject."

"You mean algebra?"

"No, I mean geometry."

Tommen puzzled over that one for a moment. Interdimensional distortions were based on geometry? Was Micah being serious or just pulling his leg? It was difficult to tell.

"Can I learn that formula, how to use it I mean?" Tommen asked.

"I expect so. You can probably ask Walter. Cai isn't the best teacher in the first place, and having to do these conversions makes him less than amiable."

His words were proven true as, no less than fifteen minutes later, the elder Durvin twin emerged from his room like an angry grizzly coming out of hibernation. He had several sheets of paper in one hand and the little slip of paper in the other. He tossed the larger sheets in the trash.

"So what did you come up with?" Micah asked. "When is our young Indiana Jones going to complete his quest to find the Holy Grail and save his dying father?"

"One hour," Micaiah replied. Micah and Tommen stared at him in stunned silence.

"One hour," he repeated severely. He pointed a finger at the clock and gave Tommen a hard regard as if he'd done something wrong. "You've got one hour to get everything packed, choose a gift, and get headed on your way to hopefully meet Sifura and get going on your little quest."

Chapter Fourteen
One Hour

Why is Micaiah mad at me?" Tommen asked as Micah reached into his closet and pulled out a dusty burlap bag for him to carry all his stuff in.

"What do you mean?" Micah shook out the bag a little and checked it for holes. Satisfied there weren't any, he handed it to Tommen, and they walked out to the living room.

"When he said I only had an hour, he sounded like he was angry at me."

Micah sighed and shook his head. "He's not mad at you. If anything, he's mad at himself for giving the Hands such an idea, and now it's looking more and more like civil war."

"But if the Hands were on their way to civil war anyway...?"

"Yes, that's true. But it's easy to forget that the bomb was already there when you know you're the one who lit the fuse."

"Then why do it at all?"

"He has a hard time showing it, but he cares a great deal for people, almost to a fault. And that fault overrode his better judgment, giving the Hands this scheme in order to save your dad."

"You don't think I should have gone before them, do you?" Tommen felt like a child realizing that his brilliant plan failed and the grown-ups had known it would all along, despite how they'd played along.

Micah frowned as he sat on the couch. "I don't know. On the one hand, we have this impending war. On the other hand, it did give us a path to a potential cure for Walter. And if the Hands are busy trying to build alliances and gain power for their own factions—if

231

indeed that is what they're doing—then it may prove useful in thwarting Cassius' plans."

"What good does that do? The other Hands are just as powerful."

"But I don't think they're as bloodthirsty as Cassius. I don't think anyone is quite as bloodthirsty as Cassius. But how that all plays in, we'll just have to wait and see."

Tommen looked up as the bathroom door opened and Micaiah headed to his bedroom. He was getting ready for work. Micah should have been getting ready as well except he was helping Tommen.

"You're sure he's not mad at me?" Tommen wondered.

Micah nodded. "I'm sure." He slapped his hands on his knees and stood. "But, that's not helping you to pack either way. So, good news for you, I guess, is that you won't have to worry about too many clothes."

"I'm still going to pack at least one set," Tommen informed him, heading to the bedroom to rummage through his suitcase.

"I don't doubt that," Micah said. "But what are you planning on taking?"

Problem was, it was winter in his world, and he hadn't exactly thought to bring shorts and a pair of flip-flops with him when he packed the first time. Clean underwear and undershirt would have to suffice, he supposed, and he was pretty set on not stripping until he was actually standing in the Red Desert sweating his balls off.

"Satisfied?" Micah asked once Tommen had shoved the clothes in the bag. It was a nice bag, actually, supposedly some local souvenir from a village in Peru. It would blend in well enough with a primitive culture.

"I guess," Tommen sighed. Seven days. He was fine with going naked around the house when no one else was home, but in front of an entire tribe and having to do so for over a week? Well, when in Rome, do as the Romans.

"Come here."

They went down the hall toward the bathroom.

"Cai, you done in here?" Micah called.

Micaiah appeared in the door of his bedroom, just tucking his shirt in his pants. "What? Oh, yeah, fine."

Micah steered Tommen to the sink where he opened the doors of the vanity and pulled out a whole doctor's office worth of small medical supplies, and even a few larger supplies. Everything from band-aids and anti-itch cream to sutures and a sterile sewing kit. He left behind the slings and splints, dumping everything else out on the counter.

"You want me to take modern medicine?" Tommen wondered.

"Cultural interference be damned," Micah told him. "If you get hurt, regardless of if you return with a cure, Walter will have my ass. Both our asses. He already had them once after the museum incident. The least I'm going to do this time is send you with something. You're going to be exposed to a number of foreign germs, viruses, bacterias, and probably fungus, too, and your immune system is not equipped to handle them."

It made sense. There was every possibility that if he did get hurt, even their medicine might do more harm than good because though they looked similar, er, vaguely, they still had very different physiology.

"Basics: band-aids and antibiotics," Micah said, picking out said items from the group and setting them aside for Tommen to stuff into his pack. "I know you don't like them, but use them if you break skin at all." He went below the vanity again and pulled out several tubes of clear liquid. "Sterile water. Not for drinking. Gauze and scissors. Even if some tribal member offers you a knife, use the scissors; you don't know where the knife has been. And even though I pray you won't have to use it, but take the sewing kit, too. Better to have it and not need it, right?"

It was times like this when Tommen thought Micah would make a good family man. He was a lover, not a fighter, and he always had a way with kids. He'd befriended Tommen even before Walter had completely earned his trust. Now he was helping Tommen pack his bag as if he was heading off to summer camp or something and fussing over every worst-case scenario, sending him with everything from band-aids to a sterile sewing kit. It was a wonder he didn't pull the tourniquet out, too. And where the fuck did they get all these supplies, and what for?

"Well, that's nice and all, but hopefully you won't have to use it as long as you keep this handy," Micaiah said. He'd disappeared at some point and now reappeared, holding a large bowie knife out to Tommen. Tommen recognized the knife as one that Micaiah kept on him at most times for self-defense. After all, what good was a gun, a long-distance weapon, when a Time-wielding opponent could just sidestep the bullet? Knives were closer, quicker, harder to dodge, or so he said.

Tommen actually kept several small pocket knives on him at all times, and he had his hunting and skinning knives at home, but this was the real deal. He took the knife and weighed it, balanced it. "Thank you."

"Try not to lose it," Micaiah told him. His tone was difficult to gauge, and he reached in his pocket again and brought out a gun. It was a tiny purse pistol, but Tommen knew he would never lower his standards to a .22. He held it out to Tommen. "I'm trusting you with this, both to not hurt yourself or anyone else." As if Tommen hadn't been shooting since he was five years old. "Primitive world and no extra clips means you use this only if your life is truly threatened. Got it?"

Tommen took the tiny gun. "I understand."

"Good. Definitely don't lose that one, or *I* will have *your* ass."

Tommen folded the gun tightly in his clothes and arranged his things so it wouldn't get jostled too much. Safeties were a neat thing, but he always planned for the event that they all failed.

"What else can you think of for gear?" Micah asked before Micaiah headed out.

The elder twin paused for a moment then shook his head.

"Nothing that I wouldn't expect the Xur to provide. If they can do it as a primitive society, I can't imagine it's actually that complicated."

"True." Micah put the rest of the medical supplies back under the sink and stood. "So, let's see about food."

Tommen followed them out to the kitchen. Micaiah got himself his own breakfast while Micah started digging through the cupboards.

"She said that most of the food should be edible," Tommen said.

" 'Most' is what worries me, and I think that's a generous estimation anyway," Micah told him. "Eat to be polite, but avoid what you can. Hopefully, you will only need a couple days' worth of food. You like trail mix?"

Tommen shrugged. "I'm not big on the raisins, but sure."

Micah tossed an enormous package on the counter. "Traveling through the desert means anything that isn't trail mix is going to go bad very fast. So what do we have?"

"What about biscuits or something? For the first day, before it all goes bad?"

The twins glanced at each other, but Micaiah was more intent on his sausage and eggs, and he left the decision to Micah who relented, but not after what Tommen assumed to be a great inner struggle.

"All right. I'll give you the biscuits," Micah told him reluctantly as he fished out a cheap store-bought roll of biscuits. "But if you see any kind of mold or something on them—"

"I'll throw them out," Tommen promised loosely.

"Yes, do so. And don't try to just pick it off either, since you don't know what kind of mold it really is. Alien world, alien fungus and so forth. Maybe it's nothing, maybe it will infect the whole biscuit, maybe it will infect you on contact."

No sooner had Micah tossed the biscuits in the oven and set the timer, than he Banded the oven and the timer went off. The younger twin grabbed a pair of mitts and brought out a fresh plate of buttermilk biscuits, or what passed for buttermilk biscuits in the modern world. He quickly put them in sandwich baggies and all but vacuum-sealed them.

"What about that jerky we got not too long ago?" Micaiah suggested, finishing off his food and heading for the sink.

"Perfect!"

Despite the stakes and the looming threat of war, packing for the trip actually put Tommen more at ease about the whole thing. It was like packing for summer camp.

Walter had sent him to summer camp once, when he was about eight or nine. Actually it was one of those summer Bible camps that ran for like a week, go in the morning, get picked up in the afternoon, repeat for five days. Except this one was specifically designed for parents who couldn't quite meet that schedule, and it was an actual overnight camp.

Overall it had been a fun camp with lots of games and the same stories Tommen had heard as a child—just with bigger, brighter, more colorful pictures. But the first day had been miserable. Not everyone adjusted to camp well, and for of the kids, it was just the daunting thought of having to be away from home for five days. For Tommen, it had been the food.

If anyone wanted advice on what constituted "organic" or "all-natural" or "pasture-raised" foods, Tommen was usually the first to jump into the conversation; he'd grown up on the stuff after all. Walter was understanding enough; when Tommen first moved in, Walter did the cooking, and he was able to make meals that were as close to what Tommen knew and had grown up on and what his system could handle.

Going to camp, Tommen was suddenly thrust into a world of fruit snacks, goldfish, and cheap meat. He'd gotten violently sick the first day, and the camp counselors had to call Walter, saying he was sick and had to go home. After some questioning and probing, Walter ended up bringing over a bit of leftover bean soup for Tommen to eat, which did make everything better. After that,

Tommen was pretty much known as the special kid who needed special foods at meal time. He was teased during meal time, and while the kitchen ladies put on a good face, he knew when he was inconvenient.

After Tommen got home from camp, Walter reluctantly started to introduce more modern foods into Tommen's diet. He still made bean soups and could dress a chicken he bought from the neighbors with the deft skill of a chef, but by the time Tommen was thirteen and in middle school having to buy school lunches, he was able to have the macaroni and cheese, the chicken nuggets, and, as he got older and Walter more or less left him to fend for himself, pizza.

"Got any dry beans?" Tommen asked now as Micah started portioning out the jerky.

"Dry beans?" Micah wondered.

"In the event we have to stop and make camp. And dried herbs would go well with it."

"He's got a point," Micaiah said, pulling his shoes on. "Send a couple bottles of water with him, too."

"And a kettle, too?" Micah shot back. "He's got three days, four max. This isn't some leisurely hiking trip."

"I know that. He's going to be Banding for seven days! That takes a lot more energy than seven days of hiking. He's going to need something more than trail mix and jerky."

"He needs to travel light."

"He needs to be strong in order to travel at all. And dry beans don't weigh that much. Besides, even primitive cultures use pots and pans to some degree; maybe they'll provide one if they have to." Micaiah went on before Micah could protest further. "If there wasn't a chance that this would work, I don't think Sifura would have suggested it. And I would expect that she planned this sensibly."

"So you trust her?" Micah asked levelly.

Micaiah sighed. "I don't know. But she's the best chance we've got at saving Walter."

Micah still hesitated for a moment.

"I'll see you at the store," Micaiah said, grabbing his coat and heading out the door.

Once he was gone, Micah glanced at Tommen, giving him an uncertain regard before shaking his head and heading to one of the cupboards. "Dry beans will take too long to soak, and I don't want to send extra water just for that." He brought out several cans of wet beans. "The cans are a little heavier, but they're already prepared. It will save you time if you have to make camp, cut down on the time you're stopped."

"Fair enough," Tommen conceded. "Do you have any dry herbs?"

"Well, in all honesty, sometimes I cheat and use the little flake shakers." Micah opened up a cupboard filled to the brim with nothing but herbs and spices. "So, what do you want?"

Tommen picked out his herbs, and Micah used a small teaspoon to scoop them into smaller baggies. By the time Tommen got all the food packed and arranged in his bag, it was almost full to bursting, and it felt awkward and heavy to sling over his shoulder.

"I'm not going to have enough room to put any kind of offering for the D'Bok," Tommen commented.

"What were you planning on giving them?" Micah wondered.

"I have no idea. I mean, I don't have any jewelry or anything, and most stuff I think would be considered too modern and outlandish."

"Modern, maybe, but outlandish wouldn't be a bad thing. What do you think a primitive tribe would want or need?"

Tommen sighed. "I don't know what they want because I don't know what they have. For all I know, I could bring them some great and awesome treasure, like a gold ingot, and it could be as common as dirt to them, and then I've insulted them."

"Then let's think about it logically. The D'Bok live in the jungle. What would people living in a jungle need or want?"

"Medicine for mosquito-borne illnesses?"

"I'll give you that one, but as a gift, what would they want?"

"I don't know. Didn't you find out anything about them in the Archives?"

Micah frowned. "Very little of use. Their so-called 'spirit animal' kind of resembles a bear, but maybe more of a bear-lizard mix. It's hard to describe."

"And they're very territorial, somewhat war-like but probably just full of themselves," Tommen recalled.

"Well, assume they're territorial and war-like. Plan for the worst and all that." Micah sat down in a heap in the recliner. "So if they are war-like, they take spoils, which means trade is less important to them because anything they want, they can take."

"Unless they can't get to their prize. Would they really cross a desert just to go bother some other people?" Tommen shook his head. "We just don't know enough about them."

They sat in silence for a few minutes, each acutely aware of the time ticking down. Tommen looked at the clock. They had only about twelve minutes before they had to get to the Wheel.

"Maybe we're overthinking this," Micah said finally.

"Probably, but how so?" Tommen asked.

"You're entering this as a whole new tribe, one they've never met, seen, or even heard of before. They don't know you as much as you don't know them. You are completely alien to each other. So it's entirely reasonable for them to expect that you don't know what they have, what they want, what they need. You are coming to them as a desperate man who is trying to find a cure for his dying people. You are willing to give up something extremely precious in order to win their favor and get this cure."

"But what would I really give? I mean, there's nothing I wouldn't give to save him, but—"

"Tommen. Listen to me. They don't know what is precious to you and your people, and what isn't. Within reason, you could probably offer anything you want as long as it has a good story to go with it about why it is precious or sacred to you and your people."

His statements put Tommen in mind of Tadashi, one of Rifun's little minions, and the one he spent the most time with in the cave. Over the course of his captivity, Tommen had been able to needle a story out of him, one about him being married and having a child. But, being a Time Agent, he was cursed with longevity and so was doomed to outlive his wife, even his children and grandchildren. So he faked his death in order to spare them that, but only wounded himself in doing so.

In the end, Tadashi had proclaimed the entire story a lie. It didn't matter, he said, what the story or the reason was. Everyone had a story, and each person would probably only hear it once. So you might as well make it a good one, even if that meant straight-up lying.

"So what do I or we have that can be made out to be that precious?" Tommen wondered aloud. "What do we have that is common and easily replaced that it's no skin off our backs but I can make a good case for it being a true sacrifice? Something that wouldn't interfere too much with their perception of the world and the universe?"

"What do we have that's common and yet so sought after that it changes men?" Micah murmured.

They seemed to come to the same conclusion as they both started to grin at the same time as they looked at each other and said, "Coffee!"

Tommen got up first, but Micah beat him to the cupboard with all the different coffee flavors. He was momentarily overwhelmed by the memories of the coffee, how amazing it had tasted and smelled, how he was sure there had to be some kind of sedative in it or something to both give him energy and yet relax him emotionally.

"You're sure Micaiah won't mind?" Tommen wondered as they pulled out half a dozen bags and mused over what flavor to send.

"If all it takes to trade for this cure is a bag of coffee, I'm pretty sure Micaiah won't mind," Micah told him.

"Which one should we send, and how many?"

"I'm thinking three bags. Different flavors. Make up some superstitious story to go with each one if you want. Like Sifura said, tell them whatever you want. It's not their business to know what it really is or anything like that. All they need to know is that they need a cup, some kind of filter, and run water through it. Hot water is best, but some might prefer it cold."

They ended up picking out a straight black blend, a peppermint flavor, and a cranberry flavor. Three distinct flavors that Tommen could explain as being ritualistically symbolic to honor different gods or whatever the fuck he wanted to tell them. It was perfect. It was more than a little difficult to try and stuff them in the bag without destroying anything else, but in the end they got everything in there and, after some finagling, they got the top flap closed and secured as well.

"With any luck, as you eat your food and take stuff out, it should clear up some space in the bag," Micah told him.

"Yeah, hopefully," Tommen mused. "No room for souvenirs then, eh?"

"Guess not."

They glanced at the clock. Only about five minutes left.

"Are you okay to open the portal on your own?" Tommen asked, suddenly realizing the implications.

"Sure," Micah told him. "Doing it together certainly helps, but I can do it by myself easy."

Tommen had his doubts, but he was more than willing to just trust Micah than try to argue. Already his nostalgia about packing for some kind of summer camp or hiking trip was wearing off. The time was here, it was coming, the time when he was risking war and even arrest in order to find a cure to save his dad. It was kind of like the anxiety he had when he went before the Hands, except this time, the Hands were stoutly against him. It was like the difference between going before a five-star general, asking for help, and getting turned down, and going on a dangerous mission knowing that he risked a court martial headed by that same five-star general afterwards.

"Nervous?" Micah asked as they watched the seconds tick by.

"A little," Tommen admitted.

"Well then, maybe I'll help you a little and remind you of what you're doing and why." Micah shifted in his seat. "You were kidnapped by a madman, and your dad came to save you, braving hell, high water, and that madman's Borelian henchman. Not only did that madman shoot your dad, but he used bullets poisoned by the Borelian. The Borelians are violent, hostile assholes who know they are extremely dangerous just to be around, but refuse to give up any sort of antidote for their poisons. When you went before the Hands to ask for help, they not only turned you down, but they stole your idea and are now going to try to use it to enrich themselves.

"Now you've been approached by a Hand who says she has a cure for your dad's illness, but it's going to take everything you've got just to make it there in time. You have three days to make a ten day journey, to impress another war-like people, albeit a primitive one, and offer them a gift to either trade for the cure or else gain permission to get it yourself. This is a very dangerous thing, because in order to get the antidote, you must also risk the poison yourself. But if you succeed, you not only save your dad, but you can snub your nose at all those other assholes who refused to help you in the first place."

Oddly enough, Micah's little pep talk helped put Tommen back at ease. Everything was so simple, at least when it was in the planning stages. He was worried about the end of the journey when he'd barely even begun. Sifura had promised to help him, which meant he was going to have to endure the feast of her people. Then they would have seven days in the desert. Seven days to do nothing. He was going to have to Band that entire time, endure fatigue and possibly sickness...

No, he couldn't think about that. *Take everything as it comes. Right now, your primary mission is to simply meet Sifura in the portal room of the Wheel—assuming she wasn't captured or arrested—and go with her to her home world. Once you're standing in the Red Desert, then you worry about everything that follows.*

Tommen took a calming breath.

"And one more thing," Micah said, interrupting his thoughts. He reached for Tommen's watch. "Keep this on at all times. Make it so it looks like whatever jewelry is the custom of their people, or make something up to be the customary jewelry of your people. But always keep it on, and check it often. You understand how it works?"

"Basically." Tommen went through the various screens. "This is what time it is now, and if there was another world I was keeping an eye on, their time would be displayed here. So I just have to keep Earth open like this—"

"Good. In theory, and if my numbers are correct, you have until Sunday, December 29th, at 8:17 p.m. to return with the cure. And believe me, Cai and I will be at the hospital as much as we can, seeing if we can't figure out if and how we can buy him more time, whether that is upping his clock as Lily sees it, or just being difficult with the doctors. We'll do everything we can to give you time to get back, but we won't be able to hold off the doctors forever. Your dad's directive is very clear. He stops breathing, they pull the plug. The most we might be able to eek out is twenty-four hours."

Tommen sighed and looked at the watch. "So I should just plan for the 29th at 8:17 p.m."

"Right."

"Okay, I think I got it set. And I'll do you one better. December 29th at noon."

"Whatever makes you feel better and whatever works," Micah told him calmly. "You've got everything?"

Tommen slung his bag off his shoulder and briefly glanced through it. "I think so. I hope so. But I'll starve for a week if I have to."

"Well, with any luck you won't have to."

Then the clock ticked the time for the rendezvous. Micah looked at Tommen. "You ready?"

"Yeah," Tommen answered, his voice breaking.

"You nervous?"

"Yeah."

"Good. I would be worried if you weren't. Just remember. For Walter."

Tommen nodded. "For Walter." He took a breath and adjusted his stance like he was going to dive through the portal into the Wheel. "Okay. I'm ready."

Micah nodded once, then opened a portal.

Chapter Fifteen
Red Desert

Being able to walk through the portal and not be arrested while lying on the floor completely sapped of strength and nearly unconscious counted as a victory in Tommen's mind, once he was able to collect himself and pull himself to a sitting position until the vertigo subsided. Micah was unconscious for a few seconds when he stepped through and was slower to recover.

"Too many times in too short a time," Micah breathed, rubbing his face and grabbing a sick bag which he did not end up needing. "All the harder for doing it myself." He sighed and closed his eyes. For a moment, Tommen was afraid he was going to pass out. "I think I'm going to have to take a few days off."

"What about the store? All the Banding you do to meet demand?" Tommen asked numbly, momentarily forgetting that it was entirely possible that they could be arrested at any moment.

"Cai will start on it," Micah said, pulling himself unsteadily to his feet. "Hopefully, by the time I get to work, I'll at least be able to manage that much."

"Are you going to be okay to drive and stuff?"

"Don't worry about me, Tommen. Worry about yourself and what you need to do. You're only a probationary now, but I have a feeling that by the time you get back, you'll be an Apprentice in skill if not in title."

Get back. Right. They had a mission to complete. Well, Tommen had a mission to complete. He stood, closing his eyes and rubbing behind his ears as his balance wavered.

"Your ears all right?" Micah asked.

"You're sure there's nothing else you can do?" Tommen wondered helplessly.

"It's only about your body healing itself. There is nothing I can do other than that."

It wasn't a pleasant thing to hear, especially since Tommen was sure his hearing had been fluctuating. Nothing extremely terrible, just enough to be noticeable. And it was both ears, not just the right one. What if they did have to defend themselves from something and he was at a disadvantage, unable to hear warnings or commands? What if he misunderstood something that was said and it turned into a huge cultural embarrassment than foiled the whole trip?

As they walked to the front of the portal room, he tried to calm himself and think logically. As long as he had the translator, he could hear and understand to the extent of the translator's ability to, well, translate. And it wasn't illogical to think the different tribes had different languages, so if he did get lost, he could fake not understanding. Couldn't he? Or would that reflect badly on his "gift of language"
 as Sifura put it?

They neared the end of the row, and tension knotted his stomach. What if Sifura wasn't there? What if she had been captured and they had to run back to the portal? What if there were Grandfathers there already waiting for them to block their escape? They couldn't hide in the Wheel forever, and Micah was in no shape to try to open an emergency portal. They were both having trouble walking straight as it was.

Then they broke the end of the row, and Tommen saw Sifura standing near the dispenser. Well, a Hand was standing near the dispenser, but being shrouded, it could have been any Hand. That was another reason Tommen disliked the shrouds of the Hands. Still, he and Micah went to the dispenser like normal, giving a courteous nod to the Hand.

"Returning a couple translators," Micah told the Hand

conversationally. "So focused on our work that we forgot to drop them off."

"The work is not yet finished, Lieutenant Micah Durvin," Sifura informed him. "Tommen and I have a long way to go yet."

"No trouble for you then?"

"Not yet. The others have not yet figured out what is going on, what we are doing. But they will, once I disappear and Tommen with me. Until then, be vigilant, Lieutenant."

"I will." Micah shifted his stance so he could look out into the Wheel. "I'm in no shape to go back through the portal just yet, and I won't be able to make one for a day or two, which means I'll be cut off from the Wheel and its news. I think I might stay for a bit and listen to some of the gossip going around."

"Your brother?"

"Working, but he's in no condition to open any more portals either for a couple days. We'll have no news of what's going on in the Wheel probably until you get back."

"I will keep it in mind and bring what news I can."

"No. Don't worry about me or Micaiah. Don't worry about the Hands or the Wheel beyond your safety. Our primary concern is getting that cure and healing Walter, or else this is all for nothing."

Sifura dipped her head. "I agree. We shall move quickly." She looked at Tommen. "You are ready?"

"Ready as I'll ever be," Tommen said, indicating the burlap bag slung over one shoulder.

"You are still covered."

"And I will be covered until we go through the portal to your world. Forgive me, but where being covered is shameful in your world, being uncovered is shameful in mine, and I would like to minimize my own discomfort."

Somewhere behind her black shrouded mask, Tommen could feel her golden eyes studying him, probably trying to digest the difference. Finally she said, "Very well. Until we return to my world, you will remain covered." She looked back at Micah. "Stay safe,

Lieutenant Micah Durvin."

"Travel safely, Great Hand," Micah said in reply, doing an imaginary tip of the hat before turning and walking into the main hub of the Wheel.

"Come," Sifura said suddenly, moving past Tommen with a renewed sense of urgency. He followed her at the head of the rows of portals before coming to a row near the outer edge and turning down it. She walked with the stealth of a hunter and warrior, and the confidence of a leader, all the while Tommen bumbled along behind her, trying to keep up.

They did not go far before she stopped in front of a portal. She waited only long enough for Tommen to get almost within arm's reach before stepping through. Blindly, Tommen followed, and darkness followed him.

Too many fucking portals. That was Tommen's first thought as he came around. His second thought was that it was way too hot to be the middle of winter. It was too hot to be the middle of summer. He also began to realize that the ground beneath him was not *terra firma*, but *terra softa.* Smooth and soft, grainy. Sand.

His thoughts came together like a bunch of small waves coming together to create a tsunami, and everything came rushing back to him at once even as sunlight hit his eyelids. He'd followed Sifura through the portal to her home world, where she lived in a desert. Right. And *fuck*, was it *hot*.

He tried to open his eyes but was only rewarded with grains of sand, blinding him even as it sent sharp stabs of pain through him. He fought to sit up, tried to rub the sand out of his eyes, found more sand on his hands that he only ground in further. Not even five minutes into his journey and he was already screwing things up. Heck, he hadn't even really been doing anything and he was already getting himself hurt. *Good going, Tommen. Explain that one to the twins.*

By the time he finally cleared his eyes enough to look around, he found that there wasn't much to look at. It was, as expected, a desert, but unlike any desert found on Earth. The sand was black, gold, and white, just like Sifura. It wasn't like a mixture where all the colors blended together in some kind of grainy static, but there were distinct color bands. Physically, Tommen could mix the different colors of sand, but as soon as the breeze came, the colors sorted themselves out again. He thought he could feel differences in the grains when he touched them, but otherwise it was a unique and very cool phenomenon.

He looked around. He was alone. Sifura had left him and no footprints. This desert was not exactly the type to have enormous dunes the size of small mountains, but neither was it a flat salt desert either. There were small rises and dips, a few scraggly bushes here and there, enough to obscure a small party of people, but not a huge obstacle to overcome.

"Well, that's just wonderful," Tommen said aloud, as if anyone could hear. "She left me. Universe's best assassination attempt ever. Offer to help, and take them somewhere to—"

"You are saying something, Tommen Forbes?"

He whirled around to see Sifura. But only just barely. If she stood still, she could easily blend in with the desert to the point where she was completely invisible. Moving, she was more noticeable, but only if the winds were calm and not whipping up sand to obscure her just as much. He couldn't decide if she truly hadn't heard him or if she was challenging his words as if he was calling her untrustworthy.

"Um, no," he said, shoving his hands in his pockets. "No. Just...I thought you'd gone."

"When you came through the portal, you fell unconscious. When you did not wake immediately, I went to make sure we were safe and not being hunted."

"How long was I out?"

"Perhaps twenty Base Minutes."

If not for the fact that they couldn't really leave until morning anyway to go and meet the D'Bok, Tommen might have been alarmed at every lost moment. It still made him uneasy, but there was nothing he could do about it.

"Oh," he said dumbly. "Thank you."

"Now we are through the portal to my home world," Sifura said. "Uncover yourself, as you promised."

So, this was a hot girl who, upon first sight, sent Tommen to the bathroom with a serious boner and an even more serious moral dilemma. Now she was asking—no, *commanding*—that he undress right there in front of her. And he had the feeling that if he didn't do it himself, she would do it for him, which was not going to help the situation.

He elected to start with his shoes and socks which were already full of sand, but he quickly came to another dilemma, that is, nothing would fit in his sack because it was already full.

"Leave it here," Sifura told him, her tone suggesting irritation.

He was able to stuff his socks in the bag, but in the end, he was forced to leave his shoes there in the sand. Who knew if he would ever be able to retrieve them, or if someone would just find them one day while out on a hunt or something. What would they think of his shoes? Would they destroy them because they were a covering? Would they send a search party to scavenge the desert, searching for someone long gone? Would a wild animal find them and devour them as a tasty, alien snack? Or would the shoes simply get buried by the sands of time, never to be seen again?

Such thought he was giving to his shoes, Tommen mused as he stripped off his coat and tossed that aside, then began working on his shirts and pants. An odd thing, too, to be concerned with something so easily replaced. Was it because he was reverting back to a school of thought that found every possession precious and difficult to replace?

He got down to his undershirt and boxers before pausing. On the bright side, he was too afraid of going further to even be concerned about getting an erection right now, no matter how hot Sifura was. On the other hand, he still had to take off his undershirt and boxers to get and stay naked. For days. Over a week in his Band even if it was really only a couple of days. But still. He was supposed to just get naked and waltz about like nothing was amiss. Would they find his hesitation and discomfort strange or upsetting? Could he (almost) lie and just say he came from a very cold land and was more accustomed to being covered? Or were the tribes from the cold lands covered in fur or some such thing? The politics and nuances of alien worlds were just so difficult sometimes.

Eventually, he did manage to get the rest of his clothes off and tossed to the side in the sand, to be devoured one grain at a time until there was nothing left. His first instinct was to use his hands to cover himself, but he refrained. At the very least, he did feel much relieved without all the layers of clothing to trap the heat next to his body, but that did nothing to shield his skin from the sharp grains of sand that whipped up in the winds, or the waves of heat beating down on him from the sun.

"Okay," he sighed. "I guess I'm ready."

Sifura studied him for a moment. "What does it do?"

He blinked. "What does what do?" He glanced at his watch, disguised as a tangle of leather thongs and beads, but he was fairly certain she should have known or had an idea what it was.

"Between your legs. What is it? What does it do?"

Come here and I'll show you, was his first thought, followed almost immediately by wordless shock at the question. For a full minute he could only stare at her. A naked society and the males did not have cock and balls between their legs. How the fuck did they reproduce, then? How did they mate? For God's sake, how did they pee?

"Um...it's...called a penis. And testicles," Tommen answered awkwardly. "They're used in human reproduction."

Fuck, was this how Walter felt when he'd finally sat Tommen down to have "the man talk"? Sure, Tommen had already known the anatomical names of things and the basic idea of sex just from having animals, but it was still strange to talk about how it related to humans, puberty and sexuality and reproduction. Fuck, Tommen was going to have to do something for Walter to show he now understood how awkward that was.

Wait, so if the males didn't have cock and balls, did that mean that the women didn't have vaginas either? So this hot wildcat alien chick standing here before him was completely out of the question in all senses? The fuck? How did they reproduce? How did anything on this world reproduce then?

"The females also have them?" Sifura inquired.

"Um, no. No, they don't," Tommen told her.

Fuck, fuck, fuck, fuck, fuck.

"I see." Sifura looked thoughtful, then became serious again. "This is a discussion for another time, one that would be interesting to dig into." *Please don't use terms like that.* "Until then, come. My people are waiting."

She turned and started off, moving swiftly across the sand. After a minute or two of struggling to keep up, Tommen saw why she was able to move so swiftly. Other than having powerful legs and paws like a tiger, he saw now that her toes, when spread, were webbed, letting her walk on top of the sand, instead of digging into it as Tommen was doing. She stopped and waited for him a couple times, but never for long.

"Why do you come out so far to open a portal?" Tommen asked as he caught up to her on top of a rise.

"I come to hunt," Sifura told him. "When I am far away and I have caught something, then I go to the Wheel."

"So you have caught something? Is it buried?"

"Yes. The hunting parties come out and hunt. The parties start out very big. If the game is small, the children take it back to the people. If the game is large, there are many hands to take it back and the party returns."

"What are you doing out here all alone then?"

"I look for small game, threats. One person moves more swiftly than a party. I am a hunter, a healer, a warrior; I can take care of myself."

She certainly could. The only princess Tommen found here was Xena, and she didn't take crap from nobody.

"So...are there any customs I should observe when we reach your...village?" Tommen inquired after a few minutes of silence and being battered by sandy winds.

"I will take you through the village so you may see my people and be seen by them." Nothing sounded more appalling at that point. "Then I will take you to the hut of the elder council." No, that had the potential to be much worse. "I will introduce you and explain our mission to seek out the D'Bok." So this was like a primitive version of going before the Hands with a case. Fantastic. "Then we will have our Sun Day feast. And in the morning, we will begin our trek."

"Yes, but are there any customs I need to observe? Titles to use, things to say or not say, proper hand gestures?"

"If you speak at all, you will address them as you address your own elders." *But I don't really have any elders, at least not in this kind of reverent sense. "Mr. Layman" is just more formal than "Orville" but it's not like I really defer to his judgment as the final authority. Or do I?* "However, it is unlikely you will speak to them directly. I will do much of the talking."

That was more than fine with Tommen. He didn't even want to see her village, really. Any other day, he would be more than happy to come and immerse himself in a truly alien culture. But now, with his dad's life on the line, all he wanted to do was turn north, south, east, west, whatever the direction was to reach the D'Bok, and get there as fast as possible. Forget the council, forget the feast, just go. Give a gift to the D'Bok to trade, whatever, just give him the damn antidote. He was chomping at the bit here.

At the same time, if he did get the directions to the D'Bok, what was really keeping him from Banding and striking out on his own? He could bypass whatever customs and rituals they had to go through and just walk through the jungle until he found the damn flower.

The only thing he could come up with was needing Sifura to

help him identify the myriad of other poisonous plants in the jungle, especially if ninety percent of them were poisonous to him. But why the delay on formality? Was it just because she was a leader and she had to, or was it just so culturally ingrained that she had to go through the motions, in the same way that Tommen could just steal anything he wanted, walk right out of any store with anything, but going through the motions of paying for stuff just for the simple fact of morality and ingrained habit?

Tommen hated it when he had these little existential crises at inconvenient times. The first time it had taken him up a mountain in the biting cold, looking for a solution to his problem. The solution he'd come up with had, in a long, drawn-out, roundabout way, led him here to the desert that was hotter than hell and his second existential crisis. And where would this one lead him?

"You are eager to go to the D'Bok," Sifura said.

"Well, it's only my dad dying," Tommen replied, hoping the sarcasm was able to be translated and she didn't actually think he wasn't all that concerned.

"You want to go yourself, get directions and Band your way just as we planned."

"Are you reading my thoughts?"

"I would be thinking the same thing if I were you."

"So other than the poisonous plants in the jungle, why shouldn't I?"

Sifura stopped, looked around at the horizon, then turned and looked at him. "Borelian poisons, the victims cannot be Banded to slow the progress of the disease because it is immune to Time. It is not affected by Bands or Time Capsules."

"That's right," Tommen said, making his way beside her.

"That is not the only thing immune to Time. Some things in this universe will hunt you and kill you and have no regard for your Bands or my Harvesting."

Tommen looked around but he saw only black, gold, and white sand. "Is that what awaits us out there in the desert? This

Time-immune creature?"

"All of the spirit animals are such. I know not why. But it makes them both mighty and feared."

"Uh...huh."

"You do not believe me."

"Oh, I believe that the animals are real. And they may even be immune to Time for some unknown reason. But I don't buy the 'spirit animal' garbage."

"Well, do not say so to my people, and do not give the elders cause to doubt you. I am the leader, but I am not all-powerful."

"What's the worst they could do to me?" As if he really wanted to know.

"Keep your mouth shut, and you will not have to find out."

It was like a slap in the face, but the refreshing kind. Like the kind one needs when the fear threatens to tear apart everything and only a good slap in the face can say, "Snap out of it!"

That wasn't to say that Tommen liked being talked to like that, but she was the leader, and he needed her. So he ran clumsily after her down the other side of the rise, bag bouncing along on his back. He was probably going to have a bruise there in the morning. That is, if it showed through the burn. He should have brought sunscreen.

"How far to your village?" he asked.

"We will reach it when the sun is midway to the horizon," Sifura answered.

Tommen looked up. It was about at its highest point now, so they still had a couple hours of walking to do yet.

"How does—?"

"Do all humans talk so much?"

"Not all of them, at least, not normally. I don't normally."

"But you talk when you are nervous or frightened."

"Not normally. Well, maybe. If the fear gets too overwhelming."

"Stop letting it overwhelm you. You are not made for the sun and the heat. The walking is hard enough. The talk will only wear you out more. Save your words and conserve your water. Remain calm, and you will remain cool, also."

Tommen closed his eyes and took a breath. She was right. The heat and the sun was bad enough; he didn't need to exacerbate himself with unnecessary stress and talk. When he opened his eyes, she was still staring at him.

"You are ready now?" she wondered.

"Just one more question," he said.

She sighed. "Yes."

"You really think this will work? You think we'll make it in time?"

"Like everything that has not yet come to pass, it is only a plan and a wish. But it is the best one we have, and so we must try."

With that, she whipped around, tail twitching irritably, and stalked off through the sand.

Chapter Sixteen
The Xresa

By the time the sun was midway to the horizon, Tommen could feel the burn on his back, and it wasn't a casual day at the beach kind of sunburn. This was like a week of shirtless hard labor, the normal burn of the sun compounded by the work and sweat to tear at his entire backside like sandpaper grating over him with every movement. If he managed to walk away without spontaneously developing skin cancer, he would be grateful.

Their pace had slowed, mostly because of him as he fought for every step. Sifura remained unfazed, still walking atop the sand with virtually no ill effect. She looked back at him from time to time, waited for him, stiffly offered an encouraging word, but never once did she suggest they stop and rest.

"Is that a mirage?" Tommen asked as they crested one of many rises they'd conquered that day.

"That is the oasis where my people stay for the Day of the Sun and the harvest," Sifura told him.

To call the landscape before them an oasis was like calling Charleston a village or a country town. An oasis was a nice little pool of water, a spring or maybe a small river if near a larger body of water or a mountain range, and there was some modest vegetation growing around it, enough to provide relief for the weary traveler so he could rest and carry on the next day, or maybe camp for a few days and recover from sunstroke or other ailment.

This was no oasis. Or if this was an oasis, Tommen feared for the size of the desert itself. How many tribes roamed this desert? Three? And they all had at least a thousand people to support, one with like ten thousand or something?

Looking at the jungle before him, Tommen could perfectly envision this "oasis" being able to support several thousand people. And it really looked like a jungle. Sand inexplicably gave way to lush grass and pathways made of dirt as average as anything found on Earth, as if there was a force field keeping the sand and the grass and dirt separated. Small bushes and some scraggly plants sent shoots out around the edge of the oasis, but they were small and starving—or they were by Earth-side standards, not that Tommen was any judge of alien plant life.

A little farther into the oasis, skimpy plants turned into full, lush bushes with huge leaves veined with black and blue. Alien flowers reached for the sky, sending out creepers and petals and even teeth like a Venus fly trap. Sifura approached a plant with a yellow flower curled tight like a tulip and picked it. She held it out to Tommen.

"This will restore your water and ease the sun pain," she told him gently.

Tommen took it respectfully, if cautiously. He sniffed it. It smelled sweet, kind of like honey. When he dared look at it, he found that a yellow juice was coming off the inside of the petals and collecting in the bottom of the cup. Did he risk it? Even if they could drink it, what would happen if it made him sick? Could he refuse it politely? Would that just make him an idiot? Finally he took a breath. "Well, *hakuna matata.*"

"*Hakuna matata?*" Sifura echoed. "Your words do not translate."

"If it kills me, then it renders it all moot anyway."

With that, he upended the cup and drank it all in one go. Immediately his taste buds came alive with the fullest, most refreshing fruit punch smoothie he'd ever had. It was like honey and melon and pineapple and strawberry and a hundred other flavors he had no name for beyond the insufficient "sweet" and "tangy" and whatever other bullshit buzzwords foodies and restaurants liked to use. This went far beyond that. Or maybe he was just dying of thirst and anything would taste good about now.

But she was right about it making him feel better, too. Rather than drinking a ton of water and waiting for his body to absorb it and cool down, it was like instant refreshment. He stopped sweating and panting. His back relaxed, and his calves released the tension they'd been holding for the last several hours of fighting through sand. Even as he processed all of this, his body relaxed even more and fatigue washed over him. Fear gripped him immediately. Of course. A flower. How fit to drag him out here and kill him with a flower. By a hot girl. Well played, Hands, well played.

"You are feeling better?" Sifura inquired, her golden eyes glittering with amusement.

"Yes, much better," Tommen replied, trying to stay alert.

"We will go to the village now, and we will meet with the council."

He started to ask where the trash was, then realized that there probably wasn't one. So he waited until she turned and started off into the undergrowth before licking the last bit of sweet refreshment and tossing the empty flower into the bushes.

The plants at the oasis came in two sizes: small bushes and gigantic trees. The scraggly things at the edge of the oasis didn't count, and there was no middle layer of the rainforest, just short and tall, and even the short bushes were almost as tall as Tommen, slapping his face and cutting his shoulders. The trees stuck out of the oasis like one feather sticking stupidly out of a duck wing. Or something. Fuck, but he was bad at analogies.

Charleston didn't really have skyscrapers, mostly because of the winds and snows; everything had to be squat and spread out. But he'd seen pictures of skyscrapers, and these looked pretty close to it, just by sheer height. An eight-lane highway could be carved through the base of the trees and still have room on either side for a couple two-lane side streets. Looking up, they did not have twisted, gnarled branches like an Amazonian tree; rather, both the bark and the leaves were more reminisce of palm trees. Huge leaves blotted out the sun over huge swaths of the ground, and despite all the heat and the tough time of the trek, Tommen found himself shivering. Was it just awe, or was there really that much of a temperature change?

"You have not seen a place like this," Sifura observed.

"No, never. I mean, Earth has deserts and rainforests, but...nothing like this," Tommen replied, still looking up at the giant trees.

"These trees have taken a thousand thousand years to grow. They provide shade from the heat and protection from the sandstorms. The wood we use for everything we need."

"How do you cut down something like this?"

"We do not cut them down. We carve what we need from the base, or sometimes we will climb to reach a piece we need."

"What happens when they die and fall to the ground?"

"They do not die. They only keep growing. And they will continue to grow."

Translation: These trees have been growing here since before anyone can remember, and none of them have actually died yet, so we don't know what happens.

But maybe it was best not to ruin every traditional belief they held. What did he care for trees?

"How far to the village?" Tommen wondered as he turned and continued following Sifura through the bushes along a narrow path.

"Not far," was the only reply he got.

It wasn't until they were right in the middle of everything that Tommen realized that the giant trees did not form a wall, as he'd initially thought just from the outside view. Rather, they formed a loose ring. There were about thirty trees in total, enough to give decent protection from sandstorms but allow for easy access in and out of the oasis in any direction.

There was no gentle thinning of vegetation, just a sudden breaking out into the open. The bushes just suddenly stopped and there was a village. Compared to Charleston, it was little more than some poor forgotten mining town way up in the mountains where only the old timers lived. Compared to the traditional (and probably heavily propagated) view of most rural African villages, this was like New York City or Chicago or something.

Strictly speaking, it was less like the cute little grass and thatch huts as portrayed in African villages and more like the Pueblo canyon dwellings. Except here, there were no caves.

Judging by one little "hut" either under construction or being repaired, the Xur were far more architecturally advanced than Tommen would have initially given them credit for. They used wood from the giant trees to build a stick-built frame as well as any new construction Tommen had seen, except it was more of a box-like frame. Rather than taking two-by-fours and running supports on the inside between the top and bottom pieces, they were run on the outside, secured using real, fire-forged nails. The planks weren't true two-by-fours with such precise edges, but given that it looked like their tool technology was somewhere between bronze and iron, it was pretty impressive.

Once the frame was built and secured using rope, nails, and wooden pegs, it lookedas though they used a special mixture of the different sands, some other plant life that might have been straw had it been Earth, and water obviously, the frames were filled in almost like cement walls, poured, set, scraped, and set again. There were no bricks baking in the sun here, just primitive concrete.

From the finished "huts" Tommen could see that leaves, flowers, and other assorted shiny goods were laid into the setting concrete, giving each one a certain unique, aesthetic appeal.

The roofs were flat, beams stretching from one side to the other, covered with woven leaves, grass, and bark. None of the huts had doors, but a few had grassy curtains. Few had windows of any form. From what he could see, most of the huts had only two rooms, some with three, others only one. Most likely, the huts were only for sleeping, not for living. Life happened outside the home, in the village as a whole.

"Did you build all this?" Tommen wondered, looking around.

"The villages are built over many generations. Old homes from old times are taken down as better homes are built, and new homes are built for the larger factions. Any faction may use a village as they come across them on their travels; no faction owns a village, and no one truly owns a home. We only borrow them for a short time. When we leave, we make sure the night furs are cleaned and replaced, and we make sure the wood is plentiful for the cooking fires, as we expect the other factions to do when they leave a village and we come upon it."

Well, it would explain why the outer edges of the village appeared deserted. If any faction could use any village, that meant that each village had to theoretically support every faction, from the smallest to the largest. Sifura's faction was by no means the largest, so these homes were just extras to them.

"So where is everyone?" Tommen asked conversationally.

"They will be at the great pit, preparing for the feast."

"What is this Day of the Sun feast all about anyway?"

"It is the longest day of the year. We come to celebrate the life and heat the sun brings. Later, we will also have our second Feast of Balance—"

"Equal parts night and day."

"Yes. You may also guess the Day of the Running Sun is the shortest day. And the first Feast of Balance when the sun begins to return to us."

"Is there anything I should know about this Day of the Sun feast? Customs, traditions, anything like that?"

"Mostly it is a feast only to celebrate the changing of seasons. As I have observed in the Wheel, the only constant throughout most of the universe is food."

That was it? So this was like Xresa Thanksgiving or something, a feast and celebration of little more than seasons, eating for its own sake because it's good? There were no gods to be worshiped or sacrificed to, no rain dances or incantations? Was there at least a witch doctor or something? Did the spirit animals come out to play? Campfires and ghost stories, marshmallows and s'mores at the bare minimum?

"You said something about the harvest. Do you farm?"

Sifura looked back at him, her expression unreadable. "The harvest is when new children are welcomed into the faction, into the tribe. It is a very joyous time, and that will happen before the feast, so the children may partake as new members."

So it was like a coming of age sort of thing, or maybe it was more like *The Lion King*. If the children were older, probably coming of age; they'd gone on the hunts and been in fights and now they were taking their place in the tribe as full hunters and warriors, respected by all and given voice in political matters. If the children were younger, it was probably more along the lines of, "Hey, you've survived heat and battle and disease before the age of five. Now it's time to begin your training."

None of it really mattered to Tommen. He was both in awe and skeptical of the fact that he happened upon this at the same time he was looking for a cure for his father. Why couldn't it ever be as simple as "Go to Place A with Person B to pick up Item C"? Why did it always have to coincide with some sacred holiday which pushed off the beginning of the quest which arbitrarily put a time crunch on the heroes? As if he wasn't under enough of a time crunch as it was. Were the D'Bok going to be doing some sacred rain dance holiday, too?

The outer reaches of the village were more like a kindly neighborhood, even if the houses were still squashed together one right next to each other. But they were sensibly laid out in street-like fashion. The closer they got to the center of the village, the more the straight and narrow streets became twisted and curved and winding, with homes jutting out first one way and then the other. Tommen could see the evolution of construction, too, as the neat little stick-frame houses gave way to houses built of sun-baked bricks. Then there were the houses made more of grass and simply patched together with mud. Several of these were in the process of being torn down, wood and nails and tools already set aside, a few framed walls already in place.

"How long does it take to build a house?" Tommen asked.

"If everything goes well, the walls can be built and filled in two days," Sifura informed him. "Then the walls must dry over a period of four days, perhaps longer. When they are dry, the roof can be set and woven, which takes only a day. Many of the homes being built would be done except for the preparations for the feast."

Tommen whistled. "Wow. If you guys are so efficient at building and so good at what you do, why do you need to roam and migrate? Why not settle down in one place?"

"It is a part of who we are. We are travelers, wanderers." She gave him a look as if he was asking why she was black, gold, and white. To most, it was just an obvious observation. "And, more practically, this oasis will not sustain everyone forever. We stay here for perhaps twenty days, maybe thirty. Then we must move on."

Looking around, he could understand that. The oasis was beautiful and bountiful, but the daily demands of thousands of people would eat this place alive if they tried to settle permanently. Taking the time to migrate from place to place and give each oasis a resting period was best for all of them.

"How many oases are there in the desert?"

"Nine. All about the same."

Tommen might have been worried that he heard no signs of life—no music or shouting or laughing or anything—except that he knew he wouldn't on account of his ears. His first sign of life came when they were just walking around a corner and three children—or what he assumed to be children as they were only about half the size of Sifura—suddenly darted out of a hiding spot and ran off down the street, laughing and shouting something to each other.

"They will be good hunters one day," Sifura said proudly, looking after the children with a certain pride in her eyes.

"Are they your kids?" Tommen dared ask.

"No. As healer, I was forbidden to have children. As leader, I have not yet found a suitable mate."

Talk about playing hard to get. But he didn't say this out loud. She was hot, a great hunter, a mighty warrior, totally hot, leader of the faction, medically trained, and super hot. She should have every available male lined up at her doorstep; surely there had to be some guy in the faction she liked.

"No doubt they will inform the rest of the faction of our arrival. There will be talk and whispers, but say nothing until you have first spoken to the council."

Tommen didn't think that would be too difficult, given that even though the translator would let him understand everything they said, it would do nothing to help them understand what he said, so conversation would be very one-sided.

They finally broke through the maze of buildings into a giant clearing where a bonfire pit the size of Tommen's house, plus a second story, sat, unlit. And it wasn't just wood in the fire, but leaves, flowers, grasses, and there were bones in there too, Tommen saw. That thing was going to get hot enough to melt his face off from a hundred feet away. Fuck, he hoped he didn't have to do anything for this feast tonight because he was going to be sitting at the far, far end of the table.

It wasn't even finished, at least as far as the villagers were concerned. They had the bucket brigade line going, standing on rooftops or ladders placed right on the pile, dumping more scraps and shavings and bits and pieces onto the mess. It was then that Tommen saw they didn't all look like Sifura. In fact, he couldn't find anyone who had the same even mixture of black, gold, and white. Most of them were predominantly black with a fair dose of either white or gold. If anyone did have all three colors, the third color was little more than rings around the eyes or on the palms of the hands.

He also noticed that some of them—maybe the males—had what looked like manes. Of course, Tommen had seen something similar in some of the old timers way up in Appalachia, where their hair was long and their beards were long and none of it washed or combed. But the way these people wore it, it put Tommen in mind of a lion's mane. Those who wore manes also had round instead of pointed ears.

It was difficult to say if the size of the mane was reflective of one's age or place in the faction as Tommen watched a couple maned males argue. One was mostly black with some white here and there and an enormous bushy mane streaked kind of like a zebra. The other was completely black with a much shorter, fuzzy mane. The bushy-maned male was doing most of the shouting and arguing, but the way the shorter-maned male carried himself said that he wasn't phased by the outburst, like a foreman waiting for a disgruntled worker to get done ranting so he could fire him.

"Purr, where are you from? Who are you? What tribe are you?"

Tommen looked down to see a small flock of children had gathered. Other than the pointed or round ears, it was impossible to tell boys from girls. Initially he was amused by the use of the word "purr" instead of "sir" until he realized that it was used seriously as a sign of deferential respect and that was just how it had been translated.

"Um, my name is Tommen," he began awkwardly, not sure if this was part of Sifura's warning not to speak to anyone. They were just curious children, right? What harm could it do? And it wasn't as if someone was going to call the cops on him for stranger danger, or even public indecency.

A few of the children touched his calves or thighs as they were tall enough to reach, feeling his single-textured skin, that is, burned to a crisp. He jumped as one poked his balls and started playing with them most immodestly.

"What are these?" the child inquired, his black mask on a gold face reminding Tommen of a raccoon.

Tommen jerked away. "Please don't touch those."

"Look, it comes out!" another said, pointing.

Well, it wasn't an erection, but it was enough of a novelty that it was drawing more and more unwanted attention. He looked around, but Sifura was gone.

"Where's your tail?" a young girl wondered, drawing one finger down his spine to his tailbone until he jumped away again.

"I like him; he's funny," a fourth child giggled.

Tommen turned as if to run and almost ran headlong into a large golden male with a bushy black and gold mane.

"I've not seen your kind before in all my travels," he said calmly, modestly. "What tribe are you from?"

"Even if I had an answer to give you, I know you won't understand what I have to say, so please let me go," Tommen said, feeling very much like a little boy lost in a huge crowd and wanting only to find his dad and go home.

"Ah, of course." The golden male took a step back and put his hands on his chest. "Shahax."

Tommen paused. He knew this game. He nodded once and put one hand to his chest. "Tommen."

"Tommen," Shahax echoed, murmuring it over and over again as if he couldn't quite get the word just right. Then he dipped his head. "Tommen."

"Yes, Tommen," Tommen said, breathing a sigh of relief. "Shahax."

"Shahax," Shahax confirmed, looking pleased.

Unfortunately, what started out to be a tentative, primitive, truly immersive experience, soon turned back into a little boy being lost in the crowd as people began coming up and introducing themselves, one by one at first, then as a whole mob.

"Enough!"

The command rang as loud and true and authoritative as any Marine drill sergeant, and immediately the mob went silent and parted. A few went back to whatever they had been doing, but most looked on, turning, Tommen included, to face an unsuspecting building where eight people stood in the doorway. Tommen assumed this was the council.

They were not as old as he might have expected from a tribal council, but as they drew near, he could see they were no longer in their hunting and fighting prime either. Maybe fifties, for a human.

The one who had spoken was like a clone of the bushy-maned male who had been arguing with the shorter-maned male, but most of his mane had gone gray, and it was thin and scraggly; his whiskers had also gone gray. Was it just a genetic coincidence that they looked similar, or could this council member be that man's father?

"What is the meaning of this?" the elder male said, his voice carrying out over the whole of the people so even those at the top of the ladders stopped and looked. "We have a visitor, it is true. But there is much preparation still to be done for the feast. Our visitor, if he be worthy, will join us then. When it is time for feast and play. Until then, return to your work."

Reluctantly, the crowd dispersed, but not without the din of whispers and giggles and not a few stolen glances. The elder approached Tommen, and the rest of the council followed suit. Sifura stood beside the first male.

"You say he will understand me if I speak?" he said.

"He will, Araf," Sifura confirmed.

"And you will understand him when he speaks."

"He has brought the gift of language and understanding. It works."

"Yes, we will understand each other," Tommen cut in.

Sifura shot him a look, but translated.

"What tribe are you from?" Araf asked.

"Um, the tribe of Ape," Tommen answered, hoping he came across only as sounding nervous and not for the liar he was. *Just take it as a distant people you've never heard of before and let's move on.*

"How many factions are you?"

"My faction is Chimp. There is also Capuchin, Orangutan, and Gorilla." Yeah, a capuchin wasn't an ape, so sue him. He just had to get through this.

"Where do you live?"

Fuck. Tommen tried to remember which way they had come. He was pretty sure it was north, which meant he came from the south, but the Red Desert extended all the way to the Southern Sea. Thankfully, before it became too obvious that he was lying, Sifura answered for him.

"South. To the Southern Sea. Then west, across the Great Grass Plains of the Darvin to the Toxic Sea and west again. He has traveled a long way to get here."

"And a long way still to go."

"Perhaps we should discuss this inside."

The elder male snorted, but agreed.

There was nothing special about the house they met in. It was about fifteen by fifteen, dirt floor, concrete wall, bark-woven roof. The only furnishings were some woven mats on which the council now sat.

There were five males and three females on the council itself. Tommen couldn't decide if Sifura was part of the council, or if this was more of a Congress-president relationship.

Two of the females were mostly gold, one with black markings, one with white. The third female was mostly white with very few black markings, and her eyes were silver. Xur albinism? None of them looked particularly old, really, just coming out of their prime. Their hair was braided and plaited similar to Sifura's, but turned back and looped around the back of the head. One of the females, Tommen saw as he stood behind her, had a scar on the back of her neck. It wasn't large, no more than the point of a knife, and it looked very old.

As for the other male council members, other than the black one who had already spoken, Araf, three were mostly gold, two with black and one with white; one of the blacks also had some white in his features.

The fifth male member was arguably the oldest of the group.

Aside from his mane going gray and his whiskers going gray, he was skinny and walked uncertainly. The only thing still youthful about him was his golden eyes, the same gold as Sifura, and the same even mixture of black, gold, and white. Was this Sifura's father or grandfather? Or were the tri-colors automatically considered to be leaders of some form? Or was it just a rare genetic mutation? Fuck, if they didn't have sex, how did they reproduce and pass on their genes in the first place, never mind worrying about special genetic mutations?

The council members arranged themselves quietly on their woven mats, murmuring greetings or hushed comments to one another. Sifura did not sit with them as part of the circle. Rather, she touched Tommen's arm and gently guided him inside the circle to sit beside her, facing Araf.

Thankfully, rather than sacrificing him to some pagan god, the council took the time to introduce themselves. Araf, the black male who had already spoken. Shashef, the white (albino?) female with silver eyes. Irura, the gold and black female. Sarabi, the gold and white female. Furix, the gold and black male with some white markings. Kurish, the gold and white male. Orin, the gold and black male with no white markings.

"And I am Sifura," the old tri-color male said.

"Sifura?" Tommen questioned. "But...she's Sifura."

"Such a balance of the three colors is very rare," female-Sifura explained. "Even more rare is two being alive at the same time." Tommen didn't miss the look of love she gave the older male. "We are automatically called Sifura. Three-heart."

"All very well," Araf interrupted, "but if your words are true, we have little time to waste on culture and sentiment."

"We have plenty of time," she-Sifura shot back. "Because of the feast, we are not able to go anywhere until morning."

"As is your duty as the leader of this faction," Shashef reminded her, Irura murmuring an agreement.

"I also have a duty to the well-being of this faction and others who come seeking need. He has brought a gift from his people and he has traveled far, looking for a cure for this ailment."

"An ailment which, if memory serves, will have killed whom it will kill, and spared whom it will spare. If he turns back now or goes on to obtain the cure from the D'Bok, he will save no one."

"Not now, but in the future."

"Tommen Forbes," he-Sifura said, his voice soft, "how did your people come to be stricken with this ailment? It is merely a poisonous plant, surely —"

"It was an attack," Tommen cut in. Sifura shot him a look, but translated. He went on. "The Ram tribe. They are not even a tribe, but a scattered people, with no factions and no honor. They attack and then disappear. They are impossible to hunt down or even fight properly. They attacked us. My father was shot with three poison arrows."

"We suffer with your loss, but he is dead now," Furix told him gently.

"He was still alive when I left. I know I can make it. I will go without you if I must, just point me in the right direction."

"It is well that you have come so far with no incidents," Sarabi said. "You are indeed a credit to your tribe and your faction. But even we can see that you are no desert skimmer. You would never make it to the jungle. And even if you did somehow survive the desert, the D'Bok are not as hospitable as we are."

"I'm sure I could make them listen and understand," Tommen told her.

"And how would you do that?" Araf inquired, unimpressed by Tommen's bravado.

Well, if I shot their leader dead with my "magic" gun, I think they might be more inclined to listen to me. If I shot you, would you waive whatever rule says we can't start traveling tonight? Short of that, I can always just Band and walk right on by with no one the wiser.

But Tommen said none of this out loud. Instead he opted for, "I don't know, but if crossing the desert takes as long as everyone says it does, I'm sure I can come up with something."

Sarabi shook her head. "If you try to cross the desert on your own, you will be thinking of nothing but the heat, the sun, and your own hunger and thirst."

Tommen tried to take an even breath and not sigh in defeat. He very clearly remembered the trek just from earlier that day, and that had only been a few hours. To do that day in and day out and day in and day out for seven days, while trying to hold a Band, they were right. He would never make it. First he would drop the Band, thereby voiding all his progress anyway and condemning Walter to death. Then he would probably drop dead from dehydration long before he ever felt hungry. That was assuming he didn't burn up like a crispy French fry first.

He thought about demanding why they couldn't leave now, or after the feast at least, why they had to wait until morning. What god of theirs told them that they would burn in hell for setting out on a life-saving journey a couple hours early? Then he decided that politics and religion were two subjects best avoided, especially when he had virtually no understanding of their belief system.

"When...is the earliest that we can leave?" Tommen asked, forcing his voice to stay calm.

"First light of the morning," Furix replied coolly.

"We will take a skimmer," she-Sifura said.

The reaction started out as all the council members protesting at once, but it died quickly. Then there was the awkward pause as everyone waited for everyone else to speak. Orin, who had been silent thus far, shifted on his mat and spoke.

"The skimmers are for emergencies only," he said. "Evacuation, or a massive assault. They are not for the leisurely transport of—"

"If our own people were attacked and dying of hasax poison, would that not be an emergency?" he-Sifura interrupted. "Would we not rush across the desert to barter with the D'Bok?"

She-Sifura gave him a grateful glance as she picked up on the line of thought. "Tommen's people are new to us, that is true. But that does not make it any less of an emergency. It is not our emergency, but it is his. He has traveled long and far, and as you can see, he is not made for the sun and the heat; you said it yourself. Walking across the desert will take twenty to thirty days, if not more depending on how he handles it. A skimmer would take seven days at most." Araf looked ready to protest, but she again cut him off. "The nearest oasis is a ten-day trek, or a three-day skim. After that, it is thirty days to the next oasis. No other tribe is able to handle the desert like we do, and if another faction decides to attack in that time, which is very unlikely, better to stand and fight here than be left in the desert to be finished off by the animals. Stand here, then the enemy must not only brave the desert to attack, but brave it again when they are forced to retreat."

The council grumbled among themselves for a short time, their words too low for the translator to pick up effectively. Tommen was forced to wonder what it was that made them so prickly about helping outsiders. Were they just mistrustful of outsiders, as isolated as they were? Were they not as peaceful with the D'Bok as Sifura had implied? Or did it all have to do with this damn feast and whatever significance it presented that must be upheld and honored?

Araf was the first to break the circle of whispers and grumbles and hisses. The black and white elder looked none too pleased, but if Tommen was any good at basic powers of observation, he-Sifura had said something to at lease soothe them even if he was unable to sway them.

"Very well," Araf said stiffly, like someone was twisting his tail or holding a gun to his head. "You will leave at first light of the morning. Orin will see to it that one of the skimmers is ready for you, and Shashef and Sarabi will oversee the gathering of provisions for your journey, including gifts to give to the D'Bok."

"I brought my own gifts to give to them," Tommen informed them.

"That is good," Kurish said with a smirk in his voice. "But not good enough. The D'Bok will always want more. They find no shame in exploiting weakness, especially in a tribe they have never met before."

Tommen glanced at she-Sifura who dipped her head once in agreement. She looked around at the council. "Thank you, wise council, for allowing this unexpected venture. Not only is it in short notice, but it comes at an otherwise very inopportune time." She stood and did a sort of cross between a bow and a curtsy. Tommen stood as well, but elected not to copy her maneuver since he did not completely understand its procedure or significance. No need to upset the Romans anymore than he apparently already had.

"Thank you, Sifura," he-Sifura said. "Thank you for your kind heart and willingness to help those in need, even when it is unexpected and at an inopportune time."

It was like addressing the Hands, Tommen thought, with all the formality involved.

The council did not move as he followed she-Sifura out of the little home. She got about twenty feet from the doorway when she paused and looked at him, her expression indeterminate.

"If I did or said something wrong, I didn't mean to," Tommen began defensively, feeling like a child who got his hand caught in the cookie jar and immediately denied doing anything wrong.

"Perhaps it was my error," she said thoughtfully. "Perhaps I assumed too much that your people and my people have much in common, enough that small things can be attributed to different tribes."

"What...did I do?"

"You speak when spoken to, or when the council allows for questions. Otherwise, you listen only. You do not offer your thoughts or opinions, and you never interrupt them."

Tommen sighed. "I'm sorry. But at least we'll be able to leave at first light, right?"

"Yes."

She started to move, but Tommen got in front of her. "I'm sorry I screwed up. Really I am. Help me understand. Okay. Who are the council members? Not their names, but who are they? What is their function in the faction?"

Sifura studied him, as if unsure how serious he was being. "Each member of the council is the leader of his or her clan. We have nine clans here. Eight form the council, and one leads the faction. When the faction leader dies or becomes too old to serve effectively, all the clans offer up their best warriors or hunters to try and claim the spot. If the new faction leader comes from the same clan as the old one, nothing changes. If the new faction leader is from a different clan, the old council member from than clan is removed, and the empty clan leader council position is filled with the candidate who tried for the faction leader position."

"At the risk of sounding ignorant, what makes a tri-color like you and other-Sifura special?"

"As the colors balance, so do our abilities. Those of greater black color are better hunters because their scent is diminished with their tougher skin. Gold makes one a better warrior, because they tolerate the heat the best. White makes the best healers, because the soft fur comforts an ailing patient. Some do cross the lines—Araf was a mighty warrior, and many whites are also either hunters or warriors—but it is best that children are trained in their strengths rather than forcing them to do something else for its own sake. A sifura is trained in all the skills, including how to lead, because we have been chosen by the xur to lead our people."

"Oh."

They looked out over the open communal area where the bonfire pit had been made as high as it could go. Few people lingered in the area now; those who did were either children at play, their parents watching them, or other villagers on miscellaneous tasks.

"The harvest will begin soon, as well as the sowing for next year," Sifura said. "Then the feast will begin."

"Is there anything I can do to help while I'm here?" Tommen asked meekly, hoping he might be able to make up for whatever screw ups he did in the council room.

"There is little to be done now. You may go. Find an empty home to sleep in tonight. Then you may wander and look around, see this new world you've stumbled into. As leader of this faction, I have responsibilities with my people, and I may not get to speak to you again tonight. If that is the case, then I will see you at first light of the morning, Tommen Forbes."

Chapter Seventeen
The Lion's Den

Walter had once taken Tommen, who was about fourteen at the time, to an amusement park, where they quickly learned that Tommen did not like amusement parks at all. He was unimpressed with the kiddie rides, but the roller coasters and other high-speed, super-G rides were not to his liking either. Actually, he liked them, but his stomach didn't. After several visits to the bathroom, the rest of the trip was little more than wandering around the park, looking at the overpriced food, overpriced sideshow games, and all the rides that Tommen couldn't or wouldn't ride.

This was about like that, as Tommen found himself wandering first around the communal area with the enormous bonfire pit and, with some further exploration, some long tables and benches. This was like seating for an army kind of long, and it still probably wouldn't be enough. Then his travels took him a little farther from the communal area, down some of the older streets where the construction was older, misshapen, haphazardly thrown together. Children darted here and there, playing some game or another. In a few huts, mothers and fathers with toddler-age children worked on some special beaded jewelry to place around a fussing child's neck or wrist.

Not a few times, Tommen was approached. Most often it was children daring each other to get close and touch him — or, as was almost always the case, his balls. He couldn't understand why they were so fascinated with them, and it only made him more self-conscious. If he hadn't already been sunburned to the point of potentially being mistaken for a tomato, he might have blushed every time a child surprised him by running up, touching his balls, and running away laughing, much to the amusement of their entire group of friends.

The first empty home that he found, he took. It was difficult to judge what was simply left behind as a courtesy for the next guy and what constituted someone's personal possessions, as he found that these people had very few personal possessions. So it was entirely possible that he had a neighbor next door to him, or that he'd mistaken possessions for courtesy and there were forty homes between him and his closest neighbor. He didn't really see how it mattered anyway, given that everyone was going to be at the feast tonight, and he would be gone by morning before anyone was awake to notice.

Tommen knew that taking a two-room hut all to himself would probably be seen as greedy, but in his view, there were more than enough empty houses to go around. And anyway, he really couldn't stand the thought of anyone just looking in and watching him sleep. Even if there weren't any doors, he just wanted to know that there were four walls at least obstructing someone's view of him while he slept.

He felt uneasy just leaving his burlap bag sitting in the corner of the little home, but he couldn't lug it around with him, could he? It had grown heavy over the course of the day, and his shoulders screamed at him every time he moved it from one to the other. Well, everything in it was pretty easy to identify as his, so he didn't have to worry too much about stuff getting stolen, he supposed. Quickly he went through everything in the bag. Set of clothes, medicines, gift of coffee for the D'Bok, assorted foodstuffs and water for the journey, bowie knife and small gun he had to make sure he got back to Micaiah. He removed the clip and did a quick inspection to make sure it had survived the first leg of the journey, which it seemed it had.

Then he sat. Alone. There in his room. In the hut he'd claimed. Bored.

Sifura had told him he was free to explore, but as far as he could tell, all the vegetation was the same, and the houses were pretty much the same. He could understand the villagers, but they couldn't understand him, so there wasn't much point in trying to mingle.

He scolded himself and shook his head. *You're on an alien world, and you're bored already? Where's the scientist in you, the one who has to learn and know and understand everything? Where's the great globetrotter, the one who wants to just go anywhere and see and do something different, something he can't do at home?*

The effects of the little honey flower were wearing off; as he stood, his burned skin screeched at him. His movements were slow and difficult as he carefully picked his way to the door facing the street. Well, Sifura had mentioned something about a harvest, and the way she kept speaking of it made it seem like it was some kind of significant thing. Maybe he could find someone heading that way and just observe. He would help if they needed hands—he knew a thing or two about harvesting and getting crops in and stored—but mostly he just wanted to watch.

He figured the best place to start was the communal area and use basic powers of observation to figure out where all the crowds were. After a few misadventures down one street and up another to no avail, he finally found a group of villagers all walking one direction. There were eight of them, and they all looked like couples. One couple had two children, another just one, and the other two couples had no children. They were chatting amiably, excitedly, but Tommen was too far away to hear them at all, never mind being in range for the translator to pick them up.

Eventually they joined a larger group, not in a field, but in a forest of smaller trees. These trees were short and fat, with trunks that reminded Tommen of morbidly obese ladies in the checkout line of the grocery store. Their branches were what might be considered normal for a small maple, with even smaller leaves. There were perhaps fifty in the grove, and every branch was weighed down with huge fruits that resembled artichokes.

Well, it would make sense, Tommen figured. They were nomadic, so they didn't have the time or tools to sit and sow wheat or whatever else. Even if they did believe in cleaning up for the next guy, nothing sewn would survive that long between tending. So for them to harvest fruit from trees which needed no help was much more practical. And given that it was a feast day probably made it all the more exciting, especially for the children who waited with all the patience of any young child.

He-Sifura was also present, standing at the entrance to the grove, but he did not appear to be any kind of guard. Rather, he appeared to be simply looking on like a kindly grandfather, watching the new youth run around with the same excitement he possessed, though they had bodies capable of expressing it, while he could only reminisce about his own youth and the wily mischief he got into.

Tommen couldn't decide if those gathered were waiting for a signal or what it was. Maybe it was like an Easter egg hunt, to see who could grab the most, a competition for the kids.

Then two of the villagers moved into the grove. They appeared to be a couple, the way they looked at each other and the way their tails flicked together in tease. He-Sifura shifted his stance and Tommen was sure he would spontaneously combust into a great ball of sunshine and happiness if he glowed any more. The couple went to one of the fruits and gently picked it; it came off the stem easily. As they did, it began moving, like a chicken that keeps flapping after its head has been cut off.

Curious, Tommen edged closer to see what was happening as the couple peeled back several layers of thick leafy material. His jaw must have hit the ground when they peeled back the last layer to reveal a tiny black and gold face. Layer after layer came off, dropping to the ground, until all that was left was the stem and a sort of umbilical cord to the back of the neck. A white and black female approached and expertly cut the cord. The little kitten-baby began wailing as some sort of salve was applied to the flesh, but the new mother held the child to her breast, and it quieted as it began nursing.

So that was why no one had any clue what Tommen's stuff was. They were grown, not born; they had no need for sex or the parts that went with them. And it explained the scar on the back of the council member's neck. If he was right, they all had the same scar, like a bellybutton but not on their bellies.

"What will you call him?" he-Sifura asked as the couple left the grove.

"Hasha," the female replied. "For my father."

Then they left the grove.

Tommen stood, rooted to the ground. It seemed to take forever for a couple to move and go into the grove to...pick their baby. After four or five, he-Sifura moved to stand beside him.

"We return to the same oasis every year for this," he explained. "Always during the Day of the Sun. A couple always remembers where they sowed their child, but they must wait until the child is ready. They know because they know. A sound, usually, a smell. Some children are late; a few will not be harvested until tomorrow. But some die on the branch, and it is a great loss for all."

The time between couples going in shortened until they were entering ten or more at a time.

"It takes a while, but once they get going, they get going." He-Sifura chuckled. "A couple may not harvest and sow in the same year. It is far too stressful to have such young children together in the same house at once. But sometimes...sometimes mother and father may be blessed with twins. Twins are lucky, and the entire family is admired."

Tommen was afraid to know what the old man meant by sowing, but he was too enthralled to look away, and soon enough, once the last of the children had been harvested, he found out.

She-Sifura, Kurish, Orin, and Irura entered the grove, dragging an enormous pelt between them. It was black, gold, and white, like the Sifuras, with one end that was bushy, which might have been a mane, and a tail that was tufted like a lion's.

Nothing was said. A whole new group of couples had

gathered at the grove, most with no children, but a few with one, maybe two. Overall, the procedure wasn't anything too elaborate, from what Tommen could gather. Each parent cut a long lock from the huge pelt, usually the mane, and then a lock of their own hair. They took the time to carefully braid the hairs together, twisting and weaving in various elaborate patterns. Once they were satisfied, they took it to a spot on the branch where the stem had lost its "fruit." All they had to do was hold the hairs to the stem and it took, the hairs seeming to melt together into a single length of rope attached to the branch. A thin, sap-like film leaked out from the branch over the hairs. Both mother and father touched the sap, then touched it to each other's lips, presumably in some sign of affection. Then the male also touched his sap-covered fingers to the female's breasts.

"The sap upon the lips is a symbol of binding the two together," he-Sifura explained. "But the sap upon the breasts lets the female body know to begin the countdown to start producing milk for the child when it is ready."

Tommen watched the whole thing, as couple after couple came forward to cut hair off the pelt and weave it with their own. Then the ceremony was over. The couple, and any children, left the grove, talking excitedly.

"Three is the most any couple can sow," he-Sifura sighed. He looked forlornly at a couple with no children who were weaving a braid of hairs, gazes more focused than they seemed to have to be. "Regardless if the children die on the branch, only three sowings."

So a child dying on the branch was like a miscarriage. While it might not be as physically painful, Tommen could see how it might still be a burden and emotionally traumatic. To only get three chances, to leave your future child hanging from a tree, to leave for a year extremely excited and fully expecting to come back to a baby, only to return and find that your little bundle of fruit had died. It couldn't be easy.

Once the couples ran out, Kurish and Orin retrieved what was left of the pelt and disappeared with it. Irura remained, walking among the trees and looking over all the new, future, fruity little kitten-babies. She-Sifura had vanished at some point, to where Tommen did not know.

Suddenly, his back was awash in heat, and his shadow stretched out long in front of him. The trees and he-Sifura turned bright yellow. Tommen whirled around but he-Sifura only stepped forward a few steps in wonder and pride, like watching fireworks on the Fourth of July. The bonfire pit had been lit, and not in the cute little Native American way with a couple of rocks and some grass, but in the modern American way of using some kind of accelerant like gasoline to light it up like a fireball, get everything burning all at once. A huge plume of smoke lifted into the air, and suddenly the whole pile shifted and broke, settling a good three feet and sending sparks and embers in all directions.

There was cheering, and people came racing from all directions toward the fire, whooping and hollering like it was spring break and time to party like it was 1999. Even he-Sifura laughed and did a little dance diddy, but he was going nowhere faster. He looked at Tommen with glowing golden eyes.

"You are new and cautious, uncertain of yourself. I am old and infirm, but as youthful as any of these children. What do you say I lead you to the feast, hm?"

Tommen found himself smiling and shaking his head. Regardless of world or species, the youth would be youthful, and the elderly would be youthful, too. So he stood beside he-Sifura and offered his arm as if he was going to escort a girl to the dance. He-Sifura did not initially understand, but once Tommen placed his hand where it should be, the old man laughed again, and together they walked toward the great fire and the feast for the Day of the Sun.

Even before they reached the communal area, Tommen felt as though his face was melting off. He suddenly understood why no plants grew within a hundred yards of the pit. He longed to run back to his little hut, which he was certain was still close enough to be more than well-heated for the night, but he-Sifura stayed staunchly on his arm, moving just a little faster the closer they got to the pit.

The sun was still hovering just over the horizon, casting long shadows across the desert, but the bonfire lit up the communal area and surrounding streets like it was midday. All the seats at the long tables had been claimed, mostly by the new parents who had just picked their kitten-babies from a tree branch, or the elderly, and the rest of the villagers found spots here and there to sit, on overturned baskets and crates, on woven sacks or woven mats, or just straight in the dirt.

"This is where I must leave you," he-Sifura said, withdrawing his hand from Tommen's arm. "The old people like me sit at the table. We could sit in the dirt, but it's unlikely we would get back up very easily."

"You got up easily enough from the council meeting," Tommen said, a split-second before he remembered that the old man could not understand him. Indeed, he-Sifura gave him an apologetic look before patting his arm and shuffling off to find a seat at one of the tables.

Tommen looked around. There did not appear to be any rhyme or reason to seating arrangement, no hierarchal code that had to be obeyed. Families sat with singles, hunters sat with warriors sat with healers, old sat with young, males sat with females. Would anyone want to sit with the stranger? Perhaps they all would, just for the novelty. And who knew what stories they would conjure up by the morning?

As he eventually found a mat to sit on against the wall of a home, Tommen reflected that this was what it must be like to be an exchange student. So familiar and yet so alien, sitting among people you don't know and don't understand, watching customs and rituals that mean everything to them and nothing to you, wondering what everyone else is doing back home, if they miss you, if they even really notice you're gone, if they're doing amazing things without you that you will never be able to do again.

He shook his head to clear it. The twins would notice his

absence, that was for damn sure. Day after Christmas and it was only them at the store? Yeah, they would miss him. Cautiously, he checked his watch, pretending to fiddle with the leather thongs of his bracelets while discreetly pushing buttons to bring up the display. It had been almost six in the morning when he left. Now his watch was telling him it was about two in the afternoon. How did the length of the days of this world compare to Earth? He tried to bring up some sort of display on this world, but only got an error message. These people didn't keep time like that, so there was no time to give.

Well, if he had to hazard a guess, he would say the days were at least equal, but even on this longest day of the year, the day itself felt shorter. Maybe his perception was messed up from spending so much time in the Wheel, but he was pretty sure the days here were shorter.

In a way, that was almost a relief. If the days here were shorter, that meant he might only be Banding for six Earth days rather than a full seven. Wasn't much, because by day four he would be dead and surviving only on coffee or some equivalent, but it was better than this world having longer days.

He jumped as a call rang out over the mild din of chatter and the raging of the bonfire. When the crowd was almost quiet, it rang out again, like the call of a banshee. He looked around and only just caught sight of she-Sifura standing up over the crowd, on a table or something else he couldn't see. When she spoke, she did not shout or strain to make herself heard; she would be any theater director's star with the way she was able to project her voice, making it so even Tommen's translator picked her up with perfect clarity.

"My people!" she began. "Today we celebrate the Day of the Sun, when all may gather and marvel at its beauty and glory, the way it brings warmth and light. Now we will feast, and begin preparing for the long nights, remembering that darkness does not come upon us suddenly like an enemy, but slowly, as a friend. And we must be vigilant against it. For though the darkness comes slowly, so also does the light, destroying the darkness just as slowly, just as cleverly."

It was a pretty speech, Tommen thought. Not anything like "four score and seven years ago" or "tear down this wall" or anything, but probably pretty good for the audience at hand. They cheered and got excited, then settled as she went on.

"No doubt many of you have seen or at the very least heard of the stranger who has come to our village today. His name is Tommen Forbes, of the Ape tribe. He is from far away, far to the south and west, across the Toxic Sea and farther still. His people have been beset by a terrible enemy who poisons them, with no cure." She paused to let that sink in. "But Tommen has come to find a cure, one that we do not possess, but that the D'Bok do possess. Tomorrow at first light, I myself shall take him to treat with the D'Bok and find a cure for his people."

That brought another round of cheering, and some looked around for the stranger in their midst. In the range of his translator, Tommen heard a number of approving statements for helping a suffering tribe, especially when one person dares to brave the Red Desert in search of a cure. But he also heard not a few statements about physically going to help the Ape tribe and crippling what deceitful people would destroy another tribe so absolutely. She-Sifura let this go on for a minute or two before calling out and regaining their attention.

"This is a long and dangerous journey," she said, bringing her speech to a close. "And it may already be too late to save those who suffer now. But it is a worthy endeavor, one that I am more than happy to assist with. In the end, once the Ape tribe has been cured and restored, though distance separates us by many days, the Ape tribe and the Xur tribe will be allies. In all times of crisis—sickness, war, famine—we will call upon one another. Let this alliance stand from this day, until our last day. May it not come swiftly with our new friends at hand."

As the villagers cheered, Tommen felt a rock settle in his gut. His gaze found Sifura's a moment before she stepped down from her stand.

Translation: You owe me. You owe all of us. Big time. It may not be today or tomorrow, or even next year, but one day I will demand a favor, and you are obligated to fulfill it. Do not cross me.

Tommen had little desire to cross her, not just for the help she was giving now, but for the sheer fact that she was a leader, a warrior, a hunter, a healer. She could take care of herself, and she would take care of Tommen if she had to, whether in the desert with no witnesses, or in Time with every political incentive. Was he right to trust her? Was there some ulterior motive at play? Was it possible she was under some sort of duress?

The food began to come around, but Tommen almost missed it in his lonely musings. Everything was done offering style, like passing the plate in church, from one person to the next, sometimes having to stand and walk things to the next man. The plates were little more than strips of bark wide enough to put a good amount of food on and strong enough to hold it without breaking. The bowls that the food came in were made of stone, as if they'd been made on a potter's wheel. It was as simple as just picking out the food one wanted, putting it on the plate, and passing it on. If the bowl was empty, take it up to the bonfire pit where several villagers were busy filling and refilling bowls, then go back and continue the passing.

Tommen had to do that once as he took the last out of a bowl of what looked and smelled like nuts of some form. He went up to the pit to get the bowl refilled and, aside from those who were doing the refilling, he saw there was another villager who stood at the carcass of an enormous beast, probably the same one whose pelt served the baby-growing grove. That villager cut off meat to send around to the people, but they were not haphazard cuts. Indeed, he seemed to be a master butcher, the way his fingers deftly handled the knife and sliced precisely through the various muscle groups. He saved the tendons and ligaments as he found them and divided the bones into several piles, throwing some of the shards and smallest bones into the fire.

The bowl of nuts refilled, Tommen returned to his spot and passed it on, reflecting on the creature whose flesh they feasted on.

The tribe was called the Xur, for its resemblance and semi-reverence for the animal of the same name. Was it possible that this creature was the xur? They used its fur for reproduction and the carcass in these grand feasts? Tommen closed his eyes and tried to picture the pelt in the grove laid over the carcass of the animal at the bonfire. He couldn't quite make it work except as a colorful lion. But that thing up there had to be two or three times the size of a lion.

Except, fundamentally, that didn't make any logical biological sense. In climates where food or water was scarce, or the weather was harsh, or both, creatures tended to be smaller in order to conserve water and energy. A giant lion was just impractical; it would starve or dehydrate.

His thoughts were interrupted as another bowl got passed along. How many courses were there? Or was it just going to be a continuous thing, just keep passing the bowls, keep taking the food, keep eating until he ended up dead in a food coma? There was certainly enough food to do that, at least to Tommen's eyes. Aside from the meat, which appeared to be roasted beautifully, he had a number of fruits he'd never seen before, several varieties of nuts, and food salads and concoctions he didn't even have names for, even to describe them.

It was probably best that he didn't understand them, actually. He was more willing to try the slimy, lumpy gray stuff when it was just slimy, lumpy gray stuff as opposed to mashed up cockroach hearts mixed with earthworm brains. Of course, that wasn't really fair to assume that just because the tribe was primitive automatically meant they went digging around in anthills. At the same time, such opinions were more reminisce of a first world attitude. He viewed eating ants and worms the same way a lot of city slickers viewed eating rabbits and coons. It just didn't happen. Not to cute, fluffy bunny rabbits and icky, trash-eating coons. Except it did. Tommen did. He trapped them and ate them. He grew up on the stuff. True, he was more leery of modern raccoons that did go through nasty garbage cans, but to him, there was nothing wrong with it.

With those thoughts in mind, he forced himself to at least try a bite of everything. Yes, there was every chance it could kill him or severely sicken him or send him on a wilder trip than the hippies ever managed on magic shrooms, but this was their sustenance. It couldn't be too bad, right? And they had healers, right? And it would be rude not to. Right?

To that end, he decided ultimately that his best bet would be to survive on nuts and berries for the duration of his visit. The xur, or whatever the creature was, tasted delicious. He was not about to deny that. But about five minutes after eating it, he had to slip away in order to throw it back up, and not voluntarily. He panicked for a minute when he saw blood in the vomit, but soon discovered that the meat itself was not fully cooked. In fact, only the outside was really done, leaving the rest of it so rare it might as well have been raw. Made sense, he figured, given that these people were probably more cat than person in their digestive system.

The nuts and berries did not seem to cause any sort of ailment and even helped his system to calm down a little, finally being fed something it knew what to do with. He took several helpings of the fruits and nuts, even the berries when they came around, trying the mind-over-matter approach to just eat and tell himself it was going to be okay. That worked until he got around to the mystery foods.

The slimy, lumpy gray stuff had a similar effect to the raw meat, except that came out the other way, moving through him like water through a straw.

By the time he got back, he felt miserable, like the time he'd gotten food poisoning from a Chinese restaurant and spent twenty-four straight hours facing one way or the other over the toilet. He found his mat and sat in a heap, not wanting to risk any more, not wanting to really eat, but forcing himself to at least eat some fruit and nuts. For normalcy if nothing else. He rubbed his face and looked up at a tap on the shoulder.

A black and gold male stood over him, holding out a cup.

"The food does not like you," he said, grinning, showing off cattish fangs. "Drink. It will calm your stomach."

Tommen took the cup, his grip weak. He nodded once. "Thank you."

Every instinct told him to take a small sip to taste, or sniff it if nothing else. But between being sick and not really giving a fuck, he just downed the whole thing in one draught.

It was as if he swallowed fire. He coughed and gasped for air, each breath stinging his throat and sinuses until it felt like his brain was on fire. Then his body started feeling tingly, as if everything had fallen asleep and was now waking up. His movements were slow and clumsy. The black and gold male was laughing riotously to the point where he had to sit down to contain himself before slapping Tommen on the back and crawling away, still laughing.

Tommen had never mastered the art of putting a finger down his throat to induce vomiting, so he settled for spitting several times, trying to clear his system but failing miserably. Between the fire and the tingly, he honestly felt drunk in body if not in mind. He was still very aware of everything going on and had his wits about him, but his body was not reacting the way he wanted it to.

After several minutes, he felt another tap on his shoulder. This time it was a black and white female. She knelt before him and offered him a cup. He regarded it suspiciously.

"It was a cruel joke," she said. "One that should not have been played. Your body is too different from ours, and if something happens, I may not understand how to treat you." She indicated the cup. "It is only water. I would give you herbs to calm your stomach, but I do not know what you can tolerate. This is all I can offer."

Tommen closed his eyes and let out a breath. Finally he nodded, opened his eyes, and took the cup. As promised, it was only water, cool and refreshing, just as if he'd gotten it out of the stream out back from the cabin. He looked at her. "Thank you."

She dipped her head once, took the cup, and headed off. Some distance away, he saw her stop and chastise the black and gold male who did not appear apologetic in the least. Well, every place has got 'em, Tommen figured.

Similarly, every place also had music. As the food stopped making rounds and people finished eating, some went up to the bonfire pit. The carcass was being divided into larger portions and taken away, leaving room for a small band of musicians. Drums were a pretty universal instrument and easy to spot, but the rest could only be guessed at. One seemed like a cross between a guitar and a harp; another resembled a clarinet but with far more finger work and rings on the fingers that moved different pieces; and still a third was like nothing he'd ever seen before, with four strings, eight keys, and a mouthpiece, like some demented lovechild between a bagpipe and an accordion.

And as with most music, there came dancing. Tommen had been to several powwows at various festivals in the area, sometimes as part of a larger celebration, sometimes just a public Native American shindig. He obviously had no Native blood in him, but he found it fascinating, to have a culture so far removed so close to home.

The dancing and the costumes put him in mind of those powwows, except the villagers here used leaves instead of feathers. The males styled their manes in all manner of wacky hairdos, some even coloring them bright colors. Even the tails of the villagers were not immune to costuming, being draped in leaves and vines and long leather thongs decorated with colored beads. A few had tiny bells made of either iron or nut shells that jingled and tinkled with every step.

She-Sifura was among them, her body draped with long leather thongs shining with beads of glass and iron and copper, the thongs seeming to run with the colored patterns on her body.

The dance itself was like a combination of Native American dancing, Irish folk, and traditional western square dancing. The steps were complex and intricate, the dancers turning on only a toe, kicking out without hitting someone else in the face, stomping hard while trying to miss a tail. Even when young children darted in and out of the dancers as they practiced uncoordinated dance moves of their own, the dance went on and the children remained unharmed. At most, it seemed as though there were probably a thousand dancers, dancing, twisting, and moving, writhing like a great leviathan unfurling its tentacles to all corners of the communal area.

And it never seemed to stop. The dance just kept going in one long procession. There was no break between songs, no change in the mood. The dancers did not need to stop and rest aching feet or knees, and the musicians did not ask for a break to catch their breath. It just kept going and going and going and going. For Tommen, just watching it was exhausting.

Finally, he could stand it no more. He looked around the area, saw a child curled up in its mother's arms, sound asleep. Elsewhere, a young woman escorted an older woman out of the area. So it wasn't an honor thing, just a matter of endurance. This party would break up on its own in its own time.

Slowly, Tommen stood, feeling slightly woozy. Fuck, had that bastard male poisoned him? Or was that just from all the food making him sick? Did it matter? Again he pretended to mess with his bracelets, glancing at the sky now dark, looking down momentarily as he finally got the display. Only seven o'clock at night on Earth. So the days were shorter here, which meant he had a better chance at successfully Banding for seven days.

He changed his watch back into leather bracelets and started down the street, not even sure if this was his street, or where his hut was for that matter. Even if he could remember certain landmarks, he would never be able to see them in the dark now.

Perhaps one of the biggest changes for Tommen when he walked out of that cave and into the modern world, was being told that he not only couldn't, but shouldn't inherently trust everyone. Yes, his pa had always taught him to be wise and cautious, but on the whole, people were generally good and trustworthy. But to have Walter tell him not to trust people or talk to strangers, and especially not to take anything from anyone he didn't know, it was very confusing and even disheartening. It was still a little disheartening, but he'd gotten used to it.

Now those same contradictory teachings were at war again as he walked through the streets in the dark. On the one hand, instinct told him to be vigilant, that danger could be lurking around every corner, and some villain could be waiting in the shadows for him to pass by where he would be jumped. He was a stupid stranger, a dumb tourist who didn't know enough to stay in after dark. On the other hand, these were good people who had taken him in and even cheered when they heard that Sifura was going to help him and a new alliance was going to come out of it. Regardless of Sifura's intentions, the rest of the village took it at face value, that they were going to have a new ally, a new friend. Would someone really be stupid enough to jeopardize that by attacking him?

Well, maybe not a direct assault, but if the drink that the black and gold male had given him was like some kind of alcohol, it could just be something that started out as a misunderstanding and went from there. No ill intentions, just an accident.

Tommen shook his head, told himself to stop being so paranoid. There were times when paranoia was good and it saved lives. There were other times when it drove someone to be an insane hermit who wore a tin foil hat and lived in a cave plated in copper. He was the stranger here, an alien who was relying every bit on the generosity of these people to survive and get the cure for his dad's illness. He was going to have to trust them a little. He had no choice.

Down one street and up another, Tommen was pretty sure he was lost. Villagers began trickling away from the feast, some still with leaves and beads and colored hair, tails drooping or dragging in the dust. No one offered to help him, though a few dipped their heads in greeting or made some respectful gesture, and he did his best to return the gesture.

Either by chance or subconscious memory, Tommen somehow found his way back to the little hut he called his own. It was devoid of life, and his bag lay unmolested in the second room. Still, he went to it and rifled through his things just to be sure. Gift of coffee, clothes, food, water, medicine, knife, gun, all still there. He ended up fishing out his clean boxers and putting them on if for no other reason than he wasn't intending that anyone would see him tonight and think him shameful, and they brought him some measure of comfort. He also checked the gun again, ejecting the clip and giving it a thorough inspection.

He checked his watch again. Barely ten after seven, but Tommen knew he'd been wandering a lot longer than that, or so it seemed. As he sat on the little woven mat with furs spread out over it, he briefly wished for his phone, as if he was going to get good enough reception to call or text the twins and let them know of his progress. Did they worry about him? Did they wonder where he was, what he was doing? Or were they so busy at the store, they hardly had time to spare a thought for anything but the next demanding customer?

Slowly, he rechecked and repacked his bag. He thought about getting into the trail mix or the jerky, just to give his body something it was familiar with, then decided against it. The desert was going to be harsh, no matter how fast they moved or how much he Banded; he would need his strength then.

As he burrowed under the furs, he was suddenly hit with homesickness as if he'd been hit in the chest with a rock. And it wasn't homesickness for his room at home, but for a little cabin in the woods on a mountain, where, on a calm night, he could hear the stream out back, and his older brother's snoring in the other bed. Tommen sighed and lay there in the darkness, looking up at nothing.

Friday

Chapter Eighteen
Scorch

Tommen did not remember his dreams precisely, but he knew he did not sleep well. From the terror that lingered every time he came close to consciousness, he could only guess that they were nightmares of the warehouse. Had it really only been Monday that it happened? It felt like so long ago, a lifetime and a galaxy away. Already the details were fading, some drifting off to be forgotten, others becoming distorted until he barely knew the truth of what really happened. And still he knew his dream ended with Rifun turning the gun on him and firing, but he knew that hadn't really happened. So why did his dream say it did?

Whatever iteration of the dream he was having, it faded away quickly when Rifun started firing. Again and again and again. No, that wasn't Rifun...

Tommen blinked open bleary eyes to see Sifura standing next to him, nudging him in the ribs. He could only just tell it was her from the faint light coming through the doorway facing the street.

"What time is it?" he whispered stupidly, sitting up and rubbing his eyes even as he was assaulted by a wave of nausea. He thought he was going to be sick, but it never came.

"Come. We must leave quickly. The first light of the morning has already passed," Sifura told him.

She said it with all the authority of a leader, but there was also that hint of exhaustion in her voice that Tommen knew well. He felt the same way. Way too much partying. If his nausea and sensitivity to even the gray dawn was any indication, he was definitely hungover. In a way he found it amusing and impressive. He could go out with Eric and Varad, have three shots—admittedly they weren't the best shots since they were cheap alcohol, but still—and wake up just fine. He comes to an alien planet, has one drink which wasn't even very big, and he's hungover like an idiot who goes out binge-drinking on his twenty-first birthday.

Well-played, sir, well-played.

Grudgingly, he pushed back the furs and reached for his bag. He stood and waited to follow Sifura who did not move.

"I'm ready," he told her.

"Your coverings," she said simply.

He looked down at his boxers and sighed. "I know it's considered shameful among your people, but I really don't like it when random people come up and touch my junk."

"Then tell them not to. With the right gestures, words are not necessary."

She said it so simply, as casually as if she were telling him to run to the store and get a gallon of milk. Could it really be that easy? Was he an idiot for not already thinking of that? Still, he relented, set the bag down, and stripped off the boxers, stuffing them in the bag and reshouldering it. Already it was growing warm outside.

"I'm ready," he said again.

"Good."

Then she turned and moved off. He followed dutifully. Neither of them moved like they had yesterday. He was still sorely burnt from the trek and exhausted from the party. Sifura had probably been one of the last to leave; had she even slept?

The streets were quiet, but not empty. A few people were out and about, probably just by force of habit at being awake with the dawn. Some were washing color from their hair, others nibbling on bits of meat, a few starting on chores, whatever they were in this village. What children Tommen saw were as dead as their parents, moving slowly, woozily. Did children drink, too? Was that healthy? Did it matter?

They passed through the communal area. Several dozen

people lay scattered about, still sleeping, some still in costume. The instruments were silent, their players asleep beside them. The bonfire itself was still going, the mountain reduced to a molehill that still stood about ten feet tall including the ashes and coal at the base, big enough that even with no tending, there were still flames. The ground had gone from packed dirt to churned mud, slick and sticky. Sifura took a wide path around the edge of the communal area, stepping lightly so as not to disturb any who were still sleeping.

Once out of the communal area, they headed north out of the main village to a smaller area that Tommen might have taken for some kind of warehouse or storage area. The buildings here were larger and had real doors made of wood that almost looked like planks. They were shut up tight, and the whole area looked abandoned.

"Stay here," Sifura commanded. "I will return."

"Where are you going?" Tommen wondered.

"I will get our supplies."

Tommen was about to tell her that he had all the supplies they would need in his bag, then decided against it. There was no harm in bringing extras, and if she had her food and he had his food, so much the better because he had little desire to have a repeat of last night's flu-like fiasco. That, and if for some reason she brought extra medical supplies, better to have and not need.

So he watched her head off toward one of the buildings and disappear, leaving him standing alone in the clearing. It was situated toward the edge of the oasis, outside the protective ring of giant trees, thick bushes on one side, scraggly bushes and grass giving way to sand on the other. Even in the dim light, he could see the differences in the sand.

Curious, he fussed with his bracelets and brought up the display of the watch.

"Fuck."

Midnight on Earth. That meant he'd only gotten about five hours of sleep, max. Fucking hell, these long days were going to kill him. At the same time, it was also probably going to be his saving grace, a way to buy more time to get the cure. But still. Fuck.

He looked up and jerked his wrist back behind him as a movement caught his eye. Sifura had returned with a golden female with slight black markings following her, also looking displeased and slightly hungover. They did not walk toward him, but another building. Sifura made a gesture towards him, and he walked over. He might have jogged over politely, but he had a feeling that anything more than he was already doing would not end well for any of them.

"Taking a skimmer," the golden female was saying, "you will need seven days of supplies. The most important of these will be food and water." She led them through the building which smelled gloriously of herbs and spices. "The xur meat of last night has not yet cured, but we do have some meat available to take." She reached up and fussed with something. Then there was the creaking of a rope and an enormous slab of cured jerky came tumbling down. The golden female simply shouldered it and kept moving. "This will be more than enough for both of you, but the Ape will need more, if last night was any indication." She gave him a knowing glance, eyes glowing with amusement. "Fruit will last the first day, so I will not give you a lot. Nuts will do well."

As she listed the foodstuffs, she brought them out of storage, putting them in small sacks and handing them to either Sifura or Tommen to carry. By the time they walked out of the building, it felt more like they were planning for the thirty-day trek instead of the seven-day trek. The golden female held out her arms, and Sifura handed over her bags; Tommen followed suit.

"Urasha will help you with your medical needs," the golden female told them.

"Thank you," Sifura said graciously.

Then they were on their way toward another building.

"Why the buildings if you guys are nomadic?" Tommen asked.

"Where else would we put our supplies between journeys?"

Sifura countered, looking at him like he was an idiot, which he probably was. "We keep everything together in case we must make a quick exit, that way we are not running here and there looking for food or supplies; we know where it is."

"What if someone steals it, like another faction or tribe? What if a wild animal breaks in?"

Sifura shook her head. "Eshi and Urasha are excellent guards themselves, and the other watchers would warn us of such a thing. And it is considered dishonorable to steal food from another faction or tribe, especially in the desert where food is so scarce."

Tommen raised a brow. "So then what do you fight over?"

"With the other tribes, the most we fight is over a disputed hunt, if two parties were hunting the same animal. Or if two come upon the same oasis and cannot both stay there. With the D'Bok in the east, it is most often over territory. What is sand is ours, whatever they claim. With the Ouin in the north, trade. We believe in quantity trade, but they trade in weight. We would trade one bow for one knife. They would trade one bow for ten knives that equal the weight of the bow." She shook her head as if in disbelief. "It is an ongoing and very frustrating thing. And with the Rupi in the west, territory again. They claim the Gin Jor take their land by force and so they must take ours. We tell them they must take back their land for they will find no free land here."

"Why not help the Rupi fight the Gin Jor and take their land back?"

"The Gin Jor are very powerful. From their land comes most of the mined metals that they trade to the other tribes and eventually reach us. That trade is worth more to us than the plight of a cowardly tribe who will not fight for themselves."

That was a new side of things. Tommen had just as soon assumed that the tribes lived more or less in peace and harmony, one with nature and kum-ba-yah and whatever else. Now Sifura was admitting that she would rather see a tribe die for their supposed cowardice than take up arms to help them and possibly lose trade with the same force that was killing said tribe. Tommen had no reason to care about tribal politics, but, damn. Criminally negligent homicide, anyone?

They reached a smaller building and entered. Before Sifura could call a greeting, the same black and white female from the night before met them.

"Sifura," she greeted. She looked at Tommen. "Tommen Forbes."

"Urasha," Sifura acknowledged. "We have need of medical supplies."

"I know." Her voice was the epitome of a gentle bedside manner, and she appeared not to suffer from any sort of hangover like the rest of them did. "When you spoke of taking a skimmer to the D'Bok, I began preparing supplies for you." She turned and began rummaging around in various bins of all sizes, shapes, and smells. "With the long days, the xur should be slow and sedentary, but you cannot be too careful. You do not want to get caught unawares."

"We must prepare for all scenarios."

"Indeed." Urasha indicated what looked like old wineskins from medieval times, all laid out on a bench. Each had a different leaf or flower burned into the leather sides. She pointed to each one, naming the plant and its uses. Tommen tried to memorize all of them, but he knew he would forget.

"Of course, I do not need to tell you all of this," Urasha finished, looking at Sifura with pride in her eyes. "You were Firix's best pupil before you became leader."

"Yes, but I know I have forgotten much of what he taught, thanks to your skills," Sifura replied, just as proud.

Urasha turned to Tommen, shooting a glance at Sifura who barely nodded. "I do not know or understand your people. The supplies I have will work for us, and if you must use them, then use them. The worst they can do is kill you, but what good is there in killing a man who is going to die anyway?" Immediately, all fuzzy thoughts about this woman being the epitome of a good bedside manner vanished. "Still, I wish you a safe journey and that you will not need these things."

Tommen cleared his throat. "If it makes you feel any better, I brought some of my own supplies for just such an occasion."

As Sifura translated, he could see the relief spreading over Urasha's face. "Very good. I am glad. You are a credit to your faction and your tribe. Travel safely. And if possible, I do wish to know how this all turns out in the end for your people."

"I'll do my best."

"Wonderful." Urasha collected the various skins. "I will take these to your skimmer. I heard you speaking with Eshi, and I know Shashef and Sarabi have already gathered the gifts you are to take to the D'Bok." She again glanced at Tommen. "If you have any hope of saving your people, I urge you to leave as soon as possible."

"We are already late," Sifura sighed. "We must leave quickly."

Urasha nodded, and they followed her out of the building and across the clearing toward the sand. It was lighter now, the sun making the golden sand glitter and the white sand blinding. Only the bands of black sand provided any visual relief.

Tommen's toes had just gone from dirt and grass to sand and grass, like an ungroomed beach, when they suddenly hit wood. He cursed softly and stopped to nurse his stubbed toes. One nail had broken off at the end and there was a little blood, but otherwise he appeared to be fine. He looked up to see both women had stopped. Urasha looked concerned while Sifura already looked exasperated.

"I'm fine," he said. "Let's keep moving."

Great. Sifura already thought he was an imbecile; she didn't need to think him a wimpering child, too. Was she having second thoughts about helping him? He hoped not because they were just about to leave.

The wood eventually appeared out of the sand and almost looked like a small sandy harbor, the wood laid out like dock sections. He followed them down a long stretch of dock where they stopped.

The thing they came upon, laden with their food and medicine and several unknown bags of what Tommen assumed to be gifts, was unlike anything he could have imagined to get them across the sand at any rate of speed, never mind turning a thirty-day walk into a seven-day ride.

The first thing that came to mind was a paddle boat, the kind old ladies sat in to go cruising around the lake because they didn't like going on speed boats. The second thing that came to mind was a modified water wheel, this thing using sand instead of water for propulsion. The third thing that came to mind was a riverboat, like the kind in New Orleans and all around the southern coast for tours around the bayous and stuff.

This thing, this skimmer as he presumed it to be, was like all of those things kind of put together. It was small like a paddle boat; with all their cargo, they would be lucky to find a comfortable sleeping position. The propulsion was big like a riverboat with the same basic concept as a water wheel. A canopy of woven leaves shaded the deck.

"The smallest and fastest of the skimmers," Urasha told them as they stepped onboard. The deck was probably the most modern-looking thing Tommen had seen. All the planks were smooth and precise, as if they'd come straight from a lumberyard. "It is designed for one person to move comfortably, or two people to move efficiently. If you reach the maximum speed with a good rhythm, it may even take some time off your journey."

It was the best news Tommen could have heard. Even if he had to row this thing by hand, he would do it. Sifura stood to one side of the enormous water wheel-esque thing and motioned for him to copy her on the opposite side.

The specific mechanics of the propulsion were a mystery as they were hidden beneath the deck, but the basic idea to make it go was, at first, once Urasha gave them a good push off the dock, similar to drilling an ice fishing hole by hand. It was strange and clunky as Tommen and Sifura worked to get into an effective rhythm, but once he caught on, they started picking up speed. With his back to the prow, Tommen wasn't sure if it was the wind from the desert or wind from the speed that whipped his hair around his face, turning a visual task into one that was accomplished by feel only.

Was his hair really getting that long?

Once they got up to a certain speed, Sifura directed him to stop turning the mechanism, and start pushing and pulling, which created a noise that sounded kind of like a blacksmith bellows, yet propelled them even faster until Tommen's back was burning from the work and the wind rather than the sun.

Eventually, Sifura, with one arm still working away at pushing and pulling her rod in time with Tommen, moved and knelt, reaching for something along one side of the skimmer. It took several tries, but eventually she pulled a third rod out of hiding. Slowing only slightly, she inserted one end of the rod into her mechanism, then lowered the other end toward Tommen so he could do the same thing.

The third rod allowed for one person to operate the skimmer while also acting as a steering mechanism. He watched Sifura for a few minutes, awed by the astounding technology of a seemingly primitive people. He looked back at the oasis, already a tiny island on the horizon.

"Rest," Sifura told him. "Sit. Band this skimmer, so we may reach the D'Bok in time."

Oh. Right. They were going fast, just not fast enough.

Reluctantly, Tommen sat, not sure if he would be getting up again anytime soon. His body relaxed as soon as he leaned back against his sack.

Don't fall asleep, he told himself.

Then he Banded. Immediately, the sand whipped up by the skimmer and distant winds stopped. The sun, hovering just over the horizon, stopped. It was as though everything stopped. Soon enough, when he looked behind them, the oasis had gone, and there was nothing but black, gold, and white sand as far as the eye could see.

He checked his watch again. Not even one o'clock on Earth. Friday morning. Technically, he had two days to accomplish a seven-day mission. He could do this. Easily.

He looked at Sifura at the stern. She was still having to push and pull the rods, but she did it with a rhythm and grace that made it look like a dance. Except she was one bad ass ballerina, with hard shoulders and a strong back. Every muscle was working, even her tail as it kept her balanced when they occasionally hit a bump or a wave in the sand.

"Um, let me know if you need a break," Tommen offered weakly, standing despite his body's protests.

She glanced back at him momentarily, then returned to her work. "I can do this for a long time. You must hold your Band for as long as you can."

"Yes, but I can still work."

"When you are becoming tired and wavering, then you will work here for a time. Then you will sleep. But we have much ground to cover and not a lot of time."

He hesitated. "Maybe we can take turns? I can't Band while I'm asleep, but I don't want to sleep for too long."

She grinned, her fangs pretty and yet horrifying at the same time. "Don't worry, Tommen Forbes. This is not the first time I have had to make such a crossing. Rest. Band."

Reluctantly, he sat down. He wished he had brought sunglasses or something. Time had stopped, which meant they were literally running into sand suspended in the air. Though, it did help that air was not affected, so they were still getting a pretty good breeze. He entertained himself by trying to judge their speed. Faster than a bicycle, that was for sure, but not quite as fast as some of the cars that zipped by on the road in front of the house, faster than the posted thirty-five. The best he could come up with was somewhere between twenty and thirty miles per hour.

So if the days here were shorter than Earth's, say sixteen hours instead of twenty-four, and if they were moving at thirty miles per hour for at least twelve of those hours...

And if another train leaves station B moving at forty miles per hour, but Train B has twenty cars where Train A has fifty cars, he thought ruefully. He grinned to himself and shook his head. Probably one of the few times math had ever meant anything outside the classroom, and even now it wasn't terribly important. Well, it probably was, if he cared to sit down and focus on the problem and actually solve for the variables and figure out their speed and then figure out the relationship of their time to Earth time. But he had neither the variables, nor the ability, nor the time, nor the patience to work out such things.

Instead, he had only the desert, the skimmer, the skimmer's hot driver, and a hope that they would make it across the desert in time to barter for only the chance that the cure was the one he needed in order to save his dad.

Tommen tried any number of things to first take his mind off his problems and the whole reason he was out in this desert in the first place. He tried thinking of all the schoolwork he still had to make up for the weeks that he was gone. Then he decided he didn't want to think about that. He tried imagining all the chaos that had gone on at the bakery the previous day, how many pissy customers there had been, how many inconsolable, how many with kids. He tried to think of their normal numbers and their holiday numbers and see if he could guess how many of each item had been sold, how many cakes and cookies and pies and loaves of bread and so forth.

When that bored him, he thought about his upcoming review. The knowledge part was the one he was most unsure of, even if he had demonstrated time and again that he knew his stuff. But what he knew and what they would ask him to know could be two completely different things. Especially if they had a vendetta against him, they could ask him questions which he shouldn't know the answers to. One way, he failed the knowledge part of the test. The other, he was indicted for being a traitor and possibly a Runner.

Eventually he found himself amazed at how much time he spent griping about being told what to do and when to do it with very little time for himself, and yet now that he was presented with a full week to basically do—or at least think about whatever he wanted, he was bored within a day. He found that he wanted someone to tell him what to do. He wanted Walter to tell him to study for his upcoming test, or Micah to tell him to think about why their new recipe hadn't turned out right and what they could do to improve.

He checked his watch, as he had been every five minutes for the last however many hours, even though he knew nothing would change. It was still barely one o'clock in the morning on Earth. Still just after dawn here on this world. And yet they had been skimming for probably six hours now, and Sifura showed no signs of slowing down.

"So how did you get mixed up in the Time industry?" Tommen asked loudly, trying to be heard over the sound of the wind and the propulsion.

Sifura looked at him, and for a second he was afraid that she wouldn't answer. Then, "It was an accident, really, long before I was the leader of my people. I was out on my first hunt as an adult of the tribe, trying to prove myself worthy of being a sifura. I was determined to be the one to bring in the xur for that year's Day of the Sun feast.

"I found a xur, but it had found something else. A Scout had come to our world and was attacked by a xur. I rushed to help him, when I saw him do something incredible. The xur had caught him by surprise, but now he was ready for its next attack, one that would have surely killed him because he was inexperienced. But as the xur charged and was on him, he had only to touch it, and it died at his feet, a snarl still upon its lips.

"Immediately I was afraid, but as you can see, there is nowhere to hide. The Scout saw me, and I had no choice but to approach, announcing my original intentions of helping him.

"He was Araxi, if you are familiar with them. In Time, he was an Intervention Harvester. Intervention and Triage Harvesters are capable of Harvesting anything at just a touch, regardless of the health of the victim. I did not know this at the time, only that he had done something miraculous. I asked him how he had done it. He asked if I wanted to learn. Foolishly, I said yes.

"He took the Time Capsule he'd gained from the xur and anointed me with it, giving me enough of an awareness that, with practice, he was able to bring me fully into Time and begin teaching me how to be a Harvester. He did not say it like that, of course, instead having me believe that his people were great and powerful, and he would teach me their secrets that I could teach my people.

"Finally, I asked him how I might teach my people. That was when he said I was now ready to begin the next step of my training, and then I could train my people. So he took me to the Wheel."

"That could not have been good," Tommen said.

"It wasn't. I was so afraid that I ran. I did not speak to him for a long time. Finally, I did return to him to ask him questions. We talked for a long time, over many days when I was able to get away, and eventually I became more involved in the Wheel and the Hands, but my people know nothing of Time. And I would intend that it says that way."

"I don't blame you."

They skimmed in silence for a time. Then she spoke again. "How did you become involved in Time?"

Tommen shifted uncomfortably. He'd never told anyone how he'd become a Timekeeper, beyond those who needed to know or knew by association, like the twins. He hesitated at first, then figured he had to get it out and move on.

"An accident, like you," he began haltingly. "I was only a child. I lived with my ma and pa and brother and sisters. I liked exploring, and I would go off on my own to explore anything and everything. There was a cave not far from our home that had been sealed off for a long time, but I got in. I explored. When I came out, I had jumped a hundred and fifty years into the future. The cave itself had been Banded, and I just got caught in the middle of it."

"None of your family survived?"

"No. Most humans won't live more than ninety years. After a

century and a half, I was alone. When I walked out of the cave, I was hit by a c—a skimmer, and taken to the hospital. When no family could be found, I went to stay with the man who found me. He ended up adopting me."

"Your father, whom you are trying to save."

"That's right."

"You have no mother?"

Tommen shook his head even though she couldn't see. "Not anymore."

"That is a terrible thing."

He shrugged. "It's all right. I've gotten by."

Thus ended the conversation. They continued to skim, flying across the sand like a boat through calm water. Eventually, Tommen felt fatigue creep up on him. He still had a hangover, hadn't slept well, and it was getting harder and harder to hold his Band. Finally, he felt a tap on the shoulder. It was Sifura's tail. Without a word, she gestured to one of the containers of water, or what he presumed to be water. Yeah, he was sheltered from the sun and the morning wasn't nearly as hot as the day, but he should still—

"It will keep you awake," she told him as he took a container. "Then you will come and pull."

Well, it wasn't the same as the nice little honey flower that she'd given him when they first reached the oasis, but he still felt the effects just as quickly, and it was like coffee got hyped up on coffee and then introduced to espresso, but without the funky jitters that coffee gave him. When he went to relieve Sifura on the rudder and start pulling, aside from the tingling and itching and pain of his sunburn, he felt like he had the energy and strength to do the job.

That sort of gung-ho willpower lasted only about twenty minutes when his body decided that nice, easy, rhythmic work was more like super intense hot pilates or something. It was a full body workout, no doubt about that, and one he'd never had to do before today. His arms killed, his back screamed, and his thighs were as tight as strings on a fiddle.

He powered through the agony for another twenty minutes to half an hour, telling himself that he needed to build strength anyway, that he shouldn't be such a wimp in front of Sifura, that he shouldn't have to rely on her completely for everything like a scared child. He ought to pull his weight on this venture, too. But even those thoughts didn't last more than the ten minutes it took for his brain to gasp them out, and soon their pace began to slow. Sifura stood and effortlessly moved him off to the side so she could take over.

"We will go a bit longer. Then we must both rest."

It wasn't a pleasant thing to do, in Tommen's mind, especially when he felt responsible for the delay. But they did not stop for very long, and it developed into a routine. Sifura would pull, then Tommen would pull, each time trying to go just a little longer until he estimated that he could go for about two hours before almost collapsing. Then Sifura would pull again, and then they would stop and rest for three or four hours before continuing.

The only time Tommen really slept was during the three or four hours of rest. It wasn't the eight or ten hours that he would have preferred, but it really was better than trying to Band for seven straight days. Combined with the magic coffee drink, he was able to stay awake and moderately strong without too much sleep-deprived crankiness.

Their conversation was limited to the point of nonexistence. Except for occasionally asking to try the food that the other brought, they were a quiet pair. Tommen finished off the fruit, and Sifura chomped away on the cured meat. She didn't care for his version of jerky. When he told her that the jerky he made instead of the stuff he bought, which was the stuff he had with him now, was much better, it turned into a conversation about his home life with his ma and pa and the old way of doing things.

Holding a conversation while pulling only exhausted him faster, however, and soon Sifura was back on the rudder. But even she did not pull as long as she normally did, and soon they were stopping.

"It is near dark," she said. "It will be too dangerous to continue until dawn."

That might have alarmed Tommen more if he didn't know that even with the sun disappearing below the horizon, it would be rising again in about four or five hours. He checked his watch. They'd been going for five days now, and it was still Friday on Earth, three in the afternoon.

"How much time do we have left?" Sifura inquired, looking over his shoulder but not understanding.

"More than enough," Tommen told her. "More than a full day, almost two full days."

She sat down beside him. "Good. Tomorrow, if we both work hard, we should reach the border with the D'Bok swiftly, the Bodek faction. Their camp is not far from the border, and we will hopefully have the cure in our hands before the day is over. Then you can return to your people and heal your father."

Tommen looked at her. "What you said the other night, at the feast, about our people being allies and coming to each other's aid and all that."

"Yes?"

"What did you mean by that? I thought you said you aren't asking anything in return for your help?"

Sifura sighed, the kind of sigh that said that something got lost in translation. "What I mean is that we are not bartering for this service. I am not saying to you, give me something and I will help you. Or if I help you, you must give me something in return. But is it unreasonable to expect that if we have some need in the future, that we can count on you to at least take notice and offer help if possible, because of how I am helping you today?"

Tommen rubbed his face. "No, it's not. It's very reasonable."

"You are exhausted. Sleep. I will rise with the dawn, and we will continue."

She stood, grabbed a rolled up woven mat that had been packed with their supplies, and found a spot on the sand. After a moment, Tommen did the same. The air had cooled, but the sand was comfortably warm, like the waterbed that Walter had slept in for years before it sprung a leak, but less wavy. He spread out his mat and lay down, but for as exhausted as he was, the moment his head hit the sand, he was wide awake.

He was thirsty. Grudgingly, he got up and rummaged around in his bag until he found a bottle of water, one of the last ones. Sifura did not drink much, he noticed, even after she'd been pulling long and hard for hours on end. Maybe her body was more efficient with its water usage. Maybe she could store it like a camel. Either way, he did not drink it all, just enough to hopefully trick his mind into shutting down enough to drift off. Then he returned to his mat. His mind was still wide awake.

He had to pee. He tried for several agonizing minutes to think of anything else before relenting. Slowly he got up and went off a short distance to relieve himself. He grinned to himself at the memory of him standing up on the skimmer and walking to the edge. Sifura calmly warned him to stand back lest they hit a bump and he fall off. The look on her face when he took his dick and started peeing over the side while they were moving was absolutely priceless. Their next rest stop entailed a fairly long and detailed explanation of human anatomy, including sexuality and reproduction. He couldn't decide if it had been sheer curiosity on her part, wanting to know how and why they were different, and her own culture's form of reproduction making her ignorant of the embarrassment of discussing such awkward and intimate topics; or if it was some sort of revenge for what he did, and in addition to learning more about him, she got to see him squirm a little.

He also couldn't decide if that counted as a simple anatomy lesson within a cultural exchange, or if he was in danger of lapsing back into his addiction. If a recovering heroin addict was asked by the DEA task force to demonstrate how to shoot up for the benefit of new recruits, and he did so with concentrated poppy seed juice—assuming that would work anyway—was that a simple lesson, or would it actually have some sort of high effect that would hinder the addict's recovery? And who would be at fault if it did? More to the point, why did he suck at analogies?

No, not the time to start thinking about that, Tommen scolded himself, shaking and then returning again to his mat. Sifura was already asleep, but even watching her slow, even breaths did nothing to put his mind to rest.

He was hungry. His stomach gave a sudden growl, loud enough that he was sure Sifura would snap awake and jump to attention, ready for whatever predator hunted them.

Crying a little on the inside, Tommen hauled himself to his feet again and went to his bag. It was a little roomier now since he'd gone through some of the waters and been able to condense the food down to a single sandwich baggie plus the bag of trail mix which was almost gone. He didn't throw any of his stuff away off the side of the skimmer, just kept it all bundled together to throw away when he got home. But empty bags took up much less room than bags full of food.

As he nibbled on some jerky, Tommen also reflected that so far, while they had seen some wildlife in the distance, they had been otherwise alone. Nothing had come sniffing around their camp at night to steal food, and they certainly hadn't been attacked by anything. Sifura remained on high alert, however. She slept lightly, deep enough to be rested, light enough that she could be ready before Tommen could shout for help twice.

Supposedly he'd done that at least once, shouted in his sleep. When Sifura finally managed to wake him and calm him down, he couldn't even remember the dream, though he could guess. They'd started out early that day. Ever since, he guessed he slept pretty well, as she hadn't had to wake him again, nor did she say anything about it.

After a time, Tommen put away the jerky, stood, and stretched. His body screamed in protest. Thanks to the canopy on the skimmer, he'd avoided making his sunburn any worse, but now it was peeling something awful, painful and beyond itchy. Plus he was putting his body through the most intense workout he'd ever had to endure.

He thought about his pa and brother, how hard they worked every day, pa on the farm, Teo in the mines. Even his ma had been a champion for working hard. Tommen had been getting to that point, dutifully following his pa around the farm and the forest, helping him in his work and chores, imitating him as best he could. At eight years old, he wasn't allowed to wield the ax yet, but he could set the log and carry and stack the firewood. He couldn't train an unbroken colt, but he could work with the gentler horses. He couldn't get the stubborn donkey to move, but he could wrestle rams and bucks well enough.

Modern life had made him soft. He probably couldn't even do an afternoon of wood if he tried, never mind doing this full body workout for more than a couple hours. Sifura could heave and haul and pull for eight hours at a time and hardly break a sweat.

After coming out of his stretch, he returned to his mat, determined to get at least a little sleep. Everything was still Banded, the Band dissipating only once he actually fell asleep. He'd gotten food, water, gone to the bathroom. He should be able to sleep now.

It had been a week since he brushed his teeth. Sparse eating had spared him too much discomfort, but it was one modern amenity he did not see a reason to protest.

Tommen rolled over and rubbed his face. No, no, no! He needed to sleep. They were finally going to get the cure tomorrow, which meant he needed to sleep so he could be on top of his game so he could work with Sifura to get the cure instead of making a fool of himself and having to run to her for help. If the D'Bok were as hostile as everyone seemed to be claiming, he could not be seen as a coward who ran away.

Guess all that fighting with Tyler Freeman does come in handy sometimes. First it helped you in a fight with Cassius — sort of — and now you're going to potentially use it when negotiating with a hostile alien race. Some things they don't teach you in school. Yes, Mr. Layman, I would like to give a presentation about how fist fighting can help you when talking to alien species.

Tommen chuckled to himself. He would get locked up in the loony bin for that one, he was sure.

He groaned and rolled over. Sleep. Not humor. No more thinking, no more thoughts. Sleep, sleep only. But his mind was swirling with a thousand things that were less than thoughts, only images and perceptions. A face, a memory, a name, a what if. Tommen sighed and rubbed his eyes. It was going to be a long night.

Chapter Nineteen
Xur

At some point, Tommen figured he must have slept because the next thing he knew, Sifura was shaking him awake. He groaned and reached down as if looking for a blanket to pull over his head. He found none. Grudgingly, he waited a second or two before opening his eyes and sitting up.

The sky was still mostly black, but there was just a streak of gray on the horizon. Looking at the sky, Tommen found crisp, black ink dotted with little white specks that were not his stars, but those of an alien world. There was no Big Dipper here, no Leo, or Taurus, or Orion. Here they had their own stars, their own names, their own mythology. He saw only a small sliver of a moon, far away.

Tommen rolled off his mat and began rolling it up. At the skimmer, he saw Sifura checking their stuff as she did every morning, though she moved with an unusually hurried pace.

"What's the rush? I don't think we overslept," Tommen said, stifling a yawn. He felt like he hadn't gotten much more than a two-hour nap or something. Given how long it took him to fall asleep and how short the nights were, he probably had only gotten two or three hours.

"We are being hunted," Sifura hissed. "We must move quickly."

"Hunted?" Tommen echoed.

He stood, mat under his arm. He looked around but everything was still dark. That was the thing about the desert, it was either all light or all dark. There was very little no vegetation to break up the view, break up the light; it was all or nothing. Right now, he saw nothing. He didn't hear anything either, but that was nothing new. With a sudden realization, he threw up a Band.

"It will do us no good," Sifura told him. "The thing that hunts us is immune to Time. Best to not Band and let the sun rise that we may see. Your night vision is poor; it puts you at a disadvantage in a fight."

Tommen dropped the Band, knowing she was right. At this time of day, he was blind and deaf. Anything that hunted them would have no trouble picking him off for a light snack. Keeping one eye on the horizon, he tossed the mat on the skimmer and joined Sifura at the rudder to heave and haul and get the thing moving again fast enough until she could take over.

"What is it that hunts us?" Tommen asked, forcing his cramping muscles to obey him for just one last stretch of skimming.

"The xur," Sifura replied.

Tommen grunted as he felt his hands slipping and he redoubled his grip. "What is the xur to you? It hunts you, you hunt it, and yet you seem to revere it. You grow your children from its hair. I don't understand."

"The xur is our enemy as much as our protector. It guides us in life, gives us wisdom and courage. But the xur is a beast also, and all beasts must hunt and eat to survive."

Sounded schizophrenic to him, but whatever made her happy. At least she was somewhat enlightened to the larger view of things, having been exposed to Time.

The pulling started to get away from him, and Tommen stepped back to let Sifura take the sole reign. She'd always worked hard to keep the skimmer moving as fast as she could, but now she seemed to really put her back, her whole body and soul into the pulling, and they skimmed and skipped along the sand faster than they had all week.

Tommen checked his watch. Just past six in the evening on Friday night. So they hadn't even slept three hours before having to leave, and Sifura was putting everything she had into their apparent escape.

"How will we know if we've escaped the xur?" Tommen inquired.

"The guardian beasts are bound by their territory," Sifura explained. "The xur cannot leave the desert as the d'bok cannot leave the jungle, nor the gin jor the mountains. We will be safe only once we are with the D'Bok."

"They're not likely to turn us away, are they?"

"No. It is dishonorable to turn a person in imminent danger away from sanctuary. Such a thing would dishonor the D'Bok in such a way that no other tribe would wish to acknowledge them for ten generations. There would be no trade, no assistance, no words spoken. They would become more isolated even than my people."

Well, it was a promising start, anyway. And hey, if simple chitchat wasn't enough to convince the D'Bok border patrol to let them in to speak to their leader, maybe running away from a ferocious xur would be enough.

Tommen glanced at the horizon where the sun had just peeked over the farthest hills and set the desert on fire in huge shining swaths of black, gold, and white. Ahead, in the distance, he saw only sand.

"How long until we reach the D'Bok?"

"Perhaps six Base Hours, less if I am able to keep up this speed."

"If you need me to take over for a while so you can rest a little more—"

"No. You are not strong enough to keep up the pace. Our only chance now is to outrun it."

Tommen looked past Sifura where they left a wide wake in the sand. "How do you know it's hunting us? How do you know where it is?"

"The xur is part of us; you saw it yourself. It is the same way new parents know when their child is ready to be taken. The same way a mother knows when her child is upset or hungry or hurt. It lives within us. So we also know when a xur is close by, and what its intentions are."

"All right, I'll bite, what are the intentions of this xur?"

"To hunt. To kill. To eat. It is very hungry; he has not eaten for many days."

Tommen swallowed. "You went from saying 'it' to saying 'he.' Is that just the translators or was that intentional pronoun choice?"

"I learn more about the xur the closer he gets."

"Do you know where he is exactly?"

Sifura huffed. "Only that he is behind us, running, gaining."

"What do you want me to do?"

"Look ahead. Tell me when you see the D'Bok territory in the distance. Once we are within range, come back and we will have to pull with everything we have."

"A sprint to the finish line."

"Exactly. Go. Do."

Tommen went to the front of the skimmer, but all he could see was sand and desert. Almost instinctively now, he put up a Band.

"Your Band will do us no good, Tommen Forbes," Sifura said over her shoulder. "Best to save your energy."

He looked back at her. "It doesn't take much energy anymore. And regardless of whatever is following us, I'm looking ahead to where we're going. We're still on a schedule, we're still racing against the clock, and I don't intend to be late for this appointment."

For a long moment, Sifura did not say anything. Finally, "Very well then. But Time means nothing to the xur. Can you fight?"

"Um, not really. I mean, I've fought other people and some goats."

"Then you mean nothing to the xur either. Look ahead."

Tommen turned his attention to the landscape ahead, which was still little more than sand and desert as far as the eye could see. With his Band in place, the only thing in motion was the air around them and, if Sifura was to be believed, a very ferocious and very hungry creature behind them.

He checked his watch again, as if expecting any difference.

Six hours to the jungle. Fuck, that never sounded like so long in his life. Six hour shift at work? Child's play compared to this. Six hour trip to the store for school supplies? Piece of cake. Six hours to reach the safety zone and not get eaten by a desert beast? Fuck no.

He kept looking behind him as much as he kept an eye on the horizon. Mostly he just wanted to make sure Sifura was still there, and she was. Finally, she'd broken a sweat. She looked as worried and exhausted as he felt after just a couple hours on the rudder. While it was nice to know she wasn't some super animal goddess who had infinite strength, there was a certain disappointment, too. And a certain kind of alarm that when she got worried and tired, something was very, very wrong, and it might just be time to bend over and kiss your butt goodbye.

More than once he thought about asking her how it was going, where the xur was, how far to the jungle. He never did, figuring it would either break her intense concentration or else annoy her, kind of like the kid asking "Are we there yet?" every five minutes of a ten-hour car ride. Not that Tommen had ever done that, of course.

Once, he thought he spotted the jungle in the distance, only to realize it was a larger than normal rise. When they safely navigated it, he turned back to see how Sifura was faring. She looked run ragged, but she was determined. Then he realized that the look in her eye was not of the leader of a great tribe or faction, but one of fear. She was a mighty warrior and hunter, but now she was the prey, and she was running like prey.

"How far do you think?" Tommen asked, hoping he sounded encouraging.

Sifura opened her mouth to speak when suddenly her ears pricked up and she turned her head. She whipped around, completely letting go of the rudder and looked about ready to say something...

Then Tommen felt himself lifting off the deck of the skimmer, still going twenty-five, thirty miles an hour, full speed through the air. He was no cat and had no instincts about which way to turn in the air to not hurt himself, but he knew enough about physics to be able to judge his trajectory. In the dim light, he could see the Predict path of his own fall. He dropped his larger Band and instead focused on a smaller Band just around himself, enough that he was able to turn himself around and try to land safely.

As he did so, he saw Sifura in full cat-twist, clawing for the right direction, spinning so she could make a smooth landing.

Tommen's landing was less smooth. Even as much as he got himself in a better position than the back of his neck, landing first on his shoulder, then his head, then his hip, then tumbling ass over head down a small depression before coming to a stop in a sand pile that partially buried him, all at approximately thirty miles an hour, was still incredibly painful. He couldn't even groan in pain for the sand in his mouth and the ringing in his ears.

He barely registered all of this before bringing his arms up to shield himself from flying debris. Wood and leaves and iron bars from the skimmer rained down around him, sticking him in several places with cuts and not a few splinters. Something moderately soft hit him in the head; it looked like one of the medicine skins. Elsewhere, supplies were scattered across the sand for probably forty yards or more. All their food, water, medicine, strewn about like candy from a piñata.

For a moment, Tommen wasn't sure it was smart to try and dig himself out. Maybe if he stayed hidden, the xur would pass him over. At the same time, if Sifura had been worried about it, that meant it was a formidable foe and probably wasn't going to back down. She'd fought these things before, she'd said, but it had probably been closer to home and with reinforcements within range of help. Here, they had no reinforcements. No one would be coming to save them, no matter how many times he shouted.

Groaning and still spitting sand, Tommen wriggled his arms free of the sand and managed to wiggle the rest of his body into a position where he could slowly pull himself out of the hole he'd buried himself in. The grit of the sand alerted him to every cut, scratch, and splinter that had been inflicted upon him from the debris, but he bit his tongue to keep from crying out. Better to assess the situation quietly than call attention to himself before he was ready. Not that he would ever be ready, necessarily.

He stood and immediately went back to his knees, head spinning. No, he couldn't have hit the ground that hard. He just needed a second to collect himself, that was all. He closed his eyes, tried to focus. The hair on the back of his neck stood up as he realized that it was way too quiet. They'd just been attacked; he should be hearing something. Snarls, screams, anything. Gritting his teeth and biting his tongue, Tommen stood again, fighting the vertigo and following his trail back to the crash site.

As he crested the hill, he paused, almost stunned by the creature before him who was currently distracted by Sifura.

Initially, just based on the physiology of the Xur tribe and seeing and understanding a little more about how they reproduced and were biologically related, he'd assumed that the xur creature was something like a lion of a different color. Well, the beast before him might have been considered a lion, if Pablo Picasso and Salvador Dali decided to collaborate on a painting of a lion, started arguing over how to do it, and each artist just began adding random elements to the lion painting according to his own style, and then both artists stormed off in an angry huff, leaving the painting ultimately unfinished.

And Tommen had seen some ugly cats in his day. Mr. Henderson down the road had a cat that always had fleas and allergies and bit and scratched at itself until it was torn and bloody, like it had mange and gotten in a fight in the alley. Plus it was old, too stubborn to die, and had a number of old injuries that had effectively maimed its body anyway, so it looked like the stuff of nightmares, and it had the personality to match.

This thing, though, was far more than any of that. It took a second for Tommen to realize that amidst the black, gold, and white fur which was stringy and tattered, it had four eyes and four ears. The ears were in two more or less symmetrical sets, one pointed like

Sifura's, and one round like the Xur males. The eyes were less than symmetrical, or matching in any way. They were distributed haphazardly across a scarred face that looked like a recovering stroke victim, and a blunt, deformed muzzle where kinky whiskers stuck out at every angle. The xur's mane looked like a coon fur that Tommen had tried and failed to tan; it had been extremely greasy, and he hadn't washed it thoroughly enough before doing the final brain tan so it came out looking and feeling like a greasy, snarled, tangled ball of hairy shit.

The rest of the xur was just as bad. At least a lion had sleek fur and smooth, rippling muscle. With this thing, even the muscles didn't seem to move correctly; there was nothing fluid about the way it moved, no feline grace at all. It was more like a drunk greyhound. Skinny hips jutted out from the fur, and bony legs supported its entire mass, talon-like toes spread wide over the sand with the same webbing that Sifura had to keep her on top of the sand. Its bony tail lashed back and forth, something like the remains of a tuft drooping sadly from the end of it.

Despite everything that was happening, that they were in the middle of a very vicious attack, Tommen found that his first thought was, This *is your spirit animal?* This *thing?*

All of this passed through his mind in the space of a second or two, then the xur sprang.

Sifura had brought several weapons with her for just such an event, but they were all lost in the debris now, and the only thing she had to hand was a long piece of wood from the skimmer, broken so the end was jagged and sharp. Rather than move to the side of the xur as it sprang, she darted forward, under the massive creature which must have stood ten or twelve feet tall. She dragged the pointed end of the spear across its belly, but it did little damage, hardly more than a scratch.

Still, she followed the xur's movements as it moved forward and back and around, trying to get her where it could attack, and still she kept jamming the wood at its belly, looking for some kind of weakness.

Finally she faltered. Whether it was a motion from the xur or she tripped over some debris, Tommen could not tell, but she went down, and the xur got her out from under him. With a snarl, it raised a paw as if to crush her or swat her away.

"Hey! Over here!" His voice sounded distant.

The xur stopped, and all four of its ears began moving, trying to pinpoint the sound. Sifura took the opportunity to scramble out of the way. When the xur looked back at her, Tommen shouted again. "Hey! Big and mangy! Over here!"

Now the beast turned and looked at him with its four eyes. One was gold, another silver, and the other two he couldn't tell. But they were all fixated on him. It didn't run towards him either, which would have made it possible to simply run away. Instead, it crouched and pounced like a regular cat.

Tommen was able to stay out of reach of the claws, but the vibration from the heavy creature's landing still knocked him off his feet. The xur was quick and soon had him pinned under one massive paw.

Instead of eating him, however, the xur lowered its big ugly head and began sniffing him, its nose almost as big as Tommen's head, sending out puffs of hot air that smelled remarkably like citrus. It bumped his head a couple times with its nose and sniffed again, clearly trying to figure out what this thing was. It was a new thing. A plaything.

Tommen swallowed and was pretty sure he wet himself as the xur opened its mouth, revealing mottled white and black gums and two rows of sharp white teeth, almost like a shark. Before it could chomp down, however, it suddenly whipped its body around, snarling, swatting Tommen and sending him skidding into the sand once more, this time burying him face-first.

His first instinct was to gasp and bring in air, but he only found sand. Immediately his body went into panic mode and he began flailing, wiggling out of the sand in good time only from the sheer fact that he wasn't buried that deep to begin with. He spit out sand, tried to suck in breath, tried to calm down.

He got to his feet, wobbled. His head ached, but at least sounds were coming back to rights. He looked around and found Sifura facing off against the xur once more. While he'd distracted it, she had gone and found a spear which she now held, as well as a couple knives which she wore around her on a loose belt. Now she was drawing real blood from the xur, puncturing skin, slicing muscle and tendon. The xur turned this way and that, but for all its size and might, the goliath was losing.

Or so it seemed. Maybe it had all been a feint; maybe the xur was intelligent enough to set its own traps. Whatever the case, it let a back leg go out from under it while Sifura was poking at its belly. She got out of dodge of the beast coming down and crushing her, but as soon as the belly made a wall, the xur curled right up around her. Sifura tried to jump and climb over the creature's belly, but the xur hooked her with a deft claw and dragged her back down so Tommen lost all sight of her.

He looked around at the debris field for something, anything that might actually help. He spotted his burlap bag. It looked more or less intact, the top flipped open and a few things tumbled out. He raced toward it, sliding in the sand and reaching it with a greedy hand. He tore through the bag, thankful it wasn't very big, until he found the knife and the gun.

This time he wasn't going to announce his presence as the xur was still curled up facing away from him. Probably snacking on Sifura. But he wasn't going to give it time for seconds. As soon as Tommen was within comfortable range, he stopped his demented hop-running through the sand, pointed the gun at the base of the xur's skull, and fired.

The xur roared and looked around, but when it tried to get up, it couldn't, and Tommen could tell that this time wasn't a feint. He took aim again, this time at an eye. Now the roar turned to a terrified scream as the beast fell in the sand. By the time he was close enough to see that his aim had been true both times, within reason, the screams had turned to pitiful whimpers, like kittens mewling for their mother's milk.

Tommen walked up close to it, always keeping one eye on its paws, but they made no hostile move, or any move at all actually. The xur watched him through its three good eyes, all ferocity gone, replaced only by fear and pleading.

That was when Tommen knew he was dealing with an intelligent being. Maybe it didn't go to school or chart stars or complete complex math equations, but the xur had a higher form of understanding; at the least, it was probably self-aware. It wasn't thinking about escape now, as prey animals did up until the point they were hunted or butchered. The xur was facing the inevitability of its death, thus the fear, pleading only for him to make it a swift end. No more little wounds, only the killing blow.

So Tommen took the knife and drove it where he hoped the beast had an artery. He stepped out of the way as blood spurted from the wound and began flowing freely over the sand like a fast-flowing river. The light went out of the beast's eyes and left Tommen to wonder if he had seen all that he'd thought in the creature's eyes, the emotion, the fear, the intelligence. Or was it something he simply wanted to see, a reflection of his own emotions? The fear of death, the pleading for it to be a swift end. As the blood stopped flowing from the neck wound, Tommen realized that even if he could know for certain, it wouldn't have mattered.

Cautiously, he went around the front legs, past the scraggly mane, toward the belly.

"Sifura!"

The word was out of his mouth before he fully registered the scene. It wasn't actually as bad as his mind told him it was at first. Initially he thought she was dead, torn open as the xur had begun snacking on her. Then he came to realize much of the blood was from the wounds she'd inflicted on the xur's belly. Just from a visual examination, her injuries amounted to claw marks of varying depths to her arms and chest, as well as a long mark across her face.

At the sound of her name, Tommen saw an ear twitch. Her head rolled his way, and her eyes opened. As he knelt beside her, she groaned and tried to move.

"Don't move," he told her lamely. "I'll bring the supplies over here and get you stitched up right."

She didn't listen to him, continuing to move around slowly even as he stood and ran off to search the debris for the medical supplies. He found only two of the medicine skins Urasha had given them, but everything Micah had sent was still in or around the burlap bag. Tommen gathered all the medical supplies and as much food as he could handily grab, and hurried back to Sifura who had managed to sit up and rest against the xur's belly.

"Okay, you're going to have to tell me what's what here," Tommen said, showing her the medicine skins.

She looked at them, more with it than he probably gave her credit for. Finally she pointed to one. "Urikanax, to keep out infection."

Tommen nodded frantically, nervously. He set down the skin and brought out a bottle of sterile water from his bag. "Let's clean that wound first."

"Don't waste water on it," Sifura chastised him.

"It's not water. Well, it is, but it's not drinkable. It's for cleaning wounds only."

It's better than peroxide, Tommen almost said, then he figured that not only would she not get the joke, but it might not be entirely true anyway. Still, he was judicious with the water, using only enough to clean the sand and fur out of the wounds before opening one of the medicine skins and pouring out a goopy orange gel.

"Does it hurt?" Tommen asked as he applied the gel more generously than he had the water.

"The medicine takes away the pain," Sifura replied, gritting her teeth at first, then relaxing as he applied the gel to all the wounds. "Are you injured?"

"I'm fine. Nothing we can do about it here."

He should have stopped after the first sentence because then she became concerned. "Where are you hurt?"

Tommen sighed as he brought out the gauze roll. "My head got bumped around a little. I'm fine."

"You can see well?"

"Yes."

"You can hear well?"

He paused for a moment, then continued wrapping her arms. "Well, that's a relative term. I already have bad hearing." *And firing two gunshots with no ear protection probably didn't help it any either. I'm going to be completely deaf by the time I get home.*

"You can stand well?"

"I'm fine. I can stand, I can walk. Listen, we've got more important things to worry about. The skimmer is destroyed and you're injured. And if this thing had friends—"

Sifura shook her head. "No. Xur do not travel together except in mating season. He will have no friends close by, at least none close enough to bother us between here and D'Bok territory."

She tried to stand but went to a knee, er, hock, putting a hand to her calf where a puncture wound was just making itself known. She hissed in frustration as she shifted to get into a position where Tommen could treat that as well.

"I wish I knew how to double-Band or pinpoint Band, that way I could heal you quickly and we could get moving," he said as he wrapped the last of the gauze around the wound and taped it. "I mean, I don't know what we're going to do now. We're sitting ducks."

But the real fear that settled in his chest was that even though they won the battle and the xur was dead, they'd lost the war. They were out of time. They didn't have any kind of transportation, Sifura was wounded, and they didn't have the resources to stay in the desert for more than a day or two. Even if they did, Tommen couldn't keep a Band long enough to heal Sifura.

"Sitting ducks?" Sifura questioned.

"We're easy prey," he clarified sadly. "You can't walk, and I..." He sat back on his heels, then on his butt. "I just lost my dad."

She studied him for a minute or two, and he willed himself not to break down in front of her. They were within a day of getting the cure, and this ugly monstrosity had to go and ruin it all. So close and yet so far. Was it really all for nothing? Was the universe so against him that no matter where he went or what he tried, he was doomed to fail and Walter doomed to die? Was he so depressed he was now composing poetry in his mind?

"Band me."

Sifura's voice cut into his thoughts, and for a moment he couldn't understand her words. He blinked, realizing that tears had started to roll down his cheeks. He quickly wiped them away. "What?"

"Band me. A Fast Band, so my wounds can heal enough that I can move and we can continue."

"But, I—"

"You are on my world and came into my faction seeking my help. That means I am your leader and you will obey my orders. Now Band me!"

Tommen took a breath and nodded. He knew how to Band other things; he just wasn't sure she understood that she would be stuck in the Band for literally days, maybe even weeks. But she couldn't be stuck in one for weeks because once she came out, all her metabolic functions would catch up to her and she could instantly die of dehydration or starvation. The metabolic suspension was what eventually fucked up Timekeepers enough to make them all but immortal, and why Tommen had needed to be constantly eating on the skimmer, so that when he came out of the Bands, he didn't keel over. Maybe...

Trying to keep a clear head, Tommen Banded Sifura. A Fast Band, but not too Fast, he saw the slight sheen of the Band, barely perceptible, hardly noticeable until it was gone. Then he tried to focus the Band, will it just around her leg. He watched the Band fluctuate. He tried harder to bend it to his will, focusing all his efforts on the size, shape, and feel of the Band. It wiggled, started to move, refused. Biting his lip and putting one hand on Sifura's leg, he tried again, bulling his will against the Band, trying to connect the physical wound with his will so the Band might better understand what he wanted. Now it bent and moved a little, at least freeing Sifura's head so she would not have to be mentally stuck in the Band for days on end.

Tommen tried several more times to get the Band to move how he wanted it, but remained unsuccessful. He released the Band and lay back in the warm sand, breathing heavily. It had been way too long of a day, and he was exhausted. And they still had far to go.

When he sat up again, Sifura was unwrapping the gauze from her leg. The wound was still obvious, but the blood had clotted, and scar tissue had begun to form, leaving the wound about half-healed. As she unwrapped her arms and peeled the pad off her chest, Tommen saw they were all about in the same stage of healing.

"I'm sorry," he said meekly. "I tried to pinpoint Band so you wouldn't be stuck in there for days on end, but it didn't work."

"You are only a probationary Timekeeper," Sifura told him gently. "You cannot be expected to know everything yet. There is much you have yet to learn, but this will suffice for now. Do you have any food left?"

Tommen looked through his bag. "Some jerky and some trail mix. I'll split it with you."

"Hand me your knife there."

He did so and watched as Sifura turned around and sliced open the xur's belly. "It is a terrible waste to leave a carcass, but we have neither the means nor the time to process it and take it with us." She cut off a chunk of meat near the ribcage. "But it still has its purpose."

Tommen thought he was going to be sick.

"When I am done, we will continue our journey. We will walk."

Chapter Twenty
Borderlands

Tommen checked his watch. Surprisingly, it was only about six-thirty on Earth. He'd been terrified that they'd somehow magically jumped ahead a day or two during the fight. But they still had time. As he scarfed down the last of his trail mix and Sifura tested out the strength and maneuverability of her injured leg, he put up the same Fast Band he'd managed to perfect over six days on the sand skimmer.

Sifura was still reluctant to leave the xur carcass, but as she herself had said, they had no way to process and carry it with them. So she merely thanked her spirit animal guardian for the meat she'd taken off him and turned east, toward the D'Bok border. The going was slow. She tried to put on the same strong face she'd always had, but Tommen could see the leg wound was paining her.

"How did the xur go from being behind us and gaining, to suddenly crashing into us and destroying the skimmer?" Tommen inquired.

"The xur is immune to Time; I have told you this," Sifura replied. "I felt the xur only in the context of the Band you insisted on having up. The xur moved around this, around us, and surprised us. If you had refrained from Banding, we would have seen it come upon us."

"Oh." He paused. "I'm sorry. I guess I'm the one who got the skimmer destroyed, huh?"

"No, it is not your fault. The xur would have attacked either way, and the skimmer would have been just as likely to be destroyed."

"Does it take much to build a new one?"

"We must trade with the Ouin for the iron bars. Some of the wood we get ourselves, some we get from the D'Bok. It is something else I can discuss and arrange when we meet with them. The actual construction is the most time-consuming. For ten skilled workers, it takes approximately eighteen days of single labor to build a skimmer that small. The larger ones take longer."

They walked in silence after that, but only until they got to the top of a rise and finally the horizon was broken. There was something out there besides sand. First, there were teeny tiny trees, but as Tommen took in the wider landscape, he also saw mountains just outlined in the far, far distance.

"There it is!" he exclaimed and burst into stupid laughter.

Tommen had been getting into fights since third or fourth grade. Always him and Tyler Freeman. When Tommen got to the end of sixth grade, and Tyler eighth grade, Tommen was sure that South Charleston High School was going to be much tougher on Tyler and he would be expelled before Tommen ever got there in two years. He endured a number of bus beatings and random acts of street violence from Tyler just in the hopes that the bully would get expelled, get arrested, get kidnapped by aliens for all he cared, just something to get him out of the way so Tommen could enjoy his high school years (if such a thing was even possible).

So when Tommen finally got to high school, he was more than happy to look at his schedule and imagine the awesome possibilities of his classes (yes, he was that young and dumb once). The first class he had was gym. He walked into the locker room the first day of class, and the first person he saw was Tyler Freeman.

He'd burst out laughing. It wasn't even funny; there just wasn't any other feasible reaction. He couldn't challenge the bully, couldn't walk out and basically run away, and he certainly couldn't cry. All that left was loud, stupid laughter. It was just so unfair and yet so predictable, it had even become comfortable.

This laugh at finally seeing the end of the desert was similar to that, except there was nothing unfair about it. They'd finally made it to D'Bok territory. All they had left to do was go in, make nice with the locals, trade for the cure, and get out. It was so simple. It had to be simple. After all the shit they just went through, how could it not be any more simple?

"Tommen! Tommen!"

Sifura cut into his thoughts just as he realized he was stumbling and hit the sand, still laughing like an idiot. Above him, Sifura looked concerned.

"Tommen Forbes, are you all right?" she asked.

He laughed for a few seconds more, then contained himself, his mind finally coming back to him and demanding to know just what the hell had been so fucking hilarious. The demented part of his brain still said it didn't know. Eventually he took a breath and said, "I am just fine, thank you. I'm just so relieved."

She helped him up and studied him severely. "Tommen Forbes, are you all right? We are meeting with the D'Bok and we must be serious, ready to attack. We cannot act like children or idiots."

He took another breath and nodded. "Yes. Yes, I'm fine."

"You said you hit your head. You have been walking well, but are you all right?"

"I'm fine. I'm sorry. It's just...it reminded me of something and...I just needed the humor to stay sane."

Finally she dipped her head and took a step back. "Very well. But we must be serious now. The D'Bok enjoy humor, but only at the expense of others. Do not try to make fun of them or play games with them. Remain serious, very serious only. And tell only the truth, whatever they ask of you."

"Are the D'Bok part of Time?" Tommen questioned smartly.

"And one more thing. Let me do most of the talking. They are wary of new people and especially new tribes. We have lost our gifts to present to them and they will not be pleased."

Tommen dropped his bag. "No, we didn't lose our gifts." He

brought out the bags of coffee. "We have them right here."

"That is only your gift. I cannot present your gift as mine. It would be improper. But let me handle it. It is my problem. We are here for one primary purpose, and that is to acquire the cure for your father's illness." She gave him an uncertain look. "Perhaps your own problems will convince you of the severity of the illness."

Tommen gave himself a once-over. Six days of reprieve under the canopy of the skimmer, all gone to waste as his skin had burned again and he was now in various stages of burning and peeling, in some places both at the same time. He looked like a fucking leper or something. But maybe it would sway the D'Bok more towards mercy, if they were capable of such a thing, which he was beginning to doubt.

He replaced the coffee and slung the bag back over his shoulder. "Shall we?"

Sifura regarded him a moment longer before turning and walking away, minding her injuries without looking like she was minding them. After a minute or two of watching her, Tommen adjusted the bag and hurried after her.

Like when he'd followed her from the middle of the desert to the oasis, Tommen was almost sure the jungle was a mirage up until the point where he began to distinguish trees and branches and leaves. As before, the desert mixed with the forest, and scraggly bushes and withered grass poked up here and there in the sand before it gave way to moist, rich soil.

Tommen stopped just before the tree line, sickly grasses itching his ankles, looking up at the jungle. He'd kind of always assumed that forests and jungles were pretty much the same, jungles being a little warmer maybe and having a few more vines. Maybe that was true of Earth-side jungles, but this was not Earth, and this jungle was much, much more than just a forest with extra stuff.

The trees in this jungle were not quite as big as the giant trees at the oasis, but they were still huge, like the California redwoods that had small roads carved through them. The bark was a rich chocolate brown, but an injury to one tree revealed the pulp to be bright yellow with an indeterminate pattern swirling within it. Some trees had low-hanging branches with little bluish fruits that put Tommen in mind of soccer balls. Other trees had branches that reached up and up for the sky and thousands of fat vines came tumbling down. Most of them were gray, but some were yellow, a couple white. When he dared to touch one, he found it remarkably squishy, though when he squeezed on it, he found a solid core.

There were more vines and creepers growing on and around the trees, some bare, others with thousands and tens of thousands of tiny flowers on them so it looked like the whole tree was in bloom, either white or blue. And there were the flowers on the jungle floor as well, everything from little flowering ivy blanketing the ground, to stalks four feet high with massive flowers of all shapes and colors and patterns.

Looking around, he also saw that what he initially mistook for a spider web was actually a type of plant, a vine perhaps, growing criss-cross between two small trees with leaves that could wrap Tommen up in a full-size burrito. He knew better than to touch the leaves, but he still tried to get close enough to study them a little bit.

He nearly jumped out of his skin as some unknown scuttling bug came running up the leaf toward him. He let out a gasp of surprise and fell backwards, scrambling to get away and not land in something far worse. When he finally got his legs under him again, he almost dove headlong into Sifura who put her hands on his shoulders and held him firmly.

"I, too, went to the Archives to research the differences in our species and how I might help you," she said firmly. "And as I recall, most of the plants here are poisonous to you. The toxic gases are held at bay by the atmospheric shell generated by the translator, but it is not impervious. And it does nothing to protect you from contact poisons. Consider yourself lucky those vines you touched were not poisonous. We are here for one cure and one cure only, so I can return you to your friends and you can help your father. We do not have time for you to get sick yourself."

Tommen nodded like a child getting in trouble in kindergarten and being devastated that he was getting his name written on the board. Thankfully he never had to endure that, but he heard it was considered cruel and unusual punishment by most kindergarteners. He sighed. "I understand."

"Follow me. Step where I step, and go where I go."

She turned and started off. Tommen remained hard on her heels, following precisely in her footsteps. "What about this border patrol or whoever we're supposed to meet?"

"It is unlikely we will meet them with you keeping a Band over us like you are, so we may walk right past them."

"You say that like it's a bad thing. Why not skip the formalities? We go in, get the cure, and get out."

"And then what?" Sifura challenged hotly. "I cannot walk back to my people alone in the desert with no skimmer, no provisions. And I cannot ask for such supplies without telling them why I have come in the first place. I had no reason to seek them out other than to bring you. If we get the cure and I send you home, I have nothing to tell them."

"What's the worst that could happen?" Tommen asked, fairly certain it was a stupid question.

"The worst is that they turn me away for all supplies and provisions. I don't even have anything to trade. I have nothing. Except a mission to help you get the cure for your father. Because I offered you the help and you saved my life from the xur, I am obligated to see it through."

Tommen took a long step over a mud puddle. "And what if they refuse us, say they're not giving us the cure?"

"Then we leave their village, wait until we are out of sight." She hesitated. "Then you may Band us, and we will be forced to take what we need." She sighed. "I do not condone such thievery, but as I have said, I am both obligated and indebted to you. I will get you the cure one way or another. I do it this way only because you are available, not because I believe it to be an honorable thing."

"Thank you."

"It is nothing to—"

"Sifura, look at me."

She stopped and turned. His words left him for a moment, but he found his tongue before the silence got too awkward. "Thank you. For helping me, for helping me help my dad. I don't understand all the politics of the Wheel or how our little ruse is going to start a whole Time Civil War, but I do understand that it is a huge risk for everyone, especially you as a Hand. And I just want you to know that I understand it and I respect you for doing it anyway, and I just want to thank you for it. And like you said to me and your people, if you ever need anything, just let me know, and I will try my best to help you however I can."

Sifura's expression softened as she closed her eyes and dipped her head. "I thank you, Tommen Forbes, for your respect and understanding. I know this is difficult for you as well, which is why we must hurry and do our best to make this work so we will not have to Band and return to do this dishonorably. Come now; we must find a border patrol and be properly escorted to their village."

She turned and stalked off, and Tommen followed dutifully. For a jungle, there was an awful lot of tall grass waving around, and it was razor sharp. When he looked down, he found thousands of tiny paper cut-like scratches all up and down his legs and butt and around his groin and belly. He probably wouldn't feel them until he got water or something on them, and then he would be writhing in agony.

"That bug back there on the leaf," he said. "Did you see it?"

"I did," Sifura replied, not turning or even slowing.

"What was that?"

"The D'Bok call it *bakadikadi*. It is extremely poisonous, even to the D'Bok. It spits venom on all intruders that will burn away the skin until it hits blood where it gets into the blood flow of the body and poison a person until they die in agony over three to four days."

"Shit," Tommen breathed. "Fucking shit." He began checking

himself. "I don't think it got me."

"If it did, you would have noticed. And then everyone in the whole jungle would have known about it too, the way you scream."

"Do you blame me?"

"No. *Bakadikadi* are not an animal you want to tease."

Tommen scanned all the leaves around them, the grass, even the trees. "Are there many of them around?"

"They feed on young sapling trees," Sifura explained. "They will not attack unless they are threatened."

"I wasn't threatening it, just looking."

"Did it know that? Was it willing to take a chance that you were just looking and not an unusual animal, potentially a predator here to eat it?"

Tommen gritted his teeth. "No," he admitted. "It was just doing what it does."

"Exactly."

"And how do you know so much about them anyway?"

"Anyone who has been to the D'Bok territory once learns about them, and it is something not easily forgotten."

Her tone laughed at him, even if she didn't, and Tommen snorted angrily. But she was right. It was a severe lesson to be learned, and he would probably never forget it.

"So does that mean you speak their language, too?" Tommen questioned.

"If I did not, I would be a poor leader of my people, and of little help to you," Sifura replied smartly. "Those who wish to enter the territory of another tribe ought to know the language, or have a good reason for not knowing. As the Xur and D'Bok share a border, it is beneficial that we have an understanding. Since you come from far away, it is not expected from you."

"Oh."

"I have noticed," she went on, "that even when using the translators, you speak differently than the Lieutenants."

"Yeah, they speak Irish and I speak Welsh. They're our native languages."

"You are from different tribes?"

"Well, no. I mean yes. Sort of. Micaiah and Micah come from Ireland. My parents came from Wales, and we all spoke Welsh at home. They all immigrated to America where English is *lingua franca*. So we all speak English just fine, and we picked up some of each other's languages, but when we have the option, we like to go back to our native tongues."

"You are from different tribes, yet you all look the same."

"Well..." Tommen mulled it over in his mind for a minute or two. "Same tribe, different factions. Each faction has its own language. Some are more closely related than others, but they're different."

"How many languages are there on your world?"

"Um...thousands. Some are spoken by millions of people, others are in danger of dying out."

She glanced back at him. "How many people are there on your world?"

"Billions. Seven billion I think was the last milestone."

She stopped in her tracks then and stared at nothing, as if trying to comprehend seven billion people. Truth be told, even Tommen had a hard time figuring that one out sometimes. Seven billion. Seven thousand million. Seven hundred thousand... thousand...thousand? Was that right? He tried to picture it in his mind. Looked right, sounded stupid.

They walked along a well-used path at the border between jungle and desert. Tommen could still feel the heat coming off the sand and on the warm winds, but the shade from the trees kept him cool and out of the sun. He picked absently at some of the peeling skin on his arms. He would have to get the twins to double-Band and heal him of this. How would it look if he walked into the hospital with a sunburn in the middle of winter? Yeah, real concern for his dying father, going to someplace warm and sunny and getting a sunburn.

"So when we do finally meet the D'Bok or their leader, what should I do?" Tommen wondered, breaking the silence. Because of his Band, with everything stopped, there was no birdsong to be heard. The most noise that came through was the wind rustling still leaves. He wasn't even sure there would be birds here to sing.

"When we come across a border patrol, stay silent." This time, Sifura made sure to emphasize the word "silent" as if he he'd done something wrong the first time.

They continued in silence again for a short time, maybe all of five minutes, before Tommen spoke again.

"So, I have a question."

He could imagine Sifura rolling her eyes as she grudgingly answered, "What is it?"

"You're a Triage Harvester, aren't you?"

"Yes."

"And Triage Harvesters can Harvest at just a touch, regardless if the victim is dying. You could Harvest me right now."

"That is correct."

"So why didn't you Harvest the xur, save yourself the trouble of fighting?"

"It is unfair to the creature, to any opponent, to possess a weapon that kills so absolutely with no effort required."

Tommen pondered this. "So...you don't like that I killed it with my gun?" Well, Micaiah's gun in all technicality, but she didn't need to know that.

"I do not know what you did or how you killed it, and I am unfamiliar with this weapon, so I cannot make a judgment."

"Well, it's kind of like that sort of Triage Harvesting, except you don't even need to touch someone to kill them, if you can aim right."

Sifura did not answer for a long time, and Tommen began to doubt she ever would. It sounded so cruel now, to describe a gun in that way, but it was true. At the same time, human condition dictated that people needed to be able to defend themselves from predators and, more importantly, each other. Once upon a time, that was with spear and rock. These days it was with a sidearm or a rifle. People didn't like it, tried to take away guns and make all sorts of laws, but the way Tommen figured it, if "Thou shalt not kill"—a command straight from a God most people professed to at least believe in somewhat—didn't deter crime, no pithy law or executive order would either.

"How far south does the border extend?" Tommen asked aloud before he realized he'd only meant to think the question.

"To the southern swamps and the Uji tribe."

Her short answer and curt tone told Tommen to shut the hell up before she shut his mouth for him, and it wasn't going to be pretty if she had to. But based on her answer, he wasn't sure if he wanted to probe further. Swamps were bad enough. Yeah, people liked to tout a diverse ecosystem and blah, blah, blah, but he saw little value to them. Sure, people lived in swamps, but who really wanted to live on or near water where your hand disappeared the instant it went beneath the surface and ran the risk of being snapped off by whatever lurked there? No thanks, give him clear mountain streams, mountain forests, and mountain meadows any day.

Sifura stopped suddenly, and Tommen almost ran into her, deep as he was in his thoughts. He opened his mouth to speak, but Sifura put a hand up.

"The D'Bok are nearby," she hissed.

"How do you know?" Tommen asked quietly.

"I smell them."

"We're Banded. They shouldn't be moving, I mean, in all technicality—"

"Stay here. Drop the Band. I will find them first and bring them."

"Shouldn't I go find them, or at least go with you? I mean, I'm the one asking for help."

"You are of a new and foreign tribe, and do not know how to handle the D'Bok. I will go and assess their condition first. There is no shame in this, Tommen Forbes."

And like that, she vanished into the bushes. Reluctantly, Tommen watched her go, waited until the leaves stopped shaking, then dropped the Band.

Instantly, the jungle came alive with all manner of noise and wildlife. Some small creature hidden behind a plant next to Tommen's ankle scurried off, screeching a warning which set off some other animal higher up in a tree that leapt off into the shadows and startled a flock of bird-like creatures which did a swirling vortex sort of pattern to get to a height where they took off through the jungle canopy, screeching and cawing and twittering warnings to all the jungle. Intruders! Intruders! Some larger beast a short distance away glomped its way through the thick undergrowth, also trying to make a run for it. Tommen only caught a glimpse of the beast, some kind of scaled llama thing.

Then all was back to what he assumed to be normal, cooler wind rustling the upper branches, warm winds from the desert tempering the shade on the floor, strange bird calls and animal noises of all sorts whistling, chirping, barking, and so forth, breaking the suffocating silence that had enveloped him and Sifura for the last who knew how long.

Nervously, habitually, Tommen checked his watch. Six-thirty-five, Friday evening. He let out a breath, almost daring to feel hopeful about the whole thing. They—well, Sifura—had found a border patrol. They would go to the D'Bok camp, village, whatever, and after whatever formalities and rituals they had to sing and dance through, they would get the cure for the illness that was plaguing poor Tommen's besieged people. He almost smiled. He was going to have this thing wrapped up by tonight. He was going to be able to go home and save Walter with time to spare.

He could only hope that he wasn't somehow dooming himself with his optimism, as if there might be some sadistic god able to read his thoughts and decide, "Nope. Not today. Way too easy. Let's just add in a few more obstacles and see how much you squirm. Because I have that power and such things amuse me."

Tommen nearly jumped out of his skin as the leaves rustled again and Sifura returned, gorgeous as ever. The things she brought with her, however, were far less than gorgeous. They barely even registered as homely in Tommen's mind.

At first glance, he figured that the D'Bok which these people were named for resembled something of a bear. At the same time, he was still trying to figure out how the hideous abomination known as the xur could produce such an exotic beauty as Sifura, but the thing had still been recognizable as some sort of feline. Therefore, the d'bok creature was probably recognizable as some sort of bear. Assuming that bear had mated with a komodo dragon and then the offspring went back and mated with their parents to produce ungodly, atrocious, incestuous offspring. But a bear nonetheless.

To compare the D'Bok scouts to anything, the first thing Tommen's mind reached for was a wookie, but upon closer inspection, that was a reach. Wookies were furry and handsome. These people had larger round ears like a bear, and a short muzzle. Overall, they looked like some first grader's art project using feathers, tissue paper, and a lot of Elmer's glue as the whole head was a hot mess of fur and scales. Where Sifura's people had different colors and markings, the D'Bok looked like they were divided more according to fur versus scale. Those with more fur were in one camp, and those with more scales were in another camp, but they were still all ugly as fuck. There was no kind way to say it; they were hideous sons of bitches, and he felt more sorry for the hideous women, too. Just...fuck.

That wasn't to say he brushed them off as immaterial. They ranged in height from about five to seven feet, but they were all as buff as a steroid-using bodybuilding quarterback who could pull a car out of a ditch single-handedly. Or maybe the conglomeration of fur and scales only made it seem that way; Tommen was not keen to find out.

The D'Bok regarded him the way he might regard an ant.

Insignificant, useful in its own limited sense, but of no value whatsoever to them. The leader was a little over six feet tall, and seemed to be in the "furry" clan as he was covered almost entirely in fur that was dark blue on top but with an undercoat of black. He—or she—looked at Tommen for a minute or two, then looked at Sifura. It said something, and to Tommen's surprise, not only was it close enough to be picked up on Sifura's translator, but the translators seemed to be programmed with the D'Bok language so it could be understood. So who among them was in Time?

"This is the one seeking help?" the leader inquired, his voice a sneer.

"He is, Karaki," Sifura confirmed, speaking in the D'Bok tongue.

"Amazing he has lasted this long, as small and skinny and hairless as he is," another one, this one almost completely scaly, hissed.

"Which is why he ought to have a chance to talk to your council."

The leader, Karaki, hesitated, stared down Sifura who did not give an inch. "You say he brought the gift of language to your people. Why not bring such a gift to the people who would help him?"

"Perhaps his gift for you is better, even than this," Sifura suggested firmly, not hesitating or faltering in her answer.

"What could be better?"

The two of them bantered for a short time, but Tommen's attention was taken more by one of the shorter members of the party, almost equal parts fur and scale, though heavier on the scale side, whose attention had been on him since the beginning, and even more so since Karaki mentioned the gift of language. Just for curiosity's sake, Tommen Banded. Not long, just long enough to judge its reaction afterwards, as if he was any master of judging the emotions of a komodo bear.

When he released the Band, the D'Bok only gave him a slow blink, then turned its attention back to the two arguing leaders. They were bulls locking horns, neither willing to give ground.

"Then that is a matter for your council to decide," Sifura was saying.

"You bring no gifts—" Karaki began.

"—but he does. And he is the one asking for help. Not I."

Tommen was no expert on the local customs, but if he was right, she was making a dangerous gamble. With no gifts, it sounded like they had every right to turn her away, tell her to make the thirty-day trek back home, good luck in the desert. After a moment of tense silence and hard stares and glares on both sides, one Xur facing off against seven D'Bok with the monkey, er, Ape in the middle, Karaki finally relented.

"We will see what the council has to say about this," he said.

Then he turned and started off along a new path away from the border and deeper into the jungle. Two of his goons followed him, then Sifura and Tommen came after, with the rest of the border patrol following close behind.

"The D'Bok have a council, too?" Tommen inquired.

Sifura started to answer, then realized the translator was still set to the D'Bok language. She discreetly fiddled with it until it was back on the Xur tongue.

"Their government is similar to that of the Xur, the Bodek faction most of all. They have six clans, one representative of each on the council, one being the leader. The difference is that if a leader dies, an entirely new council is chosen, one from each clan, and the council chooses from among themselves who the leader will be."

"How do you know so much about them? Do you visit them often?"

"Not often, but it is advantageous to be well-versed in the basic dealings and goings-on of one's neighbors."

Tommen nodded uncertainly. "How far to the village?"

"Not far. Two Base Hours perhaps."

He glanced quickly at the D'Bok who'd gotten his attention earlier, but it did not appear to have noticed the exchange or did not understand.

"Fear not, Tommen Forbes," Sifura told him. "We will save your father one way or another."

Up front, Karaki laughed and said something the translator did not catch which made the other D'Bok snicker.

"What did he say?" Tommen asked.

Sifura glared at the backs of the D'Bok before them and said, "Nothing."

So they walked. Unlike the desert which, while it had its rises and depressions, was, for the most part, flat, the jungle, after getting a fair distance from the border, became very hilly, and the thick vegetation made it difficult to traverse both in terms of general walking and trying to stay away from all the plants. The path was wide enough that Tommen was generally okay, and he quickly learned, by happenstance mostly, the few plants which were not toxic to him, but he wasn't about to take his chances. If he didn't have to touch a plant, and his only need would come from the inevitability of a trip and fall into said plant, then he vowed not to touch a plant.

The D'Bok behind them found this wildly amusing as they would randomly pick up long-stemmed plants and wave them just in front of him like a carrot on a stick. His first instinct was to swat it out of the way, except he couldn't, and more than once he had to stop only for the D'Bok to run into him from behind and force him to keep moving, clumsily dodging the plant. Sifura told them off once or twice, but Karaki made no move to stop or even scold them. It was not difficult to imagine him smirking up there at the front of the line.

"Are the D'Bok always such assholes?" Tommen growled.

"They have little love for other tribes," Sifura sighed. "New tribes they hold no love for at all. You do not share a border with them, do not threaten to share a border with them; you are not particularly intimidating or powerful. You are coming to them and asking for help, begging. They see you as little more than a child, begging for a sweet. It is unlikely that they will ever see you as anything else."

Now that he knew this, it was a little easier to tolerate. If there was nothing he could do to change their opinion of him, better to come to terms with the information, file it away in his mental filing cabinet, and move on. Understand the situation, and make the best of it. They saw him as a beggar child; the least he could do was be the most polite and respectful beggar child they had ever seen and hope it impressed them enough that they would actually help him. Be a dog and get a bone.

At the same time, similar attitudes and resolve had never helped him in his fights at school. Everyone knew him as the Chivalrous Welshman, but no one had ever come to his aid when the going got tough. They just formed a circle and watched the show until Layman came by to break it up.

They stopped once at a jungle stream which cut across the path. Karaki and the others drank like dogs, noses to the water, then refilled small canteens slung around their bodies. Sifura, too, got down and drank like a cat, lapping up the water gracefully. When she was finished, she did not ask for a canteen or lament her lack of one, simply waited for the others to be done. Tommen knew that the water in the desert was mostly good for him, but what about the jungle water? It looked like any other stream he'd seen on Earth, less a few strands of orange algae. At the same time, what sort of bacteria and microorganisms could be lurking in there? Of course, could he have really expected the desert water to have been filtered and treated and sterilized and sanitized and chlorinized before being passed to him? Fuck, he could end up in the hospital himself with some kind of alien fucking tapeworm, or worse.

In the end, he decided to risk it. After a long trek through the hot desert and now a hike through the jungle, he was thirsty and very tired. He didn't want to use up the last of his water, not here, not in front of the D'Bok. It might be seen as some kind of snubbing, if the stream was considered some kind of hospitality. It might be seen as cowardly, that he was as afraid of their water as he was of them. Better to take just a small drink to take the edge off his thirst and wait until he was alone before breaking out the bottled water. And if he did end up sick, so be it. He would be home and within reach of quality medical care soon enough. Assuming the doctors knew they would be looking for alien tapeworms and shit.

"You are well, Tommen Forbes?" Sifura asked as he slowly stood from where he drank.

"Fine," he told her, falling into place in their little formation on the path. "Let's go."

It wasn't that he was sick or anything—not yet anyway—but he was suddenly hit by a wave of fatigue. Maybe it was the stop itself, maybe it was him finally cooling down after the desert, maybe it was the clear spring water that he'd unintentionally drank more than he probably should have because it tasted so good, but he just suddenly felt exhausted. He needed a good eight hours of sleep right about now. Only Friday night on Earth; he could snag a few extra z's while he was here, right? In his thoughts, he almost ran into the D'Bok in front of him. Karaki glanced back at them and said something which Sifura unnecessarily translated.

"We are here."

Chapter Twenty-One
Treating with Bears

They crested the hill and looked down into a vast and bumpy jungle valley. Tommen might have overlooked the little village completely except for the small cookfires and the villagers running around like ants. The homes here resembled little African adobe huts except they were built into and around the various trees of the jungle. One hut had a tree growing neatly up through the center of it, while another small cluster of huts used another tree as one shared corner post. Still other huts were built higher in the branches of the trees, connected by rope-and-plank bridges. These huts were not as decorated as the Xur huts, inlaid with leaves and flowers and pretty stones. Instead, they were stick and mud only with leafy roofs, almost completely invisible amid the rest of the jungle.

In the middle was a communal area with a fire in it, though this pit was tiny compared to the monstrous thing the Xur had going for them. The D'Bok fire pit was like a cute, little, wimpy campfire at some of the camping grounds around the mountains, where the Xur fire pit was like a huge agricultural burn pile.

As they drew nearer to the village, Tommen guessed the D'Bok were not as migratory as their Xur neighbors. The hut homes were not nearly as sparse, and each one spoke more of a cozy home rather than temporary dwelling to be packed up at any given moment. There were tools of various technological advances, pots, pans, kettles and cauldrons. Some of the huts had real doors set on crude hinges while others had a woven rug of either hair fibers or various plant leaves and flowers.

"The D'Bok do not migrate like the Xur," Sifura told him,

confirming his suspicions. "They stay in a single spot and mark out territory to defend."

She said it with a tone of disapproval, Tommen thought, as if there was something wrong with settling down in one place, digging your heels in and being prepared to fight for it. Was there anything wrong about wanting to defend what's yours? Maybe it was different for her, except she did not seem to have to defend her territory because no one wanted her territory. Only her people were suited for life in the desert and the constant migration, so there was no real competition for it. More tribes were probably able to live in the jungle, so they did have to stake out a claim and defend it.

But Tommen kept his thoughts to himself as they continued walking, relaxing only once they actually set foot in the village and were relatively out of danger as far as his proximity to the plants was concerned.

Viewed from above, the Xur village was laid out in a ray pattern, with the fire pit and communal area being the point of origin, and all the streets spreading out from there. Sure, the village wasn't perfect, and there were various flaws as newer construction at the outer edges gave way to older construction in the middle, but fundamentally, that was how the village was laid out.

The D'Bok village had no such concept of organization. If there were five huts together to form a straight street, it was something to note. Otherwise it was a mass mess of huts of all sizes plopped down haphazardly here and there and everywhere, close together, like a painter doing splatter-painting, just flicking his brush wherever he felt like it.

On reflection, however, Tommen realized that it proved to be a decent tactical advantage, when dealing with small numbers. An invading force would have no easy time trying to get through the village, never mind trying to conquer it, and they would still have to fight the native population who knew their haphazard streets and huts like the back of their hand. And there was that whole bit about the huts in the trees, ready to drop rocks or arrows or something on an invading force, maybe call out the movements of the enemy.

There was something else, however, that grabbed Tommen's attention, and he didn't realize it until he was looking right at one. The D'Bok had domesticated animals.   True, they were less like chickens and goats, and more like little furry velociraptors and winged gophers, but they had domestic animals. The Xur relied solely on hunting for meat and the wild gathering of fruit and nuts, but the D'Bok had a ready supply of meat to hand. True to form, there was a rack outside one particular hut that had four carcasses hung out to cure.

"The D'Bok lure animals in and trap them here to make them breed unnaturally in order to eat," Sifura said distastefully.

"We call it domesticating," Tommen told her. "And it's not a bad thing when it's done responsibly."

"Your people have domesticated many animals, and not responsibly."

"True, but we have done it, and it supplies food for a lot of people."

"My people hunt our food, as we have always done it. We have never needed to trap animals and make them suffer with us."

Tommen did not press the matter, figuring to leave her in her own stubborn opinion. There were ups and downs to being so isolated. On the one hand, they had traditions that went back hundreds or maybe thousands of years, preserving the history of their people for generations to come. On the other hand, they would always be isolated from new ideas and so set in their ways that they would break before they bent. As Tommen looked around at some of the tools, he realized that where the Xur were dealing with crude iron and copper, some tribe, somewhere, maybe the D'Bok, maybe not, had begun forging and smithing, turning iron into steel. Someone had dared to try something new, harnessing fire and refining metals. Would the Xur be willing to trade for them? Would they be interested in forging their own metals? Or would they resist so much that one day they would be cut down by those weapons as civilization moved in and branched out? Would they really be willing to die for centuries of stone age tradition rather than take those traditions and modify them for a new era?

He didn't like to think about the answer. He told himself he didn't know enough about Sifura or her people to make a judgment, even if in the back of his mind he was starting to realize than her idealistic society would be fast-approaching its end. Isolation would keep them safe for a while, but what happened when other people began to adapt to and tame the desert? What would happen when an outside tribe did finally reach one of the oases and decide they liked it there and they weren't going to leave? Would the Xur drive them out by force? What if the new tribe had superior weaponry?

Tommen shook his head. Too many what ifs, and he was getting far too concerned about a world and a people he knew about only because of this brief moment of aid. He would be grateful, yes, and he would fulfill his promise to help them if he could in the future, but what they did and what changes they underwent after he left was all up to them. It wasn't his place to interfere.

Not that he particularly wanted to interfere. If he was going to interfere, he planned on it being with a tribe that wasn't so butt-ugly as the D'Bok. At least the Xur had feline grace, and they had beautiful colors and markings to tell them all apart. The D'Bok...there was nothing graceful or sexy or pretty about them. And they all pretty much looked the same, a failed paper maché of fur and scales ranging in color from dark blue to dark brown to dark gray and black.

Few of them took notice of the returning party. Of those that did, their gaze first went to Sifura, then to Tommen, and then back to whatever work they had been doing. Some were busy with butchering and cooking, others with the weaving of rugs or baskets, a few with repairs to a roof where it looked like a roof timber had broken. Really, they hardly looked like the hostile, war-like people Sifura had described, even with the cruel antics their escorts had played on him on the trail. Sure, most of them had knives on their person or in hand, but they were being used as tools. Only once did

Tommen actually see someone sharpening his knife, and there was nothing threatening about that.

Even the children hardly looked like they were born with a knife or ax in hand, or spewed battle tactics as soon as they could talk. Most of them ran around in one game or another, sometimes with sticks or leaves. One group of children looked like they were playing a game that resembled marbles or jacks. Another group tossed around a ball in some sort of rule-based fashion until one started shouting after he missed, the ball soaring over his head as it went out of bounds. Probably claiming it wasn't his fault or he wasn't out, or something of that sort, as all children do.

Unlike the Xur children who ran up to Tommen to poke his balls every opportunity they got, the D'Bok children seemed rather disinterested. At first Tommen thought this was because they were being escorted and there was some rule against interacting with people under escort. Then he got to thinking that the escort really shouldn't have a problem with children interfering and playing games and tricks because they'd done the same thing on the trail. Maybe it was a case of cat's away, mice will play, what happens on the trail stays on the trail. But another thought occurred to Tommen that maybe the children weren't interested because it was nothing new. Maybe they got new and strange visitors all the time, and they just didn't care anymore. The game ball was more fun than Tommen's balls.

Another fiendish thought crossed his mind that maybe his balls were nothing new because the D'Bok had their own hidden somewhere under their fur. He pushed that thought from his mind before he could go down that road and instead went to the more logical point that the D'Bok probably had similar reproductive practices as the Xur, except involving the animal d'bok. So did the D'Bok grow on trees, too, or was that unique to the Xur? Tommen thought about it for a second before deciding he didn't really want to know, nor did he particularly care. And there was no way in hell he was going to bring it up lest someone ask him how his people did it and ask him for some kind of demonstration. Fuck, but that would be embarrassing.

Eventually, they made their way to the communal area with the fire pit that, up close, was a little bigger than a wimpy campground campfire, maybe more of a small, well-contained bonfire, but it was still puny compared to the Xur fire pit.

Around the communal area, Tommen realized, were large trees, spaced pretty evenly, and each with a very long rope ladder which led to what seemed to be the nucleus of the treetop village. The nucleus, being more or less directly over the fire pit, was situated higher in the branches than the other tree huts. In the rest of the village, the tree huts were about twenty to thirty feet in the air. This cluster was somewhere between fifty and a hundred feet in the air.

Karaki led them to one of the ladders, glanced mischievously at Tommen, and said something which Sifura translated, again unecessarily.

"Are you afraid of high places?" Karaki asked.

"I live in places higher than this," Tommen replied, hoping Sifura translated that directly instead of mincing words and boiling it down. War-like or not, Tommen did not enjoy being pushed around and taunted. Sure, it only got him in more trouble at home, but here it would hopefully be seen as a sign of strength.

Although, strictly speaking, Tommen was afraid of heights, especially on unstable rope ladders. He could stand on any mountaintop, as long as he was standing there on solid ground. Swaying on a ladder that groaned and creaked under the weight of ten people, all of whom weighed around two thousand pounds collectively, that was not okay in his mind, very not okay. Still, he said none of this out loud and did not allow himself to halt, hesitate, slow down, or falter in any way that might be misconstrued as weakness. He would be strong. He would present himself bravely, resolutely.

Was it possible to beg strongly for something? How did that work? Was it like Catholicism, throwing himself at the mercy of God and slain in the Spirit and whatever, yet still retaining a firm disdain for all ye heathens who begged outside the cathedral doors? Would it be better to go full-out begging like they were his only hope, or pretend like he had better offers and make them work for his business?

When they reached the deck at the top of the ladder, Tommen decided he liked his mountains better. For one, there was an actual view and not just branches and leaves. His view was limited to about the outskirts of the village, but there was no grand view of the jungle and beyond like he'd hoped. Karaki must have noticed his expression.

"Not good enough for you?" Sifura translated.

"It's not my home," Tommen replied diplomatically. No use fighting over landscapes and scenery, he figured. If he was going to be a tough bastard, he would do it when it counted.

Karaki simply grunted and walked over to a rope bridge that led to another tree with a much larger tree hut, with at least five smaller huts clustered around it that Tommen could see. Karaki growled some orders to a couple of his minions who acknowledged him before starting across. Sifura gently touched Tommen to tell him to follow, then followed herself, two more D'Bok bringing up the rear while the rest either stayed on the first deck or moved around to other decks and outlooks.

"You are doing well," Sifura breathed so only Tommen would hear. "Proceed as if you were going before the Hands to present your case. Conduct yourself well, and consider how they may benefit. Charity is not their strongest trait."

Tommen gave a barely perceptible nod and hoped she understood. This was the moment of truth, when they would either sit down like civilized people and negotiate fairly for the cure, or they would be turned away and driven out, forced to use Time to essentially break back into D'Bok territory and steal the cure. For as much as Tommen wanted to skip all of this formality and bullshit, he wasn't too keen on the idea of breaking and entering and theft. Was it that obvious his dad was a cop?

The bridge swayed in the wind, but Tommen forced himself not to panic, just put one foot in front of the other until they reached the other side. When they did, Karaki looked back and almost seemed surprised that they were still following him. Had he hoped to mysteriously lose them over the side of the bridge, watch them plummet to their deaths in the village below? Had Tommen misjudged them? Were they as hostile as Sifura said, just in a different way?

"Stay here until I return," Karaki ordered firmly, looking more at Sifura than Tommen as he said it. "I will go in and beseech the council to meet with you."

Beseech? Tommen knew the translators weren't perfect, and sometimes the word choice was odd, but beseech was pretty far out there, wasn't it? Sifura had simply gone in and said the council was going to meet with him. Karaki had to beseech his council. Well, maybe it came from not being the leader this time.

Then it hit him.

"Was Karaki once part of the council?" Tommen asked as soon as said person was out of earshot.

"He was," Sifura confirmed. "How did you know?"

"The way he carries himself. He's proud and strong, a natural leader, but he's not in power. An aspiring leader would make good use of his time, proving himself worthy. He harbors resentment, like he'll never get another chance."

Sifura dipped her head. "Karaki was on the Council of Rurok, who was proclaimed to be a mighty warrior. He died only a year after becoming leader. It was such news that even we heard of it in the desert, that there were rumors of murder. Perhaps by his greatest competitor."

"Karaki."

"Yes. But it made no sense for Karaki to kill him, since he would never again be a candidate for leader or council member. In the end, unfortunately, the murderer, if there was one, was never caught. Karaki remains bitter that his time for being part of the council was so short-lived."

Tommen didn't blame him for being a little grouchy over such a thing, but what good did it do him to beat up on the new guy, other than for petty entertainment? Tommen might say he was compensating a little, but why have a dick-measuring contest when one party didn't even have a dick to measure?

Karaki's heavy footsteps announced his presence long before they saw him descend the stairs leading up to the third hut. His expression was flat, as if he'd gone up expecting some sort of comradery, maybe some sort of gossip and a small victory as he got them rejected from the council before they ever got in, only to be brushed aside like the leader of yesteryear and assigned to duties like an errand boy.

"They will see you," was all he said.

Sifura dipped her head respectfully, and Tommen poorly tried to emulate it. She haughtily brushed past Karaki on the steps, and Tommen meekly followed.

Whatever stone or bronze age notions Tommen had been feeling about the rest of the village, the council's hut swept those aside for something far more advanced, jumping all the way to something like a cross between Roman times and medieval times. The walls were combination mud and wood on the outside, but inside they were covered in crude metal shields, most of them plain but some with designs, attached to the wall for reinforcement. On the various limbs snaking their way through the hut, weapons were hung, everything from sharp rock knives to the first iterations of a sword, and Tommen had to duck not only under a branch, but under what looked like a failed attempt at a proper greatsword.

Where the Xur council had sat in a neat little circle on woven mats, the D'Bok council sat at a proper table carved directly from the tree, including the six seats. It was not a plain setup either, but there were intricate designs of both nature and battle carved with such fine precision that a needle could not have fallen into the cracks. The seats bore primarily nature designs while the table depicted an intricate battle scene.   Other than seeing that one side — probably the D'Bok — was significantly overpowering the other side, Tommen couldn't make heads or tails of the image, nor could he even begin to comprehend the significance it held and why it had been chosen over all other possible designs or renditions. Whoever had done it had been a true master carver.

Perhaps the most striking thing about this council was the council itself. The Xur council had been comprised of older warriors past their fighting prime and now in a position to lead by experience. This council was not that council. The D'Bok council was made up of battle-hardened warriors who had probably never lost a battle and did not intend on losing any more, instead pooling their experiences to come up with strategies that maximized the spoils while minimizing their own losses. This was not an elder council; this was a war council. Tommen felt like he'd stepped into some field commander's office on the eve of battle, a lowly messenger boy sent to tell the king that some person from a faraway land he'd never heard of was sick and needed assistance.

The council members themselves were frightening enough, even without the added decor. One was about eighty percent scales with large black eyes; Tommen wouldn't have been surprised if a forked tongue flicked out to smell him. Another was the opposite, eighty percent fur and the one to most resemble a wookie; if he'd suddenly opened his mouth and done a wookie call, Tommen would not have been surprised. The others fell somewhere in between, each one just as ugly as the rest of the D'Bok villagers.

Sifura changed her translator settings just as the council began to speak.

"Sifura Three-Heart, leader of the Xresa of the Xur, welcome," the scaly one greeted. "This visit is most unexpected."

"It is," Sifura agreed formally. "However, it is of utmost importance and urgency."

"Karaki said one has come seeking our aid," another council

member said. "Is this it?" He looked at Tommen.

"It is."

"Who are you?" the furriest one inquired.

"Tommen Forbes, of the Chimpanzee faction of the Ape tribe," Tommen introduced, hoping it was correct format but figuring Sifura's translating would fill in the courtesy gaps.

The council members took a moment to introduce themselves and speak of their greatest accomplishment, but Tommen neither cared about their accomplishments, nor would he remember their names effectively. He only needed to shmooze them long enough to get the cure. Beyond that, he didn't care for their names, their accomplishments, or their politics. The only one he remembered was Dreja, the current leader and undefeated in every battle he'd led.

"Karaki says you brought the Xur the gift of language," Dreja said. "And I see it works well. What gift do you bring for us that you may earn your right to speak here?"

Tommen intended to lower his bag slowly and nonthreateningly to the ground, but once it left his shoulder, his arm momentarily went numb with relief, and it hit the floor with a thump. None of the D'Bok reacted to that, but they craned their necks to try and see inside the bag as he rummaged around a bit until he found the bags of coffee. He breathed a sigh of relief: still intact. He closed the burlap bag, picked up the coffee bags, gingerly approached their table, and laid the bags before them.

"What are these?" one of the members asked, though Tommen could see they were all sniffing the air, sniffing the bags.

"Coffee," Tommen answered, Sifura translating. "Ground coffee beans. Put them in a filter and run hot water through them into a cup. The drink is satisfying, and it gives you energy. The wet grounds can be used to make crops grow, or burned for fuel. These three bags, they have different flavors."

One of the council members opened up one of the bags, and immediately the hut was filled with the fragrance of peppermint coffee. The rest of the council breathed deep, and Tommen saw what might have been the D'Bok equivalent of that immensely satisfied and relaxed expression one gets when walking down the coffee aisle at the grocery store. Yes, this was probably going to work out just fine. Tommen sent a silent prayer of thanks to Micah for the idea. And, since caffeine was addictive, maybe he could get the D'Bok addicted to coffee in exchange for whatever cures he ever needed. If they had the cure for one Borelian disease, who was to say they didn't have the cure for more, or even all of them?

Tommen corralled his thoughts. No time to plot and scheme now. First, he had to get the first and most important cure. Still, he couldn't help but feel a bit smug at his offering being readily accepted. One council member closed the bag while another went to the steps where, presumably, Karaki still waited. They spoke in hushed tones for a moment before the council member returned.

"We will try your coffee," he said. "Until then, why have you come to us?"

"My people were attacked by a nameless tribe that used poison arrows to try and wipe us out. We have no cure for this poison. Neither did the neighboring tribes, but one knew of you, the D'Bok, who they believed did have a cure for this poison. I have traveled many miles for many months, often alone. My people did not want me to go; they said those who were poisoned would die before the cure got to them. They said I would die before I ever found the cure. They said it would be better to stay and hope that we could beat back the invaders before the poison arrows claimed all of us. But I came anyway."

"Why?" another member asked.

"My father was one who was poisoned. I hold out hope that I can bring back the cure in time. Even if I return and he is perished, having a cure for this poison is as much a weapon against our enemy as any knife. Being able to render their greatest strength powerless, that would be worth this trek."

The council members glanced at one another for a moment, enough to make Tommen wonder if they weren't telepathic. Or maybe they just had the animal instincts combined with higher intelligence to be able to read body language and tone, trying to find the lie in his story, which, other than his dad being poisoned, was pretty much all of it. Still, he had to stand firm, and believe every word he was saying as if he had actually trekked many miles for many months, across the Toxic Sea and the Red Desert, all alone, looking for a cure which no one expected him to return with.

"Why did you come alone?" a council member wondered. "One man may perish in the Red Desert with none to mourn him. A group of men can defeat many enemies and bear the burdens of packing."

"I traveled with two others as far as the Red Desert. Then they became afraid and turned back." Well, it wasn't exactly a lie, was it? Micah and Micaiah had been with him every step of the way, even helping him pack for the trip, up until he actually followed Sifura through the portal into the desert. They hadn't joined him because first, they were too weak to go through any more portals for a while; second, they were already under heavy scrutiny by the Hands and figured Tommen could slip through the cracks easier while they dealt with the fallout from potential civil war; third, they didn't really have a whole lot of faith in the mission anyway, so they were going to let Tommen figure that out on his own; and fourth, they had a business to run, which kind of tied back into the third reason.

"You are brave," Dreja acknowledged. "Warriors are made not only in battle, but in the greater obstacles they face. The desert is as much an enemy as the Poqip. And you are right that to take an enemy's strength and use it against him is as great as strengthening your own self. You are young, we can see, but you are wise beyond your years."

Before anyone could say more, Karaki returned with cups, hot water, and something that Tommen assumed could be used as filters. The council took these things and dismissed Karaki as though he was nothing more than a servant. The old leader obeyed grudgingly, but Tommen did not miss his look of contempt. Once he was gone, the council members set the items down on the table and gestured for Tommen to show them how to make this "coffee" drink.

At first he tried to explain the different flavors, but the council did not appear to care, growing slightly impatient until he just picked one, the peppermint one they'd already smelled, and started pouring, grabbing Sifura to help hold the filters while he poured the water over the grounds. When all six cups were filled, the council took them and drank.

For a minute, it was difficult to gauge their reaction, and for a minute, Tommen was terrified that they hated it and would send him away. Well, worst case scenario, they just head out into the desert where he would Band and just walk right back in. It would eat up a lot of time, but if they had to do it... Tommen fidgeted with his "bracelets," itching to check the time.

Finally, Dreja nodded. "It is a good drink. It will suffice."

Tommen was momentarily offended by his word choice. It would suffice? Tommen knew some people who came into the bakery on a daily basis, grouchy as hell but singing the praises of coffee and practically worshiping the bean by the time they left the store. And for these people, it would "suffice"? Then he figured that it might have just been formality, or even restraint. He came asking for help and brought a good gift. They needed him to remain in their good graces, not turn it around on them so that they were begging for stuff from him.

"I am glad it pleases you," Tommen replied, waiting for them to say the words "we'll give you the cure."

"So, what do you want us to do?" Dreja asked calmly.

"I'm sorry?"

Isn't it obvious? I want the fucking cure. I'm not here to take you guys out to Starbucks just for the fuck of it.

"You brought this gift as payment to speak before this council," Dreja explained. "What do you have to trade for the cure?"

Tommen could have launched himself at the leader just then, and how he wanted to. Just take him down and beat the shit out of him like he always dreamed of doing to Tyler. Unfortunately, that dream would probably end up like all the others, on the cold floor of reality. And this time, Layman wasn't around to defend him.

"How much of it do you have?" Tommen asked instead, keeping his voice level, if stiff, trying to sound like a reasonable businessman here to negotiate a price.

Dreja grinned and chuckled. "Well, that's the catch, isn't it? We don't have any. Not on hand. We rarely do because this poison is rare to us."

"Then what good does it do to pay you for a cure you don't have?"

"But we do have it. It's sitting out there in the foothills right now, a large flowering plant whose flower holds the cure for the poison on its leaves. We do not have these flowers on hand; we do not have it ground and made into a pulp for direct application. But it is out there on our land. Therefore, you still have to give us something for it. Because of its location and the effort to reach it, you will no doubt also be taking some of our water and the foods of our forest as well."

Yes, flinging himself wildly at this asshole was looking more and more tempting.

"My people would owe you our lives," Tommen said, faltering.

"And what good are your lives?" another council member wondered lamely. "You come to us looking for help because you cannot save yourselves. What good are you?"

"I don't know. I don't know how you do things here, but my people are good at building and construction. We're good at labor."

"This is the first time we have ever heard of your people. There is no guarantee that you will not take the cure, return to your people, and never come back to fulfill your promise."

"Then you give me no reason to believe that even if I do pay you that you will not send someone after us to kill us, or at least kill me," Tommen shot back. "So either way, we're at a stalemate, and one of us is going to have to start trusting the other. Or someone is going to have to come up with some other solution."

For a moment they all sat in silence, sizing each other up, running through a hundred calculations and schemes. Finally, Sifura spoke.

"I offer a solution."

"You have not brought a gift—" one member started to say, but Dreja cut him off with, "Speak. What is your proposed solution?"

"A battle of champions," Sifura said. "On our way here, we were attacked by a xur. We lost our skimmer and almost all of our supplies, save for what is in that bag there." She indicated Tommen's burlap bag. "So I propose a battle of champions, myself against a warrior of your choosing."

"Sifura, don't—" Tommen began, but she went on as though he hadn't spoken.

"If I win, Tommen is free to collect as much of the cure as he desires, and you will supply us with the food, water, and necessary transport to make it back to my people."

The council looked at each other and spoke quietly so Tommen's translator could not pick it up. He took the opportunity to speak to Sifura.

"Are you crazy?" he hissed. "You're wounded. And what if they pit you against Karaki, or even Dreja. Fucking hell, he's a beast!"

"I am doing what is necessary," Sifura told him sharply, cutting him off with a gesture that the council was finished deliberating.

"If you win," one of the members said, "Tommen may collect his cure, and you may go with him. We will supply the necessary tools including food and water to do so. Then we will let you leave alive with the understanding that all outstanding debts with the Xur are paid, and the Ape tribe is not to return unless they have sufficient gifts and payment for future interactions."

Sifura did not look pleased, but she dipped her head. "The terms are accepted."

"And if you lose," another member interrupted, "then count yourselves lucky that we let you leave alive, assuming you survive the fight. But you will receive no food, no water, and no transport."

"Water at least," Sifura growled.

Dreja dipped his head. "Water, then."

"The terms are accepted."

"Good. Then we shall reconvene on the ground and settle this properly."

"Wait, the fight is going to be right now?" Tommen blurted.

"Of course," Sifura told him, confused. "When else should it be? We don't have time to waste on planning or thinking. If fighting is what will win you the cure, then fight I will."

Tommen shook his head. "Then I should be the one to fight."

"No. I will do it. Go now. There is work to be done."

Chapter Twenty-Two
Champion

They exited the council hut and descended the rope ladders. Karaki was nowhere to be seen, but if the gathering crowd was any indication, Tommen guessed that he'd heard the plans and come down early to find a crowd to watch the match.

He wasn't entirely certain how he felt about the whole thing; it was a dramatic turn of events to be sure, but not one that seemed to surprise either the D'Bok council or the villagers. In fact, they seemed to enjoy it as they spoke eagerly amongst themselves, forming a circle near the fire pit in the communal area. It was as though a sleepy town had awakened at the prospect of some kind of action, especially when they had the home field advantage and the champion to go with it.

Tommen hadn't heard the details of the fight, had no clue who Sifura would be fighting, didn't even understand the rules. Was there only one kind of fight to be had under such circumstances or was it more of a surprise; you didn't know the rules until you broke them sort of thing?

Whenever Tommen fought Tyler Freeman, it was always a no-holds-barred kind of fight, mostly because Tommen knew that if he didn't give it his all, Tyler would pummel him into a stain on the carpet without even a second thought. They always fought hand-to-hand, but Tommen was always vigilant, and he would never put it past Tyler to pull out a knife if he thought he was going to lose. So far, that hadn't happened as the bully usually called on his goons to step in and help in such situations.

Would the D'Bok fight like that, all dirty tricks and no honor, just to show up Sifura and snub the Xur? See, we mighty D'Bok have bested your great leader. Sifura spoke a lot about honor and respect, the honorable thing to do, the courteous thing to do, rules and formalities and all sorts of noble notions. But what happened when your opponent didn't share those values?

Easy. Tommen versus Tyler happened. Tommen held to such things as honor, nobility, dignity, respect, and Tyler still kicked his ass in every fight. Not that simple physics couldn't explain it—Tyler easily had fifty pounds on him plus a hell of a lot of training—but if honor was supposed to always triumph over dishonor, well, Tommen was still waiting for his happy ending in that story.

He followed Sifura to one corner of the communal area, outside the circle that was adding more and more spectators with each minute. She did not appear nervous or afraid, only resolute, like a warrior facing death and ready to die.

"You think I am foolish for doing this," she said before he even knew she saw him.

"Well, yeah, a little," he admitted. "Isn't there any other way to do this?"

She looked straight at him. "Tommen Forbes, you say there is nothing you wouldn't do to help your father, correct?"

"Yes. Which is why I should be the one to fight."

"And you would lose. You are not a warrior. I am."

"But it's not right."

"Why?"

Tommen didn't want to say that it was because she was female. Ingrained tradition told him that was the reason, except even in ye olde days it was sexist and wrong. Men were built to be warriors, the defenders and protectors, so women shouldn't have to be. It wasn't saying that women couldn't fight, only that they shouldn't have to, because they were far too valuable to be wasted in useless slaughter on the battlefield, or anywhere else for that matter.

Yet he really couldn't come up with a good reason. She was injured, sure, but she was still a far greater warrior than he could ever be. She was part of this world, and even if she wasn't part of this people, she still knew more about the people and their culture, their traditions and values, and possibly how to exploit them. She was the master here, and he the spectator.

He didn't like backing down, sitting on the sidelines and just watching all this happen. Sifura being female aside, this was his fight. He was the one going after the cure. He should be the one risking everything to go after it, not having someone else do the fighting for him. Even if he lost, he could still just go out, Band, and walk right back in. Where in the rules did it say that she had to be the one to fight?

"I am grateful for your concern, but I do this for your father and for your people," Sifura told him after a moment of silence.

Tommen raised a brow. "What do you mean?"

"You are the first of your people. Your people will be judged based on your actions. How you behave and perform will set the tone for all future dealings with your people."

"And I'm sitting out of the fight like a coward."

"I have offered to be your champion." Sifura's eyes blazed. "It is worse for you to fight and lose, than to have a champion fight for you and win. There is no shame in this. I will be judged according to my win or loss. You will be judged on your political interactions. If I have not explained it well enough now, I never will."

So basically, he wouldn't be thought less of by sitting this one out. Sifura would take the glory or the fall for him. It should have made Tommen feel a little better about his own standing with the council, but he still hated to see anyone else fight his battles for him. And yet, she said she would risk it. And, because he came to her for help, he came under the authority of her leadership. If she said she was going to be his champion and fight the D'Bok champion for him, he had no room to question or rebuke her.

"What does the fight entail?" he asked finally, reluctantly admitting defeat.

"The warriors will be introduced by name and accomplishments—the battles they have won and foes they have conquered," Sifura explained. "The one being put to the fight, which is me, will choose the terms of the fight."

"What terms?"

"Weapons, rules. It is easier to understand by watching than trying to explain."

It usually was. A fight that was seen in five seconds might take five paragraphs to explain. Sometimes it was better just to shut up and watch what was going on and draw his own conclusions.

"Is there a referee?" Tommen wondered. "Someone to judge the fight?"

"Only the spectators. Usually, they will call out improper actions, but it is easier just to have as few terms as possible and fight until the end."

"So this battle won't be to the death."

"No. Only until defeat, when one warrior has his opponent in such a position that he cannot hope to escape. In such a fight, I have the advantage. The D'Bok are built for brute strength and force, but they have no endurance or agility. We Xur have greater speed, endurance, and agility to break free of some positions."

Tommen could believe it, having seen her take on the xur; he could easily imagine her twisting gracefully out of an otherwise uncomfortable position. But he could also easily see the D'Bok warrior taking her whole body and giving it a single squeeze, crushing her before this cat had a chance to twist and land on all fours.

He took a breath and tried to be calm. It wasn't his fight this time. This time, he was a spectator watching the fight. This time, the fight would be between two seasoned warriors who knew what the fuck they were doing instead of two dopey adolescents hyped up on too much testosterone and foolish, narcissistic pride.

"I know you are worried, and this is probably unlike anything you experience in your culture," Sifura said, her tone softening. "But I have promised to help you, and this is how I will help you."

Tommen sighed. "So how much do I owe you?"

"Only a new skimmer and appropriate provisions."

It was difficult to judge her tone whether she was being witty and playing on his nerves, or serious and actually wanted him to somehow supply the materials to build a new skimmer, plus the provisions. He guessed the former since his confusion apparently showed on his face and her eyes glittered with amusement at his discomfort.

"Fear not, Tommen Forbes. We will get your cure one way or another."

With that, she turned her back on him and stalked off through the crowd toward the open circle. Tommen followed her movements only by the fact that she was a golden gem in a sea of ugliness. He wished he had her confidence, and the fact that he didn't seemed to show as he had a hell of a time getting through to the front of the crowd to view the circle.

Secretly he'd hoped that he wouldn't be able to get to the front, that the throng of greasy bodies would somehow impede him too much, and he would be forced to stand at the back of the crowd. And yet, that would only add to his loathing of his own cowardice, even if it wasn't called that in this culture; he would still know deep down that he'd bowed out not just once but twice. Even if he couldn't fight this battle himself, he at least had an obligation to watch his champion and cheer her on, especially since he would be the only one doing so. He had a sneaking suspicion that no D'Bok would turn against their own champion.

This was especially true when he saw that the D'Bok champion was none other than Karaki. Maybe the old bear was their go-to champion, maybe council members were not permitted to be champions, maybe it the council's way of appeasing the bitter warrior so he didn't turn on them in the future. Or maybe it was just luck of the draw. Either way, he was not someone Tommen would have enjoyed fighting. His relief at not having to fight him warred with his deep-rooted feeling of cowardice for having someone else fight for him, his emotions as much an internal battle as the impending clash of warriors was an external battle. For a moment, he thought he was going to be sick.

At some unseen cue, the crowd quieted from their chatter and their cheering, all intent on the warriors brought before them today, like sizing up a couple gladiators.

"I am the challenger!" Karaki bellowed. "Karaki, of Clan Uruk, chosen champion of the Bodek faction! I led the battle at Sundown Rocks against the Kelek faction and won with not a single loss among my men. I alone have brought the d'bok back to the clan for the tying for the last ten years. I was once the Uruk representative on the Council of Rurok, and still I fight bravely for my clan and my faction. You all know me and you know my words to be true."

The cheering and approval from the crowd was deafening, no pun intended as Tommen was forced to cover his ears for the roars and shouts that surrounded him, carrying on with seemingly no end in sight. Even when it was finally quieted, it still echoed in Tommen's ears and he almost missed Sifura stepping forward to speak.

"I am the challenged!" she said, her voice projecting as strongly and clearly as it had the night of the feast. "Sifura, of Clan Heshef, leader of the Xresa faction of the Xur tribe! I led the siege of Winded Point against the Ouin, driving back their forces with such losses that they still have not returned to that place. I have led my people through the desert on countless migrations, defended them from the dangers lurking in the sands, and have always brought them safely to the oases. I alone have brought back the xur for the tying for the last eleven years. You are not part of my tribe and yet you know my name and deeds, and you know my words to be true."

Tommen had been worried at first that the introductions were going to take forever if they had to literally recount all of their past heroics, but mentioning the most prominent or victorious ones seemed to do just as well. He allowed himself to get absorbed back into the crowd for just a second so he could Band and check his watch. Just past seven. They had to get this over with quick, whether she won or lost. If she won, they had to get a move on to wherever the cure was hiding. If she lost, they had to hurry up and leave the jungle so he could Band and they could sneak back in.

"The stakes of the match are as follows," Karaki continued. "If Sifura wins the match, she will accompany the stranger Tommen of the Ape tribe through the jungle to find the hesik flower, the cure for the illness which has befallen his people. If she loses, they will be expelled from the jungle with only their lives and some water, and they must make their way back to the oasis where the Xresa are waiting."

On Earth, some people would be utterly appalled that such a thing was even suggested. First, a barbaric fight over one little flower which was the cure for a deadly illness? It was an excellent bargaining chip to be sure, but why would anyone do such a thing except if they were cruel heathens who cared not for the value of life? Second, they professed to showing mercy by letting them leave the jungle alive, yet knowing full well that to expel them into the desert with only a tiny bit of water and a thirty day walk ahead of them was the same as killing them.

But the way the D'Bok nodded and cheered their approval told Tommen that human rights—or Xur and D'Bok and other tribe people's rights—hadn't quite made it to this planet yet, and probably wouldn't for a few more centuries.

"Challenged Sifura, name your terms," Karaki said graciously.

"I name my weapon as the knife," she decided.

Karaki went to someone in the crowd and returned with a knife. Its handle appeared to be finely polished bone, the blade glimmering steel, or so it seemed. For Sifura, a knife was tossed to the ground in front of her, one of similar style and quality, if Tommen was any judge.

"Any more terms?" Karaki questioned.

"This fight is not to the death," Sifura announced, probably more so there were witnesses to that statement, rather than just an unsaid understanding that might be conveniently "forgotten" when the blood ran hot. "If one or both opponents lose his knife, the fight will continue regardless. This fight ends only when one opponent is put in a position where he cannot hope to escape."

Tommen tried to read the crowd the way his dad had tried to teach him. There were ways to tell when a crowd was just a bunch of spectators, when they would scatter, when they would riot. Unfortunately, he'd never been too good at reading people like that, especially when they were half-bear, half-komodo dragon. But if what he knew about their culture so far said anything, they weren't likely to riot. Actually, he was more worried about them cheating.

"The terms are accepted," Karaki acknowledged, dipping his head. "Are there any more?"

"The terms are final," Sifura confirmed, also dipping her head and examining the knife. When she was satisfied, she turned and went to a spot in the circle, about three feet from the edge. Karaki did the same on the other side, and there was probably a good twenty feet between them.

Tommen wasn't sure of the rules of the beginning of the fight, if there was some signal they were waiting for before they could start, so he watched just like everyone else, almost a full minute where both warriors simply stared at each other, balancing on their feet, er, paws, shifting their weight, making small movements this way and that.

If there was a signal, Tommen didn't hear it, but he did hear the sudden uproarious cheering as Karaki made the first move, charging Sifura like a bull. If he hadn't looked so much like a bear, Tommen might have said he was a bull. He was all big, all mass, and running full steam ahead. Probably that was how he'd won the Sundown Rocks, just a straight charge, roaring and bulling his way past obstacles and through enemies, cutting down his foes right and left until none remained, even to beg for mercy. For a second, Tommen was sure that Sifura would end up just a little splotch of black, gold, and white dust on the jungle floor.

At the last second, she moved, intending to dart to Karaki's left, get out of dodge, maybe come back with some back-handed move, but where her tail lent her balance, it also gave Karaki a good point of contact. He grabbed her tail in one enormous paw and pulled. Sifura let out a purely feline screech of pain and surprise as she was jerked back and landed on her back. But she wasn't one to lay down and try to process what had happened. She kept moving, kicking her lower body out so she spun around, Karaki's knife stabbing harmlessly into dirt while Sifura managed to make contact with the back of his knees and bring him down.

Her plan initially seemed to be horribly flawed as Karaki's bulk came down on her lower legs, pinning them under his fat, furry ass, but still she kept moving, snarling at the pain but using the momentum to attach herself to his back and try to get her knife in position as if to cut his throat. But Karaki was not unused to people trying to attack from behind, and he did exactly as Tommen expected him to: he simply rolled back and laid down, squishing Sifura under him. Her arm was free however, and she again went for his throat. Karaki rolled off of her body and onto her arm, pinning it down and rendering the knife useless.

In doing so, however, he'd also sacrificed his own knife hand, and he was put in a position where he had her almost helpless, but with no real victory on his part, yet if he moved to advance himself, he gave her back the advantage. Sifura made the choice fairly easy, however, as, with a move Tommen had only ever seen in, like, Olympic gymnastics or martial arts, she brought one leg up, kicking Karaki in the jaw, and then back down, hitting first his head and then his shoulder. His position shifted just enough that Sifura was able to wiggle her arm out from under him.

Whether it was from pain or fatigue, her reflexes were slowing down, and she was unable to get a good enough grip on Karaki to keep him down before he flung her off and she landed about five feet away from him. Both were weary, that much Tommen could see. Sifura had the wind knocked out of her from Karaki landing on her while Karaki was built for a good heavy first hit, not the prolonged fight. Still, he led the second charge, again bulling his way across the circle toward her.

Sifura had learned well from the first bout. This time when she darted away, she made sure to keep her tail out of reach. Karaki slashed down into only air, but when his arm came back up, Sifura's knife met flesh. He roared in shock and pain. Sifura made a small motion with her knife and he dropped his. Then she withdrew her knife and took several steps back.

Tommen wasn't real good with detailed anatomy, and he wasn't much of a veterinarian. He knew all the organs and the major muscle groups and whatever he'd learned in health class. But from what he'd seen on TV and read on the Internet and in books, and if D'Bok anatomy was even remotely similar to human anatomy, Sifura had managed to find some muscle group, tendon, ligament, whatever the fucking difference was between the two—the one that governed the hand and allowed it to make a tight fist—and either damaged it or severed it completely. If that was true, she'd not only defeated him, but she had defeated him for life. Assuming he had any sort of decent recovery from such an injury, he would be leading no more battles. He probably wouldn't even be fit enough to skin an animal. He was done.

But as they say, it's not over 'til it's over. Once Karaki had processed what had been done to him, he stood. Slowly, wobbly, probably fighting shock and unconsciousness from the blood loss. He was in no shape to be anyone's champion or fight at all, but he knew what had been done, and if this was to be his last battle, damn it all if he wasn't going to avenge his fighting hand.

The crowd which had been so riled up and cheering for their champion was now hushed, stunned at this turn of events. They wanted to cheer, but they knew it was useless now. As the seconds ticked by slowly, Tommen watched as Karaki's movements became more sluggish and uncoordinated. He no longer charged into battle like a rabid bear, intent on killing all who stood in his path. Even his desire for revenge seemed to be fading as he fought just to stand, just to stay conscious. Truthfully, there did not even appear to be that much blood, so Sifura couldn't have hit an artery. Maybe it was all internal, or just the shock from pain.

Karaki was defeated, and he knew it. The terms had been met. Sifura hadn't killed him, only his livelihood, which, in Tommen's mind, was much worse. Take a man's life in battle and he still retains his dignity, fighting for a cause he believed in, no matter how foolishly. Take a man's livelihood, and his spirit is irrevocably crushed, and he has to drag the pieces with him for the rest of his life, the burden getting heavier and heavier with each passing year. On Earth, there was rehabilitation and programs and therapy which helped people recover their lives and, to an extent, their livelihoods. But here, in this godforsaken jungle, where survival was everything and battle even more, there was nothing for Karaki now.

Eventually, the huge bear-dragon stopped drunkenly chasing Sifura around the circle. She'd already tossed her knife away and just led the defeated warrior around and around. Now he just stood, looking at her, looking around at the crowd which waited expectantly. Was he defeated? Was it a ploy? Would their great warrior champion suddenly attack the unsuspecting outsider and win the battle when all seemed lost?

But such an attack never came. In the end, Karaki went to his knees. He brought up his arm and looked at the wound, fascinated, like how a little boy might examine a bug that had crawled on his arm. From Tommen's vantage, he could see blood soaking the fur and two severed ends of a pearly white tendon sticking out in the air. Karaki simply stared for a moment before bowing his head.

For a second, Tommen was afraid Sifura really had killed him, that she had hit an artery and he'd bled out. What did that mean for the match? Was it just considered an unfortunate turn of events and she still won? Or would she be seen in violation of the terms which she herself set down, considered the loser, and driven off? Would they suffer her to live, even, after murdering their champion?

Then Karaki looked up, looked at Sifura with a gaze almost of mutual warrior respect, one great warrior finally realizing that he'd met his match. He dipped his head once in respect, and Sifura did the same.

"I, Karaki, of Clan Uruk, champion of the Bodek faction, surrender this match against Sifura of the Xur. She has won this match according to the terms set forth and shall be declared the winner. And I, in light of injuries suffered in battle, forfeit myself as a warrior, and bear my shame in silence."

For a minute or two, it seemed like the crowd didn't know what to do. There was no cheering because the only fans in the crowd were the ones for Karaki, and he'd lost. Their greatest warrior, the one whom the parents probably told their children about and told them to emulate, had been defeated. Now they didn't know how to proceed, as if they had planned only for his victory, but were dumbstruck at his defeat. Eventually, however, the people just began to disperse and wander off. Some muttered among themselves, but most were silent. A couple villagers hurried forward to Karaki and helped him to stand. They spoke in hushed voices for a minute or two, then escorted him away.

Tommen was soon left alone to stand in the communal area like an idiot, at least until Sifura walked up and handed him one of the knives used in the match. He saw that it was hers; the blade was still bloody. She carried the one that Karaki had used.

"What's this for?" he wondered.

"Spoils," Sifura told him. "I won, so I decide what happens to what is left."

"What will happen to him?" Tommen looked around the communal area, but Karaki and his escorts were already gone.

"He will be treated as best he can be, but he will never again be a warrior."

Tommen studied her for a long minute. "Why did you do that? I understand that this is a fight between champions, but to injure him so absolutely like that, it just seems...I don't know, cruel and unusual."

"The D'Bok are not known for their mercy, Tommen Forbes. They are not known for playing by the rules. Karaki intended to end the match quickly with his first attack. When he could not, I knew he would resort to many dirty tricks which his people would not only fail to call out but help him with. I did what I had to."

"But it's more than that. You talk an awful lot about honor and respect and all that, yet you probably just condemned him to death."

Sifura looked ready to answer, then looked around suspiciously. "That is a tale to tell when we are out of this camp and on our way to find the cure."

"So, what, we just go up to the council hut and say, 'Sorry your champion's been maimed beyond any kind of usefulness. Now, about our prize...'?"

"The council will have a meeting among themselves first, to decide whether they will honor the agreement. We will join them when we are summoned."

"Wait, so you went through all that dog and pony show and we still might not get our prize?"

"It is the way of the D'Bok." She gave him a look. "I have seen your face and your body, and I have seen how you think. You think my people are primitive. Clever, intelligent, but primitive, clinging to an old way of life that will soon die out. You think that we do not know or understand the ways of the world beyond our own sands. But you are wrong. We understand very well the way of the world, how it is changing. The honor and the respect and the discipline is fading, scoffed at, as so-called 'civilization' sinks its teeth into the souls of each tribe, one by one.

"Two centuries ago, the Xur were not just confined to the desert; we also roamed where the Ouin live today. We had a more permanent village in their southern plains, where young families could reside so as not to expose a yearling to the harsh reality of the desert until they were strong enough to survive the migration.

"The Ouin attacked that village and those they did not kill, they drove into the desert with no food or water and all perished. They claimed they needed the trees, the lumber to build things. New things. They would not overcut the forests spanning the rest of their land, so they stole from others instead. All to supply their great new inventions and 'civilization.' But there is nothing civil about civilization."

"Maybe," Tommen relented, "but all peoples have to move forward at least a little. I mean, turning iron into steel is a huge deal. It's a lot stronger and more durable. And what about the differences in the architecture of your little homes in the oasis? There was a difference between the older homes and the newer ones."

"If you are going to make a weapon with which to hunt, it makes sense to improve upon that weapon. If you are going to build a house in which to live, it makes sense to improve upon that house. If you want to stay warm, you burn what is at hand. But you don't build a fire in the middle of a long desert day just because you want to see the flames."

Tommen stifled a sigh, even though he knew she would be able to detect that, too, in his expression and body language. "Some of the best inventions and innovations come out of mistakes or folly."

It was a poor rebuttal, but the only one he could offer. It wasn't that he had a thousand arguments lined up, but they were arguing different things. She was convinced that invention and attitude were the same thing, or at least irrevocably intertwined. Invention was evil. Those who thought of new things clearly weren't working hard enough or didn't want to. Tommen could see how she might perceive advancement as a threat, given that the Ouin were rude and the D'Bok dishonorable, and the Hands even more so, all of her neighbors more technologically advanced and all of them the worst representations of that advancement. Not that Tommen was going to volunteer the human race as a sterling model to be emulated.

"If the punishment were not so great—and had I understood all of this before I agreed to learn from the Araxi—I would leave Time completely," Sifura said sadly, as if reading his thoughts.

"Well, they say hindsight is 20/20." Tommen shrugged.

"Back sight is what?"

"Um, never mind. Just, you always see things better when they're behind you than when they're in front of you."

"That is very true."

"But I do have one question." Tommen shifted his stance and folded his arms. "You claim the D'Bok are dishonorable and all that, yet you willingly accept their terms and stand on their ground, metaphorically speaking. Why not take the high road, be the honorable one and play by the rules?"

"There is a saying among my people. 'When hunting kashik, think as a kashik. When walking among xur, walk as a xur.'"

"When in Rome, do as the Romans," Tommen said, nodding.

"That is what I am doing here, as much as I dare."

"And crossing the Hands? Not exactly being a very good Roman."

"There is a point where all must choose whether they are hunter or prey. If you are not hunter, you are prey."

"Problem is, some animals are both."

So there they stood in a philosophical dilemma, each in his own thoughts, pondering the mysteries of life and social hierarchy, one through the eyes of a primitive tribe leader who only wanted to do what was best for her people and keep them honest; the other through the eyes of an awkward displaced teenage boy who knew not just two, but three lives: the one of his childhood, the one as a modern teenager, and the one as a Time Agent.

Their contemplation time really only lasted a few seconds, but it felt like an eternity, and neither of them noticed the messenger who approached them. Well, he—or she or it or whatever—approached Sifura, leaving Tommen standing there like an idiot, as if he totally couldn't understand everything the messenger had to say. At the same time, Sifura was the leader of her faction and the victor in the fight. Tommen was chopped liver. Only natural that they should want to consult with her.

"The council has held a meeting to discuss the fight and its results, including the terms upon which you agreed," the messenger said. His words were supposed to be for Tommen, but he looked at Sifura and paid him no mind. As if Sifura was doing all the work for him and he had no part in it whatsoever. *No, Sifura, staying out of the fight made me look like a weak, cowardly idiot.* "They would like to meet with you again, now, for further discussion."

With that, the messenger simply walked away. He did not escort them to the council hut or even stand aside politely to watch them go.

"So, is this a good sign or a bad one?" Tommen asked.

Chapter Twenty-Three
Concession

Tommen's stomach did backflips the whole way up the rope ladder and across the bridge, and he was pretty sure it did a few cartwheels as they approached the council hut.

Immediately upon entry, Tommen knew the air was not only crackling with tension strung so thin he could cut it with a knife, but light a match and he was sure the whole place would ignite, if not just explode completely and leave nothing but ash and bits of fur and bone.

"Welcome, Sifura, victor of the fight," Dreja said stiffly.

Given how long and formal introductions normally were, Tommen got the feeling that by not using all of Sifura's titles and background and everything else that he was snubbing her in some way. Still, she took it in stride, maybe even returned the snub, acknowledging his greeting with a simple dip of the head.

"Our agreement?" she inquired coolly.

The D'Bok leader shifted in his seat, a laid-back posture that put Tommen on edge. A man has a right to be comfortable in his own castle, but Dreja just looked a little too comfortable under the circumstances.

"You know you did a grave thing, wounding Karaki in such a way," Dreja told her. "He will never again be a warrior. He will be lucky to use his hand at all."

"I fought within the rules of the match," Sifura replied. She did not say it defensively, as if being confronted, but as a simple statement of fact.

"You did. No one is denying that." Dreja stood. "Had you

faced any other warrior and done a similar thing, we on the council may not be inclined to honor the agreement. To suffer the loss of livelihood, not only as a warrior but as a productive contributor to the village and the faction as a whole, such is a fate worse than death, and one we do not tolerate lightly." While there was a measure of irritation there, his tone also suggested some sort of extra knowledge.

"Karaki is different," Sifura stated.

"Was different. He was a liability, a *tubaji* hiding in the grass and waiting to strike. He was always disquiet at not being made leader, having to submit to Rurok. When Rurok died and he was forced off the council after only a year, he went ballistic like a true d'bok." Dreja shook his head and Tommen thought he saw a look of pity cross the leader's face. "There was always speculation that he was more animal than villager, that his parents had somehow made a four-lock braid with two locks from the d'bok." Then he seemed to remember himself and was all business again. "When this council was instated and I was made leader, I sent Karaki at the head of all our war parties, hoping to use him where he was needed, where he might be fulfilled. But...it was not to be. He has had a burning resentment against us, against me, and the anger has been with him most of his life."

"Why?" Tommen interrupted a second before realizing the council wouldn't understand him. Sifura shot him a look but translated anyway. "Why? I mean, if he's off the council for good, what good does it do him?"

"What good indeed? Learn this, young warrior: there is a time for righteous anger, the burning desire to make a wrong into a right. But not all anger is righteous anger, even if we believe it so. And that which is not righteous anger is only destructive anger, and such anger cannot be controlled and reasoned with. It is a fire that must be allowed to die on its own, or forcibly snuffed out."

"So you chose Karaki to fight, hoping I'd win," Sifura concluded.

"It was a gamble, true. If Karaki won, we risked war with

your people, even if it was a fair match. And it would only add fuel to Karaki's angry fire. But we are not so foolish. We know well of your exploits and prowess in battle; few give the Xur the credit they are due. We can only be glad that the match went the way that benefited everyone."

Tommen folded his arms. So the council needed an excuse to be rid of a political rival—perhaps a truly dangerous one—but instead of dirtying their own hands (or, um, paws), they got the opportunity when he and Sifura just waltzed into their camp looking for the cure for a disease. They'd had no reason to demand the fight otherwise, except as a gamble for their own ends. It was ruthlessly clever, and Tommen had to admit he was a little impressed by it.

"You are going to honor your agreement, then?" Sifura inquired. "We are permitted to search for the hasax flower?"

"Ultimately, we were never not going to honor it," another council member informed her. "If you lost, we would give you the supplies you requested, maybe a little more, and include some medicine for you just in case. After all, those who are not Xur do not do well in the desert and we didn't want the Ape warrior falling ill." There was a mischievous glint in his eyes.

"Why not let us in on the secret?" Tommen wondered. "Why concoct this elaborate scheme and not tell us?"

"It needed to be believable," Dreja said simply. "And Karaki was always nearby, always listening; there was never a good time to tell you without him having his ear in the conversation. The plan itself had to come together over many days because Karaki always insisted on 'keeping watch' over the council hut."

So they were kept prisoners in their own castle, and now they were finally able to relax and conduct business normally again. Tommen wasn't sure what to make of all of this. He just came here looking for someone to help him find a cure for his father's illness; who knew he'd be helping those people liberate themselves from a potential psycho?

"Then you will give us the cure?" Sifura inquired. "You have some made up?"

"We must abide by the terms of the agreement," a third council member told her, perhaps a little smugly. "The Monkey warrior, Tommen Forbes, is to go into the forest to look for the cure himself, and you are allowed to accompany him."

Dreja cut in before either of them could question him. "As I have mentioned already, it must look believable. You came here for a cure which we have told you is in the forest. If it becomes known that we simply handed over the cure, Karaki may suspect something. His hand is maimed, but he still has his brute strength and notoriety. Therefore, we will proceed as agreed. You may leave whenever you wish, but I would recommend waiting until morning."

At that, Tommen Banded. Everything in the hut stopped as he checked his watch. In all the excitement, he'd almost forgotten that time was moving again. Just past eight in the evening on Friday night on Earth. If they waited until morning, which might be a little later in the jungle than the desert, it would be the wee morning hours by the time Tommen got home. Didn't matter too much, he figured, since he had pretty much forty-eight hours to accomplish a, what, maybe four hour task? But with everything that had happened so far, he didn't want to take chances. He wanted to get out and get looking as soon as possible.

He dropped the Band and life resumed.

"No. We will leave as soon as possible," Sifura told Dreja. "What supplies may we take?"

"First you should know where it is and how to get there," one of the other council members suggested. "It is not an easy climb into the foothills."

"I have been there once before."

"Years ago. Some things have changed; there have been earthquakes and rockslides and battles."

Tommen could see she was an impatient as he was to get going, but she remained calm and gestured for them to go on.

"The easiest spot to get to is a little more than half a day's travel into the foothills, just out of the main tree line. You will leave on the eastern path out of the village; when it comes to a fork in the trail, take the path heading north. Follow it until you arrive at the base of a great tree that fell over; you cannot miss it nor mistake it. Even on the ground, the tree is still taller than either of you." There was a glint of humor in some of the council members' eyes. "Attempt to scale the tree or go around it, but you must get on the old path."

"If the path is overgrown, how will we know it?" Sifura asked.

"The warriors of old, before we settled here in the jungle, they would build stone monuments to commemorate various occasions," one of the council members told her. "Such monuments were typically built along the paths leading into the old territory. The trail you will follow is one such path, and it would take more than one tree to destroy those monuments."

"Very   good.   And   when   we   find   this   path   with   the monuments?"

"Follow it still north and east. It will lead you to a rocky slope where the hesik grows. Take what you require, then return here."

Sifura dipped her head.

Tommen took a sheepish step forward. "You said that this was the easiest path. I'm all for easy routes, but is there another, closer, patch of flowers we might look into? Time is of the essence."

The council members looked at each other uncertainly.

"It is closer, true, but much more dangerous," one answered him.

"Dangerous in what way?" Sifura wondered.

"It comes very close to a known d'bok cave."

Both Tommen and Sifura hesitated. Tommen Banded.

"The d'bok are like the xur. Time does not affect them," Sifura warned him. "Our better bet is to take the longer way. With you Banding, it will not matter one way or the other if we walk for a whole day or half a day, because it will all be the same."

"They only said it was a known cave," Tommen replied, even if her argument had been completely solid and, more or less irrefutable. "D'Bok have to go out to hunt or sun themselves or, I don't know, do d'bok stuff."

But Sifura shook her head. "No. We cannot risk ourselves like that, not against a xur, and certainly not against a d'bok."

"Why? What makes a d'bok special compared to a xur?"

"It is poor luck to kill another tribe's guardian."

Fucking hell. How was it that she was able to go from stunningly gorgeous and amazingly advanced and intelligent, to primitively superstitious, in the same conversation? How could she talk to him about Time and space travel in one breath, and spirit animals who were wise and sacred and blah, blah, blah, in the next breath? It just didn't make sense to him. Pick one or the other, but you can't have both, not rationally.

But, hokey beliefs aside, her argument was sound, and he didn't particularly like the thought of running into any more wild animals, especially ones that were immune to his Banding. That part really sucked. He just wanted to be able to get in, get out, and finally go home. Camping and trekking through foreign landscapes was exciting and all, but he was ready to crawl back into his own bed, raid food from the refrigerator, maybe flip on the TV, and be a normal, lazy, modern, American human.

Reluctantly, he dropped the Band.

"In the event that the hasax is not available, or there is not enough available," Sifura began surprisingly, "where is this second patch? Or another patch near to the first?"

Dreja looked taken aback, as if questioning whether there would be enough flowers was some kind of insult. Nevertheless, he answered, "If such a thing were to happen, unlikely though it is, follow the rocky trail west. When you come to the fork leading you back to the forest, take the other trail. Follow it truly and do not divert to other trails. It will take you within a stone's throw of the d'bok cave and the second patch."

Tommen felt a little more at ease, then. Sure, he probably only needed one measly flower in order to prepare an antidote for Walter, but if they were supposed to return to the village first, they were going to have to carry enough to convince the council that they were harvesting for an entire faction. No, an entire tribe. One little flower wasn't going to be enough to convince them of that, of that much Tommen was sure.

"If that is not enough for your people, then when you return, we will discuss other locations of the plant," a council member said calmly. "However, they grow so thickly and spread so far that we would be more than surprised if there were not enough. How many people did you say were infected?"

"There are three thousand in my faction," Tommen said, picking a number off the top of his head and hoping he wasn't going to have to remember it later. "At least seven hundred were poisoned when I left."

The council member dipped his head. "One flower contains enough antidote for fifteen men. I think that once you see the plant and the flower and how far they spread, you will have no difficulty in procuring enough antidote."

"And how would you suggest we go about it?" Sifura asked innocently. "Gathering around the perimeter is easy, but if we are to collect enough, we will have to go among the plants."

"Very true," Dreja acknowledged. "Even we rarely have need for more than a couple flowers. When you prepare to leave, go to the healing hut and ask for honey. When you go to step among the plants, smear the honey wherever you fear the plants may touch: your legs, hands, arms, tail, maybe your face. The honey will do a modest job of protecting you, but it will not last forever. Gather what you need quickly. There is a stream not far from the patch, just off the trail, a mountain stream. Wash the honey from your body using a leaf or other barrier. And always save one flower for yourself just in case."

"We will remember."

"I have a question," Tommen butted in. "If the same trail directly links the d'bok cave to where we're going to be harvesting, what's to keep the d'bok from sneaking up behind us and chewing on us a little?"

"The d'bok is wary of the hesik. He can tolerate small amounts, but if you are in the middle of the patch if he comes, he will not pursue you into it. Yet he is smart enough to use it as a defense before his cave."

"Is he likely to wait us out? Is there another trail, some kind of emergency exit so we can make an escape before the honey shield runs out?"

"D'bok are not patient like xur," Dreja explained. "He may wait a short time, pace, snarl, but he will give up quickly in search of easier prey."

Tommen had heard that before. When he was six, he managed to get himself treed by the distant neighbor's bull that had escaped its pasture and gone on a small rampage. He couldn't remember exactly how it happened; maybe just a little boy antagonizing something twenty times his size and weight and ended up paying the price. At any rate, the bull charged him, chased him up a tree. It paced, circled the tree, sharpened its horns on the trunk.

His pa had found him first, not long after the incident. He might have tried to save Tommen himself except the bull was in a blind fury over something, and no one wanted to go near it. So his pa went to tell the neighbor about the incident, telling Tommen to be brave, that the bull would probably get bored after a bit, get hungry, and go off somewhere to graze.

Tommen must have sat up in that tree for an hour and a half until his pa returned with the neighbor, and the bull still hadn't given up, still pacing and circling and mooing like a hound dog howling to get the hunter's attention. It was another half hour or so before they started trying different ideas to draw the bull away safely, and then another hour before one of their ideas actually worked, and that was only after another neighbor broke four ribs — a mercy considering that if he hadn't moved at the last second, he would have been fatally gored.

When Tommen finally came down out of the tree, his hands

and feet were bleeding, his bottom was sore, his joints were aching, and his face was grubby from tears mixing with dirt and tree debris.

So now, whenever someone told him that something, that already had the potential to be very dangerous, was not going to pursue him, and even if it did, it would get bored very quickly and go away, he was reminded of that day and was very skeptical of their words. And when the current creature at hand was not only potentially dangerous, but in fact very fucking dangerous, and there was nothing he could do to really protect himself from it, Tommen almost wanted to look directly at Dreja and call bullshit.

But he refrained from saying that and instead asked, "Are the d'bok more active at certain times of day? Maybe we should avoid doing this in the dark? Or during the heat of the day?"

"D'bok are most active before sunrise and after sunset. Such is why I suggested you wait until morning." Dreja gave him a look that suggested he thought such a thing was obvious and they were idiots for not seeing it.

Sifura went to the door and looked outside. After a moment, she returned. "There is sufficient light," she decided.

Dreja merely made a motion that appeared to defer to her judgment. "If that is what you decide, we will not stop you. But everything you do or that happens to you outside of our village is upon your heads. Our agreement ends here; we converse and you walk on our land under the common laws of hospitality."

Tommen was always amused at the way some things got translated. The translators were great, nearly flawless, but every so often, something slipped through and got twisted around. Or, wait, did that actually mean that they were walking a fine line here?

"We understand," Sifura replied. "May I inquire as to supplies or provisions?"

"The journey is not long, as we have told you. Go to the healing hut and ask about honey to walk among the hesik plants. Then go to the eastern trailhead. There you will be given supplies and food sufficient for your task."

Tommen was grateful that he still had a little bit of food left. Not much, a handful of trail mix from a small package that Micah had sneaked in the bag, probably for such emergencies, and a bit of jerky. Damn, he was getting sick of jerky. He loved it, loved making it, but this was just killing him. He probably should have alternated between the beans and the jerky, but hindsight and all that.

It was just as well, though. He might try a little of their food, maybe if they had some kind of fruit or vegetable packed for them, but he could go a single day without food, two days even, if Sifura insisted that he make the return trip.

He debated that, in his mind, whether he wanted to come back to the village and go through all the niceties and formalities and charades, or if he just wanted to have Sifura open a portal to the Wheel and send him home. This wasn't his world; these weren't his people. He had no stake in this. He wouldn't lose face or standing or honor if he didn't show up. The D'bok might be a little pissy, and Sifura would probably have to take some heat for his sudden disappearance, but it wasn't his fight. His fight was against time, fighting for every second he could get in order to get the cure and get home.

At the same time, he might be able to spare an hour to go through all the formalities one last time in order to ensure that they left on a high note and with good relations. After all, if this was the only cure for Borelian poison, and if there was a war coming, he might need to be on friendly terms with the D'Bok in order to get back in with them. Or Sifura might need good relations with them for that purpose or any other, and losing the person who got you into the restricted turf in the first place probably wouldn't help her any.

"Thank you," Sifura was saying, jerking Tommen from his thoughts. "Where might we find the healing hut?"

Dreja made a motion and they left the council hut, walking out onto the main platform. The faction leader took them to a particular spot and pointed. Tommen couldn't follow where he was pointing, but he trusted that Sifura could.

"There," Dreja told her. "The healers paint it red with the blood of their patients."

"That's a little macabre, isn't it?" Tommen wondered aloud.

But Dreja only chuckled and motioned for one of the warriors on another platform to approach.

"Ready food and supplies for a three-day trip for these two," Dreja ordered. "Have them sent to the eastern trailhead."

The warrior acknowledged him and headed off to complete his mission.

"Thank you, Dreja, leader of the Bodek faction of the D'Bok tribe," Sifura told him gratefully. Tommen offered a weak echo.

"You can thank me by returning alive and bringing back some for our stores as well," Dreja informed her.

As he walked away, it was difficult to judge his tone. Was it meant as a threat that they were going to give up part of the haul or else, a demand that in exchange for the provisions they also had to provide? Or was it a simple statement of fact that one thing demanded another, being allowed on D'Bok land meant that the D'Bok people got a little cut of whatever they were intending on taking out of D'Bok land?

Sifura led the way after that, making her way across the rope bridge to the rope ladder, Tommen following uncertainly, feeling his stomach clench and not release until they were back on solid ground.

He was a bit apprehensive about going to the healing hut. It wasn't that he expected the interaction with the healers to be difficult, but he had a great suspicion that Karaki would still be there, maybe in some primitive surgery or maybe just staying there to recover. Either way, he was a huge and menacing warrior who just lost a fight, and the one who bested him was about to come waltzing in to, essentially, demand her prize.

They found the healing hut easily enough, and Tommen vaguely remembered glancing at it on the way into the village. He might have thought it was some kind of special dirt they had to use for the building, some sacred dirt maybe, or maybe it was some kind of dye or other coloring they used to distinguish the healing hut from anyone else's hut. But no, they had to go and use the blood of their patients to turn the otherwise brown mud into red mud.

While revolting, it was also fascinating to think how long and how much blood it took, not only to have colored it in the first place, but to keep it the same full red color that it was. How many hundreds of warriors had their mark upon this building? How many lay dying in this place, giving their lives for their people, their last act to give their blood to always be remembered, to leave their mark? At the same time, could it have simply been a prank by Dreja, to see how much he could make Tommen squirm?

The building itself wasn't anything remarkable. It had three rooms, a large main room that Tommen and Sifura walked into, and a room off to each side. One was separated by an animal hide curtain, the other by a more solid wooden door. Tommen could only guess at the functions of the individual rooms, but he might guess that the wooden door room was an operating room, the main room for recovery and minor injuries, and the hide curtain room where the healers themselves slept. But it was only a theory.

As he had expected and feared, Karaki was also in the healing hut, sitting up on a bed made of rough planks and covered in furs, looking a bit confused as he studied his wrapped hand and wrist, eyes a bit glassy. He did not look up at them as they entered, barely even acknowledged the healer who appeared from the hide curtain room.

"Is there something you require?" the healer asked straightly.

"Honey," Sifura told him. "We are going to harvest hasax and need to cover ourselves."

The healer considered this for a minute, and Tommen was afraid he would refuse them. In the end, however, the healer nodded and retreated back into the hide curtain room. Tommen heard the clanking and clattering of earthenware and stoneware pots and jars, the rustle of woven baskets. A moment later, the healer returned and handed each of them about a gallon-sized jar, maybe a little bigger.

Tommen couldn't decide if the pot was what made it unspeakably heavy, or if D'Bok honey was not quite like the honey found on Earth. There was a good chance it was both.

"There is enough here for each of you to cover your whole body once, or just legs and hands twice," the healer informed them. "Use it wisely as this honey is not easily gathered. It is as difficult to gather this honey as it is to gather hesik."

"Thank you," Sifura said. She stole a glance at Karaki. "Will he heal?"

The healer raised a suspicious brow. "He begged me to completely cut off his hand that he would not have to look at himself in shame ever again. The wound is not so bad, but he will never again be a warrior."

Tommen would have liked to have said that he felt smug about that, maybe even a little evil satisfaction, but he found that he couldn't muster up enough hatred or revulsion to get to that point. Karaki and his hand was like Tommen and his ears. Still there, not completely useless, but they would never fully, truly heal, and they would have to live with that for the rest of their lives, always remembering the day everything changed. And Tommen had a feeling that his lifespan was going to be much longer than Karaki's.

Sifura thanked the healer again, and they left the healing hut, heading back through the communal area and turning to the east. It took some doing, navigating the twisting streets, but eventually they came across the eastern trailhead. Or Tommen assumed it was the eastern trailhead since the same warrior Dreja had pulled aside was also just arriving with a small pack, presumably filled with provisions.

"Supplies and provisions for your journey," the warrior reported formally, holding the bag out to Sifura.

Sifura thanked him, bade him set down the pack, set down her own jar of honey, and dismissed the warrior who left promptly. Then she knelt in the dirt and opened the pack.

To Tommen's relief, it seemed as though the D'Bok had a wider variety of provisions to offer them. There was some dried fruit and vegetables, something like looked like pita or little rice cakes, strips of jerky, and a number of dry goods that might have resembled beans or nuts. And there were flasks of water, too, which Tommen guessed was moderately safe since he hadn't keeled over since drinking at the river on the way in. But still...alien tapeworms...

"Is it sufficient?" Tommen wondered as Sifura replaced everything in the bag.

"It is," she decided, standing and shouldering the bag before picking up her jar of honey. "We will use the honey to get into the flowers, then we will use the jars to carry the antidote back."

"Sounds like a plan."

Then they started off into the jungle on what Tommen hoped desperately was the real final leg of the journey to get the cure for his father's illness.

Chapter Twenty-Four
Into Darkness

It wasn't until about a mile into their journey that Tommen started considering the fact that the honey they'd procured and were now so painstakingly lugging around through the forest might be as harmful and poisonous to him as the plants they were supposed to protect themselves from. He thought about bringing up the subject to Sifura, then decided against it. She seemed to favor silence while traveling, and he didn't want to get on her bad side, not after what she'd just done to Karaki, and especially not now since they were so close to their goal.

Even if the honey did turn out to be poisonous, he figured there were some advantages to it. For one, Sifura was probably much more adept at quickly gathering flowers and herbs and such. Giving her full reign to do the harvesting would probably yield more than having him bumble around alongside her, getting spooked by this thing or distracted by that thing or stopping because he wasn't sure and had to ask a dozen questions before making a move. Plus, if this place they were going to had any kind of lookout point or even just an advantageous view, he could stand watch for any d'bok in the area. Mystical spirit animals or not, they were still animals, and even if he couldn't hear them, a good watch point would let him see them coming.

They found the first fork in the road easily enough and soon after stumbled upon a small stream that ran along the path for a good distance. They almost didn't stop, but when Sifura looked back at him, she found him looking longingly at the cool, clear water. She did not announce their stop, just stopped suddenly, and Tommen almost ran into her. Avoiding her, he then almost tripped and fell, which would have launched the honey jar from his arms, almost certainly breaking the jar. Carefully, he got his body in a position where he could slowly lower the jar versus dropping it. Groaning, he sat on the jar for a second before slithering to the ground and moving toward the stream.

"You have walked a long way today," Sifura said calmly, almost like a master praising the work of an apprentice. "Through many unfavorable conditions and weather, you have braved unfamiliar terrain and a hostile people, and you have maintained a Time Band with the skill of one above your rank. I know your people are not a warrior race, but you have demonstrated true warrior skills in your time here, Tommen Forbes, and for that I commend you."

Tommen looked up from the stream, unsure how to respond except, "Thank you. I've had a good and patient teacher."

"Your father will be proud of you."

He paused, not sure if it was a simple statement of fact or if he was supposed to say something to that. In the end, he did not say anything, simply drank his fill and reached into his pack for a couple strips of jerky. Fuck, he was sick of jerky. He loved it, but he was sick of it. First thing he was going to do when all of this was over and he and Walter were heading home, they were going to stop at the bakery. Walter was going to get his pastry, and Tommen was going to get one of everything on the menu. No more jerky, just the wonderful taste of freshly baked bread, some muffins, cookies, cake, a little bit of everything.

"You are weary," Sifura observed as she got up from her spot at the bank. "Perhaps we should wait and rest for a few hours."

"No," Tommen said, maybe a little more sharply than he meant. "No, let's keep going. Less than half a day's travel to go, and we're going to make it there before we camp."

For a minute, it almost looked like she was going to refuse and insist on camping, but ultimately, whatever she was thinking, she did not say. She simply picked up her jar of honey, waited for him to do the same, and they continued on.

Truthfully, Tommen was tired. He was very tired. He was more than tired; he was dead exhausted. Adrenaline and fear and jerky and that little orange pick-me-up flower drink had kept him going for the last seven days—approximately five Earth days if he was right—with short four hour naps here and there. Now it was all starting to catch up to him as his arms felt weak, his steps were slow, and his eyelids grew heavy. Right now, the fatigue was only still creeping up on him. By the time they reached the hasax patch, he knew it would be beating him over the head with sledgehammers, battering his muscles and his joints, sending waves of pain through his head, both from the lack of sleep and the constant Banding.

The Banding was probably what was screwing with him the most. It only let him slip into various Time Bands that moved faster or slower than the Base Time around it, but his internal clock was still functioning on that Base Time. His metabolism got a little screwy which was why most Timekeepers were prone to slowed aging, but his basic concept of time was still locked into Base Time, regardless of what kind of Band he was in. That was why he perceived seven days of Banding, or five days, but he'd only been gone for about a day as far as anyone on Earth was concerned. Double-Banding was a way to trick the mind into thinking it was back in Base Time, but Tommen hadn't learned that trick yet, creating Bands within Bands, maybe infinitely. Just thinking about it was enough for a small headache to creep into his brain. Forcing his body and mind through those kinds of differentials could give him one hell of a migraine. Staying in the Band for as long as he had, had managed to stave off the big one, but dropping out of the Band while treating with the D'Bok had given him a pretty good headache that his current Band was not helping any.

And there was that whole bit about having to go back through the portal to the Wheel, and then another portal back to Earth. That was hell on a good day. After all this, he would be grateful if he didn't end up a vegetable, sharing a room in the hospital with his dad. He doubted that such excessive Banding could actually do that; after all, he was only a probationary, and even Gatekeepers could do far worse things, and they didn't end up as vegetables. At least, not that Tommen knew about.

He let out a breath he hadn't realized he'd been holding. Fuck, he just wanted this trip to be over. No more feasts, no more long treks through any kind of obscenely and almost comically dangerous terrain, no more giant beasts waiting for them in the shadows, no more bullshit internal politics that only hindered them in their quest for the greater good. Was it really too much to ask for a part of their journey to go the way he wanted it to, the way it was supposed to go? If there was some kind of God out there, could He at least do that much? Just once?

"You are quiet back there, Tommen Forbes," Sifura said suddenly.

"Yeah, well, normally you're getting mad at me for talking your ear off, so I figured I would just stay quiet and let you take the lead," Tommen replied, stifling a yawn.

"Perhaps, but now the D'Bok know we are here, we have permission to be here, and we are not seeking prey. Therefore, silence is no longer mandatory."

"But wouldn't conversation only attract larger hunters to our position?"

"Loud conversation maybe, and we make enough noise just by moving carelessly about that any small- or medium-sized hunter would hear us. Most would not be interested. Those that might venture forth would be distracted by the small prey animals we are frightening off."

"All right, then, since you just said it's okay to talk, answer my question."

"What question?"

"Why did you maim Karaki like that? Fine, so he's arrogant, but he's not your problem; he's D'Bok, you're Xur. Why did you seem so eager to help out the council, even if you didn't know it at the time? What was all that about?"

Sifura cast him a brief glance before answering, seeming to choose her words carefully. "Karaki has been well-known among the neighboring tribes since long before the Sundown Rocks, and he was known among my people even before he was a full warrior. It was during a trading expedition, where we were to acquire some lumber in order to build a new skimmer..."

Tommen had hoped her answer would be short and to the point. Barring that, if she did have to tell a story so he got the background and details, she could have at least made it dramatic, even a little. Something that ended with "He killed my father" or "He vowed vengeance on any Xur he saw in the future."

What he got was basically Karaki's life story as it was known by the Xur from their interactions with him. Given that no one here seemed to have invented written language yet, Tommen might have expected that stories and legends and traditions were passed down orally. The casual news of the day or some lingering gossip had never entered his mind as qualifiers for stories that went on and on and on and on. He would have been afraid to ask any of the D'Bok the same question about Karaki for fear of getting a complete oral history of Karaki and the entire D'Bok tribe.

Not that he didn't get the gist of the tale she told, seemingly oblivious to how he'd almost completely tuned her out. Karaki had done this, done that, killed this person, threatened that person, overturned a desperate trade agreement, went here, went there, and on and on in went. Okay, fine, so he wasn't a very nice guy. Tommen liked villain origin stories as much as anyone, but he didn't need to know about every time Karaki stubbed his toe and so vowed vengeance on orthopedic podiatrists.

Sifura was like an endless encyclopedia. Maybe Karaki's story ran out or maybe she got distracted by something else, but when he rejoined the program briefly to find out where she was and what was going on, he found her going on about the relationship between the D'Bok and the Poqip and how that affected the relationship between the Xur and the Poqip. D'Bok territory only extended into the foothills of the mountains, but they enjoyed pushing their limits to see what the Poqip would let them get away with, which usually wasn't much. So they were always fighting. The Xur usually wanted to trade for the rare fruits and berries that grew only at the higher elevations, but because most of those fruits and berries were also used as salves and medicines, the Poqip did not part with them easily.

"Are we likely to come across any Poqip?" Tommen inquired lazily.

"No," Sifura told him, not missing a beat. "We are still too close to the flatlands."

Then why do I care about the Poqip? he wanted to ask, but he kept his mouth shut. In a way, he figured she enjoyed telling him the stories, a fresh ear for old tales.

Dreja had been right about the fallen tree; there was no way they could mistake any other tree in the forest for the one they needed. It stood, on its side, probably thirty feet tall, maybe taller. Carefully, Tommen set down his jar and went up to the tree. It smelled like fresh mulch, that sweet earthy smell before it got into full, stinking rot. He kicked at it. The wood was just soft, but not going anywhere yet.

The trail they were on diverted sharply to the right. Backing up and looking up, Tommen could see a break in the tree line where new trees hadn't completely obscured the old trail.

"Guess we'll have to go around," he said, hefting his jar, stumbling a few steps, adjusting, and moving on before Sifura could say anything about him being too tired to carry on. Fucking hell, but if he was this close, there was no way he was going to stop now because of a little fatigue.

They traveled toward the base of the tree, about forty feet away or so, where the broken stump had to be fifty feet across. The shards at the base of the fallen tree had been cut away to form a small man-sized, or rather, D'Bok-sized tunnel to the other side. It smelled even sweeter in the tunnel, like fresh cedar. Tommen and Sifura shimmied through as best they could, their packs occasionally getting hung up on one splinter or another.

When they emerged on the other side, the trees thinned noticeably after about a hundred yards, revealing craggy foothills standing guard for the endless mountains beyond. It was almost like coming home, and Tommen felt a shiver of excitement wash through him, giving him renewed energy.

Backtracking along the tree, they found the old trail and the first of a dozen stone monuments that still stood along the path. Dozens more were long since knocked down into piles of rubble, some so covered in moss and new growth that they were almost completely covered, erased from the tribe's history.

It was a wonder how they came to be knocked down, as these were not little rocks that were cobbled together like some child's plaything. These were *inuksuk*, thirty feet tall, huge slabs of rock meticulously set one way or another to create things that might have been a man-shape or an animal-shape; some looked more like abstract geometric shapes, a sort of Stonehenge. Whatever significance or symbolism or message they were revered for at one time was now long gone.

Tommen almost found it strange to think about a primitive alien world having anything that resembled ancient history, something that was talked about, sung about, speculated about, but ultimately lost. He looked around at the mountains before them and the jungles behind. Did these tribes have the equivalent of the Mayans? The Egyptians? Were the D'Bok with their crude weapons on their way to becoming the Romans of this world? Would any one tribe leave that kind of lasting impression on their entire world?

The trail soon turned from soft earth to hard-packed earth and pebbles, to stony and jagged rocks. It turned from a level cake-walk to a steep mountain climb, and more than once Tommen missed a step and almost landed face-first in razor-sharp rocks. After the first few cuts and punctures, he learned to just bite his lip each time a rock found the soft flesh of his foot. The jar of honey grew heavy in his hands as they continued up the trail, always heading west when a choice arose.

"How far?" Tommen asked once, as if he expected Sifura to know.

"We will come upon it soon, I am sure," was all she answered, but even she stumbled and limped along the trail, gaining new wounds alongside ones already sustained and only half-healed.

He was pretty sure they'd been traveling for more than half a day, but then he figured that estimation was based on a couple of young, fit warriors who ran twenty miles every morning with a hundred pound backpack, could wrestle a bear with their bare hands, could scale a mountain with no equipment and a river of lava below them, and they probably walked away from explosions on a routine basis in order to impress girls. The more he thought about it, the more Tommen considered that the D'Bok probably had scales on the bottoms of their feet, so all the sharp rocks probably didn't mean anything to them, if they registered at all.

"Fucking sons of bitches," Tommen hissed.

"What?" Sifura gave him a brief glance. In the moment she took to do so, one foot went out from under her. Carrying a big ass stone jar and having virtually no reflexes left, Tommen couldn't really do anything to help. She gasped and landed on a knee, er, hock which might not have been bad except when she got up, leaving the jar on the ground, there was a pretty good size stone cut into her hock. Not saying a word, she picked the shard out of the wound, and it bled freely.

"Can you walk?" Tommen asked.

"Yes," Sifura said shortly, trying to cover up the pain. "I saw the hasax, just over the ridge."

"Why don't you go on ahead? Find a spot to camp. I'll bring my jar and then come back for yours."

For a minute, it looked like she was going to refuse and insist on carrying her jar, but in the end, common sense seemed to win. Reluctantly, Sifura nodded and carefully picked her way up the slope and hurried off as fast as she could. Then, briefly questioning his sanity for volunteering to carry two heavy ass stone jars, Tommen followed.

His going was a little slower since the plants were near and he didn't really have to keep up with Sifura now, and he wasn't about to end up like her, not when they were so close. Bad enough he needed hearing aids; he didn't need knee surgery, too.

Getting away from the desert, out of the jungle and starting into the mountains had seen a pretty significant drop in temperature, and the cold winds coming down from the peaks didn't help things either. Sifura had found a sort of pseudo-cave and was working on building a small fire. The trail outside the cave was narrow, with a sort of rock wall on the outside, which would also help to keep the heat in. Tommen deposited the first honey jar in the cave and went back for the second without even hardly looking at the hasax.

The prospect of finally reaching the cure, finally reaching his goal, after all the stress and hassle and heartache so far, it seriously made Tommen want to break down in tears, he was just so happy. There was no other way to say it other than he was fucking happy. It was almost enough to make him think that maybe somewhere out there, there was some kind of God-like entity who'd decided to show mercy for once.

Between the rage of emotion and all the work he'd done so far to climb this mountain, he almost couldn't even pick up the jar, never mind carry it. It was all he could do to get it up to the level part of the trail that led to the cave. After that, he elected to just slide the damn thing. As he got closer to the cave, he could see a glow. Making the last turn into the cave, there was fire and warmth. Sifura had a little fire going and was cooking some kind of meat over it.

"I've never seen you cook your meat," Tommen said dumbly, surprising himself at what he'd fixated on in his exhaustion.

"It is not necessary," Sifura told him simply. "But I was cooking this for you. Your people need proteins, and you need a change in flavor. I have seen your revulsion lately as you eat your jerky."

He wasn't too keen to try alien meat, either, but he didn't say that. Actually, it sounded pretty damn good. Having a nice steak would be just the thing he needed to perk up a little. Stupidly, he sat down against one wall of the cave and closed his eyes.

Almost immediately, he was assaulted with dozens, hundreds of images and memories from being in Rifun's cave. Being alone, being there with Tadashi, being there with Isthim. Isthim telling him all about the Borelians and what each color could do, even though he couldn't see half of them. Not that it mattered since they were all dangerous. Memories of his dream about being assaulted by Borelians, of the conversation with Cassius that followed. Memories of small, sporadic meals. Memories of hunger and thirst, of sleeping on a stone floor on a blanket that did little to keep out the cold, and the only source of heat was a small fire that couldn't be allowed to get too big lest it kill them all.

Tommen wasn't sure how he got there, but he found himself at a low rock wall, looking at regurgitated trail mix and jerky splattered over the side of the wall. His entire body was shaking. He tried to tell himself he was shaking from the cold, and that the water from the stream just disagreed with him. While entirely plausible, he also knew it was entirely a lie.

Was that a panic attack? Just from walking into a cave and sitting down? Was his mind really that fucked up that he couldn't even do simple things like that? Why hadn't he felt anything when he revisited Forbes Cave? Did he actually have to be in a cave for a panic attack to trigger? Was he going to have to sleep outside in the cold tonight? He would freeze to death.

No. He wasn't going to sleep out in the cold. They were going to pick those flowers and he was going to go home and help his dad. No more of this nature channel, *National Geographic* tribal commentary, none of that shit. He was getting his cure and getting the fuck out.

By the time he stumbled back into the cave, his resolve had all but deserted him. He was tired, he was weak. He'd been going too strong for too long. He was determined not to trip at the finish line, but maybe a short nap wouldn't hurt. Of course, the hare thought that, too, and the tortoise won. If he, the hare racing to get the cure, took a nap now, the tortoise that was the slow but steady disease, would win. He couldn't have that.

Taking care to make every movement deliberate and focused, Tommen fished around in his pack for a bottle of water. One left. He went outside to rinse and spit the lingering acid and vomit from his mouth, then drank only a small portion from the bottle before returning to the cave. So far, Sifura hadn't said anything, just remained intent on turning the pieces of meat into charcoal. Tommen might have stopped her, then figured that at least it would be cooked thoroughly and he wouldn't have to worry about food-borne illnesses. Ha ha ha.

"Are you well enough to eat?" she inquired, finally handing him the stick.

He sighed, hesitated, but took the stick and started eating.

He wished he could have laughed and said it tasted like chicken. He wished he could have been amazed at incredible flavor in the meat and a gourmet rubbing of spices. He wished he could have been repulsed by some awful, bitter, gamey flavor or some obscene mixture of spices. As it was, it was burned meat that bordered on charcoal. It had virtually no flavor. Likewise, it probably had no nutrients left in it either, protein or otherwise. But it was food, something other than jerky, and his stomach was thankful.

Sifura ate her meat as it was, watching Tommen through stern golden eyes.

"What?" he wondered wearily.

"You must rest," she told him. "Sleep. I will gather the hasax."

"But I can't Band if I'm unconscious."

"What time is it on your world?"

Tommen rubbed his eyes and looked at his watch. Handy thing, that. Some small part of his brain, the conspiracy theory side, thought it was awfully convenient that he should get such a present at exactly the right time when he would need and use it the most. Then the conspiracy drifted away as he said, "A little past eight in the evening on Friday night. We've got forty-eight hours."

"And you think it will take that long to get one flower for your father?"

"No, but we do seem to have to go back to the village and talk to the council again and—"

Sifura shook her head. "No. You will take your flower back to your world and heal your father. Let me worry about the D'Bok."

"Great, so let's go get it." He shifted positions as if to stand up, but his body had had enough and was now contracting in pain in all his muscles and joints. His mouth opened in a silent gasp of pain as he went to a knee.

"Even if we did get the flower, you are not strong enough to go through the portal back to the Wheel, and then through another portal to your home."

She probably had a point. But still.

"How am I supposed to get home, anyway? Micah and Micaiah won't still be in the Wheel to do it."

Humor and mischief glittered in her eyes. "Hands may open portals where they wish."

He blinked. "So then why not open a portal directly here, to the hasax?"

"Because it would be rude to steal from the D'Bok so. And because the Wheel knows when such a thing is done, and it is reported to the secretaries and the other Hands."

Tommen sighed. "If this cure does work, better that the Hands didn't have access to the exact coordinates of the hasax."

"Yes. They would not only destroy every plant they found, but anyone who had ever touched, seen, or even heard of it. Better to think I was merely returning to my own people."

He was ready to say more, but was interrupted by a yawn.

"Sleep," Sifura commanded gently. "I will gather hasax and wake you in a little while."

Chapter Twenty-Five
A Moment with Micaiah

Micaiah leaned back in his chair in the office, exhausted from his argument with Madison and Adams and Washington and all the other dead green guys laid out in front of him. There weren't many, really, as most people preferred to use a card, but that didn't make end-of-night counting any easier. They lost more credit card receipts than dollar bills, which meant he had to go back into the register and do a full, detailed printout, then cross-reference it twice to make sure everything was in line. And really, it was more for tax purposes than any real fear of his younger brother stealing from the business. He didn't even worry about Tommen too much, not after three years of a near-perfect register record.

There was a soft knock on the door and Micah poked his head in. *"An bhfuil aon rud ort?"* (You need anything?)

Micaiah sighed, looked out at the small puddle of green, and shook his head. *"Nach bhfuil. Lean ort agus dul abhaile."* (No, go ahead and go home.)

Micah frowned, his expression perfectly capturing the same question going through both their minds. Except now Micah dared to voice it. *"Aon facal ó Tommen?"* (Any word from Tommen?)

"Níl." (No.)

Micah opened the door and leaned against the door frame, arms folded. *"Tá an Roth ag éiri níos contúirti. An bhfuil ar bhealach ar bith a sheoladh dó teachtaireacht?"* (The Wheel is getting dangerous. Is there any way to send him a message?)

"Níl. Ní mór dúinn súil a féidir leis an duillín isteach agus amach gan a bheith faoi deara." (No. We just have to hope that he can slip in

and out without being noticed.)

For a minute they stared at each other in silence. Again, Micah asked the question. *"Má tharla rud éigin dó, ar fhios againn faoi?"* (If something happened to him, would we ever know about it?)

Micaiah considered that for a minute. *"Má tharla rud éigin nuair a bhí sé le Sifura, ceapaim ar insíonn sí linn. Má tharla rud éigin den dá cheann acu agus na snáthaidí taobh thiar de sé, ní bheidh na freagraí againn go deo."* (If something happened while he was with Sifura, I think she would tell us. If something happened to both of them and the Hands were behind it, we may never know.)

"Cén uair tabhairt sinn suas?" (When do we give up?)

"An céanna a dhéanann sé. Nuair a tá Walter sé troigh faoi thalamh." (The same time he does. When Walter is six feet under.)

"Braithim ciontach, nach bhfuil ag dul leis agus cuidiú." (I feel guilty, not going with him and helping.)

"Ní féidir linn gach rud a dhéanamh. Agus má tá sé ní féidir é a dhéanamh, ar cabraigh ár láithreacht rud ar bith." (We can't do everything. And if he can't do it, our presence would help nothing.)

Micah still seemed uncertain, but finally nodded in reluctant agreement. *"Ceart go leor. Bhuail, taím ag dul abhaile."* (All right. Well, I'm going home.)

"Féach leat." (See you there.)

Micaiah waited until he heard the back door squeak shut before looking again at all the faces on the table. *"Nach bhfuil aon smaointe agaibh?"* (You guys don't have any ideas, do you?)

The bills were silent as ever. Grudgingly, Micaiah shuffled all the little papers and receipts again and began his second count. He could have Banded easily enough, but it wouldn't make the work any less tedious. He could take an extra hour or two in the morning; it was Saturday, and they would be pretty slow.

Micaiah hadn't said that he agreed with his brother, about feeling guilty for not going with Tommen. He might have been able to justify it by saying that they were doing some great work while on the home front, but that would only be a lie. After the kid left, he and

Micah had managed to Band their way through a couple of days, back and forth on each other, enough to recover enough to get back into the Wheel and check on things there. He almost wished they had stayed blissfully ignorant, called in sick as it were.

Things were not going well, to say the least. It wasn't even the Hands causing most of the trouble, but the Grandfathers. They were furious, not only that someone had potentially found a cure for their deadliest weapon, but that it was suggested that the Hands use that to control them. And on top of that, the suggestion had come from the Timekeepers, who worked the closest with the Grandfathers. It hadn't gotten to war yet, but then, by some Jewish estimates, World War II started long before Hitler ever entered Poland.

Exhausted, distracted, and not a little hungry, Micaiah finished up the counts and bundled the money appropriately, the change for the start of the till in the morning, the rest to go to the bank. Then he fished out his keys, turned off the lights, locked the doors, and headed for his car.

A storm had blown in during the afternoon, and it hadn't let up, snow falling in tiny icy flakes while the wind whipped up the soft stuff from the ground, creating a wild, hazy mess. He shivered against the cold as he backed out of the parking lot. *I hope you're enjoying that desert,* Tommen, he thought bitterly.

The going was slow, if not from the roads, then from the plows as they plodded along dutifully. Any other night, Micaiah might have been peeved, but right now, he really didn't care. For one, he wasn't in a rush. For two, he wasn't an idiot. He'd seen more than one accident outside the bakery at the intersection, and usually someone involved was going too fast.

He made it to the bank quickly enough he supposed, filling out the little receipt at the night drop box before plunking the envelope down into the abyss and driving away. As he got out to the drive at the road, he paused. Going right would take him home. But his mind was running wild, and even as tired as he was, he knew he wouldn't get to sleep, not until his curiosity was satisfied. So he turned left, toward the hospital.

Part of him hoped that Tommen had already found the cure and come back, more intent on saving Walter than calling either of them to let them know he was back. Part of him hoped that he would walk in the hospital, go up to Walter's room, and find them both there, awake and talking, putting him in the awkward position of having walked in on a special father-son moment.

He was delayed once as he came upon on accident, momentarily blinded by red, white, and blue flashing lights. A police officer stopped him and radioed something. Behind him, a firefighter guided an ambulance out of its spot and gave the all-clear. More lights, and then a siren was flipped on, and the ambulance took off. A second or two later, the officer motioned him forward. Judging by the scene as he rolled past, probably a head-on, one pickup into another, someone inadvertently crossing the center line either from weather or fatigue.

Then he was on his way, greeted two minutes later by a bright sign advertising the hospital. He just caught a glimpse of the ambulance pulling around back.

He circled the lot a time or two before concluding that everyone wanted the best parking spot. In the end he settled for something that was technically pretty close to the front of the row, but still pretty far from the doors. Then, as he pulled on his gloves, he Banded and got out of the car.

Snowflakes were frozen in midair, distant from his position. But those in the immediate vicinity were still swept this way and that in the winds that knew no bounds of Time. A step in a small snow mound showed him where a hole had formed in his shoe, as snow weaseled its way in and melted, soaking his sock. He walked around a plow that did its best to keep the lot cleared amidst cars in various stages of being buried.

Then he was inside, the blast of warm air as Micaiah forced open the automatic doors a welcome relief. He politely stomped his feet clean of snow, his eye immediately going to a small yellow "Wet

Floor" sign not ten feet from the door. Shaking his head, he went to a map of the hospital, hung on one wall, to get his bearings. Down the hall to the stairs and then up two floors. From there, he was fairly certain he knew the way. Doing a quick double-check, he took off his gloves and started down the hall.

That was the thing about Banding, he mused as he found the door to the stairwell. It was incredibly convenient and useful and very nice for being sneaky, such as sneaking around a hospital after visiting hours, but it had its limits. For example, it was entirely possible that he could extend and form his Band around the elevator, getting into all the little nooks and crannies and wires, and make it work for him while in the Band, but he had to be sure to include the entire mechanism, every gear and cable, every button and electrical switch and motherboard.

As it was, just taking the stairs was much easier, and the exercise helped him focus. Then he was on the ICU floor. It was the only floor that was always going, going, going, twenty-four hours a day. There was no rest, there was no down-time. Doctors, nurses, drugs, always moving, always going here and there.

But now they were still. A doctor flipped through a patient's file. A couple of nurses signed out some drugs from a cart. A receptionist looked at her computer screen. A couple more nurses stood around, gossiping for a minute. A janitor mopped up a spill. Yet another nurse stood just out of sight around a corner, tapping away on his phone. Micaiah bypassed all of them, weaving around them until he found the door he was looking for.

For the moment, there were no nurses in the room. But there was a familiar face, sitting in the chair, chin in hand, bloodshot eyes looking hopelessly at the man with the bushy mustache. Micaiah dropped the Band. Life resumed, but he hardly noticed as he approached.

"What are you doing here?" he asked.

Lily looked up at him, and he really couldn't say if her red eyes were from fatigue or if she'd actually been crying. How long had it been since she cried? He couldn't recall her ever crying. What was it about Walter that made her cry? Just that he'd saved her life? For a moment, she almost didn't appear to recognize him, then it came and she looked away, back at Walter.

"I'm coming to terms," she told him.

"What terms?" Micaiah demanded, suddenly fearful.

She looked at him like he was crazy. "He's going to die, Micaiah. I know you've sent Tommen out on some heroic mission, but things don't work out like that in the real world. Walter's gone. He's going. But..." She shook her head.

"How much time does he have?"

"Forty-four hours, twelve minutes, thirty-eight seconds."

Micaiah folded his arms. "How much Potential Time does he have?"

Lily shook her head again and looked at him. "It's the same. That's the thing about Borelian poisons; they wreak havoc on everything. Normally, in NICU, or with anyone, I can see their Actual Time, and then their Potential Time. So a neonate who is dying, I might see three days left in its Actual Time, but eighty years in its Potential Time, the Time and life it would have had if it had been perfectly healthy. Borelian poisons work against that, making Harvesting useless."

"So even if Tommen saves him..."

"That's a big if."

"If he did, though. If he did find a cure."

"I don't know. Micaiah, we're talking about Borelian poisons. Something there isn't supposed to be a cure for, and that the Borelians and the Grandfathers and the Hands are about to go to war over. I don't know what happens if Tommen does magically find a cure."

"And there is nothing else in the universe that does this, with the Actual and Potential Time?"

"Not that I've encountered, but in all reality, my experience is very limited. I work with dying human babies. Okay, I don't go out with the cops and firefighters on car accidents or house fires; I don't work in the ER with grandma having a heart attack or grandpa having a stroke; I don't work with cancer or AIDS or any of that. Well, no, I did have an AIDS baby once. But still. I'm not an infectious disease kind of person. I don't know."

In another life, Micaiah hated Lily, not the least for her high-horse attitude, her incredible wealth of knowledge whose vastness rivaled the Archives themselves. Never had he more wished that she had an answer, a story, even a theory. To hear her say she didn't know something was like mentally pushing Micaiah over a wall into an abyss. Walter was going to die. He and Micah could have sent Tommen to his death on the basis of some folktale medicine of a people they knew next to nothing about, his companion being part of the very institution that had all but started the war in the Wheel in the first place.

Still, he showed nothing on the outside. He wouldn't let Lily see that she'd shaken him. He just had to keep hoping, hoping that this folktale medicine not only existed but that it worked, and that his companion was as selfless as she appeared and actually helped him to get it and didn't leave his body in some godforsaken alien desert.

For a moment, they stood in silence, watching Walter as machines cranked out numbers and scans.

"Is there any way to know if and when he'll stop breathing on his own?" Micaiah inquired, electing to say it softly rather than risk his voice cracking.

"That's at a level far above me," Lily told him. "But I can't imagine it's too far from the end."

"And the doctors haven't found anything pointing them in the direction of a poison?"

"I don't get told much, but from what I've been able to glean and overhear, they found something. They just don't know quite what that something is."

Micaiah sighed. "And even if they do, it's unlikely they'll be able to do anything about it."

"Yes."

"What about a couple days ago, when we added those three or four seconds?" Micaiah asked.

"I don't know." Her expression was that of total helplessness. "I just don't know. I don't know how it happened or why it happened or what it means or how to recreate it. Honestly, for all I know, Walter could be completely aware of what we're saying, screaming an answer in his mind, and we can't hear him."

For all the havoc that the poison was wreaking on Walter, Micaiah was fairly sure that all the hospital machines were working properly. He was no neurologist, but he knew enough that the EEG said otherwise. Awareness he couldn't speak for, but the brain waves said he wasn't exactly screaming and pounding at the bars of his cell, begging to be set free.

"Are you still working, or did you take some time off?"

"No, I'm working," Lily told him. "I worked the day shift today."

She said, "I worked the day shift." Micaiah heard, "I forwent partying with my friends and getting wasted in favor of coming and sitting at the bedside of a dying friend."

"How long are you staying here?" he found himself asking.

"I don't know." He was getting really nervous about her saying that all the time suddenly. "Until I get tired. Until they ask me to leave. Until they forcibly remove me. How long until you give up?"

Micaiah's walls immediately shot up, and he answered stiffly, "Not until he's six feet underground."

She nodded slowly. "That's good. Hold out hope until the last."

She rubbed her eyes. He relented.

"Do you need a ride home?" he asked.

"No, I'm fine." Even as she said it, he could see that she was fighting a yawn. "I'm no Timekeeper who can Band his way through anything, but I'll be all right."

"You're exhausted, and you shouldn't be driving on these

roads when you're tired, or at all for that matter, but we all have to get home somehow."

She sighed. "Are you leaving right now?"

"Storm isn't getting any better. And neither is he."

He could see that she hated him for using her own words against her. In a way, he felt pretty rotten about it, too, but he was leaving and if she was coming, they had to leave now. Finally she nodded. "All right. Just give me a second."

Micaiah Banded, and she gathered her things, following him to the door where they almost walked straight into a nurse just walking in. And it wasn't like the cute little petite nurse every guy dreams of being waited on by; this was the overweight gamer-turned-nurse kind of guy that no one really wanted to wait on them, but who probably knew a lot more about nursing than Cutie Blondie in that he wasn't exactly able to sleep his way through nursing school.

"How do we get past him?" Lily wondered, her voice edged with revulsion.

Micaiah took a step back to a spot just behind the door where the nurse wouldn't see them, assuming he kept his present trajectory and didn't suddenly look to the left. With Lily beside him, Micaiah reached out and brought the nurse into the Band. As expected, he headed to the right, toward the patients. Then, Micaiah let him out of the Band, and the nurse froze.

"Just like that," Micaiah answered Lily. "Come on."

They stepped out into the hall, a 3D photograph of the daily lives of ICU techs. Lily followed him dutifully, but he saw her mouth had come unhinged as she looked around. When she saw him looking, she snapped her mouth shut and hurried to step up beside him.

"You know, I've always been a little envious of you Timekeepers," she said as he opened the door to the stairs. "Everyone thinks the Harvesters have it good. Just suck the life out of people here, suck the cash out of people there." *Isn't that all there is to it?* "But money is pretty universal; there's nothing special about it. Money is money, greed is greed." *And you, my dear, are the embodiment of such things.* "Even the Grandfathers aren't much different than the Inquisition." *And what are they inquiring about now, I wonder?* "But Timekeeping...that really is something special. That's something, like, no one else can do." *Well, you got that right, at least.*

They hit the main floor. Micaiah dropped his Band just after they exited the stairwell. Life resumed, but in this part of the hospital, it was good and quiet during the night hours. A receptionist was on the phone, giving them only a nod of acknowledgment as they walked by, heading for the doors that slid open with a crackle of ice. Cold wind blasted through, biting them in the face. Lily held her hat on her head and tread hard on Micaiah's heels. Thankfully, by Banding and cutting out probably ten minutes of time, by the time they reached his car, virtually no snow had accumulated on it, and it was still warm. When he started it up, warm air poured out of the vents.

"This is nice," Lily murmured as she clicked her belt and leaned the seat back a little. "You're sure you're okay with this? I can drive. My car's just—"

"No," Micaiah cut in. "You're tired. You shouldn't be driving, and I'm not going to see someone else I know put in the hospital or dead."

She hummed. "Only someone you know. Not a friend?"

"Haven't decided yet."

"I guess it's better than bitter enemy. But then, I don't think you would be giving a ride to a bitter enemy."

"Probably not."

She said nothing after that, and as they plodded along the streets, he figured she had probably fallen asleep. Just as well. Do his good deed for the day and get home, that was the plan. He didn't really consider her a friend, but he wasn't going to see her hurt or dead because of his stubborn pride of forcing her to drive home on icy roads when she was tired.

Truthfully, he was pretty tired himself, but he wasn't going to bother Micah who was probably already in bed anyway. And it was hell trying to wake that boy up. He was a Rip van Winkle kind of a deep sleeper. Then there was Tommen who was normally a pretty deep sleeper, but since his ordeal had turned into a very restless sleeper.

And through it all, there was Micaiah who was just about falling asleep at the wheel himself. He turned down the warm air, but couldn't quite bring himself to turn on the cold air. Anyway, Lily's condo wasn't too far. The plow had just gone down the street when he pulled onto it, forcing his way into a parking spot that was, had all the lines been crystal clear in the snow, probably halfway out in the road. But he didn't care. He reached over and shook Lily awake.

"Wake up," he said. "We're here."

She yawned and rubbed her eyes, looked around. "Oh. I think I fell asleep."

He poorly stifled his own yawn as he said. "I think you did."

"You're tired, too," Lily said. "And it's a longer drive from here to your house than the hospital to here."

"I'll be fine." He sounded just like her. Damn.

"At least let me get you a cup of coffee to keep you warm and awake. And to thank you."

Well, a cup of coffee didn't sound too bad, and he could use a little caffeine boost, enough to see him home anyway. He nodded. "Okay."

"Come on up. Once I get my shoes off, I'm not coming back out here."

He rolled his eyes but got out of the car anyway and followed her inside. The main entry wasn't as warm as his car currently, but warm enough. When they reached her penthouse, she cranked the heat, and hot air began pouring from a dozen vents. She took her snowy shoes and outer clothes off and went to the kitchen while Micaiah remained stubbornly on the welcome mat.

"Will you be able to get back to the hospital tomorrow morning to pick up your car?" he asked suddenly. He hadn't really thought of that. He wasn't sure if she had to work either.

"Yeah, I'll get a ride," Lily told him, starting the coffee maker. Like everything else in her house, it wasn't the cheap kind of coffee maker, but the kind that could make coffee, cappuccinos, take those little single serve cups in a dozen different flavors, and it connected to the Internet...so it could download different mixing recipes? Micaiah liked the old school maker they had in the shop. Filter, grounds, water. No touch screens, no electronics, no complications.

"Do you really think Tommen will actually find a cure?" Lily asked, staring intently at the small appliance as it began filling a cup.

"I don't know," Micaiah admitted. "Do you really think there's no hope?"

She didn't answer until the cup was full and she brought it to him at the entry. "I don't know. I guess I'm kind of in the spot where you are. I don't think there's hope, but I'm not giving up until he's six feet underground."

"It's a long shot, but it's the best thing we have to go on."

He took off his gloves and took a drink of the coffee. It was incredibly bitter, and he was sure his expression mirrored that, but the minty aftertaste wasn't too bad, actually.

"You don't like it," Lily stated.

He shrugged and took a drink. "Doesn't matter." He forced himself to not shudder. "I need the caffeine boost to get me home."

"You're tired."

"Yeah, but it's not that far." Another drink, another grimace.

"You could always stay."

It wasn't her words that caught him off-guard and almost made him choke, so much as her tone. Lily was not a shy woman. She made no secret of her partying and drinking and getting laid. The way she spoke now was like a high school girl asking a guy if they wanted to get it on under the bleachers, when she was a virgin and known for being goody-two-shoes teacher's pet. He slowly lowered his coffee and glanced in the mug as if looking for some hidden meaning. Then he looked at her.

"You didn't invite me up here just for coffee," he stated.

Alarm bells were going off in his mind. *Run, you dumbass! Get out of there and go straight home! Do not pass Go, do not collect $200! This is not going to end well! You have better!*

"Not exactly," she admitted. "But it is cold outside, and we've both been under a lot of stress recently with no one to turn to who would really understand. I mean, how often does your pillow talk include Timekeepers and Grandfathers and Hands and Time?"

More often than you think, some part of him said, even while another part of him was still screaming, *Bad news! Bad news bears! Get out! Get out, get out, get out! Move, move, move! Take your chances on the road!*

Those voices were quelled, but not completely snuffed out, as she took the coffee from his hands, her warm hands brushing his cold ones. "I won't make you swallow it."

Damn, but she knew just what to say. It came from getting laid every weekend, and sometimes between weekends. But then, he was no stranger to that scene, even if he hadn't been out in a while.

No! Get! Out! Dumb! Ass!

Then she took one of his hands in one of hers, and with the other, she placed his hand right where she knew it wanted to be. He let out a breath, then bent to kiss her.

Saturday

Chapter Twenty-Six
D'Bok

Tommen knew he dreamed, and he was fairly certain he mostly had nightmares, but the specifics he could not recall. He knew only that when he woke, it was completely dark outside, and the fire had burned low. The nights were short yet, so he figured he couldn't have slept more than a couple hours.

Slowly he stretched, feeling every ache, pain, and cramp. He went fetal as both calves seized in spasming charliehorses from hell. He gritted his teeth, squeezed his eyes shut, and finger-walked his hands down his legs to his calves to try and massage out the agony. It took some doing, but eventually the muscles released, and he was able to breathe again and stretch his legs properly.

It came none too soon as Sifura entered the cave just then, bearing a small armload of wood. How awful would it have been to have her walk in while he was curled up, whimpering like a baby? Sure, Tommen wasn't really one for gym class, but was he really this weak? Silently he told himself he just needed to drink more water. Next time he decided to trek across the desert for seven days and then go mountain climbing, he was going to pack at least twice the water supply.

"Did you sleep well?" Sifura inquired, dropping the wood and kneeling to bring the coals back to life.

"I think so," Tommen replied uncertainly. His body said he slept like shit, and for reasons he couldn't explain, he felt a little rattled, but otherwise he was awake and alert. "Have you gotten any sleep yet?"

"No. I have been gathering hasax. When the honey wore off, I went down to the stream to wipe clean, and gathered some firewood."

Her words set off alarms in Tommen's mind. Assuming the honey lasted more than five minutes, that kind of trip would take hours, even without the honey jars to weigh her down. Trying not to look as alarmed as he felt, he sat up and checked his watch. Three-seventeen on Saturday morning on Earth. So he'd slept about a good six or seven hours. As it had almost become habit lately, he threw up a Fast Band.

"You were weary," Sifura said, noting his expression, her face a mixture of apology and confusion. "You are not a short-sleep people. I know your days are longer than ours, so you sleep longer. We had the time, so I decided to let you sleep."

Tommen rubbed his eyes, trying to wipe away the last of the sleep and not let the frustration get to him. It was fine. He wasn't mad. He'd needed the sleep, and it wasn't like he was going to be going anywhere at three in the morning anyway. It was fine. Fine, fine, fine.

"Okay," he sighed. "Fine. Did you at least get what you needed to take back to the D'Bok?"

"I did," she answered. "One of the honey jars is now full. Half of it, I will give to the D'Bok. The rest will go with you."

"And the other honey jar?"

"Still full of honey." He eyes glimmered with amusement. Then she grew serious. "Release your Band. Dawn will be here in about two hours. We will eat, then when it is light enough, I will show you how to collect the hasax flowers."

"Yeah, about that." Tommen shifted uncomfortably. "How do I know that the honey itself isn't poisonous to me and won't kill me as soon as I touch it?"

"It will not." She went on before he could protest. "My people are primitive, Tommen Forbes, but I am not. I have done more research in the Archives, planning for this mission, than you seem to think. I cannot plan for everything, but the major elements, I looked at thoroughly. The honey will not harm you. You will have to trust me on this."

Given how many opportunities she'd had so far to kill him and leave him in the middle of the desert to rot and be lost forever, he was more inclined to trust her. Finally he nodded. "Okay. I trust you."

He dropped the Band. She gave him an acknowledging nod and opened the pack the D'Bok had given her. She pulled out some of the meat chunks and cast him an uncertain glance. "Do you want meat? I know you were sick last night."

He remembered. He remembered very well. Problem was, he still couldn't decide if that had been the meat or some kind of fucking panic attack. But his food was nearly gone and even what he had left, he was reluctant to eat, just by sheer revulsion at having to eat the same thing over and over again. Eventually, he relented. "Yeah, I'll take some meat."

He shouldn't have been so repulsed by the scraps of trail mix and jerky he had left. How many nights in a row had his ma said they were having stew for supper? And it wasn't always the stew that she got up early in the morning to prep so she could slow-cook it over a low cookfire in the hearth all day; sometimes it was the stew that she'd gotten up early four days ago to prep and put over the hearth, and it would stay there until it was gone, might be three days, might be ten. Pease porridge hot and cold and all that.

This time Sifura gave him the stick with the chunks on it, so he could cook it how he wanted. It was a little odd, really, to cook real meat over a real fire, not like roasting hotdogs over a campfire, but old school outdoorsman cooking, like he used to do with his pa and brother sometimes. Microwaves and ovens were convenient, but cooking like this, around a warm fire with good food and friends and family, that was what made memories, and that was what counted.

Tommen almost grinned. Here he was, getting all sentimental and existential and whatever else, all because of a little cookfire and a shish kabob of little meat chunks. He did get them cooked how he wanted, well done, a good medium between raw and charcoal he figured, even as Sifura popped piece after raw piece in her mouth, occasionally ripping apart a larger chunk with her bare cat teeth.

When the meat was eaten, she brought out some little fruits and nuts and berries and offered them to him. Some he recognized from the trip up, and some she explained came from the mountain itself—a small gathering expedition she'd gone on after he'd fallen asleep, just to survey the area and make sure there were no surprises waiting for them. Because the d'bok was not "her" spirit animal, she would have no idea if one was approaching except by the normal methods of watching out for wild animals, that is, sight, sound, and smell. There was no sixth sense telepathic intuition here.

"I will go look again and be sure we are safe," she announced once breakfast was over. She stood and turned as if to leave, then looked back. "Stay here until I return."

About three seconds after she disappeared from sight, Tommen had to wonder the extent of her order. Did she mean stay "here" here, as in right where he was, sitting in the cave? Problem was, now that he was awake and had eaten, he had to pee, and the more he thought about it, the worse he had to go. Maybe he could just slip outside and go down the path a short distance. He sure as hell wasn't going to pee right here in the cave; that was unsanitary. He momentarily entertained the idea of peeing into the fire, then figured he really didn't want to smoke himself out. Or accidentally put it out, at the rate the pressure in his bladder and his dick was increasing. Fuck, fuck, fuck, he had to fucking pee. Maybe he could slip outside and get back before she knew he was gone.

Eventually, nature's call won out over Sifura's order, and he darted outside, down the trail about twenty yards, and was almost ready to piss on himself before he got himself situated. There was something kind of nice, he figured, about not wearing clothes. He wasn't a fan of the nudist colonies in the area, but it was nice not to have to fumble with a belt and zipper when he was already bursting at the seams, and then there was the zipper-dick safety factor to consider.

High above, the sky was still black, but as he climbed back up toward the cave and the hasax field, the edge of the horizon was coming alive. He thought about looking around for a rock so he could try for a *Star Wars* sunrise pose, then decided against it. For one, there was only one sun. For two, he didn't have a way to take a picture of it to show his attempt, and Sifura wouldn't understand the reference. And three, Sifura had ordered him to stay in the cave anyway. Quietly, he crept back to the cave and tried to position himself naturally.

A minute or two later, Sifura returned.

"Are we safe?" Tommen wondered.

"We are," she answered coolly, and he couldn't decide if she hadn't seen him, or if she had, she was just choosing not to say anything. "Come now. I will show you how to gather hasax."

There was a time when Tommen would have been more than happy to rub something all over him in front of a hot girl. Truthfully, he had to force himself not to venture down that line of thought too far lest he embarrass himself in front of said hot girl now, and because he had to keep telling himself that he was better than that. He was more than his addiction; he was more than his hormones. Not that he wouldn't have tried to bang Sifura if she'd been willing and able to, but his body was under his control. No need to get excited at every stray thought or careless reference. Even if she removed the lid on the honey jar and the substance inside both resembled in appearance and had the consistency of lube.

Just a honey jar, he told himself, dipping one hand in the stuff and working his way head to toe, making sure to cover every inch of skin that could touch the hasax leaves. With his inexperience and lack of finesse, he judged it best to just cover every inch of himself period. Sifura, on the other hand, covered only her hands and arms, just enough to protect herself so she could show Tommen the proper harvesting of the flower, taking him to the field and using a nearby bush as an example.

In the growing light, the hasax kind of resembled a day lily, except instead of a flower on a nice, long, easy-to-reach stalk, this thing had a flower buried among an enormous bush of leaves that were not only long and spindly and seemed to be consciously reaching for him to pull him into the bush and poison him, but were also razor sharp. He thought this only briefly before blacking out.

When he blinked back to consciousness, Sifura was standing over him and the sky was almost in full daylight.

"What happened?" he asked, sitting up, momentarily overcome by a wave of nausea.

"You cut yourself on one of the leaves," Sifura told him. "The poison got in your blood, and you passed out. I had to give you antidote."

"Fuck. How long?"

"Only an hour or two. The honey has worn off. I suggest you return to the stream and wipe off what is left. In the interest of time and flowers and not wasting any more honey, I will finish the harvesting."

It was a dismissal, like a stern scolding as if he'd done something wrong, and he found himself slinking off back down the mountain like a whipped puppy. He'd tried, really. So he might have been a little distracted, but it was his first time dealing with that kind of poisonous plant. For goodness sake, the worst he'd ever dealt with at home was poison ivy. Sure, he'd gotten covered in the stuff and been in itching, screaming agony for a couple days, but it hadn't killed him.

His feet were grateful to touch soft dirt and grass again as he touched ground in the jungle and made his way among the stone sentinels lining the path toward the giant fallen tree. He had no trouble going around the tree and traveling the remaining distance to the stream.

Initially, Tommen was expecting the remainder of the lube-honey to simply wash right off. Unfortunately, this lube-honey did not appear to be water-based. Instead of washing off cleanly, as he put his hands under the water and drew them out again, the lube-honey turned into long, stringy, gelatinous slime that refused to wash off. He tried rubbing at it, using his nails to scratch at it, but for as much as he got off, just that much came right back to slap and stick to his body.

After a few minutes of unsuccessful exfoliation, he slogged out of the stream and went to find a leaf, preferably one that was not poisonous. He stared at several varieties for a minute or two before finally picking one and snatching it off a branch. He didn't keel over, so he guessed that was a good start. Already covered in sticky, slimy goo, he figured there was no real reason to return to the stream, so he just drew the leaf over his body.

It was almost like magic as the goo was drawn off his skin, sticking to the leaf. It didn't really get absorbed by the leaf, just stayed on top, so Tommen picked half a dozen more leaves and wiped himself down. Arms, legs, chest, face, the lube-honey goo sliding off like rainwater on a freshly waxed car.

It took a little doing to wipe his back, but eventually he figured he got it clean enough. When he was all done, Tommen stared at the pile of leaves. The ones on top dripped goo, while the ones on bottom were already clean, the goo having been absorbed back into the ground. What was that stuff, anyway? Wasn't like any honey he'd ever seen, and he was forced to wonder just how it was that the word got translated like that. Was it because it was made similarly, by some little insect buzzing around in the jungle? Was it sweet like honey and used in cooking? Could it be chemically similar, unlikely as it sounded?

No matter, he figured. He was done; it was off. He briefly debated whether he should pick some more leaves and take them with him, so Sifura could wash herself when she was done. He decided against it; she—or both of them—would be coming back this way when all the flowers were harvested; no need to make for extra work. Besides, there was no need to actually come all the way back into the jungle to the stream if all that was needed was leaves. There was probably some chemical reaction between the lube-honey and the water that made it easier to pull off with the leaves.

He shook his head and started back toward the mountain, going back and forth on whether he should Band his way there. On the one hand, he hadn't been gone long enough for Sifura's honey to have worn off, so he would just be waiting for her anyway. On the other hand, time was ticking and he was growing more impatient with every passing minute. He knew only what his watch told him and the information that the twins had given him prior to leaving. Anything could have happened between then and now. What if Walter's condition had deteriorated? Tommen could miss him by mere seconds! The thought twisted his stomach.

His thoughts were interrupted by an almost familiar noise as he reached the base of the mountain, where dirt turned to stone. His first thought was a grizzly bear, but hard on the heels of that thought was another thought of a mountain lion. Better judgment told him that was impossible, and his mind immediately jumped to the xur until he reminded himself that they were out of the desert now, and the only thing left that was, theoretically, in range, was a d'bok. And Sifura was up there alone, possibly cornered in a field of poisonous plants with her force field slowly wearing thin.

Ignoring the jagged stones and his own instinct to flee and not get tangled up in this again, Tommen took off like a bullet from a gun, making it about twenty steps up the mountain before tiring. He slowed and ultimately stopped to catch his breath. He was momentarily distracted as he noticed that he could see his ribs. Shit, he'd lost some weight out here, and he hadn't gained an ounce of endurance to show for it.

His first thought, as he walked up the trail, was that he should Band and surprise the beast. Then he remembered that the d'bok was impervious to Time and it wouldn't matter. So, next best thing, good old-fashioned stealth. It wasn't easy, considering how rocky the path was and how many stones he kicked. He'd probably already announced his arrival to the d'bok and he hadn't even seen it yet.

The second trip up the mountain was every bit the hell climb he remembered from the first time. He might not have been carrying a giant jar of honey this time, but he was just as tired. He almost grinned. He'd get up to the cave, look at the d'bok, probably double over in exhaustion and cramps, and put up one finger as if the d'bok was going to totally get that he needed a minute to recuperate before fighting. Tommen was chivalrous. The d'bok would not be.

Another roar—or snarl or scream or however it could be described—rang out and motivated Tommen to at least a fast walk when possible, but there was no such thing as a fast climb, not for him. He kept whispering for Sifura to hang on, as if he could just will good vibes or some shit to her, somehow let her know that he was coming.

As he got closer, his nose was tickled by a new smell, and it wasn't pleasant. It smelled like rot and dung and a festering wound. When he finally crested the last rise, he understood why.

The xur had been ugly. The D'Bok people were ugly. The d'bok itself was worse than both of them put together. He'd thought the D'Bok people were like some humanoid bear-komodo dragon mix. Throw in a little sloth, a little coyote, and a couple dozen wasting diseases, and that got a little closer to what the d'bok itself looked like.

It stood on five legs, all of them seeming to be different lengths, so it had to find various rocks and elevations in the path in order to stand levelly. And the fifth leg wasn't even a centered leg, like for balance, but acted like some redundant, useless third appendage on its right side, while the left side only had two legs. It had long, flat heels and three toes that looked more like hooves, really. Like instead of nails or claws, there were hooves, but not quite like the ones on the goats Tommen had once had. The whole creature was short and stocky, but rigidly solid, like a bear, even despite how skinny it looked, with protruding ribs and joints. Its tail was long and probably dragged in the dirt when it was down.

Tommen could only see the back of the head, and it looked as malformed as its five misshapen legs. One ear was round while the other looked like no more than a flap of gristle, as if it had been torn off in some fight from ages past.

The underbelly and backs of the legs were covered in scales, black and gray, though some looked chipped and jagged. At one time, it may have had a luscious coat of thick black and gray and brown fur, but now it was patchy and grungy with wounds and sores and insects and all manner of diseases pulsing through it. Not that Tommen was any expert on d'bok, but he might have guessed that this one was old. Old and very, very cranky about the neighbors being on his lawn.

Just through a gap between the d'bok and the mountain, Tommen caught sight of Sifura, trapped in the hasax field. As Dreja had said, the d'bok did not go into the field, but Tommen was forced to wonder whether the d'bok's patience or Sifura's lube-honey armor would wear out first.

Worst part was, the damn thing was standing right in front of the cave. Bad luck or not, Tommen was going to kill that son of a bitch before it killed his only way home. But he had no weapons.

He sucked in a tight breath as he cut his foot on a rock. Again. He hoped the d'bok hadn't heard him.

His hopes proved to be in vain as the creature swung its huge head around to look at him. Yes, it was every bit the nasty, incestuous lovechild between a bear and a komodo dragon, with some other questionable relationships in there, too. The thing had three sickly yellow eyes, two on one side of its ugly, elongated, scaly muzzle, and one on the other, placed with no symmetry, but more like the haphazard drawing of a three year old.

Tommen knew the look of excitement when a hungry person has spotted food, and this thing had spotted food, and that food was him. Tommen forced himself not to freeze as the d'bok got its legs situated and turned around, instead bending over and picking up a rock which he threw with more hope than aim. Still, the thing was big enough that he didn't miss, though the glancing shoulder blow did little to improve the thing's mood or deter its hunger.

Thankfully, the d'bok's gait was so awkward, it was unable to run, and Tommen managed to get in four more rocks, each with increasing accuracy until he finally found an eye, or an eyelid anyway. The d'bok whimpered and lifted a huge pseudo-hoof to paw at the wound, but quickly returned its attention to Tommen.

But in drawing the creature away, Tommen had created an opening for Sifura to get out of the hasax field. She came at it from behind now, wielding her knife that she'd won in the battle with Karaki. The d'bok, now assaulted from front and back, paused, confused, swinging its head to look back and forth.

Now it was no longer about food, but attack. The d'bok decided that Sifura was the larger threat and went after her. Now the ingenuity of the d'bok's lopsided frame was revealed as this creature the size of a large fuel truck managed to make a full turn in the space of about one lane of traffic by taking its shorter legs and using them almost like a spider, to find balance on the side of the mountain and the various rocks as it shifted its entire mass.

Sifura ducked under the d'bok midway through its turn, but the creature did something else astounding. It used its shorter legs to suspend itself from the rocks while its longer legs made swipes at her. She ducked and dodged, slashed with the knife as she could.

Somewhere in all the excitement, Tommen's head came back to him, and he knew he ought to help her. He just had to get under the thing and to the cave. Taking a breath, he tried to observe the d'bok's movements, see if there was a safe path through. There wasn't any that he could see; the beast had full range of motion everywhere under itself. Well, he had to get moving or else Sifura was going to die trying not to kill this thing. But Tommen had no qualms about killing it.

Before he could talk himself out of it, Tommen took off, focused only on the cave and letting Sifura do the work of distracting the beast. He growled loudly as the rocks cut his feet, but he carried on, stumbling, scraping his hands and knees, getting up, moving again, not thinking, hardly daring to breathe except that he was hyperventilating already.

And suddenly he was flying. The air was pressed from his lungs and he sucked in a panicked gasp. But his chest could not expand because his ribs and arms were trapped as the d'bok grabbed him and brought him up in front of it, like a child observing a mouse close up.

The d'bok opened its mouth and Tommen saw that while its tongue was large like a bear's, it was forked like a lizard's. Then the d'bok did something Tommen might have considered impossible. It spoke. More than that, it spoke, and the translator picked up on it and rendered it in perfect Welsh.

"You're a long way from home, Akari-bearer," it said.

"What?" Tommen gasped dumbly.

The d'bok opened its mouth, but whether to say more or eat him, Tommen couldn't say, for it suddenly snarled and dropped him. On his way down, Tommen momentarily glimpsed Sifura wrenching her knife out of the beast's leg. Then he hit the ground, his head slapping hard on the rock. The sky spun and his ears rung, but his sense of panic and self-preservation bade him get up and keep moving. By the time his head came back to him, Tommen was just grateful he'd managed to move in the right direction.

He rummaged in his bag which had grown considerably lighter, and it was much easier to find the little pistol this time around. He quickly checked the clip and turned off the safeties before running out of the cave.

The d'bok had Sifura just about pinned up against the rock face. Without thinking, Tommen shot at the d'bok, hitting it in what he thought was the shoulder, or maybe the ribcage. With the beast contorted like it was, it was hard to tell. At the shot, the d'bok lost interest in Sifura and turned its attention back to him. As soon as Tommen saw its eye, he shot again.

He wasn't sure if he missed or if the creature just got lucky or if it had some freaky Time abilities of its own, but Tommen only saw a little chink in the rock behind where he could have sworn the creature's eye had been only a second ago.

The d'bok put its longer legs down first, then lowered itself from its suspension on the rocks, bringing all five legs to the ground, turning to look at Tommen head-on. Tommen unloaded the clip, but he only counted two potential wounds, and neither of them looked particularly fatal or even serious.

"D'bok are not like xur," the thing said. "We are not so easy to kill."

Shit. Shit, shit, shit. Tommen was out of options. He had no Time and no extra clips, and a very angry old talking komodo-bear was bearing down on him. Stupidly and fearfully, Tommen simply chucked the empty pistol at the d'bok—missing by a mile—and turned and fled.

Behind him, he could hear the d'bok break into a run. Tommen could feel the ground vibrating beneath him, then it was cut short by a painful squealing. Too afraid to stop but too curious not to, Tommen turned and looked.

He barely got to see anything before Sifura was in his face, practically leaping over him onto the rock face, digging into any purchase she could, and screaming at him to climb. Tommen did so, trying to see where she found holds and reaching for the same spots.

He glanced down once at the d'bok and saw that Sifura had stuck her knife deep into its belly, right where scales met fur. He might have guessed that the scales were fairly impenetrable and protected all the major organs. But it didn't matter as the thing eventually bent and twisted and contorted itself into a position where it ripped the knife out and flung it away, over the rocks and far off the path. Then it looked up, looked at Tommen and Sifura, making a break for it.

It really was too much to ask for the thing to not be able to do something. Climbing a sheer rock face, for example, seemed to be what it was born for. And how come, when the d'bok lived in the jungle? Or was it just the way it was built that it could pretty much go anywhere and climb anything? Then Tommen figured it didn't really matter if it could climb everything, because right now, yes, it was climbing a mountain to get to them.

Tommen threw everything he had into the climbing, but Sifura had already outscaled him and he wasn't sure where he could find handholds. He took a breath. Well, he could jump and possibly die trying to escape, or not jump and definitely die because he couldn't escape.

He jumped. His fingers brushed something and he clung to it, feeling every muscle he had and didn't have stretching and groaning as he hauled himself up. Below him, the d'bok seemed to finally be having trouble with something, the smooth rock proving to be too much. It probably didn't need much for a purchase, but what little Tommen needed for a purchase was too little for the d'bok. Tommen allowed himself to relax a little and consider his options for placement.

He looked up just as Sifura disappeared from the rock face and then poked her head out of what he assumed to be another cave, or at least a shelter of some form, about twenty feet up.

When he was within ten feet, Sifura encouraging Tommen and telling him to hurry, there was a sudden vibration in the rock face and he lost his grip. He managed to stay against the face for the most part, but he slid almost halfway down before finding enough purchase to stop himself. He heard something in his right hand pop, and he cried out in pain.

The d'bok had given up climbing and was now throwing itself against the face like a battering ram.

The pain in Tommen's hand was growing worse, and he quickly found a spot for all four limbs to rest and take most of the weight off. Carefully, he removed his right hand and moved it in front of him so he could look at it. He'd been skiing for some years now, and he'd seen several knee injuries in that time—usually Eric or Eric's little brother. If anything, it didn't look or feel broken; he still had pretty good use of his fingers. Probably something dislocated, pulled apart by the fall. Well, it was something, anyway.

He pressed himself closer against the face as the d'bok threw itself at the mountain again. No time to try and pop his fingers or his hand back in place. Fuck, but this was going to suck.

Tommen tried to time his movements so they were between vibrations. When the d'bok saw this, it only moved more frequently. Instead of a couple huge hits with thirty seconds between them, it was multiple little hits. It wouldn't take much to get Tommen to fall again, and both he and the d'bok knew that. It was now a game they played, one of timing and finesse, both of which Tommen sucked at.

Actually, it kind of reminded him of Frogger, though he couldn't say why. Maybe the timing thing, or the way that he moved up the face. Since he knew the d'bok couldn't climb, he could take more time to look for better holds, especially holds that would better accommodate his right hand, and it wasn't always directly in line with the cave where Sifura watched him, pacing and poking her head in and out like a true cat.

Finally, after what seemed like forever, he reached the cave. He held his right arm up, instructing Sifura to grab by the wrist and not his hand. He scrabbled for the last footholds on the face, but eventually, he got in, just about landing on top of Sifura. He rolled onto his back, exhausted, panting, feeling very much like how a mouse must feel when it reaches the safety of its hole after being chased by a very hungry cat. For a second or two, he forgot about everything else but just the relief and the safety. He was all right. She was all right. They were alive. They had escaped.

Slowly, Tommen sat up and crawled, limping on his right hand, and peeked over the edge of the cave opening. They were about a hundred feet up, maybe more. He could see the d'bok pacing and looking up, roaring and snarling, protesting its lost meal. It threw itself against the rock face a couple more times for good measure, but the vibrations were not only diminished, they no longer mattered. They were back on solid ground inside a cave, safe from the evils that lurked below.

He burst into laughter. There was nothing particularly amusing about their new predicament, but it was all just so fucking hilarious. Like after they'd escaped the xur. Laughter for its own sake, because he was so afraid, for his life, for his sanity, afraid he would never live to laugh again. So he laughed like a lunatic, laughed until tears streamed from his eyes and he was on his back once more, gasping for breath, wondering if he hadn't had some kind of mental break.

Eventually, his laughter died down and fatigue swept over him. Still, he rubbed his eyes and went again to the mouth of the cave and looked over. Now the d'bok appeared to be sitting, still occasionally growling or sort of bark-snarling, but it did not pace, and it did not throw itself against the rock face. It just sat there, like a hound dog that has cornered a coon or a bobcat and is waiting for the hunter to come and dispatch the prey. Tommen wasn't sure how long the d'bok would sit there, how patient it really could be, but if that thing was as hungry as he suspected, it wouldn't sit there forever waiting for dinner to come to it; it would have to go out hunting again eventually.

He looked back at Sifura, grinning. "I don't think it'll be down there for long. We'll be okay. It'll be gone soon." He was blathering and he knew it, but she was right, he was a nervous talker. Or maybe that was only in life-and-death situations.

His idiotic glee was dampened when he saw her forced agreement as she scooted uncomfortably farther back into the cave.

It was not a huge cave, deeper than the one they'd been using on the ground, but only three or four feet high at most. Tommen elected to limp-crawl over to Sifura who rested against a wall, both legs out in front of her, one knee, er, hock, looking very not right.

"When did this happen?" he asked, putting a hand out as if to touch it, but too afraid to actually do so.

"I slipped," she hissed through gritted teeth. "I overextended my leg, and when the weight came down, I think it broke the joint."

So basically, she'd climbed who knew how far with a blown knee. Fuck, and Tommen thought he'd had it bad with an injured hand. Even as he thought about it, his hand began throbbing. He held his hands up so she could see where one was just slightly different than the other. "Yeah, I think we both had a hard time getting up here."

"Is your hand broken?" she asked, appearing concerned despite her own woes. Of course, faction leader, has to put her people first.

Tommen shook his head. "No. Just dislocated, I think."

"Give me your good hand."

Cautiously, he held out his left hand. She took it in both of her hands, the variety of textures in her skin and fur stirring him as she felt each bone and joint, effectively massaging his hand. She closed her eyes as she did this, doing everything by feel alone. After a minute, she dropped his left hand and held her hands out again. He gave her his right hand.

The right hand was less pleasurable. Not every movement she made with it was painful, but every so often she found that one point or one direction that send daggers up his arm. Her expression turned thoughtful, and just as he was contemplating what she was thinking or feeling, she put a knife in his hand. Not a literal one, but there was enough pain that he might have believed it. But there was also a pop and as soon as the pain came, it was gone. His hand got all tingly for a moment or two, but he could use it again.

"How did you do that?" he asked, clenching and releasing his fist until the pain and tingling had dulled to a throb to be filed away in the back of his mind.

"During my time as a healer, I had to know such things," Sifura explained. "I had to know the bones and muscles of my people, but also how to read the bones and muscles of others in case I needed to help someone I was unfamiliar with. I simply read the bones in your good hand and felt what I needed to do in your bad hand. Now your hand is fixed."

"Something tells me that your knee isn't going to be as easy to fix."

She sighed and shook her head. "No. It requires proper

treatment, and we do not even have the barest supplies to be found in this cave."

"And even if the d'bok does leave, how are you going to get down? I mean, fight or flight is great, but the swelling and damage is only going to get worse."

She shook her head again. "No, the swelling will get worse, but the damage is already done. But I will not be able to climb down."

"Great." Tommen sighed. "Just great."

"When the d'bok leaves, you must return to the village, tell them where I am, tell them I need help."

"What makes you think they'll come and help?"

"Because I know they will. They have promised us safe passage, and they are responsible for us."

"Yeah, especially when they told us this was the easier, less dangerous path." He scoffed.

"One cannot predict all the dangers of the forest."

Didn't make him feel any better about their predicament. He checked his watch. Almost ten in the morning on Earth. Fuck, he was running out of time. If Sifura hadn't been hurt, he would have been more than content to—well no, because he still had to get down to the ground and get that fucking cure.

Fuck.

He rubbed his eyes and turned to go back to the mouth of the cave.

"Tommen Forbes."

He looked back. "What?" His tone may have been a little sharper than intended.

"Come here; your head is bleeding."

Even as she said it, he could feel the pain in the back of his head. He put a hand there and it came away bloody, but also with the dry gray dust of the rock. Reluctantly, he returned to Sifura and sat with his back to her so she could pick out the rocks and clean the wound as best she could. He did not ask how, merely accepted that she was half-cat and was cleaning his wound.

"It is not bad," she told him finally. "Are you experiencing any symptoms of the concussion?"

He shook his head. "No, I'm fine. Probably just a flesh wound."

"Be gentle, and do not sleep on it until it has been properly cared for."

"Does it need stitches?"

"I do not believe so."

Well, that was the first good news he'd had all day, or at least since they got up here. With the adrenaline rush ebbing, fatigue was beginning to spread through Tommen's limbs, though he forced himself to return to the mouth of the cave and look down.

"He's still there," Tommen said.

The d'bok still sat at the base of the mountain, like a patient hound, or maybe a patient bear, looking up at the cave. When it saw Tommen, it gave a sort of snarling scream, like a coyote but with a hint of mountain lion and a touch of bear. It stood, sat, stood, paced, sat, stood, sat.

"Come away from the edge," Sifura told him. "Do not let him see you. Let him forget we are up here."

"I have a feeling that's going to be easier said than done," Tommen replied, though he did move back from the edge and join her.

They had no fire and nothing with which to build one. They were at a higher elevation sitting on cold stone. Tommen shivered and drew his knees up to his chest. He hoped the d'bok forgot about them quick. He Banded, figuring that even if the air still penetrated them and the d'bok still waited for them, at least he might be able to buy some time for his mission back on Earth. Home had never felt so far away.

"Sleep, Tommen," Sifura said gently. "We are going nowhere soon."

If it was meant as a comfort, it was a poor one, as it only

served to remind Tommen of their predicament, and the fact that it probably wasn't going to end anytime soon. He sighed and glanced longingly toward the entrance of the cave. Was anything else destined to go wrong today yet?

"I can't," he said. "I have to buy time to get back to my dad, and I can't Band if I'm unconscious."

For once, she did not argue or insist. She, too, understood how close they were cutting it, how the clock was winding down and every minute lost to frivolous waste brought them closer to the loss of his dad. He might exhaust himself; he might only just barely make it through the portals in the Wheel. But he had the ability to bend and control Time, to effectively stop it completely and buy himself as much Time as he needed to do anything, and he was going to use that ability to its maximum. Which, since he was only a probationary, really wasn't much.

But he did it anyway, setting a Band so Fast and tight and narrow, just the act took a considerable amount of energy and he began to warm up, even to sweat. Sifura gave him a concerned look, but said nothing, simply shifted her position until she got comfortable, and eventually drifted off to sleep.

They stayed that way for Tommen knew not how long. Two or three hours, maybe a little longer. It was exhausting, holding such a tight Band with such force, and watching Sifura sleep did not help in his resolve. He wanted to go and check to see if the d'bok had left, but he did not dare. He was going to hold out as long as possible, until he collapsed from sheer exhaustion.

And that was exactly what he did.

Chapter Twenty-Seven
Akari

Tommen figured he either didn't sleep long or he slept like shit, because when he woke, it felt like he hadn't slept at all. When he finally crawled his way back to full consciousness, he put up another Band, albeit a poor one. Across from him, Sifura sat with her back against the wall, eyes closed.

He looked around, eyes adjusting to the gloom, then glanced at the cave entrance. It had been late morning when the d'bok attacked; now it was nearly full dark. Uncertainly, he checked his watch. Eight-twenty-seven p.m. on Saturday night on Earth. He was down to less than twenty-four hours.

"Fuck," he hissed.

As he moved to go to the mouth of the cave, Sifura spoke quietly.

"He's still down there."

Tommen worked to bring his Band in closer and tighter. "How much longer do we have to wait?"

"I do not think it will be long. He has been howling about the hunger in his stomach and the pain in his body. He will quickly lose interest in us."

"See, that's another thing I don't get. Why did he speak to me? Not just why, but how? Why him, and not the xur?"

"The spirit animals are as much spirit as they are beast; they exist in both realms," Sifura told him. "The beast lives so that we may also live, and the spirit communicates with us to teach us. You probably thought that the translator was not only able to pick up the d'bok speaking but render it perfectly, but actually it was the d'bok

447

himself speaking to you."

"How the fuck does some ugly ass komodo-bear thing speak Welsh?"

She shrugged. "How do the spirits know anything?" Her expression turned guilty. "And you were wrong about the xur. The xur did speak, but not to you. He spoke to me, when we were separated."

"Yeah? And what did he say to you? I'm going to eat you for dinner?"

Her gaze hardened, as if she was growing weary of listening to him insult her beliefs, but she maintained an icy calm to her voice. "He asked what I was doing, escorting and helping and befriending an Akari-bearer."

Tommen studied her, trying to pick out some kind of hidden meaning, but he found none. "And what did you tell him?"

"I told him that I was helping you in order to help your people, and such a thing is not forbidden. Rather, it is encouraged." She sighed. "It is difficult to say with certainty whether it was the spirit or the beast that attacked afterwards. Initially, he was drawn to you."

"So it's entirely possible the d'bok was drawn to me, too," Tommen reasoned. "When he grabbed me, he said that I was a long way from home, and then he called me Akari-bearer."

Sifura closed her eyes. "I should have merely gotten the antidote you required and sent you home. I have no sense of the d'bok, not in the way I am aware of the xur. By delaying and insisting on following traditional protocol, now we are both injured and trapped in a cave."

Outside, the d'bok snarled, a sickening scream that made Tommen want to run back to the cabin, jump under the quilts, and burrow until he found his ma, safe and sound again.

"The spirit and the beast are at war within him," Sifura said quietly, her eyes still closed. "The spirit wishes to starve us, to starve you. The beast wishes to hunt and put food in its belly, for it is getting old, and it is becoming more difficult for him to catch prey." She nodded slowly. "Eventually, the beast will win. It always does."

Tommen wanted desperately to inch toward the mouth of the cave and look down at it, but he forced himself to stay farther back in the cave. The night was cool, and he moved to sit beside Sifura, her body warm.

"Your people are not made for hot nor cold," she observed with a wry sense of humor. "How do you claim seven billion people across a world with both such hot and cold?"

"Very carefully, and with a lot of advancements," he told her, but his mind was elsewhere. "There's something I don't get, though, about the d'bok and this whole thing."

"And what is that?" Her tone suggested she was bracing to be ridiculed again.

"When Rifun kidnapped me—" He forced his voice not to break. "—he called me an Akari-bearer. Fine and dandy, the guy is nuts anyway. How is it, though, that such an isolated world, with only the barest ties to Time itself, also has such a concept, and it has to be relayed to your people via spirit animals? What logic is there in that?"

"Again, how do the spirits know anything?" Sifura shrugged again. She shifted position. "In my opinion, my world is not so isolated from Time as you think. The Akari is known also in Time, in the Wheel and among the Hands. It is one of the things that is considered forbidden to know of, other than as an obscure and dangerous religion. Perhaps it was that in times long past, the belief or knowledge of this belief came to my people through a tribe member who was also a secret Time Agent. How it was invented or brought up, I do not know."

Now Tommen shifted position. "But something tells me that with your oral histories, you have some sort of record or rendition of how all of this came to be."

"I do. But I know you will not be interested."

"So I might not be enthusiastic about it, but if it's something that I am going to be hunted for on distant worlds, I at least want to have a little background knowledge of what it could be, or what one interpretation of it is."

Sifura studied him for a long moment as if trying to decide how serious he was being, how much she really wanted to give before she could take the insults no more. In reality, Tommen was not interested in insulting her beliefs just yet, not until he was able to piece together the truth from the myth. Eventually her countenance turned neutral once more and she dipped her head. "Very well."

"The story begins in the time of the Great Quake, when the whole world trembled, when mountains fell and valleys were ripped open to form new seas and oceans. At this time, there was only one tribe, the Umani. They were a great people, almost a hundred thousand strong, and not one of them had any reverence for the land they walked upon, so the spirits made them remember how small they were.

"The Great Quake divided the Umani into hundreds of smaller tribes. Some were separated by oceans, some by mountains. And during this time, many of them, mostly the children and the young, became very ill. Some said it was poison given up by the valleys when they opened, others said it was a curse from the spirits. But either way, there was no cure for this illness that had overtaken them, and it was unclear why some died and others survived, despite the care being the same for all.

"An old warrior named Haza, seeing his people die around him, grew angry at the spirits for their curse, and he vowed to go to the Resting Spot and slay every spirit he could find."

"Resting Spot?" Tommen interrupted, trying to keep the eyeroll out of his voice.

"It was the place where the Umani would go to commune with the spirits," Sifura explained, "except they had no reverence for anyone but themselves, so they did not commune with the spirits. It is said that the Great Quake started in the Resting Spot because when Haza finally reached the spot where it was, it was gone. Where lush, peaceful land once was, only a charred and blackened crater of rubble remained. Haza was horrified, and humbled, hit with the stunning realization that he was separated from the spirits forever. He knelt on the lip of the crater and wept.

"But in that crater, deep in the heart of it, was a small tree, a sapling that had pushed its way into the light again. Seeing this, Haza became hopeful, and he went to the tree, looking for just one spirit to speak with. And so a spirit came.

"The spirit told Haza that all people were cursed, bound forever to the land and its beasts. The older warriors who were not sick would never again bear children, and those who were sick and lived would not bear children in their likeness. They would need the hair of an animal in order to have children. Not just that, but they would also need a special tree."

"The one in the crater."

"Yes. It took many years and many families were separated as close kin were bound to different beasts. But as you have seen, we have since thrived."

"And the Akari?"

Sifura hesitated. "Haza asked the spirit if they might have a second chance to commune with them, if there could be a new Resting Spot. The spirit told him such a thing was impossible. However, the spirit did promise Haza a way to commune, that the beasts of the tribes would be of the world and of the spirit realm, to commune and protect and teach and give wisdom.

"Not all of the spirits were pleased with such an arrangement, and they blamed the first spirit for promising such a thing. They named him and any who agreed to help him Akari, which means 'friend with the mortals.' There was a war among the spirits. The beasts who were designated to help each tribe were driven insane, and so they still are, torn between their given duty and the vengeful spirits that still fight to keep them as beasts only.

"But it is said that there are some out there, sometimes beasts, sometimes a member of a tribe, who carries one of the Akari within himself, a secret, hidden from the vengeful spirits. This Akari-bearer speaks quietly with the spirit realm, listens to what the spirits have to teach, sometimes imparts their wisdom to his faction or tribe. But the vengeful spirits still seek the Akari to destroy them, using the spirit animals to do their bidding."

Tommen considered this for a minute or two, trying to put words together to formulate a question that didn't sound completely dismissive or condescending. "So basically, what you're saying, is that that thing down there that wants to kill us, is a demon-possessed komodo-bear?"

"Yes."

"Fucking hell." He shook his head. "I'm not even part of this world. I'm from a whole different quadrant. Why would that thing be attracted to me as some Akari-bearer?"

"I don't know," Sifura said simply. "Perhaps it is *because* you are not part of this world. Perhaps the vengeful spirits suspect the Akari have formed a new realm where they can be safe. Maybe it is like a new scent they are following."

Tommen shook his head. "Is there anything more to the story?"

"Like what?"

"I don't know. Anything. At least anything that relates to the Akari."

She became thoughtful for a moment. "Haza himself was rumored to be an Akari-bearer, harboring the spirit he communed with at the remains of the Resting Spot. He took the spirit and visited all the tribes he could find, telling them of the curse and how to remedy it, listening as the spirit told him which animals to seek out. Most did as he told them, and we have the tribes that you see today. A few dismissed him as crazy, and they died out. Haza himself stayed with his mate and their children, both of whom turned out to be future Kalb.

"It is said that one day, many years later, when he was an old man, Haza was out walking when he was cornered by a pack of kalb, as the animal. They were all possessed by vengeful spirits. They told him they would let him live if only he would give up the first spirit so they may have their revenge. Haza simply laughed and said, 'The spirit is become me. Fools that you are for thinking that man and spirit could be separated forever.' He also told them that he had imparted the spirit to others, that all would be Akari-bearers, and they, the vengeful spirits, would never be able to kill all of them. So the kalb murdered Haza, but they were unable to kill the first Akari." Sifura sighed. "Ever since, the spirit animals have been the creatures as you have seen them. Most often beast, sometimes driven by a vengeful spirit, but every so often, possessed by an Akari who breathes new life into an old tribe."

So basically, their gods were total schizoids. Lovely. But Tommen was smart enough to keep his mouth shut, on that at least.

"What did the Umani tribe look like?" he asked suddenly.

"No one knows for sure," Sifura answered. "Some would describe them similarly to you, but with no hair, no nose, no ears, no lips, and either completely white or completely black. Other descriptions are usually variations of their own tribe, those stories most often told to children."

"And how did they reproduce?"

"That much, no one knows. Many cannot imagine any other way of reproducing. Many animals are born of eggs, so that is one theory. Why does it matter?"

Tommen shrugged. "I don't know that it does, but it's something to think about. What do you think?"

"I do not know. The stories of the Great Quake and the Akari are known by all, but they are stories for children, to soothe them to sleep. Other than needing a xur or a d'bok to grow children, and having a good understanding of why that is, such things are largely irrelevant."

"What happens if a couple tries to just braid their own hair together and doesn't include xur hair?"

"Nothing. The tree will not accept the length, and a child will not grow."

Tommen mulled over this, fascinated by it and wanting to get a little deeper understanding of it, while at the same time reminding himself that he was running out of time and had to get home and back to real life, his life, the one with school and the bakery and saving his dad from certain death. That last bit was not only the most important, but the one that was most in jeopardy.

Tommen shifted position. "So if you think that the Akari is mostly just a myth perpetuated by some Time Agent who visited your planet however long ago, what is the Akari to Time? I mean, you said it was something forbidden, but why?"

Sifura let out a breath, unsure if she wanted to impart such knowledge now that she'd mentioned it. Finally, "Thousands of years ago—" *Because no lunacy could ever develop in recent times.* "—before the Third Rebuild—" *Because there always had to be some vague event in history, and in the end, we'll find out that the climax of this story resulted in that vague event.* "—there was a cult—" *Yeah, that's original. There's always a cult involved, isn't there?* "—called the Cult of the Akari." *Clever.* "After their defeat in the First Build—" *Love a good story of vengeance.* "—they remained mostly dormant—" *Weeds and roots and all that.* "—until the leader, called Ras—" *Al Gul?* "—came to power.

"The cult believed the Akari to be an artifact of some form—" *Cue Indiana Jones.* "—but not from our universe." *Always a catch, isn't there?* "They believed it came from some kind of alternate or parallel dimension, where the rules worked differently, where you could not only manipulate Time, but Gravity, Chemistry, the basis of life itself."

"The God particle," Tommen said. "Where did this idea come from?"

"No one knows. Not even the cult knows. It is as ingrained as any of the traditions of my people. My parents did a thing because their parents did a thing and so on. So it was with the Akari."

"All right, so what did the cult do? Or what happened?"

"The cult believed that anyone who possessed the Akari gained the abilities of that dimension, to do the things I just told you about. And the cult's whole purpose was to find it, use it, and so control the universe itself." *Nothing like a lofty goal.* "Before the Third Rebuild, the cult claimed to have found the Akari. They initially tried to blackmail the Hands—" *Because when you have the ability to mold the very fabric of the universe, obviously the first thing you do is blackmail someone.* "—but the Hands denied their claim. They publicly denounced the cult's claims on the basis of not wanting to start a panic, while privately demanding that the cult show some sort of proof that they possessed this artifact."

"Wait, so the Hands actually believe this thing exists?" Tommen interrupted.

"Even if the Hands themselves doubt its existence, with the claims of its power, many believe it wise to tread cautiously if viable evidence is given for its proof."

Well, he couldn't deny that one. He chewed on it for a second before nodding for her to continue.

"The cult showed its proof of the Akari by destroying the Wheel and everyone in it." *Well, that escalated quickly.* "However, in its destruction, the Akari itself was also believed to be destroyed." *Guess it's not possible to have your cake and eat it, too.* "And in the aftermath, when the cult had hoped to take over control of Time and rule through fear, everything just descended into chaos. Eventually, order did reestablish itself and thus the Third Rebuild."

"So the Wheel that exists today isn't the same one that's always been there for since forever ago?"

Sifura gave him a puzzled look as she said, "No," as if talking to a child who has just realized that grandma had been a child once, just like them. "If I remember correctly, the Wheel as it is today is the sixth iteration."

"Oh." Well, so much for redecorating. "Go on."

"After the Rebuild, the Hands had hoped that the cult had been destroyed along with everything else, and for almost a thousand years, that was how it seemed." *But...surprise!* "No one knows exactly when troubles began arising in the Wheel again. At first, it just seemed to be common Runners, but some scholarly Hands and secretaries revealed them as works like the cult, either the cult itself or a copycat. Rather than be dismissed again, the cult made itself fully known, that they had never died out." *Because cults never die, not really.*

"Rather than risk another Rebuild, the Hands ordered the seizure of every known member of the cult and their associates." *Can you say Red Scare?* "They also searched for the fabled Akari among the members' affects, but never found anything. When questioned about it—" *Yeah, but I doubt they just had a nice little sit-down chat, not with the Borelians around.* "—the cult members said something odd. They professed that the Akari no longer existed as an artifact. In the destruction of the Wheel, all the survivors were imbued with the power of the Akari, if they knew they had it and knew how to use it." *Ah, yes, and being exposed to radiation gives ordinary people superpowers.*

"If that was the Third Rebuild, and we're in the sixth iteration now, that's probably a long time in between. How does it get passed on?" Tommen wondered, not sure how far he wanted to take this fairy tale, moving forward only in the sense that he wanted to know, at this point, what superpowers he was supposed to have but apparently didn't. Because if he did have some cool superpowers, he was going to open a serious can of whoop-ass on that d'bok sitting there at the bottom of the mountain.

"The cult was not specific on such things," Sifura admitted. *Because who wants to really give up the secret of gaining awesome superpowers?* "Some said it could be passed on genetically, but it had to be activated by an exposure to Time." *Ah, yes, the secret powers that lie dormant until just the right moment in the hero's quest. At least they're not the kind that get all weird on you during puberty, because that's clearly not hard enough already.* "Others said it could be simply given from person to person, such as a gift at the end of life, as it was not a copy of the abilities, but a transfer."

"The one giving the abilities would lose them completely," Tommen finished.

"Yes." She shrugged. "Anyway, the Hands had them all

executed, but every so often, the cult still comes back around. So far, their story has remained consistent, that the Akari is now an internal ability and not an artifact, but few have ever demonstrated any abilities even remotely as similar or dangerous as once professed."

"Few? So there have been some."

"Over the centuries, one has gone before the Grandfathers for being a Runner, possibly a cult member, who is able to appear to manipulate gravity or the molecular structure of the interrogation rooms and is unaffected by the Time dampening field. But whatever abilities the cult members of old possessed with the ability to destroy the Wheel and everyone in it, they are long gone."

"The abilities maybe, but not the zeal," Tommen said grudgingly. "And now it looks like their leader is set to become the Zero Hour. A cult leader being voted into possibly the most powerful office in the universe. Go figure."

"Yes, it is very troubling. And as it is unclear what, if any, abilities Cassius possesses, we must be on guard with regards to not only what could happen if he wins, but also what could happen if he loses."

"And this war we've started with the Borelians and the Grandfathers probably doesn't help things either."

Sifura looked like she didn't want to agree with him, but the obviousness of the situation compelled her to agree. "It is true, this war, if it does indeed happen, will make it more difficult to track down cult members, but because Cassius has chosen to take the road of true politics, whatever makes our job more difficult also makes his more difficult."

Tommen still had his doubts. Sifura seemed to think of Cassius as a loaded gun, and instead of him shooting at a set target, this war made everything a moving target. He still had a set number of rounds, but the accuracy would generally decrease. Tommen saw Cassius as more of a bomb, nuclear, if he possessed even a fraction of the power he claimed to have or otherwise be pursuing. It didn't matter who had the hot potato at the end of the game, because everyone was going to get blown up regardless. Rather than simply keeping everything a moving target and hoping the gun did as little damage as possible, they needed to be thinking more like the bomb squad and treat everything as an all or nothing deal. Either they would all go home at the end of the day, or they would all end up exploded over a five mile radius.

"So, really, the whole point of Rifun kidnapping me," Tommen mused, "was so that he could recruit me as a new cult member?"

"I do not know his intentions," Sifura told him, "only that he is dangerous and must be stopped."

With that, she closed her eyes and shifted into as comfortable a position as she could manage. Tommen watched her for a minute or two, fascinated by and jealous of her arguably simplistic view of the world, the universe as a whole, even. She was from a world of physical and spiritual, right and wrong, black and white. Tommen came from a world of almost perpetual gray. Everyone professed to believe in right and wrong, good and evil, and yet there was always a fascination with the evil, a need to see a backstory and provide a justification. Similarly, there was always a fascination with the blemishes of good, a need to find all the dirt under the pristine white rug.

Even now, Tommen found himself wondering about Rifun and Cassius. It wasn't enough just to say they were driven by an insane ideological lust for power; he had to know why. What was the appeal? Well, okay, so the appeal was obvious when the story was glossed over—Tommen was pretty sure there was a much more detailed story to the Cult of the Akari. But after centuries of only one in a million people possessing but a tiny residual fraction of what mighty power that once existed, why did they keep going back to that well? What water could still be found there to fuel that insanity?

At the same time, some insanity could not be explained or quantified; it simply was. Sure, there might be fancy names for different types of insanity, but giving something a fancy name doesn't explain it, and it certainly doesn't cure it.

Still, there was also something kind of neat about thinking that some kind of ancient power might be residing within him. It was like his own little secret, something to hide under his bed and bring it out when no one was looking. And Tommen found his thoughts wandering to the ways in which he might have inherited this piece of the Akari.

If it was genetic, that meant that one of his ancestors—how far back this ancestor was depended on how long the gene stayed dormant in the DNA—was a Time Agent. And activated by Time? Well, there was always that little excursion into Forbes Cave. If that didn't activate something, no amount of Time exposure would.

He couldn't imagine that someone had necessarily given it to him. Then it occurred to him. Had Tommen been moving, he might have stopped so suddenly as to fall flat on his face. As it was, his lips parted just a little.

What if that was Walter's secret? What if Walter had once been this "Akari-bearer" and given it to Tommen without him ever knowing? It would explain Rifun and Cassius' fascination with him, as well as Rifun's insistence that Walter spill some secret or else die for it. Of course he'd given Tommen the Akari. How or why he had it in the first place didn't matter. Maybe he gave it to him for safekeeping, because he knew he was potentially being pursued by the likes of Rifun and Cassius. Maybe it had something to do with Cassius' story of being a guard in the same prison where Walter had been kept. Like slipping a joint in someone else's coat pocket when you know the cops are on your tail. Nothing comes up in a search, and you can go back for it later. And it made sense that, being a Timekeeper, he was charged with the arrest and turning over of Runners and cult members. Having the Akari, whether by choice or not, basically made him one of those cult members. All Cassius would have to do was blackmail Walter with being a cult member, and...

Tommen shook his head, torn between the fairy tales and the conspiracy, and what was actually going on around him. How much was true and how much was propaganda? The Hands were corrupt; who knew how much doublethinkgood they had going around, trying to scare and manipulate the masses?

He rubbed his face. It was all too much. Too much, too fast. He was too busy climbing mountains, outrunning mutated bears, and harvesting deadly flowers trying to save his dad to even worry about being pursued by a band of lunatic cult members who thought he had some kind of freaky, alternate-dimension, universe-bending superpowers. Oh, and then there was that thing about an impending civil war and being hated by the Hands, the Grandfathers, and the Borelians. And somewhere in all that mess, he still had his review coming up.

Fuck, but this was not how he'd intended to spend his Christmas break.

He looked at his watch again, but nothing had changed. He still had less than twenty-four hours to get the cure to Walter, and the d'bok was still at the bottom of the mountain. He could hear it, pacing and growling and snarling impatiently. Tommen sighed. He'd slept, but the boredom and all these stories and revelations were making him sleepy again. He might have fallen back asleep except he was hungry, thirsty, and now that he thought about it, he seriously had to pee.

Well, he wasn't going to go and show himself to the d'bok, in the event that it did encourage the beast to stay. And he certainly wasn't going to pee on it from above, however satisfying that sounded. His back screaming at him from sitting uncomfortably and now having to crouch uncomfortably, Tommen moved deeper into the cave.

It wasn't a particularly deep cave as far as he was concerned. He reached a point where the tunnel seemed to end, only a mouse-size hole giving any indication that it went any deeper. But it was far enough from their small sitting site for him to pee in privacy, if not comfort.

When he returned, he looked for anything that he could use

for entertainment, or just to keep his hands busy. A couple rocks, a stick, some grass, anything. But the cave was barren and smooth.

"How long until the d'bok leaves?" Tommen asked, knowing full well he sounded like a whiny child.

"It should not be long," Sifura repeated.

She looked like she was going to say more, but he beat her to it. "Don't tell me to sleep or rest or anything like that. I can't sleep anymore. I've already slept, and I'm not tired, and I don't have the time anymore."

Instead of pursuing an argument or being offended, she simply opened one eye. "Then don't sleep. Stay awake. Wake me when the d'bok leaves. Until then, stay quiet and let me rest."

With that, she closed her eyes, shifted her position, and went to sleep. Well, it probably wasn't actual sleep; Tommen suspected it was more like a cat nap. Either way, once again, he'd been the petulant child, and she'd simply sidestepped his small tantrum. But he wasn't going to give in to this one. He said he was going to stay awake, so he was going to stay awake and wait for the d'bok to leave, no matter how long that took.

Looking outside, Tommen knew it was going to be a long night.

Chapter Twenty-Eight
Of Thorns and Roses

"Tommen. Tommen Forbes."

Tommen blinked awake to darkness. He startled and almost panicked, but Sifura's voice broke through the shadows. "Hush, Tommen. Be still."

"What is it?" he asked, his voice tight, slowly forming a Band and bringing it in tight like a blanket.

"The d'bok is leaving," she whispered.

He let out a sigh of relief, then tensed again as he checked his watch. Just before ten p.m. So he hadn't slept long, only a couple hours.

"How long until we're safe?" he inquired.

"Perhaps an hour." He could hear her moving in the darkness. "Drop your Band and wait for daylight so you can climb down the face safely."

Well, there was no denying that logic, even if he was reluctant to give up any more time. Outside, he could hear the d'bok, growling and roaring and snarling like a couple of alley cats locked in a fight over territory, or like a possessed animal fighting to rid itself of the vengeful spirit inside it.

"Do you remember the way back to the village?" Sifura asked. She sounded close, or closer than she had been.

"I think so." Tommen racked his brain and tried to remember the way, but one jungle path was the same as any other. "Just keep heading west, right?"

"Yes." Her tone suggested that he was more or less correct

and would have a decent time trying to get back, but he had the right idea and she wasn't going to correct him. "When you climb down, take your pack and one of the honey jars. Return to the village. Present the honey jar to the council and see that they send help."

"What about the antidote that I'm actually taking with me? And how will I get to the Wheel? I mean, I know you have the power, but I'll just...disappear."

"Leave it to me," she ordered sternly, as if she was tired of being questioned and doubted. "When you get to the Wheel, unless your Lieutenants are already there, find a safe place and stay there until I arrive."

"You're coming, too?"

"Not until I have been tended. But I will come. That is why I tell you to find somewhere safe."

"Okay, so if I'm a fugitive and I'm going to walk right into a place swarming with cops, where do I hide?"

"The Archives," Sifura told him. "Go there and find the farthest corner you can. But do not take a chip. Tell the secretaries that you are there only to find someone."

"Why not take a chip? Shouldn't I start reading up on the Akari or the cult or Time Civil War?"

"Because then they can track you. Who you are, where you are, even what you are reading. When your Lieutenants were doing research on the Dispersal, that was how the other Hands found them and had them arrested."

"What's the Dispersal?"

"The story of how Cassius became the False Zero Hour, one I cannot tell you now. You must ask your Lieutenants."

Tommen didn't see a good reason why, but he was willing to let it go, just this once. "Okay, so go to the Archives, don't take a chip, find a corner to hide in."

"Yes. And wait for me."

"Unless Micah or Micaiah is already there."

"Correct."

"What about Lily? I mean, she's kind of a bitch, but Cassius was after her, too. She has the ability to open portals and stuff."

Sifura's tone was hesitant. "If you trust her. Understanding that this trust, if misplaced, could land you before the Grandfathers and a Borelian."

Tommen ran his tongue over his teeth. He didn't particularly like Lily—no one really did—but he couldn't imagine her betraying him to the Grandfathers like that. She was narcissistic and self-absorbed, but she wasn't a murderer, and handing him over would not only potentially sentence him to death or worse, but it would also mean the death of Walter. Finally he nodded, even if she couldn't see it. "Yeah, I'd trust her to help me."

"Then such is your choice, and I hope you make the right one."

Her words sent a shiver down Tommen's spine. Outside, the d'bok's cries were growing louder and far more ferocious, ranging anywhere from a stuck pig to a couple of fighting cats to an angry old bear. But if there was some form of spirit or other higher intelligence inside that ugly body, it no longer spoke to Tommen. Had he not been sitting, he might have been knocked off balance as the d'bok threw itself against the rock face.

Tommen had heard numerous stories of demon possession, most were from dusty old nuns and priests, some from small primitive African or Indian tribes. Most of them involved screaming and snarling and general rabidness, a violent physical struggle that often gave the poor conflicted soul inhuman strength while destroying anything human about the person. Tommen had thought them cruel and insensitive diagnoses for individuals who suffered from some mental illness as yet unidentified. After all, real possession involved, like, weird contortions of the body and stuff. Oh, and demons. You needed demons for that, but he had his doubts.

And yet, from the commotion going on down at the base of the mountain, Tommen might have given some credence to those old stories. What primitive people would understand what was happening to their friend or family member as they thrashed and screamed? Cultures nurtured and abandoned children who were of gentler special needs, but what could they do with something like this but call it an evil spirit and either cast it out to die on its own or kill it and declare it a mercy?

"Is it always this violent?" Tommen wondered. "When an animal tries to get rid of its spirit?"

"No," Sifura told him. "This is considerably more violent. It is a particularly vengeful spirit, one that would rather the animal die waiting than give up the wait for you to die or come down."

"What happens to the spirit when the animal gets rid of it?"

"It goes back into its own realm until it finds another animal that will take it."

"Wait, so an animal has to, like, invite it in? Why would it do that?"

"Not all spirits are evil, Tommen Forbes, but most often they look and sound the same, and you can't tell the difference until it is inside of you. The animal takes a chance, each time a spirit approaches it. If the d'bok down there survives much longer, it is unlikely that it will ever allow another spirit inside of it."

"Oh, well, that's comforting."

There was a snarl then, and then all was quiet. A minute or two later, Tommen heard some grunting and growling like a bear going through things at a campsite, and then all was quiet again.

"Is he gone?" Tommen dared ask after about five minutes of silence. He hadn't realized how much he'd missed the quiet until it was returned to him. Fuck, and if he was half-deaf, how loud would that shit have been if he'd had his total hearing?

"He is gone," Sifura confirmed, much to Tommen's relief. "Now we only have to wait for the dawn."

It was easily one of the longest waiting-for-morning waits of Tommen's life, more than Thanksgiving, more than Christmas. He was ready, more than ready. He compulsively checked and rechecked his watch just to make sure he hadn't somehow lost three days or a week or something. And as soon as he could make out his hand in front of his face, he crept his way to the mouth of the cave and looked out.

The d'bok was gone. Tommen almost could have cried. He looked down the trail as much as he could see, but the d'bok was really gone. Out across the jungle valley, the first colors of dawn streaked the sky, setting the trees as a mysterious black silhouette.

"Do not go out until you are sure," Sifura commanded behind him. "Else all is for naught, if you fall to your death."

Tommen thought of his bloody head and his dislocated hand. His hand was repaired, but when he put it to his head, it still came back a little bloody. He probably had blood all down his neck and back. What a sight he would make walking into the village. Well, it would give him a more convincing story, he thought.

He looked down at the rock face. It was facing south, a good direction for the sunrise. He barely had to wait another ten or fifteen minutes before the pre-dawn light gave way to the lights just before the sun peeked over the horizon. His mind barely registered that before he had his ass sticking out of the cave and was fishing for a foothold, slowly lowering himself down, staying as close to the face as possible. He found a hold just at the edge of his range. Taking a breath, he moved one hand down until it found a hold, then allowed himself to rest his weight. First task complete. Repeat two hundred more times.

Most of Tommen's mountain climbing experience came from his childhood and was actually closer to the realm of hiking, running out from the cabin and scrambling up the trail, over stumps and fallen trees, under low-hanging branches, scraping his hands and knees on the rocks in the trail. Very little of that had been true rock climbing.

His only exposure to actual climbing had been several years ago at a summer camp for boys. It was a week-long camp and one of the days had been devoted entirely to rock climbing. They'd spent at least forever in the classroom, going over the rules and safety precautions. When they finally did get outside, they spent at least another expanse of forever learning about the harnesses and the helmets. They talked about carabeners and knots, tied their own knots only to have an instructor come around and redo them all anyway. Then they had to watch one instructor climb the wall while the second instructor narrated all the techniques and how to find a hold and what to do if you slipped, and on and on it went, all the way up and all the way down.

By the time they actually got around to climbing, Tommen had just wanted to go home. It had been basically the same routine for each activity they had done throughout the week, whether it was climbing, kayaking, horseback riding, shooting. So when it was his turn to finally climb, he only got about a quarter of the way up the wall before he feigned a fear of heights and was gently told to simply rappel back down.

Fuck, but he wished he'd remembered more from that camp. Not that he was sure it would do any good. Back then he'd had harnesses and helmets and ropes and an instructor to tell him where he could go and how he could help himself. Here he had no equipment: if he let go, he would fall and splatter his brains all over the rocks below. And while he had no doubt Sifura was an able instructor, that was probably only relevant if she was on the ground and could see the whole picture. As it was, she simply watched him as she had before, like a cat with her head poked over the edge. She was unable to pace, but her head still bobbed back and forth like she wanted to.

Tommen tried not to think about how far up he was or how far he still had to go. All that mattered was the moment, where he was going to place his hand or foot, how comfortable he felt with a hold, how much he wanted to trust it to let go of another hold. It was nerve-wracking he felt sweat snaking down his back and in front of his eyes. The only thing that really helped was the dawn, the light getting brighter and brighter, illuminating more of the wall so he could see as much as feel, though he looked down only sparingly.

His mouth opened but his throat locked as his foot suddenly

slipped. He clenched his fingers as hard as he could on their holds and pressed himself tight against the rock. He could hear tiny rocks clattering down the face and hitting the trail below. Rather than dwell on the surprise and the fear—and the fact that he was pretty sure he'd peed a little—he tried to focus on the sound of the rocks falling and the echo, tried to judge how far to the ground. But he was no expert on the science of sound and echolocation; he didn't even have his full hearing to know what he was really hearing anyway.

Shaking his head, he put his loose foot out and swept it around a bit until he found another hold, and he continued. He glanced up at Sifura who still watched, not saying a word. He looked east, where the sun itself was hidden behind a mountain, but the light still shone all around. He looked west, across the rock face, trying to judge his distance to the ground. In his haste to escape the d'bok, he hadn't really thought ahead, about looking for markers or signs; his only thought had been to live.

Not a bad thing, he reflected as he took another step down, but it just made this second part all that much more difficult. At the same time, he was noticing that the closer to the ground he got, the less smooth and more jagged the rocks became, giving him a number of potential footholds, but most of them very painful. He cut himself more than once, his hand or foot moving wrong, his body getting a little closer to the face than he really wanted. It was a wonder his head wound wasn't worse than it had been; one of these rocks could have easily stabbed him in the neck or the back of the head and killed him right then and there.

He found another foothold, and then another handhold. Jagged or not, having an abundance of holds was giving him a little more confidence in his climbing, and looking up to see Sifura so small looking over the edge gave him hope that he wasn't as far up as he told himself he was. He paused, wondering if he wanted to risk looking down or just keep going until he landed on his ass because he reached farther than he needed to and tripped over his own feet.

He took another step down, then decided to chance it. He

looked down. He almost laughed.

Under ordinary circumstances, he probably could have just jumped the last three or four feet to the ground, but given that these were razor sharp rocks and he wasn't in the best of health, he wasn't taking any unnecessary risks. Feeling almost giddy, he hurried down, reaching for a hold and letting go of the last before firmly establishing himself. It worked for about two steps before he finally did slip and was unable to catch himself.

First he landed on a heel, then on his ass, and then he was carried onto his back where his head snapped back and reopened the old wound, if he hadn't created a new one. He lay there for a second before sitting up, feeling the rocks embedded in his skin.

"Tommen! Are you okay?" Sifura called down from the cave.

"I'm fine!" he called back, even as he winced as he found a rock in his palm and pulled it out, blood welling up from the wound. "I'm fine! Just missed the last step!"

"Get your pack and one of the honey jars! Take them to the village and get help!"

As if he had any other plans, like a nice trek through the mountains to explore all the wonders this planet had to offer. He found he was a little farther down from the camp than originally intended, probably from his choice of hand and footholds on the way down the face. It was no matter, however. By this time, he'd been through too much and gotten too close to accomplishing his mission to give a fuck about much of anything anymore. He'd traveled through Death Valley, been attacked by the ugliest cat he'd ever seen, witnessed a real warrior's duel, gone hiking through the mountains, been attacked by another ugly animal, gone freestyle mountain climbing...

"Fuck."

The word escaped his lips before his mind even registered what had happened. Whatever sounds he'd heard as the d'bok left, like a bear rifling through a campsite for food, was pretty much exactly what it turned out to be. He was less concerned about his clothes being strewn about and empty plastic baggies being torn up, but then his gaze went to the honey jars, or what was left of them.

Both jars had been destroyed, their contents splattered everywhere. Sticky orange goo was plastered all over the floor of the cave, partially down the path, interrupted only intermittently by shards of stone from the jars.

"Sifura!" he called up. "The jars are destroyed! The antidote is all over everything!"

Fear rose in him, threatening to choke him. Could the antidote be salvaged, even a little? They had no more honey for him to attempt another collection, and, when all was said and done, they were out of time. Even with Banding, there was just no time left. Maybe if Sifura wasn't injured, maybe if they didn't have to go through all the ritualistic niceties of hospitality, but they couldn't do everything.

"If you can, scrape some antidote that has not touched the ground. Just a handful will cure twenty men. Save it in one of your clear bags," Sifura called down.

Heart racing, Tommen picked his way carefully around the antidote into the little cave to his things. The burlap bag was more or less in tact, as were most of his clothes. Any food he'd had left was gone, same with the water. Most of the plastic had been shredded. Out of some ingrained sense of duty, he picked up all the garbage he could find and stuffed it all back in the burlap bag with his clothes. Then, as he made a final pass, looking for anything else that may have been scattered, he found Micaiah's bowie knife. It had been slobbered and chewed on a bit, but otherwise it was still good. No telling where the duel knives had gotten to.

Then he found the bag that the trail mix had been in. Micah wasn't much of an organic, green, vegan type of person, but the trail mix he'd sent had been of that ilk and so had been packed in a special biodegradable paper bag. That bag hadn't been touched. Maybe because it had an earthy smell to it and so it wasn't as new and interesting as the plastic sandwich bags, or maybe it had been simply passed over. Either way, it was enough.

Tommen grabbed the bag, snatching it up like a hawk, as if someone else was looking at it and he had to claim it before it was lost forever—like candy from a piñata. Then he made a beeline for the shattered jars and the goopy antidote. Handful for twenty men; fuck that. If war was coming and the Borelians were going to be coming out with a vengeance, he was going to stockpile this shit. He took the shredded plastic sandwich bags and used them to more or less line the paper bag. Once he had everything where he wanted it, he knelt and started scooping.

Only the stuff that hadn't touched the ground, Tommen reminded himself frequently, even as he pushed the line and got as close as he could. Was there no five-second rule here? Even if it had been on the ground for probably half an hour or so? Why couldn't he take the stuff that had touched the ground? Oh well, when it came to have an effective antidote, he was willing to trust Sifura on this one and skip over the majority of the antidote.

The stuff itself was more like honey than the lube-honey had been. The antidote was bright yellow and sticky to the point where it soon covered Tommen's body better than the lube-honey ever did. It filled the inside of the trail mix bag and covered the outside. Once it was full, he stood and looked back up at the cave.

"Should I wash this stuff off or what?" he called.

"Wash it or eat it," Sifura told him. "It will not harm you, but it is a sweet treat and may make you ill if you have too much."

Curious now, Tommen licked some off his fingers. It was like eating sugar straight from the bag, dark brown sugar at that. It was like a molasses cookie got baked into a sugar cookie got baked into a cake got covered in icing and then got dipped in brown sugar again. The stickiness of it was somewhere between honey on a biscuit and peanut butter that got stuck to the roof of his mouth, which only prolonged the sugary taste. Tommen liked a candy bar here and there, had never really been one for sweets, so even just this small sample of the antidote was like a sugar overload, more than he would normally have in a whole month. True to Sifura's words, it did make him feel sick. Maybe it wasn't the sugar itself, but just the general richness and the unfamiliarity of it.

Feeling slightly woozy, Tommen sat against the rock face and waited for the nausea to pass. He was going to have to wash this stuff off; there was no way he was going to eat his way out of this one. Just the thought of it was enough to make his stomach lurch. When he finally stood again, he tried to scrape off as much as he could and drizzle it back onto the jar pieces, but he might as well have been trying to escape a tar pit. Only good thing about this one was that he could just walk out of it. But he was going to have to wash in the river; of that much he was sure.

"So is that how you give it to someone?" Tommen asked. "You have to feed it to them?"

"Or you can put it directly into their bloodstream," Sifura replied.

That would make Walter diabetic, take him out of the Borelian coma, then put him back into a diabetic coma. At the same time, Tommen wondered if it would be possible to take a small sample to analyze it—how or where, he wasn't sure—and see just how similar to honey or sugar this stuff really was. If the answer to the problem was as simple as sugar, then there would be no real need to stockpile the antidote, plus it could remain humanity's dirty little secret weapon against the Borelians.

"Hurry, Tommen Forbes!" Sifura called down. "Time waits for no one!"

Oddly enough, as Tommen stood, he found himself wondering if that was a saying from her people, one of those universal truths found throughout, well, the universe, or if it was something she had more picked up from the Wheel and used now to motivate him. Well, it motivated him. He paused only once to look around and consider whether he needed to take anything with him on his way back. He went back for the bowie knife and set off down the trail.

He didn't get very far before he found the gun, abandoned where it lay after he'd stupidly chucked it at the d'bok. It did not appear to have been chewed up by the d'bok, but there were scratches and scuff marks from the impact on the animal and then on the rocks. Micaiah was going to kill him if it had been damaged beyond repair and didn't work, but Tommen figured that he had a good enough excuse for how it got that way. Hopefully then, Micaiah would only maim him instead of kill him outright.

Tommen returned to the cave once more, just long enough to stuff the gun back in the burlap sack. He hid the trail mix bag full of antidote, but didn't dare pack it yet, not until he could get it properly cleaned off. Then, with a last glance at Sifura who was sort of pacing at the mouth of the high cave, he fingered the bowie knife and set off down the trail toward the D'bok camp.

The sticky honey became painful as the sharp rocks made new cuts on the bottom of his feet, and the sugary snack soon became a salty insult. It was like walking on hot coals. Combined with everything else he'd been put through in the last however many hours, by the time he reached the end of the rocky trail and turned to look back, he found he'd left a sticky trail of blood and honey. He wiped his feet as best he could on the grass before continuing on the trail, the huge stone monuments watching his every move.

Tommen was briefly reminded of Donojok, the Grunjor sentient rock monster. He hadn't been quite as big as any of these sentinels, but there was no reason to think a Grunjor couldn't be. What if these things were secretly Grunjors? Created and deployed to keep watch over primitive worlds and report back once the people were ready to join Time? What if they were reporting on Tommen's movements, telling the Hands where he was and what he was doing? He was alone now, no gun, no super hot warrior princess to save his ass, nothing but a little bowie knife that now seemed sorely insignificant, walking along a path and surrounded by poisonous plants.

He shook his head, tried to tell himself he was being a

frightened and paranoid little boy. He'd been through a lot and now he needed to learn from it, grow because of it. When faced with adversity, tell yourself the future story of how you overcame that adversity, how you conquered that wall. In the throes of illness? Think about the speech you would give once you've been cured and are now working to help others. Dealing with financial hardships? Look forward to the story of your breakthrough into freedom and learn from the future. Walking alone on a distant, hostile planet on a timed mission to save your father while your tour guide is depending on you for help and the people you're approaching are less than friendly to outsiders?

Tommen considered that story for a second. It would be the one to tell as he and his dad and probably the twins sat around the table maybe New Year's Eve or New Year's Day, all wanting to know just how he did it, what had happened. Where would he start? What would he tell them? Walter had missed out on...five days? Was that right? Six, maybe? So he would need to hear the story of how Tommen went before the Hands to try and plead for help. And that part about starting a war? Well, maybe just skip that part for now and get right into how Sifura approached them and Tommen followed her back to her home planet.

Another thought occurred to him then, as he began piecing that story together. Walter had told him that bit of advice. Normally Tommen defaulted to advice and sayings and quips his pa had made, but in this instance, Walter's advice had come to mind. Just as it had when he was going to make a speech before the Hands.

Running through the story in his mind helped to calm him down as he found the giant fallen tree and the root tunnel leading to the main trail. Not far now. He pulled his Fast Band tighter around him, as if he was pulling a coat tighter against the rain. As far as Banding went, he only had to drop it when he got to the village and talked to the council. Once the rescue party was on their way and out of sight of the village, he could put a Band around the whole group. Well, maybe. Himself he could do easily. Himself, Sifura, and the skimmer had been a decent day's work that he had grown accustomed to, like any good workout. A group of people, depending on how many there were, that could be a challenge. But he wouldn't have to hold it for long, really. Just until they got back to the cave. He would drop it while they rescued Sifura, then reinstate it when she gave some cue that they should talk alone and then she sent him back to the Wheel.

It was a good plan, but not as foolproof as he would have preferred. With so many people around, how would she be able to sneak him back to the Wheel? There would be no sneaking. He would be there, and then suddenly he wouldn't, at least in the eyes of the D'bok. He wasn't sure of their beliefs or superstitions, but he was pretty sure that such a thing might qualify as witchcraft, or their version of it. This wasn't his world and these were not his people, but he didn't want to see anything bad happen to Sifura, not after everything she'd done to help him.

He was so deep in his thoughts, Tommen almost didn't stop when he started passing by the river. Only when a leaf came spiraling down and stuck to his sticky skin did he recall his secondary errand and stop to pick his way carefully down to the banks.

The antidote that was still sticky and pliable dissolved like sugar, and Tommen again questioned the composition of the flower nectar. Maybe it was the chemical makeup that counted, but what if it was like corn sugar versus cane sugar or beet sugar? Had he really come all this way, braved unspeakable dangers, and risked his life, for a bit of sugar that he could have gotten anywhere? Forget "the journey is what counts" and all that bullshit about personal growth. If he could have saved himself a bunch of time and worry and avoided starting a war just by making a quick run to the grocery store, he would have done that in a heartbeat. He was pretty sure Walter wouldn't have thought less of him for buying a bag of sugar at the store versus fighting lions and tigers and bears for a pixie stick. Or in this case, a fucking flower. Tommen gritted his teeth, feeling the fool for not thinking about this earlier, scrubbing maybe a little harder than necessary at the stuff that remained stuck to him.

The stuff that wasn't sticky anymore but had since hardened to an epoxy-like shell, that did not come off as easily, nor as painlessly. It was like supergluing his fingers together with the really fine, really fancy, really expensive, virtually unbreakable glue. Adding water did little to help and Tommen lost more than a few layers of skin as he finally resorted just to digging his nails under the scab-like pieces and ripping them off. He bled in a few places, but he just wanted the stuff off of him. It was a little more difficult in more sensitive areas, but eventually he was satisfied that he'd gotten everything off and he was clean again.

Still, he gave himself a quick full-body rinse before getting out. As he walked along the trail, he ran his fingers through his hair, trying to comb it just a little, amazed at not only how long it had gotten, but also how his beard had grown out again. Metabolic screwing from the Banding meant that he didn't have the same ten days' growth as he would have if he'd been in Base Time for that same ten days, but it didn't mean his hair hadn't grown at all. A memory of looking at himself in the mirror after getting home from being kidnapped flashed through his mind, and how much he'd looked like his pa.

Fuck, but if his pa or his brother could see him now, traipsing naked through some alien forest, alone with a hot girl, picking flowers. First they would be horrified. His pa would probably switch him. Teo would give him a lecture too, while their pa was looking, then later confess how jealous he was.

Tommen stopped and sighed. But he wasn't doing this for them. He wasn't risking his life for his pa or his brother. He was doing it for his dad. All of this, he did for Walter, to hopefully save him. Because he loved him.

Well, hindsight being 20/20 and all that, Tommen found a new mental clarity, walking alone there, naked, through an alien forest, toward the village of people that would help Sifura who would help him, so he could help Walter. And somehow, in spite of everything, all his fears and doubts, that was suddenly the only thing that really mattered in the universe. And he pressed on.

Chapter Twenty-Nine
Rescue

Tommen stumbled across the village more than tactfully approached it. Even being on a trail heading straight for it, and having been there once before and knowing what it looked like, the place was remarkably well-hidden and camouflaged. He found a quiet corner to safely drop his Band and was momentarily overwhelmed by the sudden tsunami of sounds and other sensations. He went from a peaceful, quiet walk through the forest, to life. Simply life. Village life happening all around him, children playing, people cooking and shouting and fixing and building and doing all manner of things Tommen couldn't even begin to understand.

Perhaps it was his mistake for not waiting to drop the Band until he'd found his way through the maze to the communal area and the council hut in the trees. But he supposed he found the area easily enough, once he figured to just pick a giant tree and keep moving in that general direction. He Banded and nervously checked his watch. Quarter after ten. He sighed and tried to find the same focus he'd had on the trail. Do it for his dad. He had time, but it was time to impose some arbitrary deadlines. Midnight. Had to be home by midnight. Which meant he had to get up there quick and speak to the council.

He wasn't actually stopped from going up the ladder to the platform, but when he started crossing the bridge to the council hut platform, a couple guards moved to block his path at the end.

Something else crossed his mind then. How in the world was he going to communicate with the council? He could understand them, but they couldn't understand him. He almost stopped and swore aloud, but he was beyond that kind of stuff now. Such would accomplish nothing. He had a goal, and he knew what he needed to do to accomplish that goal. Something as insignificant as a language barrier wasn't going to stop him now.

"I need to talk to the council," he said before the guards could say anything. When the guards looked somewhat confused, he said, "I need to speak to the council. To Dreja."

Damn, but he wished he could remember the names of the other council members. Still, the guards seemed to get the gist. One continued to block his path, stranding him on the swaying bridge, while the other went to the council hut and had a word. A few minutes later, the guard returned and made a gesture. Tommen was allowed to pass.

He tried to convey urgency but not frantic desperation as he entered the council hut, even if he felt the situation warranted desperate over urgent.

"You return alone," one of the council members observed. "And without any antidote."

Tommen remained calm as he recalled several tips he had learned about communicating around a language barrier. First, use names and cognates whenever possible.

"Sifura has been attacked by a d'bok," Tommen said simply, slowly, as if they would understand him speaking slowly versus quickly.

Tip number two: Imagery is a powerful tool and motivator. "A d'bok attacked Sifura." He knew he had their attention at "d'bok" and so only had to make like a slashing claw or something to get the point across. "Sifura is hurt." He indicated one of the wounds where the antidote had gotten stuck to his skin and he'd peeled it off bloody. "Her leg is injured and she cannot walk." Tommen indicated his knee, made like a slashing motion, and then collapsed on the floor. He was a fighter, not an actor, and the only way he knew how to go down was hard. He knew the council members heard his grand thump, maybe winced at it, probably got a good mental chuckle out of it, but he could also see by their gaze that they were understanding. Maybe not everything, but enough.

Tip number three: Tone and body language say more than words ever will. "The antidote is gone." He did his best to convey despair. "And Sifura is trapped. She needs help."

"You have told us that Sifura was attacked by a d'bok and has an injured leg, she cannot walk," Dreja said thoughtfully. "She requires assistance to return."

"Yes." Tommen did a dramatic nod. "Yes, that's right."

"Very well. We will send two warriors—"

"Please, Dreja," Tommen interrupted, knowing he was treading water. The leader gave him an unreadable look, but waited for him to continue.

Tip number four: Charades are universal. "When the d'bok attacked—" He did another slashing motion. "—we climbed the rock face—" He did his best to look like he was rock climbing, but was pretty sure he failed. "—and ducked into a cave." He crouched low and brought his arms over him like the roof of a cave. "She is very high up." He stood and stretched his arms apart vertically, one as low as he could reach, one as high.

The council members glanced around at each other, and Tommen was afraid they'd misinterpreted his motions. They murmured among themselves for a minute or two, their expressions changing from confused to thoughtful. Finally, Dreja addressed Tommen again.

"You climbed to escape the d'bok and found a cave. Sifura is there?" he asked cautiously.

Tommen did another dramatic nod. "Yes. Sifura is there."

"We know this cave," another council member told him. "It is very high up, very difficult to get to."

"Better that a healer go to her," a third said. "Fix her leg in the cave."

"And some experienced climbers go as well," a fourth chimed in. "Drive rope and hooks into the rock and lower her down safely, as the Poqip once showed us."

The others grumbled a reluctant agreement at that statement, and Tommen briefly recalled that the two tribes were apparently at war or something. No matter. *You can learn as much or more from your enemies as your friends.* Tommen forgot if his pa or his dad had told him that one.

"At any rate, we should help," the second council member said firmly. "She is here fairly, and so we are responsible both for her and to her people that she return safely."

"I agree," Dreja said, turning to look Tommen in the eye. "We will send four experienced climbers with the ropes and hooks, as well as a healer and whatever supplies he needs. I will also accompany you that I may speak with Sifura and so learn the whole story of what happened. More than just your...motions, creative though they are."

The other council members snickered at the comment, but Tommen felt only relief. It hadn't been as painful as he'd feared. This time they hadn't made him fight a warrior or eat bugs or anything; this time, without a political rival in the way, they'd gone right along with it.

"Thank you," Tommen told them, hoping he could adequately convey his gratitude. "Thank you for helping, for everything. Sifura thanks you."

But Dreja was already locked into his mission and impatient to leave, simply saying, "We ought to leave as soon as possible, and move quickly. It is not good to be left alone for long in the wilderness, especially wounded."

Tommen followed Dreja out of the council hut and across the bridge. The D'bok leader stopped at the top of the ladder and turned to Tommen. "I will summon the healer and the climbers. Wait for us at the eastern trailhead."

Tommen made a motion like he understood and was totally prepared and totally focused, when in reality, he was anything but. He understood well enough, but he felt tragically unprepared and wildly unfocused. When they hit the ground and Dreja strode off purposefully, he felt very much like the extra. The camera would follow Dreja as he gathered his closest confidants, best warriors, the wise, sagely healer, and together the band of heroes would march off into the forest to rescue the damsel in distress, with Tommen tagging along as the dopey squire, the unimportant messenger, the extra redshirt who would be killed off for dramatic purposes while the main band of heroes stayed united through the entire film.

It was one of the rare times when Tommen was glad that this was nothing like the movies. This was his mission, and he was the star of this picture. He was like the wise hero who knew when he needed to humble himself and ask for help. He'd already done it once in taking Sifura's offer. Now she was bending the knee to ask for help, and he was going along with her request, wise as it was.

His only consolation when it took so long for him to find the damn trailhead was that he at least got there before Dreja and the others, though not by much. Tommen recognized the healer, but the healer regarded him with little more than utter disdain, shifting the pack on his back and pointedly looking away. As for the climbers, two were almost as big and brawny as Karaki, probably could have taken him in a fight. The other two were lean, comparatively speaking, as the D'bok seemed to be natural-born cage fighters. Each of them also had a pack, bigger and bulkier than the healer's. Dreja himself had a pack, but what it contained, Tommen could only guess.

Dreja did not stop at the trailhead to explain their mission; likely he had done that while he gathered his troops. Instead, as soon as he confirmed that everyone was ready and had the supplies they needed, he took the lead and started off down the trail. He set a decent pace, would have made a good drill sergeant, Tommen thought. It only took about five minutes before they were at a comfortable enough distance from the village that Tommen put up a Band. Trying to hold in seven moving people was like adding a new set of weights onto an already challenging weight bar, but he told himself he was going to have to flex his muscles a little, prepare for his Apprenticeship.

He wasn't sure if any of them noticed how the forest became

silent around them or how the sun didn't move, but he wasn't going to just give up eight hours to play on the safe side and hide his abilities. They were moving at a good pace, and hopefully they were too intent on their mission to be mindful of such things, like the sun coming to a standstill in the horizon.

Only when they stopped for water at the stream did Tommen drop the Band. While the others got drinks and took a short rest, he moved a short distance upstream so he could check his watch. Barely ten thirty. He closed his eyes and breathed. Before midnight. Had to be home before midnight.

When he opened his eyes, he found one of the lean warriors squatting across from him on the bank. It took Tommen a minute to realize that they were in a Band, and not one of his making.

"It's not nice to cheat," the warrior said, holding him in a dark stare.

Tommen shook his head, tried to play it off. "Listen, I can understand you, but you can't—"

"Can't I?"

Tommen looked again. There, nestled underneath thick, greasy fur, was a collar similar to his own. He couldn't see any kind of auditory input piece, earbud or otherwise, but he had a pretty good inkling that one was hidden in there somewhere.

"So where are you really from, Tommen Forbes, of the 'Ape Tribe'?" the warrior asked.

"A planet called Earth," Tommen replied, choosing to meet his stare. "Quadrant One, Parsec Eleven, Sector Five, System Four, Planet Thirty-eight, Region Four, District Four. Probationary Timekeeper."

"Only probationary. Huh. Could have fooled me, and I congratulate you for that."

"And you?"

"S'bal. Journeyman Timekeeper."

"Your master is in your faction also?"

"No. He is from another world entirely. My exposure to Time was accidental. As was Sifura's, Hand of Scientifically Primitive and

Unengaged Civilizations."

"Does she know about you?"

"If she does, she doesn't care. And it doesn't really matter to me either. What does matter to me is why you're here. What really brings you to our little primitive world looking for flowers?"

"Looking for an antidote for poison." Tommen narrowed his glare. "I'm only a liar when I have to be. I can't tell your people that I'm from another world, but I can tell them I'm from another tribe."

"Fair enough," S'bal conceded. "But what is it that you are trying to cure?"

Something about his attitude, tone, posture, everything, made Tommen uneasy. It was like having a conversation with a panther that was crouched and ready to pounce while it asked its prey whether it liked barbecue or cajun better. Maybe he was being paranoid, but Tommen got the feeling that any kind of secrecy that he'd thought he had about being on this planet and his actions, it was all gone now, and as soon as he was out of sight, everything would get reported back to Rifun and Cassius or the Hands or the Grandfathers or the Borelians or somebody. He also got the feeling that as soon as he admitted to it, if he and S'bal were alone, S'bal would try to kill him, would probably win, and would most likely claim that Tommen had attacked him first.

So Tommen kept his mouth shut. Then, in a burst of energy and using the element of surprise—being thought weak for being a probationary had its advantages—Tommen broke out of the Band. It hadn't been a very strong Band, but it was still like trying to claw his way out of shrink wrap, or maybe one of those really expensive garbage bags that stretch forever and never seem to tear. The surprise worked, the Band dropped, and Tommen stood. Dreja looked in his direction, and S'bal lost his chance.

"Are you ready, Tommen Forbes?" Dreja asked. "Where is S'bal?"

"Here," S'bal said, following a step behind Tommen. "I am ready."

They began moving again, and again Tommen put a Band around them. He pulled it in as tight and as narrow as possible, building it up and feeling for S'bal's attacks. The lean warrior didn't know why Tommen was running around in the jungle, but he seemed to catch on that time was of the essence and was working to foil him at every opportunity, scratching and clawing at his Band, causing it to fluctuate in its speed, but never able to actually tear it down. Or maybe he chose not to, just kept giving him subtle reminders that he was there, and he was watching.

And still they moved quickly through the jungle until they came to the giant fallen tree. Tommen and Sifura had little trouble getting through the tunnel, but the D'bok warriors had to hunch and crouch and force their way through, brushing off tree fibers and picking out splinters once they emerged on the other side.

"Be alert," Dreja ordered them, "in case the d'bok is still in the area."

Despite his misgivings about the d'bok being possessed by any kind of spirit, Tommen was pretty sure that any intelligent animal wouldn't willingly attack a group of armed and trained warriors, not unless it was truly desperate. Still, he did as Dreja bade and kept his head on a swivel, eyes open, ears as open as they could be. But the stone sentinels were silent as ever, and when they reached the stony trail up the mountain, the only sound to be heard was the whistling of the wind and the clattering and echo of the sharp rocks as they scrabbled their way up the slope. The D'bok moved purposefully, but Tommen stumbled more often than not, the bottoms of his feet probably closer to hamburger than healthy flesh.

The breath was taken from his lungs and he found himself double-Banded. S'bal walked up next to him and whispered, "Careful you don't trip and fall too far. It seems as though not everyone here is as resilient as he believes."

Then the double-Band was gone, and they were moving again.

It didn't take long to reach the tiny cave where the antidote still lay spilled out of broken jars. As soon as the healer saw them, he was irate. He roared his disbelief and ran to the mess, careful not to get himself covered in the sticky goop, but still pacing and snarling his outrage.

"My jars! The antidote!" he raged. "What has happened here?!"

Before anyone could answer, there was another voice. "Dreja!"

They all looked up to see Sifura poking her head out of the cave, high above their heads, cat ears pricked forward, staring down at them intently. "You have come!"

"Yes, Sifura, leader of the Xresa," Dreja replied formally. "I have brought a healer and climbers. The healer will come and prepare you for the ropes."

"I thank you, Dreja, leader of the Bodek. And we shall speak more once I am safely on the ground."

She withdrew. Dreja turned and nodded at his warriors who all dropped their packs simultaneously and began rooting through them, digging out seemingly endless coils of rope. If they were the same ones they used for their rope ladders and bridges between the platforms, Tommen had his misgivings. At the same time, none of those things had collapsed so far. They also brought out fashioned hooks and pulleys and other modestly-forged climbing gear that Tommen almost would have dismissed as being too advanced for such a primitive people. It was foolish to think so; for all intents and purposes, while none of it was factory-made and came in twelve different colors, everything the warriors brought out of their packs and assembled was modern climbing gear.

It didn't take long for them to set up either, and soon the two larger warriors were in jerry-rigged harnesses, climbing, chipping, and anchoring their way up the rock face with expert precision and at a fraction of the speed Tommen did when coming down, to say nothing of the confidence.

"So they do this a lot?" he asked of Dreja, even as he knew the leader wouldn't understand him.

"They are impressive," Dreja said as if agreeing. "They do not do this often, but a skill a warrior learns is not soon forgotten."

So, basically, they were a bunch of amateurs who got their certification five, ten years ago and had done nothing with it since except go out for a leisure climb here and there maybe. But still, they got the job done. When they reached the cave, they did not go to Sifura immediately; they hardly paid her any mind. Instead, they turned and began rigging their ropes again, looping them through another set of metal pieces and anchoring them to the roof of the cave. It took a minute for Tommen to realize they were building a pulley system so Sifura could be lowered down instead of having to rappel.

With the system in place, the lean warrior who was not S'bal turned to the healer and began rigging him a crude rope harness, struggling to work around his pack. The healer glared at Tommen the entire time, as if he didn't understand the concept of fleeing for one's life. *Sorry, dude, but I value myself over your honey jars any day.*

The healer was no mountain climber, maybe even less than Tommen. The warriors kept yelling at him to stay still and just let them raise him up to the cave, but the idiot kept bumbling around the rock face, trying to climb on his own. Eventually they got him up there, and the two larger warriors hauled him in. Tommen could not see exactly what they were doing, but the way they stopped him before letting him pass, he could guess that they were giving the healer a good talking-to about following orders.

"I am sorry about the d'bok," Dreja told Tommen after a minute had passed. "I am sorry he attacked you and destroyed your things and injured Sifura. I truly believed he would not come this way. And I am sorry that he destroyed the jars and the antidote within. Unfortunately, we do not have anything more we can spare." Tommen hoped he could portray an appropriate amount of dejection and not give away that he had exactly what he needed stashed away in his pack. Dreja went on, "If you prefer, when we return to the village, I will have an escort for you to take you to the Kidik faction. It is six days from our village, but their territory also touches the foothills and so there will be hesik."

Tommen sighed heavily, tried to make it seem like there was extra weight being added to his shoulders. He gave Dreja an apologetic look. "Thank you, Dreja, leader of the Bodek. But the distance I have traveled was a gamble in itself. If I travel much more, I should go 'round the world and return to only an empty village. I thank you for the kindness you have shown, but I fear there is nothing more I can do at this point."

Dreja studied him, searching his tone and body language, looking for the words behind them but finding little of substance. Eventually he turned his gaze back toward the rock face, toward the cave where one guard looked out over the jungle and the other watched whatever was going on inside. Not that it was really hard to guess; Tommen remembered the unnatural angle Sifura's leg had lain at when they finally got into the cave. After this long, the muscles would have contracted and the healer would have to jerk the whole thing out of place before being able to reset the bone. Tommen's stomach twisted at the thought.

He looked at S'bal who was looking up, as if waiting for some cue. What was his story? Typically, the type of exposure to Time determined the abilities one was able to train with. So how could he have been exposed to that kind of temporal distortion, way out here in the jungle? Was it like Sifura, and he'd simply happened upon a Scout who'd gotten in a little over his head? Was it like Tommen, stumbling upon some kind of isolated distortion? Something else entirely?

Better yet, what was his motivation? A lot of the evil in the Wheel came down to two things: greed and power. Greed did S'bal little good, as the people of this world worked more on a barter system. S'bal might be able to get away with introducing a few new items to his people, but he couldn't keep it up forever—a mysterious tribe he traded with that only he could talk to, forging or other skills that no one had ever seen him work. So greed was unlikely.

Power seemed to be a more fickle thing for the D'bok than the Xur. Every time a new leader came into power, the entire governing body was changed. That was what drove Karaki over the edge, according to everyone else. And Time power wouldn't translate over into power over the faction. Unless S'bal wanted power that wouldn't change with every new leader.

On the other hand, Tommen figured, he could just be a regular, run-of-the-mill asshole. A bully in his home playing field, eager to play a little football with the new guy—*with* the new guy—especially after finding out that Tommen was of a lower rank, which meant lesser abilities. So it could be a power play, but less sinister than Cassius and more on par with Tyler Freeman.

That didn't mean that Tommen didn't get the heebie-jeebies from him, though, and feel the need to look over his shoulder even when S'bal was standing directly in front of him. His gaze drifted toward the cave where his pack lay. Should he get it now? Would that seem hopeful? Or pretentious? Or would no one care? Maybe he should wait until they got Sifura down. Would that make him seem idiotic, that he was packing up to go when the healer might still have to do some kind of work on her since they would be on solid ground?

None of the other warriors appeared fazed by how long it was taking, and Tommen almost felt guilty for fidgeting, like a small child pestering his mom in the grocery store while she stands in the aisle and chats with a friend she hasn't seen in a while. "Mom, are you done yet? Mom, can we get going? Mom, we have to go now. Mom, why are you still talking? Mom, can we get this? Mom, Mom, Mom."

His peripheral vision twitched, and he looked up to see the two larger warriors moving around just inside the mouth of the cave, dragging the rope in with them. The rope bounced a bit at the bottom of the face and did a little dance. Then the two lean warriors grabbed the ends, and it was still. A minute later, the larger warriors approached the edge of the cliff.

Sifura had been rigged into a kind of modified harness. The one rope was almost normal, holding the chest, torso, and hips in balance, while the second rope was designed to hold her hips and one leg. The two large warriors called down to the two lean warriors who shouted some kind of confirmation. Then, with four sets of hands on two ropes, they lifted Sifura up and over the edge, suspending her in mid-air.

Tommen knew that if he were the one in that position, someone down below would have ended up getting covered in piss, if not vomit too. Strange thing was, he wasn't really afraid of heights. He loved being on top of tall buildings, loved climbing trees and looking out over the mountains. If he had to hazard a guess, his biggest fear in this situation was the ropes, having to trust that they wouldn't break and send him crashing to the ground. Chains and cables were a little better, but the idea of being suspended and at the mercy of just a few threads of hemp or nylon or anything was unnerving.

Yet Sifura remained calm through the whole thing, completely trusting the ropes and those who wielded them. She did not wiggle or fidget or play with her harness or look around at things. She did not even speak, calling up or down to give orders or ask questions. It was almost as if they were carefully lowering a statue, for as calm and stiff as she appeared to be. Tommen wanted to call out some kind of encouragement or something, but didn't think it would be entirely appropriate. The warriors were in their element, doing their job as though they did do it often and not just every so often. He didn't want to break their concentration. Now, when they were lowering the healer, well, he couldn't help himself if he suddenly sneezed and startled them, right?

When she was about fifteen feet from the ground, Dreja moved under her. He gave orders and directed the two lean warriors who, through clever maneuvering of the rope, got her to a standing position. He got under one arm while the warriors loosened the harness and slipped it off. When she was free, he helped her hobble over to the cave where she sat down and leaned against the wall of the cave. Tommen was itching to go over and see how she was doing, but he did not get the chance before Dreja sat across from her, and they spoke in low voices.

So he turned his attention back to the lean warriors who sent the ropes back up to the larger warriors. The healer was standing there, waiting for his harness. The larger warriors did not move right away to rig him one, instead taking another minute to speak to him. The healer remained absolutely still, probably stiff with pride if Tommen had to guess, but he said nothing. Then the warriors made him a harness and gently lowered him over the edge. This time the healer did not twist, fidget, or try to do anything himself. He kept his arms and feet inside the ride at all times, and he did not say a word. S'bal said something in a low voice to the other lean warrior; the second warrior snickered.

The healer touched ground and still he was stiff and silent as the harness was loosened and removed. When he was finally told he could go, the disgruntled healer made long tracks over to the cave, intentionally cutting wide around Tommen who was more amused than offended, even more so when Dreja sent him away for a minute so he and Sifura could continue their conversation. The healer began to protest, but a stern look from Dreja shut him up and sent him away.

The ropes went up again one last time for the larger warriors who were working on prying loose the pulleys from the cave ceiling. Then they finagled their harnesses, set their anchors, and lowered themselves over the edge. They were as skilled as anyone Tommen had ever seen at camp or on TV, and he had to admit he was a little jealous. At the same time, he'd made that climb without any fancy equipment. Sure, he'd dislocated his hand and had the piss literally scared out of him as he held on to each hold for dear fucking life, but he'd done it.

As the warriors began packing their bags, Dreja approached them. Tommen looked at Sifura who was alone in the cave; the healer was nowhere to be seen. He went to her and sat across from her as Dreja had done.

"Are you all right?" he asked.

"I will be," she told him calmly. "The joint broke, but the healer does not believe there to be any major internal bleeding. It is wrapped now and will heal."

Apparently their idea of wrapping a joint so it healed pretty much amounted to using any old regular bandage, from what he could tell of the work. But then, he couldn't really expect there to be any decent medical facilities in the nearby area to give her a plaster cast or anything. So he just nodded. "That's good. How will you get home?"

"I will make my way," she told him simply. "Now we must get you home."

Taking his cue, Tommen Banded. "How? I mean, I can't just disappear."

"You can, and you will, but with taste. When we are returning and reach the river, simply make an excuse to go relieve yourself. Say that you will catch up. A portal will be waiting, but it will not stay open for long."

"Wait, you can do that?"

"I am a Hand. And a Triage Harvester. There are many things I can do that you cannot."

Tommen frowned. "S'bal, one of the lean warriors who was at the bottom of one of the ropes, he's a Journeyman Timekeeper."

Sifura was silent for a moment, studying him. Then she dipped her head. "I suspected as much that there were others from my world. That one should be a D'bok is no surprise."

"Yeah, but I got a bad feeling about him. He all but outright threatened me on the way here. I can't be sure, but I think that all our attempts at secrecy just went out the window."

"You think he is working for Cassius?"

"I don't know. Maybe not him, but if he tells just the right person, it could get back to Cassius."

"But not before your father is healed," Sifura told him sternly. "That is the most important thing right now. Think of nothing else until you have accomplished your mission."

"I don't want you to get burned for this."

"It is a risk we all took, me, you, and your Lieutenants, when we agreed to defy the Hands and pursue a cure for your father's illness. We can protect one another, but that protection only goes so far. But if I am to be targeted, it will be because I helped you accomplish your mission. As of this moment, you have not yet done that. And I will not be an accomplice to failure."

Her words felt both belittling and encouraging, and the best he could do was nod and say, "Yes, ma'am."

"Good. You have the antidote?"

Tommen grabbed his burlap bag and the repurposed bag of trail mix. The sticky goo that had coated the outside had dried to a crust, but the inside was still gelatinous. He stuffed it in the bag and covered it up with his clothes.

"How much time does your father have left?" Sifura wondered.

Fearfully, Tommen checked his watch. Almost midnight. A few minutes over, maybe, but the deadline had been arbitrary. He looked at her. "Sixteen hours at most."

"If possible, can you get it directly into his bloodstream?"

"I don't know; I can try."

"The longer the poison is in his system, the more damage it does, and the longer it takes to reverse. The bloodstream is the fastest way to begin the healing process. If you can't, then at least get it in his mouth, no more than what you can put on your finger, though even that is quite excessive."

"I'll keep it in mind."

"Remember, when you get to the Wheel, go to the Archives and wait for me or your Lieutenants."

"Right."

"Drop your Band, and let's go."

He did so. A minute later, the healer appeared, screeching at Tommen and shooing him violently from the cave. Tommen crept off, much to the amusement of the warriors, though he could tell from their expressions that they were not too fond of the man either. Still, they were made to wait while he did a second examination of Sifura's leg and hock, rewrapping the bandage several times before being satisfied that it would do for travel. Then he motioned for the warriors who produced, seemingly out of nowhere, a type of stretcher. Tommen guessed that when the healer had gone off to pout, he went off to build that as well.

Sifura got in it easily enough, her leg stretched out and supported as best it could be. The stretcher was designed so only one person need drag it from the front. It didn't look like a terribly comfortable ride, but Tommen figured it was better than trying to limp her along on someone's shoulder. The design also allowed for one person on each end, and the warriors carefully maneuvered the stretcher down the rocky slope, calling out warnings and barking orders, never letting Sifura touch the ground until the rocks gave way to dirt and grass.

The warriors took turns dragging her along, one taking her through the stone sentinels and the fallen tree, hunching over and awkwardly lurching through the narrow opening. Sifura bounced along, almost bouncing right out of the stretcher at one point, readjusting once safely on the other side. Then another warrior took over, and on they went.

Tommen made sure to keep one eye on S'bal, looking for any signs of malice or treachery, but the lean warrior paid him virtually no mind, instead talking and joking with his fellow warriors like any good young man. He never even flinched when Tommen threw up a Fast Band around the group. Had Tommen only imagined the threat? Had he imagined the whole conversation? No, the conversation had been real; of that much he was sure. But maybe he'd blown things out of proportion, made a mountain out of a molehill with all the stress he was under.

Still, he wasn't going to just dismiss it entirely and chalk it up to being stressed and crazy paranoid. Not until Walter was healed. Sifura would not be an accomplice to failure. Those were her words, and he was going to stick to them.

By the time they reached the river and stopped for rest,

Tommen was ready to just run upstream and dive through the portal. Instead, he turned his excitement into the happy little pee-pee dance he hadn't done since he was five years old. He glanced at Sifura who gave him the most imperceptible nod.

"Hey, listen, I have to go," Tommen said, antsing around. "Like bad. So you do what you gotta do, and I will catch up with you in a few minutes. I know the way."

He dashed off before anyone could protest, looking around like he was looking for privacy, when really he was looking for the damn portal. And there it was.

The ones that the twins or his dad made were pretty much your basic door-type portal. The one he found here was more like a Hobbit-hole. Still, as soon as he saw it, he didn't think twice, just stepped through.

Chapter Thirty
Because It's Never That Easy

There was a brief moment as Tommen entered the Wheel that everything became a jumbled mess of chaos in his mind. He thought he might have stepped through with no side effects, then that he might have been dreaming as he blinked open his eyes and stared at the black nothingness that was the ceiling, all the while suddenly aware that he was not only cold, but still stark naked. Gradually his thoughts sorted themselves out until he was able to roll over without nausea and get on his hands and knees. From there it was a short distance to his feet, and then he was rummaging in his pack for his clothes.

Actually, it was kind of a strange sensation, being dressed again, feeling the cotton and polyester against his skin. A week ago, he would have given anything just to wear underwear, but by the time he was traipsing around in the jungle, he was pretty comfortable with himself. The D'Bok had their fur and scales, Sifura had her skin, suede, and leather, and he just had his skin. Everything was totally normal. Then the sensation passed, and, once he was clothed, it was almost as though he had never been naked.

As he walked down the row toward the front of the portal room, it was like walking away from a movie. The theater was dark, and you and two hundred other people were captivated by the same story for two and a half hours, but then you get back out to the lobby, and reality kicks back in. None of it was real. The action, the drama, the setting, it was all fantasy. Yeah, you chat about it and offer critiques, but in the end, it's only water cooler talk. That was how it felt as Tommen walked away from the portal leading to Sifura's world. It was a nice break, a vacation, something that only he would understand, his own private screening of a movie no one else would see. But now he was back to reality, where he had school and work and training. Despite the knowledge that his father still lay dying in a hospital, Tommen just couldn't muster up the same sense of urgency and desperation that had driven him across a desert and through a jungle.

Perhaps the first reconciliation of his adventure and his reality was his first taste of how bad things had gotten in the Wheel. He'd almost forgotten about that part until he caught a glimpse of the Grandfathers standing at the entrance of the portal room. He ducked back in the row, hopefully before they caught sight of him.

While the Timekeepers did all the legwork to bring the Runners in, the Grandfathers were the real justice of Time. As the Hands donned glimmering white shrouds, so the Grandfathers donned black shrouds, but they did not glimmer. They weren't even like a real fabric, or so it seemed. While one might dismiss the shrouds as being black, really it wasn't like a black color so much as just the absence of color, absence of light, like the shrouds were black holes and all light and color got sucked into them. They were almost painful to look at, as if they would suck a person in, too, if he looked at them too long.

Tommen stood in the row for a few minutes, wondering what to do. Were they specifically looking for him, knowing that he would have to return at some point? Or was this like a general lockdown? Would they care about his bag or ask to check it? Could he refuse? Would they take him in? How much did he want to risk? When he was so close to getting home and helping Walter, did he really want to gamble that much?

He looked around. There had to be another portal to Earth here somewhere, hopefully to Region Four at least. It wouldn't be pleasant, but if he could brave the desert and Band for seven days, he was pretty sure he could Band for a couple hours, long enough to steal a car and get back home.

He looked at the nearest portal. Above each one was a digital readout of the galactic coordinates, but fuck if he could read them. Unless he could see obvious humans in the scene or some undeniable landmark like the Statue of Liberty, there was no way he was going to just pick a portal and hope it took him to Earth.

So instead he crept back down the row, looking at each portal, but finding little and less to definitively show him Earth. A few times, he thought he might have gotten lucky, but when he considered the village that Sifura's people built, he determined that architecture alone wasn't good enough. Once he did get lucky and found Earth. Problem was, it was in China or Japan or some such place, and there was no way he was going to make it home in time from one of those places. A rescue party was hard enough; he wasn't going to be able to Band a whole plane, never mind the logistics nightmare that would cause which would only delay them further. Better just to find either a portal closer to home or wait it out like Sifura suggested.

Maybe he could wait it out in the portal room. With a thousand rows and a thousand portals or more in each row, it wasn't like the grocery store where you only had to block a couple exits and sweep a few meager aisles. And as long as he stayed to the outer flanks, the Grandfathers would never notice him.

On the other hand, he could still be just silly about the whole thing. If they were really waiting for him specifically, Sifura said that the Hands would know about it and could easily find out. So it might just be a peacekeeping sort of measure, a way to remind folks about the potential consequences of civil war. If you stay out of it, we stay out of it. And do you really want to involve the Grandfathers and the Borelians in a war? There were no winners in that fight, no underdog come to save the day.

Still, Tommen stayed back, probably hoping that Sifura would come through the portal any minute now and be able to just wave a hand and make the Grandfathers part for both of them. But she didn't come, and when he went back to look, he couldn't find the portal. He forced himself not to panic, reminded himself that she said the portal would only be open a short time so he could get in and no one would follow — either accidentally or on purpose.

Tommen still wondered about S'bal. If he was a threat, what could he do about it? And if he was able to open portals, would he take the one or two seconds to get in the Wheel, make his report to whomever, and then go back like nothing ever happened? Or, worse, what if he'd waited for Tommen to leave so he could do something terrible to Sifura, kill her while she couldn't fight back? Had Tommen abandoned her to some lunatic? He tried not to think about it, tried to tell himself he was being silly and paranoid.

But he couldn't just stand around in the portal room forever; Sifura had told him to go to the Archives. If she didn't find him there, she might assume the worst had happened and that could have even bigger consequences. What those were, Tommen wasn't entirely sure, but it sounded ominous and dramatic and, worse, entirely realistic given the circumstances.

At the same time, he had to find some way to keep the antidote on his person and hope they were only interested in checking his bag, if they were interested in it at all. First he tried putting it in his pocket, a dumb idea considering how big the trail mix bag was. Then he tried the fat person idea, kind of trying to roll it up and tuck it into his shirt and pants, but he only made it a few steps before it started sliding out of position. He briefly entertained the idea of just scooping the sticky liquid and putting it in his pockets, then decided against it. If it didn't solidify in his pockets, it would only leak through the fabric and soak him, then solidify and render it all useless.

In the end, he was left with only two choices: stay in the portal room or hope the Grandfathers weren't interested in him or his bag. Taking a breath, he made for the front of the portal room, hoping he didn't seem nervous or otherwise acting strangely.

Instinctively he went to the translator dispenser, but remembered at the last second that he already had one on, hadn't even taken it off for ten days. He wondered if there would be any benefit to pretending to go through the motions of getting one, or if it would only tip them more that he was a suspicious character. After a second, he decided to go with the "Oops, I forgot I was already wearing one" approach, and headed nonchalantly for the opening that led to the rest of the portal.

He was almost certain he wouldn't be stopped as he walked right between the Grandfathers, until an arm or other appendage swung out and caught him in the chest. He couldn't have faked his reaction, but he did his best to try and brush it off and not freak out.

"What is your business here?" the Grandfather asked with all the softness of a cement block.

"The Archives," Tommen replied. "I have my review coming up and I want to be prepared; I'm afraid my knowledge is less then sterling, so I—"

"Your clothes. They are normal?"

Boxers and a T-shirt? Normally I'd be lucky not to be questioned for public indecency. "Yes? I mean, they're probably going out of style, but—"

"We are checking your bag."

The second Grandfather moved then and took the burlap bag right off Tommen's shoulder. He or she or it opened the flap and went through the contents which amounted to half a dozen empty plastic baggies, all shredded; Micaiah's bowie knife, somewhat chewed up; the knife he'd received from the duel, also with some teeth marks; Micaiah's gun, empty; and the trail mix bag filled with antidote.

"What is this?" the Grandfather demanded, holding up the bag of antidote.

It was an odd thing that the first thing that crossed Tommen's mind was relief that it hadn't leaked and gotten the inside of the burlap bag all sticky or crusty.

"Food while I study. I realize that the Food Court offers a vast array of foodstuffs, but there's nothing quite like the real thing."

For a moment, the Grandfathers looked at him, not saying

anything. Just like the Hands, everything about them was shrouded, so it was impossible to read expressions or body language.

"Eat it," the first Grandfather said finally. "Prove it is as you say."

Tommen was grateful that he'd already had some, first proving that it wasn't poisonous to him—which, as an antidote kind of defeated the purpose—and second so he already knew what it would taste like, and it wouldn't be a surprise. He dipped his head graciously and took the bag. He set it on the ground before opening it so as to not accidentally squish some out over the top and down the sides. Then he took a finger and made sure to do a nice big sweep to get as much as he could, then stick his finger in his mouth as if he was thrilled to have a bite.

Maybe it was the new packaging or some effect of aging on the antidote, but the flavor had changed. Now it was less like eating brown sugar right from the bag and more like a molasses cookie topped with sugar and sprinkles. It was just as tasty, and more bearable to eat. As if to prove himself, Tommen took another sweeping bite.

"Where are you coming from?" the Grandfather asked as he closed the bag and stood. "What is your designation?"

Seven of Nine, Unimatrix One, Tommen thought smugly. "Quadrant One, Parsec Eleven, Sector Five, System Four, Planet Thirty-Eight, Region Four, District Four."

"Name and rank."

"Tommen, probationary Timekeeper."

That was one of the nice things about being in the hub of Time; it was where all the different aliens and cultures collided. There were official records for every single person involved in Time, but during impromptu questioning, it was easy to get away with little details like not having a last name. Theoretically, he could lie outright, but if he got caught doing that, there was no weaseling his way out. Better to simply neglect mentioning his full name, which would probably be instantly recognizable. Unless the Grandfathers had more intimate knowledge of humanity—which was unlikely, since humans were insignificant beings in the Time industry—they wouldn't be able to call him out. At least, not until they decided to look him up, which was possible.

"When is your review?" the Grandfather wondered.

"I don't know the official Wheel date, only that it is rendered as January 2nd on my world," Tommen answered honestly.

"Who is your mentor?"

That could be a problem, Tommen figured. If they knew him by his full name, they might be suspicious by only his first name and try to connect him to his mentor, Walter. He even thought about lying and telling them Micah or Micaiah was his mentor, citing the fact that Walter was dying and he needed training. But even the twins were well-known, and he had no desire to get himself in trouble by lying or them in trouble by association.

"Walter," he replied.

"And where is your mentor? Will he be assisting your studies?"

Shit. "No. I work best when I'm alone, and it keeps me from using him as a crutch. I will learn what I know when I don't have the answers available to me."

For a minute, Tommen wasn't sure what they were going to do, whether they believed him or not. Strictly speaking, he'd done nothing but tell the truth, just not all of it. He'd given all the correct information, and while he did intend to do some studying in the Archives...well, no. Damn. He couldn't do any studying because he wasn't supposed to get a chip. At the same time, he'd just told the Grandfathers where he was heading, so did it really matter if he got a chip now? Would it look more suspicious if he didn't get a chip and do some studying? Probably. And as long as he stuck to his plan of studying, it shouldn't tip anyone off that he was doing anything other than what he said he was going to do.

"Very well," the Grandfathers said at last. "You may pass."

"Is there a problem?" Tommen wondered. "I mean, I've only

been here half a dozen times, but I don't remember anything like this in my previous visits."

"There has been a spike in Runner activity," the second Grandfather replied.

"You would do well, as a good student, to perhaps observe other Timekeepers currently in the Wheel," the first told him. "Watch and see how they do things and how justice is dispensed in the Wheel of Time."

"Thank you," Tommen told them, hoping he sounded sincere. "Maybe I will. When I'm not studying, that is. I mean, that's kind of my priority right now and—"

"Go."

They did not shout it, but there was more force behind that one softly-spoken word than a thousand drill sergeant commands. Tommen dipped his head once more and passed out of the portal room, between the Grandfathers, and into the Wheel, more or less unharmed. He still wasn't sure if the bit about watching other Timekeepers and seeing justice done was a genuine suggestion or a subtle threat, but until he was back home and Walter was alive and well again, he had little desire to test the theory either way.

The rest of the Wheel wasn't much better, Tommen observed, as he tried to remember which symbol was for the Archives. Everywhere he looked, he saw either Hands or Grandfathers. He knew there were fifty-one Hands, but he didn't know how many Grandfathers there were. What's more, he wasn't sure either if they were working together or against each other. If they were working together, they were probably looking for him. If they were working against each other, could he count either one as friend and potential protector? If so, how did he figure out who was who? He decided it best to just avoid them both if possible.

Still, it was disconcerting how many of both parties he saw. Were they assigned to various "rooms" within the Wheel, or were some of them following him? Was he just being paranoid? Looking around, he saw that maybe it was only his imagination that there were just tons of Grandfathers around. When he stopped and really considered it, there were fewer people in the Wheel. Sure, the Wheel had its ebb and flow of crowds through various rooms, but even at its slowest, it was still about as crowded as a mall on Christmas Eve.

Was it because of the threat of war? Then Tommen considered something else; how did news like that get around? If the Hands and the Grandfathers were going to war, would anyone besides the parties involved actually know why? Would they know the event that tipped it off? Would any of the Merchants or the Harvesters or even the other Timekeepers know that Tommen was the one who probably perpetuated the war? Would they be on the lookout, or did they see only a dumb probationary Timekeeper who didn't know enough to be afraid?

Truthfully, Tommen was afraid. He was very afraid. He wasn't even afraid for himself, but more for the fact that he'd come so close to curing his dad's disease that he didn't want to fuck it up now.

So when he did find the Archives, he ignored Sifura's suggestion to skip the chip, especially seeing as he already told the Grandfathers that he would be here. If they really could look that up and track his whereabouts, better to remain dumb and unsuspecting, oblivious to everything but his upcoming review. *Be a freshman*, he told himself. *Walk into school like an idiot, with bright eyes and grand dreams of the future. Focus all your efforts on that one dream of going to college and forever being a middle manager. Lick boots, kiss ass, and think only of yourself.*

By the time he walked up to the chip dispenser and gave it his pound of flesh, Tommen was smiling like an idiot. And the secretary, if questioned, wouldn't be able to say whether or not it was a convincing smile, a cheeky smile, a smug smile, or any of that, because she wasn't human, and she most likely wasn't an expert on humans. He wasn't even sure if it was a she, so how could she know his demeanor?

Tommen took his chip and entered the Archives, stopping momentarily to simply gaze upon the endless rows of books, as if everything, every topic, warranted its own library. Fuck, but even to someone like him who wasn't a huge reader like some, this was just awesome. He shook his head and turned to the left, following the balcony to the end where it opened up into the first enormous section of books. Picking up the first one he found, he inserted the chip and opened the library map.

Of course, then he was presented with another dilemma. On the one hand, he wanted to know the relationship between the antidote in his bag and basic sugar found on Earth. On the other hand, he'd told the Grandfathers that he was here to study for his review. The chemical makeup of an obscure flower hardly sounded like material that would be covered in his review.

It hit him then like a ton of bricks. Of course S'bal had been a spy, and he'd known exactly what Tommen was doing there. Tommen and the twins had been in the Archives beforehand looking up Sifura as the Hand, as well as her home world. Tommen's bullshit story about his people being attacked aside, S'bal would only have to report to confirm that Tommen was there looking for an antidote and had apparently found it. Cross-reference that with his case before the Hands and both the Hands and the Grandfathers—and possibly the Borelians—would know that there was a cure in the universe for Borelian poison.

Fuck, fuck, fuck, fuck, fuck. He was an idiot.

Next time you decide to do a secret mission, don't make it so fucking obvious.

On the other hand, how could he have known that S'bal was a spy? Wasn't it better just to assume that everything he did was being monitored?

New question: what if the antidote didn't work? Would that lessen the repercussions? Tommen wasn't willing that Walter should die, but what if they managed to fake his death? Spread the word that he had died—because the antidote had failed—and simply smuggle him away to somewhere? He would have to give up Time and Banding cold turkey, but he would be alive and no worse for wear.

No, that wouldn't work either because Cassius and Rifun were human, and they could easily check up on that story.

Fuck, but war was complicated.

Tommen rubbed his face, still staring at the map on the tablet before him. Maybe it would be better to look up the chemical makeup of sugar on Earth in an Earth-side library, where it couldn't be traced on the Wheel, then return at a later date to look up the makeup of the flower. If it worked, he would want to know why, and if it didn't work, there was no point in looking it up.

Finally, Tommen decided just to go with studying for his review. "Don't live above the law," Walter had told him once, "but live beyond reproach."

Tommen was simply there to study for his review so he could be an Apprentice Timekeeper. Yes, he'd gone before the Hands to plead his case and try to save his dad. He'd lost. Yes, he'd gone to a distant planet looking for the antidote to "something" that afflicted his people. But there was nothing to say that he wasn't going there to look for a cure to AIDS or something. In his grief, he'd gone on a humanitarian mission.

It sounded as weak as it was, but Tommen needed something to help his mind calm down, even as he did his search through the map and found the floor and the section he was looking for. It took a minute or two to commit it to memory, but soon enough he was on his way down several floors to where he suspected he needed to be.

After what felt like forever of looking through sections and subsections and rows, Tommen picked out several tablets and went to find somewhere to sit down and read. And, the way he figured it, no one had come storming in, sweeping every floor and section looking for him. Similarly, no one had sneaked up behind him and drugged him. So there was every chance that he was simply imagining things and overreacting. At the same time, it was only paranoia until it was proven true. Then the whistleblower got offed by the CIA to be blamed on someone else, or else dragged away to some godforsaken prison in the middle of the desert.

So Tommen found a good spot to sit and read. He wouldn't allow himself to get boxed into a corner, but he wasn't going to just sit out in the open with everything but a neon sign telling everyone where he was. Rather, it was just a small reading area with access to half a dozen rows of books and wasn't too far from a moving platform over the open atrium. It would allow him to see and possibly to hide.

In retrospect, Tommen also decided, as he inserted his chip into the first tablet, that being James Bond or some other international spy who was always moving and living under the gun, was not such a hot life after all. It was everything that the movies said it was, even as they tried to romanticize it: dangerous, cruel, and there was no guarantee of going home or coming out unscathed. So Tommen decided that if he did decide to pursue Timekeeping, which was turning out to be dangerous enough, he would probably spend his second life on Earth as a hermit.

Well, maybe not a hermit. Hermits usually turned out to be weird and, in most cases, insane. When a hermit died, pretty much everyone just said, "Phew. Old Man Johnson finally kicked the bucket. Now maybe we'll be able to rest in peace ourselves for a while." No one mourned a hermit.

Maybe he would go back to what he'd always known, what he'd always been good at, no matter how much modern life appeared to erode it: farming. He was bigger now, and after all of this shit he'd just gone through, Tommen was fairly confident that he could wrestle a grouchy buck goat, to say nothing of the other manual labor involved in the garden and in the woods. And people generally admired farmers. They looked out at the fields and pastures and said, "Well now, look at those fine fields and those fattened goats, and the cow with an udder as big as a sack of potatoes. Yessiree, there goes Farmer Johnson, up every morning at the crack of dawn, working hard. A fine man to be sure. With a fine wife and well-behaved children."

Well, the wife and children he would have to work on, but the rest he might be able to manage.

Tommen shook his head and rubbed his eyes. All these distractions were not helping him study; they weren't even close to what he was supposed to be studying. But it was hard to pretend to be studying while keeping an eye out for someone who might never come. If something happened to Sifura, how were the twins supposed to be able to know to come and get him? More to the point, what if someone else got here first, like the Grandfathers?

He shook his head again, determined not to let paranoia get the best of him. Caution was necessary, but paranoia paralyzed. He just had to keep calm. Keep one eye on his studying and one eye on his surroundings. Walter had taught him—or tried to teach him—how to do such a thing once, mostly in keeping an eye out for Tyler so as not to be taken by surprise.

But in doing so, his mind still wandered this way and that until he literally had no idea what he was reading, only that he was scrolling through his tablet maybe a little faster than normally necessary and having no clue what the words said. When he finally brought himself all back together and could focus for ten seconds to read the words, he found it had something to do with the way the elections worked. Fitting, given that those same elections were barely two weeks away, and yet ironic, given that they were so corrupt and rigged so as to make all the smoke and mirrors almost unnecessary. The Great Oz had lost all of his power when he'd been discovered behind the curtain, so why didn't the Hands also lose such power when everyone knew what was going on behind the scenes?

Or maybe that was exactly it. Everyone who goes to see a play knows it's a play. No one actually believes that Jean Valjean is standing there on stage singing. Everyone knows it's all an act, but the more convincing the acting, the greater the overall play. Maybe that's what all of this was: just an act. But an act for what? What play was being unfolded? How did this all end?

Tommen startled and sucked in a breath at a hand on his shoulder. He was momentarily paralyzed by fear as a human man squatted down in front of him, putting one finger to his lips.

"Tommen Forbes," he stated. While Tommen heard it well enough through the translator, being so close to the man anyway, he heard the man speak in what he guessed to be a Middle Eastern accent. It made sense as the man had bronze skin and a full head of thick black hair with a beard to match.

"Who's asking?" Tommen wondered cautiously, trying to quell his fear.

"My name is Assim Foyez; I know your father, Walter Forbes."

"Lots of people know him. One of them tried to kill him. Who are you?"

"I understand your reluctance to trust me, but know that you must. Your Lieutenants, the twins Micaiah and Micah Durvin, they sent me to fetch you home. I am a Warden Timekeeper."

"Why should I go with you?"

"Because Sifura, whom you were travelling with, is unable to come. She has been compromised. There was a spy among those with whom she was staying."

"Is she dead?"

"No, but she cannot come."

"How do I know you're telling me the truth? I've never met you before in my life."

"No, and I understand. I will tell you something that will prove your Lieutenants sent me?"

Tommen wasn't sure if there was anything that could prove such a thing. If Rifun was able to dredge up secrets about Walter, secrets that he would die for, who was to say that he couldn't just pick something that Tommen thought was private and safe and have this man parrot it to him in order to lead him into a trap?

"No harm in trying," Tommen said finally. "What is it?"

"The older twin, Micaiah, he once called you into his office at the bakery to tell you that he was disappointed in your attendance record. He gave you a lecture on discipline, that if you did not discipline yourself, others would do it for you," the man, Foyez, told him in a loud whisper.

Okay, so that was a little more private than most things Tommen would have picked. It wasn't something like, "You sell your dad a pastry every day" or something that could be gathered from basic observation and stalking. The only ones who had been present at that meeting had been Tommen and Micaiah, and the details about the lecture were a little too specific to be ignored.

"I'll give you that one," Tommen said, "but I do have one question for you."

Foyez took a measured breath and bounced a little on the balls of his feet. "Very well. What is your question?"

"I haven't personally met all of the Timekeepers in our District or our Region, but I know their names pretty well. You're Middle Eastern. How do you know my dad?"

"There was a killer—Cassius, the False Zero Hour, and Rifun—who was terrorizing your city of Charleston. Early in the investigation, in the Time-side investigation, your father's leads brought him to me, but I was too afraid to help for fear of what Rifun or Cassius might do to me. When I heard what had become of him, I blamed myself and my refusal to help. Perhaps if I had told him what I knew earlier, this could have been avoided.

"So I made the trip into the United States and met with your Lieutenants. I offered myself in any way I could, to try to help him. They told me that you had gone with Sifura, the Hand of Scientifically Primitive and Unengaged Civilizations, to find an antidote for the poison. But as you can see, the Wheel is not what it was when you left. The twins were unsure of the circumstances of your return, and suspicion of their involvement meant their time in the Wheel must be limited. They asked if I might stay and keep an eye out for you. And if something happened to Sifura and you were unable to return home, that I bring you back."

Tommen weighed his words. On the one hand, it was tough to judge whether his darting gaze was like that of cornered prey and they had to get moving five minutes ago, or if he was a bad liar and using this feigned urgency to cover it up. On the other hand, if everything he said was true, then they really did have to get going five minutes ago.

"Sorry, I lied. One more question," Tommen said. He tried to gauge Foyez's reaction, but he was terrible at the more subtle aspects of body language and facial expressions. "What is the hurry? Are you anxious for being a liar, or because of something else?"

Then Foyez got an expression that Tommen did know. It was one that adults gave to little kids when they asked something like, "Are you ugly because you don't wear makeup, or what's up with that?" It was one that basically said, "I want to punch you, but I'm not going to, even though I really, really want to."

"The Grandfathers are here, Tommen," Foyez told him seriously. "They are looking for you. And if they catch you, they will break your clock."

Chapter Thirty-One
Close Encounters

It was as if Tommen had entered a Fast Band, the way Time suddenly seemed suspended. It was the moment of truth when he had to decide whether Assim Foyez was telling the truth and they had to leave, or if this was a trap and he should make a break for it. Problem was, even if he made a break for it, there was nowhere for him to go that the Grandfathers wouldn't find him.

Foyez had mentioned the conversation he and Micaiah had when Tommen was on the verge of being fired. If Micaiah had told Foyez about that conversation as a way to reach Tommen, why that conversation? What was he trying to say? He was on the verge of being discovered? Tommen racked his brain, trying to remember the conversation, see if there might have been any hidden codes or meanings.

In the end, all he could remember was hierarchy and discipline. Hierarchy: they were above him, as Foyez was evidently above him. Problem: the Grandfathers were also technically above him. Discipline: If he didn't discipline himself, someone would do it for him. Problem: that could go either way in either submitting to the Grandfathers—and/or Foyez?—or else taking charge himself—under Foyez?

Tommen closed his eyes and let out a breath. *If you can't discipline yourself, someone will do it for you.* He opened his eyes. He couldn't open a portal by himself; Foyez would have to do it for him.

It was the hope he clung to as he finally nodded. "All right. What do we do?"

"Put your tablets away," Foyez commanded. "Act as naturally

as you can. I hope we are able to walk out of here. Better to not give them cause to think we are running."

"But we are," Tommen said quizzically, gathering his tablets and looking for the rows where they belonged.

"Have you ever herded sheep, Tommen Forbes?"

"Well, my family used to have goats. Why?"

"If one got loose, did you chase after it like a wild animal?"

"No. It would only make them—oh."

"Quick action, quick reaction. The game we play now is not one of speed or force, but finesse. All we have to do is outmaneuver them. I hope to avoid any confrontation."

"You and me both."

Tommen returned his tablets to their proper spots, Foyez keeping a casual lookout at the end of the row.

When Ryan, Tommen's foster brother for eight months, had been around, he hadn't been the best role model. He intentionally did things to spite Walter because he was a cop, and he was not above theft. Once, while they were in a store shopping for school clothes, Ryan had slipped a pair of socks in his jacket. It wasn't like the socks were expensive or anything special, but later Ryan had said he'd spotted a store security guard, the plainclothes kind.

Ryan showed Tommen who it was, and for the rest of the shopping trip, they'd kept one eye on the guard even as the guard had kept one eye on them. Tommen couldn't quite recall Ryan's expression, but he remembered his own as they went to the checkout counter, paid for their merchandise, but instead of leaving, Walter stopped.

"Anything else?" he asked, seemingly unsuspecting.

"No," Ryan and Tommen answered innocently.

"How about whatever it was you slipped in your jacket?"

"But you never said anything!" Ryan blurted.

"Didn't have to." Walter nodded to the security guard who now made himself known and approached the counter. "I know Jon very well, and I was seeing him more than I thought was coincidental.

So cough it up."

Ryan reluctantly turned over the socks even as Tommen was pretty sure he'd started to cry because he thought he was in trouble. Both of them were punished, Ryan for stealing and Tommen for not calling him out on it.

The way Foyez stood now at the end of the row of books reminded Tommen of the way Jon had followed them through the store. Even when Tommen had replaced all of his tablets and they moved through the Archives, Foyez was just like Jon. He inserted his chip at the end of the row and searched through the list of books like he was looking for something, picked a few and went down the row as if to investigate, but Tommen could see he wasn't really looking at the books.

In sixth grade, there had been a fourth member of the three amigos—Tommen, Eric, and Varad—named Kelly. She'd only been at their school for the year, but they'd learned quite a few things from her. She was the one who'd gotten Tommen into karate for a year. One of the things she'd taught them was how to look with one's peripheral vision. When people looked around, they only focused on two percent of their field of vision; she showed them how to utilize the other ninety-eight percent without actually needing to look around.

When it became clear they were going nowhere faster, Tommen tried to imitate Foyez's movements while putting those skills into practice. He kept his eyes ahead on the end of the row or on a particular tablet, but he focused on seeing through his peripheral vision, up and down the row or around him in the subsection.

Then he saw one, a black shroud. Keeping his head still and moving only his eyes, Tommen saw they had moved into a position where they could make a break for it onto a moving platform. The Grandfather was several sections away, moving with the same quiet finesse that they were.

Nonchalantly, Tommen slid down the same row that Foyez was. He gave the older man a gentle nudge in the ribs and jerked his chin in the general direction of the Grandfather. Foyez nodded almost imperceptibly and replaced the tablet he'd been staring at. Together, they moved silently down the row, toward the moving platform, keeping just out of sight until it returned, depositing several other Archive patrons. Then, when it was just about to leave, they made their move. Quick as a couple of vipers, they got on the platform and moved up.

There was no cry of alarm or calls to shoot them, but Tommen knew they were sitting ducks and as obvious as a couple of trees in the middle of a huge field. He looked around. Below them on several levels, Tommen saw more black shrouds, moving with a sort of silent urgency.

"They're coming," Foyez stated under his breath, gaze fixed firmly forward.

"Yeah," Tommen said, feeling his stomach twist and heart leap into his throat. He would have rathered to fight a dozen xurs or d'boks instead of trying to maneuver in this minefield.

"If we make it out of the Archives, we must move quickly to the portal room."

"Like, sprinting?"

"Like a snake, but no longer one who waits for its prey and darts out suddenly. We must move as one being pursued, back and forth, impossible to catch."

"Maybe it's just me, but isn't it kind of stereotypical that, like, Native Americans and Middle Easterners and stuff only talk in nature metaphors?"

"Stereotypes come from somewhere, Tommen, but for this, you must talk to the one who speaks through me."

Right. Middle Eastern. If he was any sort of religious, it was most likely Muslim. Well, Tommen didn't really want to hear about that one either.

They stepped off the moving platform on the level where the lobby was, but they couldn't make a dash for it just yet. Instead, they had to slip into a row quickly before they were spotted by another

Grandfather.

In that moment of gut-wrenching, knee-knocking fear, Tommen somehow found the time to reflect on how it was like being hunted by the Nazgul or something; for goodness' sake, the Grandfathers had black shrouds and looked like them, but with less screaming and fewer swords. Humorlessly, he put a hand to his many pockets, checking to make sure he didn't have the One Ring or something. But he had nothing except a burlap bag containing the antidote. Who knew a single flower could cause so much chaos?

Then they were moving again. Tommen kept as close to Foyez as he could, both of them acutely aware that if the Grandfathers wanted to trap them anywhere, it would be on the narrow balcony between the main section and the lobby.

But they made it to the lobby no worse for wear except for a few more white hairs, Tommen was sure. They casually returned their chips and made for the door, both trying to act natural, as if they belonged together. Behind them, Tommen felt a shadow grow and eyes on their backs. He wanted to look. Fucking hell, he wanted to look. But he didn't dare. He couldn't bring himself to turn his head, not even to look at Foyez who he was sure felt the same shadow and eyes.

Then they were out of the Archives, and Foyez abandoned the casual walk for something between a fast walk and a slow jog. Like before, the Wheel was, relatively speaking, sparsely populated. Tommen and Foyez slipped through a portal into one of the lower marketplaces, vanishing into the crowds.

"So you knew about Rifun," Tommen said as they wove their way among the many people and other alien species.

Foyez glanced back at him only briefly. "Yes, I did. When your father called me to ask questions about the Dispersal, I ran like a coward. I should have been more forthcoming, but I was afraid."

"The Dispersal?"

"The Dispersal of 1963. The elections that year were contested so hotly, it turned into a massacre. I was lucky to survive."

"What does that have to do with Rifun?"

"I was the Gatekeeper of Earth during that time. Rifun was set to become the Hand of Scientifically Advancing but Unengaged Civilizations, thus representing Earth also. I did not support Rifun in his campaigning, no matter what he threatened. He won the seat, or so he claimed. As you might imagine, some disputed the results. He was supposedly found dead in 1970, drowned. I was implicated and removed from power. Through a series of events, I was told to leave Time and never return; I was lucky my clock hadn't been broken.

"About a year later, Rifun showed up at my house. He said he bore me no ill will and that he was the reason I got off as easily as I did. He said he would have plans for me in the future as long as I sat down and obeyed like a good dog."

"And if you didn't, he would have your clock broken."

"Yes. I have lived in shame ever since. Now that I see my consequences, even if I am unable to help the father, I will help the son. Perhaps then Allah will forgive my sins."

"Well, I have my doubts about that, but I'll forgive you anyway, assuming you can get me back home," Tommen told him.

"That is where we are heading, my friend."

"So, if you were Gatekeeper during the Dispersal, and you were told to lay low, how are you a Warden now?"

"I still trained and honed my Time abilities, under Rifun's direction."

Red flags were starting to pop up in Tommen's mind. "What did Rifun say his plans were for you?"

"He never did. He stopped visiting me. I dared to hope he had somehow died or been killed, but then I would receive things in the mail. He was staying away, but he was watching."

Tommen was cut off then by someone elbowing their way through the crowd, and for a moment, he lost sight of Foyez. He found him again and caught up as quick as he could, unsure of how far he could trust the man. He decided to lay low on his own, keep his suspicions to himself, and make a run for it if he had to without tipping him off in advance.

"So we know the Grandfathers are dangerous," Tommen said. "What about the Hands?"

"We must assume they mean ill as well," Foyez decided. "Our first priority is getting you home so you can save your father."

"And going through the lower marketplaces?"

"The crowds will hide us, and they will get us closer to the portal room than any other route."

"You mean you actually understand how this place is laid out?"

Foyez chuckled. "In time, you will understand also. But you must stop thinking of it like the two-dimensional maps in a standard visitor center and start thinking in three and four dimensions. As I said, it will come in time."

So they pressed on through the marketplaces, Tommen quickly losing his ability to both keep up with Foyez and act the plainclothes security guard. Eventually, he found that he couldn't keep Foyez in sight as well as watch through his peripheral vision to keep an eye out for the Grandfathers. With luck, the Grandfathers would have just as much difficulty getting through the crowds, and a commotion would give them enough advance notice to get out of there.

"So where are you from?" Tommen wondered conversationally as they passed through a portal from one marketplace to another.

"I was born in Iran," Foyez told him matter-of-factly. "I left after Ayatollah Khomeini came into power. First I lived in Germany, then France. I was as much trying to escape oppression and prejudice as Rifun. Now I live in Canada, not far from the border with Alaska."

"Well, that's quite a change, to go from the desert to the tundra."

"Yes, but a desert of snow is still a desert. And it is not so bad. I keep animals, and they keep me busy. The slow life of farming is good enough for me; I have no need for Time when I am out in the fields with them."

Tommen knew a pang of envy then, though he couldn't say why. Maybe it was because even though he'd lived under the threat of Rifun for decades, he'd still managed to carve out a pleasant little life for himself, one where he was content. He'd found peace under a dictator while Tommen was still anxious about his freedom.

"Wife and kids?"

"No, not for many years. There are not many Muslim women where I live."

Well, there wouldn't be, Tommen figured, though he didn't say this out loud. Instead he maintained a careful silence about it.

"Your Lieutenants, they told me a great deal about your father and you," Foyez said.

"Like what?" Tommen asked suspiciously.

"They tell me that you are his world, that everything he does is for you. I do not envy him raising a child alone, but I envy you for the love he shows you. My own father was not so kind."

Tommen felt his throat get gummy and tight. "Yeah. He's a good guy."

"And you love your father. That is why you crossed half the universe to find a cure which may not even work and might even start an intrauniversal civil war."

"Gee, thanks for the pep talk."

Foyez laughed now. "Such love is not normally celebrated. Such deeds are most often reserved for romance movies, a man going to the ends of the Earth and destroying universes in order to show his love for a woman. Sometimes, it may be a parent trying to save a child. But where are the stories of children who are willing to risk everything to save a parent? Do children not love their parents? I might think so, looking around me and seeing the news of children who dishonor their parents and families. You, Tommen, are a rare child. I envy Walter, that he has you for a son."

Had he not been afraid of losing Foyez in the crowd, Tommen might have stopped in his tracks, stunned by his words. Foyez was jealous that Walter had him for a son? Normally people pitied Walter for having Tommen as a son, with the number of fights he got in, plus the little binges that everyone now knew he went on from time to time. Some of the other police officers cut out magazine articles or sent web links to him about parenting, how to manage being a single dad, how to turn uncontrollable aggression into constructive energy, how to empower his son to be a better man and stand up to bullies, those sorts of things. No one ever told Walter what a cool kid Tommen was and how they wished their kid could be more like him. And certainly no one ever straight-out said they were jealous.

It was a new sensation, as if he'd taken another step closer to not only being a good kid and not like some tantrum-throwing three year old who hit everyone, but also into being a man, a good man. Someone was depending on him, and he was determined not to let him down. Someone had faith in him, enough to keep him going. And someone was jealous of him, and not in the petty high school drama sort of way, but in a more mature sense. Was that even possible? Was there such a thing as mature jealousy? Tommen decided there was. And basically, he was the object of it. Not only that, but he didn't get that swollen ego feeling like he got when someone commented on his new shoes or something. It made him feel proud of himself, accepted, like finally he'd done something right in his life. He was doing good.

Well, he couldn't say he didn't feel his ego swell a little, and maybe that was his one major character flaw. It might not have been so major, except that in his feeling of light-headedness, he almost missed the flash of black in his peripheral vision. Whether it was from fear or some convoluted sense of thinking it was natural, he turned his head and stared. Three Grandfathers moved through the crowd, more snake-like than anything he and Foyez could have come up with. He turned his gaze forward again, noting more black shapes on the other side.

"Nine of them," Foyez said before Tommen could speak. "Three to the left, four to the right, two directly behind. No, don't look. Remember what I said about this game we play?"

"It's not about speed or force, but finesse?" Tommen wondered.

"Yes. But the time for finesse has passed. When I say so, it must be about speed and only speed. My wish is that we do not have to come to force."

"So what do we do?"

"Run to the portal room. No matter what, you must make it there. I will try to stay with you."

"And if you can't?"

"You must use your own judgment."

Tommen didn't like ambiguous and slightly cryptic statements like that. It wasn't that he didn't feel capable of acting in the moment, but he was tired of doing so. For once, he just wanted a plan to go right. No more surprise monsters or duels or being pursued by the Nazgul. He wanted to go home, so he was going to go the fuck home.

"Okay," he said, gathering his courage and hoping his legs could carry him the last distance, even as his mind panicked and said he didn't know the way.

"Go."

Foyez didn't say it any louder than a hoarse whisper and Tommen was taken by surprise at how fast the man could move. He lost probably three seconds before getting his own body to turn and go after him, barely catching sight of him as he disappeared through a portal. Tommen pushed himself, trying to close the gap.

Strictly speaking, trying to run through the lower marketplaces was reminisce of pretty much every Indiana Jones movie ever, but with more running around on walls and ceilings. The streets were full of people who were grumpy and more concerned about buying their trinkets and doodads than the life-and-death chase going on around them. They shouted and cursed, and some turned as if to punch whoever had accidentally kicked them in the face. For Tommen, it was less like track or cross country, where the course was open, if not flat, and more like an obstacle course where the obstacles were moving and sometimes violent. This was also the moment when Tommen knew he was the star of this film, had this been a film.

From the commotion behind him, he knew the Grandfathers pursued him, but they weren't having nearly as much trouble. Tommen was just an annoying human kid who was rudely shoving his way through the marketplace. But the Grandfathers were known. Not only were they known, but they were dreadfully frightening, and people parted for them like the Red Sea. Maybe there was a way to get the Red Sea to part for him like Moses, but come crashing down on the Grandfathers like they were the Egpytians.

Though an admittedly stupid idea born in the depths of a depraved and terrified mind, Tommen found himself entertaining it more and more, the more he ran. He wasn't an athlete, that was for damn sure. Yeah, ten days of braving desert and jungle and climbing a mountain with no equipment to save his life had toughened him some, but it hadn't made him much faster. Endurance, yes, that was better, but it didn't mean much when his pursuers were faster.

He followed Foyez as close as he could, but somehow he got the feeling that this wasn't the first time the man had run through a busy street while being pursued, and an image of Aladdin flickered through his mind. Soon enough, the man began pulling away and disappeared completely.

Tommen could not stop to catch his breath or ask for directions. He knew vaguely where he was, but he also knew he wasn't going to make it just by running in a straight line from A to B. He was slowed down by people and obstacles, but for the Grandfathers, he was going to have to create some obstacles.

A furious cry went up as he started grabbing things and throwing them wildly over his shoulder. He chanced a look back to see the Grandfathers had lost some momentum, briefly stunned by the turn of events. Having bought himself ten seconds—well, maybe more like three—Tommen slowed to a stop. Resisting the urge to double-over in pain, he instead grabbed the nearest Merchant booth, loaded with all number and range of Time Capsules, and overturned it. The Merchant was irate and tried to come after him, but Tommen dashed off again.

Another terrible thought entered his mind. When people asked "What would Jesus do?" it was normally in reference to kind, humanitarian things like feeding the poor and sheltering the homeless and so on. Most of them forgot that overturning tables was also a viable option. And how much better that even this, the Wheel, was like a corrupt money-changing temple to Time?

His lungs screamed at him to stop, or at least slow down. He wasn't accustomed to this. He was like a horse; his heart would burst before he made it to the portal room, assuming he even found it in the shortest route possible. Just as well, he would do like he had looking for the Archives or the Coliseum and wander around aimlessly until he either found it or the Grandfathers found him.

He didn't know how many Grandfathers there actually were, and had little desire to find out, even if there was a certain romantic notion to needing every Grandfather in the Wheel in order to catch him. But then, the more it took to take him down, the worse his punishment was likely to be. Fuck, this was like when his dad had to go after some awful criminal. Instead of surrendering peacefully, it turned into a fiasco.

He passed through another portal into another marketplace, but this one he knew. This one was familiar. Not waiting around to see how many Grandfathers still pursued him, Tommen pushed himself to his limits, forcing himself to breathe even if it came in ragged gasps. His head felt light and his vision started to blur. No, no, he had to make it.

But inevitably, bestial self-preservation of flight from a predator was pushed aside by bestial self-preservation of maintaining basic bodily functions. He began to slow. As he did, he could hear the blood thundering through his ears and pulsing in every major pulse point in his body. His whole body throbbed. He refused to let himself lapse into a walk, instead compromising with his body to maintain a fast jog as he headed for the next portal which took him to the marketplace portal hub. From there, he only had to cross two more walls and head a short ways across the room to the last portal.

He hadn't heard much commotion behind him in the previous marketplace, but he wasn't about to give up his lead now. He bulled his way through the last portal and almost collided with the two Grandfathers who guarded the entrance to the portal room. More by reflex than any help from Time, Tommen managed to dodge an outstretched hand. If the majority of Grandfathers weren't Borelians, he might have taken his chances and tried to force his way through them, but even as he stood there, staring at them, he could feel their proximal poisons start to work on him. It was then that he knew they weren't the same Grandfathers as the ones who had searched his bag, but it was a moot point.

It was all moot now. He was finished. He was cornered; they'd caught him. Now they were going to take him away. They would break his clock and lock him up, and he wouldn't even have the presence of mind to scratch out his days on the wall of his cell. If they were even a fraction as cruel as he suspected them to be, they would probably congratulate him on making it so far, commend him for wanting to help his dad. Then they would probably eat the antidote themselves, make him watch as his hard-won antidote slipped away down their gullets.

He sighed and hung his head. He almost dropped his burlap bag, but then he noticed something that was most certainly not right. Here he was, exhausted from a run, despairing that he was going to have his clock broken, and he had an erection. A rather prominent and slightly straining one at that, but still, there it was. Now how did...?

One of them was a white Borelian, master of sexual manipulation. The other he couldn't say for sure, but it probably had something to do with emotional manipulation, make him despair enough to surrender. On the other hand, it could be a pink Borelian, and he was experiencing passive compliance. If he forced his way through, he was taking a gamble that he could survive potentially being touched by one or both of them. Isthim's poisonous oils caused death; what would theirs do?

Now that he was aware of the side effects, he was in control of them. The Grandfathers apparently saw this as soon as he did, because they began moving toward him again. Making sure his burlap bag was secure on his shoulder, Tommen got in a ready stance and prepared to take the risk of his life. When they were just within striking distance, Tommen struck first.

He made a move as if he was going to push right through them standing straight up, but as soon as their arms went high to block him, he curled his body and rolled underneath. The hems of their shrouds brushed his face, but he was fairly certain neither of them had actually made skin-to-skin contact. Even before the roll was complete, Tommen had uncurled and was running again. He felt slightly dizzy and ran a little lopsided, but he made it into the portal room just the same, Grandfathers following.

He did not see Foyez immediately, briefly scanning the rows of portals, but just as he was about to dart down one row, his peripheral vision twitched and he saw the Arab man flagging him down from another row. Tommen managed to make a turn a drill sergeant would be proud of and took off in that direction.

Behind him, he could almost feel the hesitation from the Grandfathers as their steps slowed and they fell farther and farther behind. And why not? He'd won. They'd won, him and Foyez. They'd made it to the portal room, and even if they had to do an emergency dive into a portal that wasn't theirs, Foyez was a Warden Timekeeper; he could open and close portals at will. When Tommen dared slow down enough to look back, the Grandfathers were nowhere to be seen, having apparently given up.

"Did they give up?" Tommen wondered as Foyez led him to the end of the row. One portal showed a snowy landscape and Tommen couldn't decide if it was home or where it was.

"No," Foyez told him gravely. "They've gone for reinforcements. They are going to try and trace these portals."

"So what do we do?"

"Your Lieutenants gave me their most recently used coordinates; they said it would be safe. You will go there."

"What about you?"

"No doubt Rifun has already learned of my treachery. He will come for me."

"So come with me, come with us. We can fight him together."

"No, my friend. As you say in English, it would be like shooting fish in a barrel."

"And Sifura fared so well on her own?"

"Were she not injured, she would have. But I have a few tricks up my sleeve, more than just a bone knife and spirit animals."

Tommen still didn't like the idea of him going alone—either of them going alone—but then Foyez was opening a portal. Tommen had never seen one opened from this side before, and it was fascinating to watch the slot turn white and glow for a few seconds before settling into a fixed image. He recognized it instantly as the living room in the twins' house.

"Go now," Foyez told him, "before they return. Allah-willing, we will see one another again someday. Maybe sooner than you think. I will close the portal behind you, but you must go before they trace it."

Tommen was pretty sure that the Hands and Grandfathers would have no trouble tracing it, as often as the twins opened portals in their living room. Still, he grabbed Foyez's wrist. "Thank you. I'll make sure my dad knows how you helped."

Foyez dipped his head. "Thank you, my friend. Now go."

And he pushed Tommen through the portal.

Sunday

Chapter Thirty-Two
Minor Threat

Tommen lay on the living room floor for probably a good five minutes after he landed, watching the portal close behind him, just waiting for another one to open and the house to fill with Grandfathers. When that didn't happen, he scraped himself off the floor and made it to a chair where he tried to relax and get reoriented.

He was back. On Earth. In Charleston, West Virginia. In the home of his Lieutenants. Here, there were lights and technology and all sorts of things of which he had been deprived for the last ten days. Oddly enough, rather than finding his heaviest coat and rushing to the hospital, his first thought was actually whether or not he should shower and shave before going.

Now that he thought about it, he could smell himself, and it wasn't the rugged man smell that most outdoor and sporting magazines promised. This was that sort of stinking, rotting smell that lingered in the locker room all summer, no matter how often the custodians bleached it and aired it out.

He checked his watch. Just past three in the morning. After a minute or two, his senses came back to him, and he got up from the chair. He went down the hall and knocked on both bedroom doors. There was no answer for a minute, so he knocked again, louder. Still nothing. Swallowing hard, he opened both doors.

Both rooms looked relatively untouched. Micaiah was more compulsive than Micah in his cleaning and organizing, but they were both normally very clean. Neither room looked ransacked, really, just...not slept in. Tommen was just heading back out to the living room, when he saw something on the dining room table. It was a note from the twins, written in Micaiah's hand.

"Tommen," it read. "We don't know when you'll be back, so this note is just staying out in the event you come home when we're not around. When we're not working, we're usually at the hospital. We're hoping and praying you make it back in time, but if not, we're paying our respects. -Micaiah and Micah"

Tommen set it down slowly and let out a sigh of relief. So their not being home was actually a good sign; it meant that Walter was still alive. He made his way to his room, hoping they'd left his phone on a charger or something.

He couldn't find his phone, but as he looked at his suitcase, still laying out on the bed, he decided that taking half an hour to shower and shave was a good idea. Yes, he'd been through awful, harrowing trials and almost died several times, but that would be a tale to tell, not to parade around in stinking, sweaty clothes. When his dad woke up, Tommen wanted to be seen as upstanding as he could possibly be, not as a slouch who'd let himself go in his grief. So he picked out a change of clothes and headed to the bathroom.

And anyway, he told himself, the hospital wouldn't be "open" per se for several hours. When his dad miraculously came back around, Tommen couldn't just not be there one minute and suddenly there the next. Tommen did plan on Banding while he administered the antidote, but to the rest of the hospital staff, it would be a miracle cure just by his visit.

As he turned on the shower and got undressed, Tommen found a stain on the front of his boxers. He might have dismissed it, except it was still wet. He told himself it was probably just a sweat stain, even as he knew it was the result of the white Borelian. The thought on his mind, he went to the full-length mirror and checked himself, unsure if Borelian oil would show up on his skin or not. But seeing how he felt pretty in control of his emotions and wasn't currently hypersexual, he figured he'd gotten lucky. Very lucky.

Hot water and soap had never felt more heavenly. Forget all the jets and patterns and whatever other luxuries the shower purported, just the miracle of hot water was medicine in itself as Tommen scrubbed away built up dirt and grime, washed sand from spots he didn't know sand could get into—well, except if he spent all his time in the sand completely naked—and found more knicks and scratches than he remembered getting.

His last item on the to-do list was shave. He felt his beard, not quite as thick and grown out as it had been after two weeks in captivity, but it would be in a few days' time, if he let it. He considered it, actually, remembering how much like his pa he looked. The resemblance had been uncanny. Plus he kind of liked it, as if it was part of a new identity, a man's beard, showing the world that he was no longer some short-tempered child, but an adult to be respected.

He drew the razor over his cheek.

To the rest of the world, the last ten days had never happened, nor could he ever tell them. They would know and sympathize with the near-loss of his father, but they could never appreciate the lengths he'd gone to in order to bring him back. They would never believe that he'd sobered up so much as to go from fighting every other week and binge drinking and smoking with his friends, to a real man who understood the complexities of life.

Because, ultimately, he didn't understand the complexities of life. Not all of them. It wasn't as if he held some high-paying job and had to make huge decisions every day. It wasn't as if he had a family he had to protect and take care of. In the end, he was just sixteen year old Tommen Forbes, the kid who'd been kidnapped and almost lost his dad, the kid who got in fights, binge drank and smoked, the kid who didn't give a rat's ass about school, the Chivalrous Welshman.

He got out of the shower, not sure if he was sober or depressed, but being clean and dry and dressed in fresh clothes helped to revive his spirit at least a little bit. Looking in the mirror, he silently mourned the loss of his beard. But he also made it a goal, something to aspire to wear, but only once he'd earned it. No one could tell him when that would be or what he had to do, but when he reached that point, he would know.

When he was satisfied that he was as clean as he was going to get, he checked his watch again. Almost four. Well, he couldn't call for a ride, so that meant he was going to have to walk. Banding or not, it was still going to be cold, and he was going to need the heaviest coat he could find.

Tommen hung up the towel to dry and gathered his stinky clothes, not sure if he wanted to toss them in the laundry or the trash. He decided on laundry, but they would probably have to be their own separate load.

He found a plastic bag floating around his room and stuffed the rotten clothes in there before rummaging through the rest of his stuff, looking for a heavy coat. He didn't have any that he liked or trusted to get him from the house to the hospital. Only a little frustrated, he went out to the kitchen, to the little corner that housed the coats and boots. He looked through the twins' things, eventually picking out a coat that he was pretty sure belonged to Micah. As he tried it on, he heard something jingle in the pocket.

Some days, he felt the idiot. He didn't have to walk; Micah had a car. Tommen pulled out the keyring. It was the spare set, but it would start the car readily enough. Excited that something was finally going right, he hurried back to the room to grab the burlap bag, checked to make sure the antidote was still safe and sound, and started back toward the kitchen. He got halfway there when a voice almost made him jump through the roof.

"Hello, Tommen."

He looked to his right, in the living room. He almost couldn't see the shadow that sat on the couch until it moved and flicked on a lamp. Rifun stood from the spot and approached, casual, non-threatening, suspicious.

"Off to save your father?" he inquired. "How sweet."

"How did you get in here?" Tommen asked, knowing his question was far less authoritative and demanding than he'd hoped.

"How did you?" Rifun shrugged. "I'm a Warden, same as

Foyez. All I needed were the coordinates."

"Why are you here?" As if he couldn't guess.

"You know, you've caused a lot of trouble for me lately." Rifun held up his right hand. His index and middle finger were missing, and the rest was thickly bandaged, pins sticking out of the thumb. "The thumb was able to be saved, albeit just barely. The other two?" He shook his head. "Toast. Or sausages, whichever you prefer."

"You did that to yourself."

"By holding you hostage? Dear boy, did you ever really think I was going to kill you? You, who are an Akari-bearer? You're far too valuable for that."

"Well then, it was a pretty convincing act. And I don't buy that Akari bullshit either."

"Of course you don't. Not yet. But you will. As will Foyez. As will Micaiah."

Tommen shook his head. "What is it you want? Cassius wants to be the Zero Hour, King of Time or some shit. What do you want? To terrorize people?"

"Think of me as his right hand. Or his puppet master, whichever you prefer. And that reminds me, you caused quite a bit of trouble in the Wheel today, too. Now, not only are the Hands and Grandfathers out for you, but several dozen Merchants are, too. Including one very angry Urdhei who claims you completely overturned his booth and wasted probably four years' worth of Time Capsules."

"I'll be more careful next time," Tommen said through gritted teeth.

"Oh, I'm sure you will. After all, you really won't have much of a choice."

"What do you mean?" But he had a good idea where it was going.

"As of this moment, if you ever set foot in the Wheel again, you will be arrested on the spot and taken away to have your clock broken."

"On what charges?"

"Treason, of course. You openly admitted to conspiracy to overthrow the Grandfathers and bribing the Hands to help you do it." Rifun shrugged like it was common knowledge. "You're a Runner by all accounts, and a very dangerous one." He fake-gasped. "Why, what about your review coming up? You braved both hell and high water to save your father and mentor, and you lost everything to do it."

"It was worth it," Tommen informed him coldly.

Rifun pursed his lips. "Hm, the appropriate response would have been more like, 'Good golly gosh, Rifun, whatever shall I do?'"

He raised his eyebrows to cue Tommen, but Tommen wasn't playing along. Rifun sighed and rolled his eyes. "Kids these days, no respect for their elders." He tilted his head. "Oh no, Rifun, whatever shall I do if I'm considered a Runner and can't—?"

"Just skip it," Tommen cut in. "I assume you're going to say that you have some sort of bargaining chip, a way to make sure I can go back to the Wheel without being arrested?"

"Oh, better than that. I can not only make sure you can go back to the Wheel, but I can ensure that, barring egregious error and incompetence, you will pass your review with flying colors."

"Yeah? Lily can do the same thing."

"If your review were after the elections, maybe. But not before. Not now, with her influence at an all-time low. Only I can help you."

Tommen glared at him, but he couldn't come up with any other answers. There was no MacGyvering his way out of this one. Walter was dying, the twins were under just as much suspicion, and Lily had no more strings to pull.

"Is this how you controlled Foyez for decades?" Tommen asked.

"Had he waited only a little longer, he would have come to realize the plans we had for him and his full potential," Rifun answered with about as much sadness as a parent finally being able to throw away their child's once-favorite toy that had annoyed them nonstop for years. "You, however, will not have to wait so long."

He didn't want to listen to anymore of this bullshit, but he needed a way out. All of this coming from the man who'd held a gun to his head, destroyed his hearing, and then had the nerve to say that he'd never actually intended to kill him. Fuck.

"Sticks and stones, Tommen," Rifun goaded, his tone becoming strained, as if he was quickly running out of patience. "Listening never killed anyone."

"Fine," Tommen growled. "You clear me of all charges and get me through my review. What do I owe you?"

"First, a little gratitude would be nice. I don't think you realize the kind of favor I'm doing you. I'll even sweeten the deal a little by saying you don't owe me anything until after your review." Because that meant much. Then he grew serious. "You will get a sign from me. Foyez may have told you about them, but they are unmistakable nonetheless. When you get these signs, you are to see me for special training, above and beyond what Walter can teach you in the Arena."

"Special training?" Tommen wondered.

"Akari training."

Tommen blinked and shook his head. "What? You want me to study...what, comparative religion? Are you trying to make me a member of your cult or something?" He shook his head and took a step back. "No. I'll give up Time before I become a fanatic...terrorist."

He turned as if to leave, but Rifun spoke again. "Did I mention that there are consequences for not accepting my offer?"

"I said I'll give up Time," Tommen told him. "I'll never go back to the Wheel, fail my review, live life as the little probationary Timekeeper that couldn't."

"That much is a given, not a consequence. The consequences I'm talking about are much more...consequential."

Even as he spoke, Tommen felt his sinuses become congested, and it spread from his nose to his throat and into his lungs. Then he felt all leaky, like a faucet, but no matter how much he coughed, he couldn't clear it. Then it got worse, as the gunky buildup thinned and turned to water in his lungs. He tried to breathe, couldn't take a breath. Only when he was on his hands and knees, spitting water on the kitchen floor did it all release, and he was gasping for air.

Rifun got down beside him. "Walter has probably told you that the Akari is a myth. Sifura might have told you that its power has degraded over time to little pieces here and there. But I assure you, it is no myth, and it is far more powerful than anyone realizes. It can do things that should not be done."

"What did you do to me?" Tommen whispered between coughs and gasps.

"Here is your first lesson, free of charge. Consider it more of a riddle to be solved. In order for someone to wield Time, they have to be exposed to it in sufficient quantity. For you, it was making a century-and-a-half leap into the future. In order for someone to wield the Akari, it has to be within them, part of them. What am I?"

Tommen had managed to catch his breath, but his throat felt raw. "What kind of stupid riddle is that?"

"To wield Time, Time must be given to him. To wield the Akari, the Akari must be within him. What am I?"

"That makes no sense; you've already solved for all the variables. Unless you're talking about 'him' in which case it's whoever both wields Time and has the Akari."

"As I said, it's a riddle to be solved. I suggest you think about it between now and your next lesson."

Tommen sat back on his heels while Rifun stood. *Good dog.* "What do I have to do?"

"Go now, and save your father. I know you have the antidote in your bag. Hug, cry, do what you have to do. When you go to the Wheel next, you will be clear of all charges and will pass your review with flying colors to the joy of all attending. At some point in the very near future, I will send you a sign, and you will meet me for your next lesson in the Akari."

"Just one lesson."

"No, of course not. It's an ongoing thing."

"For two favors?"

"Two very big favors, unless you consider cleaning out the garage and saving your dad's life equal favors."

"Fine. How long, or how many lessons do I have to take?"

Rifun chuckled. "Dear boy, by the time you will have worked off your favors, you won't want to stop meeting for lessons."

Tommen had his doubts as he stood shakily to his feet. But the basic deal had been made. He had to get to the hospital, save his dad, and then they could work on a solution to this problem. As if reading his mind, Rifun chuckled again, more darkly this time. "And, just to make things interesting, you are not to tell anyone about this. Not your dad, not your Lieutenants, no one. Because I will know. And if you do, well, you know the phrase 'dropping like flies,' don't you?"

Oh, he knew. He knew it all too well. He also knew there was no way Rifun could be that omniscient or omnipresent. He was part of a psycho cult, but he was no god. Tommen would have to be careful and time it just right, but he would get the word out somehow. They would outmaneuver Rifun yet.

"Is there anything else you wanted while you're here? Cup of coffee, a shoe shine?" Tommen asked snidely. "Or am I free to go?"

"You're on my leash now, Tommen. You are most certainly not free to go. But if you are asking whether I am done talking and you can go to the hospital to save your dying father, then yes, by all means, you are free to go."

Tommen started to go, but stopped as Rifun interrupted him once again. "And just in case you get any funny ideas about trying to outwit me...here's a little reminder to take with you. Don't worry, it'll wear off."

Tommen waited for another drowning experience or something equally as terrifying, but it never came. Instead, the two of them just stood there, staring at each other, Rifun with a knowing look on his face that Tommen didn't like. Finally Tommen just shook his head, put his boots on as fast as he could, and headed out the door.

It was still dark out, and snow was falling in fat, wet flakes.

Ten days and Tommen had almost forgotten what snow felt like on his skin. How he'd wished for it in his trek across the desert. Now he shivered against the cold as he trudged through the snow to the little garage shelter.

It was empty. Both cars were gone. Tommen irritably fingered the spare keys in his pocket. It made sense, really, that between work and the hospital and short trips home, the twins might have both cars out. They didn't often, but today just had to be one of those days, didn't it? Because nothing about this plan was going the way he wanted it to.

Tommen shivered again and went back inside. Rifun was gone. Trying not to think about the exchange that had just happened, he grabbed another, larger jacket—presumably Micaiah's—and slipped it on over Micah's jacket. It wasn't perfect, but he just didn't have the time to sit around and wait. He was tired of waiting and delaying and having to do stupid shit just to get where he was going. With a last check in his bag just to make triple-sure that the antidote was still there, Tommen opened the door and stepped outside.

A cold wind blasted his face and buffeted his jacket, reminding him of all the joys of winter. The only good thing about it was that it eased the pain in his legs and ribs from his earlier jaunt through the Wheel. But it wasn't much farther to the hospital than it was from the bakery to home, and it was almost entirely downhill. Had he had his skis, he might have tried to ski down the hill and save time.

As it was, he could only walk, trudging through snow that, until he got to the road, was taller than his boots and fell down to his socks, first melting from the heat, and then freezing, chilling him. But he was on a mission, and this time, nothing was going to stop him.

Chapter Thirty-Three
The Return

On the way to the hospital, about every three steps resulted in a curse. Most often it was for the wind and the cold; of all days to come back, it had to be in the middle of a blizzard. Tommen didn't mind the snow too much, but the biting wind and the freezing temperatures left much to be desired, to say nothing of the ice that lay beneath the snow, which he frequently slipped on. Sometimes he caught himself; other times he went careening into a snowbank.

When he wasn't cursing the wind and the cold, he was cursing Rifun, for a variety of reasons. He started out by cursing whatever deal they'd made, and he resolved that once Walter was awake and on his way to recovery, that he would find a way to tell him about it and get out of it. Then he wound up cursing Rifun for harming Walter in the first place. Even worse was that Rifun even admitted that there had been no point to it other than to toy with him over whatever secrets he apparently thought were worth dying for. And then, when he was finished with that rant, he would curse Rifun for getting in league with Cassius, a psychotic sociopath who delighted in tearing people's throats out.

After that, he wound up cursing the Hands and the Wheel and Time in general, usually for no other reason than for being so corrupt. Not only for being so corrupt, but for being openly corrupt and still people did what they were allegedly supposed to. How could anyone get away with that, really?

By the time he was done cursing, Tommen's breaths came in ragged white puffs in the crisp night air. He did a stupid thing, then; he stopped. He wasn't far from the city, but it felt miles away. Fuck, but he was exhausted. He was no athlete, but even if he had been, even athletes had limits, and Tommen had far exceeded his own. In spite of the cold, his whole body hurt, throbbing with muscles that had gone from a casual walk to a full-sprint marathon, heavy grocery bags to world champion weightlifting. His sinuses hadn't fully recovered from Rifun's party tricks, and now his whole respiratory system felt ice cold and frozen. His head felt heavy, and he wanted nothing more than to lie down, but he didn't dare lest he not wake up.

He was momentarily confused when his shadow suddenly appeared in front of him. Even as his mind registered a vehicle coming up behind him, he had his thumb out, hoping the person was not only compassionate, but not a serial killer or something equally as terrible.

To his relief, the vehicle slowed and came to a stop. It was a four-door long bed pickup truck, heavily weighted, windows tinted dark. After a second or two, the compartment light flicked on and the passenger window rolled down.

"Need a tow?" the driver asked. Tommen didn't get a good look at his face.

"Need a lift," Tommen told him.

For a moment, the driver was silent, and Tommen was afraid he would drive off. Then, "Hop in."

The door unlocked, and Tommen clumsily scrabbled into the truck, forcing frozen hands and joints to work. The driver moved a coat out of the passenger seat so Tommen could sit and fumble with the seat belt. When he was all set, the compartment light flicked off and they were on their way.

"Where you headed?" the driver wondered, his tone wary.

"Hospital," Tommen replied, blowing on his hands even as the driver turned up the heat.

"You all right? Need me to call an ambulance?"

"No, no. Just...a family member."

Beat. Then, "Name's Jake."

"Tommen."

"I don't mean to pry, and it's really none of my business, but what's going on at the hospital that you're out in a snowstorm about ready to be the next patient yourself?"

"My dad was in an accident, and he's not doing well. They don't know if he'll survive the night." Not entirely a lie.

"Oh, shit, I'm sorry. I guess that's a good reason to be out and about."

"What about you? Heading into work?"

"Picking up my girlfriend."

"Oh. Cool."

"You got a girl? You're...what? Senior?"

"Sophomore."

"Ah. Got a girl?"

"Nah."

"Got...a boy?"

"Not even." Tommen rolled his eyes even if Jake couldn't see.

"Hey, it don't matter to me, just trying to make small talk."

Tommen wasn't really in a mood for small talk, however. Mostly he just wanted to get to the hospital and get it all over with. Even if the antidote didn't work, he needed to relieve the tension.

"So what's in the bag, if you don't mind my asking?" Jake asked after a few minutes of silence.

"Oh, um, food. In case it's a long wait."

Tommen could feel the scrutiny, even if Jake didn't turn his head. Dad gets hurt, so he rushes out the door to brave a snowstorm and get to the hospital, but he finds time to stop and pack a bag of food? Was it as crazy as it sounded, or was he lying? What was really in that bag?

"You live around here?" Tommen inquired conversationally.

"Ah, farther outside of town." Jake sounded relieved to make conversation rather than be left to sit and wonder about the bag or his passenger in general. "I live with my dad and brother and his family."

"Farmers, then."

"That's right."

"What kind?"

"Goats and sheep. We produce a lot of the goat milk you buy in stores." He told him the name of the farm. "Look for us. Unless you have animals of your own?"

Tommen shook his head. "No. My dad sometimes talks about getting chickens or something, but it never happens. Neither of us is home enough to take care of them."

"Too bad. What's your dad do?"

"He's a cop."

"No kidding? Neat. I wanted to be a firefighter when I was small, right up until I was thirteen."

"What happened?"

"My mom died, and me and my brother were needed more than ever on the farm."

"I'm sorry."

"It was a long time ago. What about you? What's your ma do?"

Tommen looked away. "I, uh, I don't have a mom. Just me and my dad for the last eight years."

Jake was silent for a moment. In the faint reflection on the windshield, Tommen could see him making quick glances his way. "I'm sorry. I know it's hard on a youngster."

"It was a long time ago."

Tommen knew his tone probably came across as brave or toughing it out, but actually, his mind was filled with awe as he studied the reflection for a moment before giving a quick glance at the dash lights. After a few more minutes, they rounded the corner and the great city of Charleston opened up before them.

And then Tommen knew what Rifun had done to him in parting. His first confirmation came when they rolled up to a stop sign. It was red. *Red.* Not gold. All the taillights of all the cars. Red. The bottom light on the stoplight. Not blue, but green. He knew those colors only by association. He looked at some coats and scarves on display in store windows, lit from the outside by street lights.

They were mostly white, but one had red accents, another blue, a third purple. He wasn't even sure how he knew it was purple, just that it was. In another window, he saw a child's coat that was pink and red, and a matching set of gloves, scarf and hat, all green and black. Even the truck they were in now was dark green. Looking at himself, he saw that the shirt he wore was green, not beige, and his coat was red.

"You okay over there?" Jake asked cautiously. "You're like, kind of freaking me out."

"What?" Tommen wondered. "No, yeah, I'm fine. Just a little anxious."

Excited was a better word, but that wouldn't exactly fit with the narrative of visiting his father who wasn't expected to live through the night. It would fit, however, with the realization that Rifun had essentially cured his deuteranopia. He'd always known he was red-green color-blind; that much had been evident since he was a small child. Honestly, he'd never thought it fair to label it red-green colorblind when he had zero clue what those colors were.

But now he knew. He could see them. Suddenly, the rest of the visible spectrum was open to him, producing an explosion of color unlike anything he'd previously been able to comprehend.

His excitement was replaced by fear. Rifun had told him it would wear off. Was that because deuteranopia couldn't be cured, or because Rifun had chosen not to cure it? Was this one of his carrots, a way to lure Tommen back into his psychotic, zealous training? How long did he have before this rainbow was taken from him and he was plunged back into a world of yellow, blue, and gray?

He didn't have long to comprehend this before they were pulling into the parking lot of the hospital, the emergency room entrance.

"This where you need to be?" Jake wondered.

"Yeah, I think so," Tommen said. "I'm sorry, I don't have any cash on me —"

"Don't worry about it. Listen, go be with your dad. I hope he pulls through."

"Thanks. If he does, we'll have a glass of goat milk and raise a toast to you."

Jake chuckled as Tommen got out of the truck, almost slipping on the icy pavement. With a last wave at Jake, Tommen turned and headed toward the emergency entrance, making sure to make every step deliberate and solid so he didn't end up the next patient in line.

He Banded just as the doors opened, just enough to get through, but before the night receptionist lifted her head to see who was coming in.

Before he moved, however, he paused to just look around the room. It was as if he was seeing everything for the first time as shades of gray turned into purples and pinks; yellow and gold became red and blue and orange. And they weren't just those flat colors, but there were shades and dimensions and everything just came alive. Just people's skin color looked different, no matter what shade of brown it was. He saw that one of the people in the emergency room wore a necklace with a ruby pendant, the stone a rich, dark red. Someone else also boasted rich, dark red, but this came from the blood leaking from a head wound as he was taken to a room. Tommen wasn't exactly a trauma junkie, but it fascinated him that he had never actually seen blood, not as it was. And then there was a nurse running around in purple and green scrubs.

Tommen let out a breath, almost afraid to move, as if by doing so, all the colors would suddenly disappear. He found himself wondering if he would be able to remember what those colors looked like, or if his brain was as color-blind as he was. Would he be able to conjure up red and green, try to mentally place them on a stoplight when he sat in traffic?

He sighed and forced his feet to move, keeping his breaths even while he walked. It was an astounding sensation, a miracle if there was one. But it was a carrot, a game, a trick played by Rifun. A bait-and-switch to get him in deeper in his obscene cult. Tommen bit his lip as he was forced to tell himself that he would rather be color-blind than part of that cult. But he liked the colors. He liked the shades and the dimensions and all the raw emotions it evoked in him, not the least of which was awe.

No. He had to remain strong, steady, and clear-headed. Rifun's tricks came from a cult, and there was nothing a cult could do that science couldn't do also. Even if it wasn't on Earth, there was probably some medical facility somewhere in the universe that could fix color-blindness. Rifun had probably just stolen that technology or that medicine and was using it on some hapless, primitive society and calling it magic. Bow down to the god of light and color.

Tommen knew roughly where ICU was, at least which floor it was on, though it took him a few laps, some backtracking, and a few map consultations before he actually found where it was.

Even at night, Intensive Care was absurdly busy as doctors and nurses moved to and fro with papers and charts and drug carts and all manner of assorted instruments and tools. There was one receptionist on duty at the moment; there would probably be more coming in later as standard business hours came around and they could get around to arguing with insurance companies and the like. One doctor was looking through a manila folder while another spoke to a nurse, and a third was just exiting a room. A few nurses huddled around a drug cart, counting out some pills and signing off on everything two and three and four times, all in the name of accountability. As Tommen rounded a corner, he almost ran into another nurse, this one pressed against a wall, trying to hide as he poked around on his phone, texting someone.

Tommen paused and looked around again, wishing he had more time to stop and just look at the color and be amazed by so simple a thing. Light. Of all things he had to suck at, it was perceiving light. But now here it was, laid out before him.

He shook his head. No, he couldn't get distracted now. Checking his watch, Tommen saw it was just before five. And given the track record of this entire mission, literally anything could happen between where he stood and where he was going. There could be a fire. There could be an active shooter. A herd of wild boar could suddenly come charging down the hall.

Or, as he found out quickly enough, his dad could have been moved. Tommen was pretty sure he had the right room, but when he walked in, his dad was nowhere to be seen, the twins either.

He slowly backed out of the room, willing himself not to panic. Micaiah had said in his note that they would be at the hospital if not at home or work. Tommen rubbed his face. Five a.m., they would already be at work. So then, where was his dad?

Tommen was determined to check every single room in Intensive Care before heading to the morgue, a thought he was not willing to entertain. He couldn't be late. It wasn't fair. Still holding the Band tight around himself, he helped himself to a nurse's station and looked over the shoulder of a nurse as he surfed a program that, thankfully, at least listed the names and room numbers of each patient, to say nothing of all the other data displayed. Tommen wished he could understand the rest of the data, but he was content with a name.

He breathed a sigh of relief when he found Forbes, W. listed. So he had been moved, and not to the morgue. Although, judging by the stats, assuming Tommen could interpret them anywhere close to correctly, he wasn't doing well, and the room he was in was basically a Last Hope for Survival room.

But he was alive, and that was all that mattered. Memorizing the room number, Tommen set out in search of it. Intensive Care was not a huge place, but each room took up quite a bit of space, and it was a minute before he got going in the right direction.

Finally, he stood outside the door to his dad's room, terrified and yet anxious to go in. He swallowed nervously, shifted his bag on his shoulder, felt the weight of the antidote, then pushed the door open. He considered dropping the Band and doing everything in real time. Banding was great for healing less-than-life-threatening wounds, but there was no telling what it could do to a Time-immune disease. In the end, he entered the room and closed the door, then released the Band.

All the activity on the floor roared back to life but was soon drowned out as the door clicked shut. Even here the lights were on, though activity was almost nonexistent. Besides Tommen, there was only one other non-hospitalized person in the room.

"Tommen," Lily said, her expression truly stunned.

She looked awful, as if she hadn't slept in days, done a lot of crying and not a lot of eating.

"Lily," Tommen said, almost as shocked. "What are you doing here?"

"Keeping an eye on him."

Tommen looked at his dad, and it was as though he was dead already. The color had gone out of his skin, and he looked terribly gaunt, his eyes sunken. All of his hair, but especially his mustache, looked dry, brittle, and unkempt. He looked as if he'd lost about fifty pounds, and his joints looked much more pronounced, far beyond what might be considered handsome. Topping it all off was an assortment of lines, wires, and IVs.

"He's got until about one o'clock," Lily told Tommen. "He's losing this battle; he's on the verge of not breathing. Do you have something for him? Anything at all?"

"Yeah!" Tommen slung the bag off his shoulder to the floor and tore open the cover flap. "Yes, I do. I have it. I have the antidote."

"Are you sure it will work?"

"No. But it's the only chance he has."

She nodded and, after a moment of thought, found her phone and dialed a number. "Micaiah said to call if and when you returned."

Tommen brought out the bag of antidote and opened it carefully. He'd just started reaching his finger toward it when there was another voice, one he never thought he'd miss.

"You got the antidote?" Micaiah said.

Tommen looked back at him. "I did."

He was about to take a generous scoop on his finger when he paused. "Is there, like, an empty syringe laying around?"

"Syringe?" Micaiah asked.

"Sifura said that the best way would be by direct injection."

Lily looked around. "I don't see any; anything they have is probably locked up."

"Worth a shot."

He jammed his finger into the sticky goo and scooped out a generous amount. He held it carefully there as he bent over his dad. He considered his options for just a second before just moving Walter's bottom lip and forcing his finger with the antidote between his teeth.

"How much does he need?" Micaiah wondered.

"That should be more than enough, but it depends on how far gone he is. I mean, I only touched the stuff, and Sifura said it took like an hour and a half for me to come back around."

"You were poisoned?"

"Accidentally, and by my own stupidity." Tommen briefly explained the paradox that was hasax, the flower being the antidote for the leaves which were poisonous. He told Micaiah about the lube-honey that had to be slathered all over in order to even get near the plants.

"Sounds like that was an adventure in itself. I expect we'll get to hear the rest of it once Walter wakes up."

"Yeah." Tommen glanced at Lily. "Has anything changed?"

"The clock has stopped," she offered. "If I had to guess at anything, it's almost like it's thinking."

"Thinking? What do you mean 'thinking'?" Micaiah wondered.

"It's difficult to describe, but...I don't know. Believe me, I'll let you know as soon as anything changes."

Tommen let out a breath and looked at Micaiah. "That reminds me. Assim Foyez."

"Yes?" Micaiah wondered.

"You know him?"

The elder twin shifted his stance and folded his arms. "Not

really, to be honest. I'd heard his name here and there, knew he used to be Gatekeeper of Earth, knew he was involved in the Dispersal of '63. When your dad was investigating the murders, Foyez's name came up, and your dad called him. According to him, the man was less than forthcoming. He's from District One.

"A day or two ago, Foyez approached Micah and me in the bakery and asked to have a word. He explained who he was and said he felt responsible for what had befallen Walter. We talked a little, but it basically came down to, he wanted to help in some way. Even if Walter didn't make it, he didn't want to see you end up in a similar situation."

Tommen knew he should have jumped in at that moment and told Micaiah about Rifun's visit and his threat, tell him that he was in exactly the same position as Foyez. But he stupidly kept silent, and Micaiah went on.

"We were still skeptical about trusting him, but we also knew that we would probably need some kind of backup plan in case something went wrong in the Wheel with you getting home. But we knew, too, that you're a smart kid and wouldn't just up and follow someone just because they said they knew us."

"So you told him about the disciplinary meeting." Tommen felt his cheeks grow hot.

"I didn't tell him about the disciplinary meeting; I told him what to say about the disciplinary meeting, enough that you would know that it really was me trying to speak to you and follow him."

"I almost didn't," Tommen confessed.

"And I wouldn't blame you. But you heard the argument, weighed the options, and trusted your gut. How was it getting out of the Wheel?"

Tommen gave them a glossed-over version of events in the Wheel, starting with Foyez approaching him and trying to convince him to follow him and escape. He told them about slipping through the Archives and sneaking out, even if the Grandfathers did catch up to them in the marketplaces. Ignoring the part about flipping over booths and angering more than a few Merchants, he told them about the chase, losing Foyez in the commotion, and having to find his way back to the portal room on his own. He told them about the Grandfathers who had been waiting for him and how he got by them. He finished by telling them about Foyez opening the portal into their living room, pushing him through, and then closing it quickly behind him.

When his tale was done, Micaiah frowned, deep in thought. For a long minute, he didn't speak. Then, "So we should assume the worst, that he has been arrested, potentially had his clock broken, potentially been killed."

Tommen didn't say anything to that, for the simple reason that he was pretty sure that Foyez, while he might have been arrested, was probably just fine. Somehow, he had a sneaking suspicion that Rifun was going to hang onto him for a while, make him sweat, make the rest of them sweat, use him as leverage somehow, ransom, like Eric and Varad, like Tommen. It was all a game, a bargain to be made, and so far, Rifun had the upper hand in everything.

"And Sifura?" Tommen wondered. "Would Rifun really go after a Hand so close to the elections?"

Micaiah sighed. "Sifura is only the Hand of Scientifically Primitive and Unengaged Civilizations. She's a nobody, politically speaking. Until she causes trouble, but I digress. The other Hands view her as insignificant. Primitive, as you might imagine. What do they care if some primitive savage mysteriously disappears or dies, whether close to an election or not? After all, her people are barbaric, killing each other over the smallest matters and exposing themselves to all sorts of diseases and such." He shrugged. "Their words, not mine. Ultimately, she will not be missed, only replaced."

Tommen could only describe the emotion that bubbled up in his gut as rage, rage against the stupidity and closed-mindedness of the other Hands against Sifura. So her people didn't have super advanced weapons and still built their houses from mud bricks, so what? They had invented skimmers that could cross a thirty-day desert in a week. They had celebrations and parties unlike anything Tommen had ever seen. The duel ritual of the D'Bok might seem primitive, yes, but it was steeped in culture and tradition. And while Sifura had every ability and opportunity to just open a portal and walk right into D'Bok territory and take their hasax without them ever knowing, there was a code of ethics, a code of honor and tradition that had to be satisfied. Primitive they may have been, but they weren't stupid.

"So S'bal really could have killed her. And we may never really know," Tommen stated. "I don't even remember if I thanked her."

"I'm sure she knew how grateful you are to her," Micaiah assured him. "And there's no reason she couldn't have survived anyway; maybe she just got delayed."

Tommen had his doubts, but said nothing out loud.

"I think he'll be okay," Lily said suddenly, cutting through the sullen silence. Though she still looked tired and haggard, she managed a small smile. "His Actual Time is climbing, and his Potential Time is realigning itself."

"How long until he wakes up?" Tommen wondered, sliding to his dad's bedside like a nail to a magnet.

"That I can't tell you. In his own time, I expect."

Tommen didn't want his dad to wake up in his own time; he wanted him to wake up now, and look at him, and know that everything was going to be okay.

Instead, he simply pulled up a chair and waited. He watched his father sleep, noting that as the clock ticked by slowly, his skin color improved, and his dismal vitals began to plateau before starting to return to where they needed to be. Several nurses who came in made notes on the improvements. Only when there had been five straight hours of nothing but improvements did the doctor himself walk in the room.

"He's going to be okay, right?" Tommen wondered. "I mean, everything is looking good."

"He is certainly showing signs of improvement," the doctor told him. "Brain activity is looking good, vitals are improving, and he looks better overall."

"So when will he wake up?"

"I don't know."

"But you're the doctor."

"Yes. But he's been in a coma for a week."

"Yeah, a week. That's not like, you know, six months or ten years or anything like that."

"The brain is a complex thing. Someone in a coma for a year is no more likely to die than someone in a coma for two days is likely to recover. It is all entirely up to the individual healing."

The doctor said more after that, but Tommen couldn't remember much of it. All he'd heard so far was that even though he'd crossed the universe and braved lions and tigers and bears to get the cure, his dad could still wake up an idiot or otherwise severely disabled. It wasn't that Tommen didn't want his dad to pull through, but he didn't want life to be just more misery. A line of duty death was noble, honorable, and dying to protect his son even more so. Living as an invalid was terrible and pitiable.

Tommen tried not to go down that road, telling himself that he'd completed his mission, and now he was going to have to take things as they came, and that applied not only for the Wheel and the political fallout, but also for daily life, the mundane day-to-day activities that made up a bulk of his life.

"What would happen if you tried to give him more?" Micaiah wondered once the doctor had gone.

"I don't know," Tommen said. "It'll either help him more or else it'll just give him a severe stomachache when he wakes up. And he'd have to go to the dentist."

"Dentist?"

Tommen offered the sticky liquid to Micaiah who got just a dab on his pinky. As soon as it touched his tongue, his face screwed up like he'd just bit straight into a lemon. He squeezed his eyes shut and shook his head as if he could shake off the flavor like a dog shook off water.

"Shit, that is some...sweet shit. The fuck." Micaiah licked his lips and swallowed several times, twisted his expression and shook his head. "Damn, even if it brings Walter out of this coma, it's going to put him in a diabetic coma right afterwards."

"Let me try some," Lily said, standing.

Tommen offered her the bag. She took a little more than Micaiah but her reaction was almost the exact same. "Holy shit." She shook her head. "That is some strong stuff right there. Wow." She headed unsteadily for the door. "Yeah, I'm sorry, I've gotta go wash my mouth out or something; that is just too strong for me."

"So is this like sugar?" Micaiah wondered, gesturing toward the antidote.

"I don't know," Tommen admitted. "I thought about researching like the chemical makeup of it or something, but I didn't want to get in too deep with the Grandfathers on my trail."

"Too bad." Micaiah licked his lips again. "Yeah, I've gotta rinse my mouth, too. But hey, if it helps him, by all means, load him up."

And he was gone, leaving Tommen alone in the room. After a few seconds, he turned back to Walter. Taking another generous helping, Tommen forced his finger into Walter's mouth and scraped the antidote against his teeth. One flower was good for fifteen men, and Walter was getting enough to save an entire village.

Tommen packed up the antidote just as a nurse walked in. She didn't seem to even be aware of Tommen's existence as she went straight for Walter, all abuzz with excitement of his impending recovery. She did some things, tweaked some things, wrote some things down, ignored Tommen the entire time, and then left.

Once she was gone, Tommen went and took his dad's hand in his own. "You're going to be okay now. You're going to wake up soon and probably be a little confused and disoriented, but we'll get you back up to speed. Me and Micaiah and Micah, and probably Lily, too. We're all out here waiting." He took a steady breath. "You just gotta come back to us."

In the movies, the dying victim would sigh softly, murmur something incomprehensible. The person at their bedside would get all excited and demand to know what the person had said. Then the person would open their eyes and repeat their words a little louder. Usually they would be words of affirmation—"You were right" or "It wasn't your fault" or something to that effect—followed by a tired smile, a cough or a yawn, and then a warm, fuzzy heartfelt moment as all was right with the world again.

But that didn't happen here. The machines puttered away, and Walter still slept. He didn't even stir to indicate any sort of reaction to Tommen's words.

Tommen sat down again and waited, hoping for something, anything. He wasn't sure how much he was willing to hope for a miracle or pray to some air spirit, but at this point, whatever helped. In the end, the only thing he actually got, was sleep.

Chapter Thirty-Four
Confession

It was one of those rare times when Tommen was asleep and dreaming, and he was perfectly aware of it. Some called it lucid dreaming, except that from everything Tommen had read, lucid dreaming involved some measure of control over one's dreams. He'd been able to manage that once, but for the most part, like now, he knew he was dreaming, but that was all. He had no real control over what or how he dreamed, only his own actions within.

Philosophically, Tommen supposed that it was his subconscious trying to bring his thoughts into perspective about life. He couldn't control the world around him, only himself and his actions.

Problem was, in this dream, he didn't even seem to have control over those. He felt the consciousness of the dream, felt the fear, but while he tried to make himself move and do things, it was like internally wiggling against shrink wrap while his body did whatever it wanted to. Left arm wanted to move, so it did. Right leg wanted to kick out wildly in some half-ass drunken dance, go right ahead. While he was able to keep his head to himself, everything from the neck down was at the mercy of whatever other forces were apparently in this dream.

He turned his head this way and that, tried to look around, up and down, but he was in darkness. Well, it wasn't really darkness so much as blackness. He saw nothing around him, but he could see his body clear as day. And it was going wild, doing things he wasn't sure it was normally physically capable of, as far as joint manipulation went, though he felt no pain.

557

"Stop!" he barked, hoping that he was able to maintain enough control that he only had to assert it for it to return to him.

As ordered, his body stopped freaking out, but he still couldn't move it willfully.

Then, out of the blackness, he heard footsteps, heavy steps like on fresh frost. He peered into the darkness beyond the blackness at a figure walking toward him with no more care than Mr. Roger. A second before the light revealed his face, Tommen knew who it was.

"Rifun," he growled.

"Tommen," Rifun acknowledged, walking nonchalantly toward him, stopping in front of him with only inches between their noses.

"Is this real?" Tommen asked. "Why would I dream you up?"

Rifun shrugged, his expression almost convincing that he didn't know. "I don't know. Because you're afraid of me? Bec—"

"I am not afraid of you."

"Of course not. You're sixteen; you know no fear."

He said it almost seriously, but Tommen could hear the mockery in it even as he felt exposed for a terrible liar. Yes, he knew fear. He'd known more fear in the last month than he had in the last eight years since coming out of Forbes Cave. And yes, if he wanted to admit it to himself, he was afraid of Rifun. But he wasn't going to admit it out loud.

"Could be that you're simply subconsciously mulling over the little discussion we had earlier. One possibility is that your subconscious thinks you know me well enough that you can conjure me up so we can have a 'safe' discussion, where you can ask me questions, get answers, and I won't throttle you without ever touching you. And so you can throttle me at will because you know you could never do such a thing in real life.

"The other possibility is that I am actually here, that I am able to enter your mind and influence your dreams, to both manipulate your dreaming body as well as hold a very real discussion with you."

"Why only the body? Why not the head, too?" Tommen

wondered.

Rifun gave him a knowing grin. "Free will is a bitch, isn't it?"

"Fine. So which is it? Are you here or not?"

"See now, there's the fear. You are afraid. You're afraid of even the possibility that this could be real, that I could be here. You're afraid that somehow I'm able to unlock all your dirty little secrets."

"What do you want?"

"But we haven't established my existence yet. On the one hand, if I'm not here, then the answer I'm about to give is simply a fabrication of your mind, what you think I would say, what you think I want, based on your limited interactions and incredibly narrow understanding of me. On the other hand, if I am here, then you're worried that either my answer is going to be a non-answer so you have nothing to tell your little friends—similar to what I did with you at the dock—or it's going to be so violent and specific that you're afraid it's going to lead into another little adventure and potentially endanger your beloved just-recovering father."

"Leave him out of this!" Tommen snapped. "Are you here or not?"

"If I said no, then you are going to be suspicious and take me for a liar. Most likely you would try to wake yourself up from this dream, or else try to find the normal river of uncontrollable dreams that everyone else experiences. But you would always be haunted by this exchange, always questioning whether or not this could have been real."

Tommen glared at him. "And if you said that yes, you are here?"

"Then you would ask me to prove it. Not because you want me to be here—which, if I did somehow prove it, you would only freak out and try to wake yourself from this dream and so on and so forth—but because you want to give yourself a fighting chance that I can't prove myself and therefore I am not actually here."

Rifun's demeanor had not changed one iota. His expressions were characteristically and infuriatingly innocent; his body language was casual, as if they were doing no more than discussing the weather.

"All right then," Tommen said, "question for you, assuming you aren't actually here."

Now Rifun grinned, and it put Tommen in mind of the Joker. "Fire away."

"Assuming you aren't actually here, why would I dream this up? Not you, but this. This whole exchange and the freaky uncontrollable body thing."

"Ah. I like how you think. Don't talk to me as me; talk to me as you, your subconscious. Very clever." He chuckled. "The uncontrollable body is your uncontrollable life. Others are pulling your strings, but they can't control your head. Like I said, free will is a bitch."

"And the double-talking exchange full of questions and non-answers?"

"Because you want to believe that you can gain the upper hand. But in order to do that, you need to get all your thoughts straight, all your little ducks in a row. So your mind puts together a physical representation of all the basic principals of logic and fallacy and leaves you to sort it out."

"So that's you," Tommen stated. "You're the physical representation of logic and fallacy?"

Rifun grinned hugely. "Child, I am the epitome of it."

"Which leads us back to square one. Are you here or are you not, and how do I know?"

"That's a good start. Is there anything else you'd like to add?"

"How do I keep myself from sliding into doubt and double-thinking?"

"Now you're starting to get it. There's just one problem with all of that, though. But I'm not going to tell you what it is."

Now it was Tommen's turn to grin. "You just did, just by not answering. I asked the questions in the wrong order. Whether or not you're here is a theory. How I know is a qualifier. The ability to stay out of the doubt is the evidence. If I solve the theory first, I'm left trying to make the evidence fit the theory. If I get the evidence first, the theory should just fall into place."

"Very good. You're a quick study. Ten days away from the twenty-first century did you good. Now then, since you've gathered all your little ducks, what are you going to do with them?"

"I need evidence. How do I keep from sliding into doubt? By reaffirming what I already know, which you already told me and I know from experience. You're right. I can't beat you. But I can beat myself any day."

Then, in a move that was somewhere between beach bodybuilder flexing his muscles and Bruce Banner turning into the Hulk, Tommen broke free of the mental shrink wrap that had bound his body. Rifun stepped back a few paces, but Tommen went forward to meet him.

"Evidence: You were controlling me, but I beat you, because you were me, and I can beat me. Theory: You're not really here. Qualifier: I just proved it."

Rifun shifted his stance from stunned back into the lackadaisical, devil-may-care smile that boiled Tommen's blood. "You're a smart kid, Tommen. We should do this more often."

Tommen shook his head. "Once is enough."

So Rifun did an imaginary tip of the hat and bowed as he backed away into the darkness beyond the blackness. "Until we meet again."

But as he backed away, Tommen noticed that his footsteps got louder and the sound got fuzzier. He was suddenly aware of the darkness closing in a second before he jolted awake, nearly falling out of his chair. He scrambled back into place and looked around.

He'd been moved from Walter's bedside to the window where late afternoon sun streamed into the room in stripes through vertical blinds. Beside him, Micaiah sat in one chair, his arm around Lily who was in another chair, uncomfortably situated with her head tucked under his arm yet on his chest. Tommen stared at them for a minute or two, wondering just what the hell had happened between the two of them. Grief and strife bring people together, but...damn. He wondered if Micah knew anything and how he felt about it.

A noise, the same one which had been in his dream toward the end and probably woken him up, sounded then. At first, he couldn't place it. Then he looked at his dad and saw that he was breathing normally, just as if he were sleeping soundly. It wasn't quite a snore, more like a huff, loose mustache hairs fluttering in the breeze. Not that Tommen was any kind of doctor, but if he had to hazard a guess, he would almost say that his vitals and other assorted machine-monitored bodily functions were normal again.

Even as he realized this, he also realized that his vision was back to normal, or normal as he knew it. He looked down at his shirt and coat which he knew were green and red respectively. Beige and gold. He closed his eyes and tried to remember what they'd looked like, envision red and green in their raw beauty, then think about all the colors that came from them that he normally missed out on. He could remember them, thankfully. He could bring red and green and purple to mind, but only in his memory. He couldn't take any of those colors and try to mentally overlay it on something he was looking at in the present moment. It was all gone.

He mentally beat himself until he stopped feeling any kind of sadness or regret about losing those colors; he would not give Rifun the satisfaction of knowing that he'd gotten to him. *Accept the gift gracefully, say thank you, enjoy it while you had it, but don't live in bondage to the one who gave it to you.*

Slowly, he stood and stretched, only to collapse back into the chair, feeling almost like he hadn't slept at all.

He didn't sit long before he got up again and headed out, looking for the nearest bathroom. After ten days of peeing pretty much wherever he wanted, bathrooms and toilets seemed almost foreign to him, but he was very thankful to be able to wash his hands again.

When he returned, he was surprised by a new person in the

room, though he was not a doctor or nurse. The man turned and Tommen recognized Greg Steggmann, Chief of Police. He nodded once to Tommen in greeting.

"We'd been told that he wasn't doing well," Steggmann said, "so I thought it only fitting that I come and pay my respects after the memorial service for the others who died. But he looks...better."

"He is," Tommen said. "He's going to make it. He'll be okay."

As he said it, the words finally sunk in and Tommen went to his knees in uncontrollable sobs. Steggmann was there to hold him up before he landed on his face, drawing him in close and holding him tight.

"He's going to be okay," Steggmann echoed. "I know, it's okay. A lot of families lost loved ones last Monday, and you were almost one of them. But your dad is going to be coming home."

"I know," Tommen whispered faintly. "I'm not sad, I'm...happy."

"And that's good. That is exactly what you should be feeling. Your dad is going to make it; he's going to come home."

Tommen took a breath and shuddered out a sigh, sniffing hard and wiping tears from his eyes, trying to collect himself. After a minute, Steggmann helped him to his feet.

"You feel skinny," Steggman said. "You been eating?"

Tommen shrugged. "Sometimes."

"Why don't we go down to the cafeteria? I'll buy you lunch."

After a moment and last glance at Walter, Tommen agreed. Together they headed down to the first floor to the cafeteria. Steggmann claimed he just ate, so Tommen sat across from him at the table and ate by himself.

"Why are you doing this?" Tommen wondered.

Steggmann started to answer, but the cafeteria was noisy, and despite sitting at the same table, Tommen found himself asking him to speak up. He felt bad, even more so when Steggmann gave him a sympathetic look, but it was his new reality. As much as he'd enjoyed seeing a full spectrum of color, deuteranopia was his reality. Hearing loss was just the newest addition to it. Either way, Steggmann obliged.

"Like I said, a lot of families lost loved ones last Monday, just a couple days before Christmas. It's not right, it's not fair, and I have no answers for them, not really. But I try to do something nice for them, help them out just a little, let them know that the world isn't ending. Most of the guys and their families believe me to be an uncaring hard ass, but police work isn't about the warm fuzzies. I can't bring back the husbands or wives or parents of those families, but I do what I can."

"But my dad is going to live."

"And that's a good thing. When did you find that out?"

Tommen sighed. "This morning."

"I'll bet the last week has been hell for you."

"Yeah."

"Like I said, I try to do something nice."

"Thanks." Tommen frowned and stared at his food, half-eaten. "The memorial was this morning. I should have been there."

Steggmann shook his head. "No. You were right where you were supposed to be: here, with your dad, so that when he wakes up, you're the first person he sees. Any idea when he's going to come around?"

"None, but it can't be too long."

"Well, I would advise you to finish your food before going up there. You're skin and bones."

Tommen nodded and did so, even though he ended up forcing down the last few bites. Then he stood and threw away his trash, leaving the tray on the stand. When he returned to the table, Steggmann had stood.

"I have more work that I have to get done today," he said. "Like I said, I came expecting to have to pay my respects, but I'm glad those plans got derailed."

"So am I," Tommen agreed.

"But listen to me, Tommen. Even after your dad wakes up,

he's still got a long way to go before he comes back to work. Coma aside, he took three bullets. Your dad is stubborn and proud, so if you need anything while he's on the mend, let me know, and I'll see what I can do. Okay?"

Tommen nodded. "Okay. Thanks."

"Good man. I'll be in touch, then."

They shook hands and went their separate ways. Steggmann headed for the exit, and Tommen the elevator. He hadn't been around Steggmann too much, and the few interactions he'd had, aside from the serious business of Rifun contacting him and making threats and plans, had been less than stellar. Usually it was when word got around that Tommen was in trouble again—not a few of the officers had kids in school with Tommen, and word spread. Steggmann himself had never said anything to Tommen, but Tommen always knew that whenever he got in trouble, Walter's reputation took a hit.

He was determined to do better now, to make his father proud instead of ashamed, glowing with pride instead of red with embarrassment. That meant no more fighting in school, or at least being a little wiser in picking his battles. It meant living less in the moment and more in the future, saving for a car, college or an apartment, instead of spending foolishly on knick-knacks, doo-dads, and other fleeting wants. Not that he wasn't already saving for a car, college, and an apartment, but he could probably dedicate more to the cause.

Tommen stepped off the elevator, trying to hold his head high even as he knew that his resolve would fail probably the second day back to school. His nobility and courage existed only in his head and he knew it. When push came to shove, he would revert back to same old Tommen, the Chivalrous Welshman who was as easily provoked as Marty McFly.

When he got back to his dad's room, Micaiah and Lily were awake. Neither was speaking, but their body language told Tommen that something had happened.

"You missed it," Micaiah said. "He opened his eyes."

"He did? He woke up?" Tommen went to Walter's bedside. "Did he say anything? Is he okay?"

"Tommen, slow down," Lily told him gently. "He's coming around slowly. Well, faster than normal, but it isn't like in the movies where they just wake up and everything is great."

Tommen wished it could be like the movies, but he wasn't complaining as long as Walter was getting better at all. He appeared to have lapsed back into sleep, but without the breathy huffs.

"Steggmann took me to lunch in the cafeteria," he said, going back to his chair, not looking at either Micaiah or Lily, but fixing his gaze on his dad so he wouldn't miss him the next time he woke up.

"We wondered," Micaiah said.

After a moment, Tommen stole a split-second glance at them. "So...are you guys an item or what happened?"

"We've made a truce."

It was a dismissive answer, probably the best one he was going to get, so he let it go. It was less important than the situation at hand, anyway. Tommen sat in his seat, got up and walked around the room, sat in his seat again, watched nurses come and go, listened to their excited chatter about the miraculous recovery, walked around the room again, then went and sat back down.

It was probably half an hour after his question to Micaiah and Lily when Tommen heard a muffled sound, somewhere between a groan and a sigh. Tommen went to his father's bedside and took his hand.

Walter's blue eyes were hazy and unfocused, looking at Tommen but not seeing him.

"Dad?" Tommen asked.

Walter blinked, but his gaze remained blank.

A nurse walked in then. She all but pushed Tommen out of the way and started interrogating Walter, taking out a pen light and shining it in his eyes. Straight verbal questions were met with blank stares, but anything physical — such as the pain in his collarbone or chest or thigh — he was able to more or less give a response, a small grunt or groan. The nurse was halfway through a question about any kind of head pain when he lapsed back into sleep.

"That was good, right?" Tommen asked. "He's getting better?"

"He is," she confirmed. "Better all the time."

Personally, Tommen thought she should have given a little better answer, more specific and descriptive. At the very least, she could send a doctor in to answer questions and reassure them and give them a spiel about what to expect moving forward. If he did recover, expect this. If he didn't recover, expect that. And so on. But she didn't. She left the room, and that was it. No answers, no reassurances, no doctors, no nothing.

So it was back to a routine of sitting, standing, and pacing. By the time five o'clock rolled around, Walter had woken up two more times, each time staying awake a little longer and, while he wasn't completely lucid, Tommen thought his eyes seemed a little more focused, a little more seeing. The last time, he was sure that his dad recognized him. He wasn't speaking yet either, but when the nurse quizzed him on movement and pain, he was able to give more specific grunts and groans. Rather than just his whole leg hurting, just his thigh hurt, and then just the area around the bullet wound.

A short time after his second waking, Tommen stuck just a tiny bit more antidote in his mouth, just to see if it would bring him around any faster or any better, not that he was any expert in alternate history theories.

Just as he was packing up the antidote, the door opened and Micah walked in.

"*Dúntar an siopa,*" Micah told his brother. "*Is fada liom go dtí é níos faide. An bhfuil sé ina lándúiseacht? Dúirt sé aon rud?*" (The store is closed. I can't stand the suspense any longer. Is he awake? Has he said anything?)

"*Mhúscail sé, ach níl sé ina chiall agus níl dúirt sé aon rud,*" Micaiah answered. (He's woken up, but he's not lucid and he hasn't said anything.)

Tommen noted that Micah did not in any way acknowledge

Lily's presence in the room. Rather, he appeared to keep his gaze fixed squarely on his brother as he spoke, far too intent on the conversation. Either it was his normal disdain for her, or else there was something going on between her and the elder twin.

"*Ach beidh sé ceart go leor?*" Micah asked. "*Bhí Tommen rathúil?*" (But he'll be all right? Tommen was successful?)

"*Go bhfios dúinn, beidh sé ceart go leor,*" Micaiah confirmed. (Yes, he'll be all right.)

Tommen could see the weight lifted from Micah's shoulders, the same weight that had been plaguing all of them. The younger twin made his way to the seat that Tommen had been occupying intermittently over the last few hours. After a few minutes of an awkward silence between the three of them, Lily stood.

"I should go," she said quietly.

"No," Micaiah said, maybe too quickly.

"You're his friends. He'll want to see you, not the one who caused all of this."

"Cassius and Rifun caused all of this, not you."

She shook her head. "No, it's okay. I'll see him later, I'm sure."

"All right. We'll see you later, then."

Lily turned to face Tommen. "I'm happy for you, Tommen. I really am. Let me know how things go."

"O...kay?"

She left the room.

"Did I miss something?" Tommen asked.

"They're having sex," Micah cut in before Micaiah could deny anything.

"Oh."

And that was that. Even though Micaiah was the one apparently in the doghouse, Tommen slipped into the empty chair like a whipped puppy. Well, it certainly explained the so-called "truce," though just the statement that they were having sex was a little more than Tommen wanted to dwell on.

He didn't remember falling asleep, didn't remember any

dreams or nightmares. The next thing he knew, he was waking up. At first, he wasn't sure what had woken him. Then, "Tommen?"

His first glance went to the twins, but their chairs were empty. Then he looked at his dad who was squinting at him like he was trying to bring him into focus.

"Dad!"

Tommen drunkenly leapt from his seat, tripped over it, and nearly went head-first into the foot of the hospital bed, catching himself at the last second on his injured hand. Shockwaves of pain lanced up his arm. Gritting his teeth, he found his footing and went straight for the big hug. His memory came back to him a second too late as Walter groaned loudly in pain. Tommen eased off and put a hand gently over the collarbone wound. "Sorry."

Walter squeezed his eyes shut and took several labored breaths before calming down. For a moment, Tommen was afraid he'd gone back to sleep. Then his eyes opened, tired but lucid.

"What the...? What happened? Where am I?" His voice was scratchy and hardly more than a tired whisper.

"You're in Intensive Care," Tommen told him, his body shaking from fear, from anxiety, from joy, from emotions he didn't have a name for. "You were shot."

He could see his dad searching his memory, looking for bits and pieces of what had happened and trying to make them all fit together.

"Oh," he finally said. He took a few breaths. "I remember."

"What do you remember?"

Before either could say more, the door opened and a doctor and several nurses rushed in. Tommen noticed that Walter's vitals had fluctuated wildly for a few seconds, probably while he'd been crushing his wounds.

"Well, look who decided to finally join us," the doctor said amiably.

What followed was about an hour of physical tests to look for any deficiencies and better assess pain, as well as tests and questions and quizzes to test his memory and cognition. Yes, he knew who he was, where he was, roughly the date.

"A week?" Walter wondered. "I've been here a week?"

"Yes. And to be honest, before this morning, we weren't sure you would make it," the doctor confessed.

"Why, what happened this morning?"

"We don't know."

Just as the doctor finished saying that, Tommen Banded, just him and his dad, saying, "I'll tell you later."

Other than a few understandable discrepancies in memory and cognition that the doctor expected to improve with time and therapy, Walter was just about as healthy as he had been when he woke up Monday morning. Tommen figured he was doing really well if he was conscious enough to come up with a healthy lie to explain away all the Time elements, instead of babbling on about Time and Banding and Borelians and whatnot.

It was after seven before the troupe of medical personnel left, promising to be back later with a plan of action, leaving Tommen and Walter alone in the room.

"I've seen guys come out of comas before," Walter murmured, clearly exhausted. "It takes a couple days, and it's never such a full recovery right off the bat. So what exactly happened this morning?"

Tommen grinned. "I've spent the last week looking for an antidote for the Borelian poison in your system. And I found it."

"There is no cure for Borelian poison."

"Obviously there is." Tommen went on before Walter could speak. "Me and you and the twins will all sit down and talk about it once you're out of here. Okay? Dad, okay?"

Walter sighed. "No, it's not okay. It's my own stupid fault I'm in here."

"It's not your fault. Cassius and Rifun did this."

"Maybe, but I'm here because of my own stubborn pride."

"What? The stubborn will to save your son?"

He sighed again and shook his head. "I'm not your father."

"Of course you are," Tommen said gently. "You are—"

"That was my secret, Tommen," Walter cut in, his voice weak but firm. "I was willing to die for my own stubborn pride because I was afraid to admit it. I'm not your father, Tommen. I'm your uncle."

Epilogue

Your pa probably never told you about me, and I really don't blame him. I was the son no parent ever wants to claim as their own. From a young age, I was a fighter. I didn't fight like you, because I believed in something and I was willing to stand up for it; I fought because I enjoyed it. I thoroughly, maniacally enjoyed it. I enjoyed dominating others. Even when I lost, I loved the feel of flesh and bone beneath my fist. Your pa, my younger brother, was honestly afraid of me.

"As I got older, I not only fought, but I drank and fought. I had a solid reputation, and it wasn't a good one. I had periods where I sobered up and thought about changing my ways, but then something would happen, and I would go right back to where I had been. Most often it was jail or the streets. I lived without a home for many years, fighting, drinking, and I added theft to my repertoire as well. I was a wanted man.

"Meanwhile, the rest of the family moved on without me. Your pa got married, our sisters got married. And I was stuck still on the streets with nothing to show for myself. Eventually, I had a prodigal son moment. I don't know exactly when it happened or what I was thinking at the time, but I was ashamed of myself. I was ashamed of who I was, what I'd done, and for the first time, I had a real resolve and a...more realistic strength to change my ways.

"I went home. My ma fled when she saw me coming up the road, and I was grateful only that my pa didn't shoot me from the doorstep. It took some doing, but I convinced them I wanted to change my ways.

" 'America,' they told me. I was too well-known in the area to be able to really change and move on, but America was the land of opportunity. I could go there and get a fresh start, be whoever and whatever I wanted to be, make a living, make a good name for myself. They told me that my brother, your pa, had already gone ahead. They suggested I seek him out, seek his forgiveness, and have him help me build a real life for myself. So I did. I hopped the first boat I could and sailed the Atlantic.

"America wasn't like Wales. I learned that as soon as I stepped off the boat on Ellis Island. No one knew anyone just by name, unless they were a wanted criminal. Asking for Teo Forbes Sr. meant nothing to anyone.

"And I had a bigger problem. I wanted to make a new life for myself, which meant I couldn't just fight or steal what I needed; I had to work. I picked up odd jobs here and there, enough to get me from one place to another. For a while, I was never able to ask around by name; I had to ask around by country. 'Where do the Welsh immigrants go?' I asked.

"Eventually I made my way to Pennsylvania, working and laboring, building a small reputation as a hard worker. I liked it, having the good reputation, having a conversation around a campfire with men who weren't deathly afraid of me, being able to sleep at night without worrying about the cops coming and arresting me in the night, beating me to a bloody pulp before they could drag me in. Honest work felt good.

"Of course, it wasn't all sunshine and roses. Working men like to socialize, and, most often, that was with a drink. One night, I got to drinking too much and somehow I ended up killing not one but three men in my rage.

"I fled into the mountains, seeking asylum in small Appalachian villages that had sprung up, offering to work for families who needed help, everything from chopping wood to breaking horses, all sorts of planting and harvesting. It was through one of those families that I finally heard my brother's name.

"After that, I was like a bloodhound, tracking your pa just as fast as I could. I never really learned survival like he did; I was too busy fighting while he was learning from our pa. So my progress was slowed because I had to work and earn my food and bed, rather than just trek alone straight through the mountains. But maybe it was better that way; the mountains are more than men, and I know I would have gotten lost or injured.

"The day I walked up to your pa's doorstep, I was more nervous than a bride on her wedding night. Your pa was understandably skeptical, but frontier life had hardened him, and he was no longer afraid of me. He had a family to protect, and he would kill his own brother if he had to in order to keep them safe. But I talked him down and told him my intentions. I asked if there was any way I could convince him or any way I could help.

"He told me that just a couple weeks prior, their youngest boy had gone missing in the old salt cave just up the mountain. He said that if I could find you and bring you home, then we'd talk. Else don't come back at all.

"So I went into the cave and fell into the same Time trap you did. It was getting late when I went in, and when I came out, it was October of 1923. I eventually bumbled my way into Charleston, and I was just as terrified as you were. I don't know what happened exactly, but I got in a fight and landed in jail—again. Most of the cops thought me insane, yammering on about it being 1855 and this, that and the other thing. But one of the jailers was a Timekeeper. When I got out of jail, he's the one who helped me make sense of what had happened and make a life for myself, again and again as needed until he finally died in Vietnam.

"I waited almost a century for you, Tommen. I knew I couldn't bring you home, but I could keep my word to your pa to find you. Since I understood what had happened with the Time trap, I knew you would be terrified. Not only that, but you would ultimately go to child services, and I wasn't going to lose you to that. I was going to keep you in the family no matter what.

"To that end, I became a cop and specialized in Missing Persons, the weirder the better, especially when it came to children. I got my foster care license, and I waited.

"I was never so happy as the day I got the call for you—a strange little boy babbling in Welsh who swore up and down he was Tommen Forbes—*the* Tommen Forbes.

"When I met you, I had hoped that somewhere, deep down, you would feel some sense of kinship, or that there might be some resemblance left of me to your pa. When there wasn't...it broke my heart. But I also resolved that because you were so torn from your family that the best break was a clean break, and I wasn't going to confuse or damage you by telling you that I was your uncle.

"Eventually, it just became so natural. I liked being your dad, and I didn't want you to think less of me if I told you the truth. I was ashamed of it, felt like I was shaming your pa, trying to take his place. And I was so determined to keep it hidden that I was willing to die for it, never mind what it would do to you, as if one secret was worse than orphaning you. Even now I'm ashamed of myself for it, that it all led to this."

For a moment, Tommen stood at Walter's bedside, silent. Walter was fully expecting—and deserving—of the anger, hurt, disappointment, and betrayal that the boy was probably feeling. But he was unprepared for Tommen putting his arms around him again, much more gently this time, and hugging him as tight as he dared.

"You're here because you were willing to die for me, your son. And I've never been more proud to call you my dad."

Keep reading for a preview of

Windup

the next exciting installment of
The Chivalrous Welshman

Chapter One
On Cochleas

Tommen was glad that Micaiah was driving, because he knew that if he'd been driving, they probably would have landed in a ditch somewhere, as distracted as he was.

Finally, his dad was coming home from the hospital. It was hard to believe that hardly ten days ago, Tommen had been taken hostage by the renegade Timekeeper Rifun, seeking to use him to get to Walter in order that he would give up the corrupt bureaucrat Lily to save him. Tommen closed his eyes and could effortlessly bring to mind standing there in the shipping yard, Rifun's gun pressed against his head, Walter hardly ten yards away trying to do his best to bring everyone home and haul Rifun and his associates off to jail.

But not everyone had gone home. Even before they'd gotten to that point, Rifun had murdered seven police officers. When all was said and done, nine officers had died, three had been maimed to the point of never returning to the force, and the rest were on suicide watch and psychological evaluation.

It was difficult to gauge where Walter fell on that spectrum. He'd gotten separated from the rest of the group, cornered by Rifun and an alien called a Borelian whose very touch was a death sentence. He'd been shot with poison bullets and left to die. While he'd made it to the ER and gotten into surgery, the poison was already working, and he lapsed into a coma with only about a week to live.

Tommen, not one to give up, had gone to the Hands of Time, seeking help. Not only did they refuse to help him, but he managed to start a civil war because of it. But one of the Hands took pity on him and told him where to find a cure. He'd ended up traipsing across a blazing hot desert, getting in a fight with the world's ugliest cat, traipsing through a jungle, getting in a fight with the world's ugliest bear-slash-komodo dragon, free-climbing a rock wall, dislocating his hand, losing all but a fraction of the antidote he'd collected, and escaping by the skin of his teeth.

When he returned, he got the antidote to Walter, and within twenty-four hours, his dad was awake and talking, almost as if he hadn't been on the verge of death.

That had been three days ago. The doctors insisted on keeping him for several more days, despite his apparent miracle recovery, or perhaps because of it. They did scans and ran tests, always doing something, trying to figure out what had pulled him back from the brink. Ultimately, they'd found nothing to explain it, and, since he he hadn't relapsed or shown any other signs of imminent medical danger, they were forced to release him.

But that wasn't to say he was going to be out dancing anytime soon. He'd still been shot three times. While it was very possible for Walter to normally Band his injuries and recover from them faster, he was unable to do so with these injuries. His best guess had been some kind of residual effect of the Borelian poison, that even as it was immune to Time, so his injuries would be also.

"Got everything?" Micaiah asked as he pulled into a parking spot. Behind them, Micah, Micaiah's younger twin brother, cruised past to find a spot in the lot. The idea was that Tommen would drive Walter home, but since he didn't have his full license yet, he still needed to catch a ride.

"Huh? Oh, um, I think so," Tommen said, perusing through the bag. That was another thing. Between multiple close-range gunshots, one set directly next to his head as close as it could get, and a number of very loud animal sounds, he'd lost part of his hearing, to the point where as soon as Walter was checked out, Tommen would be checking in to see the audiologist.

"We'll be over a little later to make sure he's settled in and make sure you don't need help or anything," the elder Durvin twin told him as they got out of the car. "Take it easy on him, Tommen; he's as shaken as you are."

At first, Tommen figured he was referring to his dad's near-death experience, which could very well have been part or a majority of it. Then he also considered that there was probably a part of Walter that still felt the shame of his dishonesty, or his perceived dishonesty, that he'd never told Tommen about just how closely related they were. Not only was Walter his adopted father, but his biological uncle as well.

The last few days, despite Tommen forgiving him completely, he could honestly say that he looked at his dad just a little differently. Not just as dad, but as uncle, too. It was a strange sensation. Family. A real, living relative, a connection to his old life, someone who could answer so many questions about his old life, his pa and their family.

Walter, for the most part, seemed to carry on as normally as could be expected, but there were times when Tommen could see not only the relief of finally sharing his secret, but also the fear of being rejected as a father. He blamed himself for a lot of things, wondering if things might have been different if Tommen had known, if he would have stayed out of trouble more or gotten in even deeper; wondering if things in the warehouse really would have turned out differently if he'd spilled as Rifun had wanted.

And there was a moment, too, during one of those conversations, when Tommen felt another sensation: equality. He loved his dad and respected him, but he almost felt a shift in their relationship, as if he'd finally been elevated from child-to-be-controlled to adult-to-be-respected. Maybe it was just him. Maybe it was still too soon to tell. Hell, his dad hadn't even left the hospital yet.

The hospital was busy, as was to be expected on New Year's Day. If people weren't getting drunk and doing stupid things, their families were constantly in and out, bringing cards and flowers and gifts and trying to make a bad holiday better. Tommen had considered it, then figured that his dad wasn't even really a card, flowers, or gift kind of person. Just getting out of the hospital and back home to sleep in his own recliner, er, bed, would be enough for him.

Tommen got to the elevator just as it was closing, someone

putting their hand out to stop the door and let him on. He thanked them briefly and bounced on his toes as the box began moving.

"Stop twitching, you're making me nervous," a lady chuckled.

"Sorry," Tommen said meekly, forcing himself to stop bouncing and settle instead for anxious toe-curling in the ends of his shoes. "My dad's coming home today."

"That's good, I'm happy for you."

The polite thing to do probably would have been to reciprocate the unasked question, ask her who she was visiting, what happened, did they have a nice Christmas, wish them well, and so on and so forth. Unfortunately, or maybe fortunately in his case, elevators don't give a lot of opportunities for small talk. So he waited out the awkward four seconds between her statement and his stop.

He shot out of the elevator with the speed of a bullet and the flexibility of water, weaving his way around doctors, nurses, assorted hospital staff, patients, and patients' families, slipping into his dad's room with minimal hindrance.

"Little early, aren't we?" Walter asked from his bed.

Before he could do much more than look around for the remote, Tommen was at his bedside, holding down the button until the head of the bed was up almost as far as it could go.

"You seem very certain they're going to let me leave."

"Aren't they?" Tommen's heart skipped a beat.

His dad chuckled softly. "Of course they are. They have no reason to keep me, and I think with me being so restless now, they'll be glad to get rid of me."

"Are you chasing nurses again?"

"Absolutely. None of them can hope to withstand my winning wobble. They want to run, but they just can't."

He was referring to the gunshot wound to his right thigh. It had severed the artery and screwed up the major muscle groups, but thankfully missed the femur. He was supposed to use a cane or walker or even a wheelchair until it healed, but his stubborn determination to walk took over just as soon as the doctor wasn't looking. He couldn't even use a cane or a walker well seeing how his right arm was in a box sling from another gunshot wound that had cracked his shoulder blade, almost splitting it up the middle. His left arm might have been in the same predicament had he woken up from surgery like he was supposed to have. That bullet had cracked his sternum, ricocheted, and taken a chip off his other shoulder blade. Other than essentially grinding down the sharp edges into more rounded ones, there was little they could do for him, and he was told simply not to exert himself to any more pain than about the equivalent of a paper cut.

At first he'd thought it silly, until he'd tried to pull up his blankets at night or reach any farther than his hip. So it was that Tommen had to help him into his clothes, everything from his boxers to his jacket.

"While you're working and whatnot, I will be figuring out a way to do this by myself," Walter assured him as he weakly fumbled with his belt and pulled it just a little tighter than it used to be and clicked it in.

"I don't mind," Tommen said. "It's the right thing to do. And it's only temporary."

His dad let out a breath and sat down on the bed. He looked at Tommen. "You know what I saw this morning out the window?"

"A car accident?"

Walter chuckled. "Good guess, but no. Two eagles and a sunrise."

He nodded slowly, and Tommen stared at him, not sure how to respond. Only when his dad's expression started to waver did he shift his stance and fold his arms. "Are you joking?"

Walter cracked up laughing for a second or two, then was forced to stop, cringing in pain. When the agony had passed, he was still smiling as he looked at his son. "I'm not dying, Tommen. You're right, it's only temporary, but what you have seen cannot be unseen. And I would just as soon not show it off any more than I have to."

Other than a few jokes between men as Tommen helped him

dress, he was more than likely referring to any number of scars that covered his body, injuries sustained long before his introduction to Time, injuries inflicted upon him by angry drunks with glass bottles or angry villagers with shotguns. The three new ones he'd gained from Rifun were nothing new, nothing truly surprising, just a few more to add to the rest.

As Tommen was helping his dad put his socks and shoes on, the doctor walked in. He was a friendly enough person, Tommen figured, though he seemed a little more intent on testing Walter for his unusual miracle cure than congratulating him on recovering at all and getting him home.

"Thought you'd sneak out on us while we weren't looking, huh?" the doctor began amiably.

"Your backs would have to be turned for quite a while for me to make that kind of getaway," Walter told him, casting a knowing glance at Tommen who turned his head so the doctor wouldn't see him smile.

"Well, I thought I would come by to wish you good luck and happy new year." He tore a script note off his pad and handed it to Walter. "One is for the pain, two as needed but not more than six in a day. The other is a muscle relaxer since you said your thigh would sometimes feel very tight."

"Like a charliehorse, yes."

"That should help. One as needed, not to exceed four in a day. And if you feel like they're not being effective, come back and we'll take a look, make sure nothing's going on either in the wound or neurologically." The doctor paused and nodded, half to himself. "Other than that, definitely take it easy. You're good to go home, but everything is still in its earliest stages of healing."

"What should I be looking for to, like, call an ambulance or bring him back?" Tommen cut in.

"Any change in his behavior, lethargy, pain that won't go away, signs of infection, excessive bruising, bleeding, that sort of thing. And as always, do not hesitate to call. If you even think you have a question or concern, get a hold of me or one of the other doctors. Better to be on the safe side than go through all of this again."

"I couldn't agree more," Walter said.

"Like I said, take it easy. A little pain is good, but do not exert yourself. No lifting, running, and I would wait on the driving, too."

"Well, there go my drag racing plans."

The doctor smiled. "Do you have any questions now while I'm standing here? I don't want to send you home if you don't feel comfortable."

Comfort had very little to do with it, and he'd been asking that question for the last two days. As usual, neither of them really had anything, and the doctor handed over a thick set of papers, the staple in the corner straining to hold them together.

"Home and work instructions, which I will let you look over at your leisure. Rachel will get you checked out at the desk. Other than that, happy new year, and I am very happy to see you walking out of here."

"You and me both," Walter said.

The doctor nodded once and finally left the room. Tommen looked at his dad expectantly.

"Well, I'm ready to get out of here," Walter decided.

Tommen helped his dad get his shoes on, no small feat considering the man had virtually no strength left in him after the coma, not to mention his thigh injury stealing what little strength he had in reserve. But the shoes went on easily enough, and Tommen positioned himself to help him off the bed.

Not that he expected to be utilized in such a way. His dad still had his pride, and after three days of being chastised by nurses for sneaking off to the bathroom on his own, Tommen figured he could get up and down well enough.

Walking was another matter altogether, however. The room offered a number of handholds and lean-tos that he'd been able to use, but there would be no such conveniences once they got out into the hallway. Well, technically there were, but there wouldn't be any in the parking lot or at home. So while Walter made it to the door with much limping and plodding along, he was then forced to choose between Tommen and an assist.

"You okay?" Tommen wondered after a few seconds of his dad staring at the door.

"I seem to be losing more and more of my dignity each day," Walter replied thoughtfully. "Lend me your arm for now; I'm probably going to have to break down and get a cane or some stupid thing before we actually get out of here."

Tommen came on his dad's left side, offering an arm and helping him out into the chaos that was the larger hospital. For a minute, his dad seemed stunned by the people and activity going on.

"A little busier than I remember," he said.

"Well, home should be quieter," Tommen told him.

"Should." Walter started ahead, gimping toward the desk. "But first we have your appointment to take care of."

Right. His appointment. The one where he would be tested and scanned and officially told that he had hearing loss and was going to need hearing aids. It was a terrible thing that, while he dreaded going to the appointment, he was also looking forward to it. He'd grown more used to his hearing loss, but he knew that he read lips and body language as much as he heard voices. Many sounds, the ones that weren't lost to him on the higher end of the audible spectrum, were muted and fuzzy.

"Checking out?" the receptionist asked.

"Finally," Walter told her.

"All right, and I'm showing your regular doctor is Roger Gerstle, correct?"

"Unless something's changed in the last two weeks."

"Okay, well, I'm showing that you should have a follow-up with him in about one week and then again two weeks after that."

"Sounds like what the doctor was telling me."

Tommen let them haggle and negotiate over dates and times, not that there was a lot to do. Wasn't like his dad was going to be returning to work first thing Monday morning; the only schedule that needed to be worked around was Tommen's school and work schedule. Theoretically, Walter could be driving himself to the second appointment, if not the first, depending on how far he wanted to push his luck.

"Great," the receptionist said, bringing Tommen back to the present. "I'll get everything sent over to him, and his office will confirm with you. But you are good to go from here. Congratulations and happy new year. Do you need help getting to your vehicle?"

"Not going out to the car yet, but thanks for the offer," Walter informed her, taking Tommen on one side and slowly limping away.

They made it to the elevator easily enough, going first to the ground floor where the pharmacy was so Walter could fill his prescriptions before heading to the second floor.

Intensive Care was busy, and the ER was even busier. Stepping onto the second floor was like a breath of fresh air, a break from the busyness. This was where the more low-key treatments were done. Optometry—or was that opthalmology?—audiology, physical therapy. The place where people made appointments, coming here for a predetermined purpose, not walking in and panicking because they didn't understand what was going to happen, or what was supposed to happen.

Down one hallway, a man no older than thirty was limping along on a prosthetic leg, using a walker and being guided by a therapist. Elsewhere, a child was experimenting with new specialized glasses, constantly taking them off and putting them back on. Tommen guessed the floor was probably a lot busier on regular days. They made their way through the maze of maps and signs to a set of large, frosted glass double doors reading Audiology.

"Good afternoon," the receptionist greeted. "What can I do for you?"

Her voice was soft, but not in the calm, reassuring manner that might have been expected. It was more like, her voice was soft because if it got any louder, she would be shouting, probably over the unfairness of having to work a holiday. Tommen bet she wouldn't be complaining about the paycheck that came her way because of it, but whatever.

"He's got an audiology appointment," Walter said, indicating Tommen. "Tommen Forbes."

Tommen didn't miss the momentary bewildered expression that crossed the receptionist's face. She'd probably been fully prepared to direct Walter to physical therapy, only to be side-swiped by the sixteen-year-old standing next to him who had the real appointment.

"Yes, I have him right here," the receptionist said after a second or two. "If you want to take a seat, I'll let the doctor know you're here."

"Busy day?" Tommen asked, trying to find some humor.

"Busier than you might expect. A lot of people have the day off, but usually that doesn't mean anything because so does everyone else. Having the doctor in today means people can get in on their schedule to see him."

Again, her words said one thing, but her tone and body language said another. She probably had any number of things she would have rathered been doing, but instead got stuck sitting behind a desk.

Still, she disappeared into the office while Tommen and his dad headed for the seats along one wall. Walter more collapsed than sat, leaning back and closing his eyes.

"You okay?" Tommen wondered.

"That's a lot of walking," his dad replied.

Any other time, Walter would not only have been able to do all that walking around the hospital, he would have been able to take the stairs instead of the elevator, too, and not even break a sweat. Tommen hoped that his strength and stamina would return with time, but there was no telling what side effects he would suffer because of Isthim's poison.

"Is there anything you want to do or anywhere you want to go before we go home?" Tommen asked conversationally.

"No," Walter said. "I just want to go home, have a nice home-cooked meal, and be able to sleep in my own bed."

"Yeah, so do I."

Tommen hadn't realized it—or maybe he had, but it just seemed unimportant until now—but he hadn't slept in his own bed either just as long as Walter hadn't been in his own bed; he'd been staying with the twins. Had it really been that long since either of them had been home? The house would need some cleaning. Worse, the refrigerator would need some cleaning.

"So how have you been coping since you lost your hearing?" Walter asked as Tommen reached for a magazine.

Tommen felt his cheeks burn hot. "Okay, I guess. I mean, I can hold a conversation just fine in a quiet room—"

"Making out sounds and hearing them as they are, are two different things." Walter still hadn't opened his eyes.

Tommen chewed his lip and let out a slow breath. "I can hear what you're saying. I know what you're saying. In a quiet room, I don't really notice a difference. But anything louder than this and it goes downhill fast. Micaiah tried to help, and it improved a little, but it's not likely I'll ever recover my full hearing. And that's why we're here."

"How'd you do on your trip?"

With nothing else to do besides sit in a hospital room for two days, Walter had managed to weasel every last little detail that Tommen could recall about his adventures with Sifura, from the oasis and the feast and the harvesting and getting drunk, to the skimmer and the desert, to the D'Bok and the warrior duel and the jungle, to the mountain and the antidote and the animal d'bok, to S'Bal's treachery and the ensuing chase in the Wheel.

In the end, they'd decided that if they ever found themselves discussing the thing in public, outside of a Band, they would simply refer to the whole thing as "Tommen's trip." What kind of trip that was, was up for speculation, but people did a lot of traveling over the holidays after all.

"If not for the translator, I probably wouldn't have survived," Tommen answered his dad's question. "And I don't mean language barrier, but I would have been so far in the dark on cultural and social niceties that..." He drew his finger across his neck. "Without that translator, I basically heard nothing but the din of voices."

Even as he spoke, Walter opened his eyes and nudged him. Tommen looked up to see the doctor standing not far away, folder in hand. Case and point, the doctor had probably called his name, and he hadn't known.

"How are we doing today, guys?" the doctor asked amiably. He was not an old man, but probably pretty close to retirement, with graying hair and wrinkled features.

"Better all the time," Walter told him. "Or at least I am. Hopefully you can help him get to that point too."

"I will certainly try. I'm Dr. Polski by the way."

"Walter Forbes. My son, Tommen. How long have you been in practice, Dr. Polski?"

"I've been in practice for about forty years now, actually. My family and I just recently moved from California where I did almost fifteen years."

"What brings you here?"

"Family, mostly. This room right here."

They entered a little exam room. Walter found a seat in the corner while Tommen assumed the spinning stool and the doctor brought out his luxury office chair.

"So, Tommen, can you tell me when you started experiencing hearing loss or what triggered it?"

"I had a gun go off next to my ear. Literally, like, right next to it. .45 revolver. There were some other gunshot incidents, but that one...I couldn't hear anything for about ten minutes, and it wasn't until the next morning that I could really say I got anything back, or enough to be really useful and not shout at everyone."

"When did this happen?"

"December 23rd."

"How has your hearing been since? I noticed you didn't respond when I called your name."

Tommen shrugged. "It has its good days and bad days. In a quiet room, I do okay. Once you start adding noise, it goes downhill pretty fast."

"And sitting here, in a quiet room in close proximity, can you describe it?"

"I can hear you; I can understand you. But I know that most computers whine and make noise if they're running, and your computer over there on the desk is running, but if I didn't see it, I wouldn't know it was there."

"Okay. That's a good description, actually. So what I'm going to do is take a peek inside your ears and look for physical damage, then start out with a standard hearing test, similar to the one you probably got when you were in grade school; that will tell me where you're at, and then we'll decide how to proceed. Sound good?" He looked first at Tommen, then at Walter.

"Sounds okay to me," Walter told him.

Tommen shrugged. "Gotta do what you gotta do."

"All right, so come over this way and we'll get started."

Tommen scooted himself over to another table set up perpendicular to the desk with the computer, this one with some unknown machine that looked like it walked straight out of 1985. He remained on his stool while Polski rummaged around in a drawer for a true old-school doctor housecall bag.

"Sit very still, Tommen," he ordered, flicking on a little light and looking in his ear.

Polski did whatever looking and poking and prodding he needed to do, first in one ear, then the other, then back to the first ear, then back to the other, back and forth probably three times before putting his stuff away and going around to the other side of the table to face him.

"I didn't see any structural damage to your ear, which is a

good thing," Polski reported.

"So then why am I half-deaf?" Tommen asked.

Polski reached for an ear model sitting next to the computer. He took several pieces and parts off. "Everyone knows the eardrum, and for as much care as people take in protecting that, it's a tough little bugger. What people forget about is the cochlea, here. Inside are millions of tiny little hairs that receive sound waves from the ear drum and send them to the brain to be interpreted. These little hairs, however, can both degrade naturally over time or they can be broken. The more hairs you have, the better you are able to perceive and interpret sound. Otherwise, there are soundwaves going in, but no hairs to catch those waves and send them to your brain."

"And there's nothing you can do? There's not like some surgery you can do to, I don't know, replace or replant or something?"

"In some cases of extreme or even complete hearing loss, there are some implants that can be used to bypass the inner ear completely and send information directly to the brain. However, this is considered a last-resort option even in those cases."

"So what happens to me, then?"

"Well, first I'm going to test your hearing, figure out your range, your highs and lows of frequency perception." He handed Tommen a pair of headphones that were almost as old as the machine they were attached to. "We're going to start off in broad increments. You are either going to hear it or you won't. Hold your hands up like this, and give me either left, right, or both as you hear the tones."

Tommen hadn't done anything like this since he entered school in third grade. The tests themselves were normally conducted in second grade, but because he had been new to the school and had no similar records to give them, he'd had to take the tests before they would let him into the classroom. He remembered being terrified of the machine, of the sounds, of the magic of technology, but he'd passed with flying colors. Well, the colors that he could see anyway.

So he went through the same motions again, except this time

there seemed to be fewer of them. He knew that Polski was sending more tones than he was hearing, but he also knew that the doctor would know if he was trying to fake his way through.

Not that he particularly wanted to fake his way through. Whether or not he liked the situation, he needed to be able to hear. It wasn't going to get better, and lying would only hurt him in the long run. Better to swallow his pride and get it over with.

"Tommen?" It was like hearing his name while he was underwater. He looked at the doctor and took off the headphones. "I'm going to change it up now," Polski told him. "This is going to be a little more specific. This time when you tell me which ear, give me a one if you think you hear it, a two if you can hear it but it's unclear, and a three if it is very clear."

And so they went through the same test again, this time with tones at frequencies that were closer together on the spectrum. Tommen was both amazed and terrified of how he could hear one tone very well, the next one okay, and by the fifth one in the sequence, it was gone. He wasn't sure if he was supposed to have heard it or where it fell on the spectrum of normal hearing, and the thought was discomforting. What if it was worse than he thought? What if the doctor wanted to have a more intimate and serious chat about moving forward?

"And we're done," Polski said suddenly.

Tommen took the headphones off and scooted back six inches from the table.

"How bad is it?" Tommen wondered fearfully, searching the man's face for any sign of encouragement or grave concern.

"Well, I don't think it's quite as bad as you're fearing, but let me gather up some numbers and paperwork and we'll have a little sit-down. How about that?"

He apparently meant it as an encouragement, but Tommen felt anything but encouraged. Polski left the room.

"So what do you think?" Walter inquired from his chair. He fumbled with a magazine he'd swiped from the waiting area.

"About what?" Tommen wondered.

"You're the physics whiz, and sound is part of physics. Any ideas?"

At first Tommen thought he was joking, then he realized that his dad was really trying to cheer him up. First it acknowledged his love of physics, then it gave him a puzzle to work through. Rather than just sitting around, his mind swirling in the unknown, it let him try to come up with a known variable to compare his experience to.

He tried to bring to mind everything he knew about sound and frequencies, the range of normal human hearing. At first it was a good puzzle to chew on, but when he tried to compare normal hearing to his hearing, what he should and could hear, it was like trying to compare his normal vision with the full visible spectrum of color.

Eventually he gave up on the puzzle. No sooner had he done that than Polski walked back in with a small stack of papers, printouts, and a couple brochures. He was kind enough to bring the conversation over to Walter rather than try and make Walter move over to one of the desks.

"So, these are your numbers," Polski began. "This is your right ear, which was the worse of the two. Your lowest range, your highest range, all indicating moderate hearing loss. Your left ear, same thing, but with better numbers, showing me only mild to just touching in the moderate hearing loss. Now then, as with any of the senses, it could fluctuate a little bit from day to day, and there is every possibility that, given time, you could recover some of your hearing. Probably not all, but some is better than none. You're only sixteen, so it is possible."

"What do you recommend?" Walter asked, his voice level.

"For his situation, I would say hearing aids. His hearing loss isn't so extreme that I believe any kind of implants or bypass to be necessary at this time. That could change, especially if it gets worse, but there is no reason that simple hearing aids won't help. Most common is a behind-the-ear style. Most people tell me that they are more comfortable and easier to manage than the hearing aids your grandpa used to wear, and with your hair as long as it is, you could cover it up and no one would be the wiser."

Tommen sighed and looked at his dad who nodded once, deferring the decision. "It's your hearing, your call. But you need something for school."

"There's nothing else you can do?" Tommen asked Polski.

Polski frowned and shook his head slowly. "Believe me, I wish there was. My sister is deaf. She's what got me into audiology because I was convinced that I could cure her. But the ear, the human body itself, is a little more complicated than that. We have the technology to boost or bypass your hearing, but not to fix it quite like that yet."

He sighed again. "What do I have to do?"

"Well, first I have to make a mold of your ear; all long-term or permanent hearing aids are custom fit, for obvious reasons. If you'd like, however, I can send you home with a trial pair just to get you used to wearing them and how to take care of them. Then, when your pair comes in, you can throw away the trial pair or save it in case something happens to yours."

"I don't want a trial pair," Tommen said.

"Yes, you do," Walter interrupted. He looked at Polski. "How long do they take to come in?"

"On a rush order, I can get them here hopefully by Monday or Tuesday."

"You have school on Monday," Walter told Tommen. He Banded the two of them. "And you still have your review tomorrow."

"If I was able to bring a case before the Hands without hearing aids, I think I can do my review without them, too." It was hard to say whether his remark came from his own stubborn pride, or from his secret that supposed he was going to pass no matter what, at least according to Rifun.

But his dad wouldn't let it go. "You're going to need every advantage you can get for your review."

Walter released the Band and looked at Polski. "He'll take the trial pair. And he'll wear them."

Polski nodded once in such a way that said he was going to send them home with a trial pair and simply let the two of them fight it out. He scribbled something on a piece of paper and stood. "So then, I will get the stuff to make a mold." He handed Tommen a couple small brochures. "And I will let you peruse." He paused. "And don't be embarrassed about saying what you do or don't like about a hearing aid. I know it's new and it might take a few tries and some discussion, but this is your hearing, and you'll be in this for the long haul. Best to get comfortable now."

The worst part was that he was right.

Tommen glowered at the brochures until the doctor left the room. Then he cautiously opened one and looked through. He'd never realized that hearing aids were such a competitive industry. He always figured that, sure, there were a couple different styles just for different fit preferences, but he'd never imagined that there would be different brands or companies. Most of the differences seemed to be purely about style—whether he wanted a solid color or a color and black. But a few boasted clearer sound or better crowd noise filtration and such.

"So what are you thinking?" his dad asked after a minute, looking through each brochure as Tommen finished and handed them off.

"I'm thinking this is a lot more complicated than it needs to be," Tommen answered honestly.

"Well, think about what you want."

"What's the insurance cover?"

"Unless you're getting the diamond-studded outlier, don't worry about the insurance. Better to pay a little more now and have hearing aids that work for ten years, than go for the cheapest pair and be back every two years to get them replaced."

Polski returned then with his ear mold making kit. Tommen sat very still once again, feeling his heart race as first one ear was done, than the other, the sticky plaster-like material being applied to his ears and then carefully peeled off when it was set, almost like when the orthodontist had made molds of his mouth over the years.

"What questions do you have for me about the hearing aids?" Polski wondered once he had the molds carefully packed away.

"Is there really any difference between one and another? Like these two, for instance?" Walter indicated a couple brochures, both behind the ear aids, but two different companies.

"There is some difference," Polski answered. "Generally, cheap is cheap, but expensive doesn't make it the end-all of hearing aids."

"Do you have any recommendations?"

The doctor pulled out a marker. "If I had to pick a top three, based on your needs, I would suggested any of these. This one comes from a brand that is known for durability and long-lasting hearing aids; some will last five, ten years, maybe more. Some people have reported, however, that the quality and clarity of sounds isn't always the greatest. This one boasts the best quality, but there have been complaints of the battery going out before the end of the day, which can be a problem if you're a sunrise to sunset kind of worker. This one is the cheapest and has good sound, but some people will tell you that physically it doesn't hold up; the plastic breaks or the earpiece comes off or something to that effect."

"What about this one?" Tommen asked, showing him one hidden in a corner of a brochure.

"That is an option." Polski ran his tongue over his teeth. "Actually, that's a very good option, why didn't I think of that before?" Beat. "Huh. Yes, that would work, too. Those guys have excellent battery life and good sound quality. They're not the cheapest, but—"

"So what are the drawbacks of it?" Walter cut in. "Is it going to break the first time he drops it?"

"No, nothing like that. However, I have heard that the average lifespan of those ones is about three years."

"How often should he be reevaluated for new ones? Does it

really matter that much?"

"In children, it doesn't matter much because they are always growing. In adults, it matters more because they've stopped growing and don't want to get new ones every few years. In Tommen's case, three years would probably be good enough because he is still growing but not at an exorbitant rate, and by the time they start to go, he'll have a better idea of what works and what doesn't."

"Sounds good to me. What about you?" Walter looked at Tommen.

He let out a breath. "I guess if I need 'em, I need 'em."

"It'll work," Walter told the doctor.

"Excellent. I will get all of this prepared and sent off, rush order so you can have them for school. Cary will take care of you guys at the desk and get you a trial pair to take home."

One thing I love about science fiction is that there is no right or wrong way to do it, and I'd like to think that *The Chivalrous Welshman* really captures that idea. Sci-fi and fantasy are genres of imagination, where you can just pick a starting point and go, adding little bits and pieces along the way.

That's what I tried to do in *Tick Tock* is add more bits and pieces—okay, fewer bits and more chunks—to the Timekeeper and Time industry universe. Earth is only one small, small player in this universe, and there is so much out there to explore yet, and it's not just about coming up with believable aliens that aren't just-humans-in-costume or CGI freaks. What politics are at play, and how do you try to more or less unify those races that are literally millions of light years apart and probably never would have seen each other if not for Time? Is it wise to make the most dangerous race known to the universe your go-to guys for executions? Who really benefits from having both the Hands and the Grandfathers shrouded like they are? And who could have guessed that the antidote for Isthim's poison would be found in the nectar of a flower halfway across the universe? Why is that? How does that work?

Writing *Tick Tock* was simultaneously a joy and a disaster to write. On the one hand, I'm like, "Finally, I can branch out and write a whole new adventure, whole new civilization and culture from scratch. It's all mine." And on the other hand, I'm like, "Oh, shoot, I have to write a whole new adventure, whole new civilization and culture from *scratch*. It's all mine." And it wasn't just one civilization, but two as they were introduced in the book, plus a myriad of little tidbits of the others given only a passing mention.

I've been asked multiple times whether we will ever revisit

Sifura and the Xur, or any of the tribes on her world. The short answer is yes, they will reappear in the future. The long answer is that it will be some time before they reappear, and their time in the spotlight will only be very brief in this main story spine. But there could be more later. Very little is set in stone when it comes to this series.

To that end, I will leave you, reader, to chomp on this while you're waiting for book three, is that there is more than meets the eye to those little tidbits. Passing comments or observations or existential crises, nothing is wasted. Well, Karaki got wasted by Sifura, but there are little gold nuggets hidden throughout, not just this book, but the first book, and each book after this. Be patient and read hard, young warrior, for none of this is for naught.